Legends of Santiago

Legends of Santiago

Santiago
The Return of Santiago

MIKE RESNICK

SCIENCE
FICTION

SANTIAGO   Copyright © 1986 by Mike Resnick
    Publication History: Tor paperback, March 1986

THE RETURN OF SANTIAGO   Copyright © 2003 by Mike Resnick
    Publication History: Tor hardcover, February 2003

First SFBC Science Fiction Printing: March 2003

Published by arrangement with:
Tor Books
Tom Doherty Associates, LLC
175 Fifth Avenue
New York, NY 10010

Visit The SFBC online at *http://www.sfbc.com*
Visit Tor online at *http://www.tor.com*

Tor® is a registered trademark of Tom Doherty Associates, LLC.

ISBN 0-7394-3215-X

PRINTED IN THE UNITED STATES OF AMERICA

Contents

SANTIAGO

To Carol, as always

And to my agent, Eleanor Wood,
For advice, encouragement, and money

Table of Contents

PROLOGUE

They say his father was a comet and his mother a cosmic wind, that he juggles planets as if they were feathers and wrestles with black holes just to work up an appetite. They say he never sleeps, and that his eyes burn brighter than a nova, and that his shout can level mountains.

They call him Santiago.

Far out on the Galactic Rim, at the very edge of the Outer Frontier, there is a world called Silverblue. It is a water world, with just a handful of islands dotting the placid ocean that covers its surface. If you stand on the very largest island and look into the night sky, you can see almost all of the Milky Way, a huge twinkling river of stars that seems to flow through half the universe.

And if you stand on the western shore of the island during the daytime, with your back to the water, you will see a grass-covered knoll. Atop the knoll are seventeen white crosses, each bearing the name of a good man or woman who thought to colonize this gentle world.

And beneath each name is the same legend, repeated seventeen times:

Killed by Santiago.

Toward the core of the galaxy, where the stars press together so closely that night is as bright as day, there is a world called Valkyrie. It is an outpost world, a place of ramshackle Tradertowns filled with dingy bars and hotels and brothels, where the explorers and miners and traders of the Inner Frontier congregate to eat and drink and embellish a few tall tales.

The largest of Valkyrie's Tradertowns, which isn't really very large, also has a postal station that stores subspace messages the way the postal stations of old used to store written mail. Sometimes the messages are held for as long as three or four years, and frequently they are routed even closer to the galactic core, but eventually most of them are picked up.

And in this postal station, there is a wall that is covered by the names and holographs of criminals who are currently thought to be on the Inner Frontier, which tends to make the station very popular with bounty hunters. There are always twenty outlaws displayed, never more, never less, and next to each name is a price. Some of these names remain in place for a week, some for a month, a handful for a year.

Only three names have ever been displayed for more than five years. Two of them are no longer there.

The third is Santiago, and there is no holograph of him.

On the colony world of Saint Joan, there is a native humanoid race known as the Swale. There are no longer any colonists; they have all departed.

Near the equator of Saint Joan, very close to where the colony once lived, there is a blackened swath of land almost ten miles long and half a mile wide, on which nothing will ever grow again. No colonist ever reported it, or if any of them did, the report has long since been misplaced by one of the Democracy's thirty billion bureaucrats—but if you go to Saint Joan and ask the Swale what caused the blackened patch of ground, they will cross themselves (for the colonists were a religious lot, and *very* evangelical) and tell you that it is the Mark of Santiago.

Even on the agricultural world of Ranchero, where there has never been a crime, not even a petty robbery, his name is not unknown. He is thought to be eleven feet three inches tall, with wild, unruly orange hair and immense black fangs that have dug into his lips and now protrude through them. And when youngsters misbehave, their parents have merely to hint at the number of naughty children Santiago has eaten for breakfast, and order is immediately restored.

Wandering minstrels sing songs about him on Minotaur and Theseus, the twin worlds that circle Sigma Draconis, and always he is portrayed as being exactly 217 years old, taller than a belltower, and broader than a barn, a hard-drinking, womanizing Prince of Thieves, who differs from Robin Hood (another of their favorites) primarily in that he takes from rich and poor alike and gives only to himself. His adventures are legion, ranging from his epic hand-to-hand struggle with a chlorine-breathing Gorgon to the morning he went down to hell and spat full in Satan's burning eye, and rarely is there a day that does not witness the addition of a few new stanzas to the ever-evolving "Ballad of Santiago."

And on Deluros VIII, the huge capital world of the race of Man, the nerve center of the Democracy, there are eleven governmental departments and 1,306 men and women charged with the task of finding and terminating Santiago. They doubt that Santiago is his given name, they suspect that some of the crimes attributed to him were committed by others, they are almost certain that somewhere in their files they possess his photograph or holograph but have not yet matched it with its proper identity—and that is the sum total of their knowledge of him.

Five hundred reports come to them daily, two thousand leads are followed up each year, munificent rewards have been posted on half a million worlds, agents are sent out armed with money and everything that money can buy, and still those eleven departments exist. They have outlived the last three administrations; they will continue to survive until their function has been fulfilled.

Silverblue, Valkyrie, Saint Joan, Ranchero, Minotaur, Theseus, Deluros VIII: interesting and evocative worlds all.

But an even more interesting world in the strange tapestry of Santiago's life is the outpost world of Keepsake, at the heart of the Inner Frontier; for Keepsake is the home, at least temporarily, of Sebastian Nightingale Cain, who dislikes his middle name, his profession, and his life—not necessarily in that order. He has fought what he believes to have been the good fight many times over, and he has never won. Not much excites his imagination anymore, and even less surprises him. He has no friends and few associates, nor does he seek any.

Sebastian Nightingale Cain is by almost every criterion a nondescript and unremarkable man, and yet our story must begin with him, for he is destined to play a major role in the saga of the man known only as Santiago. . . .

Part 1

The Songbird's Book

1.

Giles Sans Pitié is a spinning wheel,
With the eye of a hawk and a fist made of steel.
He'll drink a whole gallon while holding his breath,
And wherever he goes his companion is Death.

There never was a history written about the Inner Frontier, so Black Orpheus took it upon himself to set one to music. His name wasn't really Orpheus (though he *was* black). In fact, rumor had it that he had been an aquaculturist back in the Deluros system before he fell in love. The girl's name was Eurydice, and he followed her out to the stars, and since he had left all his property behind, he had nothing to give her but his music, so he took the name of Black Orpheus and spent most of his days composing love songs and sonnets to her. Then she died, and he decided to stay on the Inner Frontier, and he began writing an epic ballad about the traders and hunters and outlaws and misfits that he came across. In fact, you didn't officially stop being a tenderfoot or a tourist until the day he added a stanza or two about you to the song.

Anyway, Giles Sans Pitié made quite an impression on him, because he appears in nine different verses, which is an awful lot when you're being the Homer for five hundred worlds. Probably it was the steel hand that did it. No one knew how he'd lost his real one, but he showed up on the Frontier one day with a polished steel fist at the end of his left arm, announced that he was the best bounty hunter ever born, foaled, whelped, or hatched, and proceeded to prove that he wasn't too far from wrong. Like most bounty hunters, he only touched down on outpost worlds when he wasn't working, and like most bounty hunters, he had a pretty regular route that he followed. Which was how he came to be on Keepsake, in the Tradertown of Moritat, in Gentry's Emporium, pounding on the long wooden bar with his steel fist and demanding service.

Old Geronimo Gentry, who had spent thirty years prospecting the worlds of the Inner Frontier before he chucked it all and opened a tavern and whorehouse on Moritat, where he carefully sampled every product before offering it to the public, walked over with a fresh bottle of Altairian rum, then held it back as Giles Sans Pitié reached for it.

"Tab's gettin' pretty high," he commented meaningfully.

The bounty hunter slapped a wad of bills down on the bar.

"Maria Theresa dollars," noted Gentry, examining them approvingly and relinquishing the bottle. "Wherever'd you pick 'em up?"

"The Corvus system."

"Took care of a little business there, did you?" said Gentry, amused.

Giles Sans Pitié smiled humorlessly. "A little."

He reached inside his shirt and withdrew three Wanted posters of the Suliman brothers, which until that morning had been on the post office wall. Each poster had a large red X scratched across it.

"All three of 'em?"

The bounty hunter nodded.

"You shoot 'em, or did you use *that*?" asked Gentry, pointing toward Giles Sans Pitié's steel fist.

"Yes."

"Yes *what*?"

Giles Sans Pitié held up his metal hand. "Yes, I shot them or I used this."

Gentry shrugged. "Goin' out again soon?"

"In the next few days."

"Where to this time?"

"That's nobody's business but mine," said the bounty hunter.

"Just thought I might offer some friendly advice," said Gentry.

"Such as?"

"If you're thinking of going to Praeteep Four, forget it. The Songbird just got back from there."

"You mean Cain?"

Gentry nodded. "Had a lot of money, so I'd have to guess that he found what he went looking for."

The bounty hunter frowned. "I'm going to have to have a little talk with him," he said. "The Praeteep system's got a Keep Out sign posted on it."

"Oh?" said Gentry. "Since when?"

"Since I put it up," said Giles Sans Pitié firmly. "And I won't have some rival headhunter doing his poaching there and picking it clean." He paused. "Where can I find him?"

"Right here."

Giles Sans Pitié looked around the room. A silver-haired gambler on a winning streak, decked out in bright new clothes made from some glittering metallic fabric, stood at the far end of the bar; a young woman with melancholy eyes sat alone at a table in the corner; and scattered around the large, dimly lit tavern were some two dozen other men and women, in pairs and groups, some conversing in low tones, others sitting in silence.

"I don't see him," announced the bounty hunter.

"It's early yet," replied Gentry. "He'll be along."

"What makes you think so?"

"I've got the only booze and the only sportin' ladies in Moritat. Where do *you* think he's gonna go?"

"There are a lot of worlds out there."

"True," admitted Gentry. "But people get tired of worlds after a while. Ask *me*—I know."

"Then what are you doing on the Frontier?"

"People get tired of people, too. There's a lot less of 'em out here—and I got me my fancy ladies to cheer me up if ever I get to feelin' lonely." He paused. " 'Course, if you want to hear the story of my life, you're gonna have to buy a couple of bottles of my best drinkin' stuff. Then you and me, we'll mosey on out to one of the back rooms and I'll start with chapter one."

The bounty hunter reached out for the bottle. "I think I can live without it," he said.

"You'll be missing out on one helluva good story," said Gentry. "I done a lot of interesting things. Seen sights even a killer like you ain't likely ever to see."

"Some other time."

"Your loss," said Gentry with a shrug. "You gonna want a glass with that?"

"Not necessary," said Giles Sans Pitié, lifting the bottle and taking a long swallow. When he was through, he wiped his mouth with the back of his hand. "How long before he gets here?"

"You got time for a quick one, if that's what you mean," said Gentry. "Just give me a minute to check and see which of my frail flowers ain't working this minute." Suddenly he turned to the doorway. "Whoops! Here he is now. Guess you'll have to go loveless a little longer." He waved his hand. "How're you doin', Songbird?"

The tall, lean man, his face angular and almost gaunt, his eyes dark and world-weary, approached the bar. His jacket and pants were a nondescript brown, their many pockets filled with shapeless bulges that could mean almost anything on the Frontier. Only his boots stood out, not because they were new, but rather because they were so demonstrably old, obviously carefully tended yet unable to hold a polish.

"My name's Cain," said the newcomer. "You know that."

"Well, it ain't what they call you these days."

"It's what *you'll* call me if you want my business," replied Cain.

"But Black Orpheus, now, he's got you all written up as the Songbird," persisted Gentry.

"I don't sing, I'm not a bird, and I don't much care what some half-baked folksinger writes about me."

Gentry shrugged. "Have it your way—and while we're on the subject, what else'll you have?"

"He'll have Altairian rum, like me," interjected Giles Sans Pitié.

"I will?" asked Cain, turning to him.

"My treat." The bounty hunter held up his bottle. "Come on over to a table and join me, Sebastian Cain."

Cain watched him walk across the room for a moment, then shrugged and followed him.

"I hear you had pretty good luck on Praeteep Four," said Giles Sans Pitié when both men had seated themselves.

"Luck had nothing to do with it," replied Cain, leaning back comfortably on his chair. "I understand you didn't do too badly yourself."

"Not so. I had to cheat."

"I don't think I follow you."

"I had to shoot the third one." Giles Sans Pitié held up his steel fist. "I like to take them with *this*." He paused. "Did your man give you much trouble?"

"Some," said Cain noncommittally.

"Have to chase him far?"

"A bit."

"You're sure not the most expansive raconteur I've ever run across," chuckled Giles Sans Pitié.

Cain shrugged. "Talk is cheap."

"Not always. Suliman Hari offered me thirty thousand credits to let him live."

"And?"

"I thanked him for his offer, explained that the price on his head was up to fifty thousand, and gave him a faceful of metal."

"And of course you didn't then take thirty thousand credits off his body without reporting it," said Cain sardonically.

Giles Sans Pitié frowned. "The son of a bitch only had two thousand on him," he growled righteously.

"I guess there's just no honor among thieves."

"None. I can't get over the bastard lying to me!" He paused. "So tell me, Cain—who will you be going out after next?"

Cain smiled. "Professional secret. You know better than to ask."

"True," agreed Giles Sans Pitié. "But everyone's allowed a breach of etiquette now and then. For example, you know better than to make a kill in the Praeteep system, but you did it anyway."

"The man I was hunting went there," replied Cain calmly. "No disrespect intended, but I wasn't going to let four months' work go down the drain just because you think you own the deed to an entire solar system."

"I *opened* that system," said Giles Sans Pitié. "Named every planet in it." He paused. "Still, it's an acceptable answer. I forgive you your trespass."

"I don't recall asking for absolution," said Cain.

"Just the same, it's freely given. *This* time," he added ominously. "But it would be a good idea for you to remember that there are rules out here on the Frontier."

"Oh? I hadn't noticed any."

"Nevertheless, they exist—and they're made by the people who can enforce them."

"I'll keep it in mind."

"See that you do."

"Or you'll brain me with your metal hand?" asked Cain.

"It's a possibility."

Cain smiled.

"What's so funny?" demanded Giles Sans Pitié.

"You're a bounty hunter."

"So?"

"Bounty hunters don't kill people for free. Who's going to pay you to kill me?"

"I've got to protect what's mine," replied Giles Sans Pitié seriously. "I just want to be sure that we understand each other: if you go poaching on my territory again, we're going to come to blows." He slammed his metal hand down on the table, putting a large dent in it. "Mine are usually harder."

"I imagine they are," said Cain.

"Then you'll steer clear of Praeteep?"

"I'm not aware of any pressing business engagements there."

"That's not exactly the answer I was looking for."

"I'd suggest you settle for it," said Cain. "It's the best you're going to get."

Giles Sans Pitié stared at him for a moment, then shrugged. "It could be years before anyone hides there again, maybe even longer. I suppose there's no law that says we can't behave cordially in the meantime."

"I'm all for living in peace with my fellow man," said Cain agreeably.

Giles Sans Pitié looked amused. "You picked a mighty strange profession for a man who feels that way."

"Perhaps."

"Well, shall we talk?"

"What about?"

"What about?" repeated Giles Sans Pitié mockingly. "What do two bounty hunters *ever* talk about when they meet over a bottle of rum?"

And so they fell to discussing Santiago.

They spoke of the worlds where he was most recently thought to have been, and the crimes he was most recently thought to have committed. Both had heard the rumor that he had robbed a mining colony on Bemor VIII; both discounted it. Both also had heard that a caravan of unmanned cargo ships had been plundered in the Antares region; Cain thought it might well be the work of Santiago, while his companion felt he was far more likely to have been on Doradus IV at the time, masterminding a triple assassination. They exchanged information about the planets they themselves had been to without finding any trace of him, and of the other bounty hunters they had encountered who had added still more planets to the list.

"Who's after him now?" asked Giles Sans Pitié when their tallies had been completed.

"Everyone."

"I mean, who most recently?"

"I hear the Angel has moved into the area," answered Cain.

"What makes you think he's come for Santiago?"

Cain merely stared at him.

"Stupid remark," said Giles Sans Pitié. "Forget I made it." He paused. "The Angel's supposed to be just about the best."

"So they say."

"I thought he worked the Outer Frontier, somewhere way out on the Rim."

Cain nodded. "I guess he decided Santiago's not there."

"I can name you a million places Santiago *isn't*," said Giles Sans Pitié. "Why do you suppose he thinks he's on the Inner Frontier?"

Cain shrugged.

"Do you think he's got a source?" persisted Giles Sans Pitié.

"Anything's possible."

"It's more than possible," he said after a moment's consideration. "He wouldn't move his base of operations halfway across the galaxy if he didn't have hard information. What planet is he working out of?"

"How many worlds are there out there?" replied Cain with a shrug. "Take your choice."

Giles Sans Pitié frowned. "Still, he might know something worth listening to."

"What makes you think he'll talk to you, even if you find him?"

"Because the one thing bounty hunters never lie about is Santiago; you know that. As long as he stays alive, he makes all of us look bad."

"Maybe the Angel does things differently where he comes from," suggested Cain.

"Then I'll just have to explain the ground rules to him," said Giles Sans Pitié.

"I wish you luck."

"Interested in throwing in with me until we catch up with the Angel?"

"I work alone," said Cain.

"Just as well," said Giles Sans Pitié, suddenly remembering his rum and taking a long swallow of it. "Where did you hear about him?"

"In the Meritonia system."

"I think I'll head out that way later this week," said Giles Sans Pitié, rising to his feet. "It's been an interesting conversation, Cain."

"Thanks for the rum," said Cain wryly, staring at the empty bottle.

"Any time," laughed his companion. "And you *will* make an effort to keep out of the Praeteep system from now on, won't you?" He flexed his steel fist. "I'd hate to have to give you an object lesson about trespassing."

"Would you?"

"Not really," was the frank answer.

Cain made no reply, and a moment later Giles San Pitié placed the empty bottle on the bar, left enough money to cover another one he ordered for Cain, promised Gentry he'd be back to sample some nonalcoholic wares later in the evening, and walked out into the hot, humid night air of Moritat in search of some dinner.

Gentry finished serving the girl with the melancholy eyes, then brought the bottle over to Cain's table.

"What is it?" asked Cain, staring at the clear liquid.

"Something they brew out Altair way," replied the old man. "Tastes kind of like gin."

"I don't like gin."

"I know," replied Gentry with a chuckle. "That's why I'm just dead certain you're gonna invite me to sit down with you and help you drink it."

Cain sighed. "Have a seat, old man."

"Thank you. Don't mind if I do." He lowered himself carefully to a chair, uncorked the bottle, and took a swallow. "Good stuff, if I say so myself."

"You could save a hell of a lot of money by not supplying glasses," remarked Cain. "Nobody around here seems to use them."

"Savin' money ain't one of my problems," replied Gentry. "And from what I hear, makin' it ain't one of yours."

Cain said nothing, and the old man took another swallow and continued speaking.

"Did old Giles Without Pity warn you off the Praeteep system?" he asked.

Cain nodded.

"Gonna pay him any heed?"

"Until the next time I have business there," replied Cain.

The old man laughed. "Good for you, Songbird! Old Steelfist is gettin' a little big for his britches these days."

"I'm getting tired of telling you what my name is," said Cain irritably.

"If you didn't want to be a legend, you shouldn't have come out here. Two hundred years from now that's the only name people'll know you by."

"Two hundred years from now I won't have to listen to them."

"Besides," continued Gentry, "Songbird ain't on any Wanted posters. I seen Sebastian Cain on a flock of 'em."

"That was a long time ago."

"Don't go gettin' defensive about it," chuckled the old man. "I seen posters on just about all you bounty hunters at one time or another. Ain't no skin off my ass. Hell, if Santiago himself walked in the door and asked for one of my sportin' gals, I'd trot him out the prettiest one I've got."

"For all you know, he already has," remarked Cain.

"Not a chance," said Gentry. "He ain't that hard to spot."

"Eleven feet three inches, with orange hair?" asked Cain with an amused smile.

"You start huntin' for a man who looks like *that* and you're going to be out here a long, long time."

"What do *you* think he looks like?"

The old man took a small swallow from the bottle.

"Don't know," he admitted. "Do know one thing, though. Know he's got a scar shaped like this"—he traced a crooked S on the table—"on the back of his right hand."

"Sure he does."

"Truth!" said the old man vigorously. "I know a man who saw him."

"Nobody's seen him," replied Cain. "Or at least, nobody who's seen him knew it was him."

"That's all *you* know about it," said Gentry. "Man I used to run with spent a couple of weeks in jail with him."

Cain looked bored. "Santiago's never been arrested. If he had been, we'd *all* know what he looked like."

"They didn't know it was him."

"Then how come your friend knew?"

" 'Cause Santiago's gang broke him out, and one of 'em called him by name."

"Bunk."

"Here I am, offerin' to do you a favor, and you turn your nose up at it," said Gentry. "Damned good thing for you I'm an old man who ain't got the wherewithall to give you a thrashing for insulting me like that."

"What favor?"

"I thought maybe you might be interested in knowing who my friend is and where you can find him."

"There are half a dozen bounty hunters who frequent this place," said Cain. "Why give it to me?"

"Well, now, *give* ain't exactly the term I had in mind," answered Gentry with a grin. "Name like that, name of a man who actually spent some time with Santiago, it ought to be worth a little something now, shouldn't it?"

"Maybe."

There was a momentary silence.

"I didn't hear no cash offer yet."

"Let's get back to my question," said Cain. "Why *me*?"

"Oh, it ain't just you," said Gentry. "Sold it to Barnaby Wheeler a couple of months ago, but I heard on the grapevine that he got killed chasing down some fugitive or other. And I offered it to Peacemaker MacDougal just last week, but he didn't want to come up with no money. And I'll see if I can't tempt old Steelfist with it before he takes advantage of one of my poor innocents tonight." He smiled. "I got to be fair to *all* my customers."

"People have been after Santiago for thirty years or more," said Cain. "If you have any information worth selling, why did you wait until now to put it on the market?"

"I ain't got anything against Santiago," said the old man. "He ain't ever done me any harm. Besides, the longer he stays free, the longer you guys'll stay on the Frontier lookin' for him, and the longer you stay out here, the more money you'll spend at Gentry's Emporium."

"Then what caused this change of heart?"

"Hear tell the Angel has moved in. Wouldn't want no outsider picking up the bounty fee."

"What makes you think he will?" asked Cain.

"You know what they say about him," replied Gentry. "He's the best. I'll bet you Black Orpheus gives him a good twenty verses when he finally gets around to meetin' him. So," said the old man, taking yet another swig, "I'm hedging my bets as best I can. The Angel collects that money, he'll be back on the Rim before he has a chance to spend it. But if *you* get it, you'll spend a goodly chunk of it on Keepsake."

"If I don't retire."

"Oh, you won't retire," said Gentry with assurance. "Men like you and Sans Pitié and the Angel, you like killing too damned much to quit. It's in your blood, like wanderlust in a young buck."

"I don't like killing," replied Cain.

"Gonna give me that bounty hunter guff about how you only kill people for money?" said the old man with a sarcastic laugh.

"No."

"That makes you the first honest one I've met. How many men did you kill for free before you found out there was gold in it—two? Three?"

"More than I hope you can imagine," replied Cain.

"Soldier?"

Cain paused before answering. "I thought so once. I was wrong."

"What the hell does *that* mean?"

"Never mind, old man." Suddenly Cain sat erect in his chair. "All right—how much do you want for the name?"

"What kind of currency can you lay your hands on?"

"What kind do you want?"

"Credits'll do, I suppose," replied Gentry. "Though I'd be real interested in Bonaparte francs or Maria Theresa dollars if you got any."

"I haven't seen a Bonaparte franc in ten years," said Cain. "I don't think they're in circulation anymore."

"I hear tell they're still using 'em in the Binder system."

"Let's make it credits."

The old man did a quick mental calculation. "I think ten thousand would do me just fine."

"For the name of a man who might or might not have seen Santiago ten or twenty years ago?" Cain shook his head. "That's too much."

"Not for a man like you," said Gentry. "I saw the poster for the body you brought in. I know how much you got for it."

"And what if this man is dead, or if it turns out he didn't see Santiago after all?"

"Then you got a free pass to fertilize my flowers for a full month."

"I visited your garden last night," said Cain. "It needs weeding."

"What are you quibbling about?" demanded Gentry. "How long have you been on the Frontier, Cain?"

"Eleven years."

"In all that time, have you ever met anyone who's seen Santiago? Here I am offering you what you ain't never found before, for maybe a tenth of what you just picked up on Praeteep, and you're haggling like some Dabih fur trader! If you're gonna just sit there and insult the most beautiful blossoms on the Frontier and haggle with an old man who ain't got the stamina to haggle back, we ain't going to be able to do no business."

Cain stared at him for a moment, then spoke.

"I'll tell you what, old man. I'll give you twenty thousand."

"There's a catch," said Gentry suspiciously.

"There's a condition," replied Cain. "You don't supply the name to anyone else."

Gentry frowned. "Ever?"

"For six months."

"Make it four."

"Deal," said Cain. "And if you're lying, may God have more mercy on your soul than *I* will."

"Ain't got no reason to lie. Only two more of you fellers due in here in the next four months, which means one of 'em's probably dead, and there's only a fifty-fifty chance the other'd come up with the money. Not everyone makes out as well as you and Sans Pitié."

"All right. Where do I find this man?"

"I ain't seen no money yet."

Cain pulled out a sheaf of bills, peeled off the top twenty, and placed them on the table. Gentry picked them up one at a time, held each up to the light, and finally nodded his head and placed them in his pocket.

"Ever hear of a world named Port Étrange?"

Cain shook his head. "Where is it?"

"It's the seventh planet in the Bellermaine system. That's where he'll be."

"And his name?"

"Stern."

"How do I locate him?"

"Just pass the word you're looking for him. *He'll* find *you*."

"What's he like?" asked Cain. •

"A real sweet feller, once you get used to a couple of his little peculiarities."

"Such as?"

"Well, he drinks too much and he cheats at cards, and he ain't real fond of people or animals or aliens, and he out-and-out hates priests and women, and he's been known to have an occasional disagreement with the constabularies. But taken all in all, he's no worse than most that you find out here, and probably better'n some."

"Should I use your name?"

"It ought to get him to sit up and take notice," said Gentry. "When are you planning on leaving?"

"Tonight," said Cain, getting to his feet.

"Damn!" said Gentry. "If I'd of known you were that anxious, I could've held out for thirty!"

"I'm not anxious. I just don't have any reason to stay here."

"I got seven absolutely splendid reasons, each and every one personally selected and trained by Moritat's very favorite son, namely me."

"Maybe next time around."

"You got something better to spend it on?"

"That depends on whether you told me the truth or not," said Cain, walking to the door. Suddenly he stopped and turned to Gentry. "By the way, I assume your friend Stern is going to want to be paid for this?"

"I imagine so. Man sells his soul to the devil, he spends the rest of his life trying to stockpile enough money to buy it back." Gentry chuckled with amusement. "Have fun, Songbird."

"That's not my name."

"Tell you what," said Gentry. "You bring in the head of Santiago, and I'll hold a gun to old Orpheus until he gets it right."

"You've got yourself a deal," promised Cain.

2.

He's Jonathan Jeremy Jacobar Stern,
He's got lust in his heart, and money to burn;
He's too old to change, and too wild to learn,
Is Jonathan Jeremy Jacobar Stern.

They say that Black Orpheus caught Stern on an off day, that in point of fact Stern never stopped changing and learning, until he'd changed so much that nobody knew him any longer. He began life as the son of a miner and a whore, and before he was done he'd set himself up as king of the Bellermaine system. In between, he learned how to gamble and did a pretty fair job of it; he learned how to steal and became more than proficient; he learned how to kill and did a bit of bounty hunting on the side; and somewhere along the way he learned the most important lesson of all, which was that a king with no heirs had better never turn his back on anybody.

Nobody knew why he hated priests; rumor had it that the first time he'd gone to jail it was a priest who turned him in. Another legend held that he'd once trusted a couple of priests to keep an eye on his holdings while he was fleeing from the authorities, and when he'd finally come back there'd been nothing waiting for him but a note telling him to repent.

It wasn't all that difficult to figure out why he hated women. He grew up in a whorehouse, and the women he met once he went out on his own weren't much different from the ones he'd known all his life. He was a man of enormous appetites who couldn't leave them alone and couldn't convince himself that their interest in him wasn't as cold and calculating as his interest in them.

A lot of people whispered that that was the real reason he'd set up shop on Port Étrange, that since he couldn't control his passion for women he'd decided to do without them and had hunted up a world with a humanoid race that willingly allowed him to commit terrible crimes of pleasure for which nobody had yet created any words.

Port Étrange itself had a long and varied history. Originally a mining world, it had since been a glittering vacation spa, then a low-security penal colony, and finally a deserted ghost world. Then Stern had moved in, set up headquarters in a once luxurious hotel, and turned a small section of the human habitation into a Tradertown, while allowing the remainder to linger in a state of disrepair and decay. Despite reasonably fertile fields which sustained the native population, the citizens of the Tradertown imported all their food and drink from a pair of nearby agricultural colonies. When the men began outnumbering the women, they imported the latter, too, until Stern put a stop to it.

All this Cain learned during his first hour on Port Étrange. He had landed his ship at the local spaceport—only huge worlds like Deluros VIII and Lodin XI possessed orbiting hangars and shuttle service for planetbound travelers—and rented a room at the larger of the two functioning hotels, then descended to the ground-floor tavern he'd spotted on the way in.

It was crowded, and despite the chrome tables and handcrafted chairs—leftovers from the hotel's halcyon days of glory—it felt as dingy and seamy as any other Tradertown bar. The only chair available was at a small table that was occupied by a short, slender man who sported a shock of unruly red hair.

"Mind if I sit down?" asked Cain.

"Be my guest," said the man. He stared at Cain. "You new around here?"

"Yes. I just got in." Cain glanced around the room. "I'm looking for somebody. I wonder if you can point him out to me?"

"He's not here now."

"You don't know who I'm looking for," said Cain.

"Well, if it isn't Jonathan Stern, we've got a hell of a news story breaking here," said the man with a chuckle. "He's the only person anyone ever comes to Port Étrange to see."

"It's Stern," said Cain.

"Well, I suppose I can pass the word. You got a name?"

"Cain. Tell him Geronimo Gentry sent me."

"Pleased to meet you, Cain," said the man, extending a lean white hand. "I'm Terwilliger. Halfpenny Terwilliger," he added as if the name was expected to mean something. He watched Cain for a reaction, discerned none, and got up. "Back in a minute."

Terwilliger walked over to the bar, said something to the bartender, and then returned to the table.

"Okay," he said. "He knows you're here."

"When can I see him?"

"When he's ready."

"How soon will that be?"

Halfpenny Terwilliger laughed. "That all depends. Does he owe Gentry money?"

"I don't think so."

"Then it'll probably be sooner rather than later." He pulled out a deck of cards. "Care for a little game of chance while you're waiting?"

"I'd rather have a little information about Stern."

"I don't doubt it," said Terwilliger. "Tell you what. You bet with money, I'll bet with pieces of Stern's life. I'll match every credit with a story."

"Why don't I just pay you twenty credits for what I want to know and be done with it?" suggested Cain.

"Because I'm a gambler, not a salesman," came the answer.

"At a credit a bet, you're not likely to become a very rich one," observed Cain.

Terwilliger smiled. "I got into my first card game with one New Scotland halfpenny. I was worth two million pounds before it was over. That's how I got my name." He paused. "Of course, I lost it all the next week, but still, it was fun while it lasted, and no one else ever had a run of luck like that one. Been trying to do it again ever since."

"How long ago was that?"

"Oh, maybe a dozen years," said Terwilliger with another smile. "I still remember how it felt, though—like the first time I was ever with a woman, except that it lasted longer: six days and five nights. That's why I always start small—out of respect for times past. If you want to raise the stakes later, we can."

"If I raise the stakes, what can you bet to match it?"

Terwilliger scratched his head. "Well, I suppose I can start betting rumors instead of facts. They're a lot more interesting, anyway—especially if they're about the *fali*."

"What's a *fali*?" asked Cain.

"It's what the natives call themselves. I don't suppose it's the best-kept secret in the galaxy that our friend Stern's got a couple of tastes that are just a bit out of the ordinary."

"Let's stick to facts for the time being," said Cain. He nodded toward the cards. "It's your deal."

They played and talked for more than an hour, at the end of which Cain knew a little bit more about Stern, and Terwilliger was some forty credits richer.

"You know, you still haven't told me why you want to see him," remarked the gambler.

"I need some information."

"Who do you plan to kill?" asked Terwilliger pleasantly.

"What makes you think I want to kill anyone?"

"You've got that look about you. I'm a gambler, remember? My job is reading faces. Your face says you're a bounty hunter."

"What if I told you I was a journalist?" asked Cain.

"I'd tell you I believed you," replied Terwilliger. "I don't want no bounty hunter getting mad at me."

Cain laughed. "Can you tell anything from Stern's face?"

"Just that he's been with the *fali* too long. Not much human left in it."

"What do these *fali* look like?" asked Cain.

"Either pretty good or pretty strange, depending."

"Depending on what?"

"On how long you've been alone," answered Terwilliger.

"You still haven't told me what they look like."

Terwilliger grinned and ruffled the cards. "Shall we up the stakes a little?"

Cain shook his head. "They're not worth more to me than Stern is."

"They might be, when I tell you what they do."

"Hearsay?"

"Experience."

Cain cocked an eyebrow. "I thought you disapproved of them."

"Anybody's allowed to try something new once or twice, just to get the feel of it," explained Terwilliger. "What I object to is addiction, not experimentation."

"I don't plan to be here long enough to do either," said Cain. "You can put the cards away."

"Oh, we can always find a little something to wager about," said Terwilliger. "For fifty credits a hand, I could tell you where to find the Suliman brothers."

"You're too late. They were taken a week ago."

"All three?"

Cain nodded.

"Damn!" said Terwilliger. "Well, for a hundred, I might tell you about some competition that's moved into the area."

"I know about the Angel."

"News sure travels fast," commented Terwilliger ruefully.

"Tell you what," said Cain. "I'll play for a thousand a hand if you have any information about Santiago."

"You and five hundred other guys." The gambler shook his head. "It beats me how he can still be free after all these years with so many people looking for him."

Just then the bartender walked across the room and came to a stop in front of their table.

"Are you Cain?" he asked.

"Yes."

"He wants you."

"Where do I find him?" asked Cain.

"I'll show you the way," offered Terwilliger.

The bartender nodded and returned to his duties.

"Follow me," said the gambler, getting to his feet.

Cain stood up and left a few bills on the table.

They walked out through a side door, across the dusty road that had once been a major thoroughfare, and into the smaller of Port Étrange's two functioning hotels. Terwilliger led him through a lobby that had once been quite elegant but was now showing the signs of age and neglect: sleek chrome pillars were now tarnished, the ever-changing choreopattern of colored lights was out of synch with the atonal music, the front door remained dilated for almost a full minute after they passed through it.

They approached a bank of elevators and walked to the last one in line. Terwilliger summoned it with a low command.

"This'll take you right to him," he announced.

"Has he got a room number?"

"He's got the whole damned floor. Take one step out and you're in the middle of his parlor."

"Thanks," said Cain, stepping into the elevator as it arrived. As the doors closed behind him he realized that he didn't know the floor number, but then the elevator began ascending swiftly and he decided that it only went to one floor.

When it came to a stop, he emerged into a palatial penthouse. It was fully fifty feet by sixty, and filled to overflowing with objets d'art gathered—or plundered—from all across the galaxy. In the center of the room was a sunken circular tub with platinum fixtures, and sitting in the steaming water was an emaciated man with sunken cheeks and dark, watery eyes. His narrow arms were sprawled over the edges of the tub, and Cain noticed that his fingers were covered by truly magnificent rings. He smoked a large cigar that had somehow avoided becoming waterlogged.

Standing on each side of the tub were a pair of humanoid aliens, both obviously female. Their skins, covered with a slick secretion that may or may not have been natural, glistened under the lights of the apartment. Their arms seemed supple and boneless, their legs slender and strangely jointed. Each had a round, expressive face, with a generous, very red triangular mouth and pink eyes that were little more than angular slits. Both were nude and were devoid of any body hair. They had no breasts, but their genitalia, thus exposed, seemed close to human. There was a supple, alien grace to them, which Cain found fascinating and mildly repugnant. Neither of them seemed to notice him at all.

"You're staring, Mr. Cain," said the man in the tub.

"I'm sorry," said Cain. "I had heard about the *fali*, but I hadn't seen them before."

"Nice, useful pets," said the man, reaching up and giving a friendly pat to a bare *fali* buttock. "About as bright as a potted plant, but *very* pleasant in their way." He took a puff of his cigar. "I understand that you wish to see me."

"If you're Stern."

"Jonathan Jeremy Jacobar Stern, at your service," he said. "Is this going to take long?"

"I hope not."

"What a shame," he said with mock regret. "If it was, I'd invite you to join me. There is absolutely nothing like sitting in warm water to relax a man and help him shed the cares of the day. I'll be with you in just a moment." He turned to one of the *fali* and extended his arm. "Give me a boost up, my pretty."

She reached down, grabbed his hand, and pulled him to his feet, while her companion walked to a closet and returned shortly with a robe.

"Thank you," he said, slipping the robe on. "Now I want both of you to stand over there and not bother us for a while." He pointed to a spot near the farthest wall, and both *fali* immediately walked over to it and stood motionless.

"They seem very obedient," remarked Cain as Stern led him to a grouping of chairs and couches.

"Obedient and docile," agreed Stern, sprawling on a couch and staring at them with unconcealed desire.

"That oil on their skins—is it normal?"

"Why should you suppose that it isn't?"

Cain shrugged. "It just seems rather unusual."

"It is," replied Stern, smiling at the *fali*. "It smells like the finest perfume." He turned to Cain. "Go over and experience it for yourself."

"I'll take your word for it."

"As you wish," said Stern with a shrug. "It *feels* exquisite, as well—soft and sensual. Actually, I'm convinced that it's a secondary sexual characteristic. It doesn't do much for Men, of course," he added with marked insincerity, "but I imagine it drives their boyfriends right out of their minds. Seductive odor, sensual feel." He stared admiringly at them again. "It makes them look like a pair of alien mermaids emerging from the water." Suddenly he tore his gaze away from them and turned back to Cain. "So Geronimo Gentry sent you here?"

"Yes."

"I thought he'd be dead by now."

"Not quite," said Cain, finally taking a seat.

"How is he getting along?"

"He's got a bar and whorehouse out on Keepsake," replied Cain. "I guess he's doing all right. Talks too much, though."

"He always did." Stern paused. "Why did he send you here?"

"He told me that you might have some information I need."

"Very likely I do. I know an inordinate number of things. Did he also tell you that I'm not a charitable institution?"

"If he hadn't, I would have figured it out after seeing some of your trinkets," said Cain, nodding toward a number of alien artifacts that were prominently displayed.

"I'm a collector," said Stern with a broad smile.

"So I gathered."

"You haven't yet told me what business you're in, Mr. Cain."

"I'm a collector, too," replied Cain.

"Really?" said Stern, suddenly more interested. "And what is it that you collect?"

"People."

"There's a good market for them," said Stern. "But unlike *my* collection, they don't increase in value."

"There's one who does."

"So you want to know about Santiago." It was not a question.

Cain nodded. "That's what I'm here for. You're the only person who's seen him."

Stern laughed in amusement. "His organization spans the entire galaxy. Don't you think any of *them* ever see him?"

"Then let me amend my statement," said Cain. "You're the only person *I* know who's seen him."

"That's probably true," agreed Stern pleasantly. His cigar went out and he snapped his fingers. One of the *fali* immediately came over with a lighter and relit it. "That's my girl," he said, giving her boneless hand an affectionate squeeze. She wriggled all over with delight like a puppy, then returned to her position across the room. "A wonderful pet," commented Stern. "Faithful, adoring, and totally unable to utter a sound—three qualities I never found in any woman of my acquaintance." He paused and stared fondly at her. "What a sweet, mindless little thing she is! But back to business, Mr. Cain. You wish to talk about Santiago."

"That's right."

"You are prepared to pay, of course?"

Cain nodded.

"There is an old saying, Mr. Cain, that talk is cheap. I hope you do not believe in it."

"I believe in paying for value received," replied Cain.

"Excellent! You're a man after my own heart."

"Really?" said Cain dryly. "I would have been willing to bet that not a single thing in this apartment had been paid for."

"They have *all* been paid for, Mr. Cain," said Stern with an amused smile. "Not with money, perhaps, but with human grief and suffering and even human life. A much higher price, wouldn't you say?"

"It depends on who was doing the paying," replied Cain.

"Nobody very important," said Stern with a shrug. "Oh, they probably all had wives and husbands and children, to be sure, but they were merely spear-carriers in my own saga, which is of course the only one that matters to me. Certainly you must share my point of view, since the taking of lives is your business."

"I value the lives I take a little more highly than you do," said Cain. "So does the government."

"And here we are, back to discussing value and money once more," said Stern. "I think I shall charge you fifteen thousand credits to continue our conversation, Mr. Cain."

"For that, I want more than a physical description of a man you haven't seen in fifteen or twenty years," replied Cain. "I want the name and location of the jail, I want to know when you were incarcerated, and I want the name Santiago was using at the time."

"But of course!" said Stern. "Do I strike you as a man who would withhold information, Mr. Cain?"

"I don't know," said Cain. "Are you?"

"Perish the thought," said Stern.

"How comforting to know that."

"I'm so glad that we understand each other, Mr. Cain. May I first see, as we say in the trade, the color of your money?"

Cain pulled out his wallet, counted off the appropriate amount, and handed it over.

"I realize that absolutely no one uses cash anymore in the heart of the Democracy," said Stern, "but it has such a nice feel to it that I'm glad we still indulge ourselves out here in the extremities." He quickly counted the bills, then signaled to a *fali*, who came over and took them from him.

"Hold these for me, my pretty," he said, then nodded his head and watched her as she walked back to her position with an inhuman grace. "Lovely things!" he murmured. "Absolutely lovely!"

"We were talking about Santiago. . . ."

"Indeed we were," said Stern, turning reluctantly from the *fali* and facing Cain once again. "I promise to give it my full attention. For fifteen thousand credits, you deserve no less."

"My feelings precisely."

"Now, where shall I begin? At the beginning, of course. I was serving a certain amount of time in durance vile on the outpost world of Kalami Three for some imagined infringement of the local laws or customs."

"Robbery?" suggested Cain.

"Receiving stolen goods and attempted murder, in point of fact," replied Stern with no hint of regret. "At any rate, the only other prisoner at the time was a man who went under the name of Gregory William Penn. He was between forty and fifty years of age, he stood about six feet four inches tall, he was heavyset without being fat, his hair was black and his eyes brown, his face was clean-shaven. He spoke at least six alien languages—or so he informed me. I, myself, speak none, nor"—he smiled at the *fali*—"have I ever had any need to. On the back of his right hand he bore an S-shaped scar some two inches long. He seemed, overall, a pleasant and intelligent man. He didn't speak about himself or his past at all, but he proved to be an excellent chess player with a set that we borrowed from our captors."

"How do you know it was Santiago?"

"We had shared the hospitality of the Kalami jail for eleven days when suddenly five armed men broke in, subdued and bound the individual charged with our care, and set my fellow prisoner free. They were very thorough about wiping the prison's computer clean, and I later found out they had done the same over in the courtroom. Then, just as they were leaving, one of them called him Santiago."

"If that's your whole story, I want my money back," said Cain. "There's probably a thousand petty crooks on the Frontier who would like people to think they're Santiago—and if the prison records have been destroyed, you can't even prove that this one existed, let alone that he was who he said he was."

"Be patient, Mr. Cain," said Stern easily. "There's more."

"There'd damned well better be. How long ago did this little incident take place?"

"Seventeen Galactic Standard years. I bribed my way out about six months later."

"I understand that you've done some bounty hunting in your time," said Cain. "Why didn't you go after him?"

"We all have our obsessions, Mr. Cain," replied Stern. "Yours is obviously chasing criminals all across the galaxy. Mine, I soon discovered, lay in quite a different direction."

"All right. Go on."

"Shortly thereafter I noticed a sudden dramatic increase in my business."

"Which business was that?" interrupted Cain.

"I like to think of it as my wholesale redistribution network."

"Fencing."

"Fencing," agreed Stern. "By the time I reached Port Étrange I had a pretty strong feeling that I was dealing with Santiago, but of course I was never so tactless as to ask."

"Who would you have asked?"

"I dealt primarily with a man named Duncan Black—a large man, who wore a patch over his left eye—but from time to time there were others."

"Nobody wears eyepatches," said Cain sharply.

"Black did."

"Why didn't he just get a new eye? I've got one: it sees better than the one I was born with."

"How should I know? Possibly he thought it made him look dashing and romantic." Stern paused. "At any rate, I continued to enjoy a very profitable arrangement. Then, seven years ago, I received a shipment of goods that eliminated any lingering doubts I may have had that I was indeed doing business with Santiago."

"And what was that?"

"Do you see that paperweight over there?" asked Stern, indicating what appeared to be a small gold bar on a nearby table.

"Yes."

"Why don't you examine it?'

Cain got up, walked over to the paperweight, and inspected it.

"It looks like gold bullion," he said.

"Pick it up and turn it over," suggested Stern.

It required both hands for Cain to lift it. When he did so, he noticed a nine-digit number burned into the bottom of it.

"That number corresponds to part of a gold shipment that Santiago stole from a navy convoy."

"The Epsilon Eridani robbery?" asked Cain.

Stern nodded. "I'm sure you can confirm the number through your various sources. The numbers had been eliminated from all the other bars, but somehow they missed that one—so I kept it for a souvenir, never knowing when it might be of some minor use to me." He smiled. "Anyway, it was then that I knew for sure that Black and the others were Santiago's agents."

"That still doesn't prove the man you saw in jail was Santiago," said Cain, putting the gold bar back down.

"I'm not finished," replied Stern. "About a year after I received the gold shipment, a smuggler named Kastartos, one of the agents I'd been dealing with, approached me with a fascinating proposition. Evidently he was displeased with his salary or his working conditions; at any rate, he had decided to turn Santiago in for the reward. Being a prudent man, he decided not to do so himself, but offered to split fifty-fifty with me if I would approach the authorities on his behalf. I questioned him further, and eventually he gave me a description of the man I had seen in the Kalami jail. There were a few discrepancies, as might be expected with the passage of eleven years, but it sounded like the same man, and when he described the scar on his right hand I was sure."

"And what did you do?"

"I was making a considerable amount of money from Santiago's trade, and I had no more desire to be the visible partner in this enterprise than Kastartos did. After all, not only would I have faced the threat of reprisal from Santiago's organization, but once word of such a betrayal got out, most of my other clients would have felt very uneasy about dealing with me as well," explained Stern. "So I followed the only reasonable course of action: I informed Duncan Black of his proposition, and let nature take its course." He shook his head. "Poor little man. I never saw him again."

"Did he tell you where to find Santiago?"

"I felt my longevity could best be served by not knowing the answer to that particular question."

"Do you still deal with him?"

"If I did, I wouldn't be parting with this information," said Stern. "But I haven't seen Duncan Black in almost three years now, and while it's always possible that Santiago is dealing with me through someone else, I very much doubt it."

"Where can I find Duncan Black?"

"If I knew that, this little chat would have cost you fifty thousand credits," replied Stern. "The only thing I can tell you is that during the time I did business with him, his ship bore a Bella Donna registry."

"Bella Donna?" repeated Cain. "I've never heard of it."

"It's an outpost world, the third planet of the Clovis system. I'm sure that it must be listed in your ship's computer." Stern paused. "Do you still want your money back, Mr. Cain?"

Cain stared at him. "Not unless I find out you've been lying."

"Why would I lie?" asked Stern. "I haven't been offworld for seven years now, and I have no intention of leaving in the foreseeable future. You would certainly have very little trouble finding me." He stood up. "Shall I assume that our conversation is over now?"

Cain nodded his head.

"Then you'll forgive me if I immerse myself once again?"

He let his robe drop to the floor and walked over to the tub.

"Come, my lovelies," he crooned, and the two *fali* walked over and gently helped lower him into the water.

"I think I could do with a massage," he said. "Do you remember what I taught you?" The *fali* immediately entered the tub and began massaging his arms and torso with their long, sensitive, alien hands.

"Would you like to join us, Mr. Cain?" asked Stern, suddenly aware that Cain had not yet left the room. "It isn't an invitation I extend to many of my guests, and it certainly won't break my heart if you should decline, but I suppose it's the least I can do for a man who has just spent fifteen thousand credits for a useless tidbit of information."

"Useless?"

"The Angel is after Santiago now, or hadn't you heard?"

"I know."

"And yet you paid me anyway?" said Stern. "You must be a very efficient killer, Mr. Cain—or a very overconfident one." He moaned with pleasure as one of the *fali* began stroking his left thigh. "How many men have you actually killed?"

"Pay me fifteen thousand credits and I might just answer that question," said Cain.

Stern laughed hollowly in amusement.

"I'm afraid not, Mr. Cain. What you have done in the past may eventually find its way into Black Orpheus' songbook, as I myself have done, but you are simply another spear-carrier passing through my life—and an incredibly minor one at that."

"And them?" asked Cain, indicating the two *fali*.

"They represent my fall from Grace," said Stern with a smile. "Far more important than mere supporting players, I assure you. Someday I suppose I shall even give them names." He turned to one of them. "Gently, my pretty—gently." He took her hand and began guiding it gingerly.

Cain stared at the three of them for another few seconds, then turned and summoned the elevator. The sound of Stern's voice, trembling with eagerness, came to him as the doors were closing:

"Here, my pet. Lie back and let me show you how."

Cain descended to the main floor, walked out across the dusty thoroughfare, entered his own hotel, and shortly thereafter unlocked his room. He found Halfpenny Terwilliger sitting on his bed, playing solitaire.

"What the hell are you doing here?" he demanded as the door slid shut behind him.

"Waiting for you," replied the little gambler.

"How did you know this was my room?"

"I asked at the desk."

"And they gave you the combination to the lock?"

"In a manner of speaking," said Terwilliger. "Of course, they probably don't *know* they gave it to me."

"All right," said Cain. "Why are you waiting for me?"

"Because I know who you are now. You're the Songbird, right?"

"I'm Sebastian Cain."

"But people call you the Songbird?" persisted Terwilliger.

"Some people do."

"Good. Because if you're the Songbird, you ought to be leaving Port Étrange pretty soon in search of better pickings."

"Get to the point," said Cain.

"I'd like a ride."

"I don't take passengers."

"Let me word that a bit more strongly," said Terwilliger. "I *need* a ride. My life depends on it."

"Why?"

"It's a long and rather embarrassing story."

"Give me the gist of it," said Cain.

Terwilliger stared at him for a moment, then shrugged. "When I was in the Spinos system about four months ago, I passed two hundred thousand credits' worth of bad notes to ManMountain Bates."

"He's a gambler, isn't he?"

"A very large, ill-tempered one," said Terwilliger devoutly.

"I'd say that was an unwise thing to do."

"I *intended* to make them good. I was just indulging in a little deficit spending. Hell, the Democracy does it all the time." He paused. "But I just got word a few minutes ago that he's due to land on Port Étrange the day after tomorrow—and truth to tell, I'm a little bit short of what I owe him."

"How short?"

"Oh, not much."

"*How* short?" repeated Cain.

"About two hundred thousand credits, give or take a few," said Terwilliger with a sickly smile.

"I certainly don't envy you," commented Cain.

"I don't want you to *envy* me," said Terwilliger with a note of desperation in his voice. "I want you to fly me the hell out of here!"

"I told you: I don't take passengers."

"I'll pay for my fare."

"I thought you didn't have any money," noted Cain.

"I'll work it off," said Terwilliger. "I'll cook, I'll load cargo, I'll—"

"The galley's fully automated, and the only cargo I handle doesn't need loading so much as killing," interrupted Cain.

"If you don't take me, I'll die!"

"Everybody dies sometime," replied Cain. "Ask someone else."

"I already did. Nobody wants ManMountain Bates on their trail. But I figured a man like the Songbird, a man who's all written up in song and story, you wouldn't be bothered by a little thing like that."

"You figured wrong."

"You really won't take me?"

"I really won't take you."

"My death will be on your hands," said Terwilliger.

"Why?" asked Cain "*I* didn't pass bad notes to anyone."

Terwilliger scrutinized him for a moment, then forced himself to smile. "You're kidding, aren't you? You just want to see me squirm a little first."

"I'm not kidding."

"You *are*!" the little gambler half shouted. "You can't send me out to face ManMountain Bates! He breaks people's backs like they were toothpicks!"

"You know," remarked Cain with some amusement, "you seemed like a totally different man when I met you in the bar."

"I didn't have an eight-foot-tall disaster coming after me with blood in his eye when we were in the bar!" snapped Terwilliger.

"Are you all through yelling now?" asked Cain calmly.

"I arranged for you to meet with Stern," said Terwilliger desperately. "That ought to be worth *some*thing."

Cain reached into a pocket, withdrew a small silver coin, and flipped it across the room to Terwilliger. "Thanks," he said.

"Damn it, Songbird! What kind of man are you?"

"An unsympathetic one. Do you plan on leaving any time soon, or am I going to have to throw you out?"

Terwilliger emitted a sigh of defeat, gathered up the cards from the bed, and trudged to the door.

"Thanks a lot," he said sarcastically.

"Any time," replied Cain, stepping aside to let him pass out into the corridor.

The door slid shut again.

Cain stood absolutely still for a moment, then opened it.

"Hey, Terwilliger!" he yelled at the gambler's retreating figure.

"Yes?"

"What do you know about a man named Duncan Black?"

"The guy with the eyepatch?" said Terwilliger, turning and taking a tentative step in Cain's direction.

"That's the one."

"I used to play cards with him. What do you want to know?"

"Where am I likely to find him?" asked Cain.

Suddenly Terwilliger grinned broadly. "I do believe I just booked passage out of here," he said.

"You know where he is?"

"That I do."

"Where?"

"I'll tell you after we've taken off."

Cain nodded his agreement. "I'm leaving as soon as I have dinner. Get your gear together and meet me at the spaceport in two hours."

Terwilliger pulled out his deck of cards.

"I've got all the luggage I need right here," he said happily. "And now, if you'll excuse me, I think I'll go down and find a little game of chance to while away the lonely minutes before we leave."

With that, he turned on his heel and went off in search of the three or four newcomers to Port Étrange who would still accept his marker.

3.

Halfpenny Terwilliger, the boldest gambler yet;
Halfpenny Terwilliger will cover any bet;
Halfpenny Terwilliger, a rowdy martinet;
Halfpenny Terwilliger is now one soul in debt.

"Gin."

"Damn!" said Terwilliger, slapping his hand down on the table. "You caught me with nineteen." He pushed the cards over to Cain. "Your deal."

"I've had enough for a while."

"You're sure?"

"I've played more cards during the past five days than in the twenty years preceding them," said Cain. "Let's knock off for a few hours."

"Just trying to keep you amused," said Terwilliger, shuffling the deck and putting it back in the pocket of his brightly colored tunic. "Where do we stand?"

"You owe me a little over twenty-two hundred credits."

"I don't suppose you'd take a marker?" asked Terwilliger.

Cain smiled. "Not very likely."

"Mind if I mix up another pot of that coffee we broke open this afternoon?" asked the gambler, heading off for the galley. "Just as well you don't bring 'em back alive," he muttered as he searched for the coffee in the cramped confines of the galley. "This ship sure as hell wasn't built with an extra passenger in mind." He uttered a grunt of triumph as he finally found the coffee in amongst a stack of condensed rations.

"Go a little easy on that stuff," said Cain. "It's expensive."

"It *tastes* expensive. Where's it from—Belore or Canphor?"

"Brazil."

"Never heard of it."

"It's a country back on Earth."

"You mean I've been drinking coffee from Earth itself?" said Terwilliger. "I'm impressed! You do right well by a guest, Songbird."

"Thanks—and I keep telling you: my name's Cain."

"I've been meaning to ask you about that. You don't sound like you've got much of a singing voice, so how come he dubbed you the Songbird?"

"Because my name's Sebastian Nightingale Cain. He fell in love with my middle name, and I told him he couldn't use it." Cain grimaced. "I should have been more explicit."

"Come to think of it, Black Orpheus does a *lot* of dumb things," said Terwilliger. "Like that line about me being a martinet. I'm the sweetest, friendliest guy in the galaxy. He just used it to make a rhyme."

"I notice you don't object to the part about pawning your soul," noted Cain.

Terwilliger laughed. "Hell, that's the first thing a man gets rid of when he comes to the Frontier. Excess baggage, nothing more."

"Losing at cards seems to make you cynical," said Cain.

"It's got nothing to do with cards," replied the little gambler. "It's an obvious fact. You kill men for a living; where would *you* be with a soul?"

"Back on Sylaria, I suppose," said Cain thoughtfully.

"That's the world where you were a revolutionary?"

"One of them."

"You should have known better," said Terwilliger. "No matter what kind of promises a man who's looking for power makes, he's not going to turn out to be any different from the one he replaces."

"I was very young," said Cain.

"It's hard to imagine you as a callow youth."

Cain chuckled. "I wasn't so much callow as idealistic."

"Well, cheer up—the Frontier is filled with men who were going to make the galaxy a better place to live."

"So are the seats of power," said Cain wryly. "You'd think *some-body* would know how."

"You keep talking like that and you're going to convince me you still believe in all that idealistic nonsense."

"Don't worry about it," replied Cain, leaning back and propping a foot up against a bulkhead. "That was a long, long time ago."

The gambler walked over to a sensor terminal, as he had done every few hours since leaving Port Étrange, and satisfied himself that there was still no sign of pursuit by ManMountain Bates.

"You know," said Terwilliger, finally pouring himself some coffee and handing a cup over to Cain, "you never did tell me why you became a bounty hunter."

"I'd been a terrorist for twelve years. The only thing I knew how to do really well was kill people."

"How about that?" said the gambler with mock regret. "And here I thought it was because you believed in justice."

Cain patted the weapon at his side. "I learned to use this gun because I believed in truth and honor and freedom and a lot of other fine-sounding things. I spent twelve years fighting for them and then took a good look at the results." He paused. "Now all I believe in is the gun."

"Well, I've met disillusioned revolutionaries before, but you're the first one who ever fought on a free-lance basis."

"Nobody paid me for what I did."

"What I meant was that you seemed to go from one war to another."

"When the first man I thought could put things right turned out to have feet of clay, I looked around for another. It took me three revolutions before I finally realized just how much clay God put into the universe." He smiled ruefully. "I was a slow learner."

"At least you fought the good fight," said Terwilliger.

"I fought three stupid fights," Cain corrected him. "I'm not especially proud of any of them."

"You must have been a very serious young man."

"Actually, I used to laugh a lot more than I do now." He shrugged. "That was when I thought one moral man could make a difference. The only thing I find *really* funny these days is the fact that so many people still believe it."

"I had a feeling the first time I saw you that you weren't just your run-of-the-mill headhunter," said Terwilliger. "Like I told you, I've got this knack for reading faces."

"Well, if it comes to that, I had a feeling the first time I saw you that you were a lousy cardplayer."

"I'm the best damned cardplayer *you'll* ever meet."

"I thought I beat you rather handily," remarked Cain.

"I *let* you win."

"Sure you did."

"You don't believe me?" said the gambler. "Then watch *this*."

He pulled out the cards, shuffled them thoroughly, and dealt out two five-card hands on the tiny chrome table.

"Got anything worth betting?" he asked.

Cain picked up his cards, fanned them out slowly, and found himself holding four kings and a jack.

"It's possible," he answered cautiously.

"How about twenty-two hundred credits?"

"Let's make it one hundred."

"You're sure?"

"That's my limit."

Terwilliger laid his hand down on the table. It contained four aces and a queen.

"Then why did you let me win any hands at all the first time we met?" asked Cain.

"Because professional cardplayers are very careful about cheating professional killers," replied Terwilliger. "Besides, I was lonely. Once word got out that I was broke, none of the amateurs would play with me—and you can't use tricks like that on the pros."

"And why have you let me win at gin since we took off from Port Étrange?" continued Cain.

"It was just my way of keeping you in a good mood, and thanking you for saving my life." He grinned. "Besides, it's not as if I have any money to pay you with."

"Well, I'll be damned!" said Cain with a laugh. "So *that's* why you wouldn't let the computer give us random hands! All right, you little bastard. Your debt's wiped clean."

"I'd rather owe it to you."

"Why?"

"I have my reasons," said Terwilliger.

"Suit yourself," said Cain. "I've got another question."

"Ask away."

"How the hell did someone like you manage to go two hundred thousand credits in the hole to ManMountain Bates?"

"Do you know what the odds are of a man drawing a straight flush against you when you're sitting with four aces?" asked Terwilliger.

"Not long enough, I'd guess," said Cain.

"You're damned right! You know, if you play cards every day, it might happen five times before you die of old age. It was just my stupid luck that the first time it happened was against the backbreaker."

"How did you get out with your back unbroken?"

"I waited until Bates answered a call of nature, told a couple of the other players that I was going to my room to get my bankroll so I could redeem my marker, and got the hell off the planet before anyone knew I was gone." Terwilliger frowned. "I'd love to see that guy's bladder preserved for science. He must have drunk six quarts before he got up!"

"Pardon an unethical question, but now that I've seen what you can do with a deck of cards, why didn't you do it to him—exercising due caution, of course?"

"Have you ever seen ManMountain Bates?" said Terwilliger with a bitter laugh.

"No."

"Well, he's not the kind of guy you'd want to chance having mad at you, especially if he was within arm's reach."

"Not even for two hundred thousand credits?"

"It wasn't worth the risk. It'd be as dangerous as you poaching on the Angel's territory."

"From what I hear, he's about to start poaching on mine," commented Cain.

"That's different."

"Why?"

"Because he's the Angel." Terwilliger walked over to the coffee-pot and poured himself another cup. "Besides, everybody knows he's just here for Santiago. You can hardly call it poaching if nobody knows where Santiago is hiding. Which brings up another subject," he added carefully. "You came a pretty fair distance just to talk to Jonathan Stern. Usually a bounty hunter doesn't go that far beyond his own territory unless he thinks he can get a lead on Santiago. So my question is: Is there some tie-in between Duncan Black and Santiago, or not?"

"I don't see that it's any of your business," said Cain.

"Look at me," said the little gambler. "Do I look like a goddamned rival?"

"No," said Cain. "You look like a goddamned salesman."

"Just answer my question. I promise you I won't sell it to anyone else."

"Somehow, I get the distinct impression that your promises aren't exactly coin of the realm."

"Damn it, Cain—it's important!"

"To who?"

"To both of us."

Cain stared at him for a long minute, then nodded. "Yes, he's a link to Santiago."

"Good!" breathed Terwilliger with a sigh of relief.

"Why is that good?"

"Well, first I want you to remember that I still owe you a debt of twenty-one hundred credits, and that I can't pay it off if I'm dead."

"Get to the point."

The little gambler took a deep breath.

"The reason I know where to find Duncan Black is because I know where he's buried." Terwilliger held up his hand quickly, as if to fight off any possible interruption. "I should have told you back on Port Étrange, I know that. It was absolutely, positively wrong. But if I had, you wouldn't have taken me, and ManMountain Bates would be having me for dinner right about now."

"I may just take you back there and turn you over to him," said Cain.

"But everything's all right now!" said Terwilliger quickly. "Everything's all right," he repeated. "That's why I had to know if Black was a link."

"Explain," said Cain ominously.

"You see, if he had owed you money or something like that, you were out of luck and I was in big trouble. I mean, hell, the poor bastard has been dead for almost three years now." He paused for breath. "But now that I know what you needed him for, I can still help you out."

"How?"

"There was this woman he used to live with," said Terwilliger. "She handled a lot of his business for him. She probably knows everyone *he* knew, and can tell you what his connection was with each of them."

"And she's still alive?" asked Cain.

"She was two months ago."

"Where can I find her?"

"Right where we're heading—the Clovis system."

"On Bella Donna?"

"Not exactly," answered Terwilliger.

4.

She lives in a graveyard of shattered ships,
She floats through the void with her broken dreams;
But though she may long for a lover's lips,
The Sargasso Rose isn't what she seems.

Black Orpheus took one look at the Sargasso Rose and knew there was more to her than met the eye.

How he found her in the first place is a mystery, since he wasn't likely to have had any business up there, six thousand miles above Bella Donna. Probably it was the ships that attracted him, strung out in space like glittering fish on a line, some dying and some already dead. He named the station, too: he hated names like Station Number 14, and so he called it Deadly Nightshade, which was a fitting sobriquet for a graveyard of spaceships, especially one that circled Bella Donna.

He spent a couple of days up there, talking to the Sargasso Rose, jotting down her story the way he did with everyone he met. Some people say he even slept with her, but they were wrong; Black Orpheus never slept with *anyone* after his Eurydice died. Besides, the Sargasso Rose wasn't the type of woman who'd jump into bed with just anybody.

In fact, that may have been one of her problems. She was forty years old, and she had had only three lovers. The first two had left her for other women, and Duncan Black had left her to start working in the pits of hell a few years ahead of schedule. She'd always fought a lot with him, but she'd loved him as much as she would let herself love anyone after her first two experiences, and when his heart finally gave out it came pretty close to breaking hers as well.

She was still grieving a year later, when Black Orpheus stopped by—but she took the trouble to show Deadly Nightshade off to him just the same. He went deep into the bellies of the metal leviathans and spent almost a full day there, scribbling down notes as her crew gutted them and set them adrift, then watching with childlike enthu-siasm as space tugs dragged new corpses up to the station's docks. He even found time to name Bella Donna's three tiny moons—Banewort, Foxglove, and Hellebore—before he left for his next port of call.

Deadly Nightshade wasn't much to look at by the time Cain and Terwilliger arrived. Its hull was pockmarked by small, hastily repaired meteor holes, one of its docks had been damaged beyond repair by an errant tug, and it had come into contact with enough cosmic dust and debris so that the entire exterior needed refurbishing.

Still, it wasn't Deadly Nightshade that they had come to see, but rather the woman who owned it, so Cain carefully maneuvered his ship up to a dock, waited for an enclosed mobile walkway to be at-tached to his airlock, and followed Terwilliger to the interior of the station.

The floor curved gently away from them in both directions, and a narrow mat of indeterminate properties seemed to grab hold of their feet.

"You didn't tell me it was zero gravity in here," commented Cain.

"Just make sure one foot is always on the mat," replied Terwilli-ger. "You won't float away."

"I've been on G-mats before," replied Cain irritably. "I just don't like null-gravity situations too soon after a meal."

"You should have told me."

Cain was about to reply that he hadn't known that there was no gravity inside the station but decided that he didn't feel like repeating the entire conversation again.

Suddenly a humanoid being with a large cranium, deep-set golden eyes, and orange, reticulated skin began approaching them.

"What the hell is that?" asked Cain.

"An Orange Monkey," replied Terwilliger. "The Rose uses them as security guards."

"I never saw one before," said Cain. "Where is it from?"

"Varien Four," said the gambler. "They call themselves Hagibens; we call 'em Orange Monkeys. It fits them better. They work cheap, they learn the language pretty fast, and they love zero gravity. It's a hard combination to beat—especially when you consider how many alien races won't work at all and couldn't care less about money."

The Orange Monkey stopped in front of them.

"Your business, please?" it said in a lilting voice that sounded more like song than speech.

"We're here to see the Sargasso Rose," replied Terwilliger.

"The Sargasso Rose prefers not to deal personally with our customers," replied the alien. "If you will tell me what you need, I will direct you to the proper areas."

"She'll deal personally with *us*," said Terwilliger. "I'm an old friend."

The Orange Monkey looked at him. "You are Halfpenny Terwilliger, who was forcibly removed from Deadly Nightshade for cheating various staff members in a card game." It paused. "*I* was among those who escorted you to your ship."

"You were?" asked Terwilliger, surprised but unembarrassed.

"I was."

"Sorry I didn't recognize you, but all you Orange Monkeys look alike to me."

"That is perfectly understandable," said the alien. "We are all quite beautiful."

"Well, as long as we're old friends, how about telling the Rose we're here?"

"I will tell her, Halfpenny Terwilliger, but she prefers not to deal directly with the customers."

Cain stepped forward. "Do it anyway," he said in very level tones. "Tell her our business concerns a mutual friend."

The Orange Monkey stared at him for a moment, then turned and headed off to another area of the space station after summoning a companion to keep watch on them. It returned a few minutes later and walked up to Cain.

"The Sargasso Rose has instructed me to take you to her," it said in its placid, singsong voice. If it was surprised or disappointed, it kept its feelings well hidden.

Cain and Terwilliger followed it through a trio of large storage rooms and up to a small door.

"She is in here," said the Orange Monkey.

"Thanks," said Cain. He opened the door and stepped into a cluttered office, followed by Terwilliger.

Sitting behind a chrome desk that no longer gleamed, wearing a metallic gold outfit that no longer glistened, was a rather plain woman. Her hair was a dull brown, her eyes a lackluster green, her nose prominent, her chin weak. She was neither fat nor thin, but if she had ever possessed an attractive figure, that time had long since passed. Attached to her hair was a small white rose, which Cain took to be artificial.

She stared directly at the bounty hunter.

"You wished to see me, Mr. Cain?"

"You know my name?"

She smiled. "I know many things about you, Sebastian Nightingale Cain. What I don't know is who referred you to me."

"A man called Stern, back on Port Étrange."

"Jonathan Jeremy Jacobar Stern," she said. "Now *that's* a name I haven't heard in years." She gestured to a pair of chairs. "Please be seated." She turned to Terwilliger. "I understand ManMountain Bates is looking for you."

"You have excellent sources," replied the gambler uneasily.

"Indeed I do," she agreed. "Not much goes on in this part of the Frontier that I don't know about."

"Then I assume you know why I'm here," said Cain.

"I know you're a bounty hunter," she said, "and you've told me that Stern sent you, so I can make a pretty good guess as to why you're here." She paused. "But Stern wouldn't send you to *me*. He would have told you to hunt up Duncan Black." She turned back to Terwilliger. "*You* told Mr. Cain to come here, of course. Stern doesn't know Duncan is dead, but you do."

"Well, there wasn't much sense trying to have a conversation with Duncan, rest his soul," explained Terwilliger defensively.

"And doubtless he has promised to protect you from ManMountain Bates in exchange for this information." She scrutinized Cain for a moment. "You made a poor trade, Mr. Cain. You should have stayed on Keepsake."

"What makes you think I come from Keepsake?" he asked.

She smiled again. "I've known your ship's registration number since I started tracking you two days ago. In the intervening forty-eight hours I've found out things about you that even *you* may have forgotten. I know the date and planet of your birth, I know why you left the more populated worlds of the Democracy, I know how many men you have killed and who they were—and here you are, practically denying that you work out of Keepsake. If you want *my* honesty, I should think the least you can do is offer me your own."

"I apologize," said Cain.

"There's no need to," she replied. "Deceit is no more than I expect from a member of your sex."

"Will you help me?" asked Cain, ignoring her comment.

"You're wasting your time."

"I've got plenty to waste," he said. "And I can pay for yours."

"I didn't say you would be wasting *my* time," said the Sargasso Rose. "I have every intention of selling you the information you need."

"I'm not sure I understand the distinction."

"I'm quite prepared to tell you what you want to know, but it won't do you any good. The Angel has moved to the Inner Frontier."

"I'm getting a little tired of hearing about him," said Cain with a trace of irritation.

"So, I suspect, is every fugitive within ten thousand light-years," she replied. "Mr. Terwilliger, I think it is time for you to leave the room. What I have to say to Mr. Cain is for his ears alone."

"Why?" asked the gambler.

"For the same reason that you are denied free access to the goods in my warehouse: I don't want you selling something that's mine to the first qualified buyer who comes along."

"I resent that," said Terwilliger, trying to muster a show of sincerity and not quite succeeding.

"You are welcome to resent it to your heart's content," said the Sargasso Rose. "What you are *not* welcome to do is remain in my office."

Terwilliger seemed about to protest, thought better of it, and walked to the door.

"I'll be right outside," he told Cain. "Yell out if you need me."

Cain stared at him in amusement, and a moment later the door slid shut behind the little gambler.

"If you plan to hunt Santiago, you really should choose your traveling companions more carefully, Mr. Cain," said the Sargasso Rose, leaning back in her chair.

"Perhaps," replied Cain. "But on his behalf, I should point out that he brought me to you. Otherwise I'd be wasting my time hunting for Duncan Black, or else I'd be heading back for Port Étrange to beat my money out of Jonathan Stern."

"True," she admitted with a shrug. "May I offer you a drink?"

"Why not?" he said agreeably.

She pressed a button on her computer console, and a small, furry red alien, definitely not humanoid, entered by a different door and set a bottle and two glasses down on her desk.

"Do you have any Men at all on Deadly Nightshade?" asked Cain as the alien left the office.

"The race or the gender?" asked the Sargasso Rose. "In either case, the answer is no. Both tend to desert you when you need them the most—especially the gender."

"It must get lonely up here," commented Cain.

"Eventually one gets used to it." She filled the two glasses, and Cain stepped over and took one.

"Thank you," he said after returning to his chair and taking a sip. Suddenly he laughed in self-deprecation.

"What is it, Mr. Cain?"

He held up the glass. "I just realized that there's normal gravity in this room," he replied. "Some observant hunter I am! If I hadn't noticed that this stuff didn't float away, I would never have known."

"The Orange Monkeys like zero gravity. I find continued exposure to it a bit upsetting, so I tailor my office to my own needs."

"It must cost a fortune," he commented.

"It does. Thankfully, I've got a fortune to spare."

He took another sip. "This is pretty good stuff."

"It ought to be," she said. "It comes straight from Deluros Eight."

"You handle merchandise from that far away?"

"You'd be surprised at what passes through Deadly Nightshade, Mr. Cain," she replied. "Or perhaps you wouldn't. Exactly how much did Stern tell you about Duncan Black?"

"Only that Black handled stolen goods, and that he was a middle-man between Stern and Santiago," replied Cain. "I know he had access to some of the gold that Santiago picked up in the Epsilon Eridani raid."

"Now *that* was a cargo!" she said with a smile. "Six hundred million credits' worth of pure bullion!"

"I got the impression from Terwilliger that you decided to follow in Black's footsteps."

"Terwilliger talks too much."

"Most people do," agreed Cain.

"Besides, they were *my* footsteps to begin with," she continued. "I was dealing in stolen commodities long before Duncan Black ever thought of it." She paused. "I gave him a share of the business to insure his loyalty." She looked at Cain. "Does that seem manipulative and immoral to you?"

"I gave up making moral judgments a long time ago," he replied.

"Anyway," said the Sargasso Rose, sipping her drink, "Duncan liked dealing with people more than I did, so he became our front man for places like Port Étrange and people like Stern."

"Then *you* made the initial contact with Santiago, not Black."

"Actually, Santiago made the initial contact with *me*," she answered him. "Though it took a few years before I knew beyond any doubt that I was dealing with him."

"Have you ever met him?" asked Cain.

She shook her head. "No. Or perhaps I should say, not to my knowledge."

"But you might have?"

"Who's to say?" she replied with a shrug of her shoulders. "I met any number of people who delivered goods that Santiago may have stolen—though in truth I can't imagine why he would have risked exposure by coming here."

"Do you know anyone who has actually met him face to face?" persisted Cain.

"Yes, I do."

"Who?"

"Before I tell you, Mr. Cain," said the Sargasso Rose, "there are a few things I would like to know, just to satisfy my own curiosity."

"Such as?"

"You spent most of your young manhood fighting to overthrow various governments. Santiago, to the best of my knowledge, has primarily attacked and looted those enterprises that are owned or controlled by the Democracy, or are at least vital to its well-being. You were branded as a revolutionary, and once had a price on your head. The magnitude of his actions is certainly far greater, but he might also be considered a revolutionary, insofar as most of his crimes are against the State. You have so many things in common with him that I'm just a little puzzled about why you want so desperately to kill him."

"The bulk of his crimes are committed against the Democracy simply because the Democracy has more assets than any other potential target," said Cain. "As for his being a revolutionary, you might say the same for any train robber back on old Earth who ever robbed a government payroll. The man's a criminal, plain and simple."

"Have you ever known him to kill anyone?" she asked.

"He killed seventeen colonists on Silverblue just last year," replied Cain.

"Rubbish!" said the Sargasso Rose. "He hasn't been to the Outer Frontier in years."

"You know that for a fact?" he asked sharply.

"Why else would the Angel have moved into this area?" she replied.

"Maybe he's chasing him," suggested Cain.

"You don't believe that for a moment. The Angel *catches* anyone he chases."

"He's just a bounty hunter, not a superman."

"You still haven't told me why you want to kill Santiago."

"Why does *anyone* want to kill him?" replied Cain with a smile. "There's a hell of a big reward."

"That is not an acceptable answer," she said. "You are a very wealthy man, Mr. Cain, so surely money is not your primary objective."

"Money is always an objective," said Cain. "And," he added thoughtfully, "it would *mean* something."

"What would it mean?"

"That I made a difference," he replied. "That just once, something I did *mattered*."

"How about the men you helped place in positions of power?" asked the Sargasso Rose.

"They were the wrong men," answered Cain wryly. "They won't even be footnotes in the history books."

"And the criminals you've hunted down?"

"Even *I* hadn't heard of most of them before I went after them." He paused. "But Santiago is different. *He* matters, so the man who brings him down will matter, too."

She smiled. "So you want to be written up in song and story yourself."

"I've *been* in a song. I don't like it much." He finished his drink. "I don't care who else knows what I did—just so long as *I* know it."

"Well, it's a novel approach. I'll grant you that," said the Sargasso Rose.

"Now let me ask you a question," said Cain.

"We haven't settled on a price yet," she pointed out.

"That wasn't the question."

"Then go ahead."

"You've obviously made a lot of money off of Santiago. Why are you willing to help me?"

"Santiago took his business elsewhere shortly after Duncan died. I owe him nothing. Besides, I'm a businesswoman: everything I own is for sale—including information."

"Have you sold it to anyone else yet?"

"No one has asked—but if they do, I will."

"All right," said Cain. "What, exactly, do you have for sale?"

"I have the name, holograph, and current location of a man who dealt directly with Santiago. I have the names and holographs of four of Santiago's agents with whom I did business three years ago. I have some of the gold bullion with its point of origin listed on the packing crates. And I know who killed Kastartos."

"Kastartos?" asked Cain. "The man who tried to get Stern to turn Santiago in for the reward?"

She nodded. "From what I hear, it was a pretty dismal attempt."

"And what do you want for all this?"

"I want you to kill Santiago."

He looked his surprise. "That's all?"

"That's all."

"Might I ask why?"

"Duncan Black was a good man," she began. "Well, no, he wasn't. He was petty and undependable and weak—but he was *mine*. Then he found out that we were dealing with Santiago, and he thought we could make a little more money by joining the organization. I don't know what sort of proposal he made to them, but it didn't work." She took a sip of her drink. "He was found dead on Binder Ten two weeks later. The official cause of death was heart failure."

"Are you telling me Santiago had him killed?"

"Santiago probably didn't even know he existed. But *somebody* had him killed, and if it hadn't been for Santiago, he'd still be here." She paused. "He wasn't much, but he was all I had." She stared at Cain. "Santiago didn't know Duncan, and I don't know Santiago. It will be a fair trade."

"All right," said Cain. "Let's see what you have."

She rose, walked to a wall safe that was concealed behind a large, lightweight computer screen, punched out a combination on the lock, and opened it.

"You can take these with you," she said, withdrawing a number of items from the safe and returning to her chair. "I have copies."

"Somehow I was sure you did," he remarked, reaching over and taking a number of holographs from her.

"The top four are the agents I dealt with," she explained. "Their names are on the backs."

"One of them looks like a methane-breather," said Cain, holding up a holograph of a delicate crystalline being.

"He is," she said. "I only saw him once. He was very uncomfortable in his life-support paraphernalia. I suspect after his initial trip here he found a convenient drop point for his merchandise."

"Who's this?" asked Cain, holding up the holograph of a very exotic dark-haired woman with chalk-white skin.

"Altair of Altair," answered the Sargasso Rose. "She murdered Kastartos."

He studied the holograph. "She's a professional killer?"

"One of the best. I'm surprised you haven't heard of her."

"It's a big galaxy," he said. "There are a lot of people I haven't heard of." He looked at Altair of Altair again. "Are you sure she's human?"

"Who knows? But I'm sure she's an assassin."

He came to the final holograph.

"This is the man who met with Santiago?"

"Yes. His name is Socrates. I haven't dealt with him in more than a year, but I know where to find him. We do a little business together from time to time."

"Maybe it's not such a big galaxy after all," said Cain, staring at the pudgy, smiling face in the holograph.

"What do you mean?"

"I knew this man when his name was Whittaker Drum."

"The name's not familiar to me," said the Sargasso Rose.

"No, I don't suppose it would be."

"Who is he?"

Cain smiled ironically. "The man I helped put in power back on Sylaria."

"Will he recognize you?"

"I hope so," answered Cain.

5.

Socrates is hard to please:
He lives in the shade of the gallows-trees;
He prays for life on bended knees—
But he's bound for hell, is Socrates.

There weren't a lot of people on the Inner Frontier that Black Orpheus didn't like, but Socrates was one of them. You'd think that cutthroats and bandits and gamblers would have bothered him more, but for the most part they were pretty honest and aboveboard about what they did, and if there was one thing Black Orpheus couldn't abide, it was a hypocrite.

Now, there are people who say that Black Orpheus must have had some respect for Socrates or he wouldn't have given him even the single verse that he did, but Black Orpheus knew that Socrates was the ruler of an entire planet back when he was plain old Whittaker Drum—and besides, his job as he saw it was to write up the folks that he met and leave it to others to judge them.

Still, he was known to editorialize a little, and there's not much doubt that he felt Socrates was earmarked for the pits of hell. Oh, he'd said something like that about Halfpenny Terwilliger and a few others, but you got the feeling that he was joking—and he never said it at all about Schussler the Cyborg, who thought he was *already* in hell, nor even about Santiago himself. There was just something about Socrates that rubbed him the wrong way, and since most people on the Frontier were pretty much inclined to take Black Orpheus' word about characters they hadn't met, it's probably just as well that Socrates didn't survive too long after that verse was written.

Actually, nobody knows how he got the name Socrates, but it's a pretty safe bet that Black Orpheus didn't hang it on him. He was Whittaker Drum when he wrote his revolutionary tracts, he was Whittaker Drum when he took over the reins of Sylaria's government, and he was still Whittaker Drum when they threw him out a few years later; then one day he showed up on Declan IV and suddenly he was Socrates. First he caught a particularly virulent venereal disease, and then he caught an equally strong case of religion, and neither of them stopped him from making a living as an entrepreneur who specialized in providing venture capital to what could be euphemistically termed high-risk businesses.

He probably didn't know it, but he had a lot of company on Declan IV. Nobody knew what the planet's attraction was, except perhaps that it was a last jumping-off point to the Inner Frontier, but during the seven years that Socrates lived there it was also the home of five exiled planetary presidents, two kings, and a ranking member of the navy who had resigned in black disgrace.

Declan IV was a frontier society that had outgrown its origins and was uncomfortably trying to fit neatly into the pattern of the worlds of the Democracy. It had grown from two grubby Tradertowns into six sprawling modern cities, it had first pacified and later decimated the six-legged marsupials that had once been the planet's dominant life-form, it imported—always a decade after they were out of style— the latest fashions and entertainments from Deluros VIII, it bribed the major retail chains to open outlets on the planet and practically subsidized them once they arrived, it entered teams in various interplanetary sporting leagues, and it was making impressive progress at polluting its atmosphere. It was too young a colony to have much sense of its own past, so buildings, some of them quite lovely, were constantly being torn down to be replaced by newer versions of the same things, some of them quite ugly. The citizenry had also belatedly decided that killing off the native population was perhaps not the most civilized approach to take, and suddenly every business, every school, and every landlord began fighting tooth and nail to hire, teach, and house the planet's few remaining native inhabitants, who coolheadedly and cold-bloodedly hired out to the highest bidders, swallowed any humiliation they may have felt, and became almost wealthy enough to achieve a sort of second-class respectability.

Cain and Terwilliger landed at a rather large spaceport that possessed hundreds of flashing, blinking signs proclaiming that work on an orbiting hangar would be completed within the year. They spent ten minutes passing through customs, wasted another five while Terwilliger created a completely logical and totally false story to explain why his passport card was seven years out of date, and finally caught a monorail that took them into the city of Commonweal.

"Would you believe that?" complained the gambler, sitting down beside Cain. "I've been on maybe a hundred worlds in the last ten years, and this is the first time anyone's ever asked me for my passport."

"We're not on the Frontier anymore," replied Cain, staring out the window at the cultivated fields. "They do things differently here."

"How come they didn't hassle you?" asked Terwilliger.

"Mine's up to date."

"Why?"

"I never know when someone I'm looking for may head back into the Democracy," said Cain.

He pulled out a map of the city that he had purchased and began studying it. There were twenty main slidewalks in Commonweal, eight north–south, eight east–west, and four diagonal. He pinpointed the address the Sargasso Rose had given him, figured out the easiest way to reach it, and put the map back in his pocket.

They spent ten minutes on a northeasterly slidewalk, passing through a heavily trafficked, shining metal-and-glass commercial area, transferred to a westbound one for another ten, and then stepped off the moving walkways onto a brightly tiled street.

"About two more blocks," announced Cain, checking the map once more.

"I'm starting to remember what I don't like about populated planets," said Terwilliger unhappily as they began walking through a residential section topped by hundreds of transparent spires. "Too damned crowded." He looked up at the buildings. "The streets are too narrow, and you can't see the sky."

"Yes you can."

"Well, it *feels* like you can't," persisted Terwilliger. "And it's dirty."

"So are most Tradertowns."

"That's *clean* dirt. This stuff is soot and grease and garbage."

"An interesting distinction," remarked Cain.

"It's noisy, too. There's too much traffic and too many people. Hell, even the slidewalk creaks and rumbles."

"This is nothing," replied Cain. "You ought to go to Deluros Eight sometime."

"No, thanks," said the gambler. "Visiting a whole planet covered by a single building just isn't my idea of a good time."

"Actually, there are a few million buildings. They're just packed so close together that it seems like there's only one."

"I don't know how to tell you this," said Terwilliger, "but you're not exactly piquing my interest. I was born on the Frontier, and I've got every intention of dying there."

"Especially if ManMountain Bates catches up with you," remarked Cain.

"Then I'll just unleash you, and that'll be the end of ManMountain Bates," replied the gambler with a smile. He paused for a moment. "By the way, have you figured out how you're going to get Socrates to talk?"

"The same way people have always gotten him to do things—with money."

They crossed a street and Cain checked the number on the corner building. "We're just about there," he announced.

When they came to the building they sought, a sleek high rise boasting four separate penthouse towers and taking up half a block at its base, they went to the main entrance and found themselves in a spacious foyer. A uniformed alien that resembled nothing more than a six-legged kangaroo with a panda's face approached them and spoke into a translating mechanism.

"Greetings and salutations, joy be upon you,' it said. "My name is Wixtol; I am the concierge of the Tudor Apartments. How may I help you?"

"We've come to visit an old friend," said Cain. "Where can we find the building directory?"

"I will be immeasurably pleased to direct you to your party," replied the alien, "if you will only be so generous as to furnish me with its name."

"Whittaker Drum."

"Infinite sorrow, dear friends," announced Wixtol. "I prostrate myself to inform you that we have no such resident."

"He also uses the name Socrates," said Cain.

The alien gave them a delighted grin. "Joy supreme! Socrates lives in apartment twenty-nine fourteen, praise be. If you will condescend to follow your humble servant, I will lead you to the elevator."

It waddled off to the right, and Cain and Terwilliger fell into step behind it.

"Is that *him*, or is something wrong with the translator?" whispered the gambler.

"Who knows?" replied Cain. "Maybe they told him that's the way a concierge speaks."

They soon reached the elevators. Wixtol held the door open for them, pressed the button for the twenty-ninth floor, thanked them profusely for coming, and wished them a safe and happy ascent. Then the door slid shut, and a moment later they were walking down a mirrored corridor leading to apartment 2914.

When they arrived at the front door, Cain stopped and waited silently.

"I've seen you somewhere before," said a hoarse, masculine voice. "Who are you?"

"My name is Cain."

There was a pause. "*Sebastian* Cain?"

"Yes."

"Well, I'll be damned!" exclaimed the voice. "What have you been doing with yourself?"

"Hello, Whittaker. It's been a long time."

"What are you doing here?"

"The Sargasso Rose gave me your new name and told me to hunt you up. I'd like to talk to you, if you can spare me the time."

"I'd be delighted. Just move a step to your left so my security system can scan you."

Cain did so, and became aware of a soft humming noise.

"Do you think you're going to need two guns and a knife to talk to me?" asked the voice.

"No."

The door slid open a few inches.

"Toss them inside, Sebastian. I'll return them when we're done."

Cain withdrew the weapons in question and tossed them through the small gap.

"Now your friend."

"My name's Terwilliger," said the gambler, moving to the spot Cain vacated. "And I don't carry any guns."

"Okay," grunted the voice. "You're clean." There was a brief pause and then the door slid open the rest of the way. "Come on in."

They stepped into a small vestibule from which the weapons had already been removed, and walked through it to a large, opulently furnished living room. The carpeting was thick and expensive, the chairs and tables were crafted of rare hardwoods from distant Doradus IV, the lighting was discreet and indirect, a large window overlooked the city, alien art objects were displayed in abundance, and the walls were covered by literally scores of icons and gold and silver crucifixes.

A pudgy man with thinning gray hair, clad in a silk lounge suit, stood in the middle of the room, a huge smile on his face.

"How the hell are you?" said Socrates, walking over and giving Cain a friendly bear hug. "What have you been doing with yourself since the old days, Sebastian?"

"Bounty hunting."

"Well, why not?" said Socrates. "Killing people was always one of the things you did best." He smiled. "Damn, but it's been a long time! Have a seat. Can I get you something to drink?"

"Later, perhaps," said Cain, sitting down on the couch. "How come I don't see any bodyguards?"

"What for? I'm a respectable businessman, and I don't keep any cash up here."

"There are probably some people on Sylaria who'd like to see you dead," suggested Cain.

Socrates laughed. "Even if they knew how to find me, which they don't, I very much doubt that any of them even remember me. They've overthrown four or five dictators since I left." He turned to Terwilliger. "Are you a bounty hunter, too?"

"Nope," replied the gambler, amused. "I'm just a visitor who appreciates your offer of a drink."

"What'll it be?"

"Anything that's wet."

Socrates walked to a wall and touched a particular spot on it, and a moment later a panel slid back to reveal a small but well-stocked bar.

"How about whiskey?"

"Whiskey's fine," said Terwilliger, swinging a small, straight-backed chair around, throwing a leg over it, and pressing his chest against the back of it. Socrates poured the drink and handed it to the gambler, then turned to Cain.

"Damn, but it's good to see you again, Sebastian!" said Socrates, sitting down opposite him on a beautifully handcrafted chair. "It must be—what?—maybe twenty years now."

"Twenty-one," said Cain.

"I hope you're doing well."

"I've got no complaints."

"Neither have I, when you get right down to it. In point of fact, I've embarked on a whole new life—new name, new world, new money."

"I see you still have the same taste for life's little luxuries," remarked Cain, indicating the expensive furnishings.

"True," was the answer. "But then, what's life without a few luxuries?" He paused. "So tell me, Sebastian, why have you paid a visit to me after all this time?"

"Information."

Suddenly Socrates was all business.

"Buying or selling?"

"Buying."

"I've got someone coming by in a few minutes, so we'll have to make this briefer than I'd like, though perhaps we can have dinner later and talk about old times. In the meantime, what kind of information are you after?"

"I'm looking for someone. You can help me find him."

"If it's within my power. Who is he?"

"Santiago."

Socrates frowned. "I'm sorry, Sebastian. Ask me about anyone else, and there won't be any charge for the answer."

"I'm not looking for anyone else," said Cain.

"Then you should be. Leave him alone."

"A friendly warning?" asked Cain.

"A serious one. He's out of your league." Socrates paused. "Hell, he's out of *everyone's* league."

"Then what does he want with a loan shark?"

"I'm a *financier*," replied Socrates.

"I know exactly what you are," said Cain. "What I don't know is why he has to deal with you. He can't be short of money."

"I have, from time to time, arranged meetings between the various parties in a business transaction." Socrates smiled. "My calling, as I see it, is to match opportunists with opportunities."

"From what I can see, I would have thought your calling lay along different lines," said Cain, indicating the crucifixes and icons.

Socrates shrugged. "One does what one must. The good Lord is very understanding—especially when He sees the size of my weekly donations."

"I'll make a healthy donation myself if you can tell me what I need to know about Santiago."

"Out of the question."

"Name your price."

"There isn't any price," replied Socrates. "It's not for sale."

"Not to put too fine a point on it, Whittaker, everything you've ever owned was for sale."

Socrates sighed deeply. "You're referring to Sylaria, no doubt."

"As a matter of fact, I was," said Cain.

"That was an entirely different situation. I took over a corrupt and stagnant government—"

"And made it so much worse that the Democracy finally bought you off."

"That is an unfair and unjustified comment, Sebastian."

"Come on, Whittaker. I was there when your firing squads slaughtered ten thousand men and women."

"We all make mistakes," said Socrates easily. "I'll be the first to admit that was one of mine."

"I'm sure it's a comfort to them to know you feel that way."

"I should have killed thirty thousand," said Socrates seriously.

Terwilliger chuckled, while Cain merely stared at him.

"After a revolution," continued Socrates, "you either assimilate your enemies or you dispose of them. The one thing you don't do is leave them free to plot against you. There were too many to assimilate, so I should have gotten rid of them. As it turned out, I was too soft-hearted; I *believed* all that guff I used to spout. So I spent ninety percent of my time protecting my ass and ten percent trying to put Sylaria back on its feet. Is it any wonder that I failed?"

"You did more than fail, Whittaker," said Cain. "You left it a hell of a lot worse than you found it."

"I very much doubt that," replied Socrates. "I may have raised taxes and kept martial law in effect, but I got rid of the illegal searches and allowed some local elections."

"And assassinated the winners."

"Only some of them. Just the ones who were trying to sabotage my regime." He smiled. "Besides, in the long run they won, didn't they? I mean, hell, they're in control of the damned planet, and here I am, hiding out under an alias."

"After plundering the treasury," noted Cain.

"Travel expenses and incidentals," said Socrates with a shrug. "The Democracy didn't pay me all that much to vacate my position—certainly not as much as it should have." He leaned back comfortably on his chair. "You've got to learn to be a realist, Sebastian."

"I've become one," said Cain. "Thanks in no small part to yourself."

"You see? There's no need for this residual bitterness. We've each gone on to become better people. I have found God, as well as modest fortune, and you have become a successful bounty hunter and a realist. Obviously Sylaria did us both a lot of good."

"Did you *find* God, or did you buy Him off?"

"It's all a matter of viewpoint," answered Socrates. "I contribute thousands of credits to His churches and sing His praises every morning, and He pretty much protects me and helps take care of business. It's a mutually nourishing relationship."

"I'm sure," said Cain wryly. "But we're getting away from the subject."

"Sylaria?"

"Santiago."

Socrates shook his head. "I already told you: that subject is closed."

"What'll it cost to open it?"

"More money than you'll ever have," said Socrates. "All the Democracy could do was depose me. I assure you Santiago can do a lot worse."

"Santiago's not the only one," said Cain, reaching into one of his many pockets and withdrawing a small ceramic weapon, which he pointed at Socrates.

"How did you get that past my security system?" asked Socrates with no show of fear or alarm.

Cain smiled. "Do you think you're the only person in the galaxy with a security system? Bounty hunters see them every day. The molecular structure of this gun has been altered so that it won't show up on any detection device."

"Very ingenious," commented Socrates. "But it still won't do you any good. After all, if you kill me, how can I tell you what I know?" He slowly reached into a pocket, withdrew a cigar, and lit it.

"And if you refuse to tell me," responded Cain, "why should I let you live?"

"You're a bounty hunter," said Socrates confidently. "You kill for money. There's no price on my head."

"Don't push your luck," said Cain. "You're one man I wouldn't mind killing for free."

Socrates chuckled in amusement. "We turned out a strange crop of humanitarians back on Sylaria, didn't we?"

"I'd be a little more worried if I were you, friend," said Terwilliger. "That's the Songbird pointing that pistol in your direction."

"Is that supposed to mean something?" asked Socrates, puffing on his cigar and displaying a total lack of concern.

"It means he'll do what he says he'll do," said Terwilliger. "This is just business to him. He does it all the time."

"I'm counting on his being just a little bit brighter than you," replied Socrates calmly. "Killing me won't get him the information he wants, and you already know that I'm expecting company momentarily."

"There's no reason to let you live *unless* you tell me what I want to know," said Cain. "As for your visitor, you've been known to lie before."

"Not this time, Sebastian," said Socrates, checking his timepiece. "She's already a few minutes late." He smiled. "She's a reporter. You kill me now and you'll make every newscast from here to Deluros."

Cain stared at him for a long moment. Then he glanced quickly around the room.

"That's a very pretty bowl," he said, indicating a delicate fluted structure. "Made by Canphorites?"

"Robelians," replied Socrates. "Why?"

"What's it worth—about twenty thousand credits?"

"Give or take."

Cain fired off a quick shot, and the object shattered into a thousand tiny pieces as Terwilliger emitted a startled yell.

"What the hell are you doing?" demanded Socrates furiously. He jumped to his feet, then sat back down just as quickly when Cain pointed the weapon at him again.

"Negotiating," answered Cain. "How much did you pay for the gold crucifix with the jeweled Christ?"

"Damn it, Sebastian! That's a priceless work of art!"

"You've got ten seconds to put a price on it," replied Cain. "And if you haven't told me what I want to know, you've got one more second to kiss it good-bye."

Socrates slumped back in his chair. "Destroy them all," he said resignedly. "I can replace them easier than I can replace *me*."

"You mean it, don't you?"

"I do."

"Maybe I've been approaching this all wrong." Cain lowered his aim a few inches. "What's the going price on a kneecap?"

"Not high enough," said Socrates defiantly.

"Courage from Whittaker Drum? Now that *is* surprising."

"I'm no hero," said Socrates. "But there's nothing you can do to me that'll compare to what *he* can do."

"I wouldn't bet my life on that if I were you," said Cain.

"That's precisely what I'm betting. Whatever else you do, you won't kill me."

Just then there was a high-pitched beeping noise.

"That's her," said Socrates, turning his head and staring at a small holographic viewscreen. "You'd better put your gun away and leave while you can."

"Not a chance," said Cain. "What does she want?"

"Probably the same thing you do."

There was another beeping sound.

"We'd better answer it," said Terwilliger, checking the viewscreen to make sure Socrates wasn't lying. "She's got to know he's here."

Cain nodded, and the gambler walked over to a small control panel on the wall just behind Socrates' chair. The first two buttons he pushed flooded the apartment with music and dimmed the lights in the vestibule, but finally he hit the proper one and they heard the front door slide open.

A moment later a blonde woman in her midthirties entered the room. She was a few pounds overweight, though far from fat, her tunic and slacks were functional rather than stylish, and she wore no makeup at all. A leather satchel was slung over one shoulder.

She took in the situation in a single glance and immediately turned to Cain.

"Don't kill him until I talk to him," she said. "I'll make it worth your while."

"Nobody's killing anybody just yet," interjected Socrates, unperturbed. "We're still in the threatening stage."

"Who are you and what's your business here?" asked Cain, getting to his feet and backing up a few steps to incorporate both her and Socrates into his field of vision.

"I might ask you the same thing," she replied.

"You might," he agreed. "But I asked you first, and I've got the gun."

She stared at him for a moment, then shrugged. "My name is Virtue MacKenzie. I'm a journalist; I make holographic documentaries."

"What are you doing here?"

"I came here to do a feature on Socrates."

"Where's your technical crew?" asked Cain.

"I do my own tech work," she said. "And I'm all through answering questions. Now it's your turn."

"I've got one more," said Cain. "Have you talked to Whittaker Drum yet?"

"Who the hell is Whittaker Drum?"

Cain smiled with satisfaction. "Okay. You've told me everything I need to know." He paused for a moment. "Terwilliger, get her out of here."

The gambler began approaching her.

"That's close enough," said Virtue menacingly.

Terwilliger grinned and took another step forward. As he did so, she lashed out with a foot, catching him just below the knee. He dropped to the floor, cursing and groaning and holding his leg tenderly.

"You don't listen too well, do you?" she said contemptuously.

"Oh, my!" said Socrates, vastly amused. "This *is* getting interesting."

"You shut up!" snapped Cain.

"Are you ready to answer *my* questions yet?" demanded Virtue, ignoring Terwilliger and turning back to Cain.

"All right," he said.

"Who are you?"

"Sebastian Cain."

"The one they call the Songbird?" she asked.

He grimaced. "Yes."

"Why do you want to kill him?"

"I don't," replied Cain. "I want the same thing you do."

"And what do *I* want?"

"Information about Santiago."

"What makes you think so?"

"Because you didn't know that Socrates used to be Whittaker Drum—and the only important thing he's done since changing his name is to meet Santiago."

"I resent that," said Socrates.

"What's *your* interest in Santiago?" asked Virtue.

"Professional," said Cain. "And yours?"

"The same," she replied. "I really *do* produce documentaries. I convinced a couple of backers that I could get an exclusive feature on Santiago, and managed to wring a pretty substantial advance out of them."

"And now you have to deliver," suggested Cain, amused.

She nodded. "It's taken me almost a year to get this far; I don't want you killing him before I talk to him." She glanced at Terwilliger, who was getting painfully to his feet. "Who's this one?"

"Nobody very important," said Cain.

"Thanks a heap," muttered the gambler, flexing his leg and wincing in pain. "I think something's broken."

"If it was, you wouldn't be able to move it like that," said Virtue. "Now stop whining and shut up."

Terwilliger glared at her, then went back to massaging his knee.

"All right, Mr. Cain," she said, turning to the bounty hunter. "What now?"

"What do you suggest?"

"Our interests are parallel, but not identical," she replied. "I don't care if you kill Santiago, as long as I get my feature—and I assume you don't begrudge me my feature as long as you get your reward. I don't see much sense fighting to the death over who gets to extract the information we need."

He nodded. "Which brings us back to you, Whittaker."

Socrates smiled. "Nothing has changed, Sebastian. You can't afford to kill me, and I can't afford to let Santiago know I've betrayed him. So, while you can certainly cause me a great deal of pain, you're not going to get what you want."

"It's a possibility," admitted Cain. "On the other hand, finding out if you've got a breaking point is going to hurt you a lot more than it hurts me."

"Don't be an ass, Cain," said Virtue. "There's an easier way to do this."

"I'm open to suggestions," replied Cain.

"We'll shoot a couple of cc's of niathol into him and he'll tell us anything we want to know."

"Niathol isn't something that bounty hunters tend to carry around," Cain said wryly.

"Then isn't it lucky for you that I came prepared?" she said, unfastening her satchel.

"You expected to have to use it?"

"I anticipated the possibility," she replied, withdrawing a small package and starting to unwrap it.

"You couldn't have known I'd be here. How did you plan to get him to hold still for it?"

"The same way I convinced your friend to leave me alone," she replied, pulling out a small vial that had been wrapped in refrigerated tape. A moment later she had filled a small, sterile syringe with it.

"Well, Whittaker," said Cain, "are you going to make this easy on yourself, or am I going to have to hold you down?"

"All right, Sebastian," said Socrates with a sigh. "Skip the drug. I'll tell you what you want to know."

"That's very thoughtful of you, but I think as long as we have the niathol we won't bother relying on the eccentricities of your memory. Roll up your sleeve."

Socrates did as he was told, and Virtue walked across the room to him with the syringe in her hand.

"That looks like a hell of a lot more than two cc's," remarked Cain.

"It can't be refrozen," she replied. "We'll just toss the syringe into an atomizer when we're done."

"Terwilliger," ordered Cain, "get over there and hold him still, just in case he has a change of heart."

Terwilliger stared reluctantly at Socrates.

"Why don't you do it yourself?" suggested the gambler.

"My job is holding the gun," said Cain. "Yours is doing what I tell you to do. Go on; he won't kick you."

Terwilliger hobbled over to Socrates very cautiously.

"I know about niathol, but I've never used it," said Cain. "In my business, we're not usually after confessions. How long before it takes effect?"

"About ninety seconds," replied Virtue. "Maybe a little longer." She had Terwilliger hold Socrates' arm motionless, jabbed him a couple of times until she found a vein, and then began injecting the niathol.

And then things happened so rapidly that even Cain wasn't sure of the exact progression.

Socrates casually removed his cigar from his mouth with his free hand, then suddenly pressed it against Virtue's right wrist. She yelped and jumped back, letting go of the syringe, which remained stuck in his arm. Terwilliger reacted instantly, taking a roundhouse swing at Socrates. It landed on his neck, but the momentum carried the gambler's body between Cain and Socrates.

"Hit the ground!" yelled Cain, but even as the words left his mouth and Terwilliger dropped to the floor, Socrates had forced the syringe's plunger all the way down before Virtue could stop him.

"You lose, Sebastian," he said with an ironic smile as Cain realized what he had done and lowered his weapon.

"You dumb bastard!" snapped Virtue. "You'll be dead inside of a minute."

"At least it's painless this way," said Socrates, his words starting to slur.

"Well, as long as you're finally going to meet your God face to face, I hope for your sake that He's the forgiving type," said Cain.

"Not to worry, Sebastian," said Socrates with a hollow laugh. "He's in the bag."

He slumped forward.

"Shit!" snapped Virtue. "Who the hell would have thought he'd do something like that?" She opened one of his eyelids, stared at the pupil for few seconds, then let it fall shut again. "He's done."

"He's really dead?" asked Terwilliger, staring at him.

Virtue stared contemptuously at him and made no reply.

"Thanks a lot," said Cain sardonically.

"Don't you go acting so goddamned superior!" she shot back. "If you thought he was going to do that, you should have said so."

"I should have done it my way."

"Your way wouldn't have worked, either. Don't you understand that he was willing to suffer anything you could offer up rather than let Santiago know he'd betrayed him?" She paused and stared thoughtfully at Socrates. "Just what kind of man can put such fear into people?"

"Maybe you'd be better off returning your advance and not finding out," suggested Cain.

"Most of it is spent," she replied. "I can't go back without my feature. Besides, I've already spent a year of my life on this project."

"There are men who have spent thirty years hunting for Santiago," noted Cain.

"Most of them never got this far," said Virtue. "And the journalist who actually brings back tapes or holos of Santiago will be as famous as *he* is; she'll need a warehouse just to hold her awards, and she can choose her own assignments and name her own price for the rest of her career." She paused. "It's worth the effort."

"Have fun."

"I'm not beaten yet," she said with determination. "I have other leads."

"Oh?" he replied, suddenly alert.

She nodded. "Well, Mr. Cain?"

"Well what?"

"I'll show you mine if you show me yours," she said with a grin.

He shrugged. "Why not?"

"There's a condition."

"What?"

"We keep in touch, and give each other progress reports."

"How?"

She jerked a thumb in Terwilliger's direction. "Use *him*. He's not much good for anything else, is he?"

"Now just a goddamned minute!" said the gambler hotly.

"Out of the question," said Cain. "I'd have to give him his own ship."

"Let him use yours," said Virtue. "We won't be that far apart."

"What makes you think he won't just take off with it?"

"Will you stop talking about me as if I wasn't here?" demanded Terwilliger petulantly.

"Shut up," said Virtue. She turned back to Cain. "Offer him ten percent of the reward. That ought to buy the little bastard's loyalty."

"I'm not giving him any percentage right now. Why should I change that?"

"Because you don't have any information right now."

Cain lowered his head in thought for a long moment, then looked up.

"If your leads are the same as mine, the deal's off."

"Fair enough," she replied.

"Don't *I* get a say in this?" snapped Terwilliger.

"Do you want ten percent of twenty million credits enough to do what you're told, or not?" said Virtue.

The gambler glared at her, then realized what was being offered and smiled sheepishly. "I'm in," he said.

"Somehow I'm not surprised," she replied. "Well, *that's* settled. Now I suppose we'd better do something about the body."

"I'll take care of it," said Cain.

"After you visit the local post office and see if there's any paper on him?" she suggested.

"That's right."

"I think I should get half," she continued. "It was my niathol that killed him."

"Are you a journalist or a bounty hunter?" Cain asked wryly.

"Why don't we say that I'm an underpaid journalist, and let it go at that."

He stared at her and finally nodded in agreement. "Okay. If there's any reward for him, you get half."

"You know," commented Terwilliger, who had been scrutinizing her, "you could be damned attractive if you'd just go to a little effort."

"Too bad the same can't be said for you," she said, turning her attention back to Cain. "All right, Songbird—are you ready to compare notes?"

"I'm ready," he answered.

"I have a feeling that this is going to be a long and amiable re- lationship," predicted Virtue.

"I'll settle for its just being profitable," replied Cain.

"That goes without saying."

He smiled and shook his head. "That's the one thing that *never* goes without saying."

She extended her hand. "Partners?"

"Partners."

They shook hands over the unmourned corpse of Whittaker Drum.

Part 2

The Virgin Queen's Book

6.

She can drink, she can swear, can the Virgin Queen,
And she isn't a stranger to sin.
She knows what she wants, doesn't care where she's been,
And she'll do what she has to to win.

The name was Black Orpheus' idea of a joke, because while Virtue MacKenzie was a lot of things good and bad, virginal wasn't one of them.

He met her just once, out by the Delphini system—which was as close to the worlds of the Democracy as he ever tended to go—and she made quite an impression on him. She was drinking and playing cards at the time, and she wasn't even aware of his presence; but when she accused a fellow journalist of cheating and backed it up with a couple of swift kicks to his groin and a whiskey bottle slammed down on top of his head, she guaranteed herself a couple of verses in his ongoing epic.

In point of fact, she didn't even know she'd been written up until some months later, and then she was furious about the name he'd saddled her with—but after a couple of weeks she cooled down, right about the time she decided that being in Black Orpheus' song just might open a couple of doors for her out on the Frontier.

It did, too. She had to wait until the balladeer's disciples and interpreters figured out that Virtue MacKenzie and the Virgin Queen were the same woman and started disseminating the information across the Inner Frontier, but once the word got out it helped her get into a couple of previously inaccessible places on Terrazane, where she found

out about Socrates, and it got her Socrates' address from a trader on
Jefferson III.

It hadn't done her much good here on Pegasus, but this was the
Democracy, not the Frontier, and Black Orpheus wasn't much better
known here than the outcasts and misfits that he sang about. She and
Cain had traded their information in Socrates' apartment three weeks
ago, each holding back a couple of tidbits—at least, she assumed Cain
had withheld some information; she knew that *she* had—and it was
decided that Cain was better equipped to track down a professional
assassin like Altair of Altair, whereas Virtue knew her way around the
Democracy better than he did and would begin her hunt among the
Democracy's older, more established worlds.

She had spent the better part of a week searching for Salvatore
Acosta, one of the four black marketeers who had delivered Santiago's
goods to the Sargasso Rose, and had found out from her own sources
that he had been murdered on Pegasus two months earlier.

Pegasus was a former mining world, rich in gold and fissionable
materials, which was now a heavily populated member of the Democracy. It had been named for the planet's dominant herbivore, a small
horselike animal that possessed a pair of fleshy protuberances just behind its withers. (They had never been used for anything other than
balance, but they looked remarkably like vestigial wings.)

The planet itself was one of those odd scattered worlds that seemed
Earth-like, but wasn't truly habitable in the normal sense. It possessed
oxygen, nitrogen, and the various inert gases that Men needed, but
they existed in the wrong quantities, and twenty minutes' exposure to
the atmosphere left one breathless and panting; an hour could be fatal
to anyone with a respiratory problem; and even the healthiest settlers
couldn't breathe the air for two hours.

But for some reason—possibly it was the view, for Pegasus was
a gorgeous world, with snow-capped mountains and literally thousands
of winding rivers, and was possessed of gold-and-brown vegetation
that made the landscape look perpetually crisp and autumnal; though
more likely it was the location, for it was midway between the Spica
mining worlds and the huge financial center on Daedalus II—the planet
became a very desirable piece of real estate. The original miners had
lived underground, artificially enriching their air while protecting
themselves from the extremely cold nights; but once the world started
drawing crowds of permanent residents, construction began on a
domed city, then five more, and ultimately a seventh that was almost
as large as the first six combined. All of the cities bore Greek names;
the newest and largest of them was Hektor, named after the supposedly

mythical warrior who local historians had erroneously decided was either the rider or trainer of the winged horse.

Upon reaching Pegasus and taking a hotel room in Hektor, Virtue MacKenzie had immediately contacted Leander Smythe, a newsman who owed her a favor and very begrudgingly allowed her to access the raw data he possessed on Acosta's murder from her room's computer. There wasn't much information to be gleaned: Acosta had a long record of shady dealings, and more than his share of enemies. His throat had been slit as he was leaving the Pearl of the Sea, a restaurant and bar catering to the less wholesome elements of Pegasan society, and he had died instantly. It was assumed to be an underworld murder, if only because Acosta himself hadn't associated with any noncriminals in more than a decade.

Virtue then called up the shopping and restaurant guide that every hotel possessed but couldn't find any listing for the Pearl of the Sea, invariably a signal that a local pub or restaurant had a steady clientele and neither needed nor desired any new business. She then accessed a video overview of the city and homed in on the area around the restaurant. It seemed as sleek and shining and well kept as the rest of Hektor, but she noticed that the police patrolled the area in pairs—which tended to support her tentative decision that visiting it alone and asking pointed questions wasn't worth the risk involved.

Five minutes later she tied in to the local police headquarters' press department and quickly ascertained that the authorities weren't about to hand any information over to an offworld journalist. She immediately called back, asked to speak to the homicide department, identified herself as Acosta's grieving half sister, and demanded to know what progress had been made in apprehending his killer. The answer was simple enough: There had been absolutely no progress, nor was there likely to be. From the contemptuous way they spoke about Acosta, she got the distinct impression that the only thing they would do if they actually found his murderer would be shake his hand, and perhaps pin a medal on him.

Finally she had the computer check her message drop—a dumb terminal in the city's central post office—to see if there was any word from Cain or Terwilliger, found nothing waiting for her, and decided to spend a little more time investigating Acosta's murder before going after Khalythorpe, the methane-breathing smuggler who was next on the Sargasso Rose's list.

She asked the computer for a running total on her expenses thus far, found that she had run up almost three hundred credits in user and access fees, and told it to warn her when she reached the five-hundred-credit mark.

She then opened a bottle of Camorian vodka, filled a cup from the bathroom, pretended that there was an olive in it, sipped it thoughtfully, and decided upon her next step, which was to access the local library's main computer. She had it scan the past five years' worth of news reports, keying on Acosta's name, and came up absolutely empty. She then tried to find some similarity between his murder and other killings that had taken place in the same area, and discovered that of the thirty-nine murders in Hektor during the past year, thirty-two of them had occurred within a mile of where Acosta had been found, and nineteen were the result of stabbings. It was quite possible, she concluded unhappily, that Acosta simply had been in the wrong place at the wrong time; at any rate, there was no reason to assume that he had died because of his association with Santiago.

Dead end followed dead end, and finally she was faced with two alternatives: start questioning people who might have known Acosta, or give up and go after the methane-breather. She made her decision, then instructed the computer to patch in a visual connection to Leander Smythe's office.

A moment later a portly, middle-aged man with a sightly uneven hair transplant appeared on the small screen just above the speaker.

"I know I'm going to regret asking this," he said when he had recognized her, "but what can I do for you?"

"I'm up against a blank wall, Leander," she said.

"Who are you trying to kid, Virtue?" replied Smythe. "You've only been on the damned planet for four hours."

"That's all the time it takes to know I'm not going to get what I want through normal channels." She paused. "I hate calling in favors," she added insincerely, "but I need your help."

"You already collected your favor this morning," he reminded her.

She smiled. "You owe me a bigger one than that, Leander. Or would you like me to refresh your memory?"

"No!" he said quickly. "This isn't a secure channel."

"Then invite me to lunch and we'll talk face to face."

"I'm busy."

"Fine." She shrugged. "Then I'll just have to hunt up someone else from your network who'll do me a favor in exchange for a very interesting story about a local journalist."

She reached out to sever the connection.

"Wait!" he said urgently.

She withdrew her hand and grinned triumphantly.

"There's a restaurant on the top of my building," he said. "I'll meet you there in half an hour."

"Your treat," she said. "I'm just a poor working girl."

She broke the connection, ascertained that 493 credits for computer usage would be added to her hotel tab, entered a request (without much hope) for a ten percent professional discount, took the elevator down to the fourth floor of the hotel, walked out on a platform, and caught the Hanging Tube—the inhabitants' term for the elevated monorail—to Smythe's office building. She noticed in passing that a thunderstorm was in full force outside the dome and that the noonday sky was almost black, and wondered idly what the little herbivores for which the planet had been named did to shield themselves from the weather, since she had seen precious few natural shelters on her way from the spaceport to the city.

When she arrived at Smythe's building, she presented her credentials to a security guard at the door. The man gave them a perfunctory glance, nodded, and passed her through to the upper lobby, where she took an elevator to the roof.

The restaurant would have impressed anyone who had been born on the Frontier, but Virtue found it just a bit overdone: the tables were too small, the furniture too ornate, and there were too many very self-assured waiters hovering around. She ascertained that Smythe wasn't there yet, found that he had reserved a table for two, allowed the maître d' to escort her to a seat, and ordered a mixed drink from the bar.

Smythe arrived about five minutes later, walked directly to the bar, ordered a drink for himself, and then joined her at the table.

"It's good to see you again after all these years, Virtue," he said, greeting her with an artificial smile.

"How nice of you to say so," she replied dryly. "And how well you lie."

"Let's at least maintain the illusion of civility," he said, unperturbed. "Until we're through with lunch, anyway."

"Suits me."

He picked up his menu, pretended to study it for a moment, recommended a dish to Virtue, signaled for a waiter, and ordered for both of them.

"It's been a long time," he said when the waiter had gone off to the kitchen. "What is it now—five years?"

"Six."

"I've seen your byline from time to time, when some of your features have come up for syndication. That was a very nice piece you did on the war with the Borgaves."

"Ugly beasts, aren't they?" she commented.

"How did you manage to land with the first invasion wave?" he asked. "That's usually reserved for senior correspondents."

"I bribed a nice young major."

"That figures," he said with a tinge of bitterness. "You always knew how to get what you wanted."

"I still do," she said, staring directly at him.

He met her gaze for a moment, then looked away uncomfortably. "Did you ever marry that fellow you used to live with?"

"I've lived with a number of people," she replied. "I never married any of them."

"Pity." He pulled out a handsome cigarette case and offered one to her.

"No, thanks."

"They're very good," he said, removing one and lighting it up. "Imported from the Kakkab Kastu system."

"I prefer my own," she said, withdrawing a distinctive box.

"Don't you find those kind of harsh?" he asked.

"I've been smoking them since I've been on the Frontier," replied Virtue. "They grow on you after a while."

"You've been on the Frontier?"

"For almost a year."

"What were you doing out there?"

"The same thing I'm doing on Pegasus: following up a story." She paused. "I've also picked up a pretty interesting partner."

"I thought you always worked alone," said Smythe.

"This time I needed help."

"Is it anyone I know?"

"Probably not," Virtue replied. "Ever hear of the Songbird?"

He shook his head. "Is that her byline?"

"It's a him."

"I've never seen any of his features."

"That's not surprising. He's a bounty hunter."

"What the hell kind of story are you working on?"

"If I tell you, we're all through exchanging pleasantries and we start talking business."

He shifted his weight uneasily but nodded in agreement. "We're going to do it sooner or later. I suppose we ought to get it over with." He paused. "Salvatore Acosta was a small-time smuggler who died broke. He wasn't worth much more than a five-second obituary. So who are you really after?"

"Santiago."

He laughed. "You and ten thousand other journalists."

"I'm different," said Virtue seriously. "I'm going to get him."

"I wish you luck."

"I don't need luck," she replied. "I need information."

"You probably know more about Acosta than I do."

"Forget Acosta," said Virtue. "He's a dead end. I need something else."

"Such as?"

"Someone who can tell me where Santiago is."

Smythe laughed again. "Why don't you ask for a million credits while you're at it? One's as likely as the other."

"This person doesn't have to know Santiago's headquarters. He just has to point me in the right direction."

"What the hell makes you think anyone on Pegasus has any dealings with Santiago?"

"Because, with all due respect for your beautiful city, it's not exactly a vacation spa. Acosta was here to deliver some goods or some money, or else to pick something up. He probably didn't deal directly with the person I want—but that doesn't mean you can't help me find that person."

"Are you telling me Acosta worked for Santiago?" asked Smythe.

"Indirectly. I doubt that they ever met. Acosta was just a conduit for stolen goods, or perhaps money. What I need from you is the name of the biggest operator in Hektor."

"Harrison Brett," replied Smythe without hesitation.

"Does he have a criminal record?"

"Yes."

"Tell me about it."

"He's got thirty arrests."

"Any convictions?"

Smythe looked uncomfortable. "Two."

"Suspended sentences?"

He nodded.

"Who's he paying off?" she asked quickly.

Smythe shrugged. "Everybody."

She smiled. "Come on, Leander—this is Virtue you're talking to, not some slob in your newsroom. You know what I want."

"Why not just put the pressure on Brett?" he asked in a tone of voice that implied he knew the answer as well as she did.

"How do you pressure a man who knows he can't go to jail?" she replied. "The name, please."

"I don't know any other name," he said.

"Not smart, Leander," she said ominously. "Not smart at all."

"It's the truth," he replied defensively.

"*I* know another name, though," she said. "The name I know is Leander Smythe. I even know some facts to go with the name. Want to hear them?"

"No," he said, puffing rapidly on his cigarette.

"They're interesting facts," she continued. "They're all about how he falsified evidence on his first big story and helped send an innocent man to jail for eight years."

"You *covered* for me, for Christ's sake!" he hissed. "If you knew he was innocent, why didn't you block the story when you had the chance?"

"Oh, he deserved to go to jail," she said pleasantly. "He was a bastard from the word go, and the police had been trying to nail him for years." She stared seriously at him. "But the fact remains that he was innocent of the charges that were brought against him based on your information."

"Then you should have said something at the time."

"I did," she replied, finishing her drink. "I told you that you owed me a favor in exchange for my silence, and that someday I'd be by to collect it."

"You know," he said unhappily, "I never did like you much. You were always too ambitious, always scheming and plotting."

"Why should I deny it?" she said calmly. "I'll only add that it's people like you who made it easy."

"What'll you do when you finally get to the top, and there are no more bodies to climb over?"

"Mostly, I'll enjoy it," she replied. "And I'll protect myself a hell of a lot better than the rest of you ever did."

"How many other favors have you stockpiled over the years?" he asked bitterly.

"A few."

"And how many other people have you blackmailed with them?"

"I'm not blackmailing you, Leander," replied Virtue. "I have other leads. If you don't want to do me a favor, you don't have to. Just forget I asked."

"You mean it?"

"Absolutely." She paused. "Of course, I'll have to pay a visit to your superiors. After all, I'm a journalist—and what you did qualifies as news, even after all these years." She smiled. "Don't worry; you won't go to jail for it—but you'd better find a new profession."

"Have you ever done anything, even once, with no thought of a return?" he asked.

"Yes."

"How old were you? Six?"

"Younger. And I immediately decided that there was no percentage in it."

"Who did your bounty hunter have to kill for you before you teamed up with him?"

"Actually, he had to postpone killing someone," said Virtue. "But we're straying from the subject. I need a name."

He nervously lit another cigarette before his first had gone out. "You must understand: I can't be connected with it."

"You won't be," she assured him, leaning forward intently. "The name."

"This is it?" he said. "You'll never bring up that damned story again?"

"I promise."

He sighed. "Dimitri Sokol."

"How big is he?"

"Very. He's a multimillionaire, he's a director of half a dozen corporations, he's held a couple of political offices, and word is that he's about to buy himself an ambassadorship to Lodin Eleven."

"Better and better," she said with a predatory grin. "What have you got on him?"

"Officially, nothing."

"Come on, Leander. Just blurt it all out and then forget you told me. Women?"

Smythe shook his head. "Not a chance."

"Men? Little boys? Drugs?"

"Just money. He bankrolled a smuggling operation out in the Binder system, though I think it would take you a couple of lifetimes to pierce through his corporate veil. I've got a feeling that he was peripherally involved in a couple of murders six years ago—*very* peripherally—and I know he's given and taken bribes. Anyway, somewhere along the way he decided that he wanted to be respectable, and he's been cleaning up his image for the past three years."

"And now he wants an ambassadorship?"

"So I'm told."

"Okay, Leander—start giving me names and dates, and then I think we can go our separate ways."

"I don't *know* any names and dates for sure. It's all gossip and conjecture."

"I know. Now let's have them."

"Damn! I wish I could give you a suicide pill or something, just in case this doesn't work."

"I wouldn't take it."

"I know," he muttered.

Their lunch arrived, and while they ate—she enthusiastically, he totally without interest—Smythe laid out such details of Sokol's dealings as he had been able to piece together. Virtue took no notes, but he knew that she'd be able to recite the list verbatim a month later.

"I'll try to set up an appointment with Sokol for tomorrow afternoon," Virtue announced when they were finished with dessert and sipping their after-dinner drinks.

"What makes you think he'll see you?" asked Smythe.

"Turn down an interview with a journalist from Deluros with an ambassadorship in the offing?" she replied with a chuckle. "Not a chance."

"Since when are you from Deluros?"

"Since tomorrow morning."

"He'll check you out before he sees you."

"I know," said Virtue. "That's why you're going to program my new credentials into your network's computer. It's the first place he'll look if he has any doubts about me."

"The hell I will!" he exploded, then lowered his voice when he realized he was attracting the attention of the other diners. "That's above and beyond our agreement," he said, lowering his voice.

"True. I won't threaten you with your . . . ah, journalistic indiscretion again. I gave you my word, and I intend to keep it."

"Then that's settled," he said firmly. "I'm not loading false credentials in the computer."

"The choice is entirely yours," she said. "I suppose I'll just have to tell Sokol to verify my position with you personally." She shrugged. "There's always the chance that he won't put two and two together and figure out who gave me the stuff I'm going to use on him."

"You'd do it, wouldn't you?" he said furiously. "You'd really do it!"

"Nobody's going to stop me from finding Santiago—not you, not anyone. I've staked my career on it."

"Then why don't you find another career? Go raise a family or something, instead of blackmailing your old friends. Jesus, but I feel sorry for your partner!"

"He's pretty good at taking care of himself. I think your sympathy would be better spent on a sweet, innocent girl like me."

"Innocent of *what?*" he said disgustedly.

"You *will* remember to change my credentials, won't you?" she said sweetly, pushing back her chair and standing up.

"Yes," he muttered. "I'll change them."

"And one more thing, Leander."

"What other little favor can I do for you?" he asked. "Pluck out my eyeballs so you can play marbles with them?"

"Some other time, perhaps." Suddenly she was serious. "I'm sure everything will go smoothly—but just in case I don't come back, or get word to you that I'm all right, I want you to contact Sebastian Cain."

"Who the hell is that?" he demanded.

"The Songbird." She gave him the registration number of Cain's ship. "He should be in the Altair system in the next day or two."

"What message do you want me to give him?"

"I should think that would be obvious," she replied. "I may die unmourned, but I sure as hell don't plan to die unavenged."

7.

Since Black Orpheus never returned to the populated worlds of the Democracy, and Dimitri Sokol never left them, it's only natural that he gave Sokol neither a verse nor a nickname. They never met, never crossed paths, never even knew the other existed—which was probably just as well: Black Orpheus wouldn't have liked him much. Orpheus loved the uninhibited, colorful men and women of the Frontier; Sokol was calm, calculating, and self-controlled. Black Orpheus painted his word pictures in primaries; Dimitri Sokol was a pastel.

Sokol was a civilized man, and as such he indulged in the crimes of civilization. If a man had to be killed, his hand may have held the checkbook, but it never touched the weapon. If there was smuggling or black marketeering to be done, he put so many holding companies and middlemen between himself and his hirelings that he might as well have been on Deluros VIII itself. He craved respectability, which Black Orpheus disdained; and he disdained notoriety, which Black Orpheus dedicated his career to perpetuating.

Orpheus would have considered him a hypocrite, which is certainly one interpretation; but the truth of the matter was that Sokol managed to walk a very fine line between his deeds and his expectations with a skill that even the Bard of the Inner Frontier would have admired.

He had vacation homes on Seabright and Pollux IV, and a suite of offices—which he hadn't visited in years—on Canphor VII. He made large donations to charity each year and had recently paid for an addition to a hospital in Pallas Athena, the oldest of Pegasus' seven enclosed cities. He was a patron of the arts and could always be counted upon to support the local symphony orchestra and ballet with handsome contributions; he no longer donated to the opera, but it was common knowledge that he disapproved of his daughter's liaison with one of the lead tenors, and nobody thought any the less of him for it.

He had spent most of his working hours during the past two years in his penthouse atop one of Hektor's more desirable residential buildings. There were twelve rooms in all; nine served as the family's residence—a son and two daughters still lived with him—and the other three rooms, with their own private entrance, had been converted into an office suite.

It was just after noon when Virtue MacKenzie presented herself in the building's lobby, waited while a security woman announced her arrival, and then took an elevator directly to Sokol's office suite. Upon emerging, she found herself in a small reception foyer, where a secretary told her that she was expected and ushered her into an opulently furnished study.

"He'll join you in just a moment," said the secretary, returning to his post by the elevator.

Virtue took that moment to examine her surroundings. Two of the walls were covered with artwork from all over the Democracy, most of it expensive, some of it good, none of it showing any consistency of taste. A third wall, composed of floor-to-ceiling windows, afforded a dramatic view of a blue river and a deep ravine just beyond the dome. The carpet was plush, made of some wiry alien fabric which seemed to shrink from the touch of her foot, then instantly moved back and pressed against it once she had set it down. There was a large holographic videoscreen, the controls of which were built into the arm of a leather couch. There were four matching chairs, two of them almost pristine, the other two showing some signs of wear. An alien musical instrument, bulky as a piano but of a type she had never seen before, was carefully angled into a corner. Atop it were six small cubes, each containing a hologram of a member of the Sokol family. She picked up one containing the representation of a lovely young woman and examined it.

"My youngest daughter," said a firm, friendly voice, and she turned to find that Sokol had entered the room.

He was a tall man, burly without being overweight, with a well-groomed shock of steel-gray hair and a dapper mustache. His eyes were a deep blue, his nose absolutely straight, his chin square without being prominent. He wore an elegantly embroidered suit of a style that had recently been popular on Deluros VIII.

"She's very pretty," replied Virtue, setting the cube back down.

"Thank you," said Sokol. "I'll tell her you said so." He touched a concealed control behind a picture, and instantly a section of the carpet disappeared and a small but well-stocked bar rose from the floor. "Can I fix you a drink?"

"Why not?" she replied.

"What will you have?"

"What do you recommend?"

He reached for a strangely shaped bottle. "Cygnian cognac. A gift from a friend who recently returned from Altair."

"I thought you said it was Cygnian," remarked Virtue, filing the reference to Altair away for future reference.

"I did. But Cygnian cognac is in demand all across the galaxy." He paused, then smiled. "If you'd ever tasted the stuff they brew on Altair, you'd know why he brought me this instead."

He poured two glasses and handed one to her.

"Very good," she replied, taking a sip.

"Won't you have a seat?" he said, escorting her to a chair, then sitting down across from her. He pulled out a large cigar. "Do you mind if I smoke?"

"Not at all."

"It's from old Earth itself," he said proudly, lighting up. "They're very hard to come by these days."

"I can imagine."

"Still," he said, exhaling a streak of smoke, "they're worth the effort." He paused. "By the way, where's your camera crew?"

"I don't have one," she replied, opening her well-worn satchel and pulling out a small, metallic, many windowed device, which she placed on a table between them. "This has a pair of wide-angle three-dimensional lenses that can follow you anywhere in the room, and there's a built-in speaker that will pick up everything you say." She pressed a small activator button. "It's not studio quality, but one doesn't always know what conditions will be like in the field, and it's a pretty handy little gadget."

"Amazing!" he said, staring at it in fascination. "It covers a three-hundred-and-sixty-degree area without moving?"

She nodded. "That's right—which means I'll be in all the pictures, too. When I get it to the lab, they'll edit it to follow a standard question-and-answer format, cutting to each of us as we speak. No one except you and me and the lab technicians will know that there wasn't an entire crew on hand."

"And this will be aired on Deluros Eight?" he asked, his expression mirroring his interest.

"As well as half a dozen other systems."

"Can I get a copy of the final cut for myself?"

"I don't see why not," said Virtue. "Of course, you'll need professional equipment to play it back."

"I own some, and have access to still more."

"Fine. Shall we begin?"

"Whenever you're ready," said Sokol.

She proceeded to conduct a thorough and professional interview for the next thirty minutes, on the off chance that she might someday be able to sell it, if not to Leander Smythe's network, then to some other Pegasus news agency, or perhaps to Lodin XI if Sokol actually got himself assigned there.

"Well," she announced at last, shutting off the recording device, "I think that's it."

"It was my pleasure," replied Sokol. "You will let me know when it's ready, won't you?"

"Certainly," replied Virtue. "Of course, it all depends on how you answer the next question."

"I beg your pardon?"

"I have another question."

"Don't you want to turn the machine back on?" he asked.

She shook her head. "This one is off the record."

"Okay," he said, leaning back comfortably. "Ask away."

"I want you to consider it very carefully before answering."

"I think I'm pretty used to loaded questions," he replied confidently.

"I'm glad to hear that," said Virtue, staring at him. "Where can I find Santiago?"

For just a moment he looked surprised. Then his professional politician's smile spread across his handsome face. "It's my opinion that this Santiago is just a Frontier myth. If he ever did exist, he must be dead by now."

"He's alive."

"I very much doubt it."

"If you want someone who doesn't exist, Mr. Sokol," she said, "try Sidney Peru."

Suddenly the smile vanished. "Who's Sidney Peru?"

"He's a smuggler who was murdered six years ago."

"I never heard of him."

"How about Heinrich Klausmeier?" she asked.

"The name's totally unfamiliar to me."

"They both worked for you," she said. "And they were both murdered."

"What's this—some last-minute smear campaign?" he said coldly. "Because if it is, you've come to the wrong place. Anyone who wants to can go over my record. I have nothing to hide."

"I think you have a great deal to hide, Mr. Sokol," said Virtue. "Such as a smuggling ring on Binder Ten."

"I haven't been to Binder in five years," he replied. "Besides, the press tried to pin that on me the first time I ran for office. You won't get any further with it than your colleagues did, for the simple reason that I am not a criminal."

"My predecessors didn't know what *I* know."

"What do you think you know?" he asked, unperturbed.

"I know that if you don't point me in Santiago's direction, there's going to be a very interesting piece of investigatory reporting on your videoscreen before the week is out."

He looked long and hard at her, then smiled confidently. "Do your worst. I never heard of anyone called Peru or Klausmeier."

She stared at him. There was no question in her mind that he knew exactly what she was talking about; the only question was how well insulated he thought he was. She decided to take one more shot at it.

"That's not what Salvatore Acosta told me before he died," she said.

He snorted derisively. "*Another* mystery man. Who the hell is Salvatore Acosta?"

"He used to work for you, a long time ago."

"Nobody named Acosta has ever worked for me."

"I have a tape of him in which he implicates you in the murders of Peru and Klausmeier."

"I very much doubt that."

"Can you afford to take the chance?" she said. "Maybe it won't hold up in court, and maybe it will—but it will sure as hell cost you a post on Lodin Eleven."

"You don't have any such tape—and if you do, then the man's a liar."

She shrugged and walked to the door. "You're welcome to your opinion." She turned to him. "Our editing lab can't go to work on your interview until we have a signed release; I'll send over a blank form tomorrow morning."

Sokol stared at her.

"You know, you could have made this much more pleasant for yourself if you'd simply been open and straightforward with me," he said at last.

She laughed. "How much more straightforward can I be?"

"If you had just said, 'Mr. Sokol, I think you're wrong about Santiago's being dead, and I'd like any information you might have that could help lead me to him,' I'd have been happy to talk to you. But I don't like being bullied and blackmailed, especially when all you've got are lies and slander."

She stared at him for a moment, then spoke:

"Mr. Sokol, I think you're wrong about Santiago's being dead, and I'd like any information you might have that could help lead me to him."

He smiled at her. "That being the case, I'll be more than happy to help you in any way that I can. The man you want to see is a bandit out on the Frontier."

"What's his name?"

"I have no idea what his real name is—but he calls himself the Jolly Swagman."

"Where do I find him?"

"He makes his headquarters on a planet called Goldenrod, out in the Jolain system."

"What's his connection to Santiago?"

"He used to work for him."

"So did a lot of people," Virtue pointed out. "What makes him unique?"

"He knows Santiago personally."

"You'd better be telling the truth," she said ominously.

"Do what you want with your tape," he said casually. "The truth can't harm me, and lies can't help you." He walked to the doorway, waved his hand before a hidden sensor, and the door slid into the wall. "I'll be looking forward to seeing the interview after it's been edited."

"That's the very least I'll be showing you," she replied, walking through the reception foyer to the elevator.

Sokol stood staring at the spot where she had been standing, lit another cigar, and walked back to his supply of liquor where he poured himself another cognac.

"Did you hear all that?" he said in conversational tones.

"Yes," replied a disembodied voice.

"I want her followed."

"*Just* followed?" asked the voice.

"Until we find out where she's got the tape, or decide that she was bluffing. And I don't want her leaving the planet until I know one way or the other. In the meantime, I want a complete dossier on her. Not the crap they dished out at the network this morning, but the real stuff." He paused. "You've got four hours."

"It might take a little longer."

"Four hours," repeated Sokol.

In point of fact, it took only three hours and ten minutes, during which time Sokol gave out another interview, this one to a local reporter, and began preparing a speech he was to give at a political fundraiser the next evening. Finally a blond man of indeterminate age entered the room, a small notebook in his hand.

"Have a seat," said Sokol. It was not a request.

"I've put all this in the computer," replied the man. "But I thought you'd want to go over it in person, just in case you had any questions."

"What have you got on her?"

"Her name is either Virtue Patience MacKenzie or Virtue Patia MacKenzie," said the man. "The records are a little unclear. It's my own feeling that she changed her middle name from Patience to Patia when she came of age. She's thirty-six years old. She was born on Belore, grew up on Sirius Five, got her degree at Aristotle—"

"That's the university planet they created a few years ago?" interrupted Sokol.

"Right. Her grades were mediocre, but Aristotle's a pretty classy place, and she was able to hire on with a news network right after that."

"How long has she worked out of Deluros?" asked the politician.

"She's never been to Deluros in her life. She worked on salary for about ten years, mostly in the Alphard sector, then went free-lance."

"Personality profile?"

"She's always been very bright, even precocious. She drinks more than she should, and has been known to gamble—badly, I might add. She appears to have a problem forming relationships; at any rate, she's entered into six serious liaisons, none of which have lasted for as much as a year."

"That hardly sounds serious to me," commented Sokol.

"That's as serious as she gets about anything except her career."

"Then you'd better tell me a little about her career."

"She resents authority; in fact, she's been fired twice for insubordination. Her work has been pretty good, well above average, but she hasn't come within hailing distance of the kind of breakthrough story that could make her reputation. She's very success-oriented; she's afraid time is running out on her, and she's getting very impatient. About a year ago she managed to fast-talk a couple of backers into tossing almost two million credits into this Santiago project. I still don't know how; it's possible she slept with them, and more likely that she blackmailed them. She's been working on the project for about eleven months, and she's run through two-thirds of the money." He paused. "I've got a feeling that this is a make-it-or-break-it situation for her. If she comes up empty, she's through."

"Why didn't she just take the money and disappear?"

"She'd rather be rich and famous than just rich."

"I know that feeling," muttered Sokol wryly. He looked at the blond man. "Anything else?"

"Yes. She found Whittaker Drum about three weeks ago, and may even have killed him."

"What kind of half-assed statement is that?" demanded Sokol. "Either she killed him or she didn't."

"It's not that simple. While she was on Declan Four, she teamed up with a bounty hunter called Cain, who's after Santiago for the reward. From what I can tell, he's pretty good at his job. Both of them were in Drum's apartment at the same time; it's anyone's guess as to who actually killed him." He glanced at his notebook. "There's another person involved: a gambler called Terwilliger. Cain took him on at Port Étrange, and they've been traveling together ever since. I don't know if he's part of their partnership or not. My own guess is that he put Cain onto Drum, or someone who could identify Drum, in exchange for some favor or another."

"What kind of favor?"

"I don't know—but gamblers tend to make enemies. A bounty hunter is probably a pretty handy person to have nearby, especially on the Frontier."

"All right," said Sokol, lighting up a cigar and staring at the glowing tip for a moment. "Let's get back to MacKenzie. How did she get to me? Drum didn't even know I exist."

The blond man shrugged. "I don't know."

"Then I'll tell you how," continued Sokol thoughtfully. "Somebody told her—either Acosta or someone else. Who has she seen since she's been on Pegasus?"

"Just Leander Smythe."

Sokol smiled. "There's the answer. That little bastard hand-fed her all the stuff he's been trying to pin on me all these years."

"Perhaps," agreed the blond man. "But I think we'd better be sure before we move."

"That shouldn't be too hard. Who was this Acosta, anyway?"

"A smuggler. He probably did handle a little stuff for Santiago from time to time."

"Did we ever have any dealings with him?"

"Not directly."

"Could he have known my name?"

"Anything's possible."

"Let's attack it another way," said Sokol. "When was he killed?"

"A couple of weeks ago."

"Before Virtue MacKenzie landed on Pegasus?"

"Right."

Sokol smiled. "Then she never met him."

"You can't be sure of that. She didn't have to meet him on Pegasus."

"Of course she did," replied Sokol. "She'd have come straight to me the second she had that interview. She's been bluffing all the way."

"Can you afford to take the chance?"

He frowned. "Not really. She can't do any serious harm to me, but she could screw up this Lodin Eleven appointment." He paused, rolling his cigar between his fingers. "Trace Acosta's whereabouts for the past year and see if the two of them could possibly have met somewhere other than Pegasus."

The blond man was back an hour later.

"Well?" demanded Sokol.

"You were right: Acosta and MacKenzie were never within fifty light-years of each other."

"I knew it!" said Sokol triumphantly.

"What would you like done next?" asked the blond man.

"She's got to have a message drop somewhere in Hektor. There's a chance that she's already contacted Cain, so tomorrow I want you to find some way to get word to Santiago. Warn him to be on the alert, just in case Cain or this gambler actually manage to hook up with the Swagman."

"Tomorrow?"

Sokol nodded. "This afternoon you're going to hunt up Leander Smythe and see to it that he never again spreads any malicious gossip about me. We don't want to kill a member of the press, but I want you to give him a lesson he remembers. And don't say who sent you. He'll figure it out."

"That takes care of this afternoon and tomorrow morning," said the blond man. "What about tonight?"

"Tonight? Go home and go to sleep."

"What about Virtue MacKenzie?"

"She doesn't have the tape, so she's no immediate threat. I don't want any harm to come to her while she's on Pegasus."

"And once she leaves?"

Sokol smiled. "That's another matter, isn't it?"

8.

His name is Father William,
His aim is hard to ken:
His game is saving sinners;
His fame is killing men.

Whenever people would sit around talking with Black Orpheus, sooner or later the question would come up: Who did he think was the most memorable character he had met during his wanderings? He'd lean back, sipping his wine and staring off into the distance, enjoying the moment and the memories, and then, just when his listeners began to think that they weren't going to get an answer, he'd smile and say that he'd seen a lot of men and women on the Inner Frontier—killers like the Songbird and One-Time Charlie, tragic figures like Schussler the Cyborg, entrepreneurs like Descartes White (whom he had renamed Carte Blanche, a sobriquet with which he was inordinately pleased), good women like Silent Annie and Blessed Sarah, bad women like Flat-Nosed Sal and Sister Sleaze, even virtual supermen like Man-Mountain Bates—but not a one of them held a candle to Father William.

It had been love at first sight. Not a physical or personal love, but the kind of love a landscape artist feels toward a beautiful sunset. Black Orpheus painted his word pictures on a very broad canvas, and even so, Father William was almost too big to fit.

The first time Orpheus ever saw him was in the Corvus system, preaching hellfire and damnation from a pulpit, and daring anyone in his audience—which included some pretty notorious characters—not to make a donation to his personalized, monogrammed poorbox. The next time was two years later, out by the Quinellus cluster, where Father William was serenely blessing the departed spirits of four men and a woman he had just killed. Orpheus ran into him a third and final time on Girodus II and watched, fascinated, as he shot down two outlaws, turned in their scalps for the reward (the taking of scalps was unnecessary, but nobody felt obligated to argue that particular point with Father William), donated the money to the local church, and spent the next two days spreading the gospel to the elephantine natives of the planet.

Orpheus tried to find out more about his past, but it was a fruitless quest. The only thing Father William wanted to talk about was God, though with a drink or two in his massive belly he'd be willing to segue into a discussion of Sodom and Gomorrah. He was a fabulous figure, standing just under six feet five inches, weighing close to four hundred pounds, always clad in black. He wore a pair of black leather holsters, each equipped with laser pistols which he insisted contained the purifying fire of the Lord. He had forsworn all pleasures of the flesh except gluttony, explaining that a weak evangelist was an ineffective evangelist, and that he aimed to run through a lot of calories bringing Christianity to the godless worlds of the Frontier. It was his earnest belief that any world that played host to a wanted killer was more in need of salvation than most, and it was his intention to bring those worlds into the fold by eradicating the evil and spreading the Word among the survivors. The already damned would simply start serving their infernal sentences a little early, and the remainder, freed from their evil influence, would be snatched from Satan's avaricious grasp for all eternity—or until such time as the government issued paper on them.

Father William wasn't as famous as he might have been. Black Orpheus only gave him three verses, a third of what he'd given to Giles Sans Pitié, who wasn't anywhere near as colorful or interesting, but that was mainly because Orpheus figured the Bible-toting bounty hunter was so much bigger than life that there simply wasn't a lot more that could be said about him. And since the stanzas were brief and muted, and the ever-growing epic was now well past two thousand verses, people who hadn't heard Black Orpheus expound upon him could be forgiven for having overlooked his exploits.

Virtue MacKenzie was one of those people. She didn't know that Father William was preaching on Goldenrod, and wouldn't have cared even if she had known. Her only interest was in finding the outlaw known as the Jolly Swagman, and, through him, Santiago.

She landed her ship on Goldenrod, a temperate little world that was owned by a cartel of farming syndicates. The crops were harvested by robots, which worked under the direction of a handful of men and women who pretended that they were executives but knew in their hearts that they were only mechanics and caretakers. There was only one city, an ancient Tradertown that predated the farms and had expanded to the point where it now housed almost eight thousand inhabitants; and, like so many Tradertowns on the Frontier, it bore the name of the planet.

She had a feeling that she wouldn't be staying there long, so rather than reserving a room at a hotel, she left her gear in her ship and took a shuttlecart into the Tradertown. When the cart came to a stop, she found herself in the middle of a town square, surrounded by long, low buildings and standing next to a monument of the planet's founder.

Unlike Cain, who had spent two decades traveling from one Tradertown to the next and usually sought his information in bars and brothels, she hunted up the local news office—the world was too small to possess its own network and in fact employed only one stringer—presented her credentials, and asked for the Jolly Swagman's whereabouts.

"You've got more important things to worry about than meeting the Swagman," said the middle-aged man who had greeted her.

"Such as?" asked Virtue.

"You might start by giving some serious thought to getting off the planet alive."

"What are you talking about?"

"Well," he said, "it's not news, so we haven't released it—not that any other world would give a damn about what goes on here anyway—but the word on the grapevine is that you made a certain party on Pegasus very angry with you. He thought it might be bad for business to redress his grievances too close to home, so he chose Goldenrod as a more fitting setting."

"He's put a hit out on me?"

"I understand that he's hired three killers to see to it that you don't leave Goldenrod."

"Who are they?"

He shrugged. "I don't know."

"Wonderful," she muttered. She glanced out at the street, trying to guess which of the many people that she could see looked like hired killers, then turned back to the stringer. "How do I apply for police protection?"

The man shook his head. "You're not in the Democracy any longer: We don't *have* a police department."

"You must have *some* way of protecting your citizens," she persisted.

"Goldenrod is the Swagman's world—*he* protects it."

"I thought Goldenrod belonged to a bunch of corporations that own all the property."

"Well, legally it does. But they're all headquartered on Deluros and Earth and the Canphor Twins, and as long as the farms continue showing a profit they don't much care what goes on here. Besides, when you make an unofficial arrangement to let someone like the Swagman stay on your world, you expect something in return."

"So they give him sanctuary here, and in exchange he sees to it that nobody tries to hijack their goods or short-change their representatives. Is that it?" asked Virtue.

"Something like that," said the man. "I don't know the exact arrangement, but I'm sure you're pretty close to it."

"Fine," said Virtue. "Then let's get word to him that I want to see him, and get him to extend his protection to me."

"I thought you understood the situation," said the man irritably. "I guess you don't."

"What am I missing?"

"The hit men couldn't have accepted the commission without the Swagman's approval. That's the way things work here."

"I've never even met him," said Virtue. "What has he got against me?"

"Probably nothing. He's a very friendly man, actually. But the killers will pay him a commission in order to operate here, and it's not unfair to say that he likes money even more than he likes people."

"Then I'd better find *him* before they find *me*."

"You don't even know who they are," replied the man. "They *could* be those three grubby-looking men standing together across the street"—he pointed out the window to a trio of armed men who were standing together a short distance away—"but they could also be three little old ladies who are out doing their shopping, or the bartenders down the block, or even some of the mechanics at the spaceport. If I were you, I'd get back to my ship as fast as I could and take off before anyone knew I was here."

"I didn't come all this way *not* to talk to the Swagman," Virtue said firmly. "Where can I find him?"

The man shrugged.

"Damn it!" she snapped. "Are you going to help me or aren't you?"

"I don't *know* where to find him!" replied the man, exasperated. "I don't even know if he's on the planet right now. It's not in his best professional interests to announce his comings and goings."

"All right. If he *is* here, where will he be?"

"He's got a place up in the hills—a real fortress—but you can't get to it. He's got security devices all the hell over—and I mean *lethal* devices."

"How do I get in touch with him, then?"

"Well, Father William's set up shop just outside of town for the next couple of days, so I imagine the Swagman will be keeping an eye on him, just in case."

"Who's Father William?"

He stared at her disbelievingly. "Just how long have you been on the Frontier?"

"Long enough," she replied levelly. "Has Black Orpheus written him up?"

The man nodded. "Did a damned sight better on him than he did on you. You're the Virgin Queen, aren't you?"

"Yes."

"Then you ought to know what's in the song."

"I've got better things to do than commit eight thousand lines to memory. Now, are you going to tell me who he is?"

"He's a little bit of everything—preacher, bounty hunter, benefactor. I suppose it all depends on who you are."

"Would *he* know how to reach the Swagman?"

"I suppose so. There's not a lot that Father William doesn't know about outlaws."

"If he's a bounty hunter, there's a chance that he's after the Swagman himself," said Virtue. "Why would the Swagman let him land on Goldenrod?"

"Probably because he'd have a revolt on his hands if he tried to stop him. Father William's the most popular evangelist on the Frontier—and there are some who think he's the best shot, as well. He goes anywhere he wants."

"Dimitri Sokol wouldn't have hired *him*, would he?" asked Virtue thoughtfully.

"Not a chance. He's a bounty hunter, not a hired killer."

"Well," she said with a sigh, "I suppose he's the next person I have to see. Where is he?"

"He's set up his tent about a mile west of town."

She checked her timepiece. "When does he start preaching?"

"Today's sermon started about two hours ago."

"Then he should be just about through," she ventured.

He laughed. "He won't be through until nightfall."

"You're kidding!" said Virtue. "What the hell has he got to talk about that takes eight hours?"

"Anything that comes into his head," replied the stringer. "You've got to remember that he's all the flesh-and-blood religion most of these people are going to have for the next couple of years, until he passes through again, so he's got to cram a lot of hellfire and damnation into a very short space of time."

"Sounds thrilling," she said unenthusiastically. Then she stood up. "Well, I suppose I'd better be going."

"If you insist on continuing your quest, why don't you at least wait until dark?" he suggested.

"Because I don't know my way around the city," Virtue replied. "Why give them an advantage?" She paused. "Besides, they're less likely to try to kill me in the daylight. Damn, but I wish my partner was here! This is more his kind of situation than mine."

"Who's your partner?"

"Sebastian Cain. Ever hear of him?"

"The Songbird?" he said, looking at her with newfound interest. "*He's* working with you?"

She nodded.

"I agree with you. This situation is made to order for a man like Cain. Why are you here instead of him?"

"He's out in the Altair region."

The stringer looked impressed. "Allow me to hazard a guess: Is he after Altair of Altair?"

"Yes."

He let out a low whistle. "I don't know what you two are up to, but you sure aren't going about it the easy way, are you?"

"Evidently not," she said, looking out the window once more and noticing that the three men were no longer stationed opposite the news office.

"Well, I wish you luck," said the man. "You're going to need it."

"Thanks," she said, walking to the door. "One mile due west, right?"

"Right," he replied.

She pulled a small pistol out of her satchel and tucked it in her belt, then stepped out into the humid Goldenrod air. A number of people were walking down the street in twos and threes, and she stood still for a moment, scrutinizing them, trying to see if any of them seemed to be paying more than casual attention to her as they went about their business.

This is ridiculous, she thought as she watched the townspeople. *Who the hell knows what a hired killer looks like?*

She remained motionless for another minute, half expecting to hear a shot ring out or feel a laser beam searing through her flesh, then walked up to the corner and turned left. She made three more lefts, coming to a stop in front of the news office and trying to ascertain if anyone had followed her, then decided that on a world where the only law was a bandit who lived in a fortress atop a distant hill, the less time she spent presenting herself as a potential target, the better.

She headed off in a westerly direction, staying within the shadows of buildings for as long as she could. When she had traveled some two hundred yards, the town came to an abrupt end, and she could see a colorful tent set in the middle of a rolling field almost a mile away. She took one more look around, saw nobody following her, and began walking briskly toward it, checking behind her every few moments.

She had covered half the distance, and had temporarily dipped out of sight of the tent while crossing a low area of the field, when she saw an elderly couple strolling back toward town. The man was wearing a very formal suit, obviously donned in honor of Father William, and walked with a cane. The woman carried a picnic basket and a parasol. Keeping her hand very near the butt of her pistol, Virtue stopped and greeted them.

"Is Father William through speaking?" she asked.

"Oh, goodness, no!" said the old woman, obviously amused by the suggestion. "I'm just going home to take my medication, and perhaps a little nap, and then we'll be coming back."

"We haven't seen you before, have we?" asked the old man.

"No," answered Virtue. "I heard Father William was touching down for a couple of days, so I thought I'd come by to hear him. I'm from Salinas Four."

"Really?" said the old man. "I hear it's a lovely world."

"It is."

"We're from Seabright originally," said the old woman. "But we came out to the Frontier to make our fortunes."

"That was close to forty years ago," chuckled the old man. "Can't say we're any richer, but Goldenrod is a pretty nice place to retire to. And of course, it's on Father William's regular circuit."

"By the way, can I offer you a sandwich?" asked the woman, holding up her basket.

"No, thank you," said Virtue.

"I wish you would," persisted the woman. "I hate to see it go to waste, and we'll just throw it out once we get home. We're having dinner with friends."

"I appreciate the offer, but I'm really not hungry."

"Here," said the woman, fussing with the lid of the basket. "Just take a look at it, and maybe you'll change your mind. There are sandwiches, and tea biscuits, and—"

Suddenly Virtue saw a movement out of the corner of her eye and hurled herself to the ground.

The old man dropped the cane he had swung at her and began fumbling with his pocket. Virtue flung herself at his legs, heard something crack inside one of them, and leaped to her feet, her pistol in her hand. The old woman had withdrawn a gun from the inside of the basket—Virtue couldn't tell if it was laser, sonic, or projectile—and was pointing it at her.

"You have very good reflexes, my dear," said the old woman with a smile.

"What happens now?" asked Virtue, ignoring the old man as he moaned and writhed on the ground. "Do we kill each other or call a truce while you move the wounded warrior off the battlefield?"

"Well, I *could* wait for reinforcements," said the old woman. "I do have them, you know."

"Yes, I'd heard there were three of you."

The old man groaned again.

"But my dear husband is in a bad way," added the old woman. "He had trouble walking even before you so callously broke his leg. So I suppose I'll either have to dispatch you immediately, or else agree to your truce."

"If you shoot, so will I," said Virtue.

"Ah, but will a properly placed head shot allow you the opportunity to retaliate?" asked the woman, raising her aim from Virtue's chest to a point between her eyes.

"Then perhaps I'll shoot first," said Virtue, a tiny section of her mind wondering how Cain would handle the situation and deciding he wouldn't have gotten into it in the first place. "And then who will be left to take care of your husband?"

"There is *that* to consider," agreed the old woman regretfully. "We're really getting a little old for this."

"Have you done it often?"

"Twelve times," she said, not without a touch of pride. "People always expect assassins to look like they do on the videos—mean and powerful. We've made quite a substantial living from it." She lowered her voice confidentially. "Black Orpheus even wanted to write us up, but we explained that the only thing we really had on our side was the element of surprise, and that publicity could drive us out of business." She smiled. "He respected our wishes—but then, he was always a gentleman."

The old man tried to roll over, moaned in agony, and passed out.

"All right, my dear," said the old woman with a sigh. "You get your truce. I really must find a doctor."

"Not quite so fast," said Virtue. "Who's the third member of your team?"

"I can't jeopardize his life by telling you that," she said primly. "Besides, if he doesn't kill you, I'll have to come after you again once I get Henry to a doctor."

Virtue considered the problem, then nodded in agreement.

"All right—we've got a truce."

"Then please put your weapon away," said the old woman.

Virtue smiled. "You first."

"I'm counting on your being an honorable woman," said the old woman, opening the top of her basket and tossing her gun into it.

Virtue tucked her pistol back into her belt and quickly disarmed the old man. "If I were you," she said, "I'd get Henry to the house and stay there. The next time I see you I'll have to kill you."

"Help me move him into the shade, won't you?" said the woman, indicating a tree some twenty feet away. "It may take me some time to find a doctor and bring him back out here, and I don't want to leave poor Henry out in the sun."

"You're kidding, right?" said Virtue unbelievingly.

"If we leave him here, he may die. He's a very old man."

"He's a very old man who just tried to kill me."

"That was business," said the old woman. "And as you can see, he's quite unable to present any threat to you in his present condition."

Virtue shrugged and nodded her head, struck by the lunacy of helping one of her potential murderers drag another of them to shelter. "All right—but leave your basket on the ground."

"Certainly," said the old woman, placing the basket down.

The two women walked over to the old man, bent over, and began adjusting his weight so that they could pull him by his arms and shoulders. Virtue noticed the old woman's hand snaking down toward Henry's pocket and grabbed her by the wrist just as she was withdrawing a knife.

"I thought we had a bargain," said Virtue with a nasty smile.

"Business comes first," said the old woman, red-faced and panting from her exertions. "What are you going to do to me?"

"Nothing quite as bad as you were going to do to me," replied Virtue. "Let's get dear old Henry into the shade first—and if you try anything else, or go for that gun in your basket, I'll kill you."

Once she had dragged the old man over to the tree, she turned to his wife and drew her pistol.

"I'm going to ask you once more—how can I recognize the third killer?"

"That really would be a breach of my professional ethics," said the old woman. "Besides, if you shoot me, there's every possibility that he'll hear the sound of the gun and know where you are."

"True enough," said Virtue. She landed a heavy kick on the old woman's knee, felt the tendons and ligaments give way as the woman fell to the ground and let out a scream, and stood back.

"That should keep you off the playing field for the rest of the day," said Virtue, walking over to the basket and withdrawing a storage bottle. She opened it, saw that it was iced tea, closed it again, and walked back to where the old woman was sobbing and clutching her knee.

"It's a hot day," said Virtue. "There's every chance the two of you will dehydrate before someone finds you."

The old woman kept crying but offered no comment.

"Tell me what Number Three looks like and I'll leave this with you."

The old woman stared at her through tear-filled eyes. "Do your worst," she said. "I won't betray a trust."

"Last chance," said Virtue. "I can't waste any more time with you."

The woman shook her head.

Virtue shrugged and tossed the bottle on the ground about twenty yards away from them. Then she returned to the basket, removed the weapon, put it into her satchel, and headed off toward the tent.

When she arrived, she entered at the back. There were forty or fifty rows of benches on each side of a broad center aisle, and all but the last few were completely filled. Up front, at the makeshift pulpit, there was an electronic sound synthesizer that provided a soft, continuous background of hymns.

A huge man stood at a podium, staring out at his audience with fierce green eyes. He had wild red hair and a beard streaked with gray, he was clad entirely in black, and the polished handles of his laser pistols were plainly visible atop his holsters.

"And if thy hand offends thee, cut it off," Father William was intoning in a rich, resonant baritone. "For the Lord is more than an ideal, more than an object of affection, even more than a Creator." He paused for effect. "Never forget, my children, that the Lord is also a surgeon. And He doesn't use the sword of redemption. He uses the scalpel of justice!"

Virtue took an aisle seat in the next-to-last row.

"Yes, brethren," continued Father William, "we're talking about infection. Not the infection of the body, for the body is the province of the doctor, but the infection of the spirit, which is the province of the Lord and such temporal emissaries as He deigns to have represent Him."

He paused and reached for a glass that was filled with a blue liquid, took a long swallow, and then resumed speaking.

"Now, they've got a lot in common, the body and the spirit. First and foremost, they can bring pleasure to the Lord, the body by being fruitful and multiplying, the spirit by worshiping Him and singing His praises. But they've got something else in common, too. Both of them can be overrun with infection; they can become pustules of decay, unsightly in the eyes of both man and God."

A gaunt man with a handlebar mustache and thick, bushy sideburns entered the tent, looked around for a seat, and finally approached Virtue.

"Do you mind moving over just a bit?" he whispered.

She moved to her left, making room for him.

"I meant to get here sooner, but one of my harvesters broke down," he added apologetically. "Have I missed much?"

She shook her head and placed a finger to her lips.

"Sorry," he muttered, turning his attention to Father William.

"Now, if the body gets a mild infection, what do we do?" The preacher glared out at his audience, as if daring them to answer. Nobody said a word. "We give it antibiotics. And if it gets a major infection, we give it other drugs." He gripped the edges of the podium with his massive hands. "And when it gets infected by a cancer, what do we do?" He made a slashing motion with his right hand. "We cut it out!" he shouted.

He paused and drew a deep breath, releasing it slowly. "But what about the soul? What do we do when *it* becomes infected? How do we inject an antibiotic into its bloodstream? How do we amputate a piece of the soul before the infection can spread?"

"The answer," said Father William, "is that we can't and won't do any of those things, because there aren't any halfway measures when it comes to the soul, my children. Your body is just a suit that you wear for the flickering instant of your lives, but your soul is an outfit you're going to wear for all eternity, and you can't afford to take any chances with it. You can't give it an antibiotic and prescribe two weeks of bed rest for it, because it doesn't have any bloodstream and it can't lie down—and besides, it's too damned important to try to cure with halfway measures." His voice rose in volume and intensity. "Never forget this: There is no such thing as a *minor* infection of the soul! There's no breaking it down into serious and trivial, into fatal and nonfatal. There's just infection, and when you see it you've got to cut it out with the holy blade of the Lord!"

Suddenly Virtue felt the point of a knife prodding her rib cage.

"Not a sound, not a movement!" whispered the gaunt man.

Father William cleared his throat. "Some of you want to know: How can such surgery make the soul well again? Well, my children, it's a damned good question—and you're not going to like the answer, for the answer is as harsh as the wrath of the Lord." He paused for effect. "*Nothing* can make an infected soul well again." He looked out at his audience, his eyes blazing. "You think you can fool God with false contrition? Hah!" He bellowed the contemptuous laugh so forcefully that the speaker system emitted an ear-splitting whine.

"So why do we cut it out? Because—and here's the gist of it, brethren—we've got to act fast to stop that infection from spreading to other souls. We've got to stop the evil from creeping like a cancer from one soul to the next!"

"I could yell for help," whispered Virtue.

"It might start as a yell," replied the gaunt man. "I guarantee it'll end as a gurgle."

"There's nothing new about this," continued Father William. "What did the Lord do when the people of Sodom became infected? He cut out the cancer. He didn't sit up with his sick patient and tend to its illness. He used the knife! What did He do when He saw that the whole world was wicked? Did He go in and perform microsurgery? Hell, no! He flooded it for forty days and forty nights!"

He paused and wiped the sweat from his face with a black handkerchief.

"He's due to take a break soon," whispered the gaunt man. "When he does, get up and walk out very slowly. I'll be right beside you." He prodded her with the point of the knife for emphasis.

"Why should I?" she whispered back. "You're going to kill me anyway."

"I can do it quick and easy, or I can do it so you'll be in pain for hours," he replied emotionlessly. "That's all the choice you've got. It's up to you."

She considered making a break for the door, but he seemed to read her mind and suddenly grabbed her arm. She slumped back, her mind racing, searching for possibilities of escape but finding none. She had already decided that she wasn't leaving the tent like a sheep going to slaughter, and that if worse came to worst, she'd make him kill her in front of two thousand witnesses—but since he was operating with the Swagman's knowledge and consent, she couldn't be sure that anyone would lift a finger to stop him—and indeed, she suspected that they wouldn't.

"You'd think some people would learn their lesson by now, wouldn't you?" demanded Father William, his voice rising. "You'd think they'd learn that you can't pull the wool over God's eyes, that you can't hide an infection from His heavenly clinic!"

He glared out at the audience.

"That's what you'd think—but some people just never learn."

Suddenly Father William's face was filled with fury.

"You'd think they'd at least have the brains not to try to do Satan's work in the house of the Lord!" he roared, drawing a pistol and firing a blast in Virtue's direction.

Several members of the audience screamed, a few bellowed curses, and most of them—including Virtue—dove to the floor.

There was total confusion for the next thirty seconds. Then people began getting up, asking what had happened. When Virtue regained her feet, she noticed that the gaunt man was dead, his left eye socket burnt to a crisp.

"Don't touch him!" thundered Father William as other members of the congregation began noticing the victim. "There's paper on that man. He belongs to me and the Lord."

The preacher looked out over the audience.

"The Lord is my eyes and ears, and there's not a lot that escapes the two of us." Father William paused. "The Lord steadies my hand and aims my guns. Blessed is the name of the Lord!"

He replaced his pistol in its holster.

"There's an object lesson to be learned here, my children—and that is that Good can come from Evil. Once I take this sinner's scalp and turn it in, he'll have done a hell of a lot more for the Lord by dying than he ever thought of doing while he was alive." He lowered his head. "Let's say a brief, silent prayer for this poor sinful bastard's pitch-black soul, and wish Satan the best of luck with him."

He continued his sermon for another half hour, ignoring the dead body, bringing forth every reference he thought mildly appropriate to the subject at hand, from the concept of an eye for an eye to the Day of Judgment, which he promised was a lot closer at hand than most people suspected.

Finally, when he finished, explaining that he was cutting his preaching short out of respect for the dead—and also because the Democracy's post office would be closing soon—he had a young boy from the Tradertown take his platinum poorbox up and down the aisles, and he didn't dismiss the congregation until everyone had made a contribution.

"I'll be seeing you all here bright and early tomorrow morning," said Father William, signaling them that it was now permissable to rise and depart, "when the topic will be 'Sex and Sin,' for which I suggest you leave the children at home. Donations will be appreciated, and if anyone would like to bring along a couple of chocolate layer cakes with thick fudge frosting, I promise to put them to good use." Suddenly he pointed to Virtue. "You stick around, young lady. We've got some serious talking to do."

The young boy brought him the poorbox and whispered something in his ear.

"Hold it!" he hollered, and those people who hadn't yet made it to the exit froze in their tracks.

"I don't know who goes by the name of the Spike, or even what sex you are, but I've been told on very good authority that you tried passing off some Royal Yen in the poorbox. Now, as you know, the Royal Yen isn't acceptable currency anywhere but out on the Rim, and I've got a gut feeling that the good Lord is going to take it as a personal affront. So what I'm going to do is ask this handsome young man to move among you again, and see if you can't find it in your heart to come up with some coin of the realm that'll buy food and vaccines for the poor unfortunates on Kellatra Four, which is my next port of call. As for this," he added, holding up the unacceptable currency, "I'll just hang on to it in case I should run into some God-fearing missionary whose call is leading him out to where he can use it."

The boy walked into the midst of the crowd and emerged a moment later with two crisp fifty-dollar Maria Theresa notes. Father William nodded his head in approval, and a moment later Virtue found herself alone in the tent with him.

"I want to thank you," she said, approaching him and extending her hand. "I'd have been dead meat if you hadn't spotted him."

"I couldn't have done it if you hadn't come to hear my sermon," he replied, clasping her hand between both of his. "Which is just as it should be. You come to praise the Lord, and the Lord provides for you. Looks to me like He thinks you've got mighty important business somewhere up the line."

"I do."

"So important that a man with a price on his head wanted to kill you?"

"He was hired by Dimitri Sokol."

"Well, I'm sure Satan's warming up a special seat in hell for Mr. Sokol." He paused. "By the way, he had two accomplices. What happened to them?"

"They won't be bothering me," said Virtue emphatically.

Father William nodded his head approvingly. "Good. I'm glad to see you don't need this kind of heavenly protection all the time." He released her hand, picked up his glass, and took another swallow of his blue drink. "Why does Sokol want you dead?"

"I have no idea," she said, looking him full in the eye.

"You know," he said with the hint of an amused smile, "it's a damned good thing that God's got big plans for you—because otherwise He'd strike you mute for lying inside His house."

"I don't know what you're talking about," said Virtue.

"Come on, young lady," said Father William. "Dimitri Sokol's a smuggler and swindler who thinks he's worked out his own special brand of contrition." He laughed contemptuously. "As if he thinks he can keep everything he did a secret while he pretends to be a humble, churchgoing public servant!" He stared at her. "Let me suggest that you blackmailed him, he paid you off, and now he's trying to get his money back."

"Close, but no cigar," said Virtue. "I blackmailed him, all right—"

"Perfectly acceptable," he interrupted her. "Sometimes you've got to hold the cancer up to the light before you can cut it away."

"But not for money," she continued. "For information."

"Ah!" he said, his eyes lighting up. "What kind of information?"

"I'm looking for Santiago."

Father William seemed to find that uproariously funny. "If I were you, young lady, I'd find out where he was and run the other way. Now *that's* some information that's freely given, and as such ought to count for more than anything Sokol told you."

"He told me to talk to the Jolly Swagman."

"Did he indeed? Well, I suppose he was right. But you're not very likely to find the Swagman attending any sermons—and especially not when I'm doing the preaching."

"Where *will* I find him?"

"Up in the hills, about ten miles out of town. Anyone around here could have shown you the way."

"They also tell me he's a hard man to see."

"It all depends who you are and what you want to talk about."

"They say that *you* can get me in to see him," she said bluntly.

"I imagine I can, at that," replied Father William.

"Will you?"

"That's another story altogether," he said slowly.

"You mean you won't?"

"I didn't say that. I said it was another story." He looked around the room until his gaze fell on the killer's body. "That heathen came mighty close to getting you a personal meeting with God," he said. "*Mighty* close. It's a damned good thing the Lord was helping keep my eye sharp and my hand steady."

"I've already thanked you. Do you want me to do it again?"

"Well, young lady," he said, withdrawing his black handkerchief and polishing his poorbox meaningfully, "there are thanks, and then there are thanks."

She stared at him for a moment, finally comprehending. "One thousand credits," she said at last.

He smiled. "That's hardly chapter one of that other story we were talking about."

"Just remember that it's a story and not a novel," she replied. "Two thousand."

He pursed his lips and considered the offer.

"How's your cooking?" he asked at last.

"Terrible."

"Pity." He stared at her, then shrugged. "What the hell. Between the bounty money and your generous donation, we're going to see to it that five thousand children on Kellatra Four never come down with drypox or blue fever again." He bent over, raised his left pants leg, and withdrew a long hunting knife that he had strapped to his calf. "Let me just collect the proof of the pudding for the local constabulary and we'll be off." He turned to her. "You *do* have two thousand credits, don't you?"

She pulled the notes out of her satchel. "Have we got a deal?" she asked.

He took the money from her, put it in his poorbox, and grinned. "We sure as hell have, praise the Lord!"

9.

Up pops the Swagman, out pops his gun,
Down comes the money, away he does run;
There goes the posse, seeking his den—
Then up pops the Swagman, at it again!

Considering that he ran his own planet and had pretty much of a free hand on ten or fifteen others, you'd have expected the Jolly Swagman to be backed up by a veritable army of outlaws and cutthroats, but he wasn't. He had informants, of course, and a lot of contacts inside and outside the law, but for the most part he worked alone.

And considering that he worked alone, you'd have expected him to be a giant of a man, sort of a Goldenrod version of ManMountain Bates, but he wasn't. He was an inch or two shorter than normal and about twenty pounds overweight, and truth to tell he didn't have a single memorable physical feature, except maybe for his eyes, which were just about colorless.

And considering that he wasn't an imposing physical specimen, you'd have to figure that he was at the very least a sharpshooter or a demolitions expert or a master of disguise, but he wasn't. All he really had going for him were a pretty agile mind, an offbeat notion of morality, and a hunger for things that weren't his.

Now, all of that was enough to bring him to Black Orpheus' attention—but the thing that *really* interested the Bard of the Frontier was his accent.

It was the first one he'd ever heard.

Men had had accents when they were still Earthbound, and they would have them again in the future, thousands of years after the Inner and Outer Frontiers had been totally settled and civilized. But during the eras of the Republic and the Democracy and even the early Oligarchy, which spanned almost six millennia between them, every Man grew up knowing two tongues: that of his native world and Terran (and more often than not, the tongue of his native world *was* Terran). Out on the Frontier, where Men changed worlds the way their brothers back on Earth and Deluros VIII changed shirts, Terran was all anybody spoke: it had been carefully devised over a period of decades to be the kind of language any Man could pick up with ease, a language that was well-nigh impossible to speak with an accent.

So when Black Orpheus hunted up the Swagman and sat down to talk with him, the conversation wasn't half a minute old before Orpheus knew that he'd been raised by aliens.

The Swagman never denied it, but he wouldn't be coaxed into giving out any of the details. He liked the creatures who'd brought him up too much to want them to be studied and exploited by the creatures of his own race, and he knew that that was exactly what would happen if Black Orpheus incorporated them into his song.

At any rate, the balladeer was absolutely captivated by the outlaw's explosive *g*'s and sibilant *sh*'s. He stayed on Goldenrod for a week or two, and some people say that the Swagman even took Orpheus on a raid with him, just to show him what it was like. They became friends, because in spite of his penchant for lawbreaking, the Swagman was a pretty friendly person. He saw Black Orpheus a few years later and didn't even mention that Orpheus had hurt his feelings by giving him only a single verse; and Black Orpheus was so impressed that he was still on the loose that, without the Swagman's requesting it, he sat right down and added another couple of stanzas, including one about the bandit's fortress (which he insisted on calling a *schloss* in order to create a rhyme).

Schloss or fortress, Virtue decided as she and Father William stood at the massive front door, it was one hell of a structure. In a less technical age its bulk alone could have withstood an army; now its incredibly sophisticated defense systems could repel attacks from above, below, or straight ahead.

Finally the huge portal swung open with a slight humming noise, revealing the Swagman, who stood in the entry foyer, hands on hips, staring at Virtue with an amused curiosity.

Whatever it was she had expected in a bandit chief, he wasn't it. His uncallused white fingers had been meticulously manicured; his blond hair had been painstakingly styled in the latest Deluros fashion;

his face was unmarked and clean-shaven; and his clothing, from the elegant velvet tunic to the sleek lizardskin half boots, seemed to anticipate the coming fashion among the Democracy's trendsetters, rather than echoing the current one.

"Ah!" he said with a smile of greeting. "The enigmatic Virtue MacKenzie, I presume?"

"And you're the Swagman?" replied Virtue.

"The one and only," he answered. "Good evening, Father William. How's the salvation business?"

"The same as always," replied the preacher. "Satan is a full-time opponent."

"I understand that you had him down for the count this afternoon," said the Swagman in his unmistakable accent. "But where are my manners? Do come in."

They followed him down a short corridor as the door swung shut behind them, and from there into a massive great hall, complete with a floor-to-ceiling fireplace wall, a number of rugs that had been handmade on Boriga II and Kalamakii, a set of four exquisitely crafted chairs from far Antares, and numerous hardwood shelving units that housed art treasures from literally hundreds of worlds across the galaxy.

"What do you think of my trinkets?" asked the Swagman as Virtue stopped to admire a crystal globe of Bokar from the incredibly ancient days when the Bokarites were a seafaring race rather than a planet of starfaring merchants.

"They're breathtaking!" she said, turning her attention to a *praque*, the fabled torture-stick of Sabelius III.

"That's a more accurate statement than you might imagine," said Father William sternly. "A lot of good men gave their last breaths accumulating this ill-gotten wealth for the Swagman."

"Come, come, now," said the bandit with a chuckle. "You know there's no paper on me, Father William."

"There's a pile of it as high as the ceiling," replied the preacher.

"But not for murder," the Swagman pointed out. "And you leave the punishment of lesser crimes to lesser servants of the Lord."

"True," admitted Father William. "But it's immoral to flaunt your bloodstained treasures like this."

"You mean by displaying them behind locked doors in my own home?" asked the Swagman, arching an eyebrow. He paused. "Shall we change the subject? If we keep talking about my collection, we're bound to have a serious disagreement." He snapped his fingers. "Or better still, how about dinner? I had my staff start preparing it half an hour ago, when you identified yourself at the first security barrier."

"Staff?" repeated Virtue. "I didn't notice any staff."

"They're all mechanical," explained the Swagman. "And *very* discreet."

"You live alone here?" she asked, surprised.

"Is that so difficult to believe?" he replied.

"I would have thought you'd be surrounded by henchmen," she admitted.

"One of the advantages about living with nothing but robots is that you never have to count the silverware or check the display cases when they're through for the day," he said. "Besides, what would I do with henchmen?"

"Well, you do have a reputation as a master criminal."

"So I am told," he replied dryly.

"You haven't answered my question," she persisted.

"I don't know what you think a master criminal does," said the Swagman, "but in point of fact I am a large-scale employer of criminal labor, nothing more." A bell chimed twice, and he turned to Father William. "Dinner's ready. I assume you brought along your appetite?"

"I'm never without it," said the preacher heartily.

He led them into the dining hall, which was surrounded with still more displays of unique alien artifacts. The room was dominated by a table that could easily have accommodated forty people, but the three settings were all at one end of it. The chairs were all one-legged, considerably broader at the base than the top, and were much more secure than they looked.

"Won't you please sit down?" asked the Swagman, pulling out a chair for Virtue.

"Thank you," she said as Father William sat down opposite her.

"Ordinarily I'd serve such welcome guests on my Robelian dinner pieces," said the Swagman apologetically as he joined them. "But I'm having them refinished. I hope the Atrian quartz will be acceptable. It's really quite lovely in its way."

"The only thing that matters is what's being served on it," replied Father William, leaning back to allow a robot to place an appetizer of mutated shellfish before him.

"That's because you are concerned only with accumulating energy with which to fight your holy war," said the Swagman. "Those of us who are fortunate enough to be spectators at the battle of Good and Evil, rather than participants, are doubly blessed in that we also have the opportunity to admire the containers in which the energy arrives."

"Spectator, my eye!" snapped Father William, chewing and speaking at the same time. "You've got more killers working for you than Dimitri Sokol!"

"I have more bills to pay," replied the Swagman easily. "And I might add that thanks to your little fit of pique on Darius Ten, I have four less killers than I had last month." He smiled at the preacher. "You know, you've caused me so much inconvenience that I really ought to charge you for this meal."

Father William grinned back at him. "I won't ask you for a contribution to my poorbox, and we'll call it even."

"Agreed—as long as you don't make a habit of decimating my supply of menials."

"I'll take any killer who's got paper on him!" said Father William firmly, wiping the corner of his mouth with a napkin, then tying it around his neck like a bib.

The Swagman shrugged. "Serves me right for not checking them out better. Still, by taking them when you did, you cost me the possession of a shipment of art objects from Nelson Seventeen. I do wish you could have waited another week before you went on your killing spree."

"Hah!" muttered Father William, pushing his empty dish away and signaling the robot to bring him another.

The Swagman turned to Virtue. "Never don the cloth," he said with mock seriousness. "It drains away all compassion for your fellow man."

"You don't seem especially upset about losing four men," remarked Virtue.

"They were just men; I can always get more," he replied nonchalantly. "It was losing the *pieces* that hurt. There was a hand-spun Kinrossian bowl that . . ." He sighed and shook his head, then looked up. "Still, I suppose our friend here must score points with his God from time to time."

"You keep talking blasphemy," said Father William harshly "and I just may forget that all that paper on you doesn't mention murder."

"You don't really think you can harm me in my own house, do you?" said the Swagman, vastly amused. "Don't talk such nonsense, or pretty soon you'll start believing it and then we'll all be sorry. Especially you."

The preacher stared at him for a moment, then went back to demolishing the food in front of him.

. Virtue finished her appetizer, and the instant she did a robot whisked the empty plate away from her.

"They're very efficient," she said, indicating the retreating robot as well as a trio that were bringing out the main course. "I would think that household robots would cost an arm and a leg out on the Frontier."

"They do," agreed the Swagman. "Fortunately, it wasn't *my* arm or leg that paid for them."

"Totally immoral," muttered Father William between mouthfuls.

"Totally practical," corrected the Swagman. "It's a tried-and-true business axiom: Never use your own money when you can use someone else's. I just find creative ways to apply it." He turned to Virtue. "Have we pretended that we're all just good friends long enough, or do you prefer to play at it a bit more before talking about Santiago?"

She looked startled for just a moment. "We'll talk about him later," she said.

"As you wish," replied the Swagman agreeably. "Might I inquire if there's any particular reason why?"

"Whatever you've got to say," said Virtue, "I don't want you saying it in front of a rival."

"You mean Father William?" asked the Swagman. Both men seemed to find her remark enormously amusing.

"What's so funny about that?" demanded Virtue.

"Shall you tell her, or shall I?" asked the Swagman.

Father William looked across the table at Virtue. "I don't want him," he said.

"You don't want Santiago?" she repeated incredulously.

"That's right."

"But I thought you wanted any killer with a price on his head," she persisted. "And he's got the biggest price of all. Why aren't you interested in him?"

"A number of reasons," replied Father William. "First, as long as he's on the loose, there will be a couple of dozen bounty hunters on his trail. That's two dozen less competitors for *me*. Second, he's more trouble to dig out than he's worth, regardless of the price on him." He paused. "And third, I don't know for a fact that he's ever killed anyone."

"Come on," said Virtue. "He's wanted for thirty-eight murders."

"He's been *blamed* for thirty-eight murders," replied Father William. "There's a difference."

"We've been arguing about this for years," interjected the Swagman. "I keep offering to team up with him, and he keeps turning me down." He grinned. "It would appear that God is employing very selective killers these days." He turned to Father William. "Probably you're right," he said sarcastically. "Probably he only killed thirty-two or thirty-three of those men and women himself, and hired out the rest."

"Why do *you* want to kill Santiago?" Virtue asked the Swagman.

"You mean besides the fact that I'm an upstanding citizen who finds his very existence offensive?" he replied wryly. "Let's just say that I have my reasons."

Father William, who had finished his main course, pushed his plate away and got to his feet. "If you don't mind, I think I'm going to take my leave of you before he starts expounding upon all those reasons. I don't like arguing on a full stomach."

The Swagman remained seated. "Lemon pie," he said temptingly.

"With meringue topping?" asked the preacher.

"I had a feeling you'd be coming by."

Father William seemed to wage a mighty struggle within himself. Finally he sighed. "I'll be back tomorrow evening for it."

"In that case, I won't detain you," said the Swagman. "I'm sure you can find your own way out."

"You'll see to it that Virtue gets back to her hotel safely?" demanded Father William.

"But of course."

"Have you got all your infernal machines turned off?"

"All but the two at the bottom of the hill—and they've been instructed to let you pass."

"Be sure that they do."

"I will," said the Swagman. "And thank you for bringing this innocent young woman up to my den of iniquity."

Father William glowered at him, then turned and made his way out of the room.

"Interesting man," commented the Swagman.

"I'm surprised you two aren't at each other's throats all the time," remarked Virtue.

"That would be bad for *both* our businesses," said the Swagman with a chuckle.

"I don't understand."

"I allow him to set up shop on my worlds, and give him occasional information about various killers who are also in these parts. In exchange, he warns me whenever he hears of a bounty hunter who isn't as choosy about his targets as he himself is."

"Speaking of killers, why did you give three of them permission to hunt me down on Goldenrod?" demanded Virtue.

"It was strictly financial," replied the Swagman with no trace of remorse. "I allowed them to operate here in exchange for twenty-five percent of their fees—and Dimitri Sokol is offering a lot of money for you."

"So you just let anyone kill anyone on Goldenrod, as long as you get your cut of the action?" she said, her anger rising.

"It depends on the situation."

"What was it about *my* situation that made you decide I was expendable?"

"Oh, I knew that the Lance would wait for you in the tent, and that Father William would spot him. As for the other two—well, if you're not good enough to protect yourself from Henry and Martha, you're certainly not good enough to go after Santiago." He took a sip of his wine. "So if you made it here, you were worth talking business with—and if you didn't, at least I had been recompensed."

She stared at him, annoyed that her fury was evaporating so rapidly in the face of his straightforward and logical answer. Finally the last of it drained from her, and she shrugged.

"All right. Tell me about Santiago."

"Eventually," he replied. "But first of all, suppose you tell me about your interest in him—and your partnership with Sebastian Cain."

"My interest is strictly professional," said Virtue. "I'm a journalist, and I've been paid a hefty advance to come up with a feature on him." Her face suddenly became serious. "And I mean to get that story, no matter what it takes."

"Very well said," responded the Swagman. "I approve wholeheartedly. And what about Cain?"

"We decided to pool our resources and our information," answered Virtue. "Our interests are parallel, but not identical. We both want Santiago, but he wants him for the reward and I want him for the feature." She paused, staring at him thoughtfully.

"Have you something to add?" he suggested pleasantly.

"Just that nothing about our agreement is written in stone," she said, choosing her words carefully. "If I were to meet someone who was better able to help me . . ." She let the sentence hang.

"Wonderful!" laughed the Swagman. "A woman after my own heart!"

"Do we have a deal?" asked Virtue.

He laughed again. "Of course not—at least, not on those terms. If you'll double-cross one partner, you'll double-cross others—and in your mind Cain must certainly be a more formidable antagonist than I am. After all, he's a bounty hunter, and I'm just a harmless art collector."

"That's not the way I hear it."

"One mustn't believe every scurrilous rumor one hears," said the Swagman. "However, that's neither here nor there." He smiled at her. "Not to worry, my dear. We seem to have another case of parallel interests. I don't want your story, and while I'd certainly like the reward money, there are things I want even more."

"Such as?"

"Such as one less competitor," said the Swagman. "Did you know that I used to work for him?"

"No."

"I did—indirectly, for the most part. I actually met him on only two occasions."

"Why did you stop working for him?" asked Virtue.

"We had a falling-out."

"About what?"

"Methodology," he said noncommittally. "At any rate, although he himself is not a collector, and indeed has no interest whatsoever in things esoteric, he has a number of exquisite art objects in his possession on any given day. Should we reach an accommodation, I would regard those pieces as mine, if our little enterprise succeeds."

"How many pieces are involved?"

"I really couldn't say. But he has warehouses and drops all over the Inner Frontier. I'm sure that I would be satisfied with the spoils of conquest." He shrugged. "Let greedy, immoral men like Cain keep the blood money," he concluded deprecatingly.

"You'd only take the pieces you wanted to keep?" asked Virtue, suddenly aware of yet another source of income above and beyond her fee for the feature.

He shook his head. "I'm afraid my creditors have very expensive tastes, my dear. I keep the finest pieces that I find, but all the rest go to support my life-style, and not incidentally to pay for my menials. No, my fee for helping you is, as our friend Father William might state it, all of Santiago's temporal possessions. Take it or leave it."

"Why haven't you gone after him before?" asked Virtue.

"I have—or rather, I've sent men after him before," answered the Swagman. "None of them got very close before being eliminated. So now it appears that I'm going to have to take a more active hand."

"Why now?"

"Well, I suppose I should say that I admire your resourcefulness, or that I wish to establish a romantic liaison with you," he answered. "But while both are definitely true, the simple fact of the matter is that certain developments have convinced me that it might be foolish to wait any longer."

"What developments?"

"The Angel has moved to the Inner Frontier."

"Cain mentioned him," said Virtue.

"Then doubtless Cain is aware of his abilities," said the Swagman. "I had an intermediary offer him the same help I'm offering you, in return for the same considerations. He turned me down flat. This would either imply that he's as much of a loner as everyone says, or that he's getting so close to Santiago that he doesn't need my help. Probably it's the former, but I really don't think I can afford to take the chance." He paused. "So, have I entered into a joint arrangement with you and Cain, or not?"

"As far as I'm concerned, you have," replied Virtue. "I'll have to clear it with Cain after he finishes his business on Altair, but I don't imagine he's interested in anything except the reward. Besides," she lied, "I don't know why the subject of Santiago's personal possessions should ever arise."

"Excellent!" He arose and walked to a small cabinet. "This calls for a bottle of my best Alphard brandy."

He returned with the bottle and two crystal goblets.

"To your very good health and prosperous future, my dear," he said, clinking glasses with her after he had filled them. He stared admiringly at her, wondering just how many fabulous private art collections she had seen on the worlds of the Democracy, and how many of them she could help him locate in the future.

"And to a successful partnership," replied Virtue, studying him carefully and mentally adding up the awards and the money for the features he could help her obtain once they had established a working relationship.

"Virtue, my dear," he said, flashing her his most charming smile, "we have a lot to talk about in the days to come."

"I have a feeling that you're right," she replied with a predatory gleam in her eye.

He spent the next hour showing her some of his major pieces. Then, with a minimal amount of verbal thrust and parry, they went to bed together. Both of them found the experience enjoyable; each pretended to find it ecstatic.

10.

Along the road to Mother Lode
Dwells the Great Sioux Nation,
Which justifies its crimes and lies
As predestination.

Black Orpheus didn't have much use for aliens. Not that he was biased or bigoted; he wasn't. But he saw his calling as the creation and perpetuation of a myth-poem about the race of Man. In fact, the people who thought it was composed merely of unrelated four-line songs about the outcasts and misfits who managed to make an impression on him were dead wrong. By the time he died the poem was some 280,000 lines, most of it in free verse or nonrhyming iambic pentameter, and for the most part it was concerned with glorifying Man's sweeping expansion through the Inner Frontier. The little ballads about the outrageously colorful people were very little more than footnotes and punctuation marks in his epic, though they were the only parts of the poem that interested any of his contemporaries (except, of course, for the academics, who loved him when he was opaque and practically deified him on those rare occasions that he was obscure).

Anyway, while Orpheus wasn't especially interested in aliens, he had nothing against putting them in his poem if they were really unique—not in physical terms, since *all* species are physically unique; but unique in their relationship to Man. And in that regard, the Great Sioux Nation was a little more unique than most.

It wasn't really a nation at all. It possessed only eighty-four members, and only twice since its inception had all of them been on the same planet at the same time. They represented seven sentient races, all oxygen-breathers, each of them from a world that had been militarily conquered and economically subjugated either by the Republic or by the Democracy that succeeded it.

Some races were *so* alien that subjugation was meaningless to them; a goodly number of races resented it; but only a tiny handful *learned* from it.

Such a handful was the Great Sioux Nation.

They were outlaws and thieves, cutthroats and smugglers, playing Man's game on Man's turf—the Inner Frontier. But unlike their less enlightened brothers, they went directly to the source for their indoctrination. Each of them had served time as a member of some human band of desperadoes, and each had realized that if one was to play in Man's ballpark, he/she/it had better learn Man's ground rules.

And while they were studying the rule book, they studied the history books as well. They realized that before Man had turned to conquering and exploiting the races he had found among the stars, he had put in long centuries of practice back on his home planet. Their leader, a gold-feathered humanoid from Morioth II, found that he felt a special empathy toward the Amerinds, which had been methodically decimated on one of Man's last home-world frontiers. He took the name of Sitting Bull, though he was physiologically incapable of sitting and had no idea what a bull was, gave every member of his band an Indian name (oddly enough, Crazy Horse was the only other one derived from the Sioux), adopted certain practices of the Plains Indians, and named the group the Great Sioux Nation. Before long he had instilled in them the conviction that it was their destiny to adjust the balance of power on the Inner Frontier, while realizing a handsome profit in the process. They would commit no crime against any race except Man; they would accept no commission from any race except Man; and they would use no weapons against Man except those he had created himself.

Once Orpheus had written them up, neglecting to mention that they were aliens (though he revised it some years later), most of his audience thought they were a band of fanatics bent on revenge for injustices that had been perpetrated on the Amerinds in aeons past. Others held that they were a group of misguided idealists out to redress an imagined grievance on behalf of a small branch of humanity that had long since been exterminated or assimilated. Only the handful of people who had actually had dealings with them knew that they were simply alien outlaws and opportunists, trying their best to fit into a frontier culture that they could never fully comprehend.

But whatever the Great Sioux Nation's motivation, its efficiency was never in question. Sitting Bull's headquarters were on the mining world of Diamond Strike, some twenty-five miles south of Mother Lode, the planet's sole Tradertown. Through him, one could purchase contracts for anything from human contraband to human life.

One could also purchase information, which was why the Swagman had instructed Virtue MacKenzie's navigational computer to lay in a course for Diamond Strike.

Two days later Virtue set the ship down at the tiny spaceport just outside of Mother Lode. It was midmorning, and the distant sun glowed a dull orange through the heat-haze that blanketed the area.

The Swagman promptly walked to a local garage, where he spent the better part of ten minutes haggling with the proprietor over the rental price of a very old landcar.

"Why didn't you just pay him what he wanted?" Virtue asked irritably, opening a window to let in some air as they began driving the ancient vehicle down a narrow dirt road toward the Great Sioux Nation's headquarters. "Certainly we can afford it."

"Of course we can, my dear," he agreed amiably. "But this is Sitting Bull's world, just as Goldenrod is mine. By now he already knows we're here, and since he's not in the business of giving information away for free, it's not a bad idea to let him know that we don't always agree to pay the first price that's proposed to us."

"Will he offer a second one?"

The Swagman nodded. "And a third, and a fourth. He's a wholehearted believer in the barter system."

"He sounds like an interesting character," she commented, pulling out a handkerchief and wiping the sweat that was already starting to roll down her face.

"He's a *dangerous* character," the Swagman corrected her. "In fact I think it would be best if I did the talking and the negotiating for us."

"What makes you any better at it than me?" she demanded. "If you'd have let me bargain for the landcar, I'd have gotten us one with air-conditioning—or at least something with better shock absorbers."

"This was the only one available."

"You didn't answer my question: What makes you think you're better qualified than me?"

"Because he's an alien," said the Swagman.

"So what?"

"I was raised by aliens. I know how his mind works."

"Are you trying to tell me you were raised by members of Sitting Bull's race?" she said skeptically.

"No."

"Then what difference does it make?"

"I'm used to dealing with aliens."

"Apples and oranges," she replied. "That's like saying that since you're used to firing pistols, you'd be good with a saber." She grunted as the vehicle swerved to avoid an enormous pothole, then turned to him. "How the hell did you ever wind up living with aliens in the first place?"

"When I was three years old, my family was aboard a colony ship that crashed on Pellinath Four. There were only two survivors, and the other one died a couple of days later. The Bellum took care of me until I was seventeen."

"The Bellum?" repeated Virtue. "I've never heard of them."

"Most people haven't," replied the Swagman. "They keep pretty much to themselves."

"Why didn't they notify the Democracy that they had you?"

"Strange as it may seem to you, they didn't even know the Democracy existed. So I stayed there until a team from the Pioneer Corps landed and started charting the planet, and then they took me back with them."

"What was it like, growing up without any other members of your own race?" she asked curiously.

"Not that bad, all things considered. I think it was harder on the Bellum than on me."

"Oh? Why?"

"They were a dedicated communal society, and the concept of individual ownership wasn't very popular with them." He grinned. "Needless to say, this was a worldview that I didn't exactly share. I've been gone for close to thirty years now, and I'll bet some portions of their economy still haven't recovered."

"I would have thought they got you young enough to properly indoctrinate you," commented Virtue.

"That's what *they* thought," he said with an amused laugh. "But give a two-year-old child a rag doll and tell him that it's *his*, and he's got an understanding of property that even a planet filled with Bellum isn't going to shake." He paused. "Anyway, I've never been very good at taking orders, so when they told me that no right-thinking entity would ever want to possess any material goods, I immediately began accumulating things at a phenomenal rate." He grinned again. "I guess it carried over into adulthood."

"Interesting," she said, deciding that the heat was preferable to the dust and closing her window. "But I don't see that any of this makes you more qualified than me to speak to Sitting Bull."

"He's an alien who's trying to act like a human," said the Swagman. "That's much the same position *I* was in three decades ago." He paused. "Also, I've dealt with him once before, so I know the form."

"Form? What form?"

"He's very big on Amerind rituals. I suspect most of them never existed, but he's read a lot of books and tapes by a lot of half-baked anthropologists."

"And *that's* what interested Black Orpheus enough to write him up?" said Virtue, obviously unimpressed.

"He's written up less colorful characters," replied the Swagman. "You and me, for instance."

"This may come as a surprise to you, but I didn't even know I was *in* his damned song until after my verse appeared." She snorted contemptuously. "I still don't know when and where he saw me, and I don't think I'll *ever* know where he got that Virgin Queen crap."

"So you're not a virgin and you're not a queen," said the Swagman easily. "*I* was never chased by a posse, either, no matter what the song says. But Black Orpheus never lets facts get in the way of truth. After all, he's a myth-maker, not an historian."

"He's not a myth-maker *or* an historian," said Virtue. "He's just a ballad-writer, and not a very good one, at that."

The Swagman shook his head. "He may put his story in ballad form, but he's not one to let meter interfere with what he wants to say. The last time he visited me I pointed out that the meter was all wrong in his songs about Socrates and Altair of Altair and One-Time Charlie, and he just smiled and said that he'd rather have his songs ring true than scan properly."

"The man's a fool."

"If he is, then he's a very popular fool."

"You think so?" she said. "You ought to hear Cain's opinion about being dubbed the Songbird."

"Instead of complaining about it, he ought to be pleased," said the Swagman. "Orpheus has made him famous." He paused. "Hell, he's made *all* of us famous."

"You know," she said thoughtfully, wiping her forehead again, "maybe we're missing a bet here."

"In what way?"

"Maybe we ought to hunt Orpheus up and ask *him* where we can find Santiago."

"He doesn't know," said the Swagman. "He's been hunting for him for the past ten years."

"But he wrote him up!" protested Virtue. "I thought he never did that until he'd met his subject."

"Santiago's a special case. After all, an epic about the Inner Frontier that doesn't mention him just doesn't make much sense. Besides, Orpheus is like every other artist I've ever met: the further along he gets on a piece of work, the more frightened he becomes that he's going to die before it's finished and that some total incompetent will complete it for him. He wanted to make sure that the Santiago verses were done before that happened; I imagine they'll be rewritten if he ever finds him."

"Who commissioned this damned song, anyway?" asked Virtue.

"No one. He does it because he wants to."

"Then I was right the first time," she said decisively. "He's a fool."

"For doing something that makes him happy?"

"For giving it away for free."

"Maybe he's got enough money," suggested the Swagman.

She turned and stared at him. "Do you know *anyone* who's got enough money?"

The Swagman smiled. "Maybe he's a fool," he said at last.

The road suddenly dipped through a wooded hollow, and the Swagman began slowing down.

"What's the matter?" asked Virtue.

"We're almost there," he replied, pulling off to the side of the road just after it climbed out of the hollow and ran across a narrow ridge. "See that clearing about half a mile ahead?"

"What are those weird-looking structures in the middle of it?" asked Virtue, peering through the trees.

"Wigwams," replied the Swagman.

"What's a wigwam?"

"A kind of tent that Amerinds used to live in—or so Sitting Bull tells me. Personally, I doubt that anyone ever slept in anything like that. It looks much too inefficient, and it certainly doesn't afford any protection against your enemies." He shrugged. "Still, it's hardly worth arguing the point; I've got better things to do than go around researching aborigines."

He turned off the ignition.

"What now?" asked Virtue.

"Now we get out and walk," he continued, opening his door as she followed suit.

"Why? We're still almost half a mile away."

"Because Sitting Bull likes his supplicants to approach on foot. I can't really say that I blame him; there are a goodly number of ways to rig some pretty powerful weaponry to a motor vehicle, and he does have more than his fair share of enemies." He paused. "Besides, this way he gets to show off."

"I don't follow you," said Virtue.

"If the last time I came here was at all typical, we'll pick up some company along the way and march into his camp under armed guard. I imagine it makes him feel as if he's in control of the situation."

As if on cue, four aliens stepped out from behind trees and bushes. Or rather, three—tall, bald, emaciated blue beings, each carrying a multitude of weapons—*stepped* out; the fourth, which resembled a shaggy yellow caterpillar, merely *slithered*. All four aliens wore war paint and headbands. The Swagman thought they looked absolutely ludicrous, but Virtue found them interesting enough to capture with a miniaturized holographic camera that she had built into her belt buckle.

Finally one of the blue aliens, who identified himself as Cochise, pointed a sonic rifle at them. They stood motionless while the caterpillar literally sniffed out their weapons, appropriated the Swagman's two concealed pistols, and turned them over to another of the blue aliens. Finally Cochise jerked his head in the direction of the camp, and the two humans began walking toward it once again.

When they arrived, Cochise ushered them to the site of a campfire that had died sometime during the night, told them to sit down, and left them in the care of another blue alien.

"Anything out of the ordinary yet?" whispered Virtue.

"Just standard operating procedure so far," said the Swagman reassuringly.

Then the flaps of a nearby teepee were thrust apart, and Sitting Bull stepped out as Virtue surreptitiously activated her belt-buckle camera and a hidden recording device.

The first thing she noticed about him was the gold feathers. Initially she thought they were part of his costume, like the huge ceremonial headdress he wore, but she quickly saw that they were part and parcel of Sitting Bull himself.

He stood about five feet tall and was almost as broad as he was high. He covered his genitalia so inadequately with a beaded loincloth that she knew at a glance that he *was* a he and not an it; and he waddled on thick, muscular legs that were jointed so strangely that she couldn't imagine how he could possibly sit down, or even squat on his haunches.

His face, like those of the other aliens, was covered by a painted design, but seemed, if not human, at least very expressive. Virtue couldn't imagine any being with so many feathers not having a beak

to go along with them, but Sitting Bull possessed a broad, flat nose
and a narrow, puckered mouth. His eyes were umber, his pupils mere
vertical slits. If he had ears, she couldn't spot them, but she decided
that they may very well have been covered by the substantial headdress.

"Hello, Sitting Bull," said the Swagman, starting to get to his feet.
"It's good to see you again."

"Remain seated," replied Sitting Bull in a harsh, croaking voice
that grated on Virtue's ears; it seemed so out of place that she felt he
was purposely deepening it to impress them. The Swagman sat back
down and re-crossed his legs. "Who is your companion?"

"Virtue MacKenzie," said Virtue, wondering whether to extend her
hand and deciding not to. "I'm a journalist."

Sitting Bull stared at her expressionlessly for a moment, then
turned back to the Swagman and cleared his throat, a grating noise
that sounded like metal rubbing against metal and caused Virtue to
conclude that she was hearing his normal voice after all.

"What favor do you seek from the Great Sioux Nation?"

"Information," responded the Swagman promptly.

"Will the acquisition of this information bring harm to one or more
Men?" asked Sitting Bull.

"It will," said the Swagman.

The feathered alien made a sudden awkward jerking motion with
his head, which Virtue took to be a nod of approval.

"Will the acquisition of this information bring harm to one or more
members of any other race?"

"Absolutely not," the Swagman assured him.

"Are you aware of the penalty for lying?"

"Let us say that I can hazard a remarkably accurate guess."

"Do not guess, Jolly Swagman." Sitting Bull leaned forward and
stared intently at him, and suddenly Virtue decided that he looked a
lot more like an alien than an Indian. "Should any harm befall anyone
other than a Man as a result of the information that you seek, you and
Virtue MacKenzie will be found no matter where you try to hide. You
will be brought back to Diamond Strike, you will be tortured, and
eventually you will be tethered to a stake and burned to death. Is that
understood?"

"Perfectly."

"Then you may make your request."

"We're looking for Santiago. Do you know where he is?"

"Yes."

There was a long silence.

"Well?" demanded Virtue.

"This I will not tell you."

"Will not or cannot?" asked the Swagman.

"I said what I said," replied Sitting Bull stoically.

"I didn't realize you were afraid of him," said the Swagman condescendingly.

"I fear no one."

"Then why won't you tell us what we want to know?"

"Because he makes war against Men. Because he brings grief to Men. Because he brings chaos to Men. Because he is Santiago."

"Cut the crap and name your price," said Virtue irritably.

Sitting Bull turned to her, his pupils dilating and contracting as he breathed. "Women do not speak in council."

"Women with money do," she replied. "How much do you want?"

"You are very irritating, even for a member of your race," said the alien. "I begin to understand why Dimitri Sokol wants you dead." He stared coldly at her. "There is no price. I will not tell you."

"You mean you haven't got the guts!" snapped Virtue.

"We fear no one," said Sitting Bull, pulling back his lips and exposing a row of bright yellow teeth. "Even the Democracy cringes in fear of the Great Sioux Nation."

"Which in turn cringes in fear of Santiago, a common criminal with a price on his head."

"Santiago is not the only Man with a price on his head," said Sitting Bull meaningfully. "You would do well to remember that."

"Is that a threat?" demanded Virtue. "If there's a price on *my* head, it was put there by a criminal on Pegasus—and if you try to cash in on it, you're going to find out just what happens to self-important aliens who go around killing human journalists! Have you got that straight?"

Sitting Bull merely stared at her and made no reply.

"Now let's talk business," said Virtue. "We're in a hurry."

The alien continued staring at her.

"Now listen, you—" she began heatedly.

The Swagman touched her arm. "That's enough," he said. "He's not trying to jack up the price; he means what he says. And in case you've forgotten, we're surrounded by his enforcers."

"Are you trying to tell me that we came all this way for nothing?" demanded Virtue. "We talk to him for thirty seconds and just give up, is that it?"

"Not entirely," replied the Swagman. "We can at least find out how the competition is doing." He turned back to Sitting Bull. "We also seek information that does not concern Santiago."

"I will listen."

"There is a bounty hunter known as the Angel. Where is he now?"

They went through the same ritual about whom such information could and could not damage, after which Sitting Bull acknowledged that he could come up with the Angel's present location in a matter of minutes. He summoned a blue alien named Vittorio, asked him something in a tongue Virtue could not identify, dismissed him, and turned back to the Swagman.

Then the haggling began. Sitting Bull demanded 20,000 Bonaparte francs; the Swagman laughed in his face and countered with 750 credits. Ten minutes later they were still at it, 236 credits apart, and finally the Swagman gave in. The negotiated bill came to 6,819 credits, payable in advance.

The Swagman dug into his pocket and pulled out a sheaf of bills. Vittorio was summoned, emerged from a nearby wigwam, said something to Sitting Bull, collected the money, and then positioned himself a few paces behind Sitting Bull, his thin arms folded across his narrow chest.

"Now we will smoke a peace pipe," announced Sitting Bull. "And then I will give you that which you have purchased."

He nodded, and a brown, sluglike creature that Virtue had thought was a log undulated over to him and produced a long, meticulously crafted wooden pipe from somewhere within the folds of its thick, crusted skin.

Sitting Bull withdrew a tiny laser device, rekindled the logs between himself and the two humans, and gestured to the yellow caterpillar, which slithered over, picked up a burning twig, and held it just above the end of the pipe. Sitting Bull took a number of deep puffs, grunted his satisfaction, and then passed the pipe to the Swagman, who filled his mouth with smoke, seemed to analyze the taste of it for an instant, and then released it.

When it was Virtue's turn, he handed it to her and whispered, "Don't inhale."

She followed his instructions, took a couple of mouthfuls of thick gray smoke, made sure nothing went down her throat, and finally blew them out.

"What is it?" she asked, making a face and handing the pipe to the yellow alien, who ambulated away with it. "It seemed sickly sweet."

"Some kind of hallucinogenic compound," he replied softly. "It's one of his favorite parlor tricks." He grimaced. "My guess is that he insists on smoking it just so he can watch humans make asses of themselves. Get one puff of that stuff in your system and you'd still be seeing things a week from now." He turned to Sitting Bull. "May I have my information?"

"Vittorio says that the man you seek is currently on the planet of Glenovar, in the system of Zeta Halioth."

The Swagman frowned. "You're sure?"

"I am sure."

"There's no possibility of a mistake, or that you might have the wrong man?"

"None."

"All right." He paused. "I'll give you one last opportunity to talk about Santiago. We are prepared to make you a very handsome offer."

"I will not betray Santiago."

"I thought your livelihood consisted of betraying Men," interjected Virtue coldly.

"Only to the detriment of other Men," replied Sitting Bull placidly.

The Swagman stood up and helped Virtue to her feet. "Then I think it's time that we took our leave of you."

"You seek no other information?"

"No."

"Are you not curious about a shipment of anthracite sculptures in transit from Pisgah to Genovaith Four?" suggested the feathered alien, his lips curled back in what seemed to be a grin.

The Swagman smiled back at him. "I was so curious about it that I gave orders to waylay it when it passed by the Karobus system. That would have occurred, oh, about an hour ago."

"Truly?"

"Truly," said the Swagman.

"You are a very resourceful villain, Jolly Swagman," said Sitting Bull.

"In that case, perhaps I should apply for membership in the Great Sioux Nation," he replied wryly.

"You are not acceptable," said Sitting Bull. "Your weapons have been placed in your vehicle." He turned away and waddled back to his wigwam.

After the feathered alien had disappeared behind a flap in the tent, the Swagman turned to Virtue.

"We've got problems," he announced grimly.

"Oh?"

He nodded. "The Angel's a lot closer to Santiago than I thought he'd be at this time."

"Closer than we are?" she demanded.

"Probably."

"How can that be? If you know who he's seeing, why didn't we see this person first?"

"I don't know who he's seeing. What I *do* know is that there are three or four lines of pursuit for someone who's hunting Santiago. We're following the one that's tied in to his smuggling operations; if the Angel's on Glenovar, he's following a money trail." He frowned. "And he's doing a damned good job of it: he's gotten as far in four weeks as you have in almost a year—and he didn't have Cain helping him. I've got a feeling that he's within three or four worlds of someone who can probably give him Santiago's headquarters planet, and might even be able to toss in his address and room number."

"Will Altair of Altair be able to do the same for Cain?" asked Virtue.

The Swagman shrugged. "I don't know. Perhaps."

"But you doubt it."

"I really don't know," he replied.

Virtue stood up and turned to Sitting Bull's wigwam.

"Hey, Sitting Bull!" she hollered. "Come back out."

The alien emerged a moment later.

"What is your price for killing the Angel?" she asked him.

He was silent for a minute, as if weighing his expenses.

"Five million credits," he announced at last.

"Five million?" she repeated incredulously. "You must be joking! That's more than the Democracy is offering for any criminal except Santiago!"

"It will take many of my warriors, and most of them will die." He paused. "The Songbird is a killer, and he is also your partner. Why do you not ask him to kill the Angel?"

"Because I'm asking *you*," she snapped, wondering irritably if there was anyone on the Frontier who *didn't* know she had teamed up with Cain.

"I have told you my price. Will you pay it?"

"Not a chance," she replied.

Sitting Bull went back into his wigwam without another word.

"Where will the Angel be heading after he leaves Glenovar?" asked Virtue as she and the Swagman began walking back to the land-car.

He shrugged. "Who knows? The Lambda Karos system, probably. Sooner or later most money trails pass through there."

"Perhaps we should try to get there first and eliminate his contact," she suggested.

"I don't know who his contact *is*—and even if I did know, I think it's a fair assumption that from this point on, all of his contacts are pretty good at taking care of themselves. You'd need a specialist for that, someone like Cain."

"Well?" she said expectantly.

He sighed. "Out of the question. We also need him for our own line of inquiry. Of the three of us, he's the most likely to survive a meeting with Altair of Altair and some of the others who are waiting along the way. You have many wonderful qualities, Virtue—you lie and cheat and blackmail and bluff with great panache, and you're thoroughly delightful in bed—but you simply aren't a skilled professional killer."

Virtue took a deep breath, held it for perhaps half a minute, then released it explosively.

"You think the Angel is going to get there first, don't you?" she said bluntly.

He shrugged noncommittally. "The possibility exists."

Virtue stared at her companion for a long moment, and as she did so she found herself concluding that she had put her money on the wrong horse.

"Maybe I should go out to the Lambda Karos system and wait for him there," she suggested with what she hoped was the proper degree of detachment.

"Him?" repeated the Swagman. "You mean the Angel? What good would that do?"

She shrugged innocently. "Who knows? Maybe I can find some way to misdirect him, or at least slow him down." She paused. "At any rate, we'll have a clear idea of where he is and how fast he's progressing. That has to be of some use to us."

"I'm afraid you're being just a little transparent, my dear," replied the Swagman with the hint of an amused smile. "How can you possibly misdirect him if you don't know who his contact is, or what information the contact will feed him? As for having a clear idea of where he's at, that's infinitely less important than possessing a clear idea of where he's *going*." He paused, then chuckled and shook his head. "You haven't done your homework very well, Virtue: the Angel doesn't take partners. Ever."

"Who said anything about becoming the Angel's partner?" she

demanded heatedly, annoyed with herself for being so obvious. "I just want to keep tabs on him, and possibly send him off in the wrong direction."

"Or accompany him in the right one," suggested the Swagman wryly.

"You're a very distrusting man," said Virtue. "I suppose it can be blamed on your upbringing."

"How about blaming it on my present company?"

"You can waste your time assessing the blame," she said. "I intend to spend mine hunting up the Angel."

"You're being foolish, my dear," said the Swagman. "Or perhaps you weren't listening to Sitting Bull as closely as you should have been."

"What are you talking about?"

"Sokol's still got a hit out on you. In fact, the only reason that Sitting Bull didn't have you killed the minute you landed is because you were with me, and I've sent a lot of business his way over the years. As soon as you go off by yourself, you're fair game again."

"Do you think I'm going to quake in terror over a squat little alien who lives in a tent?" she said with a laugh.

"It could be anyone you might meet. You don't know who Sokol may have contacted." He paused. "As for Sitting Bull, he doesn't look like much, and he doesn't surround himself with luxury, but he's a pretty formidable antagonist."

"And if I stay with you, *you're* going to protect me?"

"Indirectly. Most people don't like to offend me."

"At least Cain has had a little experience killing people."

He smiled. "I *hire* people like Cain, my dear."

They came to a fallen tree that was blocking their way and walked around it.

"What's the greatest single piece of alien artwork in the galaxy?" she asked suddenly.

He thought for a moment. "There's a mile-long tapestry on Antares Three," he said. "Forty generations of Antareans have worked on it, and it tells the history of their race in about two thousand exquisite scenes. I'd say that's about the rarest. Why?"

"What would you risk to get your hands on it?"

"Everything I have."

"Well, Santiago's the greatest single story in the galaxy, and I'll take whatever risk is necessary to find him."

"I should add that I wouldn't risk my life for that tapestry," said the Swagman.

"That's because you're not hungry anymore," said Virtue. "I still am. I want to be the best—and if seeing the Angel can help me get what I want, then I'm willing to do it."

They reached the landcar, and the Swagman picked his pistols up off the seat and put them back into his pockets.

"You're sure you won't reconsider?"

"I'm sure."

He sighed. "Then maybe I'd better go with you."

"There's no need for both of us to go out there. I'll keep you and Cain informed of his whereabouts." She paused. "I think your best course of action is to go to Altair and hook up with him there."

"Probably," he agreed reluctantly. "A question arises, however: How am I going to get there? My ship's back on Goldenrod."

"You're a resourceful man," said Virtue. "I'm sure you'll find a way." She paused. "Now please take me back to my ship."

"And if I refuse?"

"Then I'll walk, and the result will be the same, except that I'll tell Cain that you're working for the Angel and that he should kill you on sight."

The Swagman looked at her, surprised only that he felt no surprise. "I suppose you would, at that." He paused. "The nearest major planet is Kakkab Kastu Four. Can you at least drop me there?"

She considered his suggestion for a moment, then nodded. "I suppose another few hours doesn't matter, as long as I get where I'm going." She turned to him. "But you'll pay for the extra fuel."

"We'll subtract it from your half of Sitting Bull's fee."

"I never agreed to pay Sitting Bull," she said. "I could have gotten the same information from Cain."

"If he's still alive."

"If he's not, I want half the reward if you kill Santiago."

"You're quite an operator, my dear," said the Swagman, shaking his head with mock weariness.

"One does what one must," said Virtue.

"Spare me your platitudes," he said dryly.

"I consider them words to live by."

"Only until you meet the Angel," he predicted. "Then may God have mercy on your soul, for He'll be presented with it soon enough."

Part 3

The Jolly Swagman's Book

11.

Come if you dare, come but beware,
Come to the lair of Altair of Altair.
Offer a prayer for the men foul and fair,
Trapped in the snare of Altair of Altair.

They tell a lot of stories about Altair of Altair out on the Frontier.

Some say that, like the Jolly Swagman, she was raised by aliens and grew up with a bitter hatred of her own race that the Swagman somehow avoided.

Others say she wasn't human at all, but that she could change her shape at will and enticed her victims to their deaths with an irresistible siren song.

Homer of Troy, the self-proclaimed People's Poet who spent half a lifetime trying unsuccessfully to write a saga of the Frontier that would rival Black Orpheus' epic in popularity, swore that she was a mutant who killed her enemies by the use of mental thunderbolts that shattered their minds.

There was even a group on Walpurgis III, a planet colonized by covens and devil-worshipers, that believed she was a devoted practitioner of the Black Arts who brought destruction through spells and potions.

As for Black Orpheus himself, he went directly to the source, as always. It took him almost a month to track her down after he'd reached the Altair system, and then he had to wait another week before she would agree to see him. When they finally met face to face, he took one look at her and decided that she was the most beautiful woman he had seen since the death of his beloved Eurydice.

By the time he left some twenty minutes later, he wasn't even sure that she *was* a woman—but he knew that she was the most formidable killer he had ever encountered.

He never spoke of her again, although he did write a couple of verses about her, and when others asked about Altair of Altair he always found a way to change the subject. Nobody knows what happened during their one brief meeting, but it obviously had a profound effect upon him, one that lasted for the remainder of his life.

One of the people who wished that Black Orpheus had written a little more about her was Sebastian Cain, if only so he would have some idea of what to expect when he finally reached her.

It had taken him two weeks to discover that she did not live *on* Altair III, but rather *under* it, and now he stalked, gun in hand, through the labyrinthian network of tunnels and corridors that led to her chamber. It had cost him ten thousand credits just to find out how and where to enter the seemingly endless maze, and he had then spent the better part of two days losing the trio of men who had been tailing him since he had touched down. Finally, reasonably certain that he was no longer being followed, he had entered the subterranean world of Altair of Altair.

That had been two hours ago. Since then the temperature had dropped somewhat, and the air had become dank and stale. The corridors themselves were illuminated by diffuse blue light that gave them a surreal glow, but none of them were marked or labeled, and after he found himself back where he had started, he withdrew a small knife and began carving crude directional symbols at every intersection.

He paused, wiped some sweat from his face, and cursed under his breath. There *had* to be a quicker way into her headquarters, and he decided to give himself one more hour. If he found her by then, well and good; if not, he would retrace his steps, return to the surface, take his money back from the man who had sold him his information and possibly kill him as well, and start his search all over again from scratch. If he went back to his hotel, he was sure to pick up his troika of followers once more; possibly he would separate one from the others and find some means, painless or otherwise, of extracting the information he needed.

He began walking again, wondering if he wouldn't be better off going immediately to the surface and searching for a more direct route. Then he came to yet another intersection and found that the right-hand tunnel glowed a rich red, as opposed to the usual blue. He entered it without hesitation.

It twisted to his right, then straightened out for a few hundred feet, and finally seemed to make a sweeping semicircle to the left, never once intersecting with any other corridor. Finally it broadened out, the walls gradually forming artificially perfect right angles with the floor and ceiling, and he noticed that the illumination was considerably brighter.

Suddenly the corridor came to an abrupt end, and he found himself standing in a small vestibule that led to a large, well-lit chamber. He started to enter it, then jumped back as he discovered that his way was blocked by an electronic force field.

He approached the entrance more cautiously and looked into the chamber. It was perhaps sixty feet on a side, and its smooth stone walls sparkled like polished prisms in the artificial light. He had no idea how high the ceiling was, because the room faded into darkness some thirty feet above the floor. Lining two of the walls, to a height of perhaps eight feet, were enormous water tanks filled with alien aquatic life-forms and contained not by glass walls but by translucent energy screens.

In the very center of the room was a desk with a computer console and five small screens; one of them displayed some type of readout, and the other four seemed to show various areas of the labyrinth. Just to the left of the desk were two couches. One was empty, and on the other reclined a breathtakingly beautiful woman. Her features were human, but they were so exotic that they seemed somehow alien. Her skin was chalk white, her hair was long and black, her large eyes were almost too blue beneath her oddly arched eyebrows. Her facial features, from her full lips and delicate nose to her not-quite-pointed ears, were exquisitely chiseled. Her single garment, which was draped around her supple body like a corkscrew and exposed far more than it concealed, was made of some metallic fabric that seemed to change colors every time she breathed or moved.

"Welcome, Sebastian Cain," she said in a lilting, singsong voice. "I have been watching you work your way through my labyrinth."

"You're Altair of Altair?"

"Of course."

"I've come a long way to talk to you," he said.

"I will enjoy talking to you. We have many things in common." She paused. "That is why I allowed you to find me. You are only the third person ever to enter this chamber."

"I haven't entered it yet," he noted.

"I must protect myself," she said apologetically. "After all, I have a price on my head, and you are a bounty hunter."

"I have no professional interest in you," he assured her. "I just want to talk."

"And yet you have been carrying your gun in your hand since entering my labyrinth."

"You're not the only person who feels the need for protection," he replied. "I wouldn't be the first man you've killed."

"We are *both* killers," said Altair of Altair. "Shall we declare a truce?"

"For how long?"

"You will be warned before it is over."

"I'm willing."

"Then leave your gun in the vestibule. You can pick it up when you leave."

"Not a chance," he said.

"Will you at least replace it in your holster?"

He did so, and she rose, walked to the computer, and touched a small octagonal button.

"The shield is down," she announced. "You may enter now."

"Thank you," he said, walking gingerly through the doorway and stepping into the chamber. The floor was covered by a soft yielding substance that was more resilient than it looked and glowed with different colors every time he set his foot down.

"I have been wanting to meet you for a long time," said Altair of Altair.

"Have you?"

"Yes," she said. "Killing is a lonely profession. It is so rare that one gets to visit with one's peers."

"We're not exactly peers," answered Cain. "You're an assassin; I'm a bounty hunter."

"But many facets of our work are the same," she pointed out. "The endless waiting for the prey to appear, the moment of exultation at the kill, the distrust of confederates, the craving for solitude. Do you not agree?"

"Perhaps," he said noncommittally. "But the differences are even greater, and the fact remains that you will commit murder for anyone who pays your fee, and I kill criminals at the behest of my government."

"True," she said thoughtfully. "But then, even among bounty hunters you are a unique individual."

"Oh? In what way?"

"Most of those who make their living by killing lawbreakers were once lawbreakers themselves. Peacemaker MacDougal was a smuggler, Giles Sans Pitié and Barnaby Wheeler were bandits, even the Angel was an assassin. Of them all, only you have always operated within the law."

"You're wrong," he said. "I once had a price on my head, too."

"You were fighting on behalf of what you believed to be a legal government in exile," she replied with a smile.

"How do you know that?"

"I have been studying you for a long time," said Altair of Altair. "In our business, one does not live long without knowing the face of the enemy."

"I'm not your enemy."

"And Santiago is not yours," she replied. "Why do you want him dead?"

"What makes you think I'm after Santiago?" he asked.

"Who else could have brought you this far from Keepsake?" she replied. "I repeat: Why do you wish to kill him?"

He smiled. "Have you seen the size of the reward?"

"You are a very successful bounty hunter. You have no need of money."

"Everyone needs money."

"A man like you must have another reason," she persisted.

He stared at her, then shrugged. "It would *mean* something," he said at last.

"Ah!" She smiled. "I knew you were different!" She walked back to the couch and sprawled on it. "Do you know that not a single murder I have committed has ever meant anything?"

"What about killing the governor of Alsatia Four?" he asked.

"One second later there was a new governor, and what had changed?" She shook her head. "No, the beauty of the assassin's profession is that nothing ever means anything, and hence the perceived need for assassination never diminishes. Only you, of all the killers I know, want your actions to make a difference."

"Tell me about some of the killers you know," said Cain.

"Had you someone in mind?"

"Santiago."

"I have never met him."

"I think you have," persisted Cain.

"Why?"

"Because you killed a man named Kastartos."

"What has one to do with the other?" she asked.

"Kastartos planned to double-cross Santiago," answered Cain. "He tried to get Jonathan Stern to help him. Stern didn't think it was worth the risk, and sent word of Kastartos's plans to Santiago. It stands to reason that Santiago commissioned his death."

She stared at him pleasantly but made no comment.

"If the order came directly from him, it wouldn't be unreasonable to assume that you've met him and know where he is, would it?" he continued.

"He has never directly commissioned my services," she replied. "He works only through intermediaries."

"Who are they?"

"That is not your concern."

"If you're saying that from fear of reprisal, there's no reason for Santiago to know that we ever met."

"He already knows."

"How?"

"Because he is Santiago."

"You make him sound like some kind of superman," said Cain.

"He is just a man, and he can be killed like any other man," she replied. "You have much in common with him."

"You mean because we can both be killed?" he asked sardonically.

"That, too," she said with an enigmatic smile.

Suddenly there was a flurry of motion in one of the aquarium tanks, as a bright orange eyeless fish, slim as a dagger, burrowed into the soft sand at the bottom and emerged with a yellow-and-black-striped crustacean. The orange fish tossed the crustacean up above him and darted for its soft underbelly, guided unerringly to its most vulnerable parts by what Cain assumed was some form of sonar. The water around them turned pink with the fluid that coursed through the crustacean's veins, and instantly half a hundred other marine forms of perhaps ten different species had gathered in a feeding frenzy.

"They are beautiful creatures, are they not?" said Altair of Altair, a look of almost inhuman excitement on her face. "And savage," she continued in a singsong chant. "They kill for food, and when they are sated, they kill for the love of killing."

"Interesting," he said noncommittally.

"Fascinating," she replied with conviction. "There is one you cannot see, who lives beneath the sand. Not this clumsy shellfish, but a beautiful animal, bright as the morning sun. The others hunt for him endlessly, but they cannot find him." She smiled. "I have named him Santiago."

"And which fish is Altair of Altair?" he asked.

"None of them." She stared at him through half-lowered lids. "I kill only for recompense."

"Nobody's asking you to kill at all," said Cain patiently. "I just need to know where to find Santiago." He paused. "I'm prepared to give you a percentage of the reward if your information proves useful."

"Are you indeed?"

"Ten percent of the price on his head would keep you in fish for a long time."

"Do you know what I would do if you tried to take my very bright fish?" she asked suddenly.

"What?"

"I would kill you, Sebastian Cain. I would kill you because that fish is mine, and you would be taking something that didn't belong to you."

"Are you trying to tell me that you think you have some prior claim on Santiago?"

"Santiago is mine."

"Then why is he still alive?"

"Because the reward increases every year, and I am very patient. When it becomes large enough, then I shall kill him."

"It's large right now."

"It will become larger," she said with certainty.

"And you're not worried about someone beating you to it?"

"Do you really think it is that easy to kill him?" she asked, obviously amused. "He is *Santiago*."

"If you think he can't be killed, why not give me the information I want?"

"It would do you no good."

"In that case, it would do you no harm," said Cain.

She stared at him for a long moment, then sighed. "There are more important things than information."

"For instance?"

"The gift of life," she said. "No one who has ever entered my lair has been given it. But because I lead the solitary life of a killer, I respect all others who do as well. Pledge to return to Keepsake and fish for lesser prizes, and you may leave here alive."

"After I find Santiago," he replied, suddenly wary.

"Then you are a fool," she said. "Did you know that even as we speak, Virtue MacKenzie is racing to the Angel's side to betray you?"

He looked surprised for just an instant, then shrugged. "It won't be the first time I've been betrayed," he said. "And it won't do her any good."

"That much is true," said Altair of Altair. "For when we are through here, I must hunt down the Angel and all who stand with him."

"For poaching?" he asked wryly.

"Yes."

"If you start killing every bounty hunter who's looking for Santiago, you're going to have a full-time job on your hands."

"Most of them are insignificant specks of debris in the cosmos," she replied. "Even Peacemaker MacDougal and Johnny One-Note will never find Santiago. Of them all, only you and the Angel have the ability to find him."

"What about Giles Sans Pitié?"

"The Angel killed him last week," replied Altair of Altair. "Giles Sans Pitié sought him out on Glenovar and proposed an alliance." She paused. "The Angel has no more use for competition than I have."

"I warned him to stay away from the Angel," commented Cain.

"You realize, of course, that I have every reason to do to you what the Angel did to Giles Sans Pitié."

"I wouldn't advise it," said Cain ominously.

"Forget your weapon, Sebastian Cain," she said, an unfathomable expression on her exotic face. "It will do you no good."

"You'll forgive me if I don't take your word for it," he said, withdrawing his gun and pointing it at her.

"How will you kill me?" she asked, her blue eyes alive with amused interest. "A bullet to the head? That *is* your trademark, isn't it?"

"I don't have a trademark."

"*All* good killers have trademarks," she replied. "With Giles Sans Pitié it was his metal fist, with Peacemaker MacDougal it is a pencil-thin beam of light, with ManMountain Bates it is his bare hands, with you it is a bullet. Only the Angel, who is adept with all weapons, slaughters with variety."

"And what is *your* trademark?" asked Cain.

"You shall see," she said softly.

And then, suddenly, he was no longer in a subterranean chamber on Altair III. Instead, he stood at the edge of a clear blue brook, the hot Sylarian sun beating down on his neck. He was barefoot, and the grass, long and swaying in the gentle breeze, felt like velvet between his toes.

He looked across the brook and saw a girl, her blond hair meticulously braided, her skin tanned and healthy. She wore a plain blue dress, and she gingerly held its skirt up to her knees as she stood ankle deep in the water.

"Help me," she said, her voice heavy with worry.

"It's shallow," replied Cain with a laugh. "Just walk across it."

"I'll fall."

"No, you won't."

"Don't tease me, Sebastian," she pleaded, reaching her hand out to him. "Please!"

"All right," he said with a smile.

It was funny, he reflected as he placed a foot in the brook and felt the cold water swirl around it. He had known her for years, had loved her from the first day he had met her, yet for the life of him he couldn't remember her name.

"It's Jennifer," she said.

"Right." He nodded. "Jennifer."

"Please hurry, Sebastian," she said. "I'm frightened."

"I'm coming."

He crossed the brook in five large steps, feeling remarkably invigorated by the water.

"You see?" he laughed. "There's nothing to it." He paused, momentarily disoriented. "Now what?"

"Now carry me across."

"Why don't I just hold your hand and lead you?" he asked.

"The stones hurt my feet," she said, half crooning the words. "Won't you please carry me?"

He sighed. "If that's what you want."

"You'll have to drop the stick first," she said.

He frowned. "What stick?"

"The stick you're carrying in your right hand. You can't lift me up if you're carrying a stick."

"Sure I can," he said, suddenly uneasy.

"It will hurt me," she said, "and it might even rip my dress. Please drop it, Sebastian."

He took a step back, still reluctant to drop the stick. "Something's wrong," he said, frowning again.

"What is it?" she asked innocently.

"I don't know," he said. "Maybe it's the dress."

The dress became a burgundy skirt and a frilly white blouse.

"Is this better, Sebastian?"

He stared at it. "I suppose so," he said at last.

"Then carry me across the brook. I'm late."

"For what?"

She giggled. "*You* know," she said with a sense of shared intimacy.
"Oh."

He stood motionless.

"Well?" she said at last.

"It's still wrong," he said, puzzled.

"What is, Sebastian?"

"I don't know. Let me think for a minute."

"We haven't got a minute, Sebastian. I'm *late*. Don't tease me like this."

He took a step toward her. "I've almost got it."

"Hurry, Sebastian!" she said, a note of urgency creeping into her voice.

He reached out to her uneasily.

"The stick, Sebastian," she chanted seductively. "Put it down."

He dropped the stick.

"Thank you," she said, a strange smile on her lips. "Are you happy, Sebastian?"

"I suppose so," he said, forcing himself to return her smile.

"I'm so glad."

"What's that in your hand?" he asked, peering at some shining object he hadn't seen before.

"A flower," she said. "A lovely silver flower."

"It's very pretty," he said, the uneasiness growing within him once again.

"Would you like a closer look, Sebastian?"

"Yes, I—*Shit!*" he muttered, diving for the stick. He grabbed it as he rolled over on the ground, pointed it at her, and squeezed it.

Suddenly there was a loud explosion, and he was once again in the subterranean chamber, and Altair of Altair lay on her back, blood pouring out from a small hole between her eyes, a silver dagger clutched in her hand.

Cain stood motionless, panting, sweat pouring down his body, trying to regain his bearings. It took his hands a full minute to stop shaking, and finally he put the gun back in its holster.

Then he walked over to Altair of Altair and looked down at her.

"There *aren't* any brooks on Sylaria," he said weakly.

He examined her to make sure there were no signs of life, then stood erect, his hands on his hips.

"Great," he muttered. "Back to square one again."

"Not necessarily," said a voice.

"Who's there?" he demanded, crouching down beside the corpse and drawing his pistol.

"My name is Schussler," said the voice, and now Cain realized that it was coming from the computer. "If you will retrace your steps, you'll find me waiting for you at the entrance to the labyrinth."

"How will I recognize you?" asked Cain.

"You'll have very little difficulty," said the voice with a bitter chuckle. "This I promise you."

12.

He aches for the touch of flesh upon flesh,
He wonders why Fate had to end his beguine,
He longs for a woman, all virginal fresh:
Schussler the Cyborg, unhappy machine.

Black Orpheus met many unique characters during his wanderings on the Inner Frontier. There were killers and gamblers, preachers and bounty hunters, millionaires and paupers, saints and sinners, an entire panorama of outcasts and adventurers and misfits—but not one of them measured up to Schussler the Cyborg, whose tragedy was that he didn't want to be unique at all.

Father William, for example, loved the limelight; Schussler dreaded it. Socrates enjoyed power; Schussler disdained it. Sebastian Cain sought solitude; Schussler hated it. The Angel had killed men almost without number; Schussler cherished all life but his own. The Sargasso Rose had no use for human contact; Schussler longed for it. The men and women and aliens that Orpheus put into his song were all bigger than life; Schussler was bigger than any of them, and wanted only to be smaller.

Most people saw him as a miracle of science, a shining testament to the melding of man and machine—but Black Orpheus looked beneath the gleaming surface, past the wonders of an alien technology, straight into Schussler's tortured soul, and wept at what he saw.

They met only once, on Altair III. Orpheus stayed with him for a day and a night, while Schussler poured out his strange, unhappy story. They parted the next morning, Orpheus to continue his journey among the stars, Schussler to serve his mistress and wait, without hope, for the release of death.

Things began to change when the Jolly Swagman landed on Altair. By rights he and Schussler should have had a lot in common, since one of them had been raised by aliens and the other had been rebuilt by them; but the accumulation of other people's property was the driving force in the Swagman's life—while Schussler, who *was* property, found all forms of private ownership immoral.

Still, each of them had a major stake in Cain's meeting with Altair of Altair, so they quickly reached an accommodation and awaited the outcome.

It was midafternoon when Cain emerged from the labyrinth, shielding his eyes from the pale yellow sun with his hand. He looked around the barren red landscape and saw a very small spaceship of inhuman design about eighty yards away. An elegantly dressed man was leaning against it, but when he saw Cain he immediately began walking toward him.

"I can't tell you how delighted I am that you survived!" he said with a distinct accent.

"You're Schussler?" asked Cain, starting to sweat already.

"I'm afraid not. People call me the Jolly Swagman."

"Virtue MacKenzie sent me a message that I might be running into you," said Cain. "Aren't you a little out of your bailiwick?"

"Not while you're here, I'm not," replied the Swagman easily. He looked around at his bleak surroundings. "Though one could wish for a more interesting world, I suppose. I can't imagine why anyone chooses to live here: I suspect the only things that grow on Altair Three are dust and bugs."

"Any deal Virtue may have cut with you was hers, not mine," said Cain firmly. "Where's Schussler? Aboard the ship?"

"In a manner of speaking." The Swagman grinned. "He *is* the ship."

"What are you talking about?" demanded Cain, slapping at a large red insect that had landed on his neck.

"Schussler," said the Swagman. "He's a cyborg."

Cain looked at the ship, its hull shining in the midday sun. "There's never been a cyborg like that," he said with conviction.

"Well, there is now. Orpheus gave him three verses."

"Orpheus writes so damned much, it's hard to keep up with all of it," replied Cain.

"Maybe you should have tried," said the Swagman. "Then you'd have known about Schussler."

Cain stared at the ship again. "He's *really* a spaceship?" he asked dubiously.

"Why should I lie to you?"

"Offhand, I can think of a hundred reasons." He waved his hand at a cloud of tiny, gnatlike insects, frightening them away. "How does he communicate?"

"He's got a speaker system. It sounds just the same as a ship's intercom."

"I've got to talk to him."

"He's not going anywhere," said the Swagman, turning slightly to protect his face from the dust raised by a sudden hot breeze. "Why don't you talk to *me* first?"

"About what?"

"About Santiago."

"Not interested," answered Cain.

"In Santiago?"

"In talking to you," said Cain. "I've heard about you, Swagman."

"All lies, I can assure you," said the Swagman smoothly.

"Can you now?"

"Absolutely," replied the Swagman with an amused laugh. "Anyone who can tell you the truth about me is safely dead and buried." He pulled out a thin cigar and lit it. "If you don't want to talk about Santiago, then how about Virtue?"

"What about Virtue?"

"What Altair of Altair told you is absolutely true. She's on her way to join the Angel."

"How do *you* know what she told me?" asked Cain sharply.

"I was a spectator at your little encounter," said the Swagman, dropping an ash on the ground and just missing a ten-legged purple-and-gold Altairian beetle with it.

"How did you manage *that*?"

"With the help of our cyborg friend here," replied the Swagman easily. "He's hooked into her computer." He smiled. "I would be less than candid if I didn't confess that I knew you were here to obtain information from Altair of Altair, and based on everything I knew about her, she wasn't very likely to give it to you. So, since there was no sense in both of us risking our lives, I hunted up Schussler and gave you silent moral support while we observed you from up here." The Swagman paused. "Just what did she do to you at the end there?"

"What did it look like?" asked Cain, curious.

"Nothing special. She kept urging you to cross a brook, but we couldn't see any—and I guess she tried to convince you that your gun

was a stick?" His inflection made it a question as much as an observation.

"Something like that."

"Well, I must say that you're every bit as good as Virtue said you
were. Any bookmaker would have made Altair of Altair a ten-to-one
favorite to kill you, especially on her own territory."

"Doubtless your moral support made all the difference," said Cain
dryly. "What would you have done if she'd killed me?"

"There's very little I *could* have done," admitted the Swagman.
"With you dead and Virtue gone over to the enemy, I'd have been out
of partners."

"There are worse things than being out of partners," said Cain.
"Such as *not* being out of them." He paused. "Why did Virtue go out
after the Angel?"

"I should think that would be obvious," replied the Swagman.
"She's come to the conclusion that he's got a better chance to kill
Santiago than you do."

"That's what she told you?"

"Of course not. What she told me was that she planned to spy on
him and perhaps feed him some false information."

"Bullshit," said Cain.

"My feelings precisely. On the other hand, I wouldn't take her
defection too seriously. Based on what I know of the Angel, her life
expectancy once she meets him is, not to be too pessimistic about it,
perhaps ten minutes."

"She's a lot harder to kill than you might think," commented Cain.
He was silent for a moment, then looked directly at the Swagman. "All
right," he said. "So Virtue's gone off to join the Angel. What makes
you think I'm looking for another partner?"

"You needn't look at all," said the Swagman with a confident
smile. "I'm right here in front of you."

"And what do you think *you* can bring to this proposed partnership?" asked Cain skeptically.

"A lot more than Virtue did," replied the Swagman, pulling out a
handkerchief and wiping the sweat from his face. "For one thing, I
used to work for Santiago. I can identify him for you."

"I can identify him myself."

"You mean by his scar?" The Swagman laughed. "And what will
you do if he's wearing gloves, or has a prosthetic hand?" His eyes
narrowed. "I know other things, too," he said persuasively. "I know
what world the Angel is going to run into trouble on. I know half a
dozen men who are still in Santiago's employ. I know a number of

his drop points for stolen goods." A satisfied smile crossed his face. "How does that compare with what Virtue MacKenzie could do for you?"

"What do you want in exchange for all this?" asked Cain, eyeing him warily.

"Nothing that would interest you," said the Swagman. "Though if you felt it incumbent upon you to give me a piece of the reward, I probably wouldn't refuse it."

"And just what is it that interests you?"

"Do you know what I do for a living?" responded the Swagman.

"You rob, you smuggle, and you kill," said Cain.

The Swagman laughed. "Besides that, I mean."

"Suppose you tell me."

"It would not be inaccurate to say that I'm an art collector. You want the reward money; I have no interest in it. I want certain of Santiago's possessions; you have no interest in them. Virtue, on the unlikely assumption that she was actually telling me the truth and hasn't tried to team up with the Angel, wants only a journalistic feature. None of our desires overlap at any point. Therefore, I see no reason why we shouldn't be able to work together."

"Why don't you go after him yourself?" asked Cain, rubbing his eye as some sweat rolled into it. "That way you'd have the reward *and* the art objects."

"I'm no killer," replied the Swagman. "As I said, I'm still not sure exactly what it was that Altair of Altair tried to do to you down there, but I'm certain that I wouldn't have survived it—and I can assure you that she was much easier to kill than Santiago will be. I'll supply the information; you'll supply the expertise. That's the deal."

"I'll take it under consideration."

"You'd better consider it quickly."

"Why?" asked Cain sardonically. "Will you find yourself another killer?"

"No," said the Swagman seriously. "You're the one I want. After all, you killed Altair of Altair. Do you know how many bounty hunters have died trying to do just that?" He slapped at a flying insect that was buzzing around his face. "But you're in a race, and every minute you delay is another minute the Angel gains on you."

"I thought you said something about a planet that's going to give him problems."

"I did," the Swagman assured him. "But he'll overcome them. He's the best."

"Then why didn't you offer your services to him?"

"Because he doesn't need them. You do." He reached out his hand. "Well, have we got a deal?"

Cain stared at his hand without taking it.

"What have you got to lose?" added the Swagman.

Cain stared at him for a long moment, then finally nodded his head almost imperceptibly. "All right—until your information proves wrong."

"It won't."

"Let's put it to the test. Where does Virtue MacKenzie plan to find the Angel?"

"Lambda Karos Three if she's lucky."

"And if she's not?"

"Either New Ecuador or Questados Four. It depends on what he learns on Lambda Karos."

Cain stared at him for a moment. "Halfpenny Terwilliger is waiting for me back at my ship. I think I'd better send him off to keep an eye on Virtue while she's keeping an eye on the Angel, just so we know where we stand."

"Can you trust him to tell you the truth?" asked the Swagman.

"I can trust him to act in his own self-interest," replied Cain. "And he'll get a lot richer by staying loyal to me than by deserting me."

"Just out of curiosity, if he's on your payroll, why wasn't he helping you against Altair of Altair?"

"For the same reason you weren't," said Cain. "He'd just have been in the way."

"Touché," said the Swagman with a chuckle. "By the way, if he's the same Terwilliger I've heard about, ManMountain Bates is hot on his trail."

"I know. That's another reason why he'll stay loyal to me." Cain paused for a moment while the Swagman tossed his cigar onto the red-brown dirt and ground it out with his heel. "And now, if you've got nothing further to add, I think I'd better go talk to Schussler."

"Be on your best behavior," said the Swagman, falling into step beside the bounty hunter as he headed off toward the spaceship. "He may be a little bit strange, but we need him."

"Him? You mean Schussler?"

The Swagman nodded his head. "I'm not the only one with information, and his is different from mine. He knows every place Altair of Altair has been, everyone she's seen. Even if she never met Santiago, it was almost certainly Schussler who received the order to terminate Kastartos; he has to know where it came from."

"What does one offer a spaceship?" asked Cain wryly. "He can't have any use for money."

"I'm sure he'll think of something," said the Swagman.

"I don't know," said Cain. "Any guy who wanted to become a spaceship . . ."

"I have a feeling that *want* was never the operative word."

They reached the ship and came to a halt. Suddenly a hatch door opened.

"You go ahead," said the Swagman, pulling out another cigar. "I'll join you in a few minutes."

"Why?" asked Cain suspiciously.

The Swagman held up his cigar. "He doesn't like me to smoke inside him."

Cain grimaced. "I probably wouldn't want someone smoking in *my* stomach, either, if push came to shove."

He entered the compact ship through the hatch and found himself in a brightly illuminated cabin. The control panels and terminals were like nothing he had ever seen, and even the digital readouts on the screens were in an unfamiliar language.

"Schussler?" he said hesitantly. "Are you here?"

"I am always here," replied Schussler, his melodic voice not at all what Cain had expected.

"I'm Cain."

"I know. I can see you."

"You can?" asked Cain, surprised. "How?"

"I am tied in to various sensing devices."

"So you can see inside yourself as well as outside?"

"And hear, and smell, and use senses no human can conceive of."

"It must be handy," remarked Cain.

"If one likes being a spaceship."

"Do you?"

"No."

"Then why are you one?"

"It happened seventeen years ago," said Schussler. "I was a businessman, on my way to Alpha Prego for a conference. My ship crashed on Kalkos Two."

"Never heard of it."

"It's an outpost world of a starfaring race called the Graal."

"I never heard of *them*, either," commented Cain.

"They haven't been assimilated into the Democracy yet," replied Schussler. "Anyway, I crashed, and they found me, but by the time they separated me from all the twisted metal there wasn't much left to work with." The voice stopped for a moment and was considerably shakier when it resumed. "They kept me alive, God knows how, for five months, until I came out of my coma, and then they offered me my choice: they could let me die, quickly and painlessly, or they could offer me life as a cyborg." Schussler sighed. "I was younger then, and there were many things I still wanted to see, so I chose the latter."

"But why as a spaceship?" asked Cain.

"Kalkos Two is a shipbuilding world. They used what they had."

"What about prosthetics?" persisted Cain. "I've got an artificial eye that took a day to hook up, and it sees better than the one I lost."

"They weren't human," explained Schussler.

"They could have contacted a human world."

"There wasn't enough left to work with." He paused. "Would you like to see the *real* me, the human remnant that's the driving force of this ship?"

Cain shrugged. "Why not?"

"Walk over to the computer terminal nearest the viewscreen."

"This one?"

"That's it."

"The keys don't make any sense."

"They're in the Graal's language. Touch the third from the left, top row."

Cain did as he was told, and Schussler rattled off the directions for hitting seven more keys.

Suddenly an interior wall panel slid back, revealing a small black box, no more than twelve inches on a side, with literally hundreds of wires and tubes connected to it.

"*Jesus!*" muttered Cain. "That's all that's left of you?"

"Now do you see why they didn't bother with prosthetics?" asked Schussler bitterly as the panel slid shut. "Still, they didn't do too badly, all things considered. When I try to wiggle my fingers, I alter the gyroscopes. When I feel hunger, it is assuaged by fuel for my synthetic body. When I want to speak, I activate a complex system of microscopic vibrational coils which ultimately results in what you are hearing. I am not in *control* of the ship; I *am* the ship. I monitor all my functions, navigate myself, communicate with other ships, even aim and fire weapons when the need arises. In fact, I don't yet know the full extent of my powers, since the Graal computers aren't based on binary language or any other system known to the race of Man, and I'm still learning new things about myself every day."

"It sounds like an interesting existence," said Cain without much enthusiasm.

"It is a terrible existence," said Schussler.

"Well, it's better than being dead."

"I thought so once," replied Schussler. "I was wrong." He paused. "I can analyze the air for you, break it down into so many atoms of this and so many molecules of that—but I can't breathe it. There is no meal you can conceive that I can't prepare in my galley—but I can't taste it." There was another pause, and then the beautiful voice spoke again, this time in more anguished tones. "I can count the pores in the skin on a woman's hand, give a chemical breakdown of its composition, measure the fingernails to a millionth of a centimeter— *but I can't touch it!*"

"If you're that unhappy, why haven't you killed yourself?" asked Cain. "It shouldn't be that difficult to crash into a planet, or fall right into the heart of a star."

"A *man* could choose to do that," said Schussler bitterly. "A *machine* can't."

"But you *are* a man," said Cain. "You're just wearing this ship the way other men wear clothes."

"I wish that were so, but it isn't. I am the ship and the ship is me, and when the Graal joined the two of us in this unholy alliance, they inserted two directives that are so powerful I can't override them. The first of them is to protect my own existence."

"And the other?"

"It cost the Graal a lot of money to build me. They made some of it back by selling me at auction. They explained to me that since my life expectancy is now virtually infinite, they were sure I would be happy to spend an insignificant segment of it helping them amortize my cost." He sighed, a melodic sound that somehow reminded Cain of air flowing through a pipe organ. "My other directive was to obey the commands of my owner for a period of thirty years."

"Who is your owner?"

"She was Altair of Altair," replied Schussler.

Just then the Swagman entered the ship.

"Too damned hot out there," he said, walking over to a cushioned seat and flopping down on it. He turned to Cain. "Has he popped the question to you yet?"

"What question?" asked Cain.

The Swagman laughed. "If he's got more than one, he's been holding out on me." He paused. "Well, Schussler—have you?"

"Not yet," said the cyborg.

"I repeat: what question?" said Cain.

"We still have things to discuss," said Schussler. "Then I will make my request."

"You know," said the Swagman to Cain, "I offered him good steady work back at Goldenrod, and he turned me down flat."

"I won't transport stolen goods," said Schussler firmly.

"You yourself might be considered stolen goods," noted the Swagman amiably, "since there's still thirteen years outstanding on your contract."

"I am not stolen goods," replied Schussler. "I belong to Cain for the next thirteen years."

"What?" said Cain, startled. "That's not Altairian law."

"It is one of the conditions of my contract with the Graal," said Schussler. "They understood that Altair of Altair operated beyond the scope of human law, and it was explicitly stated that should she be killed by any representative of any human government before my contract was up, I would become the possession of that representative. As a bounty hunter who will ultimately be paid by the Democracy for slaying her, you qualify as my new owner."

"I don't *want* to be your owner," said Cain.

"Just a minute," interjected the Swagman. "Let's not be too hasty about this."

"Schussler, when I was in the cavern, you indicated that you might be able to help me," said Cain, staring at the panel behind which the essential Schussler existed. "What did you have in mind?"

"I can show you where Altair of Altair has been, and who she spoke to, and many other things."

"If you'll feed it all into my ship's computer, I'll make you a free agent right now," said Cain. "I don't have any use for another ship."

"Terwilliger needs your ship, if you're really sending him to Lambda Karos," the Swagman pointed out.

"He can use yours," said Cain. "We're partners, remember?"

"It's a moot point," said Schussler. "I can't feed my information to your computer. The language my systems use is different."

"Come off it," said Cain. "You use the same language as my computer every time you receive landing coordinates. What's your real problem?"

"Please take me with you!" said Schussler suddenly, a note of desperation in his voice. "It's been so long since I've been able to *talk* with another human being!" Cain seemed hesitant, and Schussler continued: "I will serve you with complete loyalty until we find Santiago. I will guide and protect you, feed and ferry you, and I ask nothing in return except your company."

"Nothing?" repeated the Swagman meaningfully.

"Until you have found Santiago," said Schussler. "Then I have one single request to make of you."

"What is it?" demanded Cain.

"Kill me," said Schussler the Cyborg.

13.

The Songbird stalks, the Songbird kills,
The Songbird works to pay his bills.
So, friend, beware the Songbird's glance:
If you're his prey, you'll have no chance.

"Those don't belong to you," said Schussler.

The Swagman, tired of sitting in a chair that was almost comfortable, had gotten to his feet and was examining a number of alien artifacts that were attached to a wall of the command cabin.

"By the same token, they don't belong to you, either," he replied easily. He pulled at an onyx carving, breaking the magnetic field that joined it to the wall. "Interesting piece," he commented, examining it closely. "Where did your late lamented owner pick it up? Hesporite Three?"

"Neiburi Two," answered Schussler.

"Same star cluster," remarked the Swagman with an air of satisfaction. "I wouldn't have given her credit for such exquisite taste. Do you know what this little piece is worth on the open market?"

"No," said Schussler.

"Neither do you," interjected Cain, looking up from the table where he had disassembled one of his pistols and was meticulously cleaning it. "But I'll bet you can give us its black market value to the nearest tenth of a credit."

"Touché," grinned the Swagman.

"Put it back now," said Schussler.

"I'm admiring it."

"Evaluating it, anyway," said Cain dryly.

"Force of habit," admitted the Swagman, holding the carving near the wall until the magnetic field took it from him. He began studying another piece.

"I'm still watching you," said Schussler.

"How comforting."

"You'd better not try to steal anything," continued the cyborg.

"I never steal from my friends," said the Swagman.

"I know all about you, Swagman," said Schussler. "You don't have any friends."

"It *does* simplify matters," replied the Swagman with a smile. "If it will allay your fears, I also don't steal from my partners when one of them happens to be a bounty hunter." Suddenly a small carving caught his eye, and he pulled it out of the field. "Well, well," he mused. "Life is a torrent of never-ending surprises."

"What have you got there?" asked Cain.

The Swagman held the piece up.

"It doesn't look all that special."

"As a matter of fact, it's a rather mediocre work of art," agreed the Swagman. "It's where it originated that makes it interesting."

"And where was that?"

"Pellinath Four."

"Never heard of it," said Cain.

"It's the planet where I was raised. This was carved by one of the Bellum."

"Your benefactors?" asked Schussler, interested.

The Swagman nodded, studying the carving. "I think I must have sold this thing, oh, ten or twelve years ago, out by New Rhodesia. I wonder how Altair of Altair got her hands on it?"

"What were the Bellum like?" asked Schussler.

"Not bad at all, considering that we had some serious disagreements about laissez-faire capitalism," replied the Swagman. "Still, they fed me and gave me shelter, and I'm grateful to them for that."

"Not so grateful that you didn't rob them," noted Cain wryly.

"True," agreed the Swagman. "On the other hand, if God had any serious objections to what I do, He wouldn't have made insurance companies." He paused. "Besides, I didn't take very much. They were exceptionally poor artisans. I suppose it comes from being color-blind and not having thumbs." He glanced at the piece again and replaced it on the wall, then turned to the panel that hid Schussler's essence. "Tell me about the Graal."

"They were basically humanoid," replied the cyborg, "if you consider a race humanoid because it walks erect on two legs. Beyond that, they didn't have a lot in common with Men."

"That's not too difficult to believe, given the contours of the seats in here," said the Swagman with a grimace. "What kind of art did they produce?"

The ship uttered an amused, melodic chuckle. "Nothing that would interest you. They don't have any eyes; they use a form of sonar. And while I never saw their artwork, I'm sure it would reflect their limitations."

"What a pity," sighed the Swagman. "At least *my* aliens gave me a little something to remember them by, however unwillingly."

"So did mine," said Schussler, the melody of his voice conflicting with the irony of his words.

"Where *is* this world where they put you together, anyway?" asked the Swagman. "I've never heard of the Kalkos system."

"In the Corbellus Cluster," replied Schussler.

"I was out there once," remarked the Swagman. "Ever hear of Fond Hope?"

"I've heard of it," answered the cyborg, "but I've never been there."

"I've heard of it, too," said Cain. "Didn't Orpheus write it up? Something about the Deneb Arabian, or the Delphini Arabian, or something like that?"

"The Darley Arabian," said the Swagman. "Orpheus gave him his name. In fact, he gave all three patriarchs their names." He paused. "My own modest dealings were solely with the Barb."

"I don't recall any mention of him," said Cain.

"I fear I may have left him with a certain distrust of outsiders," grinned the Swagman. "He refused to speak to Black Orpheus."

"Smart man," muttered Cain.

"I didn't understand the song," volunteered Schussler. "It sounded, well, racy."

"*The Darley Arabian, tall and wild,/Has gotten another wife with child,*" quoted the Swagman. "I suppose that's as close to racy as Orpheus ever gets." He turned to the panel that hid Schussler from view. "Fond Hope was settled by three very large families, who immediately had a falling-out and began fighting with each other. Since this was a blood feud, none of the families wanted to import outside mercenaries. Then one day the Arabian conceived the notion of buying a couple of hundred mail-order brides and siring his own army—all in the line of duty, to be sure." He chuckled. "It took each of the other two patriarchs about a week to follow suit, and they've spent the past twenty years fighting all day and making little soldiers all night."

"What about the names?" asked Schussler.

"Orpheus found out that all the racehorses back on old Earth descended from three foundation sires, so he named the three patriarchs the Darley Arabian, the Byerly Turk, and the Godolphin Barb, after the three horses."

"What was your business with the Barb?" asked Cain.

"I knew that he had no need for mercenaries, but I thought he might be interested in purchasing a shipload of weapons to carry on the battle."

"Hot?"

"Lukewarm," admitted the Swagman. "The navy confiscated them a month after I delivered them."

"I wasn't aware that the navy ever got out to the Corbellus Cluster," said Schussler.

"They didn't—until someone thoughtlessly appropriated a few thousand laser weapons from one of their munitions warehouses."

"Is that why Santiago dropped you?" asked Cain.

"Why should you think so?"

"Because stealing from the navy isn't your style. You'd need Santiago's muscle for an operation like that. My guess is that he threw you out for selling weapons he wanted to keep."

"You couldn't be more mistaken," said the Swagman indignantly.

"Are you seriously trying to tell me that you stole those weapons yourself?" said Cain.

"Oh, it was Santiago's operation from start to finish," acknowledged the Swagman. "And yes, we did have some slight disagreement over their ultimate disposition. But we parted ways for a totally unrelated reason."

"The mind boggles," commented Cain wryly.

"I'm surprised that Santiago or the Godolphin Barb didn't commission your death," said Schussler.

"The Barb did," replied the Swagman. "Fortunately, my would-be assassin tried to attack me at my fortress on Goldenrod, where even the Angel would find it difficult to do me any damage."

"How do you know that it was the Barb who hired the assassin, rather than Santiago?" asked the cyborg.

"Because I'm still here." The Swagman wandered over to the table, where Cain had replaced the bullets in his first pistol and was preparing to clean and oil a second. "You know," he said, staring at the pieces that were neatly laid out on the table, "there's something I've been curious about ever since I observed you with Altair of Altair."

"Ask away," said Cain without looking up.

"Why do you use a projectile weapon?" said the Swagman.

"It's more accurate than laser or sonic pistols, and since it doesn't have an energy pack to begin with, it can't run out of power."

"But it makes such a loud noise."

"So what?"

"I would have thought stealth and silence were essential to your profession."

Cain smiled. "They're essential while I'm stalking my prey. Once I start shooting, I don't much give a damn who knows I'm there." He paused. "I'm not one of your menials, Swagman. I operate within the law; I don't have to sneak away when my work is done."

"A point well taken," admitted the Swagman.

"A laser gun is all right if you have to fan a large area," continued Cain. "But it's not a precision instrument. To each his own; I prefer bullets."

"I wonder what method the Angel used on Giles Sans Pitié?" mused Schussler.

Cain shrugged. "I suppose we'll find out in good time. I don't imagine Black Orpheus will be able to resist putting it into his stupid song."

"What's your objection to our friend Orpheus?" asked the Swagman.

"He's your friend, not mine."

"He's made you famous," noted the Swagman. "A century from now, that song is the only way people will know you and Schussler and I even existed. Consider it a form of immortality."

"Immortality is a greatly overrated virtue," interjected Schussler, the beautiful melodic tones of his voice ringing with bitterness.

"Most of the people I've known would disagree with that statement," said the Swagman.

"Most of the people *you've* known have spent their whole lives one step ahead of the hangman," replied the cyborg.

"Most of the people he's known have already met the hangman," commented Cain.

"Some of them have met less formal executioners," retorted the Swagman. "I'm still annoyed with you over that little affair on Declan Four."

"You had some use for Socrates?" asked Cain.

"Socrates?" snorted the Swagman contemptuously. "Of course not.

There are twelve million Men on Declan Four, all of them interchangeable and infinitely replaceable." He paused. "But you destroyed a Robelian bowl that I'd been after for three years."

"It was just a bowl," said Cain. "I was there for something more important."

"*Just a bowl?*" repeated the Swagman, morally outraged. "My good man, it was one of only six such bowls in existence!"

"I've seen lots like it."

For just a moment the Swagman looked interested. Then he sighed. "I suppose one bowl looks just like another to you."

"Pretty much so," said Cain, sliding the barrel of his pistol into place and turning it gently until he felt a discernible click. "Just the way people all look alike to you."

"And it means nothing to you that there are almost a trillion people spread across the Democracy, and only six Robelian bowls of that shape and design?"

"It means you'll run out of work before I do."

"It means," the Swagman retorted, "that you have destroyed an irreplaceable work of art."

"I also destroyed a man who was in serious need of destruction," replied Cain. "On the whole, I'd say the ledger came out on the plus side."

"There wasn't even any paper on Socrates."

"Then view killing him as a service to humanity."

"I wasn't aware that you were in the philanthropy business," said the Swagman.

"There are more important things than money," said Cain.

"True—but all of them *cost* money." The Swagman raised his arms above his head, emitted a loud grunt as he stretched, and then turned to Schussler's panel. "I'm getting hungry. What have you got in your galley?"

"I have a full complement of soya products," answered the cyborg.

"Don't you have any meat?"

"I'm afraid not—but I can prepare some dishes that will be almost indistinguishable from meat."

"I've heard *that* before," muttered the Swagman.

"You might as well take what he's got," said Cain. "We're not about to divert to a planet with a grocery store."

The Swagman shrugged. "Can you come up with something that tastes like shellfish in a cream sauce?"

"I can try." Schussler paused. "What would you like, Sebastian?"

"Whatever's easy," said Cain.

"How about a steak?" suggested the cyborg.

"How about a salad?" countered Cain. "I've *had* soya steaks."

"If you'll come to the galley, your dinners are ready," announced Schussler.

"What are you talking about?" said the Swagman suspiciously. "We just ordered them."

"The Graal's technology makes meal preparation almost instantaneous," explained the cyborg. "Especially when I can work with adaptable raw materials such as soya products."

Cain and the Swagman exchanged dubious glances and entered the galley, a long narrow room in which almost all of the equipment was hidden from view.

"Where are we supposed to eat?" asked the Swagman.

"I can unfold a small table," said Schussler, "but there won't be room for both of you at it."

"We'll stand," said Cain. "Where's the food?"

"I'll have it in just a second," said Schussler. "Ah, here it comes."

A shining metal panel receded, and two nondescript plates appeared on a polished counter.

The Swagman reached out for his shellfish, then withdrew his hand and muttered a curse.

"I forgot to tell you: the plate is hot."

"Thanks," said the Swagman caustically. He reached into his pocket, withdrew a monogrammed silk handkerchief, wrapped it around his fingers, and pulled the plate over. "I could use a knife and fork."

"I wish I could help you," said Schussler apologetically. "But Altair of Altair didn't use human utensils. She preferred these."

A pair of odd-looking metal objects emerged onto the counter.

The Swagman picked one up and examined it. "Wonderful," he said. "It looks about as practical as eating soup with chopsticks."

Cain picked up the other, studied it for a moment, and then began using it on his salad.

"How did you do that?" asked the Swagman.

"I've seen these things in the Teron system," said Cain, impaling an artificial tomato and twisting a piece of artificial lettuce around it. "A Teroni bounty hunter showed me how to use it. It's not too bad once you get the hang of it."

"How are they on cream sauce?" asked the Swagman, staring at his plate.

"Try it and find out," said Cain, returning his attention to his salad.

The Swagman made three or four false starts but eventually gained a rudimentary mastery of his utensil and finally managed to get a piece of pseudoshellfish all the way to his mouth without dropping it.

"Well?" asked Schussler anxiously. "What do you think of it?"

"It isn't bad," said Cain noncommittally.

"I'll tell you what it isn't," muttered the Swagman. "It isn't Goldenrod lobster." He took another mouthful. "Still, I suppose it could be worse."

"Would you do me a favor?" asked Schussler after a moment's silence.

"It all depends," replied the Swagman. "What did you have in mind?"

"Tell me what it tastes like."

"To be perfectly truthful, it tastes like soya byproducts masquerading as shellfish in cream sauce."

"Please," persisted Schussler anxiously. "I processed it and cooked it and served it—but I can't *taste* it. Describe it for me."

"As I said: a rudimentary approximation of fish in cream sauce."

"You can't be that unimaginative!" said Schussler with a note of desperation in his beautiful lilting voice. "Tell me about the sauce: is it rich? hot? sweet? Can you identify the spices? What *type* of shellfish does it taste like?"

"It's nothing to write home about," said the Swagman. "The flavors are all rather bland."

"Describe them."

"You're forcing me to insult you. The food is barely worth eating, let alone describing," said the Swagman irritably. "You're ruining what was a totally unmemorable meal to begin with."

"You owe it to me!" demanded Schussler.

"Later," said the Swagman. "It's tasting worse by the mouthful, thanks to your nagging."

Cain sighed, reached over with his implement, and picked up a piece of the artificial shellfish, after first rubbing it thoroughly in the cream sauce. He chewed it thoughtfully, then began describing the nuances of flavor to Schussler while the Swagman picked up his plate and walked back into the command cabin to finish his meal in isolation.

Cain joined him about twenty minutes later.

"Is he still sulking?" asked the Swagman.

"Ask him yourself."

The Swagman turned to Schussler's panel. "You're not going to spend all night asking me to describe how my bunk feels, are you?"

There was no answer.

"There's a first for you—a pouting spaceship."

"You hurt his feelings," said Cain.

"Not without reason. Either we nip this behavior in the bud, or he'll be spending every spare minute asking how things taste and feel."

"It's not that much effort to tell him. He's had a rough time of it."

The Swagman stared at him. "We're growing a strange crop of killers this season," he remarked at last.

"You know," said Cain, "he could always ask you how you feel after he reduces the oxygen content in the cabin down to zero."

"Not if he wants to die on schedule, he can't," said the Swagman confidently. He paused. "Are you really going to kill him if we find Santiago's base?"

"I said I would."

"I know what you said."

"I'll do what I promised."

"But you won't be happy about it."

"I'm never happy about killing things," said Cain.

The Swagman considered that remark, as well as some of the other things Cain had said since leaving Altair III, and spent the next few minutes studying his new partner, comparing him to what he knew of the Angel, and wondering if Virtue MacKenzie had made the correct choice after all.

14.

Alas, Poor Yorick, I knew him well:
He can't climb down from the carousel.
He began with dreams, with hope and trust;
Alas, Poor Yorick, they turned to dust.

His name wasn't really Poor Yorick—not at first, anyway. He was born Herman Ludwig Menke, and he stuck with that name for twenty years. Then he joined a troupe of actors that traveled the Galactic Rim, and became Brewster Moss; word has it that he even performed for the Angel, back before *he* became the Angel.

Anyway, by the time he was forty he had yet another new name, Sterling Wilkes, which is the one he made famous when he almost single-handedly brought about the Shakespearean renaissance on Lodin XI. It is also the one he made notorious, due to his various chemical dependencies.

Six years later, after he'd had one hallucinogenic trance too many before a paying audience, he was barred from the stage. It was time for a new name—Poor Yorick seemed quite apt this time around—and a new profession. Since he had an artistic bent and all he knew was the theater, he turned up on the Inner Frontier as a prop manufacturer, and in the following decade he turned out a never-ending stream of counterfeit crowns and harmless guns, bogus jewels and bogus thrones, almost real stones in almost valuable settings.

He also kept a sizable number of drug peddlers in business, and when he graduated from injecting hallucinogens to chewing alphanella seeds, he was forced to supplement his income by turning his fine forger's hand to less legitimate enterprises than the stage. As the quality of his work suffered due to his dependency, he lost his legal job and then most of his illegal commissions as well, and was reduced to selling hasty paintings of actors he had known, which were turned out during his increasingly rare periods of lucidity.

A few years later Black Orpheus came into possession of four of the paintings and instantly knew that he had stumbled onto an interesting if erratic talent.

It took him almost a year to find Poor Yorick, who was living in a ramshackle hotel on Hildegarde, still spending every credit he made to feed his habit. Orpheus tried to convince him to travel the spaceways with him and illustrate his saga, but Yorick cared more for his next connection than for posterity, and finally the Bard of the Inner Frontier admitted defeat, bought the remainder of Yorick's paintings, commissioned a painting of his Eurydice which would never be finished, and went away forever. He gave Poor Yorick only a single verse in his song; he wanted to do more, to tell his audience what a unique talent lay hidden beneath that wasted exterior, but he decided that an influx of commissions would only result in more drug purchases and hasten Yorick's death.

It must be said on Yorick's behalf that he tried to complete the painting of Eurydice, but the money he had received for it was spent within a week, and he had an ever-present hunger to feed. Since Orpheus had left him without any art to sell, he returned to forging, but every now and then, an hour here, a weekend there, he would work again on his embryonic masterpiece.

In fact, he was working on it when Schussler landed on Roosevelt III.

"Unpleasant little world," said Cain when he and the Swagman had emerged from the cyborg's interior and stood, shielding themselves from the planet's ever-present rain, on the wet surface of the spaceport.

"It's only fitting," said the Swagman, heading off for the terminal. "We're looking for an unpleasant little man." He paused. "Whoever would have thought that Poor Yorick would be Altair of Altair's most recent link to Santiago?"

"I had rather suspected *you* would," said Cain with a touch of irony. "Especially after that speech about how I needed you."

"That's why you needed both Schussler *and* me. He knew Yorick was the man we wanted, and I know where to find him."

"Isn't it about time you shared that little tidbit of knowledge with me?" suggested Cain.

The Swagman shrugged. "I can't give you an address. We'll go into the city, hunt up the cheapest hotel in the poorest area, and wait."

"And if he's not there?"

"He'll be there, or thereabouts," said the Swagman. "If we have to, we'll just follow the local dream vendor, and he'll lead us straight to him."

"What does Poor Yorick look like?" asked Cain.

"I really couldn't say. I've never met him."

"But you're sure you know where he'll be," said Cain caustically.

"I've had dealings with him before," replied the Swagman. "And I make it a habit to learn everything I can about my business associates. I know he's on Roosevelt Three, and I know that there's only one city on Roosevelt Three; finding his exact location is just a mechanical exercise."

They reached the terminal, rented a vehicle, and drove into the nearby city, which, like the planet, was named Roosevelt. Someone— an architect, a city planner, a corporate head, *someone*—had had big plans for Roosevelt once upon a time. The spaceport was built to support ten times the traffic it actually handled, the city was criss-crossed by numerous broad thoroughfares, the central square boasted two skyscrapers that wouldn't have been out of place on Deluros VIII—but some centuries back the Democracy had paused to consolidate its holdings, and when it expanded again it had been in a different direction, leaving Roosevelt III just another unimportant cog in the vast human machine, neither abandoned nor important. The proposed megalopolis became a city of diminished expectations, as modest apartment buildings, nondescript stores, unimpressive offices, and un-imaginative public structures gradually encircled the two enormous steel-and-glass buildings like jungle scavengers patiently waiting for some mighty behemoth to conclude its death throes so they could partake of the feast.

The Swagman drove once around the city, then homed in on the most dilapidated area with an unerring instinct and brought the vehicle to a stop.

"I'd say we're within four hundred yards of him right now," he said, handing a rainshield to Cain and activating one himself.

"It can't get much more rundown than this," agreed Cain, dispas-sionately eyeing a number of drunks and derelicts who peered through the driving rain at them from their safe havens inside seedy bars and seamy hotels.

"I have a feeling that I'm not properly dressed for the occasion," remarked the Swagman, looking down at his satin tunic, carefully tailored pants, and hand-crafted boots.

"You're not the only one who thinks so," commented Cain, staring at an exceptionally large, barrel-chested man who was scrutinizing them from a distance of fifty feet, oblivious of the rain that was pouring down upon his unprotected head.

"Well, we certainly don't want the riffraff rising above their stations," said the Swagman, unperturbed. "I think we'll make them your responsibility."

"What do you do when you find yourself in a situation like this and there isn't a bounty hunter around?" inquired Cain dryly.

"I'm not totally without my own resources," replied the Swagman, withdrawing a device the size of a golf ball. He tossed it casually in the air, caught it, and replaced it in his pocket.

"A fire bomb?"

The Swagman nodded. "It's more powerful than it looks. It can take out a city block, and spreads like crazy on detonation, even in weather like this." He smiled. "Still, I'd much prefer not to use it. It wouldn't do to fry Yorick to a crisp before we have a chance to talk to him."

"According to you, we're within four hundred yards of him," said Cain, looking up and down the street. "That narrows it down to fifteen or twenty beat-up hotels and boarding houses. How do you choose which one?"

"Why, we ask, of course," said the Swagman, walking into a tavern. He spent a moment exchanging low whispers with the bartender, then returned to Cain, who had been waiting just inside the door.

"Any luck?"

"Not yet," admitted the Swagman. "Not to worry. The day's still young, if a little moist."

He sloshed through the rain to two more taverns, also without success.

"Ah!" he said with a smile as they approached yet another barroom, which had a watercolor of a large-breasted nude in the window. "We're getting close! I recognize the style."

"You collect Yorick's paintings?"

"The better ones."

The Swagman entered the building, spoke to the bartender, passed a five-hundred-credit note across the scarred wooden bar, said something else, and stepped out onto the sidewalk a moment later.

"He lives at the San Juan Hill Hotel, just up the street," announced the Swagman. "When he hasn't got enough cash for alphanella seeds, he trades paintings for drinks."

"He's not bad," commented Cain, staring at the nude.

"He's damned good, considering that he probably didn't even know his own name when he painted it. I offered to buy it, but the proprietor wouldn't sell. I got the distinct impression that it's a pretty fair representation of his girlfriend."

"Or his business partner."

"The two are not mutually exclusive," said the Swagman, heading off toward the San Juan Hill. "Especially around here."

Only one man seemed intent on stopping them, but something in Cain's face convinced him to reconsider, and they made it to the hotel without incident.

It had been a long time since the lobby of the San Juan Hill had been cleaned, and even longer since it had been painted. The floor, especially around the entrance, was filthy, and the whole place smelled of mildew. There was a small, inexpensive rug in front of the registration desk, surrounded by a light area from which a slightly larger rug had been removed at some time in the past. Miscolored rectangles on the walls marked the spots that had formerly been covered by paintings and holographs. The few chairs and couches were in dire need of repair, and the camera in the sole vidphone booth was missing.

The Swagman took one look around, seemed satisfied that this was precisely the type of place where Poor Yorick was likely to reside, and walked up to the registration desk.

The unshaven clerk, his left elbow peeking out through a hole in his tunic, looked up at his visitor with a bored expression.

"Good afternoon," said the Swagman with a friendly smile. "Terrible weather out there."

"You tracked all the way across my lobby to tell me that?" replied the clerk caustically.

"Actually, I'm looking for a friend."

"Good luck to you," said the clerk.

"His name's Yorick," said the Swagman.

"Big deal."

The Swagman reached out and grabbed the clerk by the front of his soiled tunic, pulling him halfway across the counter.

"*Poor* Yorick," he said with a pleasant smile. "I hate to rush you, but we *are* in a hurry." He twisted the tunic until the seams started to give way.

"Room three seventeen," muttered the clerk.

"Thank you very much," said the Swagman, releasing him.

"You've been most helpful." He looked around. "I don't suppose any of the elevators are in working order?"

"The one in the middle," replied the clerk sullenly, pointing toward a bank of three ancient elevators.

"Excellent," said the Swagman. He nodded toward Cain, who walked across the lobby and joined him in front of the elevator. "If there's one thing I hate," he said, "it's a surly menial. You *are* protecting my back, aren't you?"

"He's not going to do anything," replied Cain.

"How do you know he hasn't got a weapon hidden behind the counter?"

"If there ever was a weapon back there, it's long since been stolen or pawned," said Cain as the doors slid shut and the elevator began ascending. "Still, I think we'll take the stairs down, just to be on the safe side."

The elevator lurched to a stop and swayed somewhat unsteadily as Cain and the Swagman emerged onto the third floor, which was in even worse repair than the lobby. Some of the rooms had no doors at all, scribbled graffiti covered the others, and the dominant smell had changed from mildew to urine.

"Three seventeen," announced the Swagman, gesturing to the last door on the floor. "Things are obviously looking up for friend Yorick; he has a corner view."

He knocked once, and when there was no answer he punched the number 317 on the computer lock.

"I always admire a complex security system, don't you?" he commented with a grin as the door slid back into a wall.

A frail, wasted man, his teeth rotted, his complexion sallow, sat totally naked on a rickety chair by a broken window, oblivious to the rain that sprayed him after bouncing off the pane. He was working on a painting with short, incredibly swift brush strokes, muttering to himself as he continually retraced the outline of a beautiful woman's face, never quite getting the proportions correct. Scattered around the floor were cheap containers filled with artificial diamonds, rubies, sapphires, and emeralds, a complex machine for covering base metals with gold plating, and a number of jeweler's tools.

The man looked up at his two visitors, flashed them a brief, nervous smile, put a few more dabs of color onto his canvas, then casually tossed his palette onto the floor and turned to face Cain and the Swagman.

"Good afternoon, Yorick," said the Swagman. "I wonder if we might have a few minutes of your time?"

Yorick stared at him for a moment, frowned, looked back at his canvas, and then turned to him once more, a puzzled expression on his face.

"You're not in my painting," he said at last.

"No," said the Swagman. "I'm in your room."

"My room?" repeated Yorick.

"That's right."

"Well," he said with a shrug, "it had to be one or the other." He stared intently at the Swagman. "Do I know you?"

"You know *of* me: I'm the Jolly Swagman."

Yorick lowered his head, still frowning. "Jolly, jolly, jolly, jolly, jolly," he murmured. Suddenly he looked up. "I don't know you, but I know *of* you," he said with a satisfied smile. He turned to Cain. "I know *you*, though."

"You do?" said Cain.

"You're the Songbird," he said emphatically, suddenly rational. "I know all about you. I was on Bellefontaine when you killed the Jack of Diamonds. That was some shootout." Suddenly his face went blank again. "Shootout," he said as if the word had lost its meaning. "Shootout, shootout, shootout." And just as quickly as it had come, the emptiness left his wasted face. "What are you doing here, Songbird?"

"I need a little information," said Cain, sitting down on the edge of Yorick's unmade bed.

"I need a little something, too," said Yorick with a wink and a cackle. "A lot of little somethings. Chewy little somethings, sweet little somethings."

"Maybe we can work out a trade," said Cain.

"Maybe maybe maybe," said Yorick, spitting out the words in staccato fashion. "Maybe we can." He paused, then suddenly looked alert. "How about a trade?" he suggested.

"Good idea," said Cain.

"Why is *he* here?" asked Yorick, gesturing to the Swagman.

"He likes your paintings," said Cain.

"Oh, he does, does he?" Yorick cackled. "He likes more than that. So you're the Swagman, are you?"

"The one and only," said the Swagman.

"Well, one and only Swagman," said Yorick, "did the museum on Rhinegold ever discover the one and only North Coast Princess that I forged for you?"

"It's still sitting right there in its display case under round-the-clock guard," replied the Swagman with a grin.

"And you've got the real stone?"

"Certainly."

"Certainly," repeated Yorick. "Lee-certain," he said, moving the syllables around. "Cer-lee-tain." He got to his feet and glared at the Swagman. "My courier was killed!" he said accusingly.

"Most regrettable," said the Swagman. "I hope you don't think *I* had anything to do with it."

"You guaranteed his safety," said Yorick sullenly.

"I guaranteed that he would gain safe entry to my fortress," the Swagman corrected him. "What he did after he left was his own business."

"I never got my money."

"I paid it to the courier. My obligation to you ended with that." He reached into his pocket. "However, I wouldn't want us to become enemies. Will this square accounts?" He withdrew a trio of small tan seeds.

"Give give give give give give!" murmured Yorick, snatching them out of the Swagman's hand. He raced to a dilapidated dresser, pulled open the top drawer, and tossed two of the seeds onto a pile of dirty clothing. The third he put into his mouth.

"Where the hell did you get those things?" asked Cain. "You didn't know back on Altair that we were going to see Poor Yorick."

The Swagman smiled. "What did you think I paid the bartender five hundred credits for?"

"Information—or so I thought."

"Information's worth about twenty-five credits, tops, on a dirtball like this. The rest was for alphanella seeds."

Yorick was sitting down on his chair again, his face suddenly tranquil as he slid the seed between his cheek and his gum and let the juices flow down his throat.

"Thank you," he said, his face relaxed, his eyes finally clear. "You know, sometimes I think the only time I'm *not* crazy is when I've got a seed in my mouth."

"Good," said Cain. "Just suck on it for a while. Don't chew it until we're through talking."

"Whatever you say, Songbird," replied Yorick pleasantly. "Oh, my, this is good. I don't know how I lived before I discovered this stuff."

"Responsibly," suggested Cain wryly.

Yorick closed his eyes and smiled. "Ah, yes—the killer who's hindered by a moral code. I know about you, Songbird." He paused. "You gave my friend a pass."

"A pass?" asked the Swagman, puzzled.

"Quentin Cicero," said Yorick, nodding his head, his eyes still closed. "Hunted him down and then let him go. Good man, the Songbird."

"You let Quentin Cicero go?" demanded the Swagman, turning to Cain.

"It wasn't that open and shut," replied Cain. "He had a hostage."

"That never stopped any other bounty hunter," said Yorick placidly. "So what if he'd have killed her? All the more reason for you to bring him in."

"You let him go?" repeated the Swagman furiously. "That bastard killed two of my menials!"

"I'm sorry to hear that," said Cain.

"*You're* sorry? One of them had fifty thousand credits of *my* money!"

"But the hostage lived," said Yorick.

"You see?" said the Swagman. "You go around letting hostages live and sooner or later it winds up costing a respectable businessman money!"

"I'll keep that in mind next time," said Cain.

"Who are you after now, Songbird?" asked Yorick. He paused. "I know where you can find Altair of Altair."

"I already found her."

"Was she human or not?" asked Yorick. "I could never quite tell."

"Neither could I," said Cain.

"Beautiful, though."

"Very," agreed Cain.

"How much did you get for killing her?" asked Yorick.

"Nothing."

Yorick smiled. "Then you're after Santiago." He sucked contentedly on the seed. "It's amazing how clear everything becomes after a minute or two, how absolutely pellucid. You killed her, and you talked to her ship, and now you're here."

"That's right."

"And now you want me to tell you where to go next?"

Cain nodded, and Yorick, not hearing an answer, cracked his eyes open.

"How are you going to kill him, Songbird?"

"I won't know until I find him," said Cain.

"What if *he* has a hostage?"

"Does he?"

Yorick laughed. "How would I know?"

"How would I?" answered Cain.

Yorick stared at Cain for a long moment. "You're a good man, Songbird," he said at last. "I think I'll tell you what you want to know."

"Thank you."

"And I'm a good man, so I think you'll pay me three thousand credits."

"Fifteen hundred," said the Swagman quickly.

"Shut up," said Cain, pulling out a wad of bills and peeling off six five-hundred-credit notes.

"Thank you, Songbird," said Yorick, looking for a pocket and then realizing that he was naked. He walked over to his dresser and tossed the money into the same drawer where he had deposited the two alphanella seeds. He then returned to his chair and sat down lazily. "The man you want is Billy Three-Eyes."

"I've heard of him," remarked Cain.

"Everyone out here has heard of him. There's a lot of paper on him, Songbird."

"What's his connection to Santiago?"

"He works for him."

"Directly?"

Yorick nodded. "When I forged a set of duplicate plates for New Georgia's Stalin Ruble, it was Billy Three-Eyes who picked them up and delivered them to Santiago. And the last time Santiago had an assignment for Altair of Altair, I was the go-between."

"Where is Billy Three-Eyes now?" asked Cain.

"On Safe Harbor. Ever hear of it?"

"No."

"It's a colony planet, out in the Westminster system."

"How do I find him?"

Yorick chuckled. "He'll be pretty easy to spot. Giles Sans Pitié caught up with him about eight years ago and put a notch in his forehead with that metal fist of his before he could escape. That's how Billy got his name; Orpheus thought it looked like a third eye."

"How many cities are there on Safe Harbor?"

"None," replied Yorick. "None none nine none nine none."

"Suck on the seed again," said Cain. "You're drifting."

Yorick sucked noisily, and his eyes became clear once more. "No cities at all," he said lazily. "There are two or three little villages. Most of the people are farmers. Just make the rounds of the local taverns; he'll be in one of them." He paused. "Do you need any more?"

"I don't think so."

"Good." Yorick smiled. "It's starting to wear off. It'll be gone in another couple of minutes unless I bite the seed."

Cain got to his feet. "Thanks," he said.

"Anything for the Songbird."

Cain walked to the door, then turned to the Swagman, who remained where he was, leaning comfortably against a filthy wall.

"Come on," he said.

"You go ahead," said the Swagman. "I've got a little business to talk over with friend Yorick."

"I'll wait downstairs."

The Swagman shook his head. "It could take days to consummate."

"What the hell are you talking about?" demanded Cain.

"I want to commission some paintings."

"Then do it and let's get out of here."

"You've seen him," said the Swagman. "If I'm going to get what I want, I'm going to have to nursemaid him while he works."

"Suit yourself," said Cain. "But I'm not hanging around this pigsty while you add to your collection."

"You go ahead to Safe Harbor," said the Swagman. "I'll charter a ship and join you there."

"If I walk out of this hotel alone, the partnership's over," said Cain.

"If you kill Santiago before I catch up with you, the partnership's over," agreed the Swagman. "But if I get to you before you reach him, it's in force again."

"For half the original deal."

"You have no use for what I want," said the Swagman.

"I'll *find* a use."

The Swagman looked perturbed. "Safe Harbor is just another stop along the way. You still need me."

"Not as much as you need me," said Cain. He frowned. "What brought this about, anyway? How much can his paintings be worth?"

"Not as much as Santiago, I'll admit," said the Swagman. "But Yorick's here now, and Santiago could still be years away. I'll catch up with you."

"For half."

The Swagman sighed. "For half." He paused. "If you leave Safe Harbor before I get there, leave a message telling me where to find you."

"Leave it where?"

"If you don't find anyone you can trust, have Schussler send it back to Goldenrod."

Cain turned to Yorick. "Once I leave here, nothing that happens between the two of you is of any concern to me—but I ought to warn you that leaving three thousand credits in the same room with the Swagman is like leaving a piece of meat in the same room with a hungry carnivore."

"I resent that," said the Swagman, more amused than offended.

"Resent it all you like," said Cain. "But if you're a religious man, don't deny it or God just might strike you dead." He walked to the dresser and stood next to it. "What about having the hotel hold it for you until he leaves?"

Yorick smiled. "This hotel makes the Swagman look like an amateur."

"Have you got any friends I can leave it with?"

Yorick shook his head.

"All right," said Cain. "What if I deposit it with the branch bank at the spaceport and tell them to release it only to you? Your voiceprint ought to be registered there."

"That would be nice," said Yorick. "But leave a thousand credits behind. I don't want to go to the spaceport the first time I run out of seeds."

"He'll take it from you," said Cain.

"A thousand credits? He doesn't need it."

"That's got nothing to do with it."

"It's *my* money. Leave a thousand credits."

Cain opened the drawer and took out four of the five-hundred-credit notes. "I'm going to tell them not to release this to you unless you're alone."

"Thank you, Songbird," said Yorick placidly.

"Are you sure you don't want to count the phony jewels before you leave?" asked the Swagman sardonically.

"No," said Cain. "But I'll have Schussler do a quick inventory of Altair of Altair's artwork before we take off."

Cain turned and walked out the door. The Swagman immediately walked over to the dresser, searched around for another seed, and brought it over to Yorick.

"Here," he said. "Don't start chewing until we've talked."

Yorick removed the first seed, now a pale yellow, from his mouth and carefully set it down on his windowsill, then inserted the new one. The Swagman stepped over to the window and stared out through the rain until he could make out Cain's figure walking back to the vehicle.

"What kind of paintings do you want, Swagman?" asked Yorick pleasantly, luxuriating in the juices of the fresh seed.

"None," said the Swagman.

"Then what was that all about?"

"Billy Three-Eyes is dead. Peacemaker MacDougal caught up with him four months ago."

"Poor Billy," said Yorick, smiling tranquilly. "I loved that notch on his forehead." He looked up at the Swagman. "Maybe you'd better go tell the Songbird."

The Swagman shook his head. "I'm just waiting for him to get off the planet before I leave."

"Well, nobody ever accused you of the sin of loyalty."

"And nobody ever will," replied the Swagman. "Just the same, I was prepared to stay with him all the way to Santiago's doorstep." He paused. "But he isn't the one."

"The one?"

"The one who can kill Santiago."

"I know," said Yorick with a euphoric smile. "That's why I told him the truth."

"What truth?" demanded the Swagman.

"About Safe Harbor. That's his next step."

"I just told you: Billy Three-Eyes is dead. Now," said the Swagman, pulling out a roll of bills and holding them enticingly before Yorick's nose, "where's *my* next step?"

"Who knows?" replied Yorick pleasantly. "Where are you going?"

"Where do you think I should go to find Santiago?"

"To *find* him?" repeated Yorick. "Go with the Songbird."

"Let me amend that," said the Swagman. "Where should I go to kill him?"

"He's my best customer," said Yorick. He paused thoughtfully. "He's my *only* customer. I don't want him killed."

"I'll buy you enough alphanella seeds so that you never need him again."

"I won't live long enough to spend the money the Songbird gave me," said Yorick placidly. "Why do I need more?"

The Swagman stared at him for a moment, then shrugged. He began walking around the room, examining the artificial gems, and finally stopped in front of the canvas.

"Are you ever going to finish this?" he asked.

"Probably not."

"I'll buy it from you if you do."

"It's already sold to your friend Black Orpheus."

The Swagman studied the portrait with renewed interest.

"Eurydice?"

"I think that's what he called her. He left a couple of holographs with me, but I lost them a long time ago."

"You could have been one hell of an artist."

"I'm happier this way," said Yorick.

"What a stupid thing to say."

"My painting brings pleasure to others. My weakness brings pleasure to me."

"You're a fool," said the Swagman.

Yorick smiled. "But I'm a loyal fool. Have you got anything else to say to me, Swagman?"

"Not a thing."

"Good." He ground the seed to pulp between his molars. "I've got about a minute before it hits. Do you mind letting yourself out?"

The Swagman picked up a number of discarded sketches from the floor and carefully tucked them inside his tunic.

"Mementos," he said with a smile, walking to the door.

"Now that you've deserted your partner, where will you go next?" asked Yorick.

"I am not without prospects," replied the Swagman confidently.

"People like you never are," said Yorick, his vision starting to blur.

"People like me get what they want," said the Swagman, taking a tentative step into the room and watching for a reaction. "People like Cain don't even *know* what they want."

Yorick was beyond replying, his frail body totally catatonic. The Swagman watched him for another moment, then walked over to the dresser and took one of the two remaining five-hundred-credit notes.

"Reimbursement of expenses," he explained to his motionless host.

He took two steps toward the door, stopped, shrugged, and went back to the dresser, appropriating the final note and placing it in his pocket.

"Filthy habit, drugs," he said, staring at Poor Yorick and shaking his head with insincere regret. "Someday you'll thank me for removing temptation from your path."

A few minutes later he was on his way to the spaceport, lost in thought as he examined every angle of his situation with the cold precision of a mathematician. He finally balanced all the diverse elements and came up with a solution just before he arrived. Shortly thereafter he began making the arrangements that would once again put him back into the heart of the equation.

Part 4

The Angel's Book

15.

They call him the Angel, the Angel of Death,
If ever you've seen him, you've drawn your last breath.
He's got cold lifeless eyes, he's got brains, he's got skill,
He's got weapons galore, and a yearning to kill.

Nobody knew where he came from. It was rumored that he had been born on Earth itself, but he never spoke about it.

Nobody knew where he got his start, or why he chose his particular occupation. Some people say that he had been married once, that his wife had been raped and murdered, and that he took his revenge on the whole galaxy. Some were sure that he had been a mercenary who had gone berserk during a particularly bloody action—but no one who ever met him and lived to tell about it thought him crazy; in fact, it was his absolute sanity that made him so frightening. Others thought that, like Cain, he was simply a disillusioned revolutionary.

Nobody knew his true name, or even how he came to be called the Angel.

Nobody knew why he chose to work the Outer Frontier, out on the Galactic Rim, when there were so many more worlds within the Democracy where he could ply his bloody trade.

But there was one thing *every*body knew: once the Angel chose his quarry, that quarry's days were numbered.

In a profession where reputations could be made by a single kill— Sebastian Cain, Giles Sans Pitié, and Peacemaker MacDougal actually had a combined total of less than seventy, and Johnny One-Note was still looking for his sixth—the Angel had hunted down more than one hundred fugitives. In a profession where anonymity went hand in glove with success, the Angel was known on a thousand worlds. In a profession where each practitioner carved out his own territory and allowed no trespassing, the Angel went where he pleased.

Orpheus met him only once, out by Barbizon, the gateway to the Inner Frontier, three weeks before he killed Giles Sans Pitié. They spoke for only ten minutes, which was more than enough for Orpheus. His audience had expected him to give the Angel no less than a dozen verses—after all, he had given three to Cain and nine to Giles Sans Pitié—but with the insight that had established him as the Bard of the Inner Frontier, Orpheus wrote only a single stanza. When asked for an explanation, he simply smiled and replied that those four lines said everything there was to say about the Angel.

Virtue MacKenzie wished he had written a little more, if only so she'd have a better idea of what to expect if she ever caught up with the Angel. She had reached the Lambda Karos system two days after he had departed, and missed him again on Questados IV. She arrived on New Ecuador three days later, checked for word of his whereabouts at the local news offices, received only negative answers, and finally returned to her hotel, where she took a brief nap, showered, changed her clothes, and went down to the main floor restaurant for dinner.

Three hours later she was sitting at a table in the back of The King's Rook, a tavern that served as the gathering place for local journalists. Two men and a woman—all newspeople—and another man, a prospector who had hit it rich in the asteroid belt two planets out from New Ecuador, sat around the table, staring at the exposed cards in front of Virtue.

"It's up to you," said the prospector impatiently.

"Don't rush me," said Virtue, sipping her whiskey and staring at her hole card until it came back into focus. "I'm thinking." Finally she pushed a one-hundred-credit note across the worn felt to the center of the table. "Call," she said.

The prospector and one of the men dropped out, the woman raised the pot another fifty credits, the other man folded, and Virtue, after still more consideration, matched her bet.

"Read 'em and weep," grinned the woman, turning her hole card face up.

"Damn!" muttered Virtue, tossing her hole card onto the table. She grabbed a nearby bottle and poured herself another drink. "You didn't learn to play from a little rodent called Terwilliger, did you?"

"Anyone for quitting?" asked one of the men, staring directly at Virtue.

"Not when I'm down almost two thousand credits," she replied pugnaciously.

"Anyone else?"

"Hell," said the prospector. "If she wants to keep on playing, I'm willing to keep on taking her money."

"I don't plan to keep losing," said Virtue.

"Then you'd better cut back on the booze," said the prospector. "She had you beat on the table."

"When I want your advice, I'll ask for it," said Virtue, trying to remember exactly what the winner's cards were.

"More power to you." He shrugged. "Whose deal?"

"Mine," said a journalist. He began shuffling the cards.

A well-dressed man entered the tavern just then, looked around, and walked directly over to the five cardplayers. They paid no attention to him until he stopped a few feet away.

"I beg your pardon," he said, "but I wonder if I might join you?"

The four locals stared at him and made no reply.

"Suit yourself," said Virtue.

"Thank you," he said. "By the way, I'm told that there is an excellent game that's in need of players."

"Oh?" asked the prospector nervously. "Where?"

"Right there," he said, pointing to an empty table at the far end of the room.

The prospector and the three journalists almost fell over each other racing to the other table. Virtue, confused, rose to join them, muttering, "What the hell's wrong with *this* table?"

"Not you," said the man firmly, seating himself on one of the hastily vacated chairs.

She stared across the table, studying him in the dim light of the tavern. He was tall, though not as tall as Cain, and quite well built without being heavily muscled. His hair was so blond that it appeared almost white, and his eyebrows were barely visible. It was impossible to guess his age. His cold, penetrating eyes were not quite blue, not quite gray, practically clear. The rest of his face was unmarked and rather handsome, but it was the almost colorless eyes that instantly commanded attention.

He was dressed in a dark gray outfit that seemed black at first glance; it was severely cut and exquisitely tailored. He wore a conservatively styled silver tunic beneath his coat, and his boots, while lacking the embellishments of the Swagman's, nonetheless seemed more expensive. On the small finger of his left hand was a platinum ring that housed a truly fabulous diamond.

"You're the Angel," she said. It was not a question.

He nodded his head.

"I thought you'd look different," she said at last, trying to buy time while everything came into sharper focus.

"In what way?"

"More like a killer."

"What does a killer look like?" asked the Angel.

"Leaner and hungrier," she said. Suddenly a thought occurred to her. "Are you here to kill me?"

"Probably not," he said, pulling out a long, thin cigar and lighting it. "You don't mind if I smoke?"

She stared into his colorless eyes and shook her head.

"Good," he continued. Suddenly he leaned forward. "You've been following me for more than a week. Why?"

"What makes you think anyone's been following you?" replied Virtue.

The Angel smiled—a cold, lifeless smile. "You reached Lambda Karos Two two days after I left and began asking questions about me. Your next stop was Questados Four. Again you inquired into my whereabouts. Now you're here. What am I supposed to think?"

"Coincidence?" she suggested lamely.

He stared at her until she began fidgeting uncomfortably.

"I must appear very stupid for you to make such an answer," he said at last. "Now, let me ask you once more: Why are you following me?"

"I'm a journalist," said Virtue. "You're a romantic figure. I thought you might make a good story."

He stared at her again, without expression, without passion, and again she found herself increasingly uneasy.

"I'm only going to ask you one more time," he said, "so I want you to consider your answer very carefully."

"You're making me very nervous," said Virtue self-righteously.

"Being followed makes *me* very nervous," replied the Angel. "Why have you been doing it?"

"I wanted to meet you."

Virtue noticed that her glass was empty and reached for the bottle, but the Angel was faster and placed it on the far side of the table.

"Why did you want to meet me?" he persisted.

"I think we may be able to help each other."

He stared at her, offering no reply, and finally she resumed speaking.

"You're after Santiago. So am I."

"Then we're competitors."

"No," she said hastily. "I'm not after the reward. All I want is the story." She paused. "And I really *could* use a story on you as well."

"I have no interest in your journalistic aspirations," said the Angel. "Why should I let you come along?"

"I have information that you may not have," said Virtue.

"I doubt it."

"Can you afford to take the chance?"

"I think so." He paused and stared at her again. "But I don't know if I can take the chance that you'll return to Sebastian Cain and tell him where I am and where I'm going next."

"Who's Sebastian Cain?" she asked innocently.

"He's a very foolish man who has taken on too much excess baggage," replied the Angel. "Did you offer him the same deal you offered me—he gets the reward and you get the story?"

"Yes. Except that the Swagman gets something, too. Santiago's art collection, I think."

"And Cain sent you here to spy on me?"

She shook her head. "Coming here was my own idea." He stared silently at her, and again she felt herself compelled to say more than she had intended. "I've sized up the candidates, and I'm going with the winner. If anyone can kill Santiago, you're the one."

"And you'll remain completely loyal to me?" he said sardonically. "Until you hear of someone else who's even better, that is?"

"That's unfair."

"But selling out your partner isn't?" he asked, a note of distaste in his voice. "I wonder what it is about Cain that makes people desert him. The Jolly Swagman has left him, too, you know."

"Who told you that?" asked Virtue, genuinely surprised.

"I have my sources. I expect him to contact me any time now to see if I've changed my mind about not requiring a partner." He paused. "I will tell him that I haven't."

"Is that what you're telling me?" she asked, suddenly apprehensive about what happened to would-be partners. She looked around for support or comfort, only to discover that one by one the customers were quietly leaving the tavern, casting frightened glances at the Angel as they did so.

"I'm not sure," he said. "You possess some information that might prove useful to me."

"I told you so," she said smugly.

"Not about Santiago," he replied disdainfully. "You know less than nothing about him."

"Then what are you talking about?"

"Sebastian Cain," said the Angel. "I'm getting close to Santiago. Three or four more worlds, another week, another month, and I'll be there." He took a puff of his cigar. "Cain is getting close, too. He's got that cyborg ship, and he's already visited the drug addict on Roosevelt Three." He paused. "And he killed Altair of Altair," he added with a touch of admiration.

"I can tell you all about him," said Virtue triumphantly.

"I know."

She paused. "What's in it for me?"

"Exclusive coverage of Santiago's death."

"And a series of features on you," she added quickly.

He stared at her once more. "Don't push your luck. I'd *like* information about Cain; I don't *need* it."

"One feature?"

He made no reply, but his cold clear eyes seemed to bore into hers.

"All right," she said at last.

"You've made a wise decision," said the Angel.

"Well, now that we're going to be traveling together, where are we bound for next?" asked Virtue.

"I'll know in a few minutes."

"Based on something I'm going to tell you?" she asked skeptically.

He shook his head. "I've already told you: you don't possess any useful information about Santiago—but there's a man on New Ecuador who does. I expect him to stop by our table momentarily."

"Why?"

"Because I asked him to."

"Does everyone do what you ask them to?" she inquired with a trace of resentment.

"Most people do," said the Angel.

"And those who don't?"

"They soon wish they had." He paused for a moment. "I think it's time you started telling me about Cain."

"Right now?"

"As soon as you sober up," he replied, signaling to the bartender, who hurried over, bowing obsequiously.

"The lady would like a cup of black coffee," said the Angel.

"And yourself, sir?"

"A white wine, I think," said the Angel. "Not too sweet. Perhaps something from Alphard."

"Right away, sir," said the bartender, scurrying off. He returned a moment later, placed a large cup of coffee in front of Virtue, and offered a glass to the Angel.

"This isn't an Alphard wine," said the Angel, taking a sip from the glass.

"No, sir," said the bartender nervously. "We don't have any. But it's from Valkyrie, which has excellent vineyards. It's a fine vintage, truly it is."

The Angel took another taste while the bartender watched him apprehensively, and finally nodded his approval. The bartender immediately signaled to an assistant, who brought the bottle to the table.

"What do I owe you?" asked Angel.

"It's on the house, sir."

"You're sure?"

"Yes, sir. It's a pleasure to serve you."

"Thank you," said the Angel, dismissing them and watching as they rapidly retreated to their posts behind the bar.

"This isn't very fair," said Virtue.

"What isn't?"

"I'm drinking coffee and you're drinking wine."

"Were you under the impression that life was fair?" asked the Angel ironically.

"I could be drinking whiskey and playing cards," she continued sullenly, glancing over toward the reporters, who were casting furtive glances in her direction.

"They don't want your company."

"What makes you think not?" demanded Virtue.

"Because you've been sitting here talking to me. They'll wait for what they think is a proper interval—perhaps another five minutes— and then leave before you can rejoin them."

"You're sure?"

"Absolutely."

"This happens all the time?" she continued.

"Yes."

"You must be a very lonely man."

"There are compensations," he replied dryly. "Surely Sebastian Cain has said as much to you."

"I'm not certain that he agrees with you."

"Then why is he a bounty hunter?" asked the Angel, suddenly interested.

"He wants to do something important," she said with a cynical smile. "Or meaningful. Whichever comes first."

"God save us from moral men with good intentions," said the

Angel. He took another sip of his wine and relit his cigar, which had gone out.

"I can see where an abundance of them might put you out of business," commented Virtue.

"I don't foresee that as an imminent danger," said the Angel. "Let's get back to Cain. The money trail is a lot easier to follow than the smuggling trail; why did he choose the latter?"

"That was where he got his first hard information."

"Information's not that difficult to come by."

"Maybe you're better at extracting it than he is."

"You make him sound something less than formidable," remarked the Angel. "This is contrary to my assessment of him, especially considering how far he's gotten."

"Bounty hunters aren't all alike," replied Virtue, reaching into her satchel and withdrawing a cigarette. "For example, I have a hard time envisioning Cain killing anyone—and I have an equally hard time picturing you letting anyone live."

"You misjudge me. I only kill fugitives."

"What about Giles Sans Pitié?"

"And fools," he amended.

"I've heard a lot of things, good and bad, about him," said Virtue, "but I never heard anyone call him a fool before."

"That's because most people were afraid of him."

"Why *did* you kill him?"

"He proposed an alliance. I refused. He threatened me." He smiled mirthlessly. "*That* was foolish."

"You killed him because he *threatened* you?"

"You doubtless feel it would have been more sporting to wait until he'd taken a few swings at my head with that metal fist of his?" suggested the Angel.

"How do you know he wasn't bluffing?"

"I don't. But when a man takes a position, he must be prepared to live—or die—with the consequences of his actions. Giles Sans Pitié threatened to kill me. There was only one possible consequence."

"How did you kill him?" she asked curiously.

"Efficiently," he replied. "Now reach into your satchel and turn your recorder off. We're supposed to be discussing Cain, not creating a biographical feature on me."

"Can't blame a girl for trying," she said nonchalantly while deactivating the recorder.

The Angel poured himself another glass of wine as the four card-players silently left the tavern.

"What was Cain's reaction when he found out that he would have to confront Altair of Altair?"

"He wasn't scared, if that's what you mean," said Virtue.

"That wasn't what I meant. Any man who's been in our profession as long as Cain has learned to master his fear." The Angel leaned forward slightly. "Was he excited?"

"Not much excites him. Resigned is the word I'd use."

"What a pity."

"Why? Does killing people excite you?"

"Killing most people is just a job to be done as quickly and efficiently as possible," said the Angel. "But killing someone like Altair of Altair . . ." His face came alive. "The highest levels of competition in *any* field of endeavor are indistinguishable from art—and I find art exciting."

"Then that's why you're after Santiago?" asked Virtue. "Because he affords you the greatest competition?"

He shook his head. "I am hunting Santiago because I need the reward. The challenge he presents is merely an added bonus."

"Come on," said Virtue skeptically. "I know your record. Do you really expect me to believe that you're after still more money?"

"What you believe is a matter of complete indifference to me," replied the Angel.

"But you've made tens of millions of credits!" she persisted.

"My creditors have expensive tastes," he said.

Suddenly his attention was taken by a small, portly, balding, red-faced man who cautiously entered the tavern. The man looked around uneasily, saw the Angel, and walked over to the table.

"Mr. Breshinsky?" said the Angel.

The man nodded, sweat dripping off his face as he did so. "I was told you wanted to see me," he said in a wary voice.

"You were also told what information I needed."

"I regret to inform you that I don't have access to it," said Breshinsky nervously.

"You *are* the account officer of the New Ecuador branch of the Bank of Misthaven, are you not?"

Breshinsky nodded again.

"Then you know on which world Dimitrios Galos initially established his business account."

"I'm forbidden by law to tell you that," protested Breshinsky. "That's privileged information."

"Which you are now going to give to me," said the Angel, staring intently at the uncomfortable banker.

"It's out of the question!"

"If it were out of the question, you wouldn't have shown up."

"I came because nobody says no to the Angel."

"Then don't say no now, or I could become very annoyed with you," said the Angel gently.

"This could cost me my job!"

"This could cost you considerably more than your job."

Breshinsky seemed to shrink within himself.

"Who is your companion?" he asked at last. "I can't divulge sensitive information like this in front of a third party."

"I personally guarantee her silence."

"You're sure?" asked Breshinsky, staring at Virtue.

"I just gave you my word."

There was another uncomfortable pause.

"Can we at least discuss some compensation?" asked Breshinsky, his hands trembling noticeably. "My entire future is at stake if this should get out."

"Of course," said the Angel. "I'm not an unreasonable man."

"Good," said Breshinsky, pulling out a silk handkerchief and mopping his forehead. "May I sit down?"

"That won't be necessary," replied the Angel. "I never haggle. I'll make one offer, and you can take it or leave it."

"All right," said Breshinsky. "What's your offer?"

"Your life, Mr. Breshinsky," said the Angel calmly.

The portly little man gasped, then emitted a nervous giggle. "You're joking!"

"I never joke about business."

Breshinsky stared at him for a long moment, then uttered a sound that was halfway between a sigh and a sob. "The account was initiated on Sunnybeach."

"Thank you, Mr. Breshinsky," said the Angel. "You've been most helpful."

"May I leave now?"

The Angel nodded, and the little banker walked rapidly to the door.

"Would you really have killed him if he hadn't told you what you wanted to know?" asked Virtue.

"Of course."

"I thought you only killed fugitives."

"And fools," added the Angel. "Eventually one comes to the realization that everyone is one or the other."

"Including Santiago?"

"*Almost* everyone," he amended.

"You're a very cynical man," she said.

"It must be the company I keep," he replied. He noticed that his cigar had gone out again, and unwrapped and lit a fresh one. "We'll leave for Sunnybeach at sunrise tomorrow morning."

"Then I'd better go back to my hotel and start packing," said Virtue. She paused. "What will I do with my ship?"

"That's not my concern," said the Angel.

"Thanks a lot."

"If you're unhappy with the arrangements, you can always remain on New Ecuador," said the Angel.

"Not a chance," she replied. "We're partners now. I'm staying with you."

"We are *not* partners," he corrected her. "We are traveling companions, nothing more. And you'll stay with me only so long as you prove useful." He stood up. "Meet me at my ship at sunrise."

"How will I know which one it is?" she asked as he began walking toward the doorway.

He stopped and turned to her.

"You're an investigative reporter," he said. "You'll find it."

Then he was gone, and Virtue MacKenzie found herself sitting alone in the almost deserted tavern. She remained motionless, lost in thought, for a number of minutes, trying to assimilate what she had seen and learned of the Angel. There was no longer any question in her mind that he would find Santiago, and very little that he would succeed in killing him. But for the first time since she had begun her search, she felt unsure of her course of action; the Angel frightened her as no other man she had ever met.

She reviewed her various options, which included finding and teaming up with Cain or the Swagman once more, proceeding on her own, or chucking the whole thing and living on the remainder of her unspent advance, compared them against remaining with the Angel, and finally concluded that while she hadn't made the safest decision, she had made the right one.

She stood up, walked to the far side of the table where the Angel had placed her bottle, downed two large swallows, and headed back to her hotel, trying to come up with various facts about Cain and Santiago that would make her of continuing value to the Angel.

16.

Come to the lair of the cold Virgin Queen!
Come and see sights that have never been seen!
Money that's piled as high as the sky,
And a bandit queen anything other than shy!

People used to ask Black Orpheus about that verse, since it seemed so different from his original stanza about Virtue MacKenzie. At first he was genuinely puzzled—after all, he hadn't written it—but after a while he put two and two together, figured out who wrote it and why, and decided to let it stand, probably to further confuse the academics who had made careers out of continually misinterpreting him.

Once the Angel had let drop that he had a constant need for money, Virtue decided to convince him that she had access to it—so she jotted down the four lines, spread some untraceable cash around, and made sure that the verse continually came to his attention.

She was guilty of overwriting a bit more than usual; at any rate, it didn't have quite the effect she had anticipated. The first time the Angel heard it he remarked that Orpheus must have discovered a second Virgin Queen; he never referred to it again. When it reached the Swagman's ears, he concluded that money wasn't the only thing Virtue was capable of piling as high as the sky. As for Cain, who heard it after he'd reached Safe Harbor, he grimaced and commented to Schussler that some of the sights referred to had been seen altogether too often. Of all the men and aliens Virtue had met on the Inner Frontier, only Sitting Bull, chief of the Great Sioux Nation, assumed that the verse had actually been written by Black Orpheus, and he found himself in full agreement that shyness was not exactly one of the Virgin Queen's more noticeable traits.

In truth, the only positive effect it ever did have was that Virtue gained another little piece of immortality when Orpheus incorporated it into his ballad.

In the meantime, it was business as usual during the two-day voyage to Sunnybeach. The Angel questioned her thoroughly about every aspect of Cain's character, every portion of his past, every hope he may have expressed for his future. She answered with the truth when she could and lied when she couldn't.

Even though he assumed that her knowledge of Cain was fragmentary at best, the picture that emerged puzzled and disturbed the Angel. He understood men who killed for profit, and men who killed for hatred, and even men who killed for ego—but Cain seemed to fall into none of those categories. And, as with anything that ran counter to his experience, he distrusted it, as he now distrusted Cain.

For her part, Virtue tried to learn more about the Angel, especially his past and his reasons for becoming first an assassin and then a bounty hunter. He didn't overtly refuse to answer her; he merely ignored her questions, and when he stared at her with his colorless eyes, she felt disinclined to force the issue.

Finally they reached Sunnybeach, which handled considerably more traffic than she had expected. On most Frontier worlds one simply decelerated and landed, but the procedure here was not unlike that back in the heart of the Democracy.

First a voice came over their radio and asked them to identify themselves.

"This is the *Southern Cross*, two hundred eighty-one Galactic Standard days out of Spica Six, William Jennings, race of Man, commanding," replied the Angel.

"Registration number?"

The Angel rattled off an eleven-digit number.

"Purpose of visit?"

"Tourism."

"Are you equipped to land planetside, or will you require use of an orbiting hangar?"

"I can land in any spaceport rated Class Seven or higher."

"Please maintain your orbit until we can confirm you," said the voice, breaking the connection.

"Who is William Jennings?" asked Virtue.

"I am—until we pass through customs."

"I assume the ship's point of origin and registration number are phony, too."

"They're untrue," said the Angel. "Which is different from being phony. I can prove they're what I say, just as I can prove that I'm William Jennings."

"Why not tell them who you really are?" asked Virtue. "It's not as if bounty hunting is illegal."

"It tends to scare off one's prey and alert one's competition."

"Then why ever identify yourself at all?" she persisted.

"I don't care who knows I've been to a world once I've left it," replied the Angel disdainfully.

The radio came to life again.

"Attention, *Southern Cross*. We need to know how many other sentient entities are aboard your ship."

"One other, besides myself," replied the Angel.

"Please identify."

"Virtue MacKenzie, passenger, race of Man, who boarded at New Ecuador two Standard days ago."

"What was your business on New Ecuador?"

"Tourism."

"Proposed length of stay on Sunnybeach?"

"I have no idea," said the Angel.

"I require a definite answer," said the voice petulantly.

"I propose to stay here for ten days."

"The Sunnybeach economy is based on Plantagenet sovereigns. Will you require the use of a currency exchange?"

"All I require is a clearance to land my ship."

"Please maintain orbit," said the voice, and again the connection was broken.

"I feel like I'm right back in the Democracy," commented Virtue.

"It's a bother," he agreed. "When I have my own planet, I won't tolerate this bureaucratic nonsense."

"Your own planet?" she repeated.

He nodded.

She laughed. "Are you laboring under the delusion that a grateful Democracy is going to give you your very own planet just for killing Santiago?"

"No."

"Then what are you talking about?"

He turned to her, and for just a moment she thought he might put a forceable end to her unwanted questioning then and there. Instead, he instructed his ship's computer to create a hologram of a cross section of the Galactic Rim.

"Do you see this?" he asked, indicating a glowing yellow star.

She nodded.

"It's a G-Four star with eleven planets, the fourth of which is named Far London. Its population has grown to almost three hundred thousand since it was initially colonized." He paused. "Far London has been ruled by a hereditary monarchy, the last descendent of which died a few years ago and left a considerable debt. The government has advertised for a new monarch."

"The stipulation being that you'll pay off the late lamented family's debts?" asked Virtue.

"In essence," said the Angel.

"How much more do you need?"

"Killing Santiago should just about do it."

"And then you'll retire to a quiet life of ruling the peasants?" she asked.

"I've always wanted to have my very own world to rule."

"Well," she said, "at least there'll be one world where we don't have these idiot delays before we can land." She paused. "Have you thought about what other improvements you'll make?"

"No. But I think I can make one guarantee."

"Oh? What is that?"

"It will be safe to walk the streets of my city."

"I don't suppose I'd like to be a lawbreaker in your city," she agreed. "What does the populace think of this idea?"

"Given the previous few monarchs, they'll approve."

"And if they don't?"

"Then they'll learn to adjust," he said softly.

Suddenly the radio crackled with static.

"*Southern Cross*, you are cleared for landing. We will now feed the coordinates into your computer." There followed two seconds of high-pitched humming, after which the ship began decelerating and heading downward toward the surface of Sunnybeach.

"I trust your passport is in order," remarked the Angel. "I don't suppose customs will be any less pompous and self-important."

"Of course," she replied.

But when they landed, she found herself the object of some ten minutes' worth of mild harassment, since her passport hadn't been scanned or registered since Pegasus. When they finally released her, the Angel was nowhere to be seen, and she walked rapidly through the spaceport, looking for him. She passed a handful of human vendors, as well as a number of aliens selling everything from indigestible sweets to incomprehensible wood carvings, and eventually found the bounty hunter at a tobacco stand, purchasing a fresh supply of cigars from a pink, tripodal being from Hesporite III.

"This place is simply lousy with aliens," she remarked. "I didn't know Sunnybeach was so cosmopolitan."

"It isn't," said the Angel. "They're not allowed to leave the free trade zone around the spaceport."

"By the way, I want to thank you for all your help back there at the customs desk," she said sarcastically.

"*My* papers were in order," he replied.

"You could have waited."

"Partners wait. Traveling companions don't."

He paid for the cigars, placed them in a lapel pocket, and began following the signs to the ground vehicle rental area. Virtue fell into step beside him.

When they arrived, he stopped and turned to her.

"You're not coming with me. Find your own transportation, and register at the Welcome Inn."

"Why can't we go into town together?" she asked. "It'll be more convenient."

"Because you're being followed."

"*What?*"

"You heard me."

"I didn't see anybody," Virtue protested.

"I did."

"Then how do you know that *you're* not the one who's being followed?"

"Because when I left customs, he stayed behind and waited for you."

"What does he look like?" asked Virtue.

"He's not that clumsy," replied the Angel. "I've only gotten two brief glimpses of him."

"How do you know he's following me if you've only had two glimpses of him?"

"I know," he said calmly.

"And now you're just going to leave?" she demanded.

"He's not after *me,*" said the Angel.

"I hope they're not expecting a chivalrous king on Far London."

"They're not," said the Angel, walking toward a rental vehicle.

"Wait!" said Virtue. "What should I do about this guy?"

"That's entirely up to you. But if I were you, I'd try to find out what he wanted before I led him to my hotel."

"It's *your* hotel, too," she said desperately. "If you don't help me lose him, he'll know where you're staying. That might be worth quite a bit of money to someone."

"It's not my hotel," he answered.

"It isn't? Then where will you be staying?"

"That's not the sort of information I share with traveling companions."

"Then how will I find you?"

"*I'll* find *you*," he replied. "I'll meet you in the Welcome Inn's lobby at sunset."

"If I'm still alive," she said bitterly.

"If you're still alive," he agreed.

He tossed his single piece of luggage into the back of the vehicle, climbed into the driver's seat, registered it to his account with an identification card, and drove off.

Virtue waited for ten minutes, casting frightened glances into the shadows, then rented her own vehicle and drove out into the bright Sunnybeach sun. When she was halfway to town she realized that she'd left her overnight kit at the spaceport, but decided not to return for it.

Her initial idea upon reaching the nearby city, which, unsurprisingly, bore the same name as the planet, was to walk up and down the streets, window-shopping, until she got a glimpse of her pursuer. That resolve lasted about thirty seconds. Whoever had named the planet had possessed a mordant sense of humor: Sunnybeach was a desert world, with about five hundred miles of beach for every foot of seashore. The heat, once she left the confines of her air-conditioned vehicle, was oppressive, and she got the feeling that the only variation in the weather was an occasional sandstorm.

She had almost collapsed from the simple exertion of walking half a block when she came to a small, elegant restaurant. She entered it, requested a table that faced the front door, and pretended to study the menu while keeping a watchful eye on the doorway.

Some five minutes later a familiar bearded face, topped by a shock of unkempt red hair, peered in through the window, and an instant later Halfpenny Terwilliger entered the restaurant and walked directly to her table.

"Goddamn it!" she snapped, both relieved and annoyed. "Are *you* the one who's been following me?"

"Yeah," he said breathlessly. "We've got to talk."

"I've got nothing to say to you."

"You've got more to say than you think," said Terwilliger, watching the door as intently as Virtue had been doing a moment earlier. He signaled to the waiter. "Has this place got another room?"

"Another room, sir?"

"One that can't be seen from the street," explained Terwilliger.

"We don't open it until dinnertime," said the waiter.

Terwilliger waved a one-hundred-credit note in front of him. "Open it now," he said. "And close it as soon as we're seated."

The waiter took the note with no sign of embarrassment and led them through a doorway into a smaller room which possessed only six lace-covered tables.

"Take money for two beers out of that and keep the rest," said the little gambler when he and Virtue had been seated.

The waiter arched a supercilious eyebrow and left the room.

"What the hell are you doing here?" demanded Virtue when they were alone.

"Waiting for you," replied Terwilliger. "I was going to give you two more days to show up, and then hop over to Hallmark."

"Why were you skulking after me like some kind of criminal?"

"I have my reasons," he said.

"You mean the Angel?" asked Virtue. "He doesn't give a damn who I talk to."

"I'm not worried about the Angel."

"Then what *are* you worried about?"

"ManMountain Bates."

"Is he still after you?"

"The man simply will not let bygones be bygones!" complained Terwilliger peevishly. "He's chased me halfway across the Inner Frontier."

"You seem to have done the same to me," remarked Virtue. "Were you on New Ecuador, too?"

The little gambler shook his head. "I followed you as far as Questados Four. Then Bates started breathing down my neck again, so I decided to jump a few worlds ahead of you, just in case he was using you to find me." He paused for breath, then continued. "The Swagman told me that the Angel would probably pass through Sunnybeach or Hallmark, depending on what he learned on Lambda Karos, and I came here first. It sounded like a vacation planet." He grimaced. "They ought to draw and quarter the guy who named it. Hanging's too good for him."

"Why were you looking for me in the first place?"

"Cain sent me."

"To spy on me?"

"Well, now, *spy* is a pretty ugly word," said Terwilliger, pulling a deck of cards out of his pocket and nervously starting to shuffle them. "Besides, if I was really spying on you, I'd stay in hiding. You'd never know I was around."

"I'd just listen for the sound of a spine snapping," she said nastily. He winced. "Don't remind me."

"All right," she said. "You're not spying. You're just here to sample Sunnybeach's delightful climate." She paused. "What *else* are you here for?"

"To appraise the situation."

"And what's your appraisal?"

"That's pretty obvious," said Terwilliger. "You've jumped ship. You're working with the Angel now."

"And you're going to run back and tell that to Cain?"

"I don't have any choice."

"Of course you do," said Virtue. "You can choose *not* to tell him."

"And risk losing my ten percent of the reward?" said Terwilliger. "Not a chance."

The waiter entered the room then and placed a glass and a container of beer in front of each of them.

"Thank you," said Virtue, immediately filling her glass.

"May I take your orders now?"

"This is all we're having," said the gambler.

"Allow me to point out that this is a restaurant, not a tavern," said the waiter officiously.

Terwilliger pulled another hundred-credit note out of his pocket and handed it to the waiter. "Point it out again in another hour," he said.

The waiter pocketed the money, picked up his tray, and pivoted toward the door in one graceful and well-practiced motion. A moment later they were alone again.

Virtue drained her glass and turned back to the gambler. "How far has Cain gotten?"

Terwilliger shrugged. "Who knows? I haven't been in touch with him since I left Altair Three."

"The Angel mentioned his having obtained some information from a drug addict on Roosevelt Three."

"It's news to me," said Terwilliger.

"If you don't know where he is, how the hell are you supposed to contact him?"

"Through Schussler."

"Schussler?" repeated Virtue. "Who's he?"

"Schussler's more of an *it* than a *he*," answered Terwilliger.

"That cyborg ship I heard about?"

He nodded.

"Schussler belonged to Altair of Altair, didn't he?"

"Yes."

"So he'd probably have had access to any information in her computer banks?"

"I don't know," said Terwilliger. "I suppose so."

"Then that means that Cain's got still another source of information," she mused aloud. "He might be closer than we thought." Suddenly she turned to Terwilliger. "Why did the Swagman leave him?"

"I didn't know that he did."

"You're not exactly a fount of information," she said caustically.

"I'm supposed to be gathering it, not dispensing it," replied the gambler.

There was a momentary silence.

"Maybe he threw him out," she suggested thoughtfully.

"Maybe *who* threw *who* out?"

"Cain," she said. "Maybe he decided he didn't need the Swagman any longer. Maybe he's come to the conclusion that this cyborg holds the key."

The waiter entered the room again.

"I thought I told you to leave us alone," said Terwilliger irritably.

"I know, sir, but if you are Mr. Terwilliger, I have a message for you."

The gambler's face turned pale. "Was it given to you personally?"

"No, sir. It came from the spaceport."

"Get out."

"But the message, sir."

"I don't want to hear it!" snapped Terwilliger.

The waiter stared at him for a moment, then shrugged and left.

"Damn!" muttered the gambler.

"What was that all about?" asked Virtue.

"ManMountain Bates," said Terwilliger. "He's landed on Sunny-beach—and he's got someone keeping tabs on me, or he wouldn't have known I was here."

"Your friend Bates isn't very long on brainpower," commented Virtue, pouring her beer into a glass. "Why announce his presence if he's hunting for you?"

"You haven't seen him," said Terwilliger unhappily. "There's no way he can *hide* his presence."

"But calling ahead, for God's sake!" she snorted contemptuously.

"He's just letting me know that he knows I'm here," said Terwilliger. "It's his idea of a joke. He thinks it'll terrify me." He paused and smiled wanly. "He's right."

"What are you going to do about him?"

He laughed nervously. "I'm going to have a couple of drinks, and then I'm going to run so fast it'll make your head spin."

"Back to Cain?"

"He's my guardian angel." He paused thoughtfully. "Unless . . ."

"Unless what?"

"Cain's a few thousand light-years from here, and you've got an angel of your own. I'll forget about my report if you'll get him to protect me."

"For how long?" she asked.

"Until I'm safely out of this system."

"There's one condition."

"What?" he asked suspiciously.

"Before you leave, you contact Cain and tell him that I'm delaying and misleading the Angel, and that I'm still loyal to him," said Virtue.

"Just in case he gets there first?" asked the gambler sardonically.

"It's always a possibility."

"I don't know," said Terwilliger dubiously. "If he finds out, I'll lose my piece of the action."

"Bates is between you and your ship," she pointed out. "What's ten percent to a dead man?"

He stared at the backs of his cards for a moment, then nodded. "It's a deal," he said at last. "You *can* get the Angel to protect me, can't you?"

Virtue flashed him a confident smile.

"He'll do anything I say," she assured him.

17.

He's bigger than big, he's taller than tall,
He's meaner than mean, and that isn't all—
He drinks straight from morning right through to the night,
He's ManMountain Bates, and he's anxious to fight.

His real name was Hiram Ezekial Bates. He was born on the colony planet of Hera, and when he was eight years old he stood six feet two inches tall.

His parents consulted with numerous specialists. The incompetent among them suggested that he had merely done his growing early; the others knew he had a pituitary system gone berserk, but after subjecting him to countless examinations and tests could recommend nothing to stop it. Finally, when he was twelve years old—he stood seven feet three inches tall by then—they found a doctor who could arrest his growth.

The problem was that nobody had asked Hiram *his* opinion, and the fact of the matter was that he relished the notion of being the biggest human being in the galaxy. When they finally took him to the doctor, he dislocated four vertebrae in the poor man's back, broke both of his legs, and quite literally tore his office apart.

That was the day that he became ManMountain Bates.

They put him in a home for disturbed juveniles. He battered down the brick wall with his bare hands and took off for points unknown, surfacing some five years later on the Inner Frontier. By then he had finally reached his full growth—eight feet seven inches, and close to 575 pounds of burly, rock-hard muscle—and he worked his way through a number of menial jobs before he chucked it all and became a gambler.

He was close to thirty years old the first time that Black Orpheus saw him. He was sitting in a poker game in the back room of a bar on Binder X, surrounded by five rugged miners. He'd been losing pretty heavily, and he was none too happy about it. Finally he glared around the table and announced in a loud, belligerent voice that his luck had just changed and he intended to win the next few hands.

The pot reached six thousand credits on the ensuing hand when Bates finally slammed his cards down on the table. He had a pair of sixes. Two of his opponents had flushes and one had a full house; all tossed their cards into the middle of the table, face down, and opined that they had nothing that could beat him. In a manner of speaking, they were right.

Two more such displays followed, and when Bates had recouped his evening's losses he took his money and left the game, heading deeper into the Frontier. It made a lasting impression on Black Orpheus.

Their paths crossed once more, about five years later, on Barios IV. Orpheus was attracted by the sounds of a barroom brawl and upon arriving at the scene found that ManMountain Bates had challenged the entire clientele of a sleazy spaceport bar. They were a hard-living, hard-drinking lot, prospectors and cargo hands and traders, but Bates threw them around the barroom as if they were so many toothpicks, laughing all the while in his deep bass. One after another was tossed through windows or into walls, until only Bates and Orpheus remained standing.

"Write *that* in your goddamned song!" he bellowed happily, tossing enough money on the bar to pay for the damages and walking off into the hazy night.

Orpheus took him at his word and gave him six verses. He also tried to line up a fight between Bates and Skullcracker Murchison, who was the unofficial freehand heavyweight champion of the Inner Frontier, but Murchison did a little checking up and decided he wanted no part of ManMountain Bates.

As he stood in the lobby of the Welcome Inn, staring apprehensively out into the street while Virtue MacKenzie registered at the front desk, Halfpenny Terwilliger found himself in complete agreement with Murchison.

"All right," said Virtue, walking over to him. "I'm all set."

"Good," replied the little gambler. "Let's go up to your room and wait for the Angel there."

"He's supposed to meet me right here."

"How soon?"

"At sunset."

"That's another two hours or more," complained Terwilliger. "Hell, Bates could walk here from the spaceport by then."

"Nobody walks in this climate."

"Damn it! You know what I mean!" He tried to regain his composure. "I'm not going to sit around this idiot hotel's idiot lobby for two hours. I might just as well stand out in the street with a bull's-eye painted on my forehead."

"Okay," assented Virtue. "Send the message and you can hide in my room."

"Message? What message?"

"To Cain."

"Right now?" he demanded.

"Whenever you want to," replied Virtue sweetly. "But you can't go up to my room until you do it."

Terwilliger glared at her, then uttered a sigh of resignation. "You win. Where do I send it from?"

"I'm sure the hotel has a subspace tightbeam transmitter. Just ask at the desk."

"What's your room number?"

"Why?" asked Virtue suspiciously.

"I'm going to have to bill it to your room."

"The hell you are."

"But I don't have any money."

"Come on, you little rodent," said Virtue. "I saw you bribing the waiter back in the restaurant."

"That was Cain's money," he said lamely.

"I don't give a damn whose money you spend, as long as it isn't mine."

"Are you sure you don't want to pay for it?" he persisted. "It seems kind of immoral to use his money to send him a phony message."

"Not as immoral as lying to me about your finances," she said firmly. "Now reach into your pocket and dig."

He shrugged, approached the desk, had the tightbeam booth pointed out to him, and began walking across the lobby to it.

"I'm sure you don't mind if I come along," said Virtue, joining him.

"You're very distrusting," said the gambler. "It'll turn you into a grouchy old lady."

"A grouchy, *rich* old lady," she corrected him with a smile.

It took him about two minutes to compose the message and another minute to issue routing and coding instructions so that Schussler would receive it. Then he paid his charges at the desk and turned to Virtue.

"Are you satisfied now?" he asked. "Or would you rather I stood on the street with a bunch of signs pointing to me?"

"Don't tempt me," she said, heading off toward the elevators. He followed her, and a minute later they were walking down the corridor of the fourth floor.

"Here we are," she said, pressing her thumb up against the lock mechanism. It took less than a second to scan her print and check it through the front desk's computer, and the door receded into the wall.

"Nice," commented Terwilliger, stepping into the room ahead of her. "Very nice."

"Not bad," she agreed, entering the room and ordering the door to slide shut behind them.

The room was large and airy, some twenty-five feet on a side, with a plush carpet, a king-sized bed, and a pair of very comfortable chairs. One wall housed a recessed cabinet which contained a holographic entertainment system that was currently displaying an assortment of paid advertisements for Sunnybeach's rather mundane night life. A small table between the chairs had instructions for expanding it into a gaming table, with boards for chess, backgammon, and *jabob*, an alien card game that was all the rage in the trendiest human gambling establishments.

"I haven't stayed in a place like this since I made my second fortune!" exclaimed Terwilliger.

"Your *second* fortune?" repeated Virtue. "What happened to it?"

He grinned ruefully. "The same thing that happened to my first one."

She looked at him, sighed, shook her head, and walked over to the closet.

"Open," she muttered.

Nothing happened.

"Open," she repeated.

Still nothing.

"Damn! It's on the blink. If I had anything to put in it, I'd call the desk and complain."

"Just a minute," said Terwilliger. "I've seen one of these before."

He walked up to the ornate door and reached his hand straight through it.

"What the hell did you do?" she asked.

"Nothing," he answered. "There's no door here. It's a holographic projection." He smiled and pointed to a pair of well-camouflaged holo lenses. "It's cheaper than actually installing a hand-carved door like that, and once you get used to it it's more convenient, too. And," he added, "you get to redecorate for the cost of a couple of new image tapes."

"How much else is fake, I wonder?" said Virtue, pacing around the room and touching various objects. "Just the closet door, I guess," she concluded.

"Try the bathroom," he suggested.

She walked to the door, tried to pass through it, and bounced off.

"I didn't mean the door," he said, ordering it to open. "But I'll bet you credits to pebbles that those gold-spun curtains around the dryshower aren't really there."

"A dryshower?" she said irritably. "Shit! I was planning to take a long hot bath tonight."

"On a desert world?" he said. "Hell, I'll bet even their suites don't supply any water except from the drinking tap."

"Oh, well," she said, returning to the bedroom and walking to one of the chairs. "We might as well relax and wait for the Angel."

"Suits me," assented Terwilliger, sitting down opposite her. He pulled out his cards and began shuffling them on the table. "Care for a little game of chance?"

"No, thanks."

"You're sure?"

"If you played games of chance instead of games with predetermined results, you wouldn't be hiding here right now," she replied.

"You can deal," he offered.

"Blackjack," she said promptly, taking the cards from him. "Ten credits a hand. Dealer wins all ties."

"Fine—as long as you'll accept my IOUs if I lose."

"You can play with Cain's money," she said. "After all, we're all partners, so we'll be keeping it in the family, so to speak."

"What the hell," he said with a shrug. "Why not?"

They played for almost two hours, during which time Terwilliger won four hundred credits without ever once being allowed to deal. Finally Virtue looked out the window, handed the deck back to him, pulled four hundred-credit notes out of her satchel, placed them on the table, and got to her feet.

"It's just about time," she said.

"Why don't you meet him and bring him back up here?" suggested Terwilliger nervously.

"What if he's been delayed and I bump into your friend first?" she replied. "Do you really want to be stuck up here in a room that has only one exit?"

"You've got a point," he admitted begrudgingly, following her to the door.

They descended to the lobby, which was considerably more crowded as dinnertime approached, and Virtue quickly scanned the faces that were assembled there.

"Is he here yet?" asked the gambler.

"No."

"Then what do we do?"

"We wait," she said.

"What if somebody has killed him?" asked Terwilliger, a blind panic starting to overwhelm him.

"If someone has killed the Angel, you'd better get down on your knees and start saying your prayers," said Virtue, "because I guarantee you that Judgment Day is at hand. Now stop shaking, and try not to wet your pants."

Terwilliger was too busy peering through the lobby windows into the darkened street beyond to make any reply.

"You can relax now," said Virtue a moment later as the Angel walked through the doorway. "He's arrived."

Terwilliger exhaled loudly with relief, and she wondered idly just how long he had been holding his breath.

"Did you learn anything useful?" she asked as the Angel crossed the lobby and approached her.

"A bit," he said noncommittally. "I'll have to see one more man tomorrow." He paused. "Who's your friend?"

"Halfpenny Terwilliger."

"Is he the one I spotted at the spaceport?"

"Yes. He works for Sebastian Cain."

The Angel stared at Terwilliger and said nothing.

"Well, actually, that's not an operative statement," said the gambler nervously. "My services are currently on the open market."

"Good luck with them," said the Angel. "Now go away."

"What?" demanded Terwilliger.

"I know all about you. You're a crooked gambler who hooked up with Cain on Port Étrange and left him on Altair Three. You have nothing that I want."

Virtue turned to Terwilliger. "Sorry," she said.

"Now just a minute!" he shouted, drawing stares from all over the lobby. "We had a deal! I kept my end of it. Now he's got to protect me!"

"Any deal you made, you made with *her*," said the Angel in level tones.

"No!" said Terwilliger desperately. "I need *you!*"

The Angel stared at him silently.

"Don't you understand?" said Terwilliger. "ManMountain Bates is coming here to kill me!"

"Not without cause, or so I've been told," said the Angel.

The gambler turned to Virtue. "You get him to protect me, or I'll tell him what you had me do."

"He might be useful to us, after all," said Virtue carefully.

"I gather he's already been useful to you," replied the Angel dryly. "He is of absolutely no use to me."

"I can tell you things about Cain," said Terwilliger urgently. "Where he's been, where he's going, things like that."

"I already know where he's been and where he's going."

"I can tell you where Santiago is!"

"You don't know where Santiago is," replied the Angel. "Now go away."

"But I—"

Suddenly Terwilliger froze, his eyes fixed on the hotel's doorway. There was an awed murmuring throughout the lobby, and Virtue and the Angel turned to see the cause of the commotion.

Standing just outside the door was a huge mountain of a man. His shaggy brown mane swirled down to his shoulders, his teeth gleamed white through his thick beard, and his blue eyes glared balefully at Halfpenny Terwilliger. He was dressed in a handmade outfit composed entirely of the cured pelts of animals he had killed with his bare hands, and his boots, except for the steel heels, were also made of animal skins.

"I want *you!*" bellowed ManMountain Bates, pointing his finger at Terwilliger.

The desk clerk quickly touched his computer panel, and the thick front door slid shut.

"You've got to help me!" pleaded Terwilliger.

"You got yourself into this situation," said the Angel. "Get yourself out."

Terwilliger began cursing in frustration and terror, his eyes glued to the door. There was a sudden thudding noise, which was repeated at regular intervals of about five seconds apiece, and he knew that

ManMountain Bates was attempting to hammer the door down with his fists.

"Can't you do *some*thing?" asked Virtue.

"There's no paper on him," replied the Angel emotionlessly.

The door began buckling, and a moment later it caved in entirely. The customers and staff scuttled for positions of safety as Bates entered the room.

"I'm ManMountain Bates!" he roared. "My father was a whirlwind and my mother was a lightning bolt! I'm Leviathan, the great beast of the murky deep!" He began pacing back and forth in front of the terrified Terwilliger. "I'm half cyclone and half tornado! I'm Behemoth, the giant hellcat of the Frontier! I was spawned in a supernova and baptized in a lake of lava! I can outfight and outdrink and outfuck and outswear any man or alien that was ever born or whelped or hatched!"

Terwilliger, tears running down his face, turned to the Angel, who had moved a few feet away from him.

"Please!" he whined.

"You think this midget is going to help you?" demanded Bates. He threw back his huge head and laughed. "Why, I'd crush him like an insect! I'd bite off his arms and legs and spit out the bones!"

The Angel stared at him with an expression of mild interest but made no comment.

"I've traveled half the galaxy to find you, you skinny little worm!" shouted Bates, turning his attention back to Terwilliger. "I've gone without food and without sleep and without women, just waiting for this moment."

He reached out with surprising swiftness for so large a man and grabbed the gambler by the front of his tunic, pulling him close.

"Now you're going to learn what happens to anyone who thinks he can cheat ManMountain Bates!"

He lifted Terwilliger high above his head with a single hand.

"Virtue!" wailed the gambler. "For God's sake, make him *do* something!"

The Angel watched, expressionless, as Bates wrapped his immense arms around Terwilliger and squeezed. There was a single agonized shriek, followed by a sharp cracking noise, and then Bates threw the gambler's lifeless body onto the lobby floor.

The huge man glared at the faces around the room, then placed a foot on Terwilliger's neck.

"I'm ManMountain Bates, and I've claimed my just and terrible vengeance!" he bellowed defiantly. "Now you've all got something you can tell your grandchildren about!"

He pivoted slowly until he was facing Virtue and the Angel.

"You!" he thundered, pointing an enormous finger at her.

"Me?" asked Virtue.

"He called to you," said Bates. "Why?"

Virtue tried to formulate an answer, found that her mouth was too dry to speak, and shrugged.

"He owed me two hundred thousand credits. What's your connection to him?"

"I hardly knew him," she managed to say.

"Who are you?"

"Oh, nobody very important," she said, taking a frightened step backward.

"If I find out that you've lied to me, I'll be back for you," he promised.

She swallowed once and nodded.

"Well?" he demanded, turning to glare at the desk clerk.

"Well what, sir?" asked the man, his voice shaking.

Bates pointed to the corpse at his feet. "Aren't you going to clean this mess up?"

"Yes, sir," said the clerk, pressing the Maintenance code on his computer. "Right away, sir."

"Good. I wouldn't want people to think that a classy hotel like this caters to ugly little worms like *that*." He emphasized the last word by spitting on Terwilliger's body, then looked up again. "All right! Everyone go on about your business."

Nobody moved.

"I mean *now!*" he roared.

Suddenly the lobby became a beehive of activity as people raced for exits and elevators. In another moment no one was left except Bates, Virtue, the Angel, the desk clerk, and two recently arrived maintenance men who were preparing to remove the little gambler's twisted body.

ManMountain Bates took a couple of steps toward Virtue and the Angel.

"You, too!" he said. "Get out."

The Angel began walking toward the front door.

"I've never seen anything like him!" whispered Virtue. "He's like some kind of primal force!"

"He talks too much," said the Angel.

"I heard that!" said Bates ominously.

The Angel continued walking, and Bates strode over, grabbed him by the shoulder, and spun him around.

"Nobody walks out on me when I'm talking to them," said Bates, a nasty smile on his face.

The Angel twisted free and met his gaze.

"I don't like to be touched," he said softly.

"You don't, eh?" Bates grinned, laying his hand on the Angel's shoulder again.

The Angel slapped his hand away. "No, I don't."

Bates suddenly shoved him on the chest, sending him careening backward into a wall.

"Leave him alone!" said Virtue. "He hasn't done anything to you!"

"He insulted me," said Bates, taking a menacing step toward the Angel. "Besides, my blood's up now! There's nothing like breaking a back to get a man's juices flowing."

"Angel, tell him you're sorry and let's get the hell out of here!" said Virtue desperately, visions of wealth and fame departing as she imagined the Angel's body lying in a crumpled heap next to Terwilliger's.

"You're the Angel?" demanded Bates, a look of uncertainty momentarily flickering across his face.

"That's right."

"Then why did you say I talked too much?"

"Because you do," replied the Angel.

"I don't care who you've killed!" bellowed Bates, suddenly enraged again. "You're going to apologize, or I'm going to be known as the man who killed the Angel with his bare hands."

The Angel stared coldly at him for a long moment. Finally he spoke.

"I'm sorry that you talk too much."

"That's it!" growled Bates. "You're a dead man! There's going to be one more angel in hell tonight!"

He took two more steps forward and was within arm's reach of the Angel.

"You can still stop," said the Angel. "There's no paper on you."

Bates roared a curse, reached back, and swung a haymaker at the Angel's head. The Angel ducked, and the huge man's fist went right through the wall. While he was trying to extricate his hand, the Angel reached forward, made two incredibly quick motions with his right hand, and stepped aside.

Bates bellowed another curse as he tried once again to pull his hand out of the wall. Then a curious expression spread across his face, and he slowly looked down to where his innards were spilling out through the slash in the front of his coat.

"I don't believe it!" he muttered, trying to hold himself together with his free hand.

The Angel retriggered his weapon to the mechanism hidden beneath his sleeve.

"But I'm ManMountain Bates!" murmured the giant incredulously, and died.

"My God!" exclaimed Virtue, staring with morbid fascination at Bates, who still hung from the wall by his hand. "What did you cut him with?"

"Something sharp," replied the Angel calmly. He walked over to the registration desk. "You'd better call the police," he said.

"I hit the alarm the second that guy broke down the door," answered the clerk, his face pale and sweating. "They'll be here any minute now."

"I trust that you'll be willing to testify that I killed him in self-defense," continued the Angel.

"Absolutely, Mr. . . . ah . . . Mr. Angel?"

The Angel stared at him for a moment, then turned to Virtue.

"This was your fault, you know," he said.

"Mine?" she repeated.

He nodded. "If you hadn't promised Terwilliger that I'd protect him, he wouldn't have waited around here until Bates showed up."

"Then Bates would have killed him two hundred feet away from here, or half a mile, or at the spaceport," said Virtue. "Don't go blaming me for that."

"But *I* wouldn't have had to kill Bates," explained the Angel patiently. "It was just wasted effort. He's not worth a credit anywhere in the Frontier."

"*That's* all he represents to you?" said Virtue unbelievingly. "Just a wasted effort? My God, he was Leviathan himself, just like he said!"

"He was just a man. He bled like any other."

The police arrived then, and the Angel spent the next couple of minutes recounting the events to a very respectful officer, who had the good sense not to ask him to produce his passport.

Finally, after he finished making his statement, and the officer was interviewing the desk clerk, and two more policemen were trying to remove Bates's hand from the wall, the Angel walked over to Virtue once again.

"By the way, exactly what was it that Terwilliger did for you in exchange for my protection?"

"Nothing."

"I asked you a question," he said. "I expect an answer."

"He sent a totally unnecessary message to a man I'm never going to see again," said Virtue earnestly, staring in awe at the huge corpse of ManMountain Bates.

"Cain?" he asked.

She turned to him and smiled.

"Who's Cain?"

18.

Simple Simon met a pieman going to the fair;
Simple Simon killed the pieman on the thoroughfare.
Simple Simon likes the taste of his new outlaw life:
It's not for pies that Simon needs his shining steel knife.

He never used a knife; that was just a case of Black Orpheus practicing a little poetic license.

And he was anything but simple.

In fact, he had degrees in mathematics and laser optics and two or three of the more esoteric sciences, and he taught at one of the larger universities on Lodin XI for the better part of a decade. He was heavily invested in the commodities market when a bumper crop of *kirtt*, the Lodinian equivalent of wheat, sent prices plummeting down and wiping out his life's savings. It was shortly thereafter that he decided a professor's salary would never buy him all the things that he wanted.

So he left the Democracy and set out for the Inner Frontier, where he embarked on a new course of studies, which included a major in murder and a minor in bigamy. He killed his first four wives and managed to collect the insurance on three of them before it occurred to him that there was a lot more money to be made if he didn't limit his killing to his spouses.

He forthwith became a free-lance killer for hire. Because he had a scientific turn of mind, he favored laser weapons of his own creation; and because he had a healthy respect for those with greater physical skills than himself, he tended to specialize in meticulously devised deathtraps rather than in personal confrontations.

His new profession forced a certain degree of modesty upon him, so much so that he took on the protective coloration of the scientific illiterate. Orpheus saw right through him, of course—seeing through façades was one of the things he did best—and named him Simple Simon as a private joke. The name stuck, and before long Simple Simon's holograph was gracing the walls of the Inner Frontier's postal stations.

The Angel stood in the spaceport's post office, glancing briefly at Simon's face while checking to see if there were any new fugitives worthy of his attention, while Virtue, her satchel slung over her shoulder, stood in the doorway and waited for him.

"I thought you were closing in on Santiago," she said as he rejoined her. "Why bother studying a bunch of second-rate villains?"

"Force of habit," he replied, heading off down the corridor that led to his spaceship. "Besides, for all I know Cain or somebody else has already killed him—and I've still got a planet to buy."

"So in effect, the post office wall is your professional trade journal," commented Virtue.

"I never thought of it that way."

"That's because you're not a journalist," she said.

There was considerably less red tape this time than during their last trip through the spaceport—Virtue guessed that the local authorities had issued orders to get the Angel off the planet as swiftly as possible—and a few minutes later they were in one of the three dozen rental hangars for private spacecraft, climbing into the ship.

"Something's wrong," said the Angel, inspecting the auxiliary control panel that was just inside the hatch.

"What do you mean?"

"The security system's been tripped. Don't touch anything."

"Is it going to explode?" she asked apprehensively.

He shook his head. "I doubt it. If they'd planted a bomb, you'd have triggered it the moment you set foot on the ship."

"Is that why you let me go through the hatch first?" she demanded.

He made no reply, but looked carefully around for another minute without moving farther into the ship, then turned back to her.

"All right," he said. "Let's get back on the ground—carefully."

She followed him through the hatch, and a moment later she was standing some fifty feet away, staring at the ship, while the Angel was speaking to spaceport security on an intercom.

"Nothing's happening," she said when he rejoined her.

"If it didn't blow up while you were walking around in it, it's not likely to blow up just because you're looking at it," he said.

"Then what was done to it?" she asked.

"That's what I intend to find out."

A moment later a harassed-looking security officer appeared.

"What seems to be the problem?" he asked.

"Someone's been in my ship since I landed," said the Angel.

"Oh? Who?"

"That's what I'd like to find out."

The security officer walked to the intercom, asked for an office extension, whispered in low tones for a moment, and then returned to the Angel.

"From what I understand, your mechanic came by just before sunrise."

"I don't carry a mechanic."

"They tell me that his papers were all in order, and that he even had a work order with your signature on it."

"Which signature?" demanded the Angel sharply.

"The Angel, I suppose," responded the officer. "Your identity isn't exactly a secret since last night."

"How did they know it was my signature?" said the Angel. "What did they compare it against?"

"How the hell do I know?" asked the officer. "My guess is that they didn't bother to check it against anything. The man works for a reputable firm. They probably took him at his word."

"What repairs did he say he planned to make?"

"I haven't the slightest idea," said the security officer.

"Why not?"

"Look—I've spent the last five hours helping the shipping department trying to track down a missing animal that was supposedly flown in from the Antares Sector. I can find out what you want to know, but I'll have to check with security and maintenance and whoever the hell else is likely to have his work order on file."

"Do so immediately," said the Angel. "Then check with his employer and see if they've ever heard of him. And then get a mechanic that you can personally vouch for and have him check my ship over from top to bottom."

"Where can I reach you?" asked the security officer.

"I'll be in the restaurant, waiting for your report."

"It may take a while."

"See that it doesn't."

The Angel headed off down the corridor, followed by Virtue. They passed several souvenir shops and a pair of alien restaurants and finally came to a large restaurant that catered to Men. The bounty hunter looked around, then walked past a number of empty tables until he came to one in the corner of the room that suited him.

"Why here?" asked Virtue, sitting down opposite him.

"Somebody sabotaged my ship," he said. "I feel more comfortable sitting with my back to the wall."

"But you don't mind having *my* back facing a doorway?" she demanded.

"Not in the least," he replied.

"Were you always this considerate of others, or did it just come with maturity?" she asked sarcastically.

"Sit anywhere you want," he said, indicating a number of empty tables. "It makes no difference to me."

She sighed. "Let's change the subject. Did you learn anything useful this morning?"

"I learned the name and location of the next world we'll be visiting."

"Would you care to share that little tidbit of information, or are we going to play guessing games?"

"I'll tell you once we've left Sunnybeach."

"This is silly!" she snapped. "Even if you tell me what planet we're going to, I don't know who or what you're looking for there. Do you really think I'll book passage out of here while you're waiting for the mechanic to check out your ship?"

"No."

"Then why are you being like this?"

"Because for a man in my profession, the most important single virtue is not the mastery of weapons or physical combat, but meticulous attention to detail."

"What has that got to do with what we're talking about?"

"Listen carefully, because I'm only going to explain it once," said the Angel, lighting up a thin cigar. "If I tell you the name of our next port of call, there are only two things you can do with that information: ignore it or use it. If you ignore it, as you almost certainly will, you didn't need it in the first place—but if you use it, you will use it to my detriment."

"But you told me back on New Ecuador that we'd be coming to Sunnybeach next," she pointed out.

"My ship was operational on New Ecuador," he replied. "If you had acted independently on that information, you would never have lived to see Sunnybeach."

"I can't tell you how touched I am by such trust," she said cynically.

"My trust isn't lightly given," he responded. "You've done nothing to earn it."

"What are you talking about? I told you all about Cain, didn't I?"

"Betraying a partner is not exactly the sort of behavior that inspires confidence," said the Angel. He paused. "Did I mention that I stopped by the information center of your hotel while you were still asleep this morning?"

"Oh?"

He nodded. "I was curious about the message you had Terwilliger send to Cain yesterday afternoon. The person on duty was kind enough to show me a copy of it."

"He's not allowed to do that!"

"Once I discussed the alternatives with him, he seemed more than happy to accommodate me."

"I told you about it last night," said Virtue defensively. "It doesn't mean a damned thing. I was just hedging my bets—but you're the one I've put my money on."

He stared at her and made no reply.

"Look," she continued. "I could have stayed at the spaceport yesterday after you left for town and caught the next ship out of here. I didn't. That ought to prove something to you."

"It proves that you have a well-developed sense of self-preservation," he replied.

"I don't know why I waste my time talking to you!" she snapped.

"Because you want to find Santiago," said the Angel, signaling to a waitress and gesturing for her to bring two coffees. "The problem," he continued, "is that *he* seems to have found *us* first."

"You think Santiago sabotaged the ship?" asked Virtue.

"Not personally, of course. But I suspect that he ordered it done."

"Why didn't he just have you killed?"

"I'm a little harder to kill than you might think," he said quietly.

"But what purpose could be gained by messing around with the ship?" she persisted. "It can't be a warning. He must know he can't scare you off."

"That's what disturbs me," said the Angel. "It doesn't make any sense—and Santiago is not a stupid man."

"Maybe it was ordered by Cain or the Swagman," she suggested. "They certainly have a stake in delaying you."

He shook his head. "They have an even greater stake in *stopping* me."

"Just because it hasn't exploded yet doesn't mean there's not a bomb."

"Nobody is going to mourn or avenge either of us," replied the Angel. "If there was a bomb, it would have exploded the instant we entered the ship."

"Speak for yourself!" she snapped. "I've got lots of friends."

"I doubt it," said the Angel.

The coffee arrived, and they waited until the waitress was out of earshot before speaking again.

"Could it have been a friend of ManMountain Bates?" asked Virtue.

"I doubt that he had any friends," replied the Angel. "Besides, one doesn't avenge a friend's death by damaging his killer's ship." He frowned. "It's got to be Santiago's doing. I just wish it made a little more sense to me."

A woman dressed in mechanic's clothing entered the coffee shop, looked around, and approached their table.

"Are you the . . . Are you Mr. William Jennings?" she asked hesitantly.

"Yes."

"I've just taken a look at your ship," she said. "I'll have to go over it much more thoroughly before I can give you a complete damage report, but you were right: someone's been tampering with it."

"I assume there were no explosives?"

She shook her head. "Not that I've been able to find. It doesn't look like anyone was out to kill you, just to keep you here for a few days."

"How many?"

"Based on what I've found so far, I'd guess that it'll take two or three days to get the parts shipped in and installed." She paused. "It could come to a lot of money. Do you want an estimate first?"

The Angel shook his head. "Just do whatever's necessary to get it working."

"Where can I contact you when it's ready?" she asked.

"You can't," he said. "But I'll be checking in a couple of times every day. Who should I ask for?"

She gave him her name and identification number, then left the coffee shop.

"You still look disturbed," observed Virtue.

"I still am," he replied. "What does Santiago think he gains by tying me down here for two or three days? I can't be that close to him yet."

He finished his coffee and ordered another.

"Why don't we go to the bar?" suggested Virtue, staring distastefully at her coffee.

"Because we want to keep our heads clear until we figure out what's going on," replied the Angel with equal distaste.

She glared at him for a moment, then shrugged and sipped from her half-empty cup.

They sat in silence for another five minutes, and then the security officer sought out the Angel.

"I've been checking up on the mechanic . . ." he began.

"His company never heard of him, and you can't find him in the directory," said the Angel. It was not a question.

The officer sighed and nodded. "Somebody really screwed up on this one." He pulled out a two-dimensional copy of the mechanic's identification card. "This is the guy. Does he look familiar to you?"

The Angel studied the photograph, which appeared just above the man's signature and thumbprint.

"No," he said. "Do you mind if I keep this?"

"Not at all," said the officer. "It's in the computer if we need another copy." He paused. "We'll keep checking from this end, and I assume that you have . . . ah, certain private sources?"

The Angel made no reply.

"Well, then," said the officer, "if you'll excuse me, I've got to get back to work."

"On the saboteur?"

He shook his head. "The scanner's broken down at one of the passenger terminals," he said apologetically. "Just one of those days. But I'll make sure that the office follows up on your mysterious mechanic."

The Angel stared at him.

"If they haven't got it solved by tomorrow morning, I'll take charge of the investigation myself," he promised with a nervous smile. He backed away, stumbled against a table, apologized, then turned and walked rapidly out of the coffee shop.

"Mind if I take a look?" asked Virtue.

"Be my guest," said the Angel, handing the card to her.

She stared at the bearded face. "Five'll get you ten that he's clean-shaven by now—if all that hair was real in the first place."

She returned the card to him. He took one last look at it, then slipped it into a pocket, threw a couple of coins on the table, and got to his feet.

"Let's go," he said.

"Where to?"

"We're not going to come up with answers hanging around here," said the Angel. "And the spaceport's bureaucracy isn't going to be of any use to us." He paused. "In a way, this may have been a blessing in disguise."

"How do you figure that?" she asked.

"Because if I can find the man who sabotaged my ship, I may be able to get a direct line to Santiago. It could save us a couple of weeks."

"Where will we start looking for him?"

"*We* aren't looking for him; *I* am," he said firmly. "You're going back to your hotel to wait for me."

"The hell I am!"

He stared coldly at her. "If I wouldn't tell you our next port of call, you may be sure that I won't allow you to come with me if there's a chance that I might actually find out where Santiago is."

She was about to protest again, but something in his colorless eyes made her decide against it.

They walked silently through the spaceport to the vehicle rental area. When they arrived, Virtue turned to the Angel.

"Separate transportation again?" she asked caustically.

He shook his head. "We'll go together."

"It can't be courtesy, and we've already ruled out chivalry," she said suspiciously.

"I want to make certain that you go directly to your hotel."

"Are you going to stand guard outside my door to make sure I stay there?"

"Once you've walked in the front door, I don't much care what you do, as long as you don't try to follow me."

The Angel rented a vehicle, and as they began the ten-minute journey into town, it became apparent that the air-conditioning system had seen better days. Virtue decided not to complain about it until he did, and was amazed to find that his face was as dry at the end of the trip as it had been within the spaceport, while she herself was soaked to the skin.

The Angel pulled up to the entrance of the Welcome Inn, where workmen were busily replacing the door ManMountain Bates had broken down, and turned to face her.

"I won't be in touch with you until tomorrow, unless I find what I'm looking for. I warn you once again not to follow me. Since I don't know where to begin, I'm going to start with the lowest examples of the local criminal element and work my way up. They're not likely to prove a very friendly or accommodating lot, and there's very little likelihood that I can protect you if you're skulking around in the shadows—so just go to your room, have dinner, and relax."

"And you think you can find out who sabotaged the ship by intimidating a bunch of small-time crooks?" she said sardonically.

"Probably not," he admitted. "Most likely the man who worked on the ship is long gone from Sunnybeach. But I'm stuck here for the next few days, and I've got to start *some*where, so—"

Suddenly he stopped speaking and stared intently out the window at a shabbily dressed panhandler who was begging for coins some fifty feet away.

Finally the Angel smiled.

"Now it all makes sense," he said softly.

"What does?"

"Never mind." He turned back to her. "When you go into the hotel, find yourself a nice, comfortable seat in the lobby."

"What are you talking about?"

"You heard me."

"I'm hot and I'm tired, and as long as I'm stuck in this hellhole, I intend to go to my room, take a dryshower, and change my clothes."

"I wouldn't advise it," said the Angel.

"I'm getting a little bit sick and tired of taking orders from you!" snapped Virtue.

"All right," he said with a shrug. "Do what you want."

"*Why* shouldn't I go to my room?" she demanded, suddenly unsure of herself.

"Because I was operating under a false premise," he explained. "I thought someone was out to stop me. It's *you* he's after." He reached forward to the control panel and hit the door latch. "Now walk into the lobby and don't look around you."

Suddenly Virtue found herself stepping out onto the sidewalk, oblivious to the intense heat, as the Angel pulled away and sped off into the distance. Forcing herself to look straight ahead, she walked past the desk, then turned left and found a chair that was partially hidden from the doorway.

She sat absolutely motionless, afraid to call any attention to herself, and wondered what to do next. She began furtively studying the people in the lobby, trying to determine which of them looked like killers, and came to the uneasy conclusion that they *all* did.

Finally, after what seemed an eternity, the Angel entered the lobby, accompanied by the panhandler, who looked terribly confused. The bounty hunter glanced in her direction and jerked his head.

She stood up immediately and gestured questioningly toward herself. He nodded, and as she joined them on their way to the elevator she noticed that the Angel had a small hand weapon pressed against the panhandler's back.

"I keep telling you, sir—you're making a terrible mistake," whined the panhandler when the three of them were alone in the elevator, ascending to Virtue's floor. "I've never seen you before in my life, honest to God I haven't."

"But *I've* seen *you*," replied the Angel grimly. "Staring out at me from the post office wall."

"I've never even been to the post office."

The Angel made no reply, and a few seconds later the elevator came to a stop.

"Who is he?" asked Virtue as they stepped out into the empty corridor.

"His name's Simple Simon," said the Angel, prodding the panhandler with his weapon until the man began walking. "And he's just a little more sophisticated than he appears to be."

"Well, there you are, sir," said the panhandler. "My name's not Simon at all. It's Brubaker, sir, Robert Brubaker. I have my identification with me."

"Keep walking," said the Angel.

"If he's really a wanted killer, how did he get past customs?" asked Virtue.

"The same way William Jennings did," said the Angel. "If I wanted, I could come up with ten authentic passports proving that *I* was Robert Brubaker."

"I suppose you could, at that," acknowledged Virtue.

"But I *am* Robert Brubaker!" protested the panhandler. "I'm an honest, hardworking man, I am."

"Hardworking, anyway," said the Angel as they came to Virtue's room. "Stop here."

The panhandler came to a halt.

"All right," said the Angel, backing about fifteen feet down the corridor. "Virtue, open the door and then step aside. *You*," he continued, gesturing toward the panhandler with his weapon, "walk in first."

"Then can I go home?" asked the man.

"Then we'll talk about it."

Virtue extended her hand, let the computer lock scan her thumbprint, and jumped back as the door slid into the wall. The panhandler, shaking his head and looking as if he truly believed he had fallen into the company of a madman, sighed and stepped into the room.

Nothing happened.

The Angel walked to the doorway.

"Go over to the window," he commanded.

The panhandler did as he was told.

"Now sit on each chair and then on the bed."

The Angel waited while the panhandler followed his orders, then nodded to Virtue. She entered the room, and then the Angel stepped inside the doorway.

"You must have been wrong," commented Virtue.

"Close the door and be quiet," said the Angel, scrutinizing the room.

"Hey!" said the panhandler irately. "You promised to let me go!"

"I promised that we'd talk," said the Angel, walking carefully around the perimeter of the room, his gaze darting from one piece of furniture to another. "Are you ready to tell me where it is?"

"Where *what* is?" demanded the man.

"My closet!" exclaimed Virtue suddenly.

"Open it," the Angel ordered the panhandler.

"It's already open," said Virtue, starting to back away from it. "This is just a holographic projection."

"How do you turn it off?"

"I don't know."

"Call down to the desk and tell them to disconnect it," said the Angel.

She did as he ordered, and a moment later the closet flickered out of existence, leaving a single metal rod stretched along a four-foot length of wall.

"That's a relief!" she breathed. "You had me believing you for a minute there."

The panhandler walked up to the Angel. "I've got a wife and three kids depending on me," he said plaintively. "Can't I go now?"

The Angel pushed him down into a chair. "You're dead meat, Simon," he said. "The only question is whether I kill you now or later."

"But my name isn't Simon!" shouted the man desperately. "I'm Robert Brubaker!"

"Shut up," said the Angel quietly. He continued his methodical inspection of the room. When he came to the bathroom door he stopped and turned to the panhandler with a smile on his face.

"Smart," he said admiringly. "Very smart, Simon."

"I don't know what you're talking about."

"The way you rigged it."

"I didn't rig anything!"

"You couldn't be sure a maid wouldn't enter the room before Virtue did, so you couldn't rig it to kill the first person to walk through the door or reach into the closet."

"Look," said the panhandler. "If I walk into the bathroom, *then* will you let me go?"

"Yes," assented the Angel. "But you look hot and uncomfortable. I think maybe you'd better treat yourself to a dryshower, first."

"I don't need a dryshower. I just want to leave."

"But I insist."

"Damn it!" yelled the panhandler. "You pull a weapon on me, drag me up here, accuse me of being someone I never heard of, and threaten to kill me! Isn't that enough? Can't you just leave me alone now?"

"After your dryshower," said the Angel.

"I'm not getting undressed in front of a strange woman."

"You can keep your clothes on."

"Ma'am?" he pleaded, turning to Virtue. "Can't you make him leave me alone? I'm just a street beggar who never did anyone any harm!"

"She's not in charge here," said the Angel, reaching out and grabbing him firmly by the wrist. "Let's get on with it."

The panhandler pulled back, and the Angel released him.

"All right," muttered the panhandler. "You win."

"Then he really *is* Simple Simon?" exclaimed Virtue.

"I told you he was."

"Why the dryshower?" she asked.

"It's the one thing a maid could reasonably be expected to leave alone, even if she cleaned the bathroom," said the Angel. "And on a planet where the average temperature is somewhere around a hundred and twenty-five degrees, it's the first thing you'd head for once you came back here." He turned to Simon. "Am I right?"

Simple Simon nodded his head wearily.

"Explosives or lasers?" asked the Angel.

"Lasers."

"Why do you want to kill *me*?" demanded Virtue.

"There's a guy on Pegasus who's put out a hit on you," replied Simon.

"Dimitri Sokol?" she said, surprised.

"Yeah, that's the one."

"But he already tried on Goldenrod," said Virtue. "I thought that was all over."

"This isn't a game, and it's not played by gentleman's rules," interjected the Angel. "Just because Sokol's failed once doesn't mean he's going to give up." He paused. "When I spotted our friend here standing outside the hotel, I realized that I had been wrong about Santiago sabotaging the ship. Simon had to scout the place out last night in order to learn your number, so he had to know that I wasn't staying here. The fact that he was here anyway meant it was *you* he was after. He was just waiting around so that he could confirm your death. Probably Sokol required a holograph, or maybe even your body itself." The Angel turned to Simon. "Obviously you sabotaged my ship to keep her on Sunnybeach until you could kill her—but why go to such elaborate lengths? Why not just pick her off when we landed at the spaceport?"

Simon made no reply.

"If I have ask again," said the Angel softly, "you'll wish you had answered the first time."

Simple Simon stared into his colorless eyes and decided that he was telling the truth.

"Sokol passed the word that she travels with bounty hunters—first the Songbird, then Father William, and now you. That meant if I tried for a hit out in the open, I'd have to go for you, too, and I didn't like the odds. So I figured the safest way to go about it was to damage your ship and kill her when she came back here. Believe me, Angel," he said sincerely, "I never intended to kill you. I did everything I could to keep you out of the way while I went about my business."

"You make it sound as if killing *me* is perfectly acceptable!" snapped Virtue.

"Well, you must have done *something* to him, or he wouldn't have ordered the hit," said Simon.

"What I did is between him and me," said Virtue.

"Not anymore, obviously," commented the Angel. He turned to Simple Simon. "I've got one last question to ask you: How much did Sokol offer?"

"Fifty thousand credits."

"That much?" said Virtue, impressed.

"Virtue, I want you to remember that figure," said the Angel. "All right, Simon. It's time for that dryshower."

"But I didn't try to kill you!" said Simon desperately.

"You're a wanted man, with a price on your head."

"Dead or alive!" protested Simon. "Contact the police and turn me over to them!"

"The dryshower," said the Angel emotionlessly.

"But why? I'm worth the same to you either way!"

"I'm in a race, and you cost me three days."

"And you're going to kill me for that? This is crazy!"

The Angel pointed his weapon at Simple Simon. "Start walking or I'll kill you right where you're sitting."

Simon, very real tears of fear streaming down his face, reluctantly got to his feet and walked into the bathroom. The Angel followed him, and a moment later Virtue heard a single shriek of utter agony. Then the Angel emerged.

"Good riddance," said Virtue. "Imagine! The son of a bitch didn't see anything wrong with killing me!"

"After I collect the reward, I think I'll inform your friend Sokol that I expect him to pay for the repairs to my ship."

"He'll never do it."

"I have ways of encouraging him," said the Angel dryly. "Now I want you to take a look at Simple Simon."

"Why?"

"Because I said to."

She shrugged and walked into the bathroom. Simple Simon lay on his back, his face and part of his torso burned away by the hundreds of tiny laser beams that had struck him when the Angel activated the dryshower. There was a smell of cooking flesh, and thin streams of black smoke rose from a number of his wounds.

Virtue resisted the urge to vomit and staggered back into the bedroom.

"God, he looks horrible!" she admitted.

"He died a horrible death," replied the Angel calmly.

"Couldn't you have turned him over to the police?" she asked. "Nobody deserves to die like that."

"I could have."

"Then why didn't you?"

"Because you needed an object lesson."

"*He* died because you wanted to give *me* an object lesson?" she said incredulously.

"He was always going to die, whether I killed him or the government did," replied the Angel. "Don't waste too many tears on him. He murdered more than twenty-five men and women, and the death he died was meant for you."

"What am I supposed to have learned from all this?" asked Virtue.

"You are a reasonably courageous and resourceful woman," began the Angel.

"Thank you," she said sardonically.

"But you are also completely unimaginative," he continued. "You act rashly, without any thought of consequences. I wanted you to see Simon's corpse, because I want you to know that you're associating with people for whom this is not an exciting adventure but a deadly serious business."

"I already know that."

"I wanted to reinforce that knowledge," said the Angel, "before I told you what I have to say next."

"And what is that?" she asked apprehensively.

"I have had to kill two men in the past twenty-four hours. Neither of them had any argument with *me*."

"Bates didn't have any argument with *me*, either," she interrupted. "He was after Terwilliger."

"Who in turn was here to see you," said the Angel. "You have caused me a great deal of inconvenience, and have cost me three days in my pursuit of Santiago."

"What are you leading up to?"

"Up until now I was perfectly willing to let you go your own way whenever you wanted," he said. "But after our stay on Sunnybeach, you *owe* me, and when we reach Santiago's planet you're going to pay off."

"How?"

"I'll let you know when we get there. But if you try to leave me before then, or disobey my orders once we're there, then I promise you that I'll accept Dimitri Sokol's commission and kill you myself."

As she looked into his cold, lifeless eyes, she knew that he was telling her the truth, and that knowledge terrified her more than anything Sokol or even Santiago could ever threaten to do to her.

Part 5

Moonripple's Book

19.

Moonripple, Moonripple, touring the stars,
Has polished the wax on a thousand bars,
Has trod on the soil of a hundred worlds,
Has found only pebbles while searching for pearls.

Beneath the grease stains and the tattered clothes, she was actually quite a pretty girl. She had blue eyes that had seen too many things and shed too many tears, square shoulders that had borne too many burdens, slender fingers that would have been soft and white in a gentler life.

If she had any name other than Moonripple, she couldn't remember it. If she had ever called any world home, she couldn't remember *it*, either.

She was nineteen years old, and she had already met Black Orpheus four times. He even began joking that he'd wander into the least likely bar on the least likely planet he could think of, and there would be Moonripple, scrubbing floors, cleaning tables, or washing dishes. The highlight of her brief life was the single verse he created about her one evening on Voorhite XIV, when he was playing his lute and singing his ballad to keep his mind off the storm that was raging through the chlorine atmosphere just beyond the human colony's domed enclosure.

She fascinated him, this waif with a future that seemed no more promising than her past. Where did she come from? How many worlds had she been to? What was she searching for? Had she no higher aspiration than to be a barmaid to the galaxy? She tried to help him, but she truly didn't know any of the answers.

The last time he saw her was on Trefoil III. She was waiting on some twenty-five tables by herself and falling increasingly behind. When her employer began yelling at her and threatening to beat her if her performance didn't improve, Orpheus stepped forward and stated that since she couldn't remember when she had been born, he was officially declaring this to be her seventeenth birthday and was taking her out to dinner. The crowd was thirsty and ill tempered, and probably not even Sebastian Cain or Peacemaker MacDougal could have taken the tavern's only barmaid away and emerged unscathed, but because he was Black Orpheus they let him lead her out of the bar without a word of protest.

He fed her, and bought her new clothes, and even offered to take her with him until he could find her a permanent job on some other world. She replied with disarming sincerity that she bore her employer no ill will and had no desire for any other type of work. Orpheus got the feeling that she was afraid to form any bond, either emotional or financial, that might tie her down to a particular world until she finally found the as-yet-undefined thing she was searching for. They talked far into the morning, the Bard who took such pleasure in the endless variety of Men and worlds he visited, completely unable to understand the wanderlust of one who seemed to take no pleasure in anything.

Finally, when it was time for him to leave, he offered her a few hundred credits, enough to book passage to another planet with another tavern, but she refused, explaining that it rarely took her more than a month or two to save enough money to move on to the next world, and that she would feel guilty about taking money from a man who had already done so much for her.

As Orpheus left for his next port of call, he was convinced that he would regularly encounter her every couple of years—but they never met again, for while he continued his aimless journey, immortalizing men and events, Moonripple finally came, after many false starts and digressions, to the colony world of Safe Harbor, which was where Cain first encountered her.

He wandered into the Barleycorn, the larger of the two local taverns, shortly after Schussler landed in late afternoon. It was totally empty. He checked the sign on the door, which proclaimed "We Never Close," shrugged, and sat down at a table.

"I'll be with you in just a moment, sir," said Moonripple, coming out of the kitchen with a huge pitcher of beer, which she carried over to a large table across the room.

She smiled at him, disappeared again, and returned half a minute later carrying an enormous roast, which she set down next to the pitcher.

"That looks like real meat," remarked Cain.

"It is," she said proudly. "We grow our own beef on Safe Harbor." She approached Cain's table. "May I help you, sir?"

"It's a possibility," he replied. "I'm looking for someone."

"Who?"

"Billy Three-Eyes. Ever hear of him?"

She nodded. "Yes, sir."

"Do you happen to know where he is?"

"He's dead, sir."

Cain frowned. "You're sure?"

She nodded again.

"When and where?"

"He was killed right out there," she said, indicating the street, "by a man called MacDougal."

"*Peacemaker* MacDougal?" asked Cain.

"Yes, sir. That was his name."

"Shit!" muttered Cain. He looked up at the girl. "Did he have any friends here?"

"Mr. MacDougal?"

"Billy Three-Eyes."

"Oh, yes," she said. "Everybody liked Billy."

"We must not be talking about the same man."

"I'm sure we are, sir," said Moonripple. "After all, how many men could have been called Billy Three-Eyes?"

"He had a big scar on his forehead?"

"Right above the bridge of his nose. Yes, sir."

"And everybody *liked* him?" continued Cain, surprised.

"Yes, sir," replied Moonripple. "He was always telling funny stories. I was very sorry when he died."

"Who would you say was his closest friend on Safe Harbor?"

She shrugged. "I don't know, sir. I only saw him when he was in here."

"Did he usually come alone?"

"Yes, sir. But once he got here, he talked to everybody."

"I see," said Cain. He sighed. "Well, I might as well stick around and talk to some of the people *he* talked to. Bring me a beer, will you?"

"Yes, sir," said Moonripple. She walked to the bar, held a glass under a tap, and returned to him.

"Thanks," said Cain.

"I should tell you, sir, that hardly anybody will show up for another three or four hours."

"How about the group that's coming by for dinner?" asked Cain, pointing toward the roast.

She smiled. "Oh, that's not a group. It's just for one man."

"There's got to be four or five pounds of meat there," said Cain. "Do you mean to tell me that one man is going to eat it all?"

Moonripple nodded. "Oh, yes, sir. And the chocolate cake that's in the oven."

Cain stared at the roast again. "Is he doing it on some kind of a bet?" he asked, curious.

"No, sir," answered Moonripple. "He has the same meal every day."

"He wouldn't happen to be eleven feet three inches tall, with orange hair, would he?" asked Cain, only half joking.

The girl laughed. "No, sir. He's only a man."

"If he can pack that much food away, there's nothing *only* about him," replied Cain. He paused. "By the way, how long has Billy Three-Eyes been dead?"

"Four or five months, sir." She paused. "Oh!" she said suddenly. "I forgot the potatoes!"

"You ought to change your sign out front," commented Cain. "I thought this place was just a tavern."

"It is."

"But you're serving food," he observed.

"Only to Father William. He's kind of a special customer."

She turned to go to the kitchen, but Cain grabbed her arm.

"Father William's on Safe Harbor?" he demanded.

"Yes, sir. He'll be by in just a few minutes."

"How long has he been here?"

"I'm not sure, sir," said Moonripple. "Maybe a week."

"I didn't see his tent on my way into town."

"Tent, sir?"

"He's a preacher."

"I know, sir, but he says he's on vacation."

Cain frowned. "Did he ask about Billy Three-Eyes, too?"

"No, sir." She looked uncomfortable. "You're hurting my arm, sir."

"I'm sorry," said Cain, releasing the girl. "You're sure he didn't say anything about Billy Three-Eyes?"

"Not to me, sir." She began walking to the kitchen. "Excuse me, but I have to get his potatoes."

"Did he mention Santiago?" asked Cain.

"Why should he do that?" asked Moonripple, stopping a few feet short of the kitchen door.

"Because he's a bounty hunter as well as a preacher."

"What does that have to do with Santiago?"

Cain stared at her, amazed by her ignorance. "He's the most wanted outlaw on the Frontier."

"You must be wrong, sir," said Moonripple, leaning forward so that the door could sense her presence and slide back to admit her. "Santiago is a hero."

"To who?" asked Cain.

She laughed as if he had just told a joke, and before he could question her further she was inside the kitchen, leaving him to sip his beer thoughtfully and stare at the door that quickly hid her from view.

She emerged a moment later, carrying a large serving dish filled with potatoes au gratin.

"Tell me about Santiago," said Cain as she walked over to Father William's table.

"I don't know him, sir," said Moonripple.

"What makes you think he's a hero?"

"Everybody says so."

"Who's everybody?" persisted Cain.

"Oh, just lots of people," she said with a shrug. "Can I get you another beer, sir?"

"I'd rather you talked to me about Santiago," said Cain.

"But I don't know him," protested Moonripple.

"He's eleven feet tall and he's got orange hair," said a deep voice from the doorway. "What else do you want to know?"

Cain turned and saw a large, extremely heavy black-clad man, his twin laser pistols clearly visible, standing in the doorway.

"You're Father William?" he asked.

"At your service," said Father William, walking over and extending a huge hand. "And you are . . . ?"

"Sebastian Cain," said Cain, surprised by the strength in the pudgy fingers.

"Ah!" said Father William with a smile. "You're Virtue Mac-Kenzie's friend!"

Cain nodded. "And you're the man who saved her life back on Goldenrod."

"The Lord was her savior," replied Father William. "I am merely His instrument."

"What's His instrument doing on an out-of-the-way little world like Safe Harbor?" asked Cain.

"You wouldn't believe me if I told you," said Father William with a smile.

"Probably not—but suppose you tell me anyway and let me make up my own mind."

"Well, the truth of the matter is that when I found out what wonderful food this child cooks"—he smiled at Moonripple—"I decided that it was time to take a vacation, and since I'm a man who likes his comforts, what better place than right here?"

"Do you really cook the food yourself?" asked Cain.

"Yes, sir," said Moonripple.

He turned back to Father William. "You still haven't told me what you were doing here in the first place."

Father William smiled again, and the fingers of his right hand drifted down toward the hilt of a pistol. "I wasn't aware that I was obliged to do so."

"Just trying to make conversation," said Cain with a shrug.

"As long as you aren't insisting, then I have no objection to telling you," said the preacher. "I set down here a few days ago because my ship needed some minor repairs." He walked over to his table. "I'll be happy to continue our conversation, but it would be sinful to let this magnificent repast get cold. Will you join me?"

"I'll sit with you," said Cain, getting up and walking over. "But I'm not very hungry."

"What a shame," said Father William insincerely. He picked up an oversized napkin, tied it around his neck, pulled the serving platter toward him, and sliced off a few large pieces of meat. He then impaled one of the pieces on his fork, brought it to his mouth, and began chewing noisily. "Perhaps you'll allow me to ask *you* the same question you asked me: What is a famous bounty hunter like Sebastian Cain doing on Safe Harbor?"

"Just sitting around drinking beer."

"God has little use for liars, Sebastian," said Father William. He turned to Cain. "And *I* have even less."

"I came here looking for Billy Three-Eyes."

"Was there paper on him?"

"Probably," answered Cain.

"Probably?" repeated Father William, wolfing down still more food and following it up with a large glass of beer.

"I don't know. I wasn't here to kill him; I was after some information."

"About Santiago?"

"Why should you think so?" asked Cain.

"Because you were talking about him when I came in."

"I thought everybody out here talks about Santiago."

"I also know of your partnership with Virtue MacKenzie," Father William pointed out. He finished the last of the meat he had sliced, considered giving himself a second helping of potatoes au gratin, decided against it, and attacked his roast with renewed vigor. "What did you think you could learn from Billy Three-Eyes?"

"Where to find him."

"So you plan to be the man who kills Santiago?" asked Father William between mouthfuls.

"I plan to try," answered Cain. He paused. "I have a feeling that I'm getting pretty close to him."

"What makes you think so?"

"Because the worst crime anyone is likely to commit on Safe Harbor is robbing a store—but three bounty hunters have landed here in the past four months: you, me and Peacemaker MacDougal. That must mean *some*thing."

Father William frowned. "MacDougal? Is *he* here?"

"Not anymore. He killed Billy Three-Eyes."

"Well, there you have it," said the preacher decisively.

"There I have *what*?"

"Coincidence. You and MacDougal were both after Billy Three-Eyes, and I'm here because my ship had a problem."

"Why was Billy Three-Eyes here?" asked Cain.

Father William shrugged. "Who knows?"

"Somebody must," said Cain. "He was a killer. What was he doing on a world like Safe Harbor?"

"Hiding out, in all likelihood." Father William took a final mouthful of meat. "Moonripple!" he called out.

"That's her name?"

The preacher nodded. "Lovely, isn't it? It evokes images of stardust and ethereal beauty."

"I've heard it somewhere before," said Cain, frowning.

"Yes, sir," said Moonripple, emerging from the kitchen.

"I think it's time for the cake, my child," announced Father William.

Moonripple stared at his plate and frowned. "I keep telling you, sir, that if you insist on finishing your meal this fast, you'll make yourself sick."

"Who says I'm through?" Father William laughed. "I've still got most of the potatoes and half a pitcher of beer. But the cake would make a pleasant change of pace."

"Wouldn't you rather rest a bit and give yourself time to digest what you've eaten?" asked Moonripple.

"It'll be digested by the time you return with the cake." He paused. "You layered it with that fudge frosting we talked about yesterday, didn't you?"

"Yes, sir."

He tossed a platinum coin to her. "That's my girl!"

She caught the coin, placed it in a pocket, and went back into the kitchen to fetch the cake.

"Delightful child," said Father William. "She's wasting her time here. I've offered her a job as my personal cook, but she turned me down flat."

"Maybe she thinks you're not likely to provide long-term employment at the rate you put food away," commented Cain dryly.

"Nonsense!" said the preacher. "The Lord's got important work for me, Sebastian. I plan to live a long, long time—which," he added, "is more than can be said for bounty hunters who try to kill Santiago."

"You're a bounty hunter, too," Cain noted.

"Ah, but I'm one of the smart ones. I'm not after Santiago."

"Why not? The price on his head could build a lot of churches."

"People have been trying to find him for thirty years or more without any success," replied Father William. "He's not worth the effort."

Moonripple reemerged from the kitchen, carrying a rich-looking chocolate layer cake.

"This has been a very interesting afternoon," remarked Cain as she set the cake down on the table.

"Has it indeed?" asked the preacher, looking down at the cake with the happy air of a child opening a present.

Cain nodded. "Yes, it has. So far I've met two people on Safe Harbor. One of them thinks Santiago is a hero, and the other is a bounty hunter who has no interest in him whatsoever."

"Moonripple, my dear," said Father William, ignoring Cain's comment, "do you think if you looked high and low you might be able to find me some ice cream to go with this luscious cake?"

"I think you finished all our ice cream yesterday, sir," she replied.

He looked crestfallen. "Check anyway, just in case."

She shrugged and headed off to the kitchen.

"Moonripple," repeated Cain. "Didn't Orpheus write her up a couple years ago?"

Father William nodded. "She's told me about him. I gather *he* offered her a job, too, and she didn't take it. She's a very independent young lady."

"And a very well-traveled one, too," said Cain. "I wonder what she's doing here?"

"Why don't you ask her?" suggested Father William, finishing his beer. "As for me," he added, rubbing his pudgy hands together, "I don't think I can wait for her to find that ice cream." He picked up a knife. "Would you like me to cut you a piece?"

"No, thanks," said Cain as the preacher cut a third of the cake away and placed it on his plate.

Father William stared at the cake for a moment, then picked up a piece and tasted it.

"Sebastian," he said, his face reflecting an ecstasy usually reserved only for his communications with God, "you don't know what you're missing!"

"Twenty thousand calories, at a rough guess," said Cain.

"I preach hard and I kill hard," said Father William seriously. "God understands that I've got to eat hard, too. You can't have a weakling doing the Lord's work, not out here on the Frontier."

"*I* believe you," said Cain. "I just hope your heart and kidneys do, too."

"The Lord is my shepherd," said the preacher, attacking the cake in earnest. "I'll make out just fine."

Moonripple approached the table again.

"I'm sorry, Father William, but there really isn't any ice cream left."

"You'll remember to get some by tomorrow, won't you?" asked Father William with childlike urgency.

"I'll try."

"Good girl!" he said, returning his attention to the cake.

"Would you like me to take the potatoes away now, sir?"

He placed a huge hand over the container. "I'll get to them, child, never fear."

"Have you ever thought of becoming a chef for the navy?" asked Cain with a smile.

"Oh, no, sir," replied Moonripple seriously. "I like my work just as it is."

"Father William suggested that I ask why you came to Safe Harbor," said Cain.

"I don't know," she said with a shrug. "I'd heard about it, and it sounded like a nice place."

"How long have you been here?"

She stared at the ceiling and moved her lips silently, totaling up the days and months.

"Two years next week, sir."

"That's a long time for you to spend in one place, isn't it?"

"What do you mean, sir?"

"Orpheus says you've been to more than a hundred worlds."

"He was a very nice man," she said. "He put me into his song."

"And he said you liked to travel all over the galaxy."

"I do."

"But you stopped here," Cain pointed out.

"I like this world."

"And you disliked all the others?"

She shrugged. "Some of them."

"And the rest?"

"They were nice enough. I suppose. I just like this one better."

"What's so special about it?" asked Cain.

She looked puzzled. "Nothing."

"Then why do you like it better?"

"I don't know. The people are nice, and I like my job, and I have a nice place to live."

"That's enough," said Father William.

"You told me to ask her," replied Cain.

"There's a difference between asking and badgering. Leave her alone now."

Cain shrugged. "I'm sorry if I've upset you, Moonripple."

"You haven't, sir," she replied. "You and Father William have both been very nice to me."

An elderly man entered and walked over to a table next to the one Cain had left, and Moonripple went off to wait on him.

"Well, Sebastian," said Father William, finishing the piece of cake on his plate and cutting the remaining two-thirds in half, "I guess you'll be on your way, now that the man you came to see is dead."

"I guess so," said Cain.

"Well, it's been a pleasure meeting you and talking to you."

"How long will you be staying here?" asked Cain.

"The way that girl cooks, I could stay forever," replied Father William. "But I think I'll be on my way in another two or three days.

There are still a lot of souls to be saved out here—and a few that need to be sent on ahead to Satan."

"But not Santiago's?"

Father William smiled. "I suppose if I were to bump headfirst into him, I might give some serious thought to it," he answered. "But I've got better things to do than chase all over the galaxy after a will-o'-the-wisp."

"To each his own," said Cain, getting to his feet.

Father William extended a chocolate-smeared hand, and Cain took it.

"You're an interesting man," said Cain. "I hope I'll see you again someday."

"Who knows?" replied the preacher. "The Lord works in mysterious ways."

Darkness had fallen when Cain walked out into the humid Safe Harbor atmosphere, and it took him a moment to get his bearings. The planet's three tiny moons were clearly visible but provided very little illumination, nor was there any lighting on the deserted street.

The town, such as it was, was only about five blocks square, and Schussler had been able to set down less than two miles away. Once the bounty hunter ascertained which way he had come, he set about retracing his steps and spent the next ten minutes walking down a dirt road that fronted an enormous field of mutated corn stalks, each some ten to twelve feet high and holding an average of twenty ears apiece.

In the distance he could hear a calf bleating. Logically he knew that imported embryos had to be born and raised before they could be slaughtered, but while Father William's roast hadn't seemed out of place to him, somehow the sound of a calf growing up on an alien world untold trillions of miles from where it had been conceived struck him as highly incongruous.

He continued walking, and after another fifteen minutes he came to Schussler, who had recognized him when he was still a few hundred yards away and opened the hatch for him.

"Did Billy Three-Eyes have anything useful to say?" asked the cyborg when Cain had seated himself in the command cabin.

"He's dead," said Cain. "Peacemaker MacDougal took him four months ago."

"I'm sorry to hear that," said Schussler. There was a momentary pause. "I'll bet the Swagman knew it all along!" he exclaimed suddenly.

"I wouldn't be surprised."

"Where will we go next?"

"Nowhere," said Cain. "There's something funny going on right here."

"Funny?"

"I ran into Father William."

"What was he doing?" asked Schussler.

"He said he was taking a vacation."

"Curious," murmured Schussler. "Still, I suppose it's possible."

"Anything's possible," said Cain. "But why here, and why now?"

"It *does* seem peculiar that so many bounty hunters have recently visited an innocuous little agricultural world," admitted Schussler.

"And I met a girl named Moonripple."

"The name is unfamiliar to me."

"She's just a barmaid," replied Cain. "Not very pretty, not very smart. Maybe twenty years old, tops."

"Then why does she interest you?"

"Because Orpheus wrote her up."

"Orpheus has written up thousands of people."

"And four of us are within two miles of each other on a little colony world in the middle of nowhere," said Cain.

"I hadn't looked at it that way," said Schussler. "That's very interesting."

"I'd say so."

"*Very* interesting," repeated the cyborg.

"Anyway, according to Orpheus, Moonripple has been to one hundred planets."

"I myself have been to more than three hundred," said Schussler. "What's so unusual about that?"

"Nothing. But it means she had to hit better than a world a month since she was ten or eleven years old—and now, for some reason, she's stayed on Safe Harbor for two years. What made her stop traveling?"

"A good question," agreed the cyborg. "What's the answer?"

"I don't have one—yet."

"Did you learn anything else about her?"

"Yes," said Cain. "She thinks Santiago is a hero."

"Why?" asked Schussler.

"I don't know," said Cain. "But I sure as hell intend to find out." He paused. "Can you get some information for me?"

"What kind?"

"I know they don't have any spaceports on this planet, but there has to be some regulatory agency that cleared you for landing and gave you the proper coordinates."

"Yes, there is."

"Contact them and see if you can find out how long Father William has been here."

Schussler had the information thirty seconds later. "He's been on Safe Harbor for almost a month."

"He told me he landed here with engine trouble a week ago. Moon-ripple said the same thing."

"I can double-check if you like."

"It's not necessary." Cain stared at the wall and frowned. "I wonder what he's waiting for?"

"We're getting close, aren't we?" asked Schussler, a note of anticipation momentarily driving the mournful tone from his musical voice.

"Very," said Cain softly.

20.

One-Time Charlie makes mistakes,
But never makes them twice.
His heart is black as anthracite,
His blood is cold as ice.

It was the name that did it.

Certainly Black Orpheus had no other reason to put him into the ballad. He wasn't a hero or a villain, a gambler or a thief, a cyborg or a bounty hunter; in fact, he wasn't anything colorful at all. He was just a drifter named Charles Marlowe Felcher, who wandered from one agricultural world to another, drinking a little too much to make up for not working quite enough.

He had a mean streak, but he wasn't a very imposing physical specimen, and his mastery of fisticuffs and self-defense left a lot to be desired. He felt no enormous compulsion to pay his debts, but since that was common knowledge nobody ever gave him a line of credit, and especially not bartenders. He carried an impressive sonic pistol on his hip, but he wasn't very accurate with it, and more often than not he forgot to keep it charged.

But he had that name, and Orpheus couldn't let it pass without putting it into a verse.

Since he wasn't a very loquacious man, nobody knew exactly *why* he was called One-Time Charlie. Some people said it was because he had been married once in his youth, left his wife behind when he came out to the Frontier, and swore he would never live with a woman again. Others created a complex legend about how he had served time for some crime or another and vowed that he would commit every criminal act in the book just once, so that the police would never again be able to find a pattern to his behavior. A third story had it that he caused such havoc on his binges that he never returned to a world he had visited. A few of his enemies—and he certainly had a number of them—said it was a name created by Flat-Nosed Sal, one of the more notorious prostitutes of the Tumiga system, after he paid for an entire weekend of her time but could only perform once.

Orpheus wasn't concerned with the origin of his name, but only with the fascinating images it evoked; and since he caught him on a bad day, when he had been drinking pretty heavily and wasn't in one of his friendlier moods, the verse came out the way it did.

One-Time Charlie's verse was a recent addition to the canon, and as a result very few people on Safe Harbor had heard it—which was probably all for the best, since sooner or later someone who had heard the song and the stories would start asking him about Flat-Nosed Sal, and as often as not he and his questioner would both wake up in the local jail or the local hospital.

He arrived on a typical Safe Harbor day—warm, sunny, somewhat humid—and spent the next few hours looking for work at the larger farming combines. He was still making the rounds when Cain awoke, shaved, showered, and walked into town.

The place had the flavor of a small village back on old Earth, with rows of frame buildings and houses divided into neat little rectangles. Even the styling was similar, with many of the houses possessing dormer windows and huge verandas. He paused to examine one of them and wasn't surprised to find that beneath the woodlike veneer was a layer of a titanium alloy, and that the house ran on fusion power.

He walked another block and saw the figure of Father William sitting on the front porch of his small hotel, swaying gently back and forth on the oversized wooden rocking chair. He shaded his eyes as he watched the bounty hunter approach.

"Good morning, Sebastian," he said. "Lovely day, isn't it?"

Cain nodded. "That it is. Good morning, Father William."

"I thought you'd be off in pursuit of Santiago this morning," said the preacher.

"There's no hurry," said Cain. "I thought I'd sample some of Moonripple's cooking myself." He paused. "Besides, Santiago's been out there for thirty years or more. Another couple of days can't hurt."

"I hear tell that the Angel is closing in on him."

"That's what they say."

"And that doesn't worry you?"

"I'm trying not to lose any sleep over it," answered Cain.

"You're a confident man, Sebastian Cain," said Father William. "If it was me, I'd have taken off from Safe Harbor last night."

"But it's not you," said Cain.

"True enough," agreed the preacher. "Well, enjoy your stay. Possibly you'd like to join me for dinner tonight?"

"Perhaps."

"You seem singularly unenthused," noted Father William.

"You eat so damned fast, you're likely to swallow my arm before you realize you've made a mistake," said Cain with a smile.

Father William threw back his head and roared with laughter. Finally he regained his breath. "I like you, Sebastian! I truly do!" Suddenly he became serious. "I hope we never have to confront each other as enemies."

"Are you planning on breaking the law?" asked Cain.

"Me?" snorted Father William. "Never!"

"Neither am I."

Father William stared at him for a long moment. "Would you care to come up here and sit beside me for a spell?"

"Later, perhaps," said Cain. "I've got to buy some supplies."

"Go in peace, Sebastian," said the preacher. He looked up at the sky. "A beautiful day—the kind of day that makes a man forget how much evil there is abroad in the galaxy."

Cain nodded to him and continued walking down the street until he came to a small general store. He entered it and was momentarily chilled by the rush of cold air.

"Good morning, sir," said the proprietor, a portly, middle-aged man who had meticulously combed his thinning hair to cover a bald spot and succeeded only in calling attention to it. "May I help you?"

"Possibly," said Cain, looking down the various aisles. "Do you carry any books or tapes here?"

"Safe Harbor doesn't have a newstape," he said. "Nothing very exciting ever happens here," he added with an apologetic smile. "But we do have a selection of tapes and magazines from nearby worlds. Is there anything in particular you're looking for?"

"Yes," said Cain. "Have you got material about Santiago?"

"Nothing worth looking at," said the shopkeeper. "Just the usual stupid speculations written by incompetents who have nothing better to do with their time." He sighed. "You'd think somebody would tell the truth about him after all these years."

"What *is* the truth?" asked Cain.

"He's a great man, a *great* man, and they keep treating him like some kind of common criminal."

"I don't mean to seem rude," said Cain carefully, "but none of the stories I've heard about him make him sound like anything but an outlaw."

"You've been listening to the wrong people."

"Are you one of the right ones?"

"I beg your pardon?"

"What can you tell me about Santiago?"

"Oh, nothing very much," replied the shopkeeper.

"Just that he's a great man," said Cain.

"That's right, sir," said the shopkeeper briskly. "You'll find our magazines and tapes in the middle of aisle three, just past the computer supplies."

"Thank you," said Cain. He wandered over to the tape section, browsed for a couple of minutes, and walked out.

His next stop was the barber shop, where he got a shave while listening to the barber tell him with a straight face that he had never heard of anyone named Santiago.

Cain spent the rest of the morning wandering through the small village, striking up conversations wherever he could. The people were divided almost equally: half of them thought Santiago was a saint, and the other half seemed not to recognize his name.

Finally he returned to Father William's hotel. The preacher was still rocking lazily in the sunlight, sipping a tall iced drink through a straw.

"Hello, Sebastian," he said. "Have you decided to join me?"

"For a couple of minutes, anyway," said Cain, pulling up a chair.

"A couple of minutes is all I've got," replied Father William. "It's getting on toward lunchtime." He paused. "Did you have a successful morning?"

"An interesting one, anyway," responded Cain.

"I notice that you're not overburdened by supplies," remarked the preacher with a lazy smile.

"I decided to carry them back after the heat of the day," lied Cain.

"Good idea," said Father William. "Will you be leaving then?"

Cain shrugged. "Perhaps."

"Where will you be going next, Sebastian?"

"I haven't decided yet. How about you?"

"Szandor Two, perhaps, or possibly Greenwillow. It's been a few years since I've preached to either of them." He paused. "I suppose

I'll stop by a post office somewhere along the way and make up my mind after I've seen the latest Wanted list."

"Haven't they got any post offices on Safe Harbor?" asked Cain.

Father William shook his head. "Not a big enough planet. The mail gets delivered every three weeks to the local chemical company. The townspeople pick it up when it arrives, and the rest of it gets passed out when they deliver fertilizer and insecticides to the farms."

"How many mail deliveries have you been here for?"

"Two," said Father William.

"Last night you told me you'd only been here a week," said Cain.

"Last night you hadn't told that unholy ship of yours to check with the local authorities," replied the preacher easily. "That was unwise, Sebastian, challenging the word of a servant of the Lord."

"Isn't lying supposed to be a sin?" inquired Cain mildly.

"God can be very understanding," answered Father William.

"Is He equally understanding of all the people who lied to me this morning?"

"Nobody lied to you, Sebastian."

"More than a dozen men told me that they had never heard of Santiago."

"*Almost* nobody," amended Father William.

"When is he due to show up?" asked Cain.

"Who?"

"Santiago."

Father William chucked. "You're letting your imagination run away with you, Sebastian."

"I thought we were going to talk," said Cain.

"We're talking right now," said the preacher.

"One of us is talking," Cain corrected him. "And one of us is still lying."

Father William smiled. "You're lucky I'm on vacation, Sebastian. I've taken men's scalps for less than that." His smile vanished. "However, I wouldn't press my luck if I were you."

"Am I to assume that our conversation is over?" asked Cain caustically.

"Not at all," said Father William, rising to his feet. "But I think we'll continue it over lunch. I'm famished!"

He walked across the unpaved street to the tavern, and Cain fell into step beside him.

Moonripple had already laid out a huge spread for Father William and looked somewhat distressed when she saw Cain enter with him.

"I didn't know you were coming, sir," she said apologetically. "I haven't made anything for you."

"He can have one of my sandwiches," said the preacher magnanimously.

Cain looked at the table. "Are you sure seven of them will be enough for you?" he asked wryly.

"God tells us that we must make sacrifices," said Father William, tying a napkin around his neck and sitting down. He turned to Moonripple. "Did you remember to buy the ice cream, my child?"

"Yes, sir," said Moonripple.

"Excellent! By the way, Mr. Cain will be my guest for dinner."

"Mr. Cain?" she repeated, staring at Cain. "Are you the one they call the Songbird?"

Cain nodded. "It's not my favorite name."

"I've heard about you all over the Frontier," she continued enthusiastically. "Black Orpheus gave you three verses!" She paused, embarrassed. "I'm sorry about not knowing who you were last night."

"There's no reason why you should have known me," replied Cain.

"But you're so famous!"

"No more so than you and Father William," said Cain. "We're all in the damned song."

She looked concerned. "Don't you like Orpheus' song?"

"Not especially," he said. Moonripple looked like she was about to cry, and he quickly added: "But the verse he did about you was lovely."

"Do you really think so?" she asked, smiling again.

He nodded. "Have you ever found those pearls that he claims you were looking for?"

"I wasn't really hunting for pearls," she replied. "That was just a thing to say."

"What *were* you looking for on all those worlds?" asked Cain.

She shrugged. "I don't know."

"Maybe we were both looking for the same thing," he suggested.

"Maybe," she agreed. "What are you looking for?"

"Santiago."

"I've never met him, sir."

"Do you know anyone who has?"

"I really couldn't say, sir," she replied. "I mean, if *you* had met Santiago, you'd hardly be likely to tell someone like me, would you?"

"Would you like to meet him?"

"A great hero like that?" she said. "He wouldn't have time for someone like me, sir."

"Moonripple, my child," said Father William, who had been eating with feverish haste during their conversation, "I think I'm ready for another pitcher of beer."

"Right away, sir," she said, walking behind the bar and holding a fresh pitcher under the tap.

"You'd better dig in, Sebastian," said Father William, "or there won't be anything left for you."

"You go ahead," said Cain. "I'm really not very hungry."

"You weren't hungry last night, either," remarked the preacher. "No wonder you're so gaunt. Don't you ever eat?"

"Aboard my ship," answered Cain.

"You couldn't get me into that unholy melding of man and machine," said Father William devoutly. "I'm surprised God allowed it to happen."

"If God didn't want Men to become spaceships, He wouldn't have created the Graal," said Cain with a smile.

Father William looked up sternly from his food. "Sebastian, you can ask all the questions you want about Santiago—but when you make fun of the Lord, you're walking on very thin ice. Do you understand what I'm saying to you?"

"I apologize if I've offended you," said Cain.

"It's not *me* you have to worry about offending," said the preacher. "It's the Lord."

"Then I apologize to both of you."

Father William stared at him for a long moment, trying to decide if Cain was making fun of him, then nodded a terse acceptance and returned to his meal.

Moonripple brought Father William's beer over to him. Cain was about to start questioning her again when the door opened and Charles Marlowe Felcher walked in, strode up to the bar, and ordered a beer and a whiskey. He looked hot and discouraged, as indeed he was.

"Good afternoon," he said, nodding to Cain and Father William.

"Greetings, neighbor," said the preacher. "I think it's still morning for a few more minutes, though."

"It feels like afternoon," One-Time Charlie replied, downing the whiskey and going to work on the beer. "I've been making the rounds all morning, looking for work."

"There's not much to be had on Safe Harbor," offered Father William.

"So I've been finding out." He signaled to Moonripple and held up his whiskey glass. "Keep this thing full, honey." He looked back to Father William. "I didn't know this joint was a restaurant, too."

"It isn't," said the preacher. "I'm a friend of the family."

"You live around here?"

"Just vacationing."

"You, too?" he asked Cain.

"Just drinking beer," replied Cain.

"What's your name, friend?" asked Father William.

"Felcher, Charles Felcher," was the reply. "But most people call me One-Time Charlie."

"Orpheus told me about you," said Moonripple disapprovingly.

"Well, whatever he told you, it was probably a lie," said One-Time Charlie. "After all, that's what he gets paid for doing, isn't it?"

"He doesn't get paid at all," she said.

"Then he's a bigger fool than I thought," laughed Charlie, downing a second whiskey and holding his glass out for a refill.

"He's not a fool!" she said hotly. "He's a great artist!"

"Didn't anyone ever tell you that the customer is always right?" said One-Time Charlie.

"Not when he says bad things about Black Orpheus, he isn't," she replied defiantly.

"Have it your way," he said with a shrug. "I'm just here to have a drink and cool off."

Father William returned to his repast, while Cain sipped his beer thoughtfully and decided not to question Moonripple any further until One-Time Charlie had left or passed out. He decided that the latter was more likely, given the rate at which he was putting away whiskey and washing it down with beer.

"Moonripple, my girl, I think I could use another two or three sandwiches before you bring out my dessert," announced Father William when he had emptied his plate. "And put a little more cheese on them this time."

"Yes, sir," she said, heading off to the kitchen.

"That looks like a nice job, being a friend of the family," commented One-Time Charlie, looking up from his drink.

"It has its advantages," agreed Father William. "Especially for a man of the cloth who donates all his money to charitable causes."

Charlie grinned. "Are you a preacher?"

"I am privileged to serve the Lord in that and other capacities," replied Father William.

"Can't be much work for you on a little backwater world like this."

"As I told you, I'm on vacation."

"Stupid place to come for a vacation."

"Ah, but *I'm* vacationing," said Father William with a smile. "Are *you* working?"

"I'm working on this bottle, is what I'm working on," said One-Time Charlie, his words starting to slur.

Moonripple returned with the sandwiches and placed them down before Father William, then went back to her post behind the bar.

"Those sandwiches look pretty good," said One-Time Charlie. "I think I'll have some, too."

"I'm sorry, sir, but they're not one of our services," said Moonripple.

"If you can make them for a preacher, you can make them for an honest worker," said One-Time Charlie irritably.

"Really, I can't, sir," said Moonripple. "These come from the owner's private kitchen."

"I don't give a damn where they come from!" growled Charlie. "If *he* can have them, so can I."

Moonripple looked across the room at Father William, who nodded almost imperceptibly.

"All right, sir," she said to One-Time Charlie. "I'll be right back with your sandwiches."

She went into the kitchen, and he turned triumphantly to Father William and Cain.

"You just have to know how to talk to these people," he said smugly.

Both of them stared silently back at him, and after a moment he returned to his drinking.

Moonripple emerged a few minutes later, carrying two platters. She set one of them down on the bar in front of One-Time Charlie and carried the other, which held Father William's dessert, to the preacher.

"Ah!" he exclaimed happily. "You found strawberries for my cheesecake! You are truly an angel, my girl!"

"That's really good cheesecake?" asked One-Time Charlie sullenly.

"The best!" enthused Father William. "The girl is an absolute artist in the kitchen!"

"I'll have a piece, too," he told Moonripple.

"I'm afraid there isn't any more," she replied.

"We're not going to go through all that again, are we, honey?" he said. "I told you I wanted a piece of cheesecake."

"She's telling you the truth," said Father William. "She only makes one a day. I prefer them fresh."

"Then make another one," said One-Time Charlie.

"I can't, sir," answered Moonripple. "I buy the makings each morning. Father William doesn't like me to use frozen ingredients."

"You're Father William?" asked One-Time Charlie, surprised.

"That's right."

"The bounty hunter?"

"When God so wills it."

"Is this girl any relation to you?"

"No."

"Then you've got no interest in anything I say to her." One-Time Charlie turned back to Moonripple. "Go out and buy some more makings."

"I'm not allowed to leave, sir."

He grabbed her arm as she walked by.

"I thought we decided that the customer was always right."

"You're hurting me!" said Moonripple, trying to twist free.

"I'm going to do a lot more than that if we don't figure out who's the boss here," he said nastily.

"Let her go," said Cain softly.

"Another party heard from," said One-Time Charlie, turning to glare at him without relinquishing his grip on the girl. "Who asked you to butt in?"

"I'm another friend of the family," said Cain.

"Yeah?" said One-Time Charlie pugnaciously. "Well, you and your goddamned family can go fuck yourselves."

"You've had too much to drink," said Cain, getting slowly to his feet. "Now let her go and get out of here."

"Are you a bounty hunter, too?" asked Charlie sarcastically.

"As a matter of fact, I am."

"Have you got a name?"

"Sebastian Cain."

"The Songbird?" said One-Time Charlie, frowning. "What have we got, some kind of convention going on here?"

"What we've got is a drunk who's asking for trouble," said Cain ominously.

"Come on," laughed One-Time Charlie. "Everybody knows you guys don't kill anyone who's not wanted by the law. This is a private discussion between me and this little girl; why don't you just keep your nose out of it?"

"Just let her go and walk out, and nobody will get hurt," said Cain slowly.

Suddenly One-Time Charlie twisted Moonripple's arm behind her and produced a knife with his free hand, pressing it against the girl's throat. "Take one step toward me and I'll slice her!" he snarled.

"Do you suppose there's any paper on One-Time Charlie?" asked Cain, never taking his eyes off the man.

Father William nodded, pulling his coat back and revealing his laser pistols. "A sinner like him? There's got to be paper on him somewhere, Sebastian."

One-Time Charlie started to realize that he was in over his head, but in his drunken state of mind he couldn't find any way out of his situation. He tightened his grip on Moonripple and began edging slowly toward the door, keeping her between himself and the two bounty hunters.

"Make a move and I'll kill her!"

Cain shrugged and turned to Father William as if to say something else. Then, in one blindingly swift motion, he spun around, drew his pistol, and placed a bullet between One-Time Charlie's eyes. The room reverberated with the sound of the gunshot.

Moonripple screamed as One-Time Charlie fell to the floor, and Cain walked over to her and put an arm around her.

"It's all right," he said gently. "You're safe now."

"Very nice work," said Father William admiringly. "You're as good as they say you are." He walked over to One-Time Charlie's body and studied his face closely. "He doesn't look familiar," he said after a moment. "But you can never tell."

"If you want him, he's yours," offered Cain.

"You mean it?"

"View it as my belated contribution to church," said Cain wryly.

"Praise the Lord, I've got another convert!" laughed Father William, pulling out his skinning knife.

"Come outside," said Cain to Moonripple. "You don't want to watch this."

"What is he going to do?" she asked, staring at the preacher with horrified fascination.

"Nothing that concerns us," replied Cain, walking her to the doorway.

She went out into the street with him, still trembling, as the townspeople poured out of their stores and houses to converge on the tavern. Cain ignored them and kept walking until he and Moonripple were well clear of the crowd.

"Will you be all right, or would you like me to take you to a doctor?" he asked.

"I'm fine, sir," she said.

"You're sure?" he asked as the sound of Father William's voice came out of the tavern, reassuring the onlookers that no crime had been committed and that another sinner had been sent to Satan a few years ahead of schedule.

"Yes, sir," said Moonripple. "I'm all right, really I am."

"Good. That was a pretty close call."

She looked up at him. "You saved my life. Why?"

"I like you," replied Cain. "And I've never been very fond of people like One-Time Charlie."

"What can I do to repay you?" she asked.

"You can tell me the truth about Santiago."

She considered his request silently for a moment, then nodded.

"If that's what you want," she said.

"Father William is waiting for him. When is he due to show up?"

"He's already here," said Moonripple.

"Santiago's on Safe Harbor right now?" asked Cain, startled.

"Yes."

"How long has he been here?"

"For years, I guess," answered Moonripple. "He lives here."

"Well, I'll be damned!" muttered Cain. "Can you take me to him?"

"No. But I can introduce you to someone who can."

"When?"

She shrugged. "Right now, if you'd like."

Cain was suddenly aware of Father William's presence and turned to find the preacher standing some twenty feet away, his grisly trophy in his hand.

"You're very persistent, Sebastian Cain," he said. "I admire that in a man."

"If he's been here all along, why haven't you gone after him yet?" asked Cain.

"I don't want him."

"Why not?"

"I have my reasons," said Father William.

"Well, I have mine for wanting to find him."

"So I've been given to understand."

"I've got nothing against you," said Cain seriously. "But if you try to stop me, I'll kill you."

"I wouldn't dream of it," said Father William, holding his hands out from his laser pistols.

"Do you plan to be here when I get back?" asked Cain.

"*If* you get back," the preacher corrected him.

"I'll see you then," said Cain. He paused. "Aren't you going to wish me luck?" he added ironically.

"God be with you, my son," said Father William sincerely.

Then Cain was following Moonripple down the street, half expecting to feel the searing pain of a laser in the small of his back. He was mildly surprised when he turned the corner intact and unharmed, with Father William's parting words still echoing in his mind.

21.

Silent Annie never speaks,
Never murmurs, never shrieks,
Doesn't whisper, doesn't call—
But someday, someday, she'll tell all.

Orpheus had a feeling about her.

There was an indefinable *something*—a look, an attitude, a way of carrying herself—that made him think she carried some enormous secret within her.

He had no idea how right he was.

Her name was Silent Annie. She wasn't mute, but she might as well have been.

All anyone knew about her was that something pretty bad had happened when she was eleven or twelve and living on Raxar II. She spent two years in the hospital, and when she emerged she was physically recovered—but she never spoke again. She was *capable* of speech, her doctors said; but the experience she had undergone had traumatized her, possibly forever.

She turned up in some mighty odd places over the years—Altair III, Goldenrod, Kalami II—but she never stayed for long. Nobody knew what she did on those worlds, and very few people knew that she called Safe Harbor home.

"Silent Annie?" repeated Cain when Moonripple told him where she was taking him. "She's here, too?"

"Yes, sir."

"It seems like half the people Black Orpheus ever wrote about are on Safe Harbor," he said.

"Not really, sir," replied Moonripple. "There's just you, and me, and your ship, and Father William, and Silent Annie."

"Didn't Orpheus say that she was a deaf-mute?"

"She doesn't talk, but she can hear everything you say."

"What's her link to Santiago?"

"She works for him, sir," said Moonripple.

"You're sure?"

Moonripple nodded her head. "Yes, sir."

"By the way," said Cain, "you can stop calling me sir. My name's Sebastian."

"Thank you, sir. It's a very pretty name."

"You think so?" he asked dubiously.

"Yes, I do. Don't you?"

"I suppose it's better than Songbird," he said. He looked around. "Does Silent Annie live in the middle of a cornfield?" he asked.

"Of course not," laughed Moonripple.

"Well, that's just where we're headed," he noted. "We're almost a mile out of town."

"She has a little house about half a mile up the road, sir."

"Sebastian," he corrected her.

"Sebastian."

"How did you meet her?"

Moonripple shrugged. "I don't even remember. At church, probably. It couldn't have been in the tavern, because she doesn't drink."

"And you're good friends with her?"

"Not *best* friends," she said, accentuating the word. "I've never had a best friend."

"How well do you know her?"

"Sometimes she stops by in the morning and we have tea together, and once in a while I visit her on my day off," answered Moonripple.

"What makes you think she'll take me to Santiago?" persisted Cain.

"Why wouldn't she?"

"Because I'm a bounty hunter."

"Santiago knows that, sir."

"Santiago knows about me?" asked Cain, startled.

"Santiago knows everything," she said.

He stared at her but made no comment, and they spent the next few minutes walking in silence.

"There it is, sir," she said, pointing to a small structure set in about fifty feet from the road.

"It looks empty," said Cain.

"Oh, she's home, sir," said Moonripple decisively.

"What makes you so sure?" he asked.

"Where else would she be?"

"Beats the hell out of me," answered Cain, turning off the road and following a narrow path up to the front door.

He waited for the security system to scan the two of them, and just as he was sure that he had been right about the home being deserted, the door slid back into the wall and he found himself facing a small, slender woman dressed in a very old military daysuit.

She was perhaps thirty years old, and her features were sharp and stark. She had a scar that began on her forehead and ran through her right eyebrow and down her cheek, which even cosmetic surgery had been unable to hide. She wore no makeup, which made her thin lips seem even thinner.

"Hello, Annie," said Moonripple. "This is Sebastian Cain. He'd like to meet you."

Silent Annie motioned for them to enter the house, and Cain followed the two women through a small foyer into a living room that was larger than it appeared from the outside. The walls were covered by shelving units, which in turn were covered by disorganized stacks of books and tapes. A dust-covered computer sat on a battered desk in one corner, and Cain could see from the text on the screen that she had been reading when they had interrupted her.

The furniture matched the decor of the room: old, not very comfortable, and arranged without any concern for design or order. Silent Annie pointed first at Cain and then at the largest of the chairs, and he sat down, while Moonripple sat cross-legged on the floor next to him.

Silent Annie made a pouring gesture.

"Yes, I'd love some tea," said Moonripple. "What about you, sir?"

"Tea will be fine," said Cain.

Silent Annie forced a smile to her lips, then left the room for a moment and returned with a chipped porcelain pot and three cups carried on a plastic tray.

"Thank you," said Cain, taking one of the cups.

Silent Annie made a squeezing gesture with her hand.

"I don't understand," said Cain.

"She wants to know if you'd like a slice of lemon," said Moonripple.

"No, thanks," said Cain as Moonripple reached out and took a cup for herself.

Silent Annie walked over to a couch that was covered by a blanket, placed the tray on a nearby table, and sat down, staring questioningly at Cain.

"He wants to meet Santiago," volunteered Moonripple. She paused for a moment. "I told him you'd take him there."

Silent Annie arched an eyebrow.

"I promised him, Annie," said Moonripple.

Silent Annie made a gesture with her hands that Cain could not interpret.

"Because he saved my life."

Another gesture.

"A very mean man came into the tavern and tried to hurt me, and he stopped him."

Silent Annie stared at Cain, appraising him.

"Will you take him, Annie?"

Silent Annie sat motionless for a moment, then nodded her head.

"Thank you!" said Moonripple happily. "I knew you would!"

Silent Annie continued to stare at Cain, who met her gaze. Finally she turned back to Moonripple and made another gesture with her hands.

Moonripple turned to Cain. "She wants me to leave now."

"How will I talk to her?"

"She's very good at making herself understood," Moonripple assured him.

"Let's hope so," he said. "I didn't know what the hell she was doing when she spoke to you with her hands."

"She's been teaching me sign language, but she has other ways of communicating."

"Then I thank you for your help," said Cain, getting up and helping her to her feet. "I hope we meet again."

"You're a very nice man, Sebastian," she said, standing on her tiptoes and kissing his cheek. Then, suddenly embarrassed, she turned and scurried out of the room.

"How soon can we start?" asked Cain.

Silent Annie held up her hand, palm outward, signaling him to wait, then walked to the window. When Moonripple reached the road and began heading back toward the village, she turned back to him.

"Soon," she said.

"What?" said Cain, startled.

"We'll start soon enough," she replied in a firm voice. "But first I think we'd better have a little speak."

"I thought you couldn't speak."

"I can, when I have something to say, Mr. Cain," said Silent Annie.

"Why do you pretend to be mute?" he asked.

"So I won't have to answer stupid questions." She sat down and sipped from her cup of tea. "You've come to kill him, haven't you?"

"Yes, I have."

"Why?"

"There's a price on his head."

"And that's the only reason?"

"How many more do you need?" replied Cain.

"I had rather hoped for something more meaningful," said Silent Annie. "I would hate to think that we had misjudged you."

"Misjudged me?" repeated Cain.

"We've been waiting for you, Mr. Cain, ever since Santiago told Geronimo Gentry to start you off on the trail that eventually led you to Safe Harbor."

"Let me get this straight," said Cain, confused. "Are you saying that Santiago *wanted* me to find him?"

"That is precisely what I am saying."

"I don't believe it."

"Believe whatever you want," said Silent Annie with a shrug. "How do *you* think you got here, after all those years of virtually no progress?"

He stared at her and said nothing.

"I shouldn't imply that he made it easy for you," she continued. "That wouldn't have served his purposes. But he did make it possible; he decided to give you the initial impetus."

"Why?"

"He's been studying you for a long time, Mr. Cain," continued Silent Annie. "Ever since you came out to the Frontier."

"Still why?"

"Because he studies everyone."

"But he doesn't allow everyone to find him."

"No," she replied. "You are only the second."

"Who was the first?"

"It doesn't matter," said Silent Annie. "He's dead now."

"What about Father William?" asked Cain.

"What about him?"

"*He* found Santiago."

"You're wrong, Mr. Cain," replied Silent Annie. "He's not hunting for Santiago."

"Then what's he doing here?"

"I'm not sure you'd believe it if I told you," she said.

"Perhaps not," agreed Cain. "But why don't you tell me anyway, and let me make up my own mind?"

"He's here to *protect* Santiago."

"From me?" asked Cain skeptically. "Then why didn't he take me on when he had the chance?"

"He's not worried about you."

Cain was silent for a moment. "The Angel?" he asked at last.

She nodded. "He'll be here before too much longer."

"I take it that he's gotten this far without any help from Santiago."

"That is correct."

"And that Santiago doesn't want to be found by the Angel?" continued Cain.

"I doubt that he's given it any thought whatsoever," replied Silent Annie. "Protecting him is Father William's idea, not his."

"Why would Father William help a man with a price on his head?" asked Cain.

"That's what I hope to show you before you meet Santiago," said Silent Annie, finishing her tea and pouring herself another cup.

"Where does Moonripple fit into all this?"

"She's just a very pleasant little barmaid, nothing more."

"But she knew Santiago was on Safe Harbor," he pointed out.

"So did everyone else you spoke to this morning."

"And no one's tried to turn him in for the reward?"

"Actually, five or six people have," said Silent Annie. "You'll find them buried in various cemeteries around the planet."

"Let's get back to Moonripple for a minute," said Cain, trying to assimilate everything Silent Annie had told him. "She's been hitting a world a month for most of her life. Why did she come here?"

"Just chance, nothing more."

"And why has she stayed?"

"For the same reason I have," said Silent Annie.

"All right," said Cain. "Why have *you* stayed?"

"Because Santiago is a great man."

"Santiago is a thief and a murderer."

"It's all a matter of viewpoint," she said.

"Viewpoint's got nothing to do with it," replied Cain. "The man has been killing and plundering since before you were born. The Democracy's managed to implicate him in almost forty murders, and

there have probably been more than a hundred they don't know anything about. And I have it on good authority that he's got warehouses
filled with stolen merchandise all over the Inner Frontier."

"May I assume that your authority is the Jolly Swagman?"

"He wouldn't be risking his life if he didn't know they existed,"
answered Cain.

"I'm not arguing their existence," said Silent Annie. "Merely your
interpretation of them." She paused. "And incidentally, I don't see the
Swagman risking his life at this moment."

"Is *he* a part of this, too?"

"Absolutely not," she replied. "He was once, but Santiago dismissed him."

"A falling-out between thieves?" suggested Cain.

"There was only one thief involved," she replied sternly. "And he
no longer works for us. I argued in favor of killing him, but Santiago
chose to let him live."

Cain leaned back and sighed. "All right," he said at last. "I've
heard a lot of talk from you and Moonripple about how Santiago is a
great man. Suppose you tell me why you think so."

"Fair enough," said Silent Annie. "You tell me that Santiago is
responsible for the deaths of a hundred and forty men. Let me begin
by telling you that the actual figure is closer to eight hundred."

"That makes him a great man?" said Cain ironically.

"How many men have *you* killed, Mr. Cain?"

"That's not at issue here," said Cain.

"Tell me anyway."

"Thirty-seven."

"You're lying, Mr. Cain," she said with a smile.

"The hell I am."

"I happen to know that you killed more than five thousand men
and women on Sylaria alone."

"That was war," he said.

"No, Mr. Cain. That was revolution."

"Are you trying to tell me that Santiago is a revolutionary?" he
asked skeptically.

"Yes, I am."

"A woman named Sargasso Rose suggested the same thing," he
said. "I didn't believe her, either. Who is he supposed to be revolting
against?"

"The Democracy."

Cain laughed out loud. "Are you seriously suggesting that he expects to overthrow the Democracy?"

"No, Mr. Cain. The Democracy controls tens of thousands of worlds, and holds some ninety-eight percent of the human population in the galaxy. There are more than thirty million ships in its navy, and it has inexhaustible wealth and resources to draw upon. It would be foolish to dream of overthrowing it."

"Well, then?"

"He seeks only to neutralize it on the Frontier, to eradicate its more heinous abuses."

"By stockpiling artwork and murdering small-time smugglers like Duncan Black?"

"Duncan Black was a traitor," she said coldly. "He was executed, not murdered."

"The end result was pretty much the same," commented Cain.

"Have you never executed anyone for deserting what you thought to be a just cause, Mr. Cain?" she demanded.

He was silent for a moment.

"Yes, I have," he admitted at last. "Keep talking."

"*You* talk about stockpiling artwork, but it's the Swagman that I hear speaking," continued Silent Annie. "In point of fact, he and Santiago had their falling-out because Santiago refused to keep certain pieces that the Swagman wanted, but sold them through the black market, where the Swagman would have had to pay competitive prices for them."

"To pay the troops?" suggested Cain.

"Were you paid on Sylaria or the other worlds where you fought?" she asked.

"No."

"Neither are we," she said. "The troops, as you call them, work for free, Mr. Cain."

"Then what does he need all that money for?"

"You shall see."

"When?"

"Soon."

"Why not now?" he insisted.

"Because you caused a bit of a commotion back in the village when you killed One-Time Charlie," said Silent Annie.

"Moonripple didn't mention anything about my killing him."

She smiled. "I'm not totally isolated here, Mr. Cain. Father William contacted me and told me what had transpired before you had covered half the distance to my house." She paused. "At any rate, while you were totally justified in your actions, it was impossible to keep your identity a secret."

"I never tried to," he interjected.

"Let me amend that," she said. "It was impossible to keep your *occupation* a secret. That was unfortunate."

"Why?"

"Because a number of the townspeople are willing to lay down their lives to protect Santiago. When Father William is certain that none of them are coming here to try to stop you, he'll contact me again, and then we can leave."

"If one of them shows up, I intend to defend myself," said Cain.

"That won't be necessary," she said. "If need be, Father William will warn them off."

"Why?"

"Because Santiago wants you intact, and Father William will honor his wishes."

"Even if it costs Santiago a couple of followers?"

"It almost certainly won't—but yes, even so."

"You're not exactly making him sound like a saint," remarked Cain.

"He's not. He's a man who has been forced to make more life-and-death decisions than any one human being should ever have to make."

"That was his choice."

"That was his calling," she corrected him.

"What makes *me* so important to him?" demanded Cain.

"I should think that would be obvious to you," said Silent Annie.

Cain stared at her for a very long moment. Finally he spoke.

"Why should I want to join him?"

"Because you yourself were once a revolutionary."

"The galaxy is lousy with men who were once revolutionaries," he said.

"Most of them have adjusted. You haven't."

"I've adjusted better than most," Cain replied with a touch of irony. "I took what I learned and put it to a new use. I used to kill men for free." He smiled mirthlessly. "Now I do it for a living."

"He's not interested in you because of the men you've killed."

"Then why *is* he interested in me?"

"Because of the men you *haven't* killed," said Silent Annie.

He frowned. "I don't think I understand you."

"You let Quentin Cicero live."

"He had a hostage."

"You've given out other pardons, too," she continued. "You spent ten weeks hunting down Carmella Sparks, and let her walk away."

"She had three kids with her," said Cain uncomfortably. "One of them was still nursing. They would all have died."

"That wouldn't have stopped Peacemaker MacDougal or the Angel," she said.

"Then maybe Santiago ought to be talking to them instead of me."

"He has no interest in men who have forfeited every last vestige of their humanity. It is *because* you are still capable of acts of compassion that he wants you."

"Yeah," said Cain. "Well, I don't know if I want *him*."

"You will," she said confidently. "He is the greatest man I know."

"How did you meet him?"

"I grew up on Raxar Two," she said. "It had a large alien population, and we had a military government in order to keep them properly pacified." The muscles in her jaw twitched slightly. "When I was eleven years old, I was beaten and raped by three soldiers. The Democracy was having trouble getting more military funding, and they didn't want any incidents that might embarrass them and cost them their money, so they covered it up. The three men were transferred to another world, and were never punished. I spent two years in the hospital."

"Is that where you got the scar?" asked Cain.

"That's just the one you can see," said Silent Annie bitterly. "Anyway, Santiago heard about what had happened, and—"

"How?" interrupted Cain.

"He's been out here a long time," she replied. "He has sources everywhere. Once he learned what they had done to me, he had the three men killed." She forced a grim smile to her face. "I believe the late Altair of Altair was my particular angel of vengeance."

"And then you joined him?"

"Wouldn't you have?" she replied.

"I'd have killed them myself."

"Not all of us are killers, Mr. Cain," she replied. "It requires a certain primal instinct that not everyone possesses."

"Does Santiago?"

"I don't know for a fact that he has ever personally killed another human being."

"Given the number of deaths that he's decreed, that might be construed as cowardice in certain circles," remarked Cain.

"I won't dignify that remark with an answer," Silent Annie said coldly.

"How did you find him?" asked Cain, declining to apologize for his comment.

"He makes it very easy, when he wants to be found."

"I think I'd be willing to debate that," he said wryly.

"Do you honestly think you could have found him if he hadn't wanted you to?" she asked.

"Based on what you've told me, no," he admitted.

"He makes the way more difficult for some than for others," she continued.

"I'll testify to that, at least," said Cain.

"For Moonripple, it was perhaps easiest of all."

"I thought you said she landed here by chance."

"It was pure chance that she landed on Safe Harbor when she did," explained Silent Annie. "But sooner or later she was bound to arrive."

"Why?"

"Her parents worked for Santiago. The Democracy captured and killed them when she was only four years old." She paused. "He couldn't reach out for her then, because there was too great a chance that she was being watched. So he became her guardian angel. Wherever she went, whatever world she worked on, there was always someone watching over her, protecting her. Finally, when we were sure that the Democracy had given up on her, it was subtly suggested that her wanderings should take her in the direction of Safe Harbor. When she finally arrived, we waited to make absolutely sure she hadn't been followed, and then she was told the truth."

"By you?"

Silent Annie shook her head. "She doesn't know I can speak."

"By Santiago himself?" asked Cain.

"She's never met him." Silent Annie paused. "She's a very sweet girl, but our battle isn't hers. She's already suffered enough casualties. The less she knows, the better."

"Then why did Santiago endanger himself by letting her know anything at all?"

"He wanted her to stay on Safe Harbor, where he could better protect her should the need ever arise."

"And if she wants to leave?" asked Cain.

"She's free to go."

"Even knowing that this is Santiago's world?"

"Even so."

Cain lowered his hand, lost in thought. Finally he looked up at Silent Annie.

"I'd like to meet him," he said.

"You shall."

"I'm also aware that this could be a trap."

"Why would we use such an elaborate one?"

"I don't know," he admitted. "But if you've been lying to me, he's a dead man."

"I'm not lying." She walked over to a communicator. "Father William should have given us the all-clear signal before this. I'd better check in at the tavern and see what the problem is."

"Maybe you'd better let me," volunteered Cain. "Moonripple might answer, and you're supposed to be a mute."

Silent Annie smiled. "If she answers, I'll just ask for Father William. Since she's never heard my voice, she's hardly likely to identify it."

"I stand corrected," said Cain.

Silent Annie spent a moment speaking in low tones, then broke the connection and turned to Cain.

"It's all right," she announced. "We can leave now."

"What was the holdup?"

"He got to drinking beer and consuming food, and totally forgot about us," she said with a semitolerant smile.

"It sounds like him," agreed Cain. Suddenly he frowned. "We'll have to put this off for an hour or so."

"What's the matter?" she asked.

"There's something I have to do first."

"Does it have to do with Santiago?" she asked suspiciously.

"Indirectly. There's a promise I have to keep."

"To whom?"

"To a friend." He walked to the door. "I'll be back."

She nodded, and he left her small house and began walking down the road that led through the little village. Within half an hour he had arrived at his destination.

"You look unhappy," said Schussler as he came through the hatch.

"I am," answered Cain.

"Then you were wrong about Safe Harbor?"

He shook his head. "I was right."

"Santiago's coming?" asked Schussler excitedly.

"He's here now."

"Thank God!" said Schussler with a sound that was as close as a thing of metal and machinery could come to a sigh of relief.

There was a momentary pause.

"Do you remember our bargain?" asked the cyborg.

"That's why I'm here."

"You're an honorable man, Sebastian."

"How do I go about it?" asked Cain, walking over to the panel that hid Schussler's essence from view. "Is there a way I can disconnect you without causing you too much pain?"

"I can't feel pain," said Schussler. "If I could, I might even choose to live."

"That's a stupid thing to say."

"Only to a man who can feel, Sebastian."

"All right," said Cain, touching the code that exposed Schussler's tiny enclosure. "What do I do now?"

"I am compelled to obey your orders, even at the cost of my own existence," said Schussler. "Simply order me to cease functioning and I'll die."

Cain stared at the small box. "You mean that's all there is to it?"

"Yes."

"I could have done that at any time."

"But we had an agreement," said Schussler. "I was also compelled to fulfill my end of it."

"Are you ready?" asked Cain.

"Yes. . . . Sebastian?"

"What?"

"I've put down on oxygen planets, and chlorine, and methane. I've been to Deluros Eight, and to the most obscure dead worlds on the edges of the Frontier. I've flown faster than light, and twisted my way through meteor storms."

"I know."

"There's one thing I've never done, one place I've never been."

"Where is that?"

"I've never seen the inside of a star."

"Nobody has."

"Then I'll be the first," said Schussler. "What a beautiful image to carry with me into eternity!"

"Then I so command it," said Cain unhappily.

"Thank you, Sebastian," said the cyborg. "You'd better leave me now."

"Good-bye, Schussler," said Cain, walking to the hatch.

"Watch for me, Sebastian," said Schussler. "It will be twilight soon. I'll wait until then, so that you can see me." He paused. "I'll be the first shooting star of the evening."

"I'll be watching," promised Cain.

And an hour later, as he and Silent Annie were finally setting out on their quest, he stopped to look up. For a moment he saw nothing out of the ordinary; and then—and it was probably just his imagination, for the sun was still quite brilliant and Schussler was some eighty million miles distant—he thought, for a fleeting instant, that he could see an unbelievably bright form streaking toward Safe Harbor's golden sun. It moved faster and faster, and then flickered gratefully out of existence.

Part 6

Santiago's Book

22.

His sire was a comet,
His dam a cosmic wind.
God wept when first He saw him,
But Satan merely grinned.

An even forty verses: that's what Black Orpheus gave him.

Nobody else ever got more than a dozen—but then, nobody else was Santiago.

Orpheus was faced with a moral and artistic dilemma when he finally confronted the subject of Santiago, for all of his verbal portraits were based on firsthand knowledge, and he had never seen the notorious outlaw. (In point of fact, he had seen him on five separate occasions over the years, and spoken to him twice, but he didn't know it, then or ever.)

On the other hand, he knew that any ballad that aspired to describe the men and events that had shaped the Inner Frontier would be laughably incomplete if it didn't include a major section on Santiago.

So he compromised. He gave him forty verses, but he never once referred to him by name. It was his way of saying that the Santiago stanzas were somehow incomplete.

Sebastian Cain was fast coming to the conclusion that the legend of Santiago was as incomplete as the ballad. He sat beside Silent Annie as her vehicle sliced between lush fields that seemed to writhe and ripple in the dim light of Safe Harbor's moons, finally coming to a halt in front of a small barn.

"First stop," she announced, opening the door and getting out.

"A barn?" asked Cain as the warmth and humidity hit him full force.

She smiled. "I was rather hoping that you'd learned not to judge anything associated with Santiago by its appearance."

She walked up to the prefabricated structure, tapped out a combination on the lock, and the door slowly opened inward.

"Come along, Mr. Cain," she said, uttering a low command that illuminated the darkened building.

Cain followed her into the cool interior of the barn and found himself facing a row of drying bins, each filled to the brim with ears of mutated corn. High above him was a loft that had once contained hay but looked as if it hadn't been used in the past twenty years.

"Well?" he said.

"Take a look in the third bin."

He walked over and stared at it.

"It looks like corn," he said.

"That's what it's supposed to look like," she replied. "Look a little more closely."

He reached in with both hands, tossing ears of corn aside, and came to a gold bar.

"The Epsilon Eridani raid?" he asked, laboriously lifting the bar with both hands and studying it.

She nodded. "We've got about forty of them left."

"All in this bin?"

"Yes."

"What happened to the rest of it?" asked Cain. "I saw one bar with Jonathan Stern back on Port Étrange, but no one seems to know what became of the others."

"Most of them have been dispersed," she replied. "Would you like to know where?"

"Why not?" He shrugged.

"Follow me."

Silent Annie walked into the barn's tiny office, which contained two vidphones, a pinup calendar printed on real paper, a small wooden desk, an ancient swivel chair, and a computer. Everything except one phone and the computer was covered by a layer of dust.

She activated the computer, waited for it to identify her retina pattern and thumbprint, and then ordered it to bring up the details concerning the Epsilon Eridani gold.

Cain studied the readout as it appeared on the small screen.

"I see that Father William got about a third of it," he noted.

"He's one of the conduits Santiago uses to feed the hungry and medicate the sick. The bulk of the Epsilon Eridani gold was sold on the Kabalka Five black market."

"Kabalka Five? That's an alien world, isn't it?"

"It doesn't take aliens long to find out what men will do for gold," she replied.

"What became of the money you got for the gold?"

She called up another chart on the screen.

"*All* of it went to hospitals?" he asked.

"Not quite. It also sponsored a raid on Pico Two."

"What the hell is on Pico Two? It's just a little dirtball of a world, out by the Quinellus cluster."

"Some of our friends were incarcerated there."

"So you got them out?"

She shook her head. "That was impossible."

"Then what?"

"We blew up the jail."

"With your friends inside it?"

"The Democracy will stop at nothing to find Santiago," replied Silent Annie. "These were loyal men, but they would have talked. If torture didn't work, there are drugs that would have."

"So much for loyalty," said Cain dryly.

"He's not a god and he's not a saint," she said. "He's just a man, and he's fighting against the most powerful political and military machine in the galaxy. Our people know what might befall them when they go out on a mission."

Cain made no comment.

"Secrecy is our only weapon," she continued. "It must be preserved at all costs." She paused, searching for the words to drive home her point. "How do you think he's kept his identity and his whereabouts hidden all these years?" she said at last. "We return from our missions, or we die—but we do not allow ourselves to be taken prisoner."

"Then what happened to your men on Pico Two?"

"They were taken by surprise, before they could destroy themselves." She stared at him levelly. "You look disapproving, Mr. Cain. I should think that you of all people would know that revolution is not a gentleman's sport and is not played by gentleman's rules."

"True enough," he said after some consideration. "I just don't like the thought of killing one's own people."

"I hope you don't think *he* does," replied Silent Annie. "This is a grim business. There's nothing romantic about harassing an overwhelming power with no hope of winning."

"If he knows he can't win, why does he do it?"

"To avoid losing."

"That sounds profound, but it doesn't make a hell of a lot of sense," said Cain.

"I'm sure he'll be happy to expand upon it for you."

"When?"

"Soon," she replied, deactivating the computer and heading back toward the vehicle. "Come along, Mr. Cain."

He fell into step behind her, and a moment later they were once again driving through the humid night air on a single-lane country road.

"Was he born on Safe Harbor?" asked Cain after a momentary silence.

"No."

"How long has he been here?"

"Safe Harbor has been his headquarters for about fifteen years now, though he spends about half his time off-planet."

"Have I ever seen him?" he asked, curious.

"I really couldn't say," she replied. "It's possible." She smiled. "Black Orpheus has, though he doesn't know it."

"There are a lot of things that damned folksinger doesn't know," said Cain.

"You're a very disapproving man, Mr. Cain," said Silent Annie. "Your life must have been filled with disappointments."

"No more than most," he answered. Then he smiled wryly. "On the other hand, there has been a noticeable lack of triumphs."

"Let's have no false modesty. You're a very successful bounty hunter."

"You've been watching too many video fictions," he said. "I don't call villains out to fight in the midday sun. There's nothing very challenging about walking up to a man who's never seen you before and blowing him away before he knows what you're up to."

"And is that what you did to Altair of Altair and the Jack of Diamonds?" she asked with a smile.

"No," he admitted. "I was careless in one case and clumsy in the other."

"What about Alexander the Elder? He had six men protecting him when you took him."

"Four," he corrected her.

"You're evading the point."

"I thought the point was that you were interested in me because of the people I *didn't* kill."

"That's true. But you're a man of many talents, and I'm sure Santiago can make use of all of them."

"We'll see," he said noncommittally.

They rode in silence for another half hour, the corn and wheat fields broken only by an occasional methane production plant, where the waste of Safe Harbor's farm animals was converted into energy. Finally she turned off the road and approached a row of silos.

"More spoils of conquest?" he asked as the vehicle came to a halt.

"A medical center," she replied.

"Why camouflage it?" he asked. "The Democracy has got better things to do than make raids on hospitals."

"Because Safe Harbor's population isn't large enough to support a facility of this size," explained Silent Annie. "A complex like this would draw unwanted attention to ourselves."

He got out of the vehicle and followed her into one of the silos. She led him to an elevator, and after a brief descent he found himself in a white, sterile environment some sixty feet beneath the ground.

"How big is this place?" he asked, looking down the polished corridors that radiated in all directions.

"I don't know the square footage," she replied, "but it extends beneath the entire silo complex. We have twenty-three laboratories, half a dozen observation wards, a pair of surgeries, and four isolation wards. There's also a commissary, as well as extensive staff quarters so that our people aren't seen arriving and leaving every day."

They began walking past the laboratories, each with its white-frocked medics and scientists, and finally came to the first of the observation wards Cain paused to look in through a thick, one-way glass and saw nine men and women lying in beds, plugged in to life-support and monitoring units. They reminded him of burn victims with blackened skins that blistered and peeled away from their bodies.

"What happened to them?" asked Cain, staring at an elderly woman whose cheekbones were both exposed.

"They're from Hyperion."

"Never heard of it."

"It was opened up five years ago," she said. "There were about five thousand initial settlers, all of them members of an obscure religious sect."

"They look like they believe in walking through fire," he commented.

She shook her head. "They believe in living in peace with their neighbors. In this particular case, their neighbors were a very aggressive humanoid race, and it took them almost two years to reach an accommodation—but they finally did." She paused. "Then the Democracy decided that Hyperion was strategically desirable as a military base. There were a couple of incidents involving the native population, and Hyperion was declared off limits to civilians. The colony, which had made its peace, refused to leave."

"And the navy did *this* to them?"

"Indirectly," she replied. "After the navy came to the conclusion that pacifying the native humanoids was more trouble than it was worth, they released a chemical agent in the atmosphere which killed off the entire race. It's far from the first such instance out here." She looked through the glass at the nine humans. "Unfortunately, it also caused a bacterial mutation that resulted in a virulent skin disease among the colonists. Since they had been warned to leave, the navy refuses to take responsibility for them."

"How many colonists survived?" asked Cain.

"Of the original five thousand, a little less than half of them are still alive."

"And how many of them are here?"

"Just those that you see. We haven't the room or the money to treat them all, so we brought a representative sample here to see if we could effect a cure. If we can come up with a serum or a vaccine, we'll ship it back to Hyperion with them."

"And you do this for how many worlds?"

"As many as we can."

"It must cost a small fortune to run this kind of operation," he commented.

"A *large* fortune," she corrected him. "We have four other facilities on the Inner Frontier."

"All functioning covertly?"

She nodded. "If the Democracy knew about them, they'd be that much closer to finding Santiago." She looked directly at him. "And if they find him, the people of Hyperion and a hundred other worlds of the Inner Frontier will have no place to turn."

They walked out into a corridor leading to the next ward, and Cain immediately stepped back to allow an orderly to wheel an enormous, elephantine being into one of the surgery rooms.

"What the hell was *that?*" he asked.

"A native of Castor Five," she replied.

"You work on aliens, too?"

"Her race is sentient, and it has been oppressed by the Democracy. We have no third qualification."

"You start treating all the aliens the Democracy has oppressed, and you won't be able to build enough hospitals to hold them," said Cain.

"I know," she said. "But we do what we can. It's just a gesture, but a very important one." She eyed him carefully. "Or are you of the opinion that it is Man's manifest destiny to rule the galaxy alone?"

"I never gave it much thought," he answered. "I suppose if might makes right, he's got a jump on the rest of the field."

"*Does* might make right?" she asked.

Cain shrugged. "No. But it makes it pretty difficult for anyone to tell you you're wrong."

"But not impossible," she pointed out. "And that's precisely what we're doing—by example." She stared at him again. "I hope this is making some impression on you, Mr. Cain. It's very important that you understand exactly what we're fighting for."

"It's making an impression," he said noncommittally.

"I hope so," she repeated.

They walked through the remainder of the complex in silence, then returned to the elevator.

"How many more public works do I have to see before I get to meet Santiago?" asked Cain as they ascended to the surface.

"There aren't any more," said Silent Annie. "At least, not on Safe Harbor. We don't want to do anything that might call attention to this planet."

She stepped out into the interior of a silo, and he followed her as she made her way to the vehicle. A moment later they were once again speeding across the countryside.

"How much farther?" he asked after a few minutes.

"About fifteen miles," she replied. "It's been dark for almost three hours now. Are you getting hungry?"

"I can wait."

"I can signal ahead and have dinner waiting for you when we arrive."

"It's not necessary."

"Do you still intend to kill him?" she asked suddenly.

"I don't know."

She made no further comment, and they drove the next twenty minutes in silence. Then she took a hard left turn and began driving down a bumpy dirt road. In the distance Cain could see a white pre-fabricated house with a huge veranda that seemed to circle it completely.

"That's it?" he asked.

"That's it."

"He's not very well protected," he commented. "I've only spotted three sensing devices since we turned onto this road."

"You're not supposed to see *any*."

"It's my business to see them."

She shrugged. "It's dark out. Probably some of them have escaped your attention."

"I doubt it."

"You must also remember that he has no enemies on Safe Harbor," said Silent Annie. "Except perhaps for you."

"Just the same, his security's lousy," said Cain. "That guy on the roof stands out like a sore thumb."

"What guy?"

"The one with the laser rifle. He let the moonlight glint off his infrared scope a minute ago."

"I don't see anyone," she said, peering into the darkness.

"He's there, big as life—and twice as easy a target. It's going to take more than this to keep the Angel out."

"Is that your professional opinion?"

"It is."

"I'll tell him you said so."

"I'll tell him myself," said Cain.

They pulled up to the house and climbed out of the vehicle. Silent Annie led the way to the front door, which slid back into the wall before she reached it, letting out a burst of cool dry air in the process.

Cain followed her into the foyer, which was empty, and then into the large living room. There were a number of slightly shabby, very comfortable chairs and couches arranged in little groupings, and a heatless pseudofire roared in a brick fireplace. There was also a portable bar, a large holo screen, and a trio of elegantly framed mirrors—but it was the books that overwhelmed everything else in the room. They were everywhere—stacked neatly in floor-to-ceiling cases, piled on tables, casually tossed onto window seats, spread open over chair and sofa arms, even laid out on the hearth.

The only person in the room was a man dressed in a tan lounging suit. He sat on an easy chair, reading a leather-bound book and sipping an Alphard brandy.

He appeared to be in his late forties or early fifties. His hair was brown and thinning, and had started to turn gray at the sides. His eyes, too, were brown, and stared curiously at Cain from under long, thin eyebrows that sloped gently upward, giving him a perpetually questioning look. His nose had been broken at least once, possibly many times, and his teeth were so white and straight that Cain immediately decided they weren't his own. There was an S-shaped scar on the back of his right hand.

He was a burly man who was starting to put weight on a once powerful figure, but when he stood up he did so with an athletic grace.

"I've been waiting a long time to meet you, Sebastian," he said in a deep voice.

"Not as long as *I've* been waiting to meet *you*," said Cain.

Santiago smiled. "And now that you're here, which do you propose to do—talk or shoot?"

"We'll talk first," said Cain. He looked around the living room. "You've got quite a library. I don't think I've ever seen so many books in one place before."

"I like the heft and feel of a book," replied Santiago. "Computer libraries are filled with electronic impulses. Books are filled with *words*." He patted his book fondly and tossed it onto his chair. "I've always preferred words."

"You've also got a lot of mirrors," noted Cain.

"I'm a vain man."

"Tell whoever's behind them not to get overeager. I could have taken them out the second I entered the room."

Santiago laughed. "You heard him," he said, turning to the mirrors. "Leave us alone." He turned back to Silent Annie, who had been standing quietly behind Cain. "You can leave us, too. I'll be quite safe."

"You're an optimist," said Cain as Silent Annie left the room.

"A realist," said Santiago. "If you kill me, you'll do it in such a way that you live to spend the reward." He paused. "Can I offer you some brandy?"

Cain nodded, and Santiago walked over to the bar and poured out a glass while the bounty hunter studied him.

"Here you are," said Santiago, approaching him and handing him the brandy.

"You're too young," said Cain.

"Cosmetic surgery," replied Santiago with a smile. "I told you I was a vain man."

"You're also a *wanted* man."

"Only by the Democracy," said Santiago. "Let me suggest that sometimes it's not a bad idea to judge a man by his enemies."

"In your case it's an absolute necessity," said Cain sardonically. "I've *met* your friends."

Santiago shrugged. "One works with what's at hand. If I could have enlisted better allies than Poor Yorick and Altair of Altair and the others, I assure you I would have." He paused. "In fact, that's why you're here."

"So I've been told."

"We're very much alike, Sebastian. We hold the same values, we fight against the same oppression, we even subscribe to the same methodology. I very much want you on my side."

"I've retired from the revolution business," said Cain.

"You fought for the wrong causes."

"The causes were right," said Cain. "The *men* were wrong."

"I stand corrected."

"What makes you any better than they were?"

Santiago stared at him for a moment.

"I have a proposal," he announced at last. "You've had a long, hard day, Sebastian. You've killed a man, you've seen things that no member of the Democracy has ever seen, and you've finally come face to face with the most wanted man in the galaxy. You must be hot and tired and hungry." He paused. "Let's declare a truce for tonight. We'll have dinner, we'll get to know each other a little better, and tomorrow morning, when you're feeling rested, I promise that we'll talk business—mine *and* yours."

Cain stared at him impassively, then nodded. "I think I'll skip dinner, though," he said.

"You've only had one sandwich all day."

"You're very well informed," remarked Cain.

"And *you're* worrying needlessly," said Santiago. "I've had numerous opportunities to kill you since you landed on Safe Harbor. I didn't permit you to come all this way just to poison you."

"Makes sense," admitted Cain.

Santiago led him into the dining room, which was as cluttered with books as the living room.

"I trust you'll be a little easier on my pantry than Father William," said Santiago. He shook his head wonderingly. "The way that man eats, I don't know why he isn't dead by now."

"A lot of people are wondering the same thing about you," said Cain, seating himself across from Santiago.

"A lot of people think I *am* dead," said Santiago. Suddenly he chuckled. "You wouldn't believe some of the stories they tell about me, Sebastian. I've heard that I was killed three different times last year, and that I laid waste to a little world called Silverblue out on the Galactic Rim. One story even had me assassinating some diplomat on Canphor Seven."

"You're also eleven feet tall and have orange hair," remarked Cain wryly.

"Really?" asked Santiago, interested. "I hadn't heard that one." He shrugged. "Well, I suppose that's the price of anonymity."

"I'd hardly call you anonymous," said Cain. "There are hundreds of men making full-time careers out of trying to hunt you down and kill you."

"And here I am, alive and well," said Santiago. "I'd say that's a pretty good definition of living anonymously."

"If you really want to be anonymous, why not scotch some of these myths and legends that have sprung up about you?"

"The more crimes the Democracy thinks I've committed, the more manpower they'll divert from people who can't defend themselves," he replied. "But here we are, talking business again, after I promised to let you relax."

"I don't mind," said Cain.

"We'll have ample time for it tomorrow," said Santiago. "Shall we talk about literature?"

Cain shrugged. "Whatever you like."

"Good," said Santiago as a pair of young men emerged from the kitchen and began serving them. "Have you ever read anything by Tanblixt?"

"I never heard of him."

"He's an *it*, not a *him*," said Santiago. "A Canphorite, in fact— and an absolutely brilliant poet."

"I've never been interested much in poetry," said Cain.

"Excellent soup," commented Santiago, sipping a spoonful. "Father William drinks it by the gallon."

"It's very good," agreed Cain, taking a taste.

"I've also been rereading a number of novels written in the days when we were still Earthbound," continued Santiago. "I've developed a special fondness for Dickens."

"*David Copperfield*?" suggested Cain.

"Ah!" Santiago smiled. "I *knew* you were a learned man."

"I just said I'd read it," replied Cain. "I never said I liked it."

"Then let me recommend one I've just finished: *A Tale of Two Cities*."

"Maybe I'll give it a try tomorrow," said Cain. "*If* we're still talking."

"We will be," Santiago assured him. "A few minutes ago you asked how I differed from all the other revolutionaries you've fought for. We'll discuss it in detail tomorrow, but I'll give you a hint right now, if you'd like."

"Go ahead."

"My cause was lost before I ever joined it," replied Santiago with an enigmatic smile.

Cain was still considering that remark when he got up from the dinner table and went off to discuss literature with the King of the Outlaws.

23.

He lives on a mountain, a mountain of gold,
With a temper that's hot and a heart that is cold.
He issues his orders, makes known his demands,
Then sits back to watch while his empire expands.

It wasn't a mountain of gold, of course—but it was as beautiful a farm as Cain had ever seen.

There were some 1,800 acres, divided equally between wheat, mutated corn, soybeans, and livestock, crisscrossed with streams, dotted here and there by ponds.

"Actually, the ground rolls a little too much to be truly efficient farmland," remarked Santiago as the two men sat on the veranda, looking out over the sloping fields. "It's a fact that realtors all over the galaxy have learned to appreciate: the prettier the landscape is, the harder it is to farm it effectively. Proper farmland is flat." He sighed. "But I took one look at this place and fell in love with it."

"It's restful," agreed Cain.

"It broke my heart to bulldoze the trees that were in the field. I kept the prettiest grove intact, and erected the house right next to it." Santiago pointed to a pair of nearby trees. "I have a hammock that I tie between those two," he said. "I love to lie on it, sipping an iced drink and feeling just like a proper country gentleman."

"You're an odd kind of revolutionary," remarked Cain.

"I'm fighting an odd kind of revolution," replied Santiago.

"Why?"

"Why is it odd?" asked Santiago.

"Why are you fighting it?"

"Because somebody has to."

"That's not much of a reason."

"It's the best reason there is," said Santiago. "The first duty of power is to perpetuate itself. The first duty of free men is to resist it."

"I've heard this song before," said Cain dryly.

"Ah, but it was sung by people who wanted power themselves, people who wanted to remake their worlds or even the Democracy."

"And you don't want to do that?"

"Remake the Democracy?" said Santiago. He shook his head. "The second you attain power, you become what you've been fighting against." He paused. "Besides, I'm enough of a realist to know that it can't be done. The Democracy has more ships than I've got men. It will still be abusing its power a millennium after you and I are dead."

"Then why persist?" asked Cain.

Santiago stared at him thoughtfully for a moment.

"You know, Sebastian, I have a feeling that you'd be happier if I were a gentle, white-haired old man who called everyone 'my son,' and told you that utopia was just around the corner. Well, it isn't. I persist in fighting because I see something that's wrong, and the alternative to fighting is to submit."

Cain made no comment.

"If you want a philosophic justification, you'll find it in my library," continued Santiago. "I've got a much simpler explanation."

"What is it?"

He smiled a savage smile. "When someone pushes me, I push back."

"It's a good feeling," admitted Cain. "But . . ."

"But what?"

"I'm tired of losing."

"Then join me, and fight on my side," said Santiago.

"You've already admitted you can't win."

"But that doesn't mean I have to lose." He paused. "Hell, I wouldn't want to overthrow the Democracy even if I could."

"Why not?"

"First, as I said, because I don't want to become part of the establishment that I'm fighting. And second, because the Democracy isn't truly evil, or even especially corrupt. It's simply a government that, like all governments, makes its decisions based on what will result in the greatest benefit for the greatest number. From their point of view, and given their constituency, they're a moral and ethical institution. They undoubtedly feel that they have every right to plunder the

Frontier and abrogate the rights of its citizens—and in the long run, if it strengthens their position in the galaxy, they may even be correct." He paused. "On the other hand, those of us who bear the brunt of these abuses don't have to stand idly by and hope that everything will work out for the best. We can fight back."

"How?" asked Cain, staring intently at him.

"By understanding the nature of the enemy," said Santiago. "This isn't some planetary military machine we're talking about. This is the *Democracy*. It encompasses more than a hundred thousand worlds, and it's not going to change—not overnight, not ever." He paused. "But if we harass and harry them enough, we can convince them that it's less expensive in terms of money and human life to leave us alone than to continue to oppress us." He took a deep breath and exhaled it slowly. "After all, what do we really have that's worth such an expense? We're a mass of insignificant, underpopulated worlds."

"To say nothing of disorganized," commented Cain.

"That's part of our strength."

Cain arched an eyebrow.

"You look skeptical," noted Santiago.

"I never thought lack of organization was a virtue."

"It never was before. But if we organized, if we had an army and a navy and a chain of command, the Democracy would know where to strike, and we would be decimated within a week. In fact, the nature of the enemy makes it impossible for a leader to emerge from the masses and rally men to his banner."

"Except for you."

Santiago chuckled. "I'm not a leader," he said. "I'm a lightning rod. I raid and I loot and I kill, and the Democracy wrings its hands and offers rewards for the King of the Outlaws." A satisfied smile crossed his face. "If they *knew* why I was doing this, if they had the slightest inkling what I was financing with the spoils of my conquests, they'd have fifty million men out here, scouring every inch of every world for me." He paused. "I'm good at hiding, but I'm not *that* good. I'd much rather be thought of as a successful villain than a successful revolutionary."

"*Are* you a successful revolutionary?" asked Cain.

"You were at the medical center," replied Santiago. "You've seen what we're trying to do."

"Any team of doctors could do the same thing."

"True," admitted Santiago. "But any team of doctors couldn't pay for the facility, and they certainly couldn't mine the area where the navy plans to build its base on Hyperion."

"Silent Annie says it was an accident."

"Was it also an accident that they killed off a native population of millions of sentient beings?" demanded Santiago. "That scenario has been played over and over again all across the Inner Frontier. I'm trying to convince them that there's a better way—and failing that, I'll damned well convince them that there's a less painful way."

"Is it working?"

"It depends on your point of view," answered Santiago. "Hundreds of colonies exist that would have been decimated. Tens of thousands of Men are alive who otherwise wouldn't have been. A handful of alien races who hated all Men have learned that some of us are a bit less hateful than others." He smiled. "It's a matter of proportion. I would say it's working; the Democracy would probably wonder why we had wasted so many lives and so many years to produce such insignificant results."

A man in his early thirties, with a streak of white running through his coal-black hair, emerged from the interior of the house just then and approached them.

"Yes?" said Santiago. "What is it?"

The man looked at Cain hesitantly.

"This is Sebastian Cain," said Santiago. "While he is my guest, I have no secrets from him." He turned to Cain. "Sebastian, this is Jacinto, one of my most trusted associates."

Cain nodded a greeting.

"I am pleased to meet you, Mr. Cain," said Jacinto, inclining his head slightly. He turned back to Santiago. "Winston Kchanga has refused to deliver our merchandise to us."

"I'm sorry to hear that," said Santiago, frowning. "Has he offered any reason?"

Jacinto snorted contemptuously.

"I'm afraid Mr. Kchanga has outlived his usefulness to us," said Santiago.

Jacinto nodded and went back into the house.

"I suppose I should explain."

"It's none of my business," replied Cain.

"Hopefully it will be before much longer. Winston Kchanga is a smuggler operating out of the Corvus system. He made a commitment to us, money was exchanged, and he has elected not to honor that commitment. He doesn't know that *I* am involved, but that's neither here nor there." He sighed. "Regrettable."

"Not *that* regrettable," said Cain. "There's paper on him."

"Perhaps I should clarify my statement," said Santiago. "I find it regrettable that one of the people we are fighting for should try to swindle us. I have no regrets whatsoever about ordering his death." He looked sharply at Cain. "I'm fighting a war, and whenever one fights a war there are going to be casualties. My main concern is that they aren't innocent ones."

"From what I hear, there's wasn't a hell of a lot that Kchanga was innocent of," said Cain. He paused. "There's paper on your friend Jacinto, too. He used to go under the name of Esteban Cordoba."

"Jacinto hasn't left Safe Harbor in seven years," said Santiago. "You have a remarkable memory, Sebastian."

"It's that white streak in his hair," replied Cain. "It's pretty hard to forget."

"He's the most trusted associate I have," said Santiago. "He's served me loyally for almost fifteen years." He stared at Cain again. "What do you propose to do about him?"

Cain shrugged. "Nothing."

A broad smile spread over Santiago's face. "Then you're joining us?"

"I didn't say that. We've got a lot more to talk about."

Santiago got to his feet. "Shall we walk while we talk?" he suggested. "It's too beautiful a day to just sit in the shade."

"Whatever you want."

"Then come with me, and I'll show you the farm while we speak." Cain followed Santiago down off the veranda.

"Are you a fisherman, Sebastian?" asked Santiago.

"No."

"You should try it sometime. I've stocked three of the ponds."

"Maybe someday I'll take it up."

"You should. It's very relaxing." He began circling one of the ponds. "I believe you had some questions to ask me?"

"A few," said Cain, falling into step beside him. "For starters, when did you decide you needed a bodyguard?"

"Is that what you think I have in mind for you?"

"If it isn't, then it should be," said Cain. "The Angel can't be too far away."

"I already have bodyguards."

"They couldn't stop me if I decided to kill you right now."

"True—but I know that you won't. And I have no intention of giving the Angel a tour of my farm."

"I assume that you haven't helped *him* to find you?"

Santiago frowned and shook his head. "No. He's a remarkable man."

"And as I said last night, you're a wanted one."

"He won't get past Father William."

"He's gotten past better men than Father William," said Cain.

"There *are* no better men than Father William," replied Santiago.

"If you don't want me as a bodyguard, just why *am* I here?" asked Cain.

"I've been a very fortunate man, Sebastian," said Santiago. "But nobody lives forever. I would like to think my work will go on after I'm gone. It can't do that unless I leave good people behind me— people like Jacinto and Silent Annie, and people like you."

Cain stared at him. "You *do* think he's going to kill you."

Santiago shook his head. "No, I truly don't. But I can't conscript men to my cause the way the navy can. I have to study them carefully and then try to convince the best of them to join me."

"Why now?"

"It took me this long to be sure you were the man I wanted."

"How many others have you asked?"

"Recruiting people is nothing new, Sebastian. I've been doing it ever since I came out here. You're the most recent, but you're not unique."

"How many of them have I met?"

"More than you might suppose," replied Santiago. "How else would I have known about you?"

"I know Geronimo Gentry is one of them."

"That's correct."

"What about Terwilliger?"

Santiago shook his head. "No."

"Stern?"

"No." Suddenly Santiago laughed. "I suppose I'll have to recruit him if I ever want to organize the *fali*."

"He says he met you when you were in jail on Kalami Three."

"Then I suppose he did."

"You don't match his description of you."

Santiago shrugged. "As I told you, I've had cosmetic surgery."

"Did it take four or five inches off your height?"

"That was many years ago, and Stern has been with the *fali* for a long, long time—and he was a much smaller man than you are." He looked amused. "Or are you suggesting that I'm an imposter?"

"No," said Cain. "Are you suggesting that *I* become one?"

"I don't think I follow you."

"I looked at your *Tale of Two Cities* last night," said Cain. "It occurs to me that the Angel has never seen either of us."

"And you think I want you to impersonate me if and when he arrives?"

"Do you?"

"Absolutely not. I fight my own fights." He paused. "Other than that, how did you like the book?"

"Other than that, it was pretty boring."

"I'm sorry that you didn't enjoy it."

"I had other things on my mind," said Cain. "I still do."

"Such as?"

"Such as whether or not I can believe you," replied Cain. "I've killed an awful lot of people for men I believed in, and I've always been disappointed."

"I'm not asking you to kill anyone for *me*, Sebastian," said Santiago. "That would be presumptuous. I'm asking you to help me *protect* people from the abuses of a distant government that couldn't care less about them."

"Not ten minutes ago you ordered Jacinto to kill someone for you," Cain pointed out.

"That was for the cause, not for me," answered Santiago. "Since I can't fund my operation through legitimate means, I must resort to questionable tactics. Winston Kchanga cannot be allowed to cheat us and escape punishment for his actions. If word got out that we didn't protect our interests, it wouldn't be long before the criminal element preyed upon us just as the Democracy does." He turned and began walking alongside a field containing row upon row of huge, mutated corn. "Revolution is no place for the squeamish. Surely you must understand that."

"I understand that," said Cain. "How many men will you want me to kill?"

Santiago stopped and met his gaze levelly. "I'll never ask you to kill anyone who doesn't deserve killing."

"I do that now, and I get well paid for it."

"If you come with me, you'll continue doing it. You'll get paid nothing, there will be a price on your head, and even the people you're fighting for will want you dead." Santiago smiled wryly. "That's not much to offer, is it?"

"No, it isn't."

"Then let me sweeten the pot," continued Santiago. "You'll have one benefit that you don't have in your present occupation."

"What?"

"The knowledge that you'll have made a difference."

"It would be nice to have, just once," said Cain sincerely.

"Nobody will know it but you," said Santiago.

"Nobody *has* to."

There was a momentary silence.

"What are you thinking, Sebastian?"

"That I'd like to believe you."

"Do you?"

"I haven't made up my mind." He paused in the shadow of a twelve-foot-high cornstalk. "What if I decide not to?"

"I'm unarmed, and my bodyguards are back at the house."

"I was more concerned with what *you* might do to *me*."

"We'll worry about that when the time comes."

"You'll have to kill me," said Cain. "Or try to, anyway. I know what you look like and where to find you."

"There are a few others who do, too," said Santiago. "It would make things much less complicated if you joined me, though."

They continued walking, Santiago listing his grievances against the Democracy, telling Cain of the actions he had taken and the people he had saved and failed to save. Cain listened thoughtfully, asking an occasional question, making an occasional observation.

"It's the judgment calls that age you," said Santiago as they walked alongside a stream that made a natural boundary between two of the fields. "There's an enormous amount of work to be done, and we have very little money and manpower. Do we spend it on salvation or retribution? Do we put everything we have into patching up the Democracy's victims and sending them back to be stomped on again, or do we let them lie where they've fallen and take steps to see that the same thing doesn't happen to their neighbors?"

"You prevent it from happening again," said Cain firmly.

"Answered like a bounty hunter," replied Santiago. "Unfortunately, it's easier said than done. The Epsilon Eridani raid was atypical. We don't have the firepower to stand up to the navy." He sighed. "Oh, well, that's what keeps it challenging. We do what we can, where we can. It's a balancing act—saving people when it's possible, punishing others when we can get away with it, and financing the whole thing with enterprises and associates that make the Swagman look honorable by comparison."

"How did you miss killing Whittaker Drum?" asked Cain.

"Socrates?"

"Yes."

"Because I'm not some kind of phantom avenger, righting all the wrongs of the galaxy," said Santiago. "I knew what he had done on Sylaria, even before I knew that you had fought for him." He turned to Cain and stared at him. "But that was twenty years ago, and Sylaria is thousands of light-years away. Socrates was useful to me, so I used him, just as I've used hundreds of men who are far worse than him."

He stopped and inspected an enormous ear of corn.

"Three more weeks and it'll be ready to harvest," he announced. "Four at the most. Have you ever been on a farm at harvesttime, Sebastian?"

Cain shook his head. "No, I haven't."

"There's a sense of accomplishment, of nature fulfilled and renewed," said Santiago. "Even the air smells better."

Cain smiled. "Maybe you should have been a farmer."

"I suppose I am, in a way."

"I meant full-time," said Cain. "I wasn't referring to this."

"Neither was I," replied Santiago. "Saint Peter was a fisher of men. I'm a sower of revolution." He seemed pleased with himself. "I rather like that."

They walked another quarter mile or so. The cornfields were supplanted by long rows of soybeans, which in turn dwindled into nothingness as they reached the top of a ridge.

"What's that down there?" asked Cain, pointing to a neatly manicured clearing within a small dell. There was a wooden bench facing a pond that was dotted by colorful water plants.

"My very favorite place," said Santiago, leading him over to it. "I often come here to read, or simply meditate. You can even see some of the livestock from here." He took a deep breath, as if even the air tasted better in this clearing. "I've planted some flowers, but they've already blossomed and died; they won't bloom again for another five or six months."

"Flowers aren't all you've planted," commented Cain, gesturing to two mounds of earth.

"They were two of the best men I ever knew," said Santiago quietly.

"Then why put them in unmarked graves?"

"Nobody ever comes here except me, and I know who they are," replied Santiago.

Cain shrugged, then noticed a flash of motion out of the corner of his eye. Turning, he saw a man walking toward them. The sun caught the white streak in the man's hair, and Cain realized that it was Jacinto.

"I thought I'd find you here," said Jacinto when he finally joined them. He turned to Cain. "Rain or shine, he spends a couple of hours a day here."

"It's a pretty place," said Cain.

"Are you just visiting?" asked Santiago.

Jacinto shook his head. "Father William is at the house."

"It's unusual for him to come out to the farm. I suppose he's just making sure that Sebastian hasn't killed me."

"He *did* say that he's here to talk to Mr. Cain," said Jacinto.

"He's about as subtle as an earthquake," remarked Santiago. He stepped away from the graves. "Well, I suppose we shouldn't keep him waiting."

He began walking back toward the house, and Cain and Jacinto fell into step behind him.

"Will you be staying with us for any length of time, Mr. Cain?" asked Jacinto.

"It's a possibility," replied Cain.

"I hope so. We've needed someone like you."

"We need about a thousand people like him," said Santiago. "However, we'll settle for the one we've got."

"May I ask a question that requires your professional expertise, Mr. Cain?" said Jacinto.

"Go ahead."

"What do you think of our security?"

"It stinks."

Jacinto shot a triumphant smile at Santiago. "That's what I've been trying to tell *him* for months." He turned back to Cain. "How would you change it?"

"Triple your manpower and put them on round-the-clock watches, for starters. And try to explain to them that if *they* can see in the dark, so can the Angel."

"You see?" Jacinto demanded of Santiago.

"We've been through all this before," said Santiago irritably. "I won't be a prisoner on my own planet." He increased his pace, and Cain and Jacinto lagged behind.

"I apologize for involving you in this argument," said Jacinto softly. "But he simply will not bring any more men back to Safe Harbor."

"How many has he got here?" asked Cain.

"You mean on the planet?"

"Not counting doctors and technicians and the like."

"Perhaps fifty."

"And on the farm?"

"Fifteen, counting myself."

"That won't stop the Angel."

"I know. Hopefully you will be all that we need."

"I haven't said I'm staying."

"Then perhaps Father William . . ."

"I doubt it." Cain paused. "By the way, there's one other bit of professional advice I can give you."

"Yes?"

"If you ever leave Safe Harbor, dye your hair."

Jacinto looked surprised. "I will," he said. "Thank you."

They caught up with Santiago shortly thereafter, and the three men walked the remaining distance to the house together, Santiago pointing out various facets of the farm to Cain as they passed them. Father William was waiting for them on the veranda.

"Good morning, Santiago," said the preacher. "Jacinto." He turned to Cain. "Hello again, Sebastian. Have you enjoyed your stay?"

"It's been interesting," replied Cain.

"Are you getting along well with your host?" he asked sharply.

"So far."

"I'm glad to hear it."

"I was sure you would be."

"I understand you want to talk to Sebastian," said Santiago. "If you wish, we'll leave you two alone."

"That won't be necessary," said Father William with a curious smile. "Actually, I'm just here to deliver a message from a new arrival."

"The Angel?" asked Cain, suddenly tense.

Santiago shook his head. "He's out by the Cantrell system."

"Who is it, then?" persisted Cain.

"Why don't you just read this?" said Father William, handing him a folded sheet of very expensive stationery.

Cain saw that it was written in an elegant, near calligraphic script, and read it aloud:

> *"The Jolly Swagman sends Greetings and Felicitations to his Partner, Sebastian Cain, and cordially invites him to the Barleycorn Tavern for aperitifs at four this afternoon, at which time they will renew their Friendship and also discuss certain Matters of Business."*

Cain tossed the note onto a table. "That's the Swagman, all right," he said.

"Silent Annie urged me to kill him while I had the chance," said Santiago. "I think she may have been right."

"Is there any reply?" asked Father William, still amused.

"I'll deliver it in person," said Cain grimly.

24.

He robs and he plunders, he kills and he loots,
He stealthily sneaks up and suddenly shoots.
He never forgets and he never forgives;
He never relents while an enemy lives.

One of the things Black Orpheus never understood was why the Jolly Swagman, who was his friend, refused to give him any information about Santiago, denying him even a physical description. He was sure the Swagman knew Santiago, had overheard two of his associates say as much, but that was the one subject upon which the loquacious criminal refused to speak.

It made a lot more sense from the Swagman's point of view. What nobody understood about him, not Orpheus, not even Father William or Virtue MacKenzie, was that money was just a tool, a means to an end—and that end was his collection of alien artwork. He kept his own counsel about Santiago not out of any loyalty or friendship for him, but simply because Santiago alive and free was plunderable, if he could just come up with a method, whereas Santiago captured and incarcerated was the property of the Democracy, as were all his possessions.

The third alternative was Santiago dead, and that was what he had come to Safe Harbor to discuss.

He sat in the tavern, sipping an iced mixture of exotic liqueurs from Antares and Ranchero, a small alien puzzle-game in his hand. He manipulated the oddly shaped pieces with a sureness that came from long hours of practice, looking up every now and then to admire

Moonripple's face and figure—what he could distinguish of them beneath her unkempt hair and the ragged clothing.

Finally he tired of the puzzle, put it back in the pocket of his elegantly tailored satin tunic, pulled out a small, transparent cube from another pocket, and spent the next few minutes admiring the tiny blue-and-white beetlelike insect, crusted with jewels, that resided there.

He had just put it away when Cain and Father William entered the tavern and approached him.

"Good afternoon, Sebastian," said the Swagman with a friendly smile. "I see you got my message."

Cain sat down opposite him. "What the hell are you doing here?"

"In a moment," said the Swagman, holding up his hand. "First I have a gift for your chauffeur."

"I assume you're referring to me," said Father William, amused.

"That I am. Moonripple!"

"Yes, sir?"

"Father William's present, if you please."

She went into the kitchen and emerged a moment later carrying an enormous tray, which contained a large roasted waterfowl in a cream sauce. It was surrounded by dumplings and potatoes.

"Where shall I put it, sir?" asked Moonripple.

"As far from this table as possible." He smiled apologetically at Father William, who was eyeing the waterfowl greedily. "I'd like to speak to my partner privately. This will give you something to do with your mouth."

"I'm not even going to take offense at that remark, given the magnitude of this thoroughly Christian gesture," said Father William, rubbing his hands together and walking over to the table where Moonripple had placed the tray. He signaled to the girl. "I think I'm going to need a pitcher of beer to wash this down, my child." She began to protest, but he held up a finger for silence. "I know what we discussed last night, but God understands that the flesh is weak. I'll begin my diet next Monday."

"For sure this time?"

"Unless Providence intervenes."

She looked her disbelief but brought him his beer, and a moment later he was attacking his dinner, oblivious to the rest of the universe.

"It's good to see you again, Sebastian," said the Swagman, lowering his voice just enough so that it wouldn't carry across the room.

"I wish I could say the same," responded Cain. "What are you doing here?"

"Simple. You followed a smuggling trail and the Angel followed a paper trail." He grinned. "I decided to follow the easiest trail of all—bounty hunters."

"There are a lot of worlds with more bounty hunters than this one."

"True," admitted the Swagman. "But they don't have you and Father William on them. You killed a man yesterday, but you didn't leave—and Father William has been here for more than a month."

"Santiago's not here," said Cain.

"Allow me the courtesy of asking if he is, before you start lying to me," said the Swagman. He paused. "If he *isn't* on Safe Harbor, Orpheus must be having a reunion of all the killers he's ever written up. You know that the Angel's on his way here, don't you?"

"How close is he?" asked Cain.

"Two or three days away," replied the Swagman. "And he's got another of your partners with him."

"Virtue or Terwilliger?" asked Cain.

"Hadn't you heard? Terwilliger, alas, has gone to that great gambling parlor in the sky."

"Who killed him—the Angel?"

The Swagman shook his head. "ManMountain Bates finally caught up with him."

Cain shrugged. "He shouldn't have cheated him."

"I knew you'd be heartbroken," said the Swagman with a chuckle. "If it'll make you feel any better, the Angel avenged his death."

Cain frowned. "There wasn't any paper on Bates."

"I guess the Angel must be one of nature's noblemen," commented the Swagman. "He gives work to incompetent journalists and he avenges crooked gamblers." He scrutinized Cain from beneath half-lowered lids. "Have you met any similarly public-minded citizens lately?"

"Who did you have in mind?" asked Cain expressionlessly.

"You know who," said the Swagman. "Has he enlisted you in the Great Crusade yet?"

"I don't know what you're talking about."

"If you play the fool, Sebastian, we're never going to get anywhere. I know he's here, and I can't believe that you've been on this world for two days without finding him."

Cain stared at the Swagman for a long moment.

"I found him," he said at last.

"And of course you didn't kill him."

"No, I didn't."

The Swagman smiled. "I knew you wouldn't. So did Yorick." He shook his head. "I would have thought you'd have gotten all that idealism out of your system after getting the hell pounded out of you in your impetuous youth."

"I thought so, too," admitted Cain.

"There's no drunk like an old one," said the Swagman. He signaled to Moonripple, who had just brought Father William a pan of hot biscuits. "A refill, if you please."

"Yes, sir." She looked at Cain. "Will there be anything for you, sir?"

"Maybe a change in company."

"I beg your pardon?"

He sighed. "I'll have a beer."

"Right away, sir."

"I can't imagine what Orpheus saw in her," commented the Swagman as he watched Moonripple walk to the bar.

"No, I don't suppose you can," said Cain.

The Swagman smiled. "I have a feeling that I've just been insulted."

Cain stared at him and made no reply.

"By the way," continued the Swagman, "I didn't see Schussler on my way into town."

"He's dead."

"That was stupid, Sebastian. You receive an absolutely free spaceship with an enormous bank of interesting information, and you destroy it? How wasteful."

"I gave him my word."

"I sincerely doubt that a promise given to a machine is legally binding."

"All the more reason for keeping it," said Cain.

"You're sounding more like him every day," said the Swagman, amused.

"Like Schussler?" asked Cain, puzzled.

"No. Like *him*."

Moonripple arrived with their drinks.

"I want to thank you once again for saving my life, sir," she said to Cain.

"I was happy to do it," he replied.

"I hope Silent Annie was able to help you."

He nodded.

She smiled. "I'm glad. That means I've done something good for you, too."

"Yes, you have."

She smiled again and went back into the kitchen to work on Father William's dessert.

"That's a very touching mutual admiration society you two have going," commented the Swagman.

"If you say so."

"If *I* save her life, will she take *me* to see Santiago, too?"

"I very much doubt it."

"What commitment have you made to him?"

"None, as yet."

"But you will?" he persisted.

"Perhaps."

The Swagman grimaced and shook his head sadly. "Stupid. Just plain stupid."

"Then I suggest you don't join him," said Cain dryly.

"The man is sitting on the biggest collection of artwork on the Frontier!" said the Swagman in exasperation. "And nobody seems to care about it except me!"

"He's also sitting on the biggest collection of bluefever vaccine," answered Cain calmly.

"Who the hell cares about vaccine?" demanded the Swagman. "We're talking about irreplaceable objects of art!"

"Talk about them a little more softly," said Father William from across the room. "You're spoiling my digestion."

"You're a bigger fool than *he* is," said the Swagman, lowering his voice and nodding his head toward Father William. "At least he thinks he's serving the Lord."

"Maybe he is," said Cain.

"You're in danger of becoming a bore, Sebastian," said the Swagman distastefully. "A newfound sense of purpose is one thing; a newfound religious conviction is another."

Cain stared across the table at him. "Just what the hell is it that you want, Swagman?"

"You know perfectly well what I want."

"You'll have to get it yourself."

"Nonsense. We're partners."

"Our partnership is dissolved."

"That doesn't change a thing," said the Swagman.

"Oh? Just how do you figure that?"

The Swagman leaned forward. "Santiago is a dead man, Sebastian. If you don't kill him, the Angel will. It's as simple as that." He withdrew the cube from his pocket and began examining the jewel-encrusted beetle again. "Why let *him* pick up the reward for doing what you can do right now?"

"He won't."

The Swagman smiled. "Who's going to stop him—Father William?" He chuckled. "Killing run-of-the-mill sinners is one thing; killing the Angel is another." He stared intently at Cain. "Or do you think that *you're* going to stop him?"

"It's a possibility."

The Swagman snorted contemptuously. "You haven't got a chance."

"I didn't have a chance against Altair of Altair, either."

"This is different," said the Swagman earnestly. "He's the *Angel*."

"I'm getting tired of hearing about him," said Cain.

"You're going to get a lot more tired of it when everyone starts talking about how he killed Santiago."

"Santiago has stayed hidden for the past three decades," Cain pointed out. "He strikes me as a man who can take care of himself."

"What are you talking about?" demanded the Swagman. "Do you think you're the first bounty hunter to set foot on Safe Harbor?"

Cain shook his head. "Peacemaker MacDougal was here four months ago. He killed Billy Three-Eyes right in front of this tavern." He smiled grimly. "But of course you knew that, didn't you?"

"I'm not talking about Peacemaker MacDougal!" snapped the Swagman. "Hell, half a dozen bounty hunters have gotten this far. Two of them even made it out to his farm."

"What farm?" asked Cain innocently.

"The goddamned farm where Father William gave you my note," said the Swagman, holding the cube up to the light. "I told you: I'm not totally without resources."

"You didn't even know he lived on Safe Harbor when I left you two weeks ago," said Cain, unimpressed.

"Not until yesterday," admitted the Swagman. "But I knew that he lived on a farm, and I knew that he buried the two bounty hunters who found him out there in one of his wheat fields. I just didn't know where the farm was."

"Who told you that?"

"Someone who worked for him and saw the graves."

"That bespeaks a certain ability to defend himself, doesn't it?"

"If ordinary bounty hunters could get that close, the Angel will kill him," said the Swagman. He paused. "Unless you kill him first."

"Not interested," said Cain.

The Swagman smiled. "You haven't let me make my offer yet."

"Make it and then leave me alone."

"Half," said the Swagman with a confident grin.

"Half of what?"

"Half of the artwork. You keep all the reward and we split the artwork fifty-fifty."

"Stop playing with that damned beetle and go away," said Cain.

"Do you realize what I'm offering you?" asked the Swagman, putting the cube back in his pocket.

Cain nodded. "Do *you* realize that I'm rejecting your offer?"

"You're crazy!" snapped the Swagman. "Even after I take the pieces I want, the rest of it is worth millions on the black market!"

"Maybe I'm just not an art collector."

"You've made a very foolish career decision, Sebastian."

"Is that a threat?" asked Cain.

The Swagman shook his head. "Just a prediction."

"All right. You've made your offer, I've turned it down. Now what?"

"Now we wait."

"For what?"

"For you to change your mind."

"I'm not going to," said Cain.

"Then we wait for the Angel to kill Santiago."

"*He* won't deal with you, either."

"Probably not," agreed the Swagman. "But he also won't know where the artwork is, and I've got as good a chance of finding it as he does."

"Then why make an offer to me at all?" asked Cain, puzzled.

"Because you're a reasonable man, and we've already got a partnership agreement, whether you choose to acknowledge that fact or not. The Angel might take a different view of my confiscating the artwork."

"Then let me set your mind to rest," said Cain seriously. "If you try to take anything that belongs to Santiago, whether he's alive or dead, I'll kill you myself."

The Swagman stared at him. "He *has* made an impression on you, hasn't he?" he said, amused.

"You heard what I said."

The Swagman sighed. "Then I guess I'll just have to check into the boarding house where Father William is staying and await developments."

"Like a scavenger waiting around a kill," commented Cain distastefully.

"An apt comparison," agreed the Swagman with no show of anger. "You'd be surprised how few scavengers die hungry when they follow the right predators."

Cain turned to Father William, who had finished his fowl and was just in the process of polishing off the various side dishes with great enthusiasm.

"We're through talking, if you'd like to join us now," he said in his normal voice.

"Or you could continue to pretend you weren't listening," said the Swagman.

Father William looked across the room and smiled.

"*I* was eating. *God* was listening." The preacher spent another moment sopping up the last of the cream sauce with a piece of a biscuit, then walked over to join them. "Did you conclude your business?"

"We agreed to disagree," said the Swagman.

"Are you planning to leave today, or are you going to blacken your immortal soul still further?" asked Father William.

"Oh, I think I'll stay around for a few days." The Swagman suddenly grinned. "Nice place for a vacation."

"Much as I like you, Swagman, if you lift a finger against Santiago, I'll hunt you down like an animal," said Father William.

The Swagman chuckled. "You'll have to stand in line. Everyone seems to have become terribly single-minded."

"Just remember: there's paper on you."

"But not for murder," said the Swagman.

"Don't count on that saving your sinful scalp," said the preacher. "You wouldn't be the first man who got killed for resisting arrest."

"Arrest?" repeated the Swagman with a laugh. "Since when did you become a minion of the law?"

"What do you think bounty hunters are?" demanded Father William. "Out here on the Frontier, we're all the law there is. We may not keep the peace, but we punish the lawbreakers—and even that leads to a proper respect for the law after a time."

"I never looked at it that way," admitted the Swagman. "Still, I suppose there's some truth to it."

"More than you know, Swagman," said Father William seriously. "I suggest that you keep it in mind."

"Maybe you'd better tell my partner here," said the Swagman. "He's thinking of helping a wanted criminal."

"You know," said the preacher, "it might be best for all parties concerned if you just went back to Goldenrod and admired your ill-gotten gains."

"I thought it might be more fruitful to try to add to them."

"The only reason you're still alive is because *he* hasn't told me to kill you yet," continued Father William. "This is his world, and you're trespassing."

"I'll try not to lose any sleep worrying about it," said the Swagman.

"Maybe you'd better *start* worrying about it," suggested Cain.

"Kill me, and *Santiago* had better start worrying," retorted the Swagman confidently. "If I don't report in to Goldenrod every day, one of my robots will tell my menials where I am."

"They won't care," said Cain.

"They will when the robot informs them that this is Santiago's world." The Swagman grinned. "You don't really think I'd come here without taking some precautions, do you?"

"I've seen your menials," said Father William. "They're not much."

"But they talk incessantly," replied the Swagman. "You know, for years I've been trying to figure out how to get them to keep a secret. Now I'm glad that I never found an answer."

Father William and Cain exchanged glances.

"All right," said the preacher after some consideration. "You can stay."

"How hospitable of you," said the Swagman ironically.

"But you'd better be on your ship five minutes after we kill the Angel, or you're a dead man." He paused. "Santiago wasn't born on Safe Harbor; he doesn't have to live out his life here, either. If I were you, I'd keep that in mind before I did anything rash."

"Well," said the Swagman, getting to his feet. "I hate to drink and run, but I think I'd better arrange for my accommodations." He turned to Cain. "Once you've calmed down, I trust that you'll reconsider my offer."

"I wasn't excited the first time I heard it," said Cain.

"Think about it," urged the Swagman, walking to the doorway. "Fifty percent."

"Go away," said Cain, turning his back on him.

The Swagman shrugged and walked out the door.

"Well, Sebastian," said Father William, leaning back on his chair, "I must say that I'm proud of you."

"Oh?"

"You looked into the face of the enemy and didn't blink."

"*He's* not the enemy," said Cain. "He's what you're fighting to protect."

"A sobering thought," admitted Father William with a grim smile.

"How much worse can the Democracy be?" mused Cain.

"It's not how much worse," replied the preacher. "It's how much more powerful—and hence, how much more capacity for harm?"

Cain nodded. "I know."

"Things aren't as clear-cut as they were when you were a young man, are they?" chuckled Father William.

"No, they're not."

"It's easy to decide to remake a world," said the preacher. "It's more difficult to choose between evils."

Cain sighed. "It is that," he agreed. He paused. "How did *you* meet him?"

"Santiago?"

"Yes."

"He recruited me, just like he recruited you."

"You knew that was why I was here, didn't you?" asked Cain.

Father William nodded. "I knew almost a year ago that he had decided he wanted you." He chuckled again. "I'll confess I had my doubts when I learned that you were hooked up with the Swagman and that young woman."

"Virtue?"

"That's the one."

"She's an interesting lady," said Cain. "Sometimes I have the feeling that she's going to come out of this better off than anybody."

"She knows how to get what she wants. I'll grant her that," said the preacher.

"And now she's got the Angel," said Cain.

"I have a feeling that she's going to learn that he's a little *more* than she wants," said Father William, not without a note of satisfaction.

"Tell me something," said Cain.

"If I can."

"Who's buried in those two graves?"

"Two men who gave their lives to Santiago's cause."

"The Swagman said they were bounty hunters."

"Once upon a time they may have been. I really couldn't say."

"He told me they were after Santiago, and they made it all the way out to the farm before they were killed."

"The Swagman's wrong," said Father William firmly.

"What were their names?"

Father William shrugged. "Who knows? Nobody uses their real

names out here—and especially not if they work for Santiago." He paused. "Why are you so curious about them?"

"Inconsistencies bother me."

"Then don't talk to the Swagman. He's never seen the farm in his life. Santiago has no reason to lie to you; the Swagman has no reason to tell you the truth." He leaned forward. "What did he offer you?"

"Half of the artwork."

"That's very generous," said the preacher. "I wonder how he planned to cheat you out of it?"

"I'm sure he's given it considerable thought," said Cain.

Moonripple emerged from the kitchen and approached Father William.

"How soon will you be wanting your dessert, sir?" she asked.

"Right now," said Father William. "Will you join me, Sebastian?"

"Why not?" said Cain.

"You're sure?" asked Father William, surprised.

"I could use a little snack."

Father William looked as if his heart was about to break. Finally he turned to Moonripple. "My child, how long will it take you to cook up another chocolate cake?"

"I have three more in the kitchen, sir," she replied.

"Good. Bring two of them out here." He turned to Cain. "That way neither of us will leave the table hungry."

"Moonripple's right, you know," said Cain.

"About what?"

"You're going to eat yourself to death."

"I need energy for the work ahead," answered Father William seriously.

Cain shrugged. "It's your life."

"No, Sebastian. It belongs to the Lord, just as yours belongs to Santiago now."

"What makes you think it does?" asked Cain.

"I don't think so," replied the preacher. "I know so."

"I don't know any such thing."

"Yes, you do. Sebastian," said Father William. "He chooses his recruits very carefully, and he's never been wrong about one yet. You could have killed him last night or this morning and cashed the biggest reward you ever dreamed about; you didn't. You could have dealt with the Swagman just now: you didn't." His booming voice became almost gentle. "Your mind may be undecided, but your heart knows where you stand."

Cain looked momentarily surprised.

"I suppose it does, at that," he said thoughtfully.

25.

A riddle inside an enigma,
Wrapped up in a puzzle or two.
What man fits these specifications?
The King of the Outlaws—that's who!

"How did your meeting with the Swagman go?" asked Santiago, looking up from his book as Cain joined him on the veranda.

"About as expected."

Santiago seemed amused. "He was that obvious?"

"He was that hungry," replied Cain.

"By the way," said Santiago, "I sent one of my men to Silent Annie's house for your belongings. I hope you don't mind."

"It's all right," said Cain, sitting down and looking out over the vast expanse of farmland. "I'll be staying."

"I'm delighted to hear it."

"You knew it all along."

"Yes, I did," admitted Santiago. "But I'm glad that you know it, too. We can use you, Sebastian."

"Sooner than you think," replied Cain. "The Swagman says that the Angel will be here in two or three more days." He paused. "It might be a good time to select a target and go off on a raid."

"Somewhere far away?" asked Santiago with a smile.

"The farther the better."

"I thank you for the thought, Sebastian, but Safe Harbor is my home. I don't propose to run away from it at the first sign of danger."

316 *Legends of Santiago*

"*Is* it the first sign?" asked Cain. "The Swagman told me that half a dozen bounty hunters had made it this far."

"He was wrong," said Santiago. "The actual number is four—and if I didn't run from them, you may rest assured that I won't run from the Angel. Besides," he added, "would you want to serve a leader who flees from his enemies?"

"I don't suppose it's any worse than serving a leader who's got a death wish," said Cain seriously.

"Believe me, Sebastian—it will take more than the Angel to kill Santiago." He gazed at the horizon and sighed contentedly. "Look at that sunset. Isn't it glorious?"

"If you say so."

"I do." Santiago turned to Cain. "I assume the Swagman is staying on Safe Harbor?"

Cain nodded.

Santiago chuckled. "He's not as inspiring as the sunset, but he's every bit as predictable. What did he offer you to kill me—a third of his profits in addition to the reward?"

"Half."

Santiago looked amused. "Well, why not? He doesn't intend to pay you anyway."

"I know," replied Cain. He paused. "How did you ever get mixed up with him in the first place?"

"The same way you did, I suspect. He had something that I needed."

"What?"

"Certain business contacts."

"And he asked to join your organization in exchange for them?"

Santiago shook his head. "That was *my* idea."

"Why?" asked Cain, puzzled.

"Some men have a lean and hungry look about them," replied Santiago. "If you're going to have any dealings with them, it makes sense to put them where you can keep an eye on them."

Cain smiled ironically. "If that's your criterion for employment, I'm surprised you don't have a standing army of ten million."

"If there were ten million Swagmen out there who could help me accomplish my goals, rest assured that I would hire them all," said Santiago. "However, it has been my experience that truly competent criminals are almost as rare as truly competent heroes." He stood up suddenly. "But where are my manners? Here it is evening, and you haven't eaten yet. Come into the house."

Cain stood up and followed him inside. "I'm not really hungry," he said. "Watching Father William demolish a ten-pound bird can kill anyone's appetite." He grimaced. "I'm surprised he left the bones."

Santiago laughed. "I know the feeling." He paused. "Well, at least let me offer you a drink to celebrate your joining us."

Cain nodded his assent, and they walked to the living room, where Jacinto was sitting on a couch, reading one of Santiago's books.

"Have you heard the news?" Santiago asked him. "Sebastian has decided to stay with us."

"I know," replied Jacinto. "Father William told me when he dropped him off a few minutes ago."

Santiago walked over to his bar and studied the array of bottles. "Something special," he muttered, half to himself. Suddenly his face lit up. "Ah! The very thing." He reached up and grabbed a bottle. "Korbellian whiskey," he said, displaying the label. "It's made from a plant very similar to barley that they have growing up the sides of their mountains. There's nothing else quite like it." He poured out three glasses and began passing them around. "What do you think of it?" he asked as Cain took a tentative sip.

"Unusual," replied Cain. He took another taste. "Interesting, though. I think I like it."

"You *think* you like it?" laughed Santiago. "Sebastian, you've been on the Frontier too long."

Cain downed his drink and held out his glass for a refill. "I'll need another to make up my mind."

"Happy to," said Santiago, filling his glass again. "But be careful. It packs quite a wallop."

Cain finished the second, and suddenly, for the first time in years, felt a little light-headed. "I see what you mean." He grinned. "I think I'd better quit while I'm ahead."

"Good," said Santiago. "I like a man who knows his own limitations."

"Maybe you should suggest that to Father William the next time he comes to dinner," said Jacinto sardonically.

"As far as his capacity to put away food is concerned, the man *has* no limitations that I've been able to discern," replied Santiago. He shrugged. "Well, I suppose bounty hunters, like revolutionaries, come in all shapes and sizes."

"I suspect that his size gives him an added advantage," said Jacinto.

"Oh?" asked Cain, interested. "What is it?"

"He looks like he's too slow and fat to draw those laser pistols of his. It breeds overconfidence in the enemy."

"I doubt it," said Cain. "What you have to remember is that any man who carries a gun out here is undefeated. You can't afford to get overconfident in this business."

"That's probably why you're still alive when so many men who view things differently are dead," said Santiago.

"Perhaps."

"Have you another explanation?" asked Jacinto.

"When I was a very young man I wasn't afraid of death, and that gave me an advantage over the men I fought. As the years went by, I realized that there was nothing fair or reasonable about death, that it could come to anyone, so I became very careful; that gives me an advantage of a different kind."

"Which you've used with remarkable success," interjected Santiago. "I suppose all good bounty hunters do."

"There *are* no bad bounty hunters," replied Cain. "Just good ones and dead ones."

"Why did you become a bounty hunter in the first place?" asked Jacinto.

"When I realized that I wasn't going to make the galaxy a better place to live in in one bold stroke, I decided to try doing it one small step at a time."

"Have you ever regretted it?"

"Not really," replied Cain. "We all make choices; most of us get pretty much what we deserve." He paused thoughtfully. "I used to think, years ago, that someday I'd like to settle down. I was always going to find the right woman when I got a little spare time." He smiled ruefully. "I never even began looking for her." He shrugged. "I suppose if it had meant more to me, I would have."

Santiago nodded knowingly. "With me it was children. I'd been an only child, and a very lonely one at that. I always wanted a house filled with kids." He chuckled ironically. "So now I have one filled with killers and smugglers. Every now and then I stop and wonder how the hell it happened."

"People don't come out to the Frontier to raise families," said Cain.

"Unless they're colonists," agreed Santiago. "Or shopkeepers. Or merchants. Or farmers." He sighed ironically. "Or anyone but us."

"It's just as well," said Jacinto. "None of us expects to die of old age."

Santiago turned to Cain. "Second-guessing himself is not one of Jacinto's strong points." He smiled. "As for dying of old age, I personally plan to live forever. There's too much work yet to do to worry about dying."

"Then don't take foolish chances," replied Cain.

"You're referring to the Angel again?"

Cain nodded.

Santiago sighed. "How can I ask my supporters to risk their lives if I'm not willing to do the same thing?" he said seriously.

"The operative word was *foolish*," said Cain.

"He can't run from the Angel," said Jacinto.

Cain turned to him. "I thought you were the one who wanted to tighten his security."

"I still do," replied Jacinto. "But if word gets out that Santiago can be frightened off, then before long everyone we deal with will be surrounding themselves with killers and refusing to honor their commitments to us." He paused. "We don't do business with honorable men, Mr. Cain. It is their fear of Santiago that keeps them in line, nothing more."

"It's probably all for the best that you don't have children," remarked Cain ironically. "Being the most feared man on the Frontier isn't much of a legacy to leave them."

"It *would* be more satisfying to lead my troops into glorious battle," agreed Santiago. "Unfortunately, that's not the kind of war we're fighting—and my troops, for the most part, are a bunch of misfits, reprobates, and criminals who don't even know they're involved in financing a revolution."

"How often do you deal with them directly?" asked Cain.

"Very seldom. Things seem to work much more smoothly when they think I'm some kind of unapproachable demigod. Even in this day and age there's a considerable amount of primal mysticism in the human soul; it would be foolish not to capitalize on it." He paused. "This doesn't mean that I don't take a very personal interest in my operation. I'm away from Safe Harbor about half the time—but since only a handful of people know what I look like, I can usually check up on my employees without any danger of disclosure."

"No one's ever suspected you?"

"Let's say that no one's ever been so bold as to voice their suspicions to my face," replied Santiago with a satisfied smile. "Every now and then I let them know—always well after the fact—that they've been in my presence without being aware of it; it helps to convince them that I'm a mysterious criminal kingpin from whom nothing can be kept hidden." He paused. "I would say that takes up most of my time abroad."

"And the rest of it?"

"I do have other business to conduct," answered Santiago. "I search for potential recruits, look for weak spots in the Democracy's defenses, and try to determine which worlds can best use our money and our manpower."

"Always without their knowledge, of course," added Jacinto. "If we let them know, then the Democracy would realize what Santiago really is."

"So it's like a chess game," said Cain. "Move and countermove."

"I really couldn't say," said Santiago. "I've never played chess."

"Never?" asked Cain sharply.

"Never," replied Santiago. "You say it like I've committed some kind of sin."

"I apologize," said Cain. "I was just surprised."

"No offense taken," said Santiago. He paused. "You're sure I can't offer you some dinner?"

"In a little while, perhaps."

"Or another drink?"

Cain shook his head. "No, thanks. I'd like to ask you a question."

"Go right ahead."

"Were you ever in jail on Kalami Three?"

"I think if you'll go there and check the records, you won't find any mention of me," replied Santiago.

"That isn't what I asked."

Suddenly Santiago grinned. "I've got it!" he announced. "Stern told you that I played chess with him!"

"Did you?"

"I've already told you: I don't play chess."

"Why would he have said you did?"

"Probably to embellish a story for which he was receiving a considerable amount of money."

"But you *were* imprisoned on Kalami Three?"

"For a very brief period. My memory of Stern is that he bragged about the men he'd swindled and killed, and kept relating grandiose schemes about how he intended to find a solar system of his own to rule. It seems to me that we played cards until one of the prison attendants took away his deck." Santiago smiled. "As I recall, he still owes me money from that game." He looked at Cain. "Were there any other questions you wanted to ask?"

"Just two."

"Ask away."

"First, now that I've joined you, there's no sense keeping me here on Safe Harbor once we've taken care of the Angel. What will you be wanting me to do next?"

"To tell you the truth, I haven't decided," replied Santiago seriously. "There's the little matter of getting our money back from the late Mr. Kchanga's heirs. The sooner we do it, the sooner we can purchase food and ship it to Bortai."

"Bortai?" asked Cain.

"A mining world about two hundred light-years from Bella Donna," replied Santiago. "They've only got a three-week supply of food remaining."

"Can't they import more?"

Santiago shook his head. "The Democracy's tied up their funds."

"Why?"

"Because a month ago they sold two hundred tons of iron ore—perhaps a week's output, certainly no more than that—to a pair of alien worlds that have refused to join the Democracy's economic network. This is the Democracy's way of telling them never to do so again." A savage expression crossed his face. "In the meantime, more than a hundred and fifty human children stand an excellent chance of starving to death."

"When do I leave?"

"*If* you leave, it will be in about a week," answered Santiago. "We'll give Kchanga's associates every opportunity to honor his commitment first."

"That's cutting it awfully close," said Cain. "Once I get the money, you'll still have to buy and ship the food."

"I know. As I told you before, it's a balancing act. It's worth the delay if we can find someone in Kchanga's organization that we'll be able to deal with in the future. And if not," he added with a quiet ferocity, "we'll show them what it means to play fast and loose with Santiago."

"And if they *do* come up with the money?"

"What do you think, Jacinto?" asked Santiago.

"Zeta Piscium," answered Jacinto promptly.

Santiago shook his head. "Too risky."

"What about Zeta Piscium?" asked Cain.

Santiago studied the bounty hunter for a long moment, and then began speaking. "The navy has a large base on the fourth planet of the Zeta Piscium system. We have a number of reports on it somewhere." He paused. "All their supplies for the entire Quartermaine Sector are purchased through the Zeta Piscium office and routed through the supply base there."

"And?"

"If someone were to destroy their computer system, it would be months before they could bring their records up to date," explained Jacinto. "Arms shipments couldn't be forwarded, payrolls couldn't be processed, they couldn't purchase so much as a cup of coffee until their accounting department was able to determine how much money was in their various accounts." He paused. "We would have to lay the blame elsewhere, of course; Santiago is a criminal, but he cannot be perceived to be a revolutionary."

"Everyone knows he was responsible for the Epsilon Eridani raid," Cain pointed out.

"But that was a gold robbery," explained Jacinto with a smile. "He was merely a cunning criminal who robbed the navy of its bullion." He paused. "But no conceivable profit will accrue from destroying the computer complex at Zeta Piscium Four. Therefore, he can't be associated with it."

"What's their security like?" asked Cain.

"Very tight," said Santiago. "That's why I'm not inclined to try it, despite Jacinto's enthusiasm."

"But think of the lives we'll be saving if we can disrupt their system for even two months!" urged Jacinto.

Santiago stared at him. "I appreciate your arguments, but passionate advocacy is no excuse for rashness. The odds are hundreds to one against success."

"But—"

"We can't join *every* battle," interrupted Santiago. "Our purpose is to perform meaningful actions, not to die with poetic futility. The subject is closed." He turned back to Cain. "You had a second question, Sebastian?"

"It's not quite of the same magnitude," said Cain apologetically.

"Good. One question of that magnitude is all I really care to discuss before dinner. What was it that you wished to know?"

"I was curious about that scar on your hand."

Santiago held up his right hand, staring at the S-shaped scar on it. "I wish there was a heroic story to go along with it, but the simple truth is that I caught it on a fishhook when I was a small boy."

"I would have guessed that it was a knife wound."

Santiago chuckled. "Nothing so exciting. Shall we adjourn to the dining room now?"

"I haven't asked my question yet."

Santiago looked puzzled. "I beg your pardon. What, exactly, did you wish to know about it?"

"Why do you still have it?" asked Cain. "It's the only physical feature of yours that seems to be known beyond Safe Harbor. Why didn't you get rid of it when you underwent your cosmetic surgery?"

Santiago stared at his hand for another moment, then laughed. "I'll be damned if I know," he replied. "It's been a part of me for so long that I never even mentioned it to the surgeon."

"I hope you wear gloves when you're traveling incognito," said Cain.

"I always do. I was born in the Democracy; my fingerprints are on file there somewhere. I wear contact lenses that distort my retina pattern for the same reason." He rose to his feet. "Shall we eat now?"

They went off to the dining room and spent the rest of the evening talking about Santiago's immediate and long-range plans for the future. Cain went to bed with another book—Tanblixt's poetry, which he found totally incomprehensible—and continued his discussion with Santiago and Jacinto the next day, his enthusiasm for their enterprise growing by the hour.

Then, just before sunset, Virtue MacKenzie showed up on Santiago's doorstep, and all of the revolutionary's plans for the future were forcibly put on hold.

26.

He burns brighter than a nova;
He stands taller than a tree;
He shouts louder than the thunder;
He flows deeper than the sea.

"Actually," Santiago was saying as he leaned back in his easy chair and sipped his brandy, "I'm told that he was the patron saint of the oppressed Spanish nobility. They used to invoke his spirit before doing battle to drive the Moors out of their country."

"Santiago means Saint James in Spanish, a language they used to speak on old Earth," added Jacinto, who was sitting on a large, comfortable couch with Cain.

"Not quite as biblical as your own name, Sebastian," remarked Santiago.

"It's my middle name that bothers me," said Cain. "I should never have let Orpheus know what it was. Then I wouldn't have to put up with this Songbird nonsense." He sighed. "Still, I suppose we can't choose our names."

"Everyone out here does just that," noted Santiago.

"Those are names for the Frontier," replied Cain. "They're not official."

"If you stay on the Frontier, they're official enough."

Suddenly the security system warned them that a vehicle was approaching. It was identified as Silent Annie's, and a moment later the door slid back to reveal her slim figure.

"Annie—what a pleasant surprise!" said Santiago, getting to his feet. "To what do we owe the pleasure of this visit?"

"We have a bit of a problem on our hands," replied Silent Annie, remaining in the doorway.

"Oh?"

Silent Annie nodded her head. "She's sitting in my vehicle."

"Who is it?" asked Santiago.

"Virtue MacKenzie."

Cain stood up and walked to a window, saw Virtue sitting blindfolded inside the vehicle, then turned to Santiago and nodded. "Where's the Angel?" he demanded.

"In orbit," replied Silent Annie.

"Why did you bring her out here?" asked Santiago, more curious than annoyed.

"She landed a couple of hours ago, found Father William, and told him that she had a message for you from the Angel." Silent Annie paused. "He figured that if she was telling the truth, you'd probably want to hear what it is."

"And if she's lying?" asked Cain.

"Then she'll never leave Safe Harbor alive," promised Silent Annie coldly.

"Why didn't Father William bring her himself?" asked Santiago.

"He wants to be in town when the Angel lands," answered Silent Annie.

"It's a big planet," said Cain. "What makes him think the Angel will land near the town? I wouldn't."

"You *did*," replied Silent Annie.

"But I didn't know Santiago was here," Cain pointed out.

"He'll land there because he'll need Virtue to guide him to me, and she landed there," said Santiago.

Cain considered the statement for a few seconds, then nodded. "You're probably right," he conceded.

"Well, let's not keep our guest waiting," said Santiago to Silent Annie. "Bring her in."

Silent Annie went back outside and returned a moment later with Virtue MacKenzie. Her blindfold was removed, and she looked around the room, studying each of the three men confronting her.

"Hello, Cain," she said at last.

Cain nodded a greeting but said nothing.

She looked at Jacinto. "You're too young," she said decisively and turned to Santiago. "It must be *you*."

Santiago smiled and bowed. "At your service. Won't you sit down?"

"Can I have a drink first?" she asked.

"Of course. What would you prefer?"

"Anything with alcohol."

Santiago turned to Silent Annie. "Would you do the honors, please?"

She nodded and walked to the bar, while Santiago escorted Virtue to a chair.

"You're a very courageous woman to come here by yourself," said Santiago, sitting down opposite her.

"After you've traveled with the Angel, not much else can scare you," she replied sincerely.

"Just a minute," said Cain, walking over and taking her satchel from her.

"Hey!" she snapped, grabbing futilely at it. "What's the idea?"

"You're delivering a message," said Cain, reaching in and withdrawing a small recording device, "not getting an interview." He held the bag up to a light, examined it minutely, then returned it to her with his hand outstretched. "Where is it?"

"I don't know what you're talking about," said Virtue.

"You've got to have a camera hidden somewhere. You can hand it over or I can strip you naked. There's no third way."

"I don't have to put up with this!"

Cain turned to Jacinto. "Hold her," he ordered.

Jacinto took a step in her direction and Virtue held up a hand. "All right," she said. "Just a minute." She fumbled with her jacket and plucked off a large button, handing it to Cain. "Are you satisfied now?" she demanded.

"For the moment," he said, deactivating the incredibly miniaturized holographic mechanism and putting it in his pocket.

"I'll want that back when I leave," she added.

"We'll see," said Jacinto ominously.

"What's this 'we'll see' shit?" said Virtue heatedly. "I came under a flag of truce!"

"As a message carrier, not a journalist," responded Jacinto.

"You have my word that your property will be returned to you," said Santiago. "And now," he added, glancing firmly at Cain and Jacinto, "if my friends can control their enthusiasm, I would be interested in hearing what you have to say."

"The Angel wants to meet you tomorrow morning," she said.

"I'll just bet he does," said Silent Annie, returning with Virtue's drink.

"The Angel wants to kill me," said Santiago. "Why should I care to present myself to him?"

"He's willing to discuss it," said Virtue.

Santiago looked amused. "To discuss killing me?"

"To discuss *not* killing you," she replied.

"A subject near and dear to my heart," replied Santiago. "What does he propose to say?"

"That he's willing to be bought off," said Virtue.

"For how much?"

"It's negotiable," answered Virtue. "I get the feeling that he's talking in the neighborhood of two or three million credits."

"The reward for me is up to twenty million credits. Why should he settle for so much less?"

She grinned. "Nobody knows what you look like. He can turn in the body of the first derelict he finds, claim that it's you, and still get the reward."

"I'm sure it's been tried before," said Santiago.

"Probably," she agreed. "But people tend not to argue with the Angel."

Santiago studied her thoughtfully. "Where does he want to meet me?"

"A place called the Barleycorn Tavern."

"How did he find out about it?"

"It's where Peacemaker MacDougal killed Billy Three-Eyes," replied Virtue. "It's the only location on Safe Harbor that he knows."

"What time does he want to meet me?" asked Santiago.

"Nine o'clock."

"You're not seriously considering meeting with him?" demanded Cain.

"I haven't decided yet," said Santiago.

"It's a setup," said Cain.

"Perhaps," agreed Santiago.

"Then don't go. Make him come out here."

"And kill ten or twelve of my men?" said Santiago with a smile. "I can't spare them."

"They can't spare *you!*" snapped Cain.

"Possibly the Angel really wants to make a deal," said Santiago. "After all, twenty-three million credits is better than twenty."

Cain shook his head vigorously. "He'll have to go into the Democracy to collect it—and they won't give a damn if he's the Angel or God Himself. They're going to want proof."

"How soon does he need an answer?" Santiago asked Virtue.

"I'm supposed to contact him tonight and let him know your decision," she replied.

"And if I decide against meeting with him?"

She shrugged. "Then I suppose he'll come out here and kill you."

"What do *you* get out of all this?" asked Jacinto.

"I'm a journalist. I get a story." She turned to Santiago. "Perhaps you'd like to give me an interview right now?" she suggested.

Santiago chuckled. "I admire your dedication."

"Then you'll do it?" she persisted.

He shook his head. "I'm afraid not."

"If you'll give me an interview, I'll tell the Angel you're not here."

"She's lying," said Cain.

"The hell I am!" snapped Virtue irately.

Cain turned to her. "Come on," he said. "You tell him that, and the second the interview appears, he'll come after you and hunt you down."

"He'll never find me."

"If he could find Santiago, he can find a journalist who'll be making the most of her publicity."

"I'll take my chances," replied Virtue.

"No you won't. You'll take your interview, and then you'll tell the Angel everything you saw and heard."

Santiago cleared his throat.

"I'm going to take a little walk," he announced, "and consider the Angel's proposition. I'll give you my answer when I return."

"I'll go with you," said Silent Annie.

He shook his head. "I'd rather go alone. I'll be back in a few minutes."

He walked out the door.

"Where is he going?" asked Cain.

"Down to the dell," answered Jacinto. "He always goes there when he wants to think."

"What the hell is there to think about?" said Cain, puzzled. "He can't actually be considering going through with this!"

Jacinto shrugged. "Who knows?"

Cain walked over to Virtue, grabbed her by the wrist, and yanked her to her feet.

"Come on," he said.

"Where are you taking her?" demanded Jacinto.

"Out to the veranda," said Cain. "I want to talk to her."

"You can talk to her right here."

"Alone," said Cain.

Jacinto stared at Cain for a moment, then nodded his head.

Cain led Virtue through the dining room and out onto the veranda, then commanded the door to close behind him.

"I can't believe it!" she said, her face flushed with excitement. "I've finally found him!"

"And now you're going to kill him," said Cain.

"I'm not killing anyone," she said. "I'm just a journalist." She look at him sharply. "But while we're on the subject, how come *you* haven't killed him?"

"The situation has changed," said Cain. "I've joined him."

"How much is he paying you?" she asked, curious.

"Nothing."

She stared at him disbelievingly. "Are you going to give me all that crap I heard from Silent Annie about what a great man he is?"

"I don't know if he's a great man," said Cain slowly. "But he's a *good* man—better than I'll ever be, anyway. And he's working for a good cause."

"He's a goddamned outlaw."

"He's a good man," repeated Cain. "And I'm not going to let him be killed."

"I seem to remember that we made a deal back on Pegasus," said Virtue.

"You broke it when you joined the Angel."

"Didn't you get Terwilliger's message?"

Cain nodded. "Was it sent before or after ManMountain Bates killed him?" he asked sardonically.

She glared at him. "It was the truth!"

"Then why are you running the Angel's errands?" he shot back.

"Because he got Dimitri Sokol to take the hit off me," she replied.

"And when do you stop working for him? When he kills Santiago?"

"He's just going to talk to him."

"That's a bunch of shit and you know it," said Cain. "This thing's got trap written all over it."

"What difference does it make?" demanded Virtue defiantly. "I've got a story to get, and you've sold out to the enemy. If I can't get an interview, I'll cover his death."

"The enemy isn't Santiago," said Cain. "It's the Angel."

"The Angel is a bounty hunter who's working within the Democracy's law. Santiago is a criminal who's broken it time and again."

"It's not that simple," said Cain.

"It's precisely that simple," she said triumphantly. "You've joined a gang of killers and bandits, and you're castigating me for working with the man who's trying to bring their leader to justice."

"You never gave a damn about justice in your life!" snarled Cain. "All you care about is your goddamned story and what you think it will do for you."

"Don't you go getting high and mighty with *me*, Cain!" she snapped back at him. "I know how many men you've killed—and not just as a bounty hunter, either. There's still a price on your head back on Sylaria." She paused to catch her breath. "We both set out to find Santiago. You were going to kill him, and I was going to get my story. It's hardly my fault that you've forgotten what you're supposed to be doing here!"

"I'll give you a story to take home with you," he said savagely. "You can cover the death of the Angel."

She glared at him, and then her expression changed as all the rage seemed to drain from her.

"You can't kill him," she said, shaking her head slowly. "Don't throw your life away trying."

"I won't let him kill Santiago," said Cain doggedly.

"Nobody can stop him. Believe me, Cain—I've seen him in action. I know what he can do." She suppressed a shudder. "He's inhuman!"

Cain stared at her. "If you're that afraid of him, why are you working for him?"

"Because he can get what I need," she said with a tight smile. "And because I'm that afraid of him." She stared directly into Cain's eyes. "Have you got anything else to say, or can I have another drink?"

He stared back at her, seemed about to speak, thought better of it, and led her back inside. Jacinto and Silent Annie were still in the living room, waiting for them.

"Is he on his way back yet?" asked Jacinto.

"I didn't see him," said Cain. "What's he doing out there, anyway—communing with the dead?"

"That's in very bad taste, Mr. Cain," said Jacinto. "The men in those graves were fine men."

"Then maybe *they'll* talk a little sense to him," said Cain. "He's got to know this is a trap."

"He knows."

"Then what's the problem?"

Jacinto sighed wearily. "Billions of people in the Democracy may fear his name, but there are tens of thousands out here who practically worship it, who know that he's the only thing that stands between them and their oppressors. He's all they've got, he and the myth that has grown up around him—and he doesn't want them to think that he's betrayed their faith in him by becoming a coward."

"There's nothing cowardly about running away from a fight you can't win," said Cain.

"When you're Santiago, there is."

"No one will ever know."

Jacinto nodded toward Virtue. "We'd have to kill *her* to keep the story from spreading, and he won't do it."

"Then you and I will have to stop him," said Cain decisively.

"How?"

"By force, if necessary."

"You'll do whatever Santiago tells you to do," interrupted Silent Annie. "He's your leader."

"We're trying to *keep* him our leader," answered Cain.

She stared harshly at him. "When you make a commitment to follow a man, you make a *total* commitment. You don't just obey those orders you approve of, and disregard the rest." She paused for emphasis. "Whatever he decides, we'll support it."

"We'll see," said Cain noncommittally.

There was an uneasy silence which Virtue finally broke.

"Does anyone mind if I pour myself a drink?"

Jacinto gestured toward the bar. "Fix it yourself."

She walked over and began inspecting the rows of bottles. "This is a pretty well-stocked little bar," she said, impressed. She noticed one bottle in particular and picked it up. "Korbellian whiskey!" she exclaimed. "I haven't had any of this in, oh, it must be five years!" She poured herself a glass and took a quick swallow. "He's got good taste, I'll give him that."

"I consider that a great compliment," said a voice from the dining room doorway, and they all turned to see Santiago standing there.

"Well?" said Cain, looking at him.

Santiago walked across the room to where Virtue was standing, glass in hand.

"Tell the Angel I'll be there," he said.

"You're crazy!" exploded Cain.

"Nevertheless, that's my decision." He turned back to Virtue. "If you'll wait in the vehicle that brought you, I'll have one of my men take you back to town. I'm sorry, but I'll have to tell him to blindfold you again."

"And my camera?"

"It will be returned to you after we've destroyed whatever it recorded here."

Virtue finished her whiskey and walked to the door. "Cain's right, you know."

"Thank you for your opinion," said Santiago, dismissing her.

She shrugged and left the house. Santiago nodded to Silent Annie, who went off to find a driver.

"You can't do it!" said Cain.

Santiago smiled. "Are you giving me orders, Sebastian?"

"She as much as said that the whole thing is a setup," continued Cain. "If you really feel you've got to give the Angel a crack at you, stay here at the house, and at least make him work for it."

"To what purpose?" asked Santiago. "If he truly intends to kill me, why let him kill all of you as well? He's good enough to do just that, you know."

"He won't kill *me*," promised Cain.

"Even you, Sebastian," said Santiago. "I've followed his career as closely as I have your own. I don't mean to hurt your pride, but you haven't got a chance against him."

"If that's true, then you've got even less of a chance," said Cain as Silent Annie rejoined them.

"*If* he wants to kill me," said Santiago. "There's a chance that he only wants to talk."

"There's two chances—slim and none."

"Then," said Santiago calmly, "perhaps he'll discover that it's harder to kill me than he thinks."

"You're just flesh and blood like anyone else," said Cain.

"No, Sebastian," said Santiago. "I may be flesh and blood, but I am also myth and mystery and legend."

"It won't do you any good."

"It has before."

"You've never faced anyone like the Angel before," said Cain.

"If it ends, it ends," said Santiago. "I've led a satisfying life. I've seen hundreds of worlds, I've had the pleasure of owning this farm—and, in some small way, I've made a difference." He shrugged and forced a smile to his lips. "And before you go writing my epitaph, I wish at least one of you would consider the possibility that I might not die."

"I beg you not to do this," said Jacinto earnestly.

"I appreciate your concern," replied Santiago, "but my decision has been made."

"Then let me go in your place," said Cain suddenly. "The Angel has never seen either of us. At least I'll have a chance against him."

"I thought we decided that you didn't want to become Sydney Carton," noted Santiago.

"I've changed my mind."

"Well, I haven't changed mine," said Santiago. "I appreciate your offer, Sebastian, but I have more important things in mind for you."

"What could be more important than saving your life?" demanded Cain.

"There's still work to be done, whether I'm here or not," said Santiago gently. "And now, if no one minds, I think I'd like to have dinner."

Cain and Jacinto spent the entire meal trying to argue Santiago out of his position, but he remained adamant. When he had finished eating he went out to the dell by himself and returned at about midnight, seemingly content. He invited Silent Annie to spend the night in one of the guest rooms, bade the three of them good night, and went off to bed.

Cain retired to his room, pulled two pistols out of his luggage, and spent the next hour oiling and cleaning them. He set his alarm for twenty minutes before sunrise and was totally dressed and checking his ammunition when he heard a knock at the door.

"Open," he commanded in a low voice, and Santiago and Silent Annie entered the room.

"I was afraid of this," said Santiago, staring at the pistols that Cain had laid out on the dresser. "Sebastian, what are you doing?"

"I'm going into town," replied Cain, making no attempt to hide his weapons.

"I've told you not to."

"I know what you told me," said Cain. "I'm going anyway."

"Annie?" said Santiago, stepping aside, and suddenly Cain was looking down the barrel of a sonic pistol.

"What the hell is this?" demanded Cain.

"I appreciate what you want to do, Sebastian," said Santiago, "but I can't allow it." He turned to Silent Annie. "I'm leaving in ten minutes. You'll keep him here?"

She nodded.

"Good-bye, Sebastian," said Santiago.

He walked down the hall, and the door slid shut.

"You know he's going off to get killed, don't you?" said Cain bitterly.

She stared unblinking at him. "Santiago can't be killed."

"Santiago could do with a few more realists in his organization, and a few less fanatics." He got to his feet. "If you let me pass, I can still stop him."

"Stay where you are," she warned him.

"You're letting him drive off to his death!" snapped Cain. "Why?"

"Because it's his decision, and I plan to abide by it."

"Why the hell is he doing it?" said Cain, still mystified.

"To save the lives of everyone here," she replied. "If the Angel wants to kill him, he'll kill him wherever he is."

"We could have tightened our security."

"In one night?" said Silent Annie, shaking her head and smiling sadly.

"We could have laid a trap for him." He glanced desperately at the door. "We still can."

"The die has been cast."

"That's a feeble thing to say," replied Cain. "He's going off to face the Angel, and all I get from you is platitudes!"

She stared at him. "He rescued me from a life of despair, and gave meaning to it. I love him more than you ever could. If I can let him do what he has to do, then so can you."

Cain heard the sound of Santiago's vehicle starting off down the farm's long, twisting driveway.

"He's gone," he said, his emotions draining away. "And you've helped to kill him."

"I told you: Santiago cannot die."

"Be sure you write that on his tombstone!"

"Why are you so enraged?" she asked, honestly curious. "You've only known him for two days."

"I've been searching for him all my life," said Cain bitterly. "And now, thanks to you, I've lost him."

She smiled. "He would approve of that answer."

"He's not going to be around to approve of anything much longer."

They sat there in silence for the next five minutes, Cain glaring at her with a growing sense of futility and frustration, Silent Annie watching his every movement with a fanatical intensity.

Suddenly there were footsteps in the hall, and then they heard Jacinto's voice.

"Are you in there, Annie?"

Silent Annie turned her head toward the door for just an instant—

and in that instant Cain dove across the room and sent the pistol flying against a wall. She leaped toward it, but he was faster, grabbing her and hurling her roughly onto the bed.

"What's going on in there?" demanded Jacinto, pounding on the door.

Cain picked up the sonic pistol, disconnected the charge, and tossed it onto the dresser. Then he picked up his own guns and loaded his pockets with ammunition, never taking his eyes off her. Finally he walked to the door and commanded it to open, only to find himself confronted by Jacinto, whose face was streaked by tears.

"I'm going into town," Cain announced.

"I know," said Jacinto. He took a step forward, and Cain saw that he held a wicked-looking knife in his hands.

"Don't try to stop me," Cain growled ominously.

"That was never my intention."

"Then let me pass."

"There is one thing that I must do first," said Jacinto, still approaching him.

27.

There are those who will say he's a sinner,
There are those who will say he's a saint;
There are those who will swear he's as strong as a bear,
But whatever they tell you—he ain't!

Black Orpheus wasn't so much prophetic as he was just plain lucky. He wrote that verse for pretty much the same reason that he wrote Silent Annie's—because he had a feeling that there was a lot more to his subject than met the eye.

He never knew just how right he was.

Virtue MacKenzie was already seated in the tavern when Father William and the Swagman showed up. The preacher greeted her coldly, then sat down at his usual table and asked Moonripple to prepare some breakfast for him, while the Swagman walked over and joined her.

"Good morning, my love," he said. "I knew we were destined to meet again."

"It's a little early in the day for you, isn't it?" she responded, setting her 360-degree holographic camera on the table and checking her microphone.

"What would life be without new experiences?" he said with a smile. "I've always wondered what the world looked like before noon."

"Which world?" she inquired dryly.

"*Any* world."

"Pretty much the same, I'd imagine," said Virtue.

"Blurrier," he replied, blinking his eyes. "Where's your traveling companion?"

"He'll be along," she assured him.

"Well, in his absence, I suppose it wouldn't hurt to talk a little business," said the Swagman.

"I've got nothing to discuss with you," said Virtue, inserting the microphone into its slot in the camera.

"We *do* have an agreement concerning the disposition of the artwork," persisted the Swagman.

"That agreement's only valid if Cain kills Santiago," replied Virtue. "And in case you hadn't heard, Cain has joined him."

"Then put in a good word for me with the Angel."

She stared at him. "Swagman, I don't know any good words about you."

"This is no time to deal in acrimony," said the Swagman. "Neither you nor the Angel knows how to dispose of the artwork; I do. You need me."

"I don't care about the artwork," she said. "I'm getting what I want."

"You think so?" asked the Swagman, amused.

"The Angel wants the reward money, I want the story. Our interests don't overlap."

"Ah, Virtue," he said with a sigh, "I wish you were as bright as you think you are."

"What are you talking about?"

"Do you really think he's going to let you live?" asked the Swagman.

"Why shouldn't he?"

"Because Dimitri Sokol's put a price of one hundred thousand credits on your pretty little head."

"The Angel had him take the hit off," she said.

He shook his head. "The Angel had him stop advertising it. There's a difference."

"Then why hasn't he killed me already?" she demanded.

"Because he needed you to get Santiago to come here. Once he kills Santiago, he doesn't need you for anything—unless you can convince him that he can make a healthy profit by letting you and me dispose of the artwork."

"You and me?" she repeated skeptically. "Why are you suddenly being so generous?"

"Because he knows you, whereas my reputation has been besmirched by numerous small-minded parties who are jealous of my success." He leaned forward. "I'll cut you in for ten percent."

"Ten percent?" she said with a harsh laugh. "Your generosity knows no bounds."

He shrugged. "All right—fifteen. And you'll still have your story."

"Not a chance."

"You're making a big mistake," said the Swagman.

"Somehow, as frightening as the Angel is, I find him more trustworthy than you."

"It's your funeral," he replied. "Just think about what I said." He signaled to Moonripple, who emerged from the kitchen carrying Father William's breakfast on a huge tray. "A cup of coffee when you get the chance, my dear."

"Right away, sir," she answered.

"Coffee?" asked Virtue, grinning.

"They tell me it contracts the pupils," said the Swagman. "I'm certainly willing to give it a chance."

"It steadies the nerves."

"Whatever," he shrugged. Suddenly he noticed that Father William had clasped his hands before him and lowered his head. "I've never seen you do that before," he said.

"I pray all the time," replied Father William.

"Not before a meal, you don't," said the Swagman. "Usually you just dig in like you're trying to break a speed record."

"Maybe he's nervous," suggested Virtue.

Father William stared sternly at her. "I was praying for the Angel's soul. I plan to remand it to Satan's custody this morning."

"Maybe you'd better put in a good word for yourself, if you plan to go up against him," said Virtue.

"I don't ask the Lord for personal favors," said Father William. He continued staring at her. "I think I'd better pray for you next. You've done a wicked thing, Virtue MacKenzie."

"Don't you go blaming *me* for this," she said defensively. "I never even heard of Safe Harbor until yesterday. The Angel found this place without any help from me."

"But you convinced Santiago to meet him."

"All I did was deliver a message," she replied. "Hell, I told him he was crazy to come."

"I'll pray for you anyway."

"While you're at it," said the Swagman, "you might say one for me, just to be on the safe side."

"It wouldn't do any good," answered Father William.

Moonripple arrived with the Swagman's coffee, while Father William said a brief prayer for Virtue and then attacked his meal with even more gusto than usual.

Moonripple placed the tray behind the bar, then hesitantly approached Father William.

"Excuse me, sir," she said tentatively.

"Yes, my child?"

"I realize it's none of my concern, but I couldn't help overhearing what you said, and I just wanted to know if it was true?"

"That the Swagman's going to hell?" replied Father William. "Absolutely."

"No," she said. "That wasn't what I meant." She paused, nervously fidgeting with her apron. "Is it true that *he* is coming here today?"

"I hope not," said Father William.

She started to ask something more, then shook her head and retreated to the kitchen while Father William returned his attention to the diminishing pile of food on his plate.

Virtue busied herself rechecking her equipment, while the Swagman sipped his coffee and tried unsuccessfully to pretend that it was Cygnian cognac.

Then the door opened and the Angel, clad in a strikingly somber outfit, stepped into the tavern. His pale, no-color eyes surveyed the room, missing no detail.

"You're a few minutes early," said Virtue.

He made no answer but chose a table that was next to a windowless wall and walked to it, elegant and catlike, never taking his eyes from Father William. When he reached it he pulled out a chair and sat down.

"I assume from your demeanor that you're the Angel?" said the Swagman cordially.

"I am."

"Good. They call me the Jolly Swagman. I have a mutually beneficial business proposition to put to you."

"Later," replied the Angel.

"It could mean a lot of money to you," continued the Swagman persuasively.

"I said later."

The Swagman looked into the Angel's cold, lifeless eyes.

"I'll tell you what," he said hastily, getting to his feet and keeping his hands in plain view. "I think I'll just go across the street and relax for a little while. We'll talk later."

The Angel paid no attention to him as he hurried out the door, but stared intently at Father William.

"I won't let you kill him," said the preacher, glaring at him while continuing to eat.

"I'm only here to talk to him," replied the Angel.

"I don't believe you."

The Angel shrugged. "Believe what you want—but don't do anything foolish."

Father William continued glaring at him as Moonripple came through the kitchen door and approached the Angel.

"May I help you, sir?" she asked.

The Angel shook his head, never taking his eyes from Father William.

"He should be here any minute," said Virtue.

"Will Cain be with him?" asked the Angel.

"No." She paused nervously. "I have to ask you a question."

"Go ahead."

"Has Dimitri Sokol still got a hit on me?"

"No."

"You're sure?"

"Who told you otherwise?" asked the Angel.

"I was just curious."

"It was the Swagman," said the Angel.

"Was he telling the truth?"

"Does he ever?"

"Damn it!" snapped Virtue, her anger overcoming her fear. "I want an answer!"

He turned his head toward her slightly, still keeping Father William in his field of vision. "I already answered your question. If you didn't believe me the first time, you won't believe me now."

They sat in silence for another minute. Then Father William finished the last of his breakfast, took the napkin he had tied around his neck, wiped his mouth off, and tossed it onto the table.

"You've had your warning," growled the preacher ominously.

"You don't have to die," said the Angel. "There's no paper on you."

"The Lord is my shepherd, I shall not want!" intoned Father William, rising to his feet, the handles of his laser pistols glinting in the tavern's artificial light.

Suddenly Moonripple, her eyes wide with horror, took a step toward the Angel.

"You can't kill Father William!" she said in hushed tones. "He's a servant of the Lord!"

"It's his choice," replied the Angel calmly, his gaze never leaving the preacher's hands.

"Stand back, child!" said Father William.

"You can't!" she repeated, rushing toward the Angel.

Father William reached for his pistols, and three long metal spikes appeared in the Angel's right hand as if by magic. Moonripple hit his arm just as he was hurling them, but all of them found their way into Father William's massive body before he could draw his pistols, and he collapsed with a surprised grunt.

The Angel got to his feet and swept Moonripple aside with his arm. She careened off the wall and fell to the floor, motionless.

"See if she's still alive," he ordered Virtue while he walked across the room and crouched down next to Father William. One of the spikes was buried in his chest, another protruded from his right arm, and the third was lodged in the left side of his neck, but he was still conscious.

"You were lucky," said the Angel dispassionately, appropriating Father William's pistols. "You owe your life to that child. Try not to move too much and you may not bleed to death."

"Kill me now!" rasped Father William. "Or as God is my witness, I'll hunt you down to the very depths of hell!"

"Stupid," muttered the Angel, shaking his head. He frisked the preacher for concealed weapons, carefully withdrew the three spikes, stood up, and walked over to Moonripple.

"She's breathing," said Virtue. "But she's got a hell of a bump on her head."

He felt her head and neck with expert hands. "She'll be all right," he said.

"What about Father William?"

"He's in better shape than he has any right to be," replied the Angel. "That fat gives him a lot of protection."

"Will he live?"

"Probably."

"Shouldn't we get the pair of them to a doctor?"

"Later," said the Angel.

She looked at the semiconscious preacher. "He's bleeding pretty badly."

"You do what you want," replied the Angel, returning to his chair. "I'm here to meet Santiago."

She stared at Father William for another moment, then shrugged and went back to her recording equipment.

They sat without speaking for a few minutes, the silence broken only by Father William's hoarse breathing and occasional curses. Then the door slid open once again, and Santiago entered.

"What's been going on here?" he demanded, kneeling down next to Father William.

"Are you Santiago?" asked the Angel.

"I am," replied Santiago without looking up.

"Your associate made an unwise decision."

"Is he alive?"

"I'll outlive *that* spawn of Satan!" rasped Father William, regaining consciousness.

Suddenly Santiago saw Moonripple.

"What have you done to the girl?"

"She'll be all right." The Angel gestured toward the chair opposite him. "Take a seat."

"In a minute," said Santiago, walking over and examining Moonripple. His hands found the swelling on the side of her head. "That could be a fracture there." He turned to Virtue. "Have you summoned a doctor?"

"All in good time," interjected the Angel. "We have business to discuss first."

Santiago glanced back at Father William, then turned to the Angel.

"I want your word that you won't kill them, however our negotiations turn out."

"You have it."

Santiago sighed. "All right," he said, sitting down. "Let's get on with it."

"You realize that you are the most wanted man in the galaxy," began the Angel.

"I do."

"This is because you are the most successful criminal in the galaxy," he continued.

"Get to the point," said Santiago.

"The point is simply this: A criminal who has been as successful as you have been undoubtedly has accumulated a considerable amount of money. I wonder if you would be interested in spending some of it to purchase your continuing good health?"

"How much did you have in mind?"

"The reward is currently twenty million credits," said the Angel. He paused thoughtfully. "I should think that thirty million will do nicely."

"Thirty?" exclaimed Virtue. "I thought you were talking about three!"

The Angel smiled mirthlessly. "That was talk," he said. "This is business." He stared directly into Santiago's eyes. "The amount is payable in full before you leave this table."

Santiago smiled grimly. "You never had any intention of making a deal, did you?"

"I am a man of my word," replied the Angel. "I said that if you came here I would make you an offer, and I have. What is your answer?"

"You go to hell," said Santiago.

The Angel reached out with an incredibly swift motion, and an instant later Santiago fell out of his chair, blood spurting from his throat. He was dead before he hit the floor.

Father William emitted a hideous gutteral yell, tried to get to his feet, and actually got one leg planted before he grabbed at his chest and collapsed, panting heavily.

Virtue closed her eyes and fought the urge to vomit as the Angel got to his feet, walked over to Santiago's body, and looked down at it, studying the contorted face.

"Well, you've got your story," he said at last.

"It was gruesome!" she said weakly.

He turned to her. "Death usually is."

Suddenly a single gunshot rang out.

For a moment nobody moved. Then the Angel, a trickle of blood starting to run out of his mouth, turned to the door, swaying slightly.

"Fool!" said Cain softly. "Do you think Santiago can be killed that easily?"

He fired another shot, and the Angel dropped to his knees.

Father William laboriously raised himself onto his elbows.

"You poor dumb bastard!" he rasped with a derisive laugh. "You murdered the wrong man!"

Cain advanced slowly across the room.

The Angel, puzzlement and pain reflected on his face, tried to speak, coughed up a mouthful of blood, and finally forced the words out.

"Then who is Santiago?"

Cain held up his right hand and displayed an S-shaped wound that was still oozing blood.

"*I* am now," he said.

"Poor sinner!" grated Father William. "Everybody knows that Santiago can't die!" He roared with laughter and was still laughing when he passed out.

The Angel reached inside his coat for a sonic weapon, and a third shot rang out. He flew backward as if hit by a sledgehammer, then lay still.

Cain turned to Virtue. "Go get a doctor," he ordered.

She got up and began putting her camera into her satchel.

"Leave it," said Cain.

"Not a chance," she said, glaring at him. "I risked my life to get what's in there."

"It'll still be there when you get back."

"Then why can't I take it?"

"Because I want to make sure you return. We've got things to discuss."

She looked at the camera, then back at Cain again. "You promise you won't touch it?"

"Unless someone dies because you stood here arguing," he replied. "If that happens, I swear to you that I'll blow it to pieces."

She seemed about to argue with him, then turned and went out the door. Cain briefly examined the four bodies on the floor, two of them living, two of them dead, then walked to the bar, poured himself a drink, and waited.

Virtue returned alone about two minutes later, her face flushed from running.

"There's quite a crowd gathering outside," she remarked.

"Where's the doctor?" asked Cain.

"I told him he was going to need a lot of help," she replied. "He's getting his staff together, and hunting up a vehicle that can transport everyone to the hospital."

"How soon will he get here?"

"I don't know. About five minutes, I suppose."

"Wait here," he said, walking to the door. He stepped out onto the street and found himself facing about twenty onlookers.

"There's been some trouble," he said, "but it's under control now. There will be a medical team arriving shortly. I think it would be best if all of you would go back to your homes."

Nobody moved.

Cain held up his right hand and turned it so they could see the wound on the back of it.

"Please," he said.

They stared at his hand, and then, one by one, they began dispersing. One man lagged behind the others, then walked up and asked if there was anything he could do to help; Cain shook his head, thanked him, and sent him on his way.

"That was pretty impressive," said Virtue when he came back into the tavern. "How long is this charade going to continue?"

"What charade?" he asked.

"Pretending to be Santiago."

He stared at her expressionlessly. "I'm not pretending."

"What about the reward?" she asked.

"I imagine it'll go up," he replied. "The Angel was working for the Democracy."

She met his gaze and was surprised at what she saw there. "You're serious, aren't you?"

He nodded silently.

"Then what about my story?" she asked.

"What story?"

"I've got a recording of the Angel killing Santiago."

He shook his head. "*I'm* Santiago. You have a recording of a bounty hunter killing an imposter."

"We'll let the viewers judge for themselves."

Cain shrugged. "It's a pity, though," he said softly.

"What is?" she asked suspiciously.

"That your story has to end here."

She looked at him curiously.

"And that you never got your interview," he added.

"Oh?"

"There were so many things you could have learned," he continued. "Enough for ten pieces."

"Enough for a book?" she asked meaningfully.

"Who knows?"

"I'll have to think about it," said Virtue.

The door opened and a doctor, flanked by three assistants, entered the tavern.

"Not for too long," Cain told her.

The medics carried Father William and Moonripple out on air-cushioned stretchers, and the doctor walked over to Cain.

"I'll be back for the other two later," he said. "But I'm going to have to work fast to save Father William."

Cain nodded. "Just come back for this one," he said, gesturing to the Angel. "I'm taking the other home with me."

The doctor looked down at Santiago, then at Cain, and nodded his head.

Cain waited until he and Virtue were alone again before speaking.

"I'd better pull my vehicle up and load him into it," he said. He walked to the door, then turned to her. "I'll need your decision before I go."

He turned back and found himself facing the Jolly Swagman.

"I saw everyone else leaving, so I decided that this might be an opportune time to come over," he said with a smile. "I'm glad to see you're still alive."

He walked past Cain and stared at the two corpses.

"Well, I'll be damned!" he muttered. "Both of them!" He turned back to Cain. "I thought I saw two bodies being carried out."

"Father William and Moonripple," said Cain. "They're still alive."

"I'm glad to hear it. I've got a sneaking fondness for that fat old man." He rubbed his hands together. "Well, here we are—the Three Musketeers! Who would have thought that we'd actually make it?"

"What do you want?" asked Cain.

"What do you mean, what do I want?" laughed the Swagman. "You've got the reward, Virtue's got her story—I want the artwork."

"No deal," said Cain.

The Swagman frowned. "What are you talking about, Songbird?"

"My name's not Songbird."

"All right—Sebastian."

"It's not Sebastian, either."

"Well, what *do* you want to be called?"

"Santiago."

The Swagman laughed heartily. "He's got *that* much stashed away?"

"What I have is none of your business."

"All right," said the Swagman. "This has gone far enough. We made a deal. The artwork's mine!"

"You made a deal with a man who no longer exists," said Cain.

"Now listen to me!" said the Swagman. "I don't know what kind of double cross you're trying to pull, but it's not going to work. You've got the reward; I want the artwork."

"What you want doesn't interest me."

"Do you think that just because you're the one who killed him you're entitled to everything?" demanded the Swagman. "It doesn't work that way, Sebastian!"

"His name's Santiago," said Virtue.

"You, too?" he said, turning to face her.

"I'm his biographer," she said with a smug smile. "Who knows Santiago better than me?"

The Swagman turned back to Cain. "I don't know what kind of scam you two have worked out, but you're not getting rid of me that easily. I've put as much work into this as you have; I deserve something for my time."

"Some alien artwork?" suggested Cain.

"Of course some alien artwork! What the hell do you think I've been talking about?"

"All right," said Cain. "You're entitled to something."

He walked to Santiago's body, knelt down, and removed a gold ring from one of his fingers.

"Here you are," said Cain. "Now go away."

The Swagman looked at the ring, then hurled it against the wall.

"I'll tell what I know," he said threateningly.

"Do whatever you think you have to do," said Cain.

"I'm not bluffing, Sebastian. I'll tell them he's dead."

"And next month or next year another navy convoy will be robbed, and everyone will know that Santiago is still alive," replied Cain calmly.

The Swagman stared at Cain. "This isn't over yet," he promised.

"I know," said Cain. "For one thing, you're going to be protecting me."

"What are you talking about?"

"There's still a price on my head, and you know I live on Safe Harbor. If any bounty hunter makes it this far, I'm going to assume that you told him where to find me." He smiled grimly. "I would take a very dim view of that."

"How can I keep tabs on every bounty hunter who's looking for Santiago?" demanded the Swagman in exasperation.

"You're a clever man," said Cain. "You'll find a way."

The Swagman seemed about to protest, then sighed and turned to Virtue.

"You're really going along with this deception?" he asked.

"What deception?" she replied innocently.

"Wonderful," he muttered. "You know," he added thoughtfully, "it occurs to me that you've run through most of your advance already. You're not going to do much more than break even."

"Have you any suggestions?"

He smiled with renewed self-confidence. "Hundreds of them, especially for a famous art critic like yourself."

"We'll talk about it later," she said, unable to completely hide her interest.

"I'll be at the boarding house for a few more days. That is," he added sardonically, "if it's all right with Santiago?"

"Two days," said Cain.

"Then, if there are no further objections, I think I'll take my leave of you," he said, walking to the door. "I crave the company of honest men and women."

"I doubt that the feeling is mutual," said Cain.

The Swagman chuckled and left the tavern.

"I was afraid that you were going to kill him," remarked Virtue.

"Cain might have. Santiago will find a use for him."

"But all he has to do is tell the navy where to find you."

"But he won't," said Cain confidently as he walked to the door. "If the navy kills me, the Democracy will appropriate all my belongings, including the artwork."

It took Cain another five minutes to load Santiago's body into his vehicle. Then he and Virtue drove the fifty miles out to the farm.

Jacinto was waiting for him, and while Virtue remained at the house, the two men gently carried Santiago down to the dell, where a third grave had been dug that morning.

"He loved this place," said Jacinto after they had filled in the grave. He looked around. "It *is* beautiful, isn't it?"

Cain nodded.

Jacinto stared down thoughtfully at the unmarked grave. "He was the best of them all."

"Was he a bounty hunter, too?" asked Cain.

Jacinto shook his head. "He came here as a colonist almost twenty years ago, and built the Barleycorn Tavern."

"What about the one before him?"

"A professor of alien languages."

"And a chess player?" asked Cain.

Jacinto smiled. "A very fine one."

Cain walked to a shaded area beneath a gnarled tree. "When you bury me, I want it to be right here," he said.

Jacinto drew himself up to his full height and looked into Cain's eyes. "Santiago cannot die," he said firmly.

"I know. But when you bury me, remember what I asked."

"I will," Jacinto promised.

Cain walked back to the three graves.

"Go on up to the house," he said. "I'll join you in a little while."

Jacinto nodded and began walking away, while Cain lowered his head and stared at the three mounds of earth. He stood there silently for almost half an hour, then sighed deeply and returned to the house.

Virtue was waiting for him on the veranda, camera in hand.

"Are you ready?" she asked eagerly.

"In a minute. I've got to say something to Jacinto first." He turned to her. "By the way, there's a condition."

"What is it?"

"You're to take no holograph of my face. You'll use the little camera I took from you yesterday and aim it at my hands." He paused. "That's my ground rule. Do you agree to it?"

"Of course," she replied easily. "It may actually extend my term as your biographer."

"I'm glad we understand each other."

He sought out Jacinto and asked for a status report on Winston Kchanga's organization.

"We've had no reply from them," said Jacinto.

"And the Democracy is still freezing Bortai's funds?"

Jacinto nodded.

"Then I'm going to have to pay our associates a little visit," said Cain grimly. "Load their coordinates into my ship's navigational computer. I'm leaving tomorrow."

"Yes, Santiago."

He returned to the veranda.

"All right," he said. "Let's begin."

"Suppose you start by telling me about this movement of yours," said Virtue, focusing her camera on the back of his right hand. "Who are you fighting against?"

"Movement?" he repeated, puzzled. "I don't know anything about any movement." She opened her mouth to protest. "But I can tell you about the seventeen men and women that I robbed and killed on Silverblue."

She grinned and activated the microphone, and he spoke far into the night, telling her the bloody history of the most notorious criminal in the galaxy.

EPILOGUE

Some say that he's a hundred,
Some say that he is more;
Some say he'll live forever—
This outlaw commodore!

That was the last verse Black Orpheus ever wrote.

Shortly after setting the words down, he landed on the fourth planet of the Beta Santori system. It was a beautiful world, a pastoral wonderland of green fields and cool clear streams and sturdy ancient trees, and the moment he stepped out of his ship he decided to spend the rest of his life as its only inhabitant.

He named it Eurydice.

Of course, even without Black Orpheus, life—and death—continued on the Inner Frontier.

Geronimo Gentry, Poor Yorick, and Jonathan Stern were all dead within a year—one from old age, one from too many alphanella seeds, and one from a plethora of sins that still had no names.

The Sargasso Rose remained a lonely and bitter woman, cursing Sebastian Cain nightly for not fulfilling his promise to her. Skullcracker Murchison lost his unofficial title, regained it, and finally retired after taking one blow too many to the head.

Peacemaker MacDougal hunted down Quentin Cicero and Carmella Sparks, then went deeper toward the core of the galaxy in search of Santiago. Dimitri Sokol served as ambassador for two years on Lodin XI, resigned when he felt he had accumulated enough political favors, and moved to Deluros VIII, where he ran successfully for a minor office and later was offered a major post within the government.

Father William was slow to heal from his wounds. He remained in the hospital for the better part of six months, invoking the wrath of God upon all the doctors who refused to release him until he had lost half his body weight. The day he walked out he began regaining his lost bulk with a vengeance, but his stamina was gone, and he finally settled on Safe Harbor, the pastor of that planet's only church.

As for the Swagman, he actually did team up with Virtue MacKenzie for a brief period. After they had yet another falling-out, he returned to Goldenrod and sat down to write his memoirs. His enthusiasm soon waned, though he never completely abandoned the project, and before long he had hired a new batch of menials and was once again adding to his collection in his inimitable way.

Virtue had left the Democracy in obscurity, but she returned as a celebrity. Her series of interviews with Santiago won her three major awards, and her biography of the notorious bandit made her wealthy. She returned to the Inner Frontier every couple of years for fresh material on the King of the Outlaws and never failed to come up with it. She drank too much, slept with too many men, and spent too much money—and enjoyed every minute of it.

Cain carried on his campaign for nine more years, spending what his network of illicit enterprises accumulated where it would do the most good, fighting only that handful of battles he knew he could win, and spreading the myth of Santiago even farther across the Frontier.

He had always felt that when the end came it would be at the hands of Peacemaker MacDougal—but it was Johnny One-Note, making only his ninth kill, who finally hunted him down. He was sitting on his veranda, gazing tranquilly across the rolling fields of corn and wheat, when it happened, and he never knew what hit him. Johnny One-Note got to within half a mile of his ship before they tracked him down and killed him.

That afternoon there was a fourth unmarked grave in the small dell by the pond—under the gnarled tree, as Cain had requested. In the evening Moonripple came all the way out from town on foot.

A slender man, with sad eyes and a brilliant streak of white running through his dark hair, stood on the front porch and watched her approach.

"Yes?" he said.

"I've come to see Santiago."

"Why?" he asked.

"I've been a barmaid all my life," she replied. "Father William says that it's time to do something more." She paused uneasily. "He says that Santiago might be able to help me."

"It's possible."

"Where can I find him?" asked Moonripple.

"Come, child," he said gently, reaching out his bandaged right hand to her. "I am Santiago."

THE RETURN OF SANTIAGO

To Carol, as always

And to the members of the Resnick Listserv
(Join it at www.mikeresnick.com), who keep me
amused, stimulated, alert, and reasonably sane

Table of Contents

PROLOGUE

Some people say he was killed by the Angel. Others say that Johnny One-Note gunned him down. Most think he died at the hands of Peacemaker MacDougal.

Nobody knows exactly when he met his fate, or where. It just slowly began dawning on his enemies—he didn't have any friends, not that anyone knew about—that he hadn't made any trouble for some time.

Now, that doesn't mean men weren't still killed and banks weren't still robbed and mining worlds weren't still plundered. After all, Santiago wasn't the only outlaw on the Inner Frontier; he was just the biggest—so big, some say, that his shadow blotted out the sun for miles around.

Long after the Angel and Johnny One-Note and Peacemaker MacDougal had all gone to their graves, men and women—and aliens—were still arguing about Santiago. Some held that he was just a man, a lot smarter and more ruthless than most, but a man nonetheless. Others said that he was a mutant possessed of extraordinary powers, or else how could he have held the Navy at bay for so many years? There were even a few who thought he was an alien, with undefined but awesome alien abilities.

There was no known holograph of him, no retinagram or fingerprint anywhere in the Democracy. There were a few eyewitness accounts, but they differed so much from each other that no one took any of them seriously. A long-dead thief who called himself the Jolly Swagman swore he was eleven feet three inches tall, with orange hair and blazing red eyes that had seen the inner sanctum of hell itself. A preacher named Father William claimed he was an alien who always wore a face mask because oxygen was poison to his system. Virtue MacKenzie, who wrote three books about him, never described him, and the only holograph she took was of the S-shaped scar on the back of his right hand. According to one description he was a purple-skinned alien with four arms. Another had him a mechanized, gleaming metal cyborg, no longer capable of any human emotion.

There was even a school of thought that argued that there never was a Santiago, that he was merely a myth—but there were too many graveyards on too many worlds to lend any credence to that belief.

They say that Black Orpheus, the poet and balladeer who wandered the spaceways, writing his endless epic of the larger-than-life heroes, villains, adventurers and misfits that he found there, spent half a dozen verses of his *Ballad of the Inner Frontier* describing Santiago in detail, but those verses were never codified and were lost to posterity.

The one thing everyone agreed upon was that the last time he had manifested his presence was in the year 3301 of the Galactic Era, and with the passing decades it was generally assumed that Santiago, whoever or whatever he may have been, was dead.

Which simply goes to show, as has been shown so many times in the past, that a majority of the people can be wrong.

For in 3407 G.E., 106 years after he vanished, Santiago returned to the Inner Frontier, to once again juggle worlds and secrets as in days of old, to bring death to his enemies, to stride across the planets in all his former glory.

This is his story. But to fully understand it, we must begin with Danny Briggs (who is not to remain Danny Briggs for long), a simple thief, physically unimpressive, artistically wanting, morally ambiguous, a young man of seemingly unexceptional gifts and abilities, and yet destined to play a central role in the return of Santiago. . . .

Part 1

The Rhymer's Book

1.

Some say that he's a hundred,
Some say that he is more;
Some say he'll live forever—
This outlaw commodore!

That was the last verse ever written by Black Orpheus, the Bard of the Inner Frontier. Though Santiago's name doesn't appear in it, it is generally considered to have been about the notorious King of the Outlaws.

And with that, Black Orpheus' history of the Frontier was done. Not finished in the sense that it was complete, but done. Shortly after writing those words he disappeared forever. Some say he found an idyllic world on which to live out his life. Others say that Santiago himself gunned him down. A handful believe that he found the task of codifying the entire history of the Inner Frontier in verse too daunting, and that he simply gave it up and went off to live out his years in solitude.

At the moment that he became a catalyst for history, Danny Briggs knew little of Santiago and even less of Black Orpheus. Like most kids, he'd grown up thrilled by legends about both, but that was the extent of his knowledge and his interest. On the third night of the fifth month of the year 3407 of the Galactic Era, Danny Briggs had other things on his mind as he scaled the end of a long, low building, a cloth bag slung over his right shoulder.

He moved slowly, carefully, trying not to make a sound—but then the wind shifted, carrying his scent to the creatures below, and all his precautions were for nothing. A huge Moondevil, two hundred pounds of muscle and sinew, saw him creeping across the roof and began howling. A Polarcat, glistening white in the moonlight, leaped up from its own enclosure and tried to dig its claws into Danny's leg.

As the young man sidestepped the Polarcat, two more animals of a type he'd never seen before launched themselves toward him, falling back as they hit the edge of the gently pitched roof.

Danny cursed under his breath. There was no sense moving cautiously any longer. The only way to shut all the animals up was to get out of their sight as quickly as possible. He raced the length of the roof, ignoring the increasing din, and finally jumped down to a small atrium. He adjusted his pocket computer to set up a signal that disrupted the security cameras, found the door he was looking for, used the code he had stolen months earlier, and entered the office.

He ignored the safe and instead activated the computer. In seconds he had accessed the data he needed. He pulled out his tiny scanner, transferred the data to it, and put it back in a pocket. Then he deactivated the computer. The entire operation took less than a minute.

He considered killing the security system and just walking out the front door, but that would have given away the fact that he'd been there, and all his efforts would be wasted if the police suspected that anyone had invaded this particular office—especially when they discovered that no money had been taken.

Instead he went back the way he'd come. The animals were silent now, but he knew they wouldn't stay that way for long. Choosing speed over stealth, he climbed onto the roof of the long, low building again and raced the length of it in the face of the ever-increasing howls, growls, and screams. When he came to the Moondevil, he reached into his cloth bag, withdrew a small dead animal, and tossed it into the Moondevil's enclosure. Now if enough neighbors reported all the noise and the police investigated, they'd find the remains of the animal and assume that it had somehow wandered into the kennel and caused all the commotion.

An hour later he was sitting at his usual table at the Golden Fleece, a tavern on the outskirts of New Punjab, a small city that had nothing in common with the original Punjab except the subjugation of its natives, in this case the orange-skinned humanoids of Bailiwick. The world wasn't a very large or very important one: it held no fissionable materials, few precious stones or metals, and the farmland wasn't the best. But it did have two million natives—it had had close to five million before the Navy pacified them—and three human cities, of which New Punjab, with almost forty thousand residents, was the largest.

It was said that Black Orpheus had once spent a night on Bailiwick, but there were no holograms or other records to prove it. Bailiwick's main claim to fame was Milos Jannis, who had been born there and was now the Democracy's middleweight freehand champion. Two minor actors and a second-rate novelist were the only other things Bailiwick had to brag about.

Danny Briggs didn't want to add to that total. He was content to remain relatively unknown and unapprehended. He shunned publicity the way bad politicians seek it out. Even when he turned a profit at what he considered to be his business, he always made sure to deposit and spend it offworld.

He ordered a drink and sat there, staring at himself in the mirror behind the bar. He wasn't thrilled with what he saw: He stood a few inches under six feet in an era when the average man stood two inches over six feet. He was thin; not emaciated, but somewhere between slender and wiry. His head was covered by nondescript brown hair. He didn't like his chin much; too pointy. For the hundredth time he considered growing a beard to cover it, but his mustache was so sparse he hated to think of what a beard would look like. His ears stuck out too far; he figured one of these days he was going to lose one or both in a fight.

No, on the whole, there wasn't much about Danny Briggs that he liked. Hell, he didn't even like the way he made his living. He didn't believe in God, so he didn't believe that God had some nobler purpose for him. He had no fire burning in his belly, but rather a certain unfocused dissatisfaction, a desire to make some kind of mark, to scratch his name on the boulder of Time so people would know he'd been here. Not that he was a hero, because he wasn't; not because he would someday make a difference to the handful of misfits and criminals that formed his circle of friends, because he knew he was incapable of making one; but simply to show those who came after him that once upon a time there was a man named Danny Briggs, and he had lived right here on Bailiwick, and that, just once, he'd done something worth remembering.

Except that everything he'd done up to now was aimed at letting no one know he'd been here, and far from remembering him, he wanted nothing more than for the police and the Democracy to completely ignore his existence.

Interesting conflict, he thought wryly. The urge to be known versus the need to be hidden. Perhaps someday he'd resolve it, though he doubted it.

A grizzled, white-haired man with a noticeable limp entered the Golden Fleece, looked around, and walked directly to Danny's table.

"I'm not too early, am I?" he asked.

"No, I've got it," said Danny.

"The usual price?"

"Three hundred Maria Theresa dollars up front and twenty percent of whatever you make."

"It was two hundred fifty last time," grumbled the man.

"Success breeds inflation."

"You sure you won't take Democracy credits?" asked the old man.

"I don't want anything to do with them," said Danny. *Besides,* he added mentally, *you start spending too many Democracy credits, you start attracting a little too much Democracy attention—but I guess you haven't figured that out, have you?*

"Okay, okay," said the old man. He removed a prosthetic hand, pulled a wad of money out of it, counted out three hundred Maria Theresa dollars, and pushed them across the table.

"Thanks," said Danny. He pulled out a tiny computer, retrieved an address, and transferred it to a hologram for the old man to study. "This is it."

"You're sure?"

"Have I ever been wrong yet?" asked Danny, nodding to another client, who had entered the Golden Fleece and caught his eye.

"No, you never have been," said the old man. "I don't know how you do it."

That's because you and every other fool I deal with would have broken into the kennel's safe tonight and come away with a couple hundred credits if you were lucky. Not one of you would ever think of stealing a list of the animals' owners, complete with their addresses and the dates that they're gone.

"Memorize it," said Danny, indicating the hologram that the tiny computer was projecting.

The man studied it, then nodded his head. Danny wiped the information from the machine and deactivated it.

"Thanks, Danny," said the old man, getting to his feet. The next client sat down opposite him.

Jesus! I rob the data from that computer every three or four months and don't take any other risks, and I get twenty percent of three hundred robberies a year. It's almost too *easy. Doesn't anyone else on this dirtball have a brain?*

Their negotiation completed, the man got up and left, and Danny was alone with his drink once again. A redhead, a bit overweight but still pretty, smiled a greeting at him from a nearby table.

"Hi, Danny," she said.

"Hi yourself, Duchess," said Danny. "I just finished tonight's business. Why don't you come over and join me?" He flashed a wad of money. "I'm solvent tonight."

"You never give up, do you?" she said, amused.

"Of course not," replied Danny. "You don't hit the moon if you don't shoot for it."

. "Am I the moon?"

"You'll do."

"Boy, you sure know how to turn a girl on," she said sardonically.

He smiled. "It works with all the other girls."

"So turn your charm on one of them."

"Anything worthwhile takes effort," he replied. "*You* take effort."

"I suppose I'm flattered," said the Duchess.

"So join me."

"I said I was flattered, not interested."

"One of these days you're going to say yes, and it'll be a race to see which of us drops dead from shock first."

"One of these days you'll get an honest job, and maybe I'll say yes."

"If I had an honest job, I couldn't afford you." He smiled. "I'm sure someone somewhere has based an entire philosophical system on a paradox just like that one."

"Not funny, Danny."

"Look, some people are great rulers of men, some are great cleaners of stables. I found out what I was good at early on."

"I think it's criminal that you feel that way."

He smiled again. "Criminal's the word. Still, I'm willing to be shown the error of my ways. Come have a drink."

"No, thanks."

"You really won't join me?"

"I really won't."

"But your heart would be broken if I hadn't asked, right?"

"Try not asking some night and we'll see."

"You drive a hard bargain, Duchess," said Danny. "But one of these days you'll see me as I really am."

"Maybe I already do."

"Fate forfend," he said in mock dismay.

A moment later he got up and made his way to the men's room.

As he was washing his hands the door dilated and two burly men entered the small cubicle.

"Hi, Danny," said the taller of them.

"Hi, Mr. Balsam," replied Danny, trying to hide his apprehension. "Hi, Mr. Gibbs."

"That's *Commander* Balsam."

"And *Lieutenant* Gibbs," added the shorter, wider man.

"That's only when you're on duty," said Danny. "And if you were on duty, you wouldn't be drinking in a tavern."

"We're not drinking," said Balsam. "And it's still Commander."

"Whatever makes you happy," said Danny. "Good evening, Commander."

"Well, it didn't start out that way, but it's improving," replied Balsam. A grin that boded no good spread across his face. "You fucked up big time tonight, Danny."

"I don't know what you're talking about. I've been in the bar all night."

"No, you've been swiping data from a kennel. We've got you cold."

"You have holograms of me breaking into a kennel? I doubt that."

"Of course we don't have any holos, Danny. You disabled the cameras, remember?"

"Fingerprints, then? Or maybe voiceprints, or a retinagram?" suggested Danny.

"We know you've wiped your prints, and you've got contacts that give a false retina reading," said Gibbs.

"Well, you're certainly welcome to search me for this mysterious data you're referring to."

"You're a bright lad, Danny," said Balsam. "You've either got it hidden away or committed to memory."

"I wish I could help you," said Danny with a smile, "but aren't you supposed to have evidence before you start making accusations?"

"Oh, we've got it, Danny. Holograms, retinagrams, voiceprints, everything."

Danny frowned. "But you just said—"

"We didn't get it at the kennel," said Balsam. "We got it at the market."

"What market?"

Balsam grinned again. "For a smart guy, you did a really dumb thing, Danny. You went to the biggest, best-protected market in town, and you bought a dead *minipor* to feed the animals if they got noisy."

"I assume you're going to get to the point sometime this evening," said Danny, already scanning the room for some means of escape.

"The *minipor*'s a rare item, Danny. And the reason it's a rarity is because it comes from Churchill II. The store has security cameras showing you buying the only *minipor* imported to Bailiwick in the past half year—and there was enough of its skeleton left in the Moondevil's enclosure so that we could identify it." He paused. "It was a nice scam, Danny. Of all the scum I deal with, only *you* would have figured out there was a hundred times more profit in a list of empty houses than in the kennel's cash box."

Danny glanced at the small window on the back wall of the washroom.

"Don't even think of it," said Gibbs. "You'd never fit through, and we'd tack on another two years for trying to escape."

"Who's escaping?" said Danny pleasantly. "I hope you have a comfortable cell. My lawyer doesn't like getting up before noon, so I'll be spending the night with you."

"This night and the next thousand," said Balsam. He withdrew a pair of glowing manacles. "Hands behind your back, Danny."

"Can I get a drink of water first?"

"Okay, but no funny stuff."

"You tell me what's funny about a glass of water," said Danny, pulling a cup out of the wall and holding it beneath the faucet. "Cold," he ordered.

Cold water filled the cup, and Danny drank it down.

"One more?"

"Come on, Danny. You had your drink."

"You know what the water's like in jail," said Danny. "Let me have one more drink. How can it hurt?"

Balsam shrugged. "Yeah, okay, go ahead."

"Thanks," said Danny. He turned to the sink and held the glass under the tap as the two officers relaxed and waited for him.

"Hot!" he croaked.

Boiling hot water filled the glass, and in a single motion he hurled it in Balsam's face, grabbed the manacles, connected Gibbs' wrist to the sink, and raced out the door.

Danny had a three-step lead on Balsam as he raced to the door of the Golden Fleece. The commander pulled out a screecher, a sonic pistol that would put him out for the rest of the night and give him a headache for a week, but as he was running after Danny and taking aim, the Duchess stuck out a foot and tripped him. He fell with a bone-jarring thud.

Danny raced back to the table, took her hand, and began pulling her toward the door.

"I didn't mean to do that!" she said, panic-stricken. "It was instinct! I just didn't want him to shoot you!"

"I believe you!" said Danny urgently. "*He* never will! Come on! He's not going to stay down forever, and he's got a partner!"

Suddenly Gibbs, the manacle hanging from his wrist, burst into the tavern.

"*Now!*" said Danny urgently. The Duchess took a quick glance at Gibbs, screamed, and actually beat Danny out the door.

"Left!" he whispered as he caught up with her. They reached the corner and had just turned out of the line of sight when the two policemen emerged, weapons in hand, from the tavern.

"Now they're going to kill us!" whispered the Duchess, terrified.

"They're never going to find us," answered Danny. "Just trust me and do what I say."

They ran through the streets, turning frequently, never seeing any sign of their pursuers, always moving farther and farther from the center of the small city. After a few minutes the buildings took on new and different shapes: some were triangular, some trapezoidal, some seemed to follow no rational plan at all.

"Where are we?" asked the Duchess, as Danny led her down narrow winding streets that seemed totally patternless.

"The native quarter," he said. "They won't follow us here."

"Is it dangerous?" she asked, looking around.

"It is if they know you work for the Democracy. They'll leave us alone."

"How do you know?"

"I've spent a lot of time here," said Danny, nodding to an orange-skinned being who stared right through him as if he didn't exist. "They know I won't do them any harm."

"You have alien friends?"

"They're not aliens, they're natives," answered Danny. "And yes, I have friends here."

She began looking panicky again. "I can't believe it! I'm a fugitive, and I'm hiding out in the alien quarter!"

"Calm down," said Danny. "You're safe now."

"*You* calm down!" she snapped. "Maybe you're used to having the police after you, but it's a new experience for me, and I don't like it very much!"

"They won't come to the quarter," he said confidently.

"Are we going to spend the night here?"

He shook his head. "We'll give the police half an hour to figure out where I went, and another couple of minutes to decide it's not worth the effort to search for us here."

"Then what?"

He smiled. "Then we have our choice of fifty-three empty houses."

She lit a smokeless cigarette. "So it's not enough that I helped a criminal escape capture," she said bitterly. "Now the police can add breaking and entering to the charges."

"I'm grateful that you stopped my friend Commander Balsam from shooting me," said Danny, "but no one asked you to. It was your choice to hinder a police officer in the pursuit of a criminal, so don't blame me."

"I told you: I wasn't thinking clearly," she said. "I was just reacting."

"Believe me, no one's going to arrest you," Danny assured her. "Any red-blooded man who was at the tavern will swear that Balsam tripped over you."

"Do you really think so?"

"I do. Besides, if *I* don't know your real name, neither do they. If you choose to stay with me, all they know is they're after someone who called herself the Duchess. Correct me if I'm wrong, but I'll give plenty of ten-to-one that that's not the name on your ID disk or your passport."

"It isn't. I didn't like my name, so I changed it."

"They do that on the Inner Frontier, not here on the Democracy worlds. How can the government keep tabs on you if they don't know who you are?"

"I never thought of it that way," she said, "but maybe choosing a new name wasn't a bad idea."

"Beats the hell out of being a Myrtle."

"Do I look like a Myrtle to you?"

He stared at her and shook his head. "You look like a Duchess who saved my life. Of course, you won't drink with me, but if I have to choose between your doing one or the other . . ." He ended with a smile.

"Well, you look exactly like a Danny Briggs."

"That bad, huh?"

"If you don't like the name, change it like I did."

"What would I change it to?"

"That's for you to decide."

"I never had a hero," he admitted. "I guess I'll keep it and stay who I am."

They stood in silence for a few more minutes, engulfed in angular shadows. Then Danny checked his timepiece.

"We've been here almost an hour," he announced. "I think we can start hunting up a place to stay while we figure out our next move."

"Where are we going?" she asked as he began walking back toward the city.

"Where do you want to go?"

"You know that little hill at the south end of town, the one overlooking Lake Belora?" she said. "Have you got anything there?"

"I've got two houses in the area," he replied. "I won't know if either of them has a lake view until we get there."

The first house was actually in a valley just beyond the hill, but the second, still luxurious but less impressive, looked like they would be able to see the lake from the second level.

"It's too bad I didn't know this would be happening," remarked Danny. "There's an empty villa fronting the lake. It even has a dock and a couple of boats."

"So let's go there."

He shook his head. "It's going to be robbed sometime tonight. We don't want to be anywhere near it, just in case."

"How will we get in?" asked the Duchess as they approached the front door of the house they had chosen. "I don't know *how* to break into a house. Won't it have a security system?"

"Have a little trust in the man whose life you saved," he replied, kneeling down to study the computer lock. *"Shit!"*

"What is it?"

"I can crack the combination in a couple of minutes, but it's got a bone reader."

"A bone reader?"

"Yeah. I can get around almost any retina ID system, but bone readers are tough. They scan your skeleton and compare it to anyone who the computer's been programmed to accept. I've got a couple of healed fractures that won't match up against anyone else's."

"Then we'll do without our lake view and go to the other house."

"Give me a minute," he said. "There's never been a security system that couldn't be penetrated."

"By you?"

"By somebody." He flashed her a smile. "I am but a talented amateur."

"Sure," she retorted. "And I'm a millionaire virgin."

"That gives me all the more reason to find a way into the house."

He touched the lock, and a holographic screen appeared in the air, filled with dozens of icons. His fingers began moving expertly over the lock, and the icons began racing across the screen in near-hypnotic patterns.

"How's it coming?" asked the Duchess after a few minutes.

"Oh, it's been unlocked for a while," he said.

"But you can't hide your fractures."

"I'm not trying to."

After another minute he stood up. "Okay," he said. "I'm done."

The door dilated, and she began to step through it. He grabbed her arm and held her back.

"Gentlemen first," he said, stepping through.

The door slammed shut in her face. He disappeared for a moment, then opened the door and invited her in.

"What was that all about?" she said, entering the house.

"I fed the computer the data about my skeleton and told it I'd been approved. But I didn't know what your skeletal history might be, so after I went in I deactivated the security system." He paused. "I also ordered all the windows to polarize. We can see out, but no one on the outside can see in, even if we have the lights on."

"Do you do this kind of thing often?" she asked.

"Certainly not," he replied. "I get people who are hungrier than I am to do it for me."

She stared at him with an expression that was a cross between concern and admiration. "There's a lot more to you than meets the eye."

"Thank you," said Danny. "I won't even offer an obscene rejoinder." He looked around. "So what do you think of our new quarters?"

"Elegant," she said, walking through the entry room. The carpet anticipated her steps and thickened as she walked, and the mural on the wall slowly, almost imperceptibly, began turning into a three-dimensional scene, then gradually added motion. It went back to being a flat painting as they passed into the next room.

"This is some house!" she said. "I've never been close to anything like this!"

"Yeah, a person could get used to this without much effort," agreed Danny, as a chair positioned itself to accommodate him.

"As long as we're going to be stuck here for a day or two, let's go upstairs and see if we can see the lake," suggested the Duchess.

"Why not?" assented Danny, following her to a staircase. As they put their feet on the first wide stair, it metamorphosed into a carpeted escalator, totally silent, and gently transported them up to the second floor.

They walked to a window and stared out.

"You can *almost* see it," she said. "If we were even one floor higher we'd have a magnificent view."

"I saw a third level of windows when we were outside," said Danny. "There's probably an attic above us somewhere. We should be able to see it from there."

They searched through the rooms, and finally came to an airlift next to a storage closet.

"This has got to be it," said Danny. "It's the only thing leading up."

"What do we stand on?" asked the Duchess nervously as she looked down to the basement some thirty feet below.

"Just step into the shaft," explained Danny. "It'll sense your presence, and you'll stand on a cushion of air that'll take you up to the attic."

"You're sure? I've never seen one of these things before."

"They're all the rage on Deluros VIII and the bigger worlds," said Danny. "Give it another twenty years and they'll be just as popular here."

She looked skeptical, so he stepped into the shaft first. When she saw him standing on air she joined him, and they floated gently up to the attic.

"Lights," he ordered, and suddenly the attic was illuminated with soft, indirect lighting. As tidy as the house had been, the attic was that chaotic. Books, tapes, disks, and cubes were stacked awkwardly on the floor; paintings were piled against a wall, each leaning on the next. Piles of old wrinkled clothes sat beside piles of unmarked plastic boxes.

"Take a look, Danny!" she enthused, staring out a window. "You can see the whole lake. It's gorgeous!"

"Just a minute," he replied, walking to another window. He knelt down, pushing a few plastic boxes aside. One of the ancient boxes literally cracked open and fell apart.

"Don't you just love the way the moonlight plays on the water?" said the Duchess.

"Oh, Jesus!" whispered Danny.

"I didn't hear you."

There was no answer, and she turned to him.

"I thought you were looking out the window," she said, staring at him as he fingered through a stack of ancient, crumbling papers. He paid no attention to her. *"Danny!"* she said irritably. "What's the matter with you?"

Finally he looked up, the strangest expression on his face. "Who'd have guessed it?" he whispered. "I mean, this is just another house. Nothing special, nothing to indicate . . ." His voice trailed off.

"What are you talking about?" she demanded.

He held up a sheet of paper.

"We just hit the mother lode," he said in awed tones.

2.

Come if you dare, come but beware,
Come to the lair of Altair of Altair.
Offer a prayer to the men foul and fair,
Trapped in the snare of Altair of Altair.

That was the first thing Danny read. Soon he was making his way through the thousands of verses.

"They don't even know what they've got here!" he said excitedly. "If they did, it would be under lock and key in a vault, not out in the open in a plastic box that's falling apart."

"What is it?" asked the Duchess.

"Listen," said Danny. He picked up another page and read to her:

"They call him the Angel, the Angel of Death,
If ever you've seen him, you've drawn your last breath.
He's got cold lifeless eyes, he's got brains, he's got skill,
He's got weapons galore, and a yearning to kill."

"Is that supposed to mean something to me?" she asked.

"That's the Angel he's writing about!" enthused Danny. "*The Angel!* Haven't you heard of him?"

She shrugged.

"He was the greatest bounty hunter of them all! They say he killed more than two hundred men!"

"So you found a poem about the Angel," said the Duchess, her interest fading. "So what?"

"You don't understand!" said Danny. He held up a sheaf of papers with the same scrawl on all of them. "This isn't just *any* poem! This is Black Orpheus' original manuscript!"

"Yeah?" she said, walking over to look at it. "What makes you think so?"

"The verses themselves. They're all about the characters he met on the Frontier. And I've heard about these characters—Altair of Altair and the Angel. Heard about them, read about them. They've even made some videos about them."

"But anyone could write a few verses."

He opened three more ancient boxes, and pulled verse-covered pages from each. "A few verses, sure. Ten thousand verses, I don't think so. This is *it!*"

"What's it worth?" asked the Duchess.

"Who knows? Ten million, thirty million. What's history worth to a people who don't have any?"

"I don't know what you're talking about," she said.

"He was the Bard of the Inner Frontier. There's no law on the Frontier, no government, and there's sure as hell no historians. He was all they had, him and this poem. Bits and pieces have been printed here and there, but no one's ever seen the whole thing." He patted the pile of papers. "Until tonight."

"Who would buy a bundle of crumbling old papers?"

"Every museum and every library in the galaxy," answered Danny. "And probably every collector." He held up a long, thick feather. "This is the quill pen he wrote with. This alone ought to bring half a million."

"You're kidding!"

"The hell I am. All I have to do is check through the whole man-uscript and make sure it's authentic."

"And you can really auction it for that much?"

"Not publicly," he said. "I'm stealing it, remember?"

"Well, if the people who own this place don't know what they've got . . ."

"It makes no difference. The bidders—well, the *legitimate* bidders, the ones I plan to avoid—will want to know how I got it. They'll want to take it away to authenticate it, and once it's out of my possession, I can't control what happens to it."

"So it'll be a private sale?"

"A very limited auction, let's call it," he corrected her. "Market value could be fifty million credits. I'll take twenty million and be happy with it."

"I hear a lot of 'I's," she said suddenly. "What happened to 'we'?"

"I thought you didn't want to be a criminal."

"I'm *already* a criminal. I might as well be a rich one."

"I'll take care of you," promised Danny.

"I don't want to be taken care of," complained the Duchess. "I want to be a partner—an *equal* partner."

"I don't have equal partners," said Danny.

"You'd never have found it if I hadn't wanted a view of the lake," she persisted.

"And you still wouldn't know what it was if I hadn't told you," retorted Danny. "I said I'd take care of you and I will. Now get off my back and let me look at what we've got here."

"We should pack it up and leave Bailiwick tonight," said the Duchess.

He shook his head. "Too soon. They'll have men posted at the spaceport, and I don't own a private ship."

"What makes you think they won't still have men posted in another day or two?"

"Look, I embarrassed them, but it was a small-time crime. Pretty soon there'll be a nice juicy murder or two, and they'll decide to go after bigger fish."

"You'd better be right," she said.

"You're free to leave any time you want," said Danny. "But I stay here, and so"—he patted the boxes—"do *these*."

She stared at him sullenly for a long moment, then walked to the air shaft. "I'm going down to the kitchen to see what kind of food they've got." She paused, then added reluctantly, "Do you want anything?"

"Yeah. Bring me back a beer if they have any."

She disappeared down the shaft, and returned five minutes later with a pair of beers. She walked across the cluttered floor to hand one to Danny.

"Listen to this," he said excitedly:

> *"The Songbird stalks, the Songbird kills,*
> *The Songbird works to pay his bills.*
> *So, friend, beware the Songbird's glance:*
> *If you're his prey, you'll have no chance."*

Danny looked up, his face aglow with excitement. "You know what I think? I think he's writing about Sebastian Cain!"

"Never heard of him," said the bored Duchess.

"What kind of education have you had?" he said contemptuously.

"Math, science, computers, literature—the usual."

"Sadly lacking."

"Not everyone studies killers and cutthroats," she shot back.

"They should. They're much more interesting than vectors and angles."

"So who was the Songbird?"

"I told you: Sebastian Cain."

"That's what I meant: who was Sebastian Cain?"

"Another bounty hunter. And a revolutionary early in his life."

"Why is he the Songbird?" she asked. "And don't tell me something silly like he whistled whenever he killed a man."

"His full name was Sebastian Nightingale Cain. I think Orpheus took it from his middle name."

"And everyone knew him as the Songbird?"

Danny shook his head. "No, I don't know if anyone did." He paused and stared at the paper in his hand. "I could be wrong, but I'd bet the farm that the Songbird was Cain!"

"Why is that so important?"

"Cain was a major figure on the Frontier a century ago. There's nothing written about it here, but I've got a feeling he's the one who killed the Angel."

"You got all that from a few verses?" she asked skeptically.

"Like every kid, I grew up learning everything I could about the Inner Frontier. *That's* where the action was, where all the bigger-than-life heroes and villains lived and died. I'm just adding what I already knew to what I've read here." He paused. "Black Orpheus hid a lot of things inside those verses. It's like putting together a very complex jigsaw puzzle."

"Well, you play detective," said the Duchess, making no attempt to feign interest. "I'm going to find a bedroom."

"Fine, you do that," he said, never looking up from the manuscript.

When she awoke in the morning, she went up to the attic and found him still sitting there, poring over the manuscript.

"I take it you haven't been to bed yet," she said.

He looked up, his face aglow with excitement. "Listen to this:

> *"His name is Father William,*
> *His aim is hard to ken:*
> *His game is saving sinners;*
> *His fame is killing men.*

"Father William was a preacher. They say he tipped the scales at more than four hundred pounds. According to legend, he was also a bounty hunter."

"It sounds like your friend Black Orpheus went to a bounty hunters' convention," she observed.

"That's all the law there was on the Inner Frontier," replied Danny. "All the law there is even today." He looked up from the papers. "I've been piecing things together all night, and you know what I think?"

"What?" she asked in bored tones.

"I think Father William actually worked for Santiago. In fact, I think he was a conduit for most of the money that Santiago stole."

"That doesn't make any sense," said the Duchess.

"Why not?"

"Santiago was the greatest outlaw in the galaxy, right? Why would he use this preacher as a conduit to move money he stole? Move it *where*? You don't steal money just to give it away again. You keep it, or else you spend it on yourself. So it makes no sense." She made no attempt to hide her annoyance.

"I've still got thousands of verses to read," said Danny, "but there's something very strange about this manuscript, and it has to do with Santiago. I'm not sure what, but I'll find out before I'm done."

"Well, at least you know now that Santiago existed."

"I always did."

"You took it on faith," she said.

"And now my faith has been rewarded."

"Good. Now let's pack up and get the hell off the planet and sell the damned thing."

"Too soon," said Danny. "We'll give Balsam and Gibbs another day to get tired of looking for us."

"Just one day, and then we go!"

"Probably."

"What's this 'probably' shit?" she demanded. "One day and we're out of here!"

"There's no rush," he replied. "The owners aren't coming home for two more weeks."

"I'm not staying here two weeks!"

"Just a day or two."

"*One* day. And even so, I don't like it."

"You're free to go any time you want," said Danny. "But the manuscript stays with me."

"Don't get so cocky," she warned him. "I might leave right now and turn you in for the reward."

Danny smiled. "You might, but you won't."

"Why not?"

"Because whatever the reward comes to, it's peanuts next to what I'll give you once we've sold the poem." His smile vanished. "Now leave me alone and let me get back to work."

He spent the day poring over the manuscript. At sunset the Duchess insisted he come down to the kitchen for dinner. He ate quickly and unenthusiastically, then went back to the attic to continue reading.

She heard a loud *thump!* in the middle of the night and went upstairs to see what had happened. Danny had been sitting on the floor, reading, and finally fell asleep. He had fallen over on his side, and now lay, snoring gently, a page still clutched in his hand. She figured he was out for the next twelve to sixteen hours, but when she checked on him again in the morning he was up and reading.

"Danny!" she insisted. "Put it down for a few hours. You'll kill yourself!"

"I didn't know you cared."

"I don't want you dying before we sell the poem. I wouldn't begin to know how or where to do it."

"You sure know how to flatter a guy," he said.

"So are you going to get some sleep?" she said, ignoring his remark.

"Not right away," he said. "I'm getting close."

"Close to what? Finishing?"

"To understanding."

"What's to understand? They're all just four-line verses. There's nothing very difficult about them. In fact, I thought Black Orpheus would be a better poet. The things you've read to me sounded wimpy and literary and kind of lame."

"It's *what* he says, and what he *doesn't* say, not *how* he says it," replied Danny. "This thing is nothing short of the secret history of the Inner Frontier up to a century ago."

"Everything's a mystery," she said with no show of interest. "Why does it have to be a *secret* history? Why not a public one? After all, the public read it."

"The men and women and aliens he wrote about were alive when he wrote these verses. Many of them had prices on their heads. Still more confided in him, told him of deeds, some good, some bad, that no one knew about. You have to understand: Black Orpheus was the Bard of the Inner Frontier. He was welcomed everywhere he went. No one ever turned away from him—but to earn that kind of trust, he couldn't openly say anything more than you might find on a Wanted poster." Danny paused, his eyes still bright with excitement. "So he found secret ways to say what he wanted to say. This manuscript is to the Inner Frontier what, oh, I don't know, what Homer was to the Trojan War. Except that Homer exaggerated like hell and told everything out in the open, and Orpheus is concealing things all over the place. Including something huge, right in the middle."

"You said that yesterday. What is it?"

"I don't know. I think I'm getting close to piecing it together, but I won't know what it is until I'm done. It's as if he were holding someone for ransom, and I had the money, and he wanted to make sure the police weren't tailing me, so he ran me all over the city to make sure I was clean." He emitted an exhausted sigh. "He's running me all over the history of the Inner Frontier before I can discover what he's hiding."

"Maybe you're not supposed to find it."

"That would make a mockery of the whole thing. No, it's there—but he didn't want it to be easy." Danny looked at her. "That means it's something *big*. Otherwise, he wouldn't have taken such trouble to hide it. I spotted Cain and some of the others right away, but this whatever-it-is is taking a lot more work. Still, another few hours, another day or two, and I'll have it."

"Hey!" she shouted. "We're leaving today, remember?"

"We'll see."

"You promised!"

"You *wanted* me to promise," answered Danny. "That's not the same thing."

"Every day we stay here we increase our risk. A neighbor could report us. The police could find us. The owners could return early. We've been pushing our luck, Danny. Why can't we leave?"

"I'm still piecing things together," he said. "I don't want to stop, not even for a day."

"You act like it's some kind of treasure map."

"I doubt it. Legend has it that Orpheus died broke on an uninhabited world that he named after his dead wife, Eurydice."

"He doesn't sound all that brilliant to me," said the Duchess. "He writes little rhymes that anyone can do—"

"I *told* you—" Danny interrupted her.

"I know what you said. But you haven't discovered any deep dark secrets yet, so maybe there aren't any. He's famous all over the Frontier, all over the Democracy too, and he died penniless." She snorted contemptuously. "Some genius."

"Most poets die penniless," said Danny. "Anyway, I envy him."

"Why?"

"He traveled the Frontier, saw a new world every few days, lived every kid's dream, every romantic's dream. He did important work—and look at the people he got to meet, men and women like the Songbird, Father William, the Jolly Swagman, Peacemaker MacDougal, Johnny One-Note, the Angel, the Sargasso Rose. Just the names alone conjure up such fantastic pictures." He picked up another sheet and began reading:

> *"Moonripple, Moonripple, touring the stars,*
> *Has polished the wax on a thousand bars,*
> *Has trod on the soil of a hundred worlds,*
> *Has found only pebbles while searching for pearls.*

"Listen to her name: Moonripple. A girl named Moonripple, who's been to a hundred worlds. Now, *that's* evocative—especially when you live on a dirtball like"—he grimaced—"Bailiwick."

The Duchess was unimpressed. "Read the rest of the verse. She found only pebbles while searching for pearls."

"She found a lot more than that," said Danny. "You just have to know where to look and how to read it."

"It sounds to me like she died as broke as Orpheus," said the Duchess with finality, walking to the shaft. "I'm not kidding, Danny. I want to leave here today. I keep looking out the windows every five minutes, expecting to see the police surrounding us."

"Soon," he said distractedly, his attention already back on the manuscript.

Two hours later he went down to the kitchen and made some coffee.

"Well?" she demanded.

"I just need a little time away from the poem, time to think."

"To think about what, or am I going to be sorry I asked?"

"There's stuff there even Orpheus didn't know about," said Danny. "He was too close to the forest to see the trees."

"Whatever *that* means."

"I don't know what it means." He paused, swaying slightly from lack of food and sleep. "But I *will* know," he promised as he downed his coffee and went back up to the attic.

He was back down an hour later, a triumphant smile on his face.

"All right," he said. "Now we can leave."

"Why now?" she asked. "What do you think you've learned?"

"*The* secret."

"This is about the poem?"

"This is about the Inner Frontier," he replied. "It's all there in the poem, but even Black Orpheus didn't know how to interpret it." He shook his head in wonderment. "The greatest character of all, and he never knew!"

"Orpheus was the greatest character?" she asked, puzzled.

"No," he said distractedly. "I'm talking about Santiago!"

"*That's* what you learned?" she said incredulously. "Everyone knows that Santiago was the greatest outlaw in the history of the Inner Frontier."

"But he *wasn't*," said Danny, still smiling. "*That's* what I learned."

"What are you talking about?" demanded the Duchess.

"Santiago," explained Danny. "He wasn't an outlaw, not in the normal sense of the word. Oh, he did illegal things, but he was actually a revolutionary. I knew that yesterday afternoon."

"That's rubbish! Everything I've ever heard about him—"

"—was what he *wanted* people to hear," concluded Danny. "You asked once about bounty hunters. Here's your answer: if the Democracy had known he was a revolutionary, they'd have sent the whole fleet, five billion strong, to the Inner Frontier to hunt him down—so he made them think he was an outlaw, and all he had to deal with was a handful of bounty hunters. Orpheus guessed at that, but he never knew for sure."

"So Santiago killed all the bounty hunters?" she said.

Danny smiled again. "He tried, but he didn't always succeed— and *that's* the secret that's hidden in the poem, the secret even Orpheus didn't know."

"You're not making sense. How could he have stayed in business if he *hadn't* killed them?"

"There wasn't just *one* Santiago!" said Danny, unable to contain his excitement. "There was a series of them! I'm sure Sebastian Cain was one, and I think his successor was Esteban Cordoba." He paused for effect. "There were at least six Santiagos, maybe as many as eight!"

"You're crazy!"

"I'm right! Virtue MacKenzie, his biographer—she tried to hide it, but she was so sloppy that scholars never put much stock in her books, even though they sold tens of millions of copies." His arms shot up in a sign of triumph. "The most important single thing in the history of the Inner Frontier, and we're the only two people who know it!"

"So now we can leave the planet and then sell the manuscript?" she asked with a look of relief.

"We'll leave the planet," he agreed.

"And sell the manuscript."

He shook his head. "I'm not selling anything, not yet."

"Then what are you going to do with it?" she demanded.

"Add to it."

"What are you talking about?"

"Maybe it's time for the Inner Frontier to have a chronicler again."

"You?" said the Duchess incredulously.

"Why not?"

"I thought you were a criminal."

"I've *been* a criminal. I've never tried being a poet or a chronicler."

"What does the job pay?"

"What's the going price on immortality?"

"Immortality?"

"I plan to create something that outlasts me, just as Orpheus did." He looked off into the distance, at some exotic place only he could see. "Think of all those worlds I've never seen—Serengeti, Greenveldt, Walpurgis III, Binder X, the Roosevelt system, Oceana . . . worlds I only heard about and dreamed about when I was a kid. You know," he added confidentially, "this is the first time I've been excited—really *excited*—about anything since I was that little kid, dreaming of those worlds."

"You're really considering it, aren't you?" she said.

"I'm done considering it," he said with a sudden decisiveness. "I'm *doing* it."

"But why?" she demanded, as visions of the auction receded into the distance.

"There are hundreds of thieves here on Bailiwick. There are millions in the Democracy, dozens of millions in the galaxy. But there was only one Black Orpheus, and there will be only one me. A century after I'm dead, someone will read my poem the way I'm reading *his*, and I'll have made my mark on the universe. I'll have done something that outlasts me. People will know I was here."

"And is that so important to you?"

"It always was."

"And what about me?" she said bitterly. "Three days ago I was a law-abiding citizen. Three minutes ago I was a fugitive, but one who'd been promised a substantial amount of money from selling Orpheus' poem. Now I'm still a fugitive, but with no financial prospects again! You owe me something!"

"I said I'd take care of you. I will."

"How?"

"I don't know yet—but a million opportunities are opening up, and one thing I've always been good at is seizing opportunities."

"You'd damned well better be," the Duchess shot back. "In the meantime, you'd better work at making the name of Danny Briggs worth something."

He shook his head. "That's no name for a Bard."

"Did you have one in mind?"

"Give me a few minutes," he said, walking to a computer and activating it.

She went to the kitchen to pour herself a beer, and she drank it before returning. When she entered the room he looked up at her, a happy smile on his face.

"You found one," she said.

"We may be going to worlds that seem like paradise, and we may be going to worlds that reek of hellfire. Now I'm prepared for both." He paused. "From this day forward, my name is Dante Alighieri."

3.

They call him the rhymer, a wordsmith by trade,
He can bring you to tears or use words like a blade.
He roams the frontier writing down what he sees,
And he makes men immortal, dotting i's, crossing t's.

That was the first verse Dante Alighieri ever put to paper. Internal evidence suggests he wrote it while still on Bailiwick, though of course that is impossible to prove.

It wasn't true when he wrote it. No one had yet called him the Rhymer (or even Dante), and he had never been to the Inner Frontier. But before long the verse would gain an aura of absolute truth, and eventually it was so widely accepted that people forgot that it was merely a prediction when it first appeared.

Finding Black Orpheus' manuscript may have given him his initial impetus to go to the Frontier, but it was the arrival of the police that gave him a more immediate reason.

"Hey, Danny!" hissed the Duchess, staring out the kitchen window.

"I keep telling you," he replied irritably, looking up from his coffee cup, "the name's Dante."

"I don't care what the name is!" she snapped. "Whoever you are today, you'd better know a way out of here!"

"What are you talking about?" asked Dante.

"Take a look," she said. "We've got company."

"You must be mistaken. The owners aren't due back for almost two weeks!"

"These aren't the owners! They're the police!"

He raced to the window and saw two policemen standing about fifty feet away, staring at the house and speaking to each other. *"Shit!"*

"I thought you told me no one could see in!" said the Duchess accusingly.

"They can't," answered Dante. "But I should have figured once Balsam knew what I'd stolen from the kennel, he'd put a lookout on every house that was boarding an animal there."

"So they're just going to set up shop out there and watch the house?" she asked.

"Probably," he said. "But we can't count on that. They might decide to check and see if anything's been stolen."

"They don't seem to be moving any closer."

"They could be waiting for orders to enter, or for a backup team, or for some heat and motion sensors that will tell them we're here." He stepped back from the window. "We're not going to wait for that."

"What will we do?"

"Leave, of course."

"You're crazy!" she said. "It's broad daylight, and neither of us is armed."

"I don't like guns. If you carry one, sooner or later you have to use it. I'm a thief, not a killer." He paused. "By nighttime they'll definitely have the place under electronic surveillance. We're better off leaving right now."

"You think we can just go out the door and wave to them as we walk past?" she said sardonically.

"They're both in front," said Dante. "We'll go out the back. With a little luck and a little maneuvering, we can keep the house between us and them until we make it to the next street." He saw the doubt on her face. "Trust me. I've gotten out of worse scrapes than this."

He walked to the airlift.

"What are you doing?"

"I've got to get the manuscript."

"Five boxes? Do you know how heavy that will be?"

"Then you can help me carry it."

"What if we have to run?" she persisted. "I know what you think it's worth—but it's not worth a thing to us if they throw us in jail."

"I'm not leaving without it. Look through the closets and see if there's something we can carry it in. Most of the boxes it's in now are falling apart."

He returned a moment later, and found her waiting for him with a small overnight bag.

"You're going to look damned silly walking through our neighbor's yard and down the street carrying that," she noted.

"Not as silly as I'd look carrying three thousand pages in busted boxes," he replied, transferring the manuscript to the bag. "One thing I've learned over the years: act as if whatever you're doing, no matter how aberrant, is normal, and nobody will give you a second glance." He examined the bag. "Has this thing got a strap?"

"I didn't see one."

"Then let me rig something with one of our host's belts. I'll be a lot happier if I can sling it over my shoulder and have both hands free."

"Why bother? As you pointed out, you're unarmed."

"Don't get too melodramatic," he said. "I'm more likely to need my hands to solve a computer lock or even hold a sandwich than to shoot anyone."

She walked to a closet, found a belt, and tossed it to him. "You got me into this," she said. "I hope to hell that you can get me out."

"Just don't lose your head and you'll be fine."

He connected both ends of the belt to the bag, slung it over his shoulder, was surprised at how heavy it was, and walked to the back door.

"Okay," he said. "Take one last look to make sure they haven't moved, and then we'll leave."

She walked to the window, peered out, then turned to him. "They're in the same place," she informed him.

"Good," he said. "It's less than one hundred feet to all that shrubbery our neighbor planted at the back of his yard. See the tallest bush there? Just walk to it in a straight line from the back door, and I guarantee that no one on the street will be able to see you."

"And when I get there?" she asked, staring at the bush.

"I think there's room to walk around it on the left without getting tangled up in any thorns. Then walk straight through, and if anyone sees you just act like you've got a perfect right to be there. I promise no one will challenge you."

"What if someone does?"

"Not to worry—I'll be right behind you."

"Then what?"

"Then we walk to the nearest public conveyance, take it to the spaceport, and figure out a way to get the hell off this dirtball."

"Have you got any money?"

"You know I do. You saw me getting paid at the Golden Fleece."

"Then let's take a private aircab to the spaceport," she said. "For all you know, our faces are plastered all over the public transports."

He considered her suggestion, then nodded his assent. "Yeah, probably we're safe either way, but there's no sense taking chances."

"If we're safe, why are the police watching the house?"

"If they thought there was even a one-in-a-hundred chance that Danny Briggs was in the house, they'd have blown the door away and come after me," answered Dante confidently. "They're the crime-prevention unit, not the criminal catchers." He opened the back door. "Now let's go."

The Duchess walked out into the warm dry air and he followed her. They made it to the largest shrub undetected, then circled it, walked through the neighbor's yard—not undetected, but unhindered by an orange-skinned native gardener who stared at them for a moment and then went back to work—and then they were on the next street.

They walked to a corner and summoned an aircab, then rode in silence to the spaceport. Dante waited while the robot driver scanned the cash he'd given it and made change. He looked around for the Duchess and saw that she was walking toward the spaceport's entrance. He quickly caught up with her, linked his arm with hers, and turned her so they were walking parallel to the large departure building.

"What's the matter?" she complained.

"If they're watching houses, they're watching the spaceport too," he said. "Don't be in such a hurry to walk right into their hands."

"You've spotted them?" she asked as they walked past an upscale luggage store flanked by a pair of restaurants, one catering to humans, one to aliens.

"I don't plan to get close enough to spot them. It's enough that I know they're there."

"Then how are we going to get on the spaceliner that takes us away from here?" demanded the Duchess.

"We're not going to take a spaceliner."

"We're not?"

"We never were," said Dante. He glanced carefully around to make sure they weren't being followed. "It's too dangerous to book passage on it—and why tell them where to find us? Even if God drops everything else and we make it out of here on a liner, they'll simply signal ahead to wherever it's bound and have their counterparts waiting for us."

"I thought most Frontier worlds don't have police forces," she said.

"So you'll be met by a couple of bounty hunters," he replied with a grimace. "Is that any better?"

"Come on, Danny," she said, annoyed. "Why are you trying to scare me? You know we didn't do anything to put a dead-or-alive price on our heads."

"You know it and I know it, but I don't think they're real fussy about that on the Frontier. If the reward isn't big enough, it's not cost-effective to keep you alive and deliver you back into the Democracy. That's another reason we want a private ship: we don't want anyone knowing where we're going."

She frowned as the logic of his answer registered. "What the hell have you gotten me into?" she asked in panicky tones. "All I did was trip a man—and suddenly we're leaving Bailiwick and you're telling me that bounty hunters may want to *kill* me!"

"*I* didn't get you into anything at all," said Dante. "I'm grateful that you tripped Balsam, but it was your idea. I think it was a fine idea, and it kept me out of jail, but it wasn't mine." He paused. "Try to calm down. Neither of us was doing all that well here. Maybe it's time to go to the Frontier and start over."

"I was doing just fine!" she snapped.

"Well, you can stay if you want . . ."

"*No!*" she shouted.

"Well, *that's* settled."

"Some hero!" she muttered.

"I'm no hero. I'm just a guy who's trying to get the hell off the planet before the police catch up with me." He spotted a small hotel that catered to travelers who were changing flights on Bailiwick, and began walking toward it. "And it's time I started putting the wheels in motion."

"What are you going to do?" she asked, unable to slow down while their arms remained linked.

"I thought I'd warn the spaceport that we're coming in," he said with a smile.

"You're kidding, right?"

"I was never more serious in my life."

They reached the hotel, and Dante approached the front desk.

"May I help you?" asked the robot clerk in obsequious tones.

"Yeah. I want to contact the spaceport about my connecting flight. Where's a communicator?"

"There is a row of communication booths on the west wall, sir," said the robot. "Allow the booth of your choice time to scan your retina and verify your credit rating, and then follow the instructions."

"I know," said Dante. "I've done it before."

"In that case, have a most pleasant day, sir," said the robot as Dante walked to an empty booth.

"Wait here," he said to the Duchess. "There's only room for one in a booth."

He went in and emerged less than a minute later.

"Okay, that takes care of Step One," he announced.

"What did you do?"

"I reserved two seats on the spaceliner to Far London. It leaves in about two hours."

She frowned, trying to comprehend. "Correct me if I'm wrong, but I thought we were trying to escape from Bailiwick. Why did you announce our presence?"

"So that every spaceport official, every security guard and policeman, will be alerted that we're going to show up in the next hour or so and board the liner." He smiled. "I didn't stay connected long enough for them to trace my location."

"Okay, so now the spaceport is swarming with men and women whose sole desire is to capture us. Now what?"

"Now, while they're all trying to hide themselves near Passport Control or the boarding gate and appear unobtrusive, we choose a private ship to steal." He looked out the window. "You'll notice that they're all at this end of the spaceport."

Suddenly she smiled. "Maybe you should stay a thief. I don't know how good a poet you'll be, but you were born to be a thief."

"Well, it's still not that simple. We won't move until dark."

"Why not? By then they'll know we're not showing up for the Far London flight."

"We've got them all tense. The next step is to make them relax so they don't react as quickly."

"I'm not following you at all."

"In about an hour and a half, I'm going to cancel Far London and book us on a flight to Deluros VIII. Then I'll cancel that and book it to Sirius V. By the time I've changed flights six or seven times, they'll be convinced we're just having fun with them, and most of them will go home. The ones who are left behind will assume we're not showing up, and if anything alerts them, they'll be reasonably sure it's not us."

"So we're staying here for what, another eight or nine hours?" she asked.

"Yeah, about that. I don't know what the robot's programmed to think of as unusual behavior, so I think we'd better rent a room for three or four days."

"Three or four?"

"Right. We're not going to pay for it regardless, but I'm sure the police are monitoring every hotel desk. If someone takes a day room, or even a room for one night, anywhere near the spaceport, alarms are going to go off in every police station within fifty miles."

"All right, that makes sense," she agreed. "Now, how do we know which ship to take?"

He handed her his pocket computer. "I've put all the proper codes in for you to get past any security walls. Find out which ships have been fueled in the past six hours. Then check the registry; we're not interested in any ships that are owned by citizens of Bailiwick."

"Why not?"

"Because they have to file new flight plans, so if we take one we'll run a pretty fair chance of getting shot out of the sky. But a ship that's just stopped for fuel, or business, will already have a flight plan filed. They might *think* it's been stolen, but unless the owner reports it within two minutes of our taking off, they won't *know* it before we're at light speeds and out of the system, and they really aren't about to blow away a ship on a suspicion."

Dante approached the desk and rented a room, then went up to the fourth floor with the Duchess. A moment later they were inside the room, and she was starting to assemble her list of possible ships on Dante's computer while he stood by the window, looking out at the rows of private ships across the street. There was a sparkling force field surrounding the area, but he spotted the entrance, recognized the locking mechanism, knew he could break its code, and nodded in satisfaction.

Then he walked over to the large bed and lay down on it, cupping his hands behind his head. He wanted to read more of the poem, but he knew it would only annoy the Duchess, so he simply stared at her as she worked. Finally she put the computer down and turned to him. "I've got the perfect ship," she announced.

"Perfect in what way?" asked Dante.

"It's a six-man ship, so there will be plenty of room. Three sleeping cabins and a fully-equipped galley. Owned by a mining baron from Goldstrike, which is way into the Inner Frontier. Refreshed its atomic pile this morning, but it's not due to leave until tomorrow afternoon." She paused. "And best of all, it's *close*! You can see it from the window!"

He walked over.

"See that row?" she continued. "It's the fourth one back from the fence. We won't have to walk a hundred yards once we're inside the fence."

"Okay," said Dante. "Let's go for a walk."

"Now? I thought you wanted to steal it after dark."

"I do. But if I can disable that lock on the fence right now, it'll be even easier tonight."

"You can't just kneel down and work on a computer lock in broad daylight!" protested the Duchess.

"I don't plan to," he said. He walked to the door and ordered it to open. "Come on."

They emerged in the lobby a moment later. He stopped by the desk to speak to the robot clerk, then rejoined her.

"What was all that about?" she asked.

"I told it we're going shopping."

"Why does a robot care?"

"It doesn't—but if the police start searching all the hotels near the spaceport, and it won't be too long before the thought occurs to them, I don't want it to respond that it doesn't know where we are. It should take them a day to figure out that I used a phony ID to register—but if they have a reason to want to learn more about us, they'll break that identity in five minutes." He looked out into the street, then slung the bag containing Orpheus' poem over his shoulder. "Okay, let's go."

"Are you planning on stealing the ship now?" she asked, indicating the manuscript.

"No, I'm just not willing to leave it in a spaceport hotel."

They walked out, arm in arm, and began window-shopping up and down the street. Dante kept looking for an excuse to cross to the spaceport's side of the thoroughfare if anyone was watching them. He needed a stray animal, a child who might step into traffic while his parents were concentrating on each other, anything like that—but nothing turned up.

"Okay, we'll do it the bothersome way," he said after about ten minutes.

"What way is that?"

"We walk about a mile down the road, far enough that no one from the spaceport is still watching us, and then cross the street and walk back. We're no longer window-shopping; now we're taking our afternoon constitutional."

They walked away from the spaceport for ten more minutes. Then, as they reached the outskirts of the small city, they crossed the street and began walking back.

As they neared the spaceport, Dante, looking straight ahead, said,

"When we get opposite the entrance through the force field, twist an ankle."

"What?"

"Twist an ankle. Fall to one knee. Make a bit of a fuss about it. I'll kneel down and examine it."

"What does this have to do with the lock?"

"Just trust me."

They walked another two hundred yards. Then, when they were within five yards of the door, the Duchess lurched forward, fell to her knees, and began holding and massaging her left ankle.

Dante knelt down beside her, his back to the entrance, his hands shielded from any onlookers by her body.

"What's that?" she asked as she heard a faint beeping.

"Quiet!"

She fell silent, and concentrated on her ankle.

More beeps, and suddenly he looked at her and grinned. "Okay, we can walk through it any time we want."

"You could do that with your pocket computer?" she asked, surprised.

"Well, it's not an ordinary computer. It's been jury-rigged by experts. Well-paid experts, but on days like today I decide they were worth the money."

"Why don't we walk through right now? We could be at the ship in less than a minute."

He shook his head. "If anyone's been watching, your being able to walk or run without a limp will be a dead giveaway."

"So I'll limp."

He looked up and down the force field. "We'll wait until dark."

"But the place is deserted."

"It's *too* deserted," he said. "I haven't made any more reservations yet. They're all still here. *Someone's* got to be watching the private ships."

"Why? They're waiting for us to show up for the spaceliner to Far London."

He shook his head. "It's already taken off. Besides, *most* of them will be there, but the bright ones—and that includes Balsam—will know we'll never show up at the public terminal, and the only other way off the planet is to swipe a ship."

"But there's no one here! *Now* is the perfect time. We don't have to take off until you want, but they're more likely to search our room than the ship."

"It's too easy," he said, frowning. "I don't see a single guard. Do you?"

"No. That's why—"

"It's wrong," he said. "It's almost as if they're inviting us to try to steal a ship." He helped her to her feet. "Come on, lean on me and limp back to the hotel. I'll start making some more reservations."

"I don't want to," said the Duchess. "You've unlocked the entry, and there's no one around. I say we go to the ship. Even if they know we're there, we can take off before they can do anything about it."

"They'll blow us out of the sky."

"It's owned by Schyler McNeil. Just call the tower and tell them you're McNeil and you've got an emergency back on Goldstrike. They may not believe you, but they'll hesitate about destroying the ship until they find the real McNeil."

Dante studied the area once more, then shook his head. Something felt wrong, and he always listened to his instincts.

"Tonight," he said, still scanning the spaceport. "Now let's go back to the hotel."

She made no reply, so he turned back to her—and found that she was gone.

"*Shit!*" he muttered, trying and failing to grab her arm as she darted through the entrance and raced toward the private ships.

He didn't know how they would stop her, but he knew in his gut that she'd never make it to McNeil's ship. Then he heard a hideous roar, and he turned to see a huge animal, almost four feet at the shoulder, not canine and not feline but clearly a predator, racing toward the Duchess.

"Get into a ship now!" he yelled, breaking into a run.

The Duchess turned back to him, startled, then saw the creature bearing down on her. It was possible that she couldn't even have made it into the ship she had just passed, but she didn't even try. She screamed and raced toward McNeil's ship, and the animal swerved to run her down.

Dante saw that he couldn't reach her in time, even if he hadn't been carrying the huge manuscript. He looked for a weapon, even something as primitive as a club, as he ran, but the spaceport was neat as a pin, and he couldn't see anything he could use. Then he saw another motion out of the corner of his eye—the animal's keeper.

It made sense. Someone had to be able to control it, or it might savage someone with a legitimate reason for being there. The keeper, armed with a pulse gun, was walking leisurely after the animal, obviously in no hurry to call it off. Dante raced to him, knocked him down just as the creature reached the Duchess. It took about ten seconds to wrestle the pulse gun away from the keeper and crack him across the head with it—and those were ten seconds the Duchess didn't have.

Dante whirled and fired at the animal, killing it instantly—but it fell across the Duchess's torn, lifeless body.

"Damn you!" yelled Dante at the senseless body by his feet. "She didn't do anything worth dying for!" He stared at the main terminal. "Damn you all!"

He knew he couldn't stay where he was or return to the hotel. A sweeping security camera or another beast and keeper would spot the Duchess in a matter of seconds. He tucked the gun into his belt and ran to McNeil's ship.

He followed the Duchess's instructions, claiming to be McNeil. That bought him enough time to reach the stratosphere. Then came all the warning messages, which meant they'd either found the Duchess or McNeil or both. He alternately lied and threatened for the next thirty seconds, spent another fifteen seconds admitting that he was Danny Briggs and promising to return to the spaceport—and while they were debating whether to shoot him down his ship passed through the stratosphere and reached light speeds.

And because he was Dante Alighieri and not one of the larger-than-life characters he planned to write about, he did not vow to avenge the Duchess. *Someone* would avenge her; that much he *did* promise himself. When he found the right person, he would tell him the story of the Duchess and point him toward Bailiwick, and he would enjoy the results every bit as much as if he had physically extracted his vengeance himself.

Then he was on his way to the Inner Frontier, where he would assume his new identity and his new career among legendary heroes and villains who, he suspected, couldn't be any more dangerous than the Democracy's finest.

4.

Hamlet Macbeth, a well-named rogue,
Loves the women, when in vogue.
Loves the gents when no one cares,
Gets rich off his perverse affairs.

That was the first poem that Dante Alighieri wrote once he reached the Inner Frontier. There was nothing very special about Hamlet Macbeth except his name, which fired Dante's imagination. He decided he couldn't leave anyone named Hamlet Macbeth out of his history, so he began finding out what he could about the man.

What he found out was a little embarrassing to both parties, because it turned out that Hamlet Macbeth was a gigolo who rented himself out to both sexes. The people of Nasrullah II, his home world, didn't much give a damn what Macbeth did as long as he didn't do it to or with them, but some of the men who were just passing through found that they were expected to pay not only for Macbeth's sexual skills, but also for his silence.

Nasrullah II was the first world that Dante touched down on. He stayed only long enough to refuel his stolen ship and have a drink in a local bar, which was where he heard about Macbeth. He didn't write the poem until he had landed on New Tangier IV, in the neighboring system, where he proceeded to recite it in a couple of taverns.

He spent a couple of days on New Tangier, a dusty, ugly reddish world with nothing much to recommend it except one diamond mine about ten miles east of the planet's only Tradertown. There was one hotel—a boardinghouse, actually, since not enough people visited New

Tangier to support a hotel; one casino, which was so obviously rigged
that the humans gave it a wide berth and the only players were the
Bextigians, the mole-like aliens that had been imported to work the
mine; and the two taverns.

Dante was standing at the bar in the larger of the taverns, sipping
a beer and idly wondering how Orpheus had been able to spot colorful
people when they weren't doing colorful things, when a slender man
with sunken cheeks, dark piercing eyes, and braided black hair sidled
up to him. Everyone else instantly moved away.

"Hi," said the man, paying no attention to anyone but Dante.

"Hi," replied Dante.

"I heard your little poem yesterday. Have you written any others?"

"Some," lied Dante. "Why?"

"Just curious. I like poems. Especially erotic ones. You ever read
anything by Tanblixt?"

"The Canphorite? No."

"You should. Now, *there's* someone who truly understands the
beauty of interspecies sex."

"If you say so."

"I also like epic poems of good and evil, especially if Satan himself is in them." He smiled. "It gives me someone to root for."

"You have interesting taste in poetry."

"I have interesting taste in everything." The man paused. "What's
your name, poet?"

"Dante. But people call me the Rhymer."

"They do?"

"They will."

The man smiled. "I think I'll call you Dante. We were made for
each other."

"Oh?"

"I'm Virgil Soaring Hawk." He paused, waiting for the connection
to become apparent. "Dante and Virgil."

"Virgil Soaring Hawk—what kind of a name is that?"

"It's an Injun name."

"Okay, what's an Injun?"

"It takes too long to explain. But once, when we were still Earthbound, white men and Injuns were mortal enemies—or so they say."

Dante frowned. "White men? You mean albinos?"

"No," replied Virgil with a sigh. "The Injuns were redskins, except
that our skins weren't really red. And the white men weren't really
white, either—they ranged from pink to tan. But a lot of people died
on both sides because of what they thought their color was."

"You're making all this up, right?" said Dante.

"Yeah, what the hell, I'm making it all up." Virgil signaled to the bartender. "Two Dust Whores."

"What's a Dust Whore?" asked Dante.

"You're about to find out."

"I don't understand."

"You've got Democracy written all over you, poet," said Virgil Soaring Hawk. "Virgil was Dante's guide through Heaven and Hell. I figure a new Dante needs a new Virgil to show him the ropes. Right now I'm going to introduce you to one of our local drinks."

"What the hell, why not?" agreed Dante.

"Let's go sit at a table," suggested Virgil.

"What's wrong with standing here at the bar?"

"I don't like turning my back to the door. You never know what's going to come through it."

"Whatever you say," said Dante, walking to a table in the farthest corner of the tavern.

"Glad you agree," said Virgil, sitting down opposite him. The men at the two nearest tables immediately got up and moved to the other side of the tavern.

"Why does everyone move away from you?" asked Dante.

Virgil sighed deeply. "They don't like me very much."

"Have they got some reason?"

"Not any that I agree with," said Virgil.

"What the hell did you do?" asked Dante.

"I don't think I'm going to tell you."

"Why not?"

"I don't want you making a rhyme out of it and reciting it in bars all over the Frontier."

"I can always ask someone on the other side of the tavern," said Dante.

"You'd do that to the only friend you've made on the Frontier?" asked Virgil.

Dante stared at him in silence for a long moment. Virgil stared right back.

The bartender dropped off the drinks and left immediately.

"What goes into them?" asked Dante, staring at the purple-green liquid that was smoking as if on fire. "They look like they're going to explode."

"It varies from planet to planet," said Virgil, taking a long swallow of his own drink. When he didn't clutch his throat or collapse across the table, Dante followed suit, and promptly grimaced.

"Jesus! This stuff'll take the enamel off your teeth!" He paused. "Still," said Dante at last, "it's kind of warming. Got an interesting aftertaste." He frowned. "I don't know if I like it."

"After you've had a few more, you'll know," said Virgil with conviction.

"All right," said Dante. "Now the drinks are here and I've had half of mine. So why did you approach me and what do you want to talk about?"

"I want to talk about you."

"Me?" repeated Dante, surprised.

"And me."

"So talk."

"What are you doing out here?" asked Virgil. "Why have you come to the Inner Frontier? You're no settler, and you don't strike me as a killer. No human comes to New Tangier IV to play at the casino, so I know you're not a gambler. You haven't offered to trade or sell anything. So why are you here?"

"Did you ever hear of Black Orpheus?"

"Everyone out here has heard of Black Orpheus," answered Virgil. He grimaced. "He was probably about as black as you are white."

"I'm here to finish his poem."

Virgil Soaring Hawk stared at him expressionlessly.

"Well?" said Dante.

"Why not choose something easy, like going up against Tyrannosaur Bailey?"

"Who's Tyrannosaur Bailey?"

"It doesn't matter. Black Orpheus was one of a kind. He was unique in our history. What makes you think you can be another Orpheus?"

"I can't be," admitted Dante. "But I can follow in his footsteps." He paused, then added with conviction: "It's time."

"What do you mean?"

"I take it Tyrannosaur Bailey is a formidable figure?"

"He's about fifteen formidable figures all rolled into one ugly sonuvabitch."

"You make him sound fascinating—but I've never heard of him until just now. No one in the Democracy has, and probably ninety percent of the Inner Frontier hasn't either." Dante took another sip of his drink. "The Democracy is so damned regimented! All the really interesting characters are out here on the Frontier. It's time someone wrote them up the way Orpheus did, before they're gone and we have no record of them."

"You don't think the Secretary of the Democracy is interesting? What about Admiral Yokamina, who has six billion men under his command?"

"They got where they are by following the rules and fitting the mold," replied Dante. "All the men who broke the mold are out here, or on the Outer Frontier."

"Or dead," said Virgil.

"Or dead," agreed Dante. "Killing is one of the Democracy's specialties. They killed a friend of mine as we were preparing to come here."

"Did he have it coming?"

"Nobody has it coming—and it was a she."

"What was her crime?"

"She tripped a man," said Dante.

"That's all?"

"That's all," repeated Dante. "The Democracy doesn't seem to care who trips it these days."

"What uniquely individual crimes did you commit?" asked Virgil.

"Nothing that deserved that kind of retaliation."

"They obviously saw it differently."

"They always do. That's why I'm here. The Democracy stops at the borders to the Inner and Outer Frontiers."

Virgil stared at him as one would stare at a child. It was a look that seemed to say: *If you're that dumb, is it even worth the effort to set you straight?* "The *law* may stop," he said at last. "But the *Democracy* doesn't."

"What are you talking about?"

"They come out in force and take what they need," said Virgil, "whether it's fissionable material, or food for newly colonized worlds, or conscripts for the military. Any Man or planet that objects gets the same treatment that any alien or alien planet would get."

"I didn't know," admitted Dante. "None of us do."

Virgil shrugged. "Maybe I'm being a little hard on them. Sometimes they pay for what they take, though it's never what it's worth. And if they come to a mining world with, say, thirty miners working it, and grab a couple of hundred pounds of plutonium, well, they'll probably use it to fight off some alien army that would otherwise subjugate a planet with ten million Men on it." Virgil paused. "But we don't *know* that. We just know they come and they take and they leave and no one can stand up to them. So maybe it's comforting to think they have some noble purpose for plundering the Frontier whenever they want."

"Are they on New Tangier IV?"

"The Democracy?" Virgil shook his head. "You might go years without running into them. Or you might run into them three times in a month. It depends on where you are and what they want at the moment."

"Okay, forewarned is forearmed. But in the meantime, I still need material for my poems, so I still plan to travel the Frontier."

"I was hoping you'd say that."

"Why?"

"Because we're going to make a deal," said Virgil. "You'll need a guide, and I've worn out my welcome in the New Tangier system."

"How?" asked Dante.

"How," replied Virgil, holding up his right hand in a sign of greeting.

"I beg your pardon?"

"An old Injun joke. Forget it."

"How did you wear out your welcome?"

"How can I put this delicately?" said Virgil. "I indulge in certain, shall we say, unmentionable acts with members of . . ."

"The opposite sex?" Dante offered.

"The opposite species," Virgil corrected him.

"Is that against the law?"

"We don't have too many laws on the Frontier," answered Virgil. "It's against at least four hundred laws back in the Democracy."

"What species do you perform these unmentionable acts with?" asked Dante.

"Why should I limit myself to one species?"

"So what you're saying is . . ."

"What I'm saying is that I've worn out my welcome," answered Virgil. "We'll talk it more after you've adjusted to the Frontier."

"Okay—but I'll probably spend all my spare time wondering who you did what with."

"It'll give you something to do while we're traveling between planets."

Dante finished his drink and slapped some bills on the table. "I'll have another one of these."

"Credits," noted Virgil. "They'll take them here, but most Frontier worlds don't have much use for Democracy currency."

"Speaking of Frontier worlds, where are we going next?"

"As I remember my *Inferno*, I guide you through the nine circles of hell." Virgil paused. "Of course, you were in hell when you lived in the Democracy. You just didn't know it."

"I knew it. That's why I came out here."

"Oh, you're still in hell. It's just a less structured, less orderly one."

At that moment a tall, burly man appeared in the doorway. He was covered with reddish dust, which he brushed from his heavy coat.

"I'm looking for the poet," he announced.

"You mean the Rhymer," Dante corrected him.

The tall man glared at Dante. "I'm Hamlet Macbeth," he said furiously. "Does that mean anything to you?"

"I know who you are."

"Have we ever met before?"

"No," answered Dante.

"Then why are you spreading lies about me?"

"What I wrote was the truth and you know it," said Dante.

"Hi, Hamlet," interjected Virgil. "Come join us."

Hamlet stared at Dante. "You're with *him*?" he demanded, jerking a thumb in Virgil's direction.

"That's right," answered Dante.

"You don't choose your friends any more carefully than you choose your subject," said Macbeth. He stepped into the tavern, and two more men entered with him. "How many worlds have you been kicked off of, Injun?"

"I stopped counting when I ran out of fingers and toes," replied Virgil easily.

"I hear tell you turned a couple of your mutant ladyfriends into corpses," added one of the other men, staring at Virgil through narrowed eyes.

"That's a lie," replied Virgil. "They were corpses *before* I met them."

"Did you hear that?" roared the man. "Did you hear what he just said?"

"Excuse me for a moment," Virgil said softly to Dante. "I'll be back as soon as I clear up this little misunderstanding." He got up and began walking toward the three men. "I know you don't mean what you say, but I wish you wouldn't embarrass me in front of my new friend."

"Your new friend ain't gonna be around that long, Injun," said Macbeth. "We got nothing against you, at least not today. If you're smart you'll keep out of our way."

"Come on over to the bar," said Virgil. "I'll buy you a round of drinks, and then maybe we can all be friends."

"Keep your distance, scumbag!"

"You really shouldn't call people names like that," remarked Virgil, still approaching them. "Even scumbags have feelings."

"What are you going to do about it?" demanded Macbeth pugnaciously, his right hand resting on the butt of his holstered burner.

"This," said Virgil softly.

His hands moved so fast that Dante couldn't follow them, but suddenly he had a knife in each, and an instant later all three men lay writhing on the floor, gagging and clutching their necks as blood spurted forth. None of them had had a chance to draw a weapon.

Virgil calmly walked back to the table, paying no attention to any of the other patrons, who stared at him but made no move to stop him. By the time he rejoined Dante, all three men had stopped thrashing and were still, each lying in a widening pool of his own blood.

"You killed them!" exclaimed Dante, staring in fascination at the corpses. "All three of them!"

"They would have killed you," said Virgil. "And me, too, if they thought they could get away with it."

"You just walked right over and killed them!" repeated Dante. "In front of witnesses."

"So what?"

"So they'll report what they saw."

Virgil stared at him. "To who?"

Dante blinked rapidly. He tried to come up with an answer but realized he had none.

"Welcome to the Inner Frontier, poet."

"Just who the hell are you?" demanded Dante.

Virgil got up to leave. "You're the new Bard of the Inner Frontier," he said. "I'm sure *you'll* tell *me* before we hit the next world."

5.

The Scarlet Infidel is odd—
He has no quality of shame.
He spits into the eye of God,
And commits sins that have no name.

Virgil Soaring Hawk's skin wasn't really red, but Dante decided to exercise some poetic license, especially since Virgil kept referring to himself as a redskin.

Besides, the Scarlet part didn't interest Dante anywhere near as much as the Infidel part. Virgil would never discuss any details, but from what Dante heard on his first few worlds, the poet concluded that if a race of oxygen breathers—*any* race—was divided into sexes, Virgil had spent a night or two with a female member of that race and another night with a male. There were a few races that boasted more than two sexes, and Virgil had sampled some of their wares as well.

Virgil also didn't speak much about his other areas of physical prowess, but Dante noted that most people were content to disapprove of the Scarlet Infidel from afar, that no one wanted any part of him in a fight.

As for Virgil, he was thrilled to be written up by the new Orpheus, and was constantly nagging Dante to give him more verses.

"Come on, now," he was saying as Dante's ship neared Tusculum II. "Orpheus gave Giles Sans Pitié nine verses. Giles Sans Pitié, for Christ's sake! Take away his metal hand and he was nothing, a second-rate bounty hunter. I mean, really, who the hell did he ever kill?"

"Who did you?" asked Dante.

"I'm not a bounty hunter, so I'm not in a position where I can brag about it without certain legal repercussions. But the things I've done, the places I've been, surely they're worth as many verses as Giles Sans Pitié!"

"He only gave one verse to the Angel," Dante shot back. "And Peacemaker MacDougal and Sebastian Cain got just three apiece. Are you sure you *want* all those verses?"

Virgil grimaced. "Well, I was sure until about twenty seconds ago. Now I have to think about it."

"While you're thinking, suppose you tell me why we're going to the Tusculum system?"

"You said you wanted to meet Tyrannosaur Bailey."

"What makes you think he'll be on Tusculum II?"

Virgil smiled. "He owns it."

"He owns the whole world?"

"Well, there's not that much to own—a couple of Tradertowns and a landing field."

"How did he get to own a world?" asked Dante. "Did he win it in a card game?"

"Nothing so romantic," replied Virgil. "He killed the man who owned it before him."

"I take it the laws of inheritance don't work quite the same out here as in the Democracy."

"Well, yes and no."

"What does that mean?"

"It means they might very well work the same, but no one felt compelled to argue the point with Tyrannosaur."

"No one hired any mercenaries?" asked Dante. "I mean, hell, with a whole planet at stake . . ."

"Tyrannosaur Bailey eats mercenaries for breakfast," answered Virgil.

"Has he got a price on his head?"

"A big one," said Virgil. He smiled. "He eats bounty hunters for lunch."

"How did you get to know him?"

"I met him at a gaming table out on the Rim, years ago. One of the players accused him of cheating, and he killed him. Literally ripped his head off his body."

"*Was* he cheating?"

"Absolutely."

"But you didn't complain?"

"I don't have that kind of death wish," said Virgil.

"So you just kept playing?"

"For another hour or so," replied Virgil. "I won forty thousand New Stalin rubles. He asked me if I was cheating, and I said of course I was, that after playing a couple of hands I just naturally assumed everyone at the table was supposed to cheat. Well, he could have killed me for that, but instead he laughed so hard I thought he'd bring down the ceiling, and we've been friends ever since."

"How many men has he killed?"

"You'll have to ask him. First, I don't know, and second, even if I *did* know it's been better than a year since I've seen him, and he's probably added to his total since then."

"If he's such a fearsome killer, why does anyone else live on Tusculum II?" asked Dante.

Virgil stared at him. "The Bard of the Inner Frontier doesn't ask stupid questions."

"*Was* it a stupid question?"

"Figure it out."

Dante considered it for a moment, then nodded. "Of course. They're there for protection." He paused. "How does it work? They pay him a fee to live there, and he doesn't allow any bounty hunters to land?"

"Well, you got the first part right. They pay for the privilege of living on Tusculum. But Tyrannosaur will let anyone land. He owns a casino, and he doesn't much care whose money he takes. He just makes it clear that if you kill a resident, one of his 'children,' as he calls them, you won't live to enjoy the reward."

Dante chuckled. "I take it Tusculum II is a pretty peaceful place."

"So far. But you never know what'll happen tomorrow."

"You made it sound like no one could kill this Tyrannosaur."

"You're on the Inner Frontier now, where just about every man and woman carries a weapon and can be hazardous to your health."

"What are you getting at?"

"If they're alive and they're carrying weapons, what does it imply to you?"

"Stop with the guessing games," said Dante irritably. "What is it *supposed* to mean to me?"

"That every last one of them is undefeated in mortal combat," said Virgil. "They don't all have big reputations. In fact, mighty few have reputations to rival Tyrannosaur's. But there's fifty, maybe sixty million people out here, all of 'em undefeated. It seems unrealistic to assume a few dozen of them couldn't kill Tyrannosaur if push came to shove." He paused. "That's why you have to be a little cautious out here. You know the odds, but you never can tell *which* of those nondescript men has it within him to be the next Santiago."

"Hey, I'm just a poet and an historian," said Dante. "I don't plan on challenging anyone."

"And I'm a lover," said Virgil wryly. "Problem is, you don't always have a choice."

"As far as I know, no one ever called Black Orpheus out for a duel to the death."

"Yeah—but he was the real thing. You're just an apprentice Orpheus."

"Keep talking like that and I may tear up your verse," said Dante.

"Keep thinking you're above the fray and you may not live long enough to write a second one."

The ship jerked just then, as it entered Tusculum II's stratosphere at an oblique angle.

Dante stared at his instrument panel. "Now what?"

"Now you land."

"But no one's fed any landing coordinates into the navigational computer."

"You're not in the Democracy anymore," said Virgil. "Have the sensors pinpoint the larger Tradertown, and then find the landing field just north of it."

"And then?"

"And then tell it to land."

"Just like that?" asked Dante.

"Just like that."

"Amazing," said Dante after issuing instructions to the sensors and the computer. "Have you ever been to Deluros VIII?"

"Nope."

"It's got more than two thousand orbiting space docks that can each handle something like ten thousand ships. There are dozens of passenger platforms miles above the planet, and thousands of shuttles working around the clock, carrying people to and from the surface. I don't think a ship has actually landed *on* Deluros VIII in two millennia." He shook his head in wonderment. "And here we just point and land."

"You'll get used to it."

"I suppose so."

The ship touched down, and the two men soon emerged from it.

"I assume there's no Customs or Passport Control?" asked Dante.

"You see anything like that?" responded Virgil, walking over to a row of empty aircarts. "We'll take one of these into town."

"Fine," said Dante as he climbed in.

"Uh . . . you want to let it read your retina?" said Virgil.

"Is something wrong with your eye?"

"Something's wrong with my credit. It won't start until the fee has been transferred to the rental company's account."

"No problem," said Dante, walking up to the scanner. His credit was approved in a matter of seconds, and shortly thereafter they were skimming into town, eighteen inches above the ground.

"Tell it to stop here," said Virgil as they cruised along the Tradertown's only major street.

"Why don't you tell it yourself?"

"Your credit, your voiceprint. It won't obey me."

Dante ordered the aircart to stop. "The casino's up the street."

"Yeah, but we need a place to stay. We'll register at the hotel first, and then go hunting for dinosaur."

They entered a small hotel, and Dante ordered two adjacent rooms, both of which were to be billed to his account.

They decided to stop at the hotel's restaurant for lunch before going to the casino, and they emerged half an hour later, ready to meet Tyrannosaur Bailey.

A nondescript man of medium height and medium build was standing outside the hotel, leaning against a wall. As Dante and Virgil emerged, he stepped forward and faced them.

"You're Danny Briggs, right?" he said.

"I'm Dante Alighieri."

"Well, yeah, you're him, too," agreed the man. "But it's Danny Briggs I want to speak to."

"Never heard of him," said Dante, trying to walk past the man, who took a sidestep and blocked his way again.

"That's too bad," said the man. "Because I have a business proposition for Danny Briggs."

"I know who you are," said Virgil. "Get the hell out of our way."

"Now, is that any way to talk to a businessman?" asked the man. His hand shot out and pushed Virgil backward. The Scarlet Infidel took a heavy flop onto the street, and his hand snaked toward his pocket.

"Don't even think about it, Injun!" said the man harshly. "If you know who I am, you know I don't die as easily as those assholes you took out on New Tangier."

Virgil tensed, then looked into the man's eyes, and slowly, gradually relaxed again.

"Good thinking, Injun," said the man. "You get to live another day and deflower another corpse." He turned to Dante. "My name is Wait-a-bit Bennett. Does it mean anything to you?"

"No," said Dante.

"We have something in common, Danny. You come from the Democracy, and I work for the Democracy. On a freelance basis, anyway."

"Get to the point."

"The point is that the bank account the aircart computer okayed was in the name of Danny Briggs, not Dante Alighieri." Bennett smiled. "It seems that the Democracy has issued a fifty-thousand-credit reward for you, dead or alive."

"Bullshit!" said Dante. "That dead-or-alive crap is for killers. I never killed anyone."

"Sure you did," said Bennett. "You killed Felicia Milan, alias the Duchess, back on Bailiwick."

"*I* didn't kill her!" snapped Dante. "The police did!"

"The Democracy says you did," replied Bennett. He smiled. "What's a poor bounty hunter to believe?"

"You're going to believe whoever's offering the money, so why are you wasting both our time talking about it?"

"I do believe you've got a firm grasp of the situation, Danny, my boy," said Bennett. "I always believe the man with the money. That could be you."

"What are you talking about?" demanded Dante.

"A business deal," said Bennett. "A transaction, so to speak." Suddenly he turned to Virgil. "Keep those hands where I can see 'em, Injun!" Then back to Dante: "Before I can get paid, I have to take your body back to the Democracy for identification, or to one of the Democracy outposts, and I think the nearest one is fifteen hundred light-years away. That's a lot of bother."

"My heart bleeds for you," said Dante.

"It doesn't have to. Bleed, I mean."

"So what's the deal?"

"Pay me the fifty thousand credits and I let you walk."

"When do you need an answer?" asked Dante.

"I'm a reasonable man," said Bennett. "If I wasn't, you'd be dead already." He looked up toward the sky. "It's getting toward noon. I'll give you until noon tomorrow. Either you hand me the money then, or I'll kill you and your pal."

"Why Virgil?"

"I don't like him very much."

"He hasn't done anything to you."

"No corpse is safe around him. That's reason enough." He turned to Virgil. "I'm going into the hotel now. I think it might be a good idea for you to stay where you are until I'm inside."

He turned and walked through the hotel's doorway and vanished into its interior.

"Wait-a-bit Bennett," said Dante, staring after him. "You never mentioned him to me."

"I didn't know he was in this part of the Frontier."

"Tell me about him."

"There's not much to tell," said Virgil, finally getting to his feet. "He's a bounty hunter. A good one. He's up around twenty kills, maybe twenty-five."

"Then let's go meet Tyrannosaur Bailey and get the hell off the planet before morning," said Dante.

Virgil shook his head. "You're fifty thousand credits on the hoof. You don't think he's going to let you walk just because you can't pay him the reward, do you?"

"He can't watch us forever."

"Forever ends tomorrow at noon."

"I meant that he's got to sleep sometime. We'll sneak out tonight."

"He knows that nobody comes to Tusculum without a reason. He's gone off to take a nap while you take care of whatever business brought you here. He'll be awake by dinnertime, and he'll seek out your ship and wait there until noon, just in case you're thinking of leaving."

"This is ridiculous!" said Dante. "I came here to get *away* from the Democracy and now they're paying bounty hunters to kill me!"

"The only difference between here and where you came from," said Virgil, "is that out here there are no voters and no journalists to restrain the Democracy's worst instincts."

"Is Wait-a-bit Bennett as good at his trade as he thinks he is?" asked Dante.

"Better," answered Virgil. "You didn't see me move when he told me to be still, did you?"

"How am I going to get fifty thousand credits to buy him off by noon?"

"You've got a bigger problem than that."

"Oh?"

Virgil nodded. "Even if you get the money, you don't think he's the only bounty hunter who reads Wanted posters, do you?"

Suddenly Dante's stomach began to hurt.

6.

Wait-a-bit Bennett, calm and cool,
Sips his drink by the swimming pool.
His prey appears, all unaware;
He'll wait a bit, and then—beware!

Virgil Soaring Hawk hit the roof when he sneaked a look at the poem. Here was this bounty hunter who had already manhandled the notorious Scarlet Infidel himself and was preparing to extort money from the poet in the morning or (more likely) kill him, and Dante was actually writing him into the poem.

Even worse, he gave three verses to Bennett—but of course, Bennett was the first man on the Frontier to threaten Dante's life, so Virgil reluctantly admitted that it made sense in a way.

Bennett had threatened a lot of lives, and had taken more than his share of them. Rumor had it that he'd been a hired killer before he started doing his killing for the Democracy. They said he'd been shot up pretty badly on Halcyon V, but he certainly didn't move like a man who was supposedly half prosthetic, and he never ducked a fight.

Somewhere along the way, he'd decided that it was easier to make money for not killing men than for killing them, and from that day forward, he always offered to let a wanted man walk free if the man paid him the reward. And he was a man of his word: more than one man paid the price, and none of them were ever bothered by Bennett again. (Well, none except Willie Harmonica, who went out and committed *another* murder after buying his way out of the first one. He refused to pay Bennett the reward the second time, and wound up paying with his life instead.)

And now Dante Alighieri had less than a day to raise fifty thousand credits or somehow escape from one of the deadlier bounty hunters on the Inner Frontier.

"I can't spend all day working on the poem," he announced after giving Bennett his third verse. He put down his quill pen and got up from the desk in the corner of his room. "Let's go visit your friend."

"I've been ready for an hour," remarked Virgil.

"I had to write those verses," explained Dante. "Who knows if I'll be alive to write them tomorrow?"

"Son of a bitch doesn't deserve three verses!" muttered Virgil, ordering the door to dilate.

"Kill him tonight and maybe I'll give you four," said Dante, stepping through into the hallway.

"Mighty few people out here can kill him," answered Virgil. "And I'm honest enough to admit I'm not one of them."

"I saw what you did to those three guys in the bar back on New Tangier."

"Those were two miners and a gigolo. This guy is a professional killer. There's a difference."

"He didn't look that formidable."

"Fine," said Virgil. "*You* kill him."

"I'm no killer," replied Dante. "I'm a poet. I can outthink him, but I have a feeling that won't help much in a pitched battle."

"Look around the galaxy and you'd be hard-pressed to prove that intelligence is a survival trait," agreed Virgil.

They reached the street and walked out of the hotel, turned right, and headed to Rex's, which was the name Tyrannosaur Bailey had chosen for his establishment.

"Anything else I should know?" asked Dante as they reached the door to the casino.

"Yeah," said Virgil. "No dinosaur jokes."

"I don't know any."

"Good. You'll live longer that way."

They entered, and Dante was surprised at the level of luxury that confronted him. From outside, Rex's seemed like every other nondescript Tradertown building. Inside it was a haven of taste and money. The floors gripped his feet, then released him as he took another step, and another. The gaming tables were made of the finest alien hardwood, meticulously carved by some unknown race, while the matching chairs hovered a few inches above the floor, changing their shapes to fit each player's form—and the players were not merely men, but giant Torquals, tripodal beings from Hesporite III, Canphorites and Lodinites and a couple of races that Dante had never seen before.

Atonal but seductive alien music filtered into the casino, and nubile young men and women dressed in shimmering metallic outfits ran the tables.

Sitting alone in the farthest corner was a huge man, easily seven feet tall, muscled like an athlete. His hair was the color of desert sand, and tumbled down to his shoulders. His nose had been broken at least twice, maybe more, and looked irregular from every angle. One ear was cauliflower; the lobe of the other was stretched enough that it was able to hold an unwrapped cigar that had been placed in an exceptionally large hole there. When he smiled, he displayed a mouthful of ruby and sapphire teeth, all carefully filed to dangerous-looking points.

His shirt was loose-fitting, which added to the impression of enormous size. Dante couldn't see his legs or feet, but he managed to glimpse the tops of three or four weapons stuck in the man's belt.

The man looked up, saw Virgil, and smiled a red-and-blue smile. "Virgil, you corpse-fucking old bastard, how the hell are you?"

"Hi, Tyrannosaur. I've got a friend who'd like to meet you."

Tyrannosaur Bailey studied Dante for a long moment. "You're the one that Wait-a-bit Bennett is after?"

"How did you know that?" asked Dante.

"This is *my* world," answered Bailey. "Not much goes on here that I *don't* know."

"Then you know who I am and why I want to see you," suggested Dante.

"I know who both of you are," laughed Bailey. "You're Danny Briggs, a thief from the Democracy, and you're Dante Alighieri, the self-proclaimed successor to Black Orpheus." He gestured to a pair of chairs. "Have a seat. You too, Virgil."

"*He's* the one who wants to speak with you," replied Virgil. "I could go spend a little money at your gaming tables, if you wish."

"You don't want to gamble," said Bailey.

"I don't?"

Bailey shook his head. "No, you don't. What you want is to get my Stelargan bar girl into the sack while I'm paying attention to your friend."

"What a thing to suggest!" said Virgil with mock outrage.

"Virgil, the last time you were here, two of my human girls and one of my Tilarbians had to seek psychiatric help to get over the experience. Next time it happens, you pay the bill."

"It was worth it."

"That's it!" snapped Tyrannosaur. "You sit here or you wait outside. There's no third way."

"I thought we were friends."

"We are—but we're not close friends. Now make your choice."

"I think I'll get a breath of air," said Virgil with all the dignity he could muster. He turned and slowly walked out into the street.

"Have a seat, poet," said Tyrannosaur after Virgil had left the casino.

"Thank you," said Dante, sitting down opposite the huge man.

"I approve of what you're doing," continued Bailey. "That poem is all the history we've got—and there's tens of millions of us out here. It's time someone added to it. I'm just as loyal to the Frontier as all those people we left behind are to the Democracy."

Dante didn't quite know what to say except to thank him again, so he remained silent.

"Interesting friend you've picked up," continued Bailey. "They're going to have to write two or three books just to cover the new perversions he's invented." He paused. "How many verses did you give him?"

"One."

Bailey nodded thoughtfully. "Who else have you written up?"

"Not too many," said Dante noncommittally. "I'm still getting my feet wet, so to speak."

"Well, assuming you live past tomorrow, you should find it a pretty easy job."

"Being the only historian for a third of the galaxy isn't all that easy. I suspect it can be quite a burden from time to time."

"I'm sure it was a burden for Orpheus," agreed Tyrannosaur. "But that's because someone had to be first. He paved the way. It should be a cakewalk for you."

"It'll be harder for me."

"Don't have the talent, huh?"

"I don't know. That's for others to judge. But Orpheus had a unifying theme."

"What theme was that?" asked Bailey.

"He had Santiago."

"Santiago wasn't a theme. He was a man."

"He was both. Everyone in the poem is valued based on how he related to Santiago."

"What are you talking about?" said Bailey. "I grew up on that poem! I can quote whole sections of it to you, and we both know that most of them never even knew Santiago!"

"The outlaws were compared to him, never very favorably. The bounty hunters and lawmen were measured based on how close they got to him. Preachers, thieves, aliens, even an itinerant barmaid, they all formed a kind of nebula around him. They were caught in the field generated by his strength and his charisma; Orpheus knew it, even if they didn't."

"So who's *your* Santiago?" asked Bailey.

"I don't have one . . . yet." The poet sighed. "That's why my job's harder."

"And you may not live past noon tomorrow."

Dante smiled ruefully. "That's another reason why my job's harder."

"So what's your name—Danny or Dante?"

"Dante Alighieri—but they call me the Rhymer."

"Who does?"

Dante made a grand gesture that encompassed half the universe. "Them."

"Them?"

"Well, they will someday."

"We'll see," said Bailey dubiously.

"What makes you an expert on poetry?" demanded Dante.

"I'm not," answered Bailey. "I'm an expert on survival." He stared at Dante. "You've already made a lot of mistakes. You're lucky you're still alive."

"What mistakes?"

"You hooked up with my friend Virgil, who attracts outraged moralists everywhere he goes. You made some kind of mistake at the spaceport, or Wait-a-bit Bennett would never have spotted you. You made a third mistake by sticking around after he made you that offer. He probably has a confederate watching your ship, but by tonight he'll be there himself, and I guarantee he's more dangerous than anyone he might hire." He paused. "How long have you been on the Frontier, poet? A week? Ten days? And you've already made three fatal blunders. Tomorrow you'll probably make a fourth."

"I don't know what I can do about it," said Dante. "I can't raise fifty thousand credits by tomorrow morning."

"Sell your ship."

"Uh . . . it's not exactly *my* ship," said Dante.

"Make that *four* fatal blunders. The spaceport's got to have reported the registration back to the Democracy. You'll have another warrant out on you by dinnertime, and you've almost certainly got a squad of soldiers already flying out here to reclaim the ship—after they kill you for putting them to the trouble."

"So what do you think I should do?"

"I thought you'd never ask," said Tyrannosaur with a grin. "What you should do is hire a protector, someone who can stomp on Wait-a-bit Bennett as easily as you stomp on an insect."

"If I can't afford to buy him off, I can't afford to pay you to protect me," explained Dante.

"I don't want your money."

"What do you want?"

Bailey learned forward. "How many verses did you give Bennett? I want the truth, now."

"Three," said Dante.

"Then the man who kills him ought to get at least four, right?"

"At least," agreed Dante.

Tyrannosaur extended an enormous hand. "You've got yourself a deal, poet."

Dante shook the giant's hand. "Call me Rhymer," he said with a smile.

"Rhymer it is!" said Bailey, gesturing to the purple-skinned Stelargan barmaid. "This calls for a drink!"

This calls for more than that. It calls for some serious thought. Here I am, the objective observer, the nonparticipant, the man who reports history but doesn't make it, and I've just commissioned a man's death. Sure, it's a man who's planning to kill me, but that's his job, and he did offer me a way out.

And then:

I'm the only historian out here, as well as the only poet. What I write will become future generations' truth. Is Tyrannosaur Bailey worth four verses? Was Bennett worth three? What criteria do I apply—who saves me and who threatens me? Is that the way history really gets created?

And because he was nothing if not a realist, he had one last thought:

What the hell. Orpheus didn't leave any guidelines for the job, either. I'll just have to play it by ear and do the best I can—and how can I serve history or art if I die tomorrow at noon?

"Here you are, Rhymer," said Tyrannosaur, taking a drink in his massive paw and handing another to Dante.

"Thanks."

"Here's to four verses!"

"You've got 'em, even if he runs."

"Bennett?" asked Tyrannosaur. "He won't run."

"But he can't beat you." Suddenly Dante frowned. "Can he?"

"Not a chance."

"Well, then?"

"A man in his profession can't run," said Bailey. "He's got to believe he's invincible, that nothing can kill him, even when he knows better. Otherwise he'll never be able to face a wanted killer again. He'll flinch, he'll hesitate, he'll back down, he'll run, he'll do *something* to fuck it up."

"But *if* he wants to back down, if it's his last day as a bounty hunter, let him walk," said Dante. "You'll get your verses anyway."

"Whatever you say," agreed Tyrannosaur. "But he won't back down."

"Against a monster like you?" said Dante, then quickly added: "Meaning no offense."

"None taken," said Bailey. "But size isn't everything. They say the guy who killed Conrad Bland wasn't much bigger than you are. And I know the Angel was supposed to be normal in size, maybe even a little undernourished. Men have developed more than two hundred different martial arts, and we've picked up dozens more from aliens. Those are great equalizers." He uttered a sigh of regret. "Size just isn't what it used to be."

"Then why does everyone come here to live under your protection?"

"Because I've mastered seventy-two of those martial arts, and I'm the best shot you ever saw with a burner or a screecher."

"Yeah, those are good reasons," agreed Dante. "And the fact that half the guys you fight can't reach your head probably doesn't hurt either."

"Neither does spreading the word."

"I beg your pardon?"

"When I was a young man, I was an adventurer," answered Bailey. "I wanted to pit my skills against the best opponents I could find. I was a mercenary, and for two years I was the freehand heavyweight champion of the Albion Cluster, and I even put in some time as a lawman out in the Roosevelt system. But eventually a man wants to settle down."

"What does that have to do with spreading the word?" asked Dante, confused.

"I still needed an income, so I passed the word that anyone who was willing to tithe me ten percent of their income and their holdings could live here under my protection. My reputation drew more than a thousand immigrants to Tusculum II and kept an awful lot of bill collectors and bounty hunters away."

"I see."

"You're a man of letters," continued Bailey, "so let me ask you your professional opinion about something."

"Shoot."

"I think Tusculum II is a really dull name for a world. I'm thinking of changing it."

"To what?"

"I don't know. Tyrannosaur's World, maybe." He looked across the table. "You don't like it."

"It's a little too, well, egomaniacal."

"I'm open to suggestions."

"How many planets are there in the system?"

"Six."

"Okay," said Dante. "As long as you're a Tyrannosaur, name them after periods in Earth's prehistory."

"I *like* that. What are the periods?"

"Damned if I know—but there were dozens of them. Have you got a pocket computer?"

"Sure. Don't you?"

"No."

"How do you write?"

"With a quill pen, just like Orpheus."

Bailey withdrew his computer and slid it across the table to Dante, who instructed it to list the various prehistoric eras.

"All right, this should work," announced Dante. "Call the first planet Cambria. This world is Devonia. The next four, in order, are Permia, Triassic, Jurassic, and Cretaceous. If any of them have moons, name the moons after the animals that existed in their eras."

"You've got a head on you, Rhymer!" enthused Bailey. "It would have been a shame to let Wait-a-bit Bennett remove it from your shoulders." He paused. "What'll we call the star?"

"Well, it's on all the charts as Tusculum, but that shouldn't matter. The planets are Tusculum I through VI, but if you're giving them names that appeal to you, there's no reason why you can't do the same to the star. How about Dinosaur, since that's the idea that gave birth to all the names?"

"Sounds good to me," said Bailey. "Tomorrow I'll have the space-port computer start signaling ships that we're Dinosaur."

"Make sure it adds that you were formerly Tusculum or you'll drive 'em all crazy."

"Right. I'm sure glad I ran into you, Rhymer."

"Not half as glad as *I* am," said Dante as Wait-a-bit Bennett entered the casino.

Bennett saw Dante and walked over to him.

"Got my fifty thousand credits yet, Danny?" he asked pleasantly.

"No."

"Well, you've got a little over half a day left. I'm sure a bright young lad like you can come up with the money." Bennett paused. "But until that happy moment occurs, I'm not letting you out of my sight."

"You've made two mistakes, Wait-a-bit Bennett," said Tyrannosaur.

"Oh?"

"First, his name's Rhymer, not Danny. And second, no one's laying a finger on him as long as he stays on Devonia."

"Where the hell's Devonia?" asked Bennett.

"You're standing on it."

"You don't have to stand up for him, Tyrannosaur," said Bennett. "The kid's not worth it."

"This is *my* world!" bellowed Bailey, getting to his feet. "I'm the only one who decides who lives and who dies!"

"I have nothing against you," persisted Bennett. "My business is with Danny Briggs and no one else."

"You have no business on Devonia."

"Like I say, my business is with Danny here . . . but if you try to hinder me in the pursuit of my legal livelihood, I'll have to kill you too."

Tyrannosaur smiled. "Is that a threat?"

"You may consider it such," acknowledged Bennett.

His hand moved slowly down toward his burner, but before he could reach it Tyrannosaur's hands shot out with blinding swiftness, one grabbing him by the neck, the other holding his hand away from his weapon.

Bailey lifted Bennett straight up two, then three, then four feet above the ground. The bounty hunter struggled to free himself. His free hand chopped at Tyrannosaur's massive arm. He landed a pair of devastating kicks in his attacker's stomach. Bailey merely frowned and began squeezing.

Soon Bennett was gasping for air. He landed two more kicks, and poked a thumb at Bailey's right eye, but Bailey simply lowered his head, and Dante could hear the bounty hunter's thumb break with a loud cracking sound as it collided with Bailey's skull.

Bennett's struggles became more desperate, and finally Bailey released his grip on Bennett's arm, used both hands to lift the bounty hunter above his head, and hurled him into the wall. There was a strange, undefinable sound as all the air left Bennett's lungs, and he dropped to the floor, where he lay motionless.

Suddenly a cheer went up from the assembled gamblers and drinkers.

"What the hell are they applauding?" asked Dante, staring at the dead bounty hunter.

"They're paying for my protection, remember?" said Bailey, who wasn't even panting from his efforts. "They're cheering because I've just shown them they're getting their money's worth. Bennett came after you, but he could have been *any* bounty hunter coming after any of *them*."

Virgil stuck his head in the door in response to the cheering, and gazed impassively at Bennett's corpse.

"Couldn't wait till tomorrow, huh?" he said.

"Out!" ordered Bailey, and Virgil removed himself from the doorway. Tyrannosaur then ordered two of the men on his staff to remove the body and dispose of it.

"The usual method, sir?" asked one of the men.

"Unless you've got a better way," answered Bailey. He turned back to Dante, who was staring at him intently. "I thought I just solved your problem. Suddenly you look like you've got another one?"

"No." *Just a question.*

"Good. And don't forget our bargain: I get four verses."

"At the very least," said Dante.

Who knows? You may get a hundred or more. It's become clear to me that I can't be an Orpheus without a Santiago. Could I possibly have found you this soon?

7.

Tyrannosaur, Tyrannosaur,
Whatever you give him, he wants more,
The world is his oyster, the stars are his sea;
He fishes for souls, a man on a spree.

That was about as political as the Rhymer ever got to be.

The first three verses were about Bailey's size, his strength, his mastery of martial arts and martial weapons. It glorified his fighting abilities, and in time it made his name a household word.

But it was the fourth verse, the one you see above, that was written with a purpose, for the new Orpheus sought a new Santiago, and the mythic proportions he drew—"the stars are his sea" and "He fishes for souls"—were written expressly to get Tyrannosaur Bailey thinking along those lines, to consider himself as something unique and special, a man not so much on a spree as on a holy mission.

"I like it," said Bailey enthusiastically after Dante had read it aloud to him the morning after he killed Wait-a-bit Bennett. "I don't know that I understand it, especially that last bit, but I like it. You've fulfilled your end of the bargain, Rhymer."

"Maybe I could explain the parts you don't understand," offered Dante.

"Sure, why not?"

"It means you collect lost souls, just as you've been doing here on Devonia. But you don't just collect them here; like the poem says, the stars are your sea."

"Well, that's right," agreed Bailey. "They come from all over."

"I don't see you being so passive, just sitting here and waiting for them to come to you," said Dante, selecting his words carefully. "As a matter of fact, I can see you going out and recruiting them."

"Devonia can't support that many more people," Bailey pointed out.

"Then you'll leave Devonia," said Dante. "Maybe you'll come back here from time to time for spiritual refreshment, but you'll find you have a greater purpose and you'll have to go abroad to fulfill it."

"I doubt it," said the huge man. "I'm happy with the purpose I've got."

"The choice may not be yours. It may be thrust upon you by powers that are beyond your control."

"I still don't know what you're talking about, Rhymer," said Bailey. "You almost make it sound like I'll be recruiting an army."

"Not the kind anyone else would recruit."

"We've already got the Democracy protecting us from the rest of the galaxy."

Dante leaned forward. "Who's protecting you from the Democracy?"

Bailey stared at him for a long moment, then laughed. "You're crazy!"

"Why?" demanded Dante. "Exceptional times call for exceptional men. You're an exceptional man."

"I'm a *live* man. I plan to stay that way." The huge man paused. "And you'd better get off the planet soon if *you* want to stay a live man. The Democracy's got to have traced your ship by now."

"Send them packing when they show up."

"Me? Take on the whole Democracy?"

"Just one squad. How the hell many men are they going to send to find a thief and his ship?"

"You don't understand much about geometrical progressions, do you, Rhymer?" said Bailey. "Say they send ten men, and I kill them all. Next week they'll send fifty to exact revenge. Maybe I'll hire some help and kill *them*, too. Then they'll send five hundred, and then thirty thousand, and then six million. If there are two things they can spare, they're men and ships—and if there's one thing they can't tolerate, it's having someone stand up to them."

"There are ways," said Dante.

"The hell there are!" growled Bailey.

"It's been done before."

"Never!"

"It has!" insisted Dante.

"By who?"

"Santiago."

"Come off it—he was just an outlaw!"

"He was a revolutionary," Dante corrected him. "And what kept him alive was that the Democracy never understood that he *wasn't* just an outlaw."

"What do you know about it?"

"Everything! If the Democracy had ever guessed what his real purpose was, they'd have sent five billion men to the Frontier and destroyed every habitable world until they were sure they'd killed him. But because they thought he was just an outlaw—the most successful of his era, but nothing more than that—they were content to post rewards and hope the bounty hunters could deliver him."

"Let me get this straight," said Bailey. "You're saying that you want me to pretend I'm Santiago?" He snorted derisively. "They may be dumb, Rhymer, but they can count. He'd be close to a hundred and seventy-five years old."

"I don't want you to *pretend* anything," said Dante. "I want you to *be* Santiago!"

Tyrannosaur Bailey downed his drink in a single swallow and stared across the table. "I never used to believe all artists were crazy. You've just convinced me I was wrong."

Dante was about to argue his case further when Virgil Soaring Hawk burst into Rex's and walked directly over to him.

"Time to go," he said, a note of urgency in his voice. "Say your good-byes, pay your bar tab, and let's get the hell out of here!"

"What's your problem?" asked Dante irritably.

"You haven't paid any attention to the news, have you?" said Virgil.

"What news?"

"Remember New Tangier IV, that pleasant little planet where you and I met?"

"Yeah. What about it?"

"It's become a piece of uninhabited rock, courtesy of the Democracy."

"What are you talking about?" demanded Dante.

"They sent a Navy squadron to find you and your ship," explained Virgil, figiting with impatience. "No one there knew where you'd gone. The Navy didn't believe them, so to punish them for withholding information they dropped an exceptionally dirty bomb in the atmosphere." He paused. "Nothing's going to live on New Tangier IV for about seven thousand years."

Dante turned to Tyrannosaur. "Did you hear that? The time is ripe!"

"The time is ripe to get our asses out of here, and to lose that fucking ship as soon as we can," said Virgil.

"*Shut up!*" bellowed Dante, and Virgil, startled, fell silent. "It's time for him to come back."

"The Democracy does things like that all the time."

"Then it's time to stop them."

"Maybe it is," agreed Bailey reluctantly. "But I'm not the one to do it."

"You've got all the attributes."

"You don't even know what his attributes were," said Bailey. "And neither do I. No one does."

"Someone has to stand up to the Democracy!"

"And have them do to Devonia what they did to New Tangier IV?" snapped Bailey irritably. "How do you stand up to a force like that?"

"*He* found a way. *You* will, too."

"Not me, Rhymer. I'm no revolutionary, and I'm no leader of men."

"You *could* be."

"I've *done* my time in the trenches. You'd better listen to the Injun and get the hell out of here, because if it comes to a choice between fighting the Navy or telling them where you've gone, I'll be the fastest talker you ever saw."

Dante stared at him, as if seeing him for the first time. "You mean it, don't you?"

"You bet your ass I mean it. *You* may have a death wish; *I* don't."

Dante blinked his eyes rapidly for a moment, as if disoriented. Then he sat erect. "I'm sorry. I was mistaken. You're not the one."

"I've been telling you that."

"But I'll find him."

"If he exists."

"If the times call exceptional men forth, they're practically screaming his name. He exists, all right—or he will, once I find him and convince him of his destiny."

"I wish you luck, Rhymer."

"You do?" said Dante, surprised.

"I live here. I know we need him." Bailey paused. "Are you going to keep my four verses?"

"Yes."

"Even that last one?"

"Even the last one," replied Dante. "It's not your fault you're not Santiago."

"Okay," said Bailey. "You played square with me. Maybe I can do you a favor."

"We're even," said Dante. "You killed Bennett, I gave you four verses."

Bailey shook his head. "A couple of hours from now the Navy is going to show up and ask me what I know about you, and I'm going to tell them. So I owe you another favor."

"All right."

"If you want to find a new Santiago, you'd better learn everything you can about the old one."

"I know everything Orpheus knew."

"Orpheus was a wandering poet who may never even have seen Santiago," said Bailey dismissively. "If you really want to know what there is to know about Santiago, there's a person you need to talk to."

"What's his name and where can I find him?"

"He's a she, and all I know is the name she's using these days—Waltzin' Matilda. She's used a lot of other names in the past."

"Waltzin' Matilda," repeated Dante. "She sounds like a dancer."

Bailey smiled. "She's a lot more than a dancer."

"Where is she?"

"Beats me. She moves around a lot."

"That's all I have to go on—just a name?"

"That's better than you had two minutes ago," said Bailey. Suddenly he looked amused. "Or did someone tell you that defeating the Democracy was going to be easy?"

The giant's laughter was still ringing in Dante's ears as he and Virgil left the casino and hurried to their ship.

Part 2

Waltzin' Matilda's Book

8.

Matilda waltzes, and she grinds.
Matilda gets inside men's minds.
Matilda plunders and she robs;
Matilda's pulled a thousand jobs.

It was an exaggeration. At the time Dante found her, Matilda had
pulled only 516 jobs, which was still sufficient to make her one of the
most wanted criminals on the Frontier.

Her specialty was that she didn't specialize. Gold, diamonds, artwork, fissionable materials, promissory notes, she stole them all. She'd
done two years in the hellhole prison on Spica II, and another four
months on Sugarcane. She escaped from both, the only prisoner ever
to break out of either penitentiary.

She was a lot of things Dante wasn't—skilled in the martial arts,
skilled in the ways of high society, exceptionally well read—and a
few things that Dante was, such as an outlaw with a price on her head.
It didn't bother her much; she figured that if she could survive Spica
II, she could survive anything the Democracy or the Frontier threw at
her.

The most interesting aspect of her past was that she came from
money, and had every whim catered to. At eight she was so graceful
a ballerina that her family mapped out her entire future—and at nine
she proved to be even more independent than graceful by leaving the
Democracy forever. She stowed away on a cargo ship bound for Roosevelt III, somehow made her way to the carnival world of Calliope,

bought a fake ID with money she'd stolen from her brother, and soon found work dancing in various stage shows.

As she grew older she learned every dance from a tango to a striptease, and made her way from one world to another as an entertainer, dancing solo when possible, with partners when necessary. She changed her name as often as most people changed clothes, and changed her worlds almost as frequently—but she never left a world without some trinket, some banknote, some negotiable bond, *something*, that she hadn't possessed when she arrived.

Just once she made the error of stealing within the Democracy's borders. That was when she was apprehended and incarcerated on Spica II. She never went back again.

No one knew her real name. She liked the sound of Matilda, and used it with half a hundred different surnames. She was Waltzin' Matilda just once, on Sugarcane, but that was where she was arrested the second time, and after she escaped from jail, that was the name that was on all the Wanted posters.

She still used a different name, sometimes more than one, on every world, but she was resigned to the fact that to most of her friends and almost all of her enemies she had become Waltzin' Matilda, despite the fact that she could not recall ever having performed a single waltz onstage.

It was a pleasant life, punctuated only by the occasional narrow escape from the minions of the Democracy or those bounty hunters who wished to claim its reward. She liked appearing onstage, and she found her secret vocation as a thief sexually exciting, especially when she knew that her movements were being watched.

Like tonight.

Dimitrios of the Three Burners was in the audience. He hadn't come to Prateep IV to find her—he was after other prey—but he had a notion that Matilda Montez was really Waltzin' Matilda, and since he hadn't turned up his quarry yet, he'd dropped in to check her out, maybe keep an eye on her in case she was up to her usual tricks.

She watched him out of the corner of her eye as she spun and dipped, jumped and pirouetted. It was Dimitrios, all right, with two of his trademarked burners in well-worn holsters and the handle of the third peeking out from the top of his boot. He seemed relaxed, sipping his drink, staring at her with the same appreciative smile she'd seen on so many other men in so many other audiences.

Well, you just keep drinking and smiling, bounty killer, because before you leave here I'm going to be two million credits richer—and even you, who's seen it all and heard it all, won't believe the only eyewitness.

She spun around twice more, then stopped and bowed, perfectly willing to let the audience think her smile was for them. They were informed that she would take a twenty-minute break, and then return for the evening's finale.

She waited for the applause to die down and bowed one last time, then began making her way to her dressing room. A drunken man jumped up from his chair and tried to climb onstage. She dispatched him almost effortlessly with a spinning kick to the chest, and got another standing ovation as she finally left the stage.

Once there, she locked the door behind her, peeled off her clothes, and donned a thin robe. She picked up a tiny receiving device and inserted it in her ear, then hit the control on her makeup table.

"Twenty minutes . . . nineteen minutes fifty seconds . . . nineteen minutes forty seconds . . ." droned a mechanical voice.

She slid her feet into a pair of rubber-soled shoes, then ordered her window to open. She climbed up onto the ledge and leaped lightly to the roof of the adjoining brokerage house with the grace of an athlete. A cloth bag was suspended on a very thin line from her room. She walked over to it, removed a pint of hard liquor from the neighboring system of Ribot, walked to a door leading to the building's interior, whispered the code that opened it, and stepped inside.

"Eighteen minutes, thirty seconds . . ."

She removed her shoes, took off her robe, and unstrapped the shocker from her leg. Then, totally naked, she descended two levels on the airlift.

A middle-aged man, dressed in a guard's uniform, suddenly looked up from the musical holo he had been watching on his pocket computer. His jaw dropped when he saw Matilda.

She smiled at him and began walking straight toward him.

"My God!" muttered the man. "Who . . . what are you doing here?"

Her smile widened, promising no end of wonders as she approached him, her hands behind her back.

"You . . . you . . . you shouldn't be here!" he stammered.

She considered replying, but decided that total silence would be more effective as she continued walking toward him.

"This is . . ." he began, and then seemed to run out of words for a moment. He blinked his eyes. "Things like this don't happen to me!"

Her left hand held the whiskey. She stretched it out to him, offering it, and as if in a dreamlike trance, he took a step toward her and reached out his arms.

And then, before he quite knew what hit him, she brought the shocker out in her right hand, aimed it at him, and felt it vibrate with power as it sent its voltage coursing through his body. For a moment he seemed to be a life-sized puppet dancing spasmodically on strings; then he fell to the floor in a silent heap.

She knelt down next to him, poured as much of the whiskey as she could into his mouth without choking him, spilled the rest on his clothes, and, after carefully wiping her fingerprints from the bottle, tossed it onto the floor, where it broke into pieces. She then raced to his desk and began manipulating his pocket computer.

"Fifteen minutes, ten seconds . . ."

She was still trying to find what she needed five minutes later. Then, finally, she broke through the encryption, found the code words she needed, walked to the safe, uttered the words in the proper order, and a minute later was thumbing through a score of negotiable currencies. She finally settled on New Stalin rubles and Far London pounds, since they were the largest denominations, took two huge handfuls, and raced to the airlift. Once she reached the third level she donned her robe and shoes and walked out onto the building's roof.

The guard would be out cold for at least five more hours. More to the point, he'd stink of booze, and no one on this or any other world would believe his story about a gorgeous naked woman entering the building and turning a shocker on him. It sounded too much like a drunken fantasy—and the remains of the drink were there to prove it.

She went to the bag that was suspended from her window, the one where she'd found the whiskey, and put the money into it. Then she tested the line that held it to make sure it was secure. It was, and a moment later she scrambled up the wall, feet on the slick metal exterior, hands on the line, until she reached her window.

She climbed back into her dressing room, raised the line high enough so that in the unlikely event someone else were to walk on the brokerage house's roof, they wouldn't be able to reach the bag, then removed her shoes and robe, put them in a closet, and began climbing back into her costume.

"Four minutes, twenty seconds . . ."

She felt proud of herself. She didn't believe in repeating her methods—that was the quickest way to give the police and the bounty hunters a line on you—and she thought tonight's job was one of her most creative to date. She'd stolen the equivalent of two million credits in currency that would be almost impossible to trace, and the only witness was an old man stinking of alcohol and raving about a naked lady. It was beautiful.

"Two minutes, thirty seconds . . ."

She took the receiver out of her ear, deactivated it, and placed it in a jar of face cream, covering it so no one could see it—not that anyone had a reason to look for it, but she hadn't made it this far by not being thorough.

Then, nineteen minutes after she left the stage, she walked out again and stood in the wings, waiting to be introduced, her take suspended from a window where no one could see it, and another perfect crime to her credit. If she was a little flushed from her efforts, well, that could be written off as excitement at appearing onstage, or satisfaction at the wild applause she generated.

She waited for the emcee to run through her intro, then stepped out and faced the audience, smiling and bowing before beginning to dance again.

Yes, he was still there: Dimitrios of the Three Burners. *I pulled it off right under your nose, bounty killer, and it's almost a pity that I did it so well you'll never know what happened. That's the only part of this business I don't enjoy; I can never let anyone know how good I am at what I do.*

She was on such an adrenaline high that she gave them not only a five-minute dance but a four-minute encore, and then another four minutes in which she and the band improvised wildly but in perfect harmony. When it was finally over, she bowed again, gave Dimitrios a great big smile, and returned to her dressing room—and found a small, slightly-built man sitting there on her chair.

"Hi," he said. "My name's Dante Alighieri. We have to talk."

"Who let you in here?" she demanded.

"I let myself in. It's one of the things I do really well."

"Well, you can let yourself right out!"

"Look," he said, "I'm not a bounty hunter, I'm not a security guard, I don't work for the Democracy or any police agency. I don't give a damn that you robbed the office next door."

Her eyes widened. "How . . . ?" She forced herself to stop in midthought.

"Because robbery is another of the things I do really well. I have nothing but professional admiration for you." Suddenly he smiled. "I wonder if Dimitrios knows how close he is to a *real* outlaw?"

"Probably not," she said, still eyeing him suspiciously.

"Where are my manners?" said Dante, suddenly getting to his feet. "This is your chair."

"I'd prefer to stand."

"All right," he said. "But hear me out before you start hitting and kicking. That's *not* one of the things I do well—though I'm learning."

"Just what the hell is it that you want?"

"I told you—I want to talk to you."

"If you think I'm going to pay you to keep quiet about tonight, you can forget it. They can question that old man all they want, his story will never hold up."

"I don't care about him or about what you stole."

"Then what *do* you want to talk about?"

"Santiago."

9.

He was a cop on the make, a cop on the take,
As corrupt as a cop gets to be.
The very same men that he saved from the pen
Are now owned by Simon Legree.

His name was Simon Legree, and he'd been after Matilda for a long, long time. She was the One Who Got Away, and it was a point of honor with him that he bring her to the bar of justice—or at least threaten to do so.

For Legree had his own profitable little business, not totally dissimilar from Wait-a-bit Bennett's. It was trickier, because he didn't have the advantage of a price on his prey's head—but when it worked, it was far more lucrative.

Oh, he took bribes, and he always managed to stuff a few packets of alphanella seeds in his pocket for future resale when there was a major drug bust—but what Simon Legree lived for was to catch a criminal in the act of committing a crime. Then it was a choice between jail and turning over a third of their earnings for the rest of their lives—and Legree had enough working capital to hire agents to make sure his new partners fulfilled their obligations.

He made millions from Billy the Whip, and millions more from the New Bronte Sisters, and he had almost fifty other partners out there earning money for him—but the one he wanted the most, the one he was sure had amassed the greatest fortune, Waltzin' Matilda, had thus far eluded him. Oh, he knew where she worked and where she lived, and whenever she changed planets—which she did on an almost weekly basis—his network of informants always let him know where she came to rest. But she was so damned creative in her lawlessness that he had yet to catch her in a compromising position, and she remained his Holy Grail.

He knew she was on Prateep IV. He knew she was dancing at the Diamond Emporium. He knew that she had signed a six-day contract, and had already been there five days. He knew that this was the night she figured to strike. He knew that by morning someone would be short hundreds of thousands, maybe even millions, of credits, and that her alibi would be airtight.

He tried to think like her, to predict what she might do, but he had nothing to go on, no past performance, no modus operandi. The damned woman never operated in the same way twice, and trying to predict and outthink her was driving him to distraction.

He sat in the audience, aware that Dimitrios of the Three Burners was there too, and wondered if Dimitrios had come for Matilda. He had no desire to go up against Dimitrios—no one in his right mind did—but he wasn't going to give Matilda up without a fight.

So Simon Legree sat there, silent, motionless, going over endless scenarios and permutations in his mind, and wondering how long it would be before Matilda emerged from her dressing room and returned to her hotel.

But Matilda had more important things on her mind—or confronting her from a few feet away. She stared curiously at the young man who knew she had just plundered the brokerage house but wanted only to talk about Santiago.

"He's been dead for more than a century," she said at last. "What makes you think I know anything about him?"

"Tyrannosaur Bailey seems to think you know more about him than anyone else alive," answered Dante.

"Probably I do," she agreed. "So what? He's still been dead for over a century."

Dante met her stare. "*All* of them have been," he said.

She looked her surprise. "I thought I was the only one who knew!"

"You were, until a few weeks ago."

"What happened a few weeks ago?"

"I found Black Orpheus' manuscript."

"The whole thing?"

Dante nodded. "Including a bunch of verses no one's ever seen or heard."

"Okay, so you know there was more than one Santiago," said Matilda. "So what? That was *his* secret, not mine."

"Tell me about them," said Dante. "And tell me why you're the expert."

"I'm the only living descendant of Santiago."

"*Which* Santiago?"

"What difference does it make?"

"It would help me to believe you."

"I don't give a damn if you believe me or not."

"Look, I have no reason *not* to believe you, and I want very much to. It's in both of our best interests."

"Why?" she insisted. "Who the hell are you, anyway?"

"My name is Dante Alighieri. The name I plan to be remembered by is the Rhymer."

"So you're the new Black Orpheus."

"You're very quick, Miss . . . ah . . ."

"Matilda." She frowned. "Okay, you're Orpheus. That doesn't change anything. Santiago still died more than a century ago."

Dante stared at her for a long minute. "I think it's time for him to live again," he said at last.

Her eyes widened, and a smile slowly crossed her face. "Now, *that's* an interesting idea."

"I'm glad you think so."

"Just a minute!" she said. "I hope to hell you're not thinking of *me!*"

"I'm not thinking of anyone in particular," said Dante. "But if we can talk, if you have any memorabilia, anything at all, I might get a better idea of what I'm looking for. As far as I can tell, of them all only Sebastian Cain could be considered truly skilled with his weapons, so they obviously had other qualities."

"They did."

"Qualities such as you exhibited tonight."

"I told you—I'm not a candidate for the job!" she snapped. "I'd like a Santiago, if only to take some of the pressure off me and give the law and the bounty hunters an even bigger target—so why in the world would I volunteer?"

"All right," he said. "I won't bring it up again." He paused. "*Do* you have any records or other memorabilia—letters, holograms, anything at all?"

"My family has lived like kings for three generations on what he chose to leave us—probably about two percent of what he was worth—but whatever we started with, it was converted into cash over a century ago. I've never seen any documents or anything like that."

"Did they ever speak of him?"

"How else would I know I was his great-great-granddaughter?"

"What did they say?"

"When people were around, the usual—that he was the greatest bandit in the galaxy, that he was a terrible man, that he might not have even been a man at all."

"And when people weren't around?"

She studied his face again, then shrugged. "What the hell. Who cares after this long?" She leaned back against a wall. "They told me that he was a secret revolutionary, that he was trying, not to overthrow the Democracy, but to hold it in check, to stop it from plundering the human colonies on the Frontier when there were so many alien worlds to plunder." She paused. "Does that agree with what Orpheus said?"

"No," replied Dante. "But Orpheus didn't know. It agrees with what I pieced together after reading the manuscript. Orpheus was too close to things. He studied all the people, but he never stepped back and really looked at the picture." He looked at her. "What else did they tell you?"

"That he had to do some morally questionable things, that he killed a lot of men because he felt his cause was just. Since it was essential that the Democracy think of Santiago as an outlaw rather than a revolutionary, almost everyone who worked for him was a criminal. Some looted and murdered on their own and let him take the blame—and some did terrible things on his orders." She paused. "They all served his cause, one way or another."

"Sounds about right. He came into existence because we needed him. I think we need him again."

"And if you and I select him and train him and control him, there's no reason why we shouldn't get a little piece of the action," she agreed.

"I don't want it," said Dante. "I just want *him*."

She looked at him like he was crazy. "Why?"

Dante shrugged. "It's difficult to explain. But he helps define me: there can't be an Orpheus without a Santiago. And God knows the need still exists. I've seen more brutality practiced in the name of the Democracy than I've ever seen practiced against it. Nothing's changed. They still don't seem to remember that they're in business to protect us, not plunder us."

"They would say they're doing just that."

"They're doing that if you're a citizen in good standing," replied Dante. "But out here, on the Frontier, they prevent alien races from running roughshod over us only so they can do it themselves. It's time to remind them just what the hell the Navy is *supposed* to be doing out here."

"What makes you think one man can stand up to them?" asked Matilda.

"Your great-great-grandfather did."

"*They* didn't know that, or they'd have used the whole Navy to hunt him down," she replied. "I know he robbed a lot of Navy convoys, and I know he ran the Democracy ragged trying to hunt him down— but what good did it do? All the Santiagos are dead, and the Democracy's still here."

"They stopped it from being worse," said Dante. "They built hospitals, they misdirected the Navy, they saved some alien worlds from total destruction. That's *some*thing, damn it."

"And who knows it besides you and me?" said Matilda. "Everyone he fought for thought he was a criminal out for *their* property."

"You know who knows it?" shot back Dante. "The *Democracy* knows it. They were scared to death of him—of them—for more than half a century . . . and if Santiago comes back, they'll be scared again."

She grimaced. "You know why there are no more Santiagos?"

"Why?"

"Because the Democracy blew Safe Harbor to smithereens when they got word that an alien force was hiding there. They never knew it was Santiago's headquarters, or that they'd killed him and his chosen successors. We live out here on the Frontier, so we think of him as King of the Outlaws—but if you're the Democracy, he's no more than a bothersome insect that's hardly worth swatting."

"You're wrong," said Dante. "I've studied it. The Democracy had eleven different agencies charged with finding and terminating him. Even today there's still one agency whose job is to find out who he was, how he got to be so powerful, and to stop history from ever repeating itself."

"Really?" she asked, interested.

He nodded. "Really." He paused. "So are you in or out?"

"Like I told you, I could use a Santiago to take the heat off me. Hell, I could use a couple of dozen. I'm in. Now what do I do?"

"Now we pool our knowledge and try to find the next Santiago."

"We could do a lot worse than the Tyrannosaur," she suggested.

"He's out. Doesn't want any part of it—and he's not what we need anyway."

"Why not? He's well named."

"Santiago wasn't just a physical force, or even primarily one," answered Dante. "He was a *moral* force. Men who never gave allegiance to anyone laid down their lives for him." He paused. "Do you see anyone giving up their lives because Bailey tells them to?"

"If that's your criterion, we'll never find a Santiago," she complained.

"We'll find him, all right," said Dante firmly. "The times will bring him forth."

"They haven't brought him yet."

"He's out there somewhere," said Dante. "But he doesn't *know* he's Santiago. It was easier for most of the others, all of them except the first one; they were recruited by the man they succeeded. *Our* Santiago doesn't know that the Santiago business still exists."

"All right, we'll proceed on that assumption," said Matilda. "I'll see what I can remember from my childhood." She paused. "I'm leaving Prateep tomorrow, for New Kenya. What should I be looking for?"

"I don't know. They were all different. Reading between the lines, I figure the original collected animals for zoos, and he was followed by a chess master, a farmer, a bounty hunter, and a bank robber. You'll just have to use your judgment, look for the kind of qualities you think he should have."

"That's not much to go on."

"We're planning to take the Frontier back from the Democracy. We can't put too many restrictions on the man who will lead us."

"All right," she said. "Where will you be? How can I contact you?"

"*I'll* contact *you.*" She stared at him curiously. "I'm a little hotter than you are right now," he explained. "I've got to keep moving."

"What did you do?"

"Nothing," he said wryly. "*That's* one of the things I have against the Democracy."

"I saw Dimitrios in the audience," she said. "Is *he* looking for you?"

"I doubt it," answered Dante. "If he was, I'm sure he'd have found me by now."

"He's one hell of a bounty hunter," Matilda noted. "You don't seem very worried about it."

"I'm not without my resources."

"They must be formidable."

"They're okay." He got to his feet. "I think I'd better be going now. I'll contact you again before you leave New Kenya."

"I don't know where I'll be staying yet."

"I'll find you."

He turned toward the door, which opened before he could reach it—and Simon Legree, dressed in his trademark navy blue, entered the dressing room, a burner in one hand, a screecher in the other.

"What have we here?" he said. "A carnival of thieves?"

"Go away," said Matilda contemptuously. "You don't have any-thing on me."

"I will soon, Tilly," he said.

"The name's Matilda, and you can tell me about it when you have it. Now get out of my dressing room."

"When I'm ready," he said with a smile. "As it happens, I didn't come for you." He turned to Dante. "Hello, Danny Briggs, alias Dante Alighieri, alias the Rhymer."

"All three of us bid you welcome," said Dante with no show of fear or alarm.

"Got a nice price on your head, Danny Briggs," continued Legree. "I could blow you away right now and take what's left to the nearest bounty office for the reward."

"The nearest office is halfway across the Frontier," said Dante. "I'd spoil."

"That wouldn't do either of us any good," said Legree. "Perhaps we should consider alternatives."

"I'm always happy to consider alternatives."

"What do you do for a living, Danny Briggs?"

"My name's Dante, and I'm a poet."

Legree made a face. "Poets don't make any money, Danny. You're going to have to learn another skill if you want to live." He paused. "Do you rob or kill?"

"I write poems about colorful characters like you before history has a chance to forget them."

"Damn it, I'm trying to give you a chance to buy your way out of this!" snapped Legree. "Usually I take thirty percent of your earn-ings for life—but what the hell does a poet earn?"

"I'm rich in satisfaction," replied Dante. "I love my work and I have loyal friends. What more does a man need?"

Legree shook his head. "No good, Danny. If you know a short prayer, you've just got time to say it."

Dante looked him in the eye. "I pray that you die quickly and painlessly," he said.

And before the words were out of Dante's mouth, Simon Legree blinked and frowned, as if he couldn't quite understand what had just happened. His weapons fell from his hands. He cleared his throat and opened his mouth to speak; nothing came out except a stream of blood.

"I *told* you I have loyal friends," said Dante, just before Legree fell to the floor with a knife protruding from his back, and Virgil Soaring Hawk entered the room, stepping over the lawman's corpse.

"Ma'am," said Virgil, staring at her with unconcealed lust, "you are unquestionably the most gorgeous creature to grace this forsaken world since the Maker of All Things set it spinning in orbit."

"Matilda, this is Virgil Soaring Hawk," said Dante.

"Dante's Virgil at your service." The Injun bent low in a stately bow. "Or the Scarlet Infidel, if you prefer."

"The Scarlet Infidel?" she repeated.

"It's a long story, ma'am," said Virgil. Suddenly he smiled. "But it's an interesting story, if you've got time to hear it over a couple of drinks."

"Leave her alone," Dante said. "She's one of us."

"What better reason to initiate her?" said Virgil.

"Don't," said Dante, and something in his voice made the Injun back off. The poet jerked his head toward Legree. "Get him out of here before someone sees him."

Virgil smiled apologetically at Matilda. "If you'll excuse me, ma'am, I'll just pick up this poor gentleman's body and put it somewhere where it won't bother anyone." He lifted Legree's corpse to his shoulder. "If you need anything, ma'am, now or anytime I'm around, just holler."

Dante stared at him for a moment, then turned back to Matilda. "If he lays a hand on you, tell me."

"I'm not the complaining type," she said. "Anything either of you try to do with me, you do at your own risk."

"Fair enough," said Dante.

Virgil vanished into the hallway.

"He seems to work for you."

Dante shrugged. "He attached himself to me the moment he heard my name. He insists that Dante needs a Virgil to get through the hell of the Inner Frontier." He smiled wryly. "So far he's been right."

"Does he do anything you ask, or is it limited to killing and disposing of bodies?"

"I don't know. I suppose I'll find out someday."

An uneasy silence followed, broken at last by Matilda.

"I'm sure you have things to do," she said. "You'd better be going."

"I will be. We can cover twice as much territory and consider twice as many candidates if we split up. I'll be in touch every week or two until we've finally found our Santiago." He paused. "I'm just giving the Injun a couple of minutes to get the body safely away. Don't let me keep you from doing whatever it is you have to do."

"You're not."

"Of course not." He smiled, walked over to the window, opened it, and pulled up the bag containing the currency. Matilda surreptitiously picked up a nail file from her vanity and held it behind her back as she watched the poet. He hefted the bag without opening it, then tossed it on her dressing table. "You can drop the knife," he said. "We're partners now—and partners don't rob each other."

She placed the file back on the vanity, opened the bag, pulled out the money, checked to see that it was all there, then turned to him.

"How did you . . . ?" she began—but Dante Alighieri was already gone.

10.

He has no future, he has no past,
His eye is sharp, his gun is fast,
He lives for the moment, he lives for the kill,
He's Dimitrios, and he's angry still.

Men aren't all cut from the same cloth. Many bounty hunters started out as lawmen, and when they decided they were good enough, they went out to the Rim or one of the Frontiers to ply their trade for far more money than a lawman makes.

Some were outlaws who decided that killing other outlaws was far more profitable than killing the agents of the law who pursued them.

And then there were men like Dimitrios of the Three Burners. No one knew his last name. No one knew where he came from. Some said he grew up on a small world in the Spiral Arm, others say he spent his youth on the Outer Frontier. There was one point where the speculation ended, and that was the day Johnny the Wolf shot his wife and infant daughter. He wasn't aiming for them. In fact, he probably never even knew they were there. He had just finished robbing the bank of Marcellus III, and they blundered between him and the law.

Dimitrios had never fired a hand weapon in his life, but he bought a matched set that afternoon, and spent the next hundred days working from sunrise to sunset at becoming proficient with them. When he felt he was ready, he went out hunting for the Wolf, and finally caught up with him in a casino on Banjo, an obscure little world in the Albion Cluster.

That fight was the stuff of legends. Dimitrios walked right up to

Johnny the Wolf as he sat at a table playing cards, placed the muzzle of his burner in Johnny's ear, and fired. Johnny never knew what hit him—but six of his hired killers did, and Dimitrios shot four of them down before one of his burners shorted out and the other was blown out of his hand. He began throwing whiskey bottles, chairs, spittoons, anything he could get his hands on. The two men were no cowards. They fought back gamely, but they were no match for the vengeful Dimitrios, and within a few minutes of Dimitrios entering the casino the Wolf and all six of his men were dead.

Most men would have considered themselves lucky to have survived and returned to their normal lives, but Dimitrios had nothing to return to. He also had the feeling that for the first time in his life, something he'd done had made a difference, that given the geometrical permutations involved, he might have saved as many as a hundred lives by killing those seven murderers, and he decided then and there to go into the bounty-hunting business. The first thing he did was buy an extra burner to stuff in his boot, just in case one of the two he wore in holsters should ever short out again, and since he never offered his last name to anyone, before long he was known simply as Dimitrios of the Three Burners.

He didn't talk much, socialized even less, rarely drank, never drugged. If he ever felt like hanging it up and going back to his former life, he just forced himself to remember how it felt when he learned his wife and child had been killed, and he rededicated himself to preventing others from sharing that terrible, aching emptiness, that undirected hatred at the universe.

He wasn't interested in bringing anyone back alive. If the rewards didn't specify dead or alive, he ignored them. He was even particular about the types of killers he went after. He much preferred to go after those who had killed unarmed women and defenseless children, and he frequently passed up closer, easier, and far more lucrative prey to go after the ones who fit his criteria.

He lived very simply. His clothes were commonplace; even his weapons were not of the best manufacture. His ship was old and unimpressive. Most people felt he was hoarding his rewards. They would have been surprised to know that he kept only enough to live and travel on, and sent the rest to handpicked charities that gave help and comfort to women who had survived violent attacks and children whose parents had been murdered.

He was on Prateep because he'd been given a tip that Hootowl Jacobs was there, but he hadn't seen any sign of him. He'd heard about this new character called the Rhymer, but when he looked into it, he found it far more likely that the Democracy had killed the Duchess than that the young poet had.

He knew all about Matilda, too, but he had no interest in bringing her down. In fact, he admired her. He liked the way she drove the Democracy and the Frontier's authorities crazy. He knew that she plundered every world she visited; what impressed him the most was that everyone else knew it too, and no one had been able to prove a thing. He'd stopped by the Diamond Emporium to watch her dance—he'd seen her before, and was intrigued by her combination of grace and athleticism—and to see if there was anyone in the crowd who might point him in the direction of Hootowl Jacobs. As usual, he didn't socialize; there was no one there that he either trusted or respected—there were mighty few of either in the galaxy—and so he simply relaxed and enjoyed his drink.

When the show was over, he got to his feet. He'd seen the Rhymer sneak into Matilda's dressing room, but that was no concern of his. He walked two blocks to his hotel, stopped at the bar for a nightcap, and went up to his room.

A few minutes later he heard a single knock at the door. He was still dressed, but his weapons, all three of them, were on the dresser. He quickly walked over, grabbed one, and trained it on the door.

"Come in," he said, uttering the code words that unlocked it.

"Thank you," said Matilda, entering the room. "I think it's time we met."

He shrugged. "I know who you are—and I know what you're supposed to have done. Makes no difference to me. As far as I'm concerned, you're free to keep on doing it."

She smiled. "That's very comforting."

"Is that what you came to find out?" asked Dimitrios.

"No."

"Then have a seat. Can I get you something to drink?"

"No, thanks."

"I don't do drugs, and I don't let anyone around me do them," he said.

"That's all right. I don't drug."

"You're a cheap date," he said, finally lowering the burner and stuffing it in a boot.

"I believe in making every credit count."

"Really? I've heard that you've got money you haven't even counted yet."

"Oh, no—I always count it. How else would I know that I'm not being ripped off?"

"I like you, Waltzin' Matilda," said Dimitrios. "I like the way you dance. I like the fact that you drive the Democracy crazy. And now I find that I like your wit." He paused. "But I still don't know what the hell you're doing here."

"I want to get to know you."

"That's a line I usually hear from some floozy the hotel manager sends up to make sure I don't shoot up the place," he said.

"I'm sure it is," she replied. "But I really *do* want to get to know you."

"Why?"

"Because from everything I hear you're an honorable man, and they're pretty rare."

"All right, I'm an honorable man. Now what?"

"Now I want you to tell me about the other honorable men you know: who they are, what they do, what they believe in?"

"You want to talk to a minister, not a bounty hunter."

"I know what I want to talk to," said Matilda. She sighed. "Okay, forget honorable. Who's the most formidable man on the Inner Frontier?"

"*I* am," he said, and when she made no comment, he continued: "I know it sounds egomaniacal, but if I didn't think so, if I didn't truly believe it, then I'd never be willing to go up against some of the men I have to face."

"Who else?"

"There are a lot of formidable men out here," answered Dimitrios. "Hootowl Jacobs, for one. I've heard about a character called Silvermane, out in the Quinellus Cluster. There's the Plymouth Rocker, there's Mongaso Taylor, there's the Black Death, there's a woman they call the Terminal Bitch who's supposed to be as deadly as any of them." He lit a thin smokeless cigar. "And there are some mighty formidable aliens too. From what I hear, there's a pair named Tweedledee and Tweedledum that might be deadlier than any of them."

"Well, that's a start," said Matilda. "How many of them are honorable?"

"Maybe one, maybe none, who knows? Mind if I ask you a question?"

"Go ahead."

"Why is the most accomplished thief on the Inner Frontier looking for an honorable man? That's kind of like mixing oil and water, isn't it?"

She laughed. "I don't think you'd believe me if I told you."

"Probably not, but why don't you tell me and I'll decide for myself."

"Fair enough. I'm looking for an honorable man to train and finance."

"What will you train him to be?"

"A dishonorable man."

He stared at her for a long minute. "That's an interesting notion. What are you looking for—a bodyguard or a partner?"

"Something much more than that," said Matilda. "I'm looking for a leader."

"Leaders are in short supply these days," replied Dimitrios.

"That's why we need one so badly."

"We?" he repeated. "As in you and me?"

"As in the whole Inner Frontier."

"We've never had one."

"Yes we have," said Matilda.

He stared at her curiously. "You're getting at something. I wish you'd come right out and say it."

"It's time for Santiago to return."

He chuckled. "You wouldn't like it much. He's been a rotting corpse for over a century."

"Maybe not," she said.

"Oh?"

"Maybe I'm looking at him right now."

"You've got me all wrong, Waltzin' Matilda," said Dimitrios. "Santiago was the King of the Outlaws. That's just the kind of person that I'm in business to hunt down and kill."

"What if I told you he wasn't what you think?"

"I'd ask what special insight you had into him."

"I'm his granddaughter."

He stared at her, then shook his head. "The numbers are wrong."

"All right," she said with a shrug. "His great-great-granddaughter."

"And you want me to go out and pillage and steal and kill for you?"

"No, I want you to do it for *us*."

"You and me?"

"The entire Inner Frontier."

"You keep saying that, but it doesn't make any sense."

"Have you got any coffee?" she asked. "Because what I have to tell you is going to take a while."

He ordered the kitchenette to prepare it, then handed her a cup and finally sat down on a chair that hovered a few inches above the ground, and changed its shape to accommodate his long, lean body.

"All right," he said. "I'm listening."

She proceeded to tell him about Santiago—everything she knew about him, everything her family had said when no one was around to overhear, everything Dante Alighieri had found hidden in the pages of Black Orpheus' poem. It took her close to two hours. When she was done she stared at him, waiting for a reaction.

"I believe you," he said at last.

"Good. That means I haven't wasted either of our time."

"Let me finish," he said. "I believe what you said. I believe Santiago was a secret revolutionary. I'm even willing to believe there was more than one Santiago." He paused, considering his words. "I believe that the time is right for another Santiago. But I'm not your man."

"Why not?"

"I'll help you look for him," continued Dimitrios. "I'll work for him and I'll fight for him." He stared unblinking into her eyes. "But I won't *become* him."

"Think of the difference you could make."

"Someone else can make it. Not me."

"But why?" she insisted.

"Because I'm not willing to do the things Santiago has to do if he's to *be* Santiago. I won't give orders to kill innocent men and women. I won't be the one who sends out men to kill young soldiers who are only trying to protect the Navy's payrolls or weapons. I understand why it has to be done, but it's contrary to everything I believe in, everything I *am*. I'll help you as far as I can, I'll protect you while you and the Rhymer are searching for the next Santiago, I'll never betray you—but I won't be Santiago, not now, not ever."

"You're sure?"

He smiled again. "Santiago is capable of lying. I'm not."

"But you *will* help us?"

"I said I would."

"Have you any suggestions where we should go next?"

"It'll take some thought," answered Dimitrios. "Santiago has to be able to lie, as I said. He has to send men to their deaths. He has to commit enough crimes to convince the Democracy that he's a criminal and not a revolutionary, and he has to be brutal and efficient enough to discourage any criminals on the Frontier from trying to take over his operation." He shook his head and added wryly, "He could be every scumbag I've ever hunted down."

"But he's not," she pointed out. "With him, it's a facade."

"I know. But they're not traits you're likely to find in a minister."

"That's why we decided to start with lawmen or bounty hunters," said Matilda.

"Maybe," said Dimitrios dubiously. "The question is who you trust more: a man who's been an outlaw all his life, or a man who's willing to become an outlaw on five minutes' notice."

"I see your point."

"Tell me about the one they call the Rhymer," he said. "I know he spent some time in your dressing room on Prateep. What's *his* interest in all this?"

"He's the one who sought me out in the first place."

"Why?"

She shrugged. "He wants to write poems about Santiago."

Dimitrios considered her answer for a moment, then nodded his head. "I suppose Orpheus needs a Santiago as much as Santiago needs an Orpheus."

"And what do *you* need?"

"I need men who deserve to die for what they've done. Right now I need one named Hootowl Jacobs. I heard a rumor tonight that he might have gone to Innesfree II. That's where I'll be heading tomorrow."

"If he's the one we're looking for, you won't kill him, right?"

"If he's the one you're looking for, I'll have to reevaluate my pledge to you," said Dimitrios.

"What has he done?"

"You don't want to know."

"Whatever it was, he did it to a woman," she said. "I know that much about you. That's why I was willing to come alone to your room."

"I saw you take that drunk out with a spinning kick," said Dimitrios. "You handle yourself just fine."

She got to her feet. "Tell me where your ship is and I'll meet you there in the morning."

"You're coming along?" he said. "Don't you have any professional engagements?"

"I'll cancel them and pick up work wherever you're going."

"We might do better going in three directions—you, me, and the poet."

"I'm coming with you," she said adamantly.

He shrugged. "Suit yourself."

"So where's your ship?"

"There's only one spaceport. Be there an hour after sunrise."

She got to her feet and walked to the door, then turned back to him. "I can't help thinking it should be you. You're such a goddamned moral man."

"You don't want such a goddamned moral man," he assured her. "You want a man who understands his purpose and will do whatever he has to do to succeed. I'm not that man."

"Well, you might at least look a little sad about it."

"Why?" he said. "Whoever he is, he is—or soon will be—the most important man on the Inner Frontier. We both know he's out there somewhere. What could be more challenging than finding him?"

"Convincing him that he's Santiago?" she suggested.

"When we find him, he'll know," said Dimitrios with certainty. "Hell, he's probably busy *being* Santiago right now. All we have to do is find him and tell him what his true name is."

"You really believe that, don't you?"

"If he's Santiago, the one thing he's not is a fool. If he's got the abilities we're looking for, he's been honing them, getting ready to meet his destiny. Our job is to point it out to him and convince him we're right."

"Do you really think we will?" asked Matilda.

"As sure as my name is Dimitrios of the Three Burners."

11.

Hootowl Jacobs loves his life.
Hootowl Jacobs takes to wife
A woman here, a woman there—
A bigamist, but one with flair.

Dante wrote that verse about Hootowl Jacobs, but he was still new
at the job, and he made a major mistake, one Black Orpheus never
made: he relied upon other people's descriptions and recollections. He
never met Hootowl Jacobs himself, and that was the real reason the
verse was so flawed.

Hootowl Jacobs loved his life, all right, and he certainly was a
bigamist from time to time, but therein lay the rub: Hootowl tended
to fall in love only with ladies of property, and since he was aware
that he wouldn't be awarded that property in a typical divorce proceeding, he "divorced" his wives in his own unique way: with a ser-
rated hunting knife across their windpipes.

No one knew how many wives he had taken, though there were
doubtless records of it somewhere. No one knew how many he had
dispatched either, but he came to the attention of Dimitrios of the
Three Burners when the total reached double digits.

Dimitrios was nothing if not thorough—it was the best way to
keep alive in his line of work—so he began checking up on Jacobs.
The man had killed women on Sirius V and Spica VI in the Democracy, on Silverblue out on the Rim, and on Binder X, Roosevelt III,
Greenveldt, and at least four other worlds of the Inner Frontier.

His method was always the same. He'd show up on a world, a

well-to-do widower (as indeed he was), and because of his economic and social station he tended to meet more than his share of well-to-do widows. He wasn't all that much to look at, and his manners weren't the type that would sweep a woman off her feet . . . but he would stress what they had in common, which was money and loneliness, and it wasn't long before wedding bells would be ringing and Hootowl Jacobs (who, after the deaths of his first three wives, never used his own name again) was a husband again.

He never rushed into his "divorces." The fastest was five months, the slowest almost three years. But sooner or later it was inevitable. A distraught, hysterical Jacobs would seek out the authorities, claiming some passing stranger had killed his wife. She was always missing some jewelry, so the motive was apparent. The legalities were usually concluded in two or three weeks—a new John Doe warrant, and a quick property settlement in favor of the grieving widower.

Hootowl Jacobs was not just the kind of man that Dimitrios longed to catch, he was the kind that the bounty hunter wanted to kill slowly and painfully with his bare hands. He knew that he was unlikely to get the opportunity, but he could hope.

It took two days for Dimitrios and Matilda to get to Innesfree II. She had wanted to question him further about potential Santiagos, but he had his own priorities and preferred to go into Deepsleep, which would eventually extend his life by two days provided he beat the odds and lived to an old age. And as he explained, "If I didn't plan to live my full span of years, I wouldn't be in this business to begin with."

To which she thought, *The hell you wouldn't*—but had enough tact to keep her mouth shut, and after reading the opening chapters of an exceptionally unthrilling thriller she climbed into her own Deepsleep pod, awakening when the ship went into orbit around Innesfree II.

"Get up," said Dimitrios, who was already awake and alert.

"I'm starving!" said Matilda.

"Of course you are. You haven't eaten in two days. We'll eat when we land."

She climbed out of the pod, amazed at how stiff her joints could become in just two days.

"Any messages for me?" she asked.

"Yeah. The ballet doesn't need a prima ballerina, stripping is outlawed on Innesfree, but if you can dance the flamenco, whatever that is, there's a joint that can give you four days' work." He paused. "Four days is plenty. If Jacobs is here, I'll find him in less time than that."

"Okay, I'll take it."

"Don't tell *me*," said Dimitrios. "Send a message to *them*."

"I will," she said. "Give me a minute to wake up."

"All right," he said. "I've booked two rooms for us at a hotel in the center of what seems to pass for the planet's only city."

"Fine. I hope they have a restaurant."

"I hope Hootowl Jacobs is staying there."

"You act like it's a personal vendetta," said Matilda. "Have you ever met him?"

"No. He deserves to die; that's all I need to know."

"How many women has he killed?"

"Too many."

"You know," she said, "I could represent myself as a wealthy widow, or an heiress . . ."

"Forget it. There's a price on his head. We don't need to set him up."

"I thought it might draw him out."

"If he can find a wealthy widow on Innesfree before I find him, then it's time for me to retire."

"Do you even know what he looks like?" asked Matilda.

"Computer, show me Hootowl Jacobs," ordered Dimitrios.

Instantly a life-sized holographic image appeared. It was a man with bulging blue eyes, a widow's peak of brown hair, an aquiline nose, medium height, medium weight, dressed expensively.

"That's him," said Dimitrios.

"He's certainly distinctive," she said.

"If you mean easy to spot, yes, he is."

"I gather he's inherited a number of fortunes," said Matilda. "What the hell is a man with that kind of money doing on a little backwater world like Innesfree II?"

He shrugged. "Who cares? It's enough that he's here—*if* he is."

"If I were you, *I'd* care. He might have hired a small army."

"What for? He's never killed anyone but middle-aged women."

"Aren't you even curious?"

He shook his head. "Not a bit."

Santiago would be curious, she thought. *And cautious. He'd want to know what business Hootowl Jacobs had on this world. You're so intent on killing him that you're not even interested in what makes him tick, and yet that knowledge could be the advantage you need. I know, I know, all he kills are his wives, but you still should look for any edge you can get. This is life and death, after all.*

She began to appreciate the problem of finding Santiago. He was one tiny needle in the haystack of the Inner Frontier, and he probably had no idea of who and what he was to become. Just finding him could take a few lifetimes; convincing him to fulfill his destiny could take almost as long.

She was still considering her problems when the ship touched down. Shortly thereafter they passed through Customs—they had to purchase one-month visas for fifty credits apiece—and Dimitrios rented an aircar, which skimmed a foot above the ground and got them from the spaceport to the city in a matter of a few minutes.

"Here we are," said Dimitrios, deactivating the aircar. "The Shaka Zulu Hotel."

"Who or what was Shaka Zulu?" asked Matilda.

"Who knows? Probably some politician or poet." He paused. "Let's check it out before we unload our luggage."

The doors faded into nothingness as they approached the entrance, and a moment later a small, rotund purple alien was escorting them to their rooms. He stopped when he reached the end of the corridor. For a moment Matilda thought he had forgotten where to take them, but then Dimitrios flipped him a coin, which he caught in his mouth, and he toddled away.

"I'd have asked him if Jacobs was here, but I don't think he speaks Terran," said the bounty hunter.

"Why not ask at the front desk?"

"Clerks don't keep their jobs long if they reveal their guest lists to bounty hunters." He smiled. "Some of them don't live long, either."

She turned to the doors. "Which is mine?"

"Whichever you want. Just let it read your handprint and retina once, and it'll be programmed for you for the next four days."

"I don't know which one I want until I see them both."

"They're identical."

"Okay, this one is fine then," said Matilda, letting the security system scan her readings. The door dilated a moment later and she passed through it. "Not bad," she said. "Larger than I expected."

"Space isn't at a premium on Innesfree," remarked Dimitrios.

She walked back out into the corridor. "It'll do. Now I have to pop over to El Gran Señor and see about a job."

"I'll come with you," he said.

"Why don't you just stay here and relax? I'll be back in a few minutes."

"I didn't come here to rest."

They walked back to the front of the hotel, where Dimitrios

brought their luggage in from the aircar and tossed another coin into another blue alien's mouth after telling him their room numbers.

"I hope he understood," she said as they walked out onto the street.

"They wouldn't let an alien hang around the lobby and collect tips if he couldn't."

They walked two blocks north to El Gran Señor. It was closed for the afternoon, but a doorman let them in. The interior was starkly decorated, with a bar in one corner, a number of tables with uncomfortable-looking chairs, and a small stage. A second, even smaller stage held a single stool, obviously for the guitarist.

"Good afternoon," said a balding, pudgy man with a reddish face. "My name's Manolete. You must be my new dancer."

"Matilda," she said, extending her hand.

"Got a last name?" he asked as he took her hand and shook it.

"Not lately," said Matilda with a smile.

"No problem. Just need something for our records."

"Pay me in cash and use any last name you like."

"Done." He turned to Dimitrios. "*You're* sure as hell no dancer," he said, staring at the bounty hunter's weaponry.

"Just looking for a friend," said Dimitrios.

"Well, I'm as friendly as they come," said Manolete. "What can I do for you?"

"You're not the friend I'm looking for," said Dimitrios. "I hear that Hootowl Jacobs is on Innesfree."

"Could be," said Manolete. "What do you want with him?"

"I'm his attorney, here to deliver an inheritance."

"I hear tell he's had his share of them."

Dimitrios nodded. "Poor fellow *does* seem unlucky," he agreed.

"Not as bad as his luck is now, Dimitrios of the Three Burners," said Manolete with a grin. "I've heard about you. They say you're one of the best."

"So is he on Innesfree?"

"He is."

Dimitrios stared coldly at Manolete. "You wouldn't be so silly as to warn him?"

"Me?" laughed Manolete. "Hell, no! I want you to take him out right here in El Gran Señor! We can use the publicity. Maybe I'll even catch it on my holo cameras." He outlined the entertainment with his hands. "Last show each night. For an extra two hundred credits, watch the fabled Dimitrios of the Three Burners take out that notorious ladykiller Hootowl Jacobs! Now, why the hell would I warn him away?"

Dimitrios was silent for a long moment. Finally he spoke: "Draw up a contract."

"A contract?" repeated Manolete. "What for?"

"*If* Hootowl Jacobs shows up here, and *if* I kill him, and *if* you capture it on your holo cameras, and *if* you start charging customers to watch it, then I want fifty percent of the gross to go to these two charities." He wrote the names down on a counter, then looked up. "Is it a deal?"

Manolete sighed. "Okay, I'll have a contract ready tonight."

"If I should ever find out that you were cheating my charities," said Dimitrios, "I would be seriously displeased with you. Do we understand each other?"

Manolete nodded, and Dimitrios turned and walked back out into the street. The club owner turned to Matilda.

"Nice company you keep."

"We get along."

"I hope Jacobs kills *him*!" said Manolete passionately. "Hootowl would never charge me half just for showing holos of it." He paused. "Where does he get off, charging me for showing holos of what happens in my own club?"

"It hasn't happened yet."

"It will."

"Probably," agreed Matilda. "Killing's *his* job. Mine is dancing. Where's my costume?"

"In your dressing room," said Manolete, getting to his feet. "Come on, I'll show you." He escorted her backstage. "We haven't got time to teach you a number. I hope you can improvise."

"I usually do."

"We've got a Borillian playing the guitar," continued Manolete.

"A Borillian?" she repeated. "Why?"

"It's a fourteen-string guitar, and he's got seven fingers on each hand. You won't believe the music he can make."

"As long as it's flamenco, we won't have a problem."

"Here we are," he said as they reached a small dressing room. "Usually we have two or three women backing up the lead male, but that asshole went and got himself shot last week."

"And the other women?"

He shrugged. "You know how women are."

"No," said Matilda. "How are we?"

"Easy come, easy go."

"Right," she said. "We're so flighty we don't hold still long enough to get shot like your male dancers."

He glared at her, but made no reply. She looked around the room, checked out the costumes to make sure they'd fit her, examined the vanity, and finally nodded. "All right, I've seen it. When do you need me?"

"We're pretty informal here. Show up after you've digested your dinner. You'll do three shows, maybe four." He paused. "Don't you want to try on the shoes?"

"I'll wear my own."

"They won't match."

"But they'll fit."

"You know," said Manolete, "you're as disagreeable as *he* is."

"I'm not here to be agreeable," said Matilda. "You wanted a dancer. You've got one."

"As long as you're hired, I'd better tell you the rules."

"There's only one rule," said Matilda. "No one enters my dressing room when I'm in it."

"There's no drinking, no drugging, no—"

"You'll get your money's worth," she said, walking to the exit. "I'll see you later."

Before he could say a word, she'd shut the door in his face and headed out to the street. Once she was outside she looked around for Dimitrios, couldn't spot him, and walked back to the hotel. She checked the bar before going to her room, and saw him sitting there, the only customer in the place in midafternoon, a tall cold drink on the table in front of him.

"Don't drink too many of those," she said, sitting down opposite him. "I've got a feeling Jacobs will show up tonight."

"There's no alcohol in it," he replied. "I don't indulge when I'm working. You want one?"

"Sure. What is it?"

"I don't know what it's called. It's a mixture of three or four citrus fruits native to Innesfree. Nice tang to it."

She signaled the bartender, yet another rotund blue alien. "I'll have one of those," she said, pointing to Dimitrios' glass.

"Yes, Missy," growled the alien.

"Are those creatures the original inhabitants of Innesfree?" she asked. "They seem to be omnipresent."

"Only in the hotel," answered Dimitrios. "They're native to Halcyon II. The ones you see are indentured servants, working off their debts."

"How do you know that?"

"I've been to Halcyon II, and I know the policy of the corporation that owns this chain of hotels."

"And you put up with it?"

"It's not up to me," said Dimitrios. "They sign the papers, they work off their debts. It's the law."

"Didn't you ever want to break a bad law?"

"Lady, I represent the law out here. If you don't break it, you'll never have a problem with me."

"And good or bad law, it makes no difference to you?" she persisted.

"You're looking for Santiago," he said. "I've got my own priorities."

"I know," said Matilda. The alien arrived with her drink, set it down, and scuttled away. "Strange little beasts, aren't they?"

"Not to a lady Halcyoni," said Dimitrios.

"Point taken." She sipped the drink. "It's very good."

"Most fruit drinks are," he said. "I don't know why, but the human body seems to metabolize alien fruits and vegetables easier than alien protein."

"Are you saying you're a vegetarian?"

"No, I like meat. But I try not to eat it on days that I'm likely to work. Wouldn't want to get stomach cramps or worse at the wrong time."

"You keep saying it so impersonally: 'days that I'm going to work.'"

"You can't humanize these bastards," answered Dimitrios. "You can't ever do anything that'll make you pause, or hesitate, or listen to a plea or an explanation or an excuse. They killed the innocent and the helpless; they have to die."

"Do you ever have second thoughts, or regrets?"

He shook his head. "I might have, about a man who killed another man in a fair fight. Or a man who robbed a bank and killed a guard who was trying to kill him. Or about you. But not about the men I go after."

"So you never feel remorse, or regret?"

"Only satisfaction." He paused. "Why do you care?"

She shrugged. "I don't know. I'm trying to make a list of traits I need to find in Santiago."

He laughed softly.

"What's so funny?" she asked.

"If you get close enough to ask 'em, he's probably not Santiago."

They spent the rest of the afternoon in the bar, sipping fruit drinks and waiting for night to fall. When it had been dark for more than an hour, she got up and made her way back to El Gran Señor.

"You're early," said Manolete. "I like that in a performer."

"Not much to do in this town," she replied.

"And I like *that* in a town," he said. "This is the only excitement there is." He paused. "We should be full all night long. Everyone knows Dimitrios of the Three Burners plans to kill Hootowl Jacobs here tonight."

"Just how many people did you tell?"

"Enough."

"If word reaches Jacobs, you'll be in for a disappointing evening."

"You don't know the Hootowl," said Manolete. "He doesn't back down from anything."

"I thought all he didn't back down from were middle-aged wives who trusted him."

"That's because you've been listening to Dimitrios."

She considered sending a warning to Dimitrios, then changed her mind. His rejection of her offer hadn't discouraged her, but failure to take Hootowl Jacobs would decide it once and for all: if he couldn't kill Jacobs, then he could never be Santiago.

She changed into her costume, put on her makeup, then sent for the Borillian guitarist. His name could not be pronounced by any human, so she decided to call him José. He seemed friendly enough, and spoke in tinkling chimes, which his T-pack translated into a dull monotone. After learning the extent of his repertoire, she felt confident that she could improvise to anything he chose to play.

She had some time to kill, so she left her dressing room and began wandering around the building, trying to acquaint herself with it. She found the staff's bathroom and kitchen, and a small room with a card table, then went out front. A few men and women were already sitting at tables, drinks in front of them, and a hologram of a quartet of guitarists was projected on the stage, with the music coming from everywhere, or so it seemed.

"You look good," said Manolete, approaching her.

"Thanks."

"I mean really good."

"I mean really thanks," she said.

"You know, maybe we could work a little something out here," he continued.

"I doubt it."

"It would mean more money for you."

"It'd mean a quick kick in the balls for you," said Matilda. "Are you sure you want to pay me extra for that?"

He glared at her. "Maybe I'll just turn you over to Hootowl."

"First, I'm not rich enough for him, and second, his life expectancy is probably about an hour."

"We'll see," said Manolete, walking off.

She walked over to the bar, introduced herself to the two bartenders, and sat on a stool for a while listening to the recorded music.

A few moments later a man with bulging blue eyes and a distinctive widow's peak entered and took a table in the farthest corner, his back to a wall, and she knew Jacobs had arrived. Before long the room was full and she went back to her dressing room, awaiting her signal to perform.

It came after another half hour, and shortly thereafter she was dancing to the music of José, her fourteen-fingered Borillian guitarist. He took it easy on her, building his speed and rhythm slowly until he saw that she could keep up with him.

She spun around as José reached the final few bars of his song, then stopped and bowed to mild applause. As she looked up, she saw that Dimitrios had entered the room and was walking calmly toward Hootowl Jacobs. She began stamping her feet and whirling around again, with no accompaniment, hoping to attract Jacobs' attention, to keep him looking toward the stage.

She dared a glance in his direction, and saw that he was indeed watching her. Then Dimitrios was next to him, placed a burner in his ear, and fired.

There was a shrill scream from a nearby table as Hootowl Jacobs pitched forward on the table, blood pouring out of his ear.

"There's no cause for alarm," said Dimitrios in a loud, clear voice. He held up a small titanium card. "I am a licensed bounty hunter. This man was wanted for a minimum of ten murders. I'm sorry to have disrupted your evening. I'll have him out of here as soon as possible."

A man at a nearby table stood up.

"You didn't even give him a chance!"

"This is a business, not a sporting event," answered Dimitrios.

"But you just walked up to him and shot him!"

"He was wanted dead or alive. Given the crimes he had committed, I prefer dead."

"I wonder how good you are against someone who knows you're there and can fight back." The man pulled his jacket back, revealing a matched pair of screechers in his gunbelt.

"Well, friend," said Dimitrios, "I'm about to show you. Keep your hands away from those pistols."

Dimitrios whirled and fired three blasts into the upper corners of the room, and three holographic cameras melted.

"Do you still want to see how good I am against someone who knows I'm here?" asked Dimitrios.

The man held his hands out where everyone could see them and then sat down.

"Hey!" yelled Manolete, approaching the bounty hunter. "You destroyed three very expensive cameras."

"You didn't prepare the contract we discussed," said Dimitrios. "I told you I wouldn't let you make those holos if you didn't turn half over to the charities I named."

"You said I couldn't *show* them."

"Well, now you can't."

"I'm going to remember this!" promised Manolete.

"I hope so," said Dimitrios. "And the next time you promise a contract to someone, you'd better deliver it."

Some of the customers began leaving, giving Dimitrios a wide berth.

"Look at this!" growled Manolete. "Now all my clients are leaving! Get that body out of here!"

"You didn't mind that body when you thought you could rerun his death every night," said Dimitrios.

"Just get him out of here and don't come back!" yelled Manolete. He turned to Matilda. "*You* get out of here too! You're fired!"

Matilda climbed down from the stage and approached Manolete. "Why are you firing me?" she asked.

"You're connected with *him*!" he said, jerking a thumb toward Dimitrios. "That's reason enough."

"Well," she said, "as it happens, I would have quit tonight anyway. He's going on to another world, and I'm going with him, so I don't mind being fired. But I mind your reason for it, and I mind your attitude."

"What are you going to do about it?" demanded Manolete pugnaciously.

"I'm going to give you a present."

He frowned in confusion. "What present?"

"Remember the trade we talked about earlier?" she said. Before he could react, she kicked him hard in the groin. He groaned and dropped to his knees. "You don't even have to pay me extra for that."

She turned her back on him and walked to the door, then waited for Dimitrios to sling the corpse over his shoulder and join her.

He summoned a robot car, loaded Jacobs into the back, and ordered it to take them to the spaceport.

"You know," she said, "that's just the way I think Santiago would dispatch an enemy."

He shook his head. "What I did was legal and moral. You've watched too many bad holodramas. I don't know how good Jacobs was with his weapons, so why give him a chance to prove he's better than me?" He paused. "Or take that man who got up and half-threatened me. It's easier to frighten him off with a display of marksmanship than kill him to prove a point."

"Yeah, I suppose so," she said.

"Don't look so depressed," he said. "I *told* you I'm not a candidate for the job. You ought to be pleased that I'm good at what I do, and that I'm willing to join your army."

"I am," she said. "But . . ."

"But what?"

She sighed deeply. "But I still need to find a general."

"Finding him won't be so hard," replied Dimitrios. "Recruiting him will be the difficult part."

Which was as wrong a pair of predictions as he'd ever made.

12.

He used to be a lawman, a master of his tools;
His name was the Rough Rider, his game was killing fools.
He used to be a hero, backing up his boasts—
But now he lives a private life, hiding from his ghosts.

His real name was Wilson Tchanga, and there was a time when
he' was the most feared lawman on the Inner Frontier.

They tell the story of the day he followed eight members of the
notorious Colabara Gang into a small warehouse on Talos II, and less
than a minute later he was the only living soul in the building.

They talk about the evening he saved an entire Tradertown from
Pedro the Giant, a nine-foot mutant who had gone on a rampage with
a laser pistol and was in the process of burning the place down when
Tchanga showed up to stop him.

It was when he rode an alien steed halfway across Galapagos V
to hunt down an escaping killer that he picked up the sobriquet of the
Rough Rider, for the terrain was positively brutal. Men envied him,
women loved him, children worshipped him, and criminals all across
the Frontier feared him.

He never did become a bounty hunter, because he wasn't in the
game for the money. He believed that when you saw Evil you stood
up to it, and for twenty years he never flinched, never backed down,
never once worried about the odds before he marched into battle, burners blazing, screechers screaming.

And then one day Varese Sarabande, who was only twenty-six at
the time, called him out, just like a cowboy in the Old West, and

because he was the Rough Rider he stepped out into the street the way Doc Holliday or Johnny Ringo might have done a few millennia earlier. They went for their guns together, but Varese Sarabande was faster, and a moment later Tchanga lay writhing in the street, blood spurting from an artery in his neck.

They saved him—barely—but as he lay in the hospital recuperating, he finally came to the realization that he was mortal, and that whatever guardian angel had been protecting him over the years had taken up residence on some other lawman's shoulder. He was forty-three years old, and he had painful proof that he couldn't outgun a twenty-six-year-old outlaw like Sarabande. And he knew in his gut that he couldn't beat a strong young man—or woman—in any kind of a fair fight, with weapons or without.

His body, which had resisted age for so many years, suddenly felt decades older as he lay there. He was just a day from being released when a gang of three men burst into the hospital, shot two security guards, and began robbing the pharmacy of its narcotics. A young nurse suddenly entered his room, tossed him a burner, and told him what was happening.

He refused to leave his bed.

They almost had to pry him loose from the hospital the next morning. He resigned his job before noon, withdrew his savings—he didn't transfer them to another world, because he didn't want anyone to know where he was going—and left before the day was over.

He set up housekeeping under a new name on Bedrock II, but the Spartan Kid found out he was there and went gunning for him to pay him back for killing his father and two brothers.

He ran.

He wound up on Gingergreen II. No one knew who he was, no one bothered him, and he lived in total obscurity for three years. Then a thief tried to sneak into his house under cover of night, and he killed him. Shot him dead as he stood there, then shot him thirty or forty more times. And since he was using a burner, he inadvertently set the house on fire.

They saw the blaze and found him still firing into the charred, unrecognizable corpse. He went berserk when they tried to take his weapon away, threatened to kill them all, and finally collapsed as he was about to turn the burner upon himself.

He spent a year in an asylum, and when he came out he was fifty pounds lighter and his eyes were still haunted by visions that no one else could see. This time they knew who he was, but even the young toughs who wanted to make a reputation knew that they couldn't make one by killing this emaciated, fear-ridden old man, and so he was left to live out his years in a kind of peace.

The Rhymer heard about him and was touched by his story, and even though they never met, no one who knew Tchanga ever argued with the truth of the poem.

"So what makes this Rough Rider so special?" asked Matilda as Dimitrios directed their ship to Gingergreen II after dropping Jacobs off at the nearest bounty station. "The word I get is that he's lost his nerve."

"He was my hero when I was a kid."

"That was a long time ago."

"The qualities that made him a hero haven't changed," said Dimitrios.

"But other things have changed *him*," she said. "So why, of all the people you might have suggested, are we seeing the Rough Rider?"

"To give him a chance to save his soul."

"We're not in the salvation business," said Matilda.

"Really?" said Dimitrios wryly. "I thought Santiago was going to be the salvation of the Inner Frontier."

"You know what I mean."

"Yeah, I know."

"Then why him?"

"When I was a kid, I wanted to grow up to be the Rough Rider," said Dimitrios. "A man who couldn't be bought off or scared off. A man who knew that the humanists are wrong, that there is good and there is evil, and both are abroad in the galaxy, and that someone had to confront evil and destroy it. You slept better knowing there were men like Wilson Tchanga."

She got to her feet and walked to the small galley. "I'm getting hungry. Do you want anything before we land?"

"Yeah, might as well," he said, joining her.

"I hope this Tchanga is everything you think he is."

"He was once."

"That's not much of a recommendation," said Matilda. She sighed. "I've never recruited a Santiago before. I don't know if I'm doing it right." She ordered beer and sandwiches for both of them. "I hope you've got the right man, but somehow I can't believe it's this easy."

"We'll know soon enough," said Dimitrios. "And don't forget, all but the first Santiago had an advantage ours won't have—a ready-made organization. Maybe they had to take it over, convince it, mold it to their needs, but it was there. Our man will have you, me, and the poet. That's not much of an army to stand against the Democracy."

"Then we'll get more."

"Where?"

She shrugged. "Where we got you."

"Bounty hunters?" he replied. "There aren't that many of us, and most bounty hunters don't have any reason to be unhappy with the Democracy."

"No, not bounty hunters," answered Matilda. "Just men and women who know the time has come for Santiago to walk among us again."

"When you describe him like that, he sounds bigger than life," noted Dimitrios.

"He is."

"That's a lot to ask of one man."

"Maybe that's why it's been a century since he last manifested himself."

"You make him sound like he's still alive."

"He is," said Matilda. "He's an idea—and it's harder to kill an idea than a man."

Dimitrios took a bite of his sandwich, then tossed the rest of it into the atomizer. "Next big one I bring in, I'm using the money to buy a ship with a better galley," he announced.

She stared at her sandwich. "It's not spoiled."

"No. It's just not good enough. Like most of your candidates for Santiago. They won't be evil, and they won't be stupid. They just won't be good enough."

"Well, *I* like it," she said, taking another bite.

"I hope you're choosier when it comes to Santiago."

"You worry about your Rough Rider; I'll worry about my decision."

"Fair enough."

They finished their beer and returned to the control cabin just as the ship went into an elliptical orbit around Gingergreen II. A moment later they received their landing coordinates from the sole spaceport, and shortly thereafter they were on the ground.

"So where do we find the Rough Rider?" asked Matilda when they had cleared Customs.

"I've got directions to his place," answered Dimitrios. "It's out in the country."

She looked around. "Except for maybe a square mile, the whole damned planet's out in the country."

"It's an agricultural world," said Dimitrios. "They grow food for seven nearby mining worlds."

"They don't need a whole world for that. Most of the mining's done by machine."

"Then they sell what's left to the Navy at rock-bottom prices ... or maybe they just give it to them in exchange for being ignored."

"Ignored?" she repeated.

"At tax and conscription time."

"Were you ever in the Navy?"

"The Army."

"For how long?"

"Fifty-three days."

"And then what?" she persisted.

"And then I wasn't in the Army anymore," said Dimitrios, and for the first time since she'd known him, she felt a trace of fear.

She followed him in silence to a ground vehicle, and a moment later they were speeding out of the planet's only town, skimming a few inches above a dirt road that took them through blue-tinted fields of mutated corn. Finally, after about twenty miles, Dimitrios instructed the vehicle to take the shortest route to a location that consisted only of numbers, no words.

It turned onto a smaller, narrower road, bore right through two forks, and finally came to a halt before a small one-story home. Dimitrios and Matilda got out of the vehicle and approached the front porch.

"That's far enough!" said a voice from within the house. "Who are you?"

"I'm Dimitrios of the Three Burners," said the bounty hunter, holding his hands out where they could be seen. "This is Waltzin' Matilda, a dancer."

"What's your business here?"

"We want to talk to you."

"What about?"

"Why don't you invite us in and give us something to drink and we'll be happy to tell you," said Matilda.

"The man drops his burners where you stand," said the voice.

Dimitrios unfastened his holster and let it fall to the ground.

"And the one in your boot."

"Good eyes for an old man," said Dimitrios with a smile. He removed the third burner and placed it atop the other two.

"You got any weapons?"

"I just took them off," said Dimitrios.

"Not you. The lady."

"None," said Matilda.

"You'd better be telling the truth. You'll be scanned when you walk through the door, and I'll have the punisher set on near-lethal."

"Well, let me check and make sure," said Matilda. In quick order she found two knives and a miniature screecher and left them next to Dimitrios' pile of weapons. "I must have forgotten about them," she said with an uneasy smile.

"Can we come in now?" asked Dimitrios.

"Yes—and keep your hands where I can see them."

They obeyed his instructions, got past the scanner without incident, and found themselves in a small, modestly furnished living room. Standing against the far wall was a tall black man, his face ravaged by illness and inner demons, his body emaciated, a pulse gun in his right hand.

"Sit down," said Wilson Tchanga.

They sat on a couch, and he seated himself on a chair about fifteen feet away.

"Why don't you come a little closer?" suggested Matilda. "We're not here to harm you."

"I'll be the judge of that," said Tchanga. "Now talk."

"Do we call you Wilson, or Mr. Tchanga, or Rough Rider?" asked Dimitrios.

"You know who I am?" said Tchanga.

"Why else would we be on your doorstep?" said Dimitrios. "Before we begin, let me tell you that you've been my hero since I was old enough to *have* a hero. Meeting the Rough Rider is quite an honor, sir."

"I haven't been the Rough Rider in a long, long time."

"You're my hero just the same."

Tchanga stared at him, his face expressionless, for a long moment. "What did you say your name was?" he said at last.

"Dimitrios of the Three Burners."

"Lawman?"

"Bounty hunter."

"I suppose you have your reasons."

Dimitrios nodded his head. "Valid ones."

Tchanga turned to Matilda. "And you are?"

"Matilda."

"Got a last name?"

"Got a couple of dozen of them," she said.

He smiled. "*You're* no lawman or bounty hunter."

"No, sir, I'm not."

"All right, now we know who we are," said Tchanga. "Why have you sought me out?"

"I want to see if you're the man I'm looking for," said Matilda.

"If you're looking for Wilson Tchanga, I'm him." He smiled grimly. "If you're looking for the Rough Rider, I used to be him."

She shook her head. "I'm looking for Santiago."

He stared at her curiously. "Santiago's been dead for a century or more—if he ever really existed in the first place."

"He was my great-great-grandfather," said Matilda.

"I know I've aged," said Tchanga, "but do I look like anyone's great-great-grandfather?"

"No," interjected Dimitrios. "But you might look like Santiago." Tchanga frowned. "I think I'm missing something here."

"Santiago is more than a name or a person," continued Dimitrios. "It's an idea, a concept, maybe even a job description. And the job has been open for a century. We're looking for someone to fill it."

"He was the King of the Outlaws," said Tchanga. "I was an honest lawman. I may not be much these days, but I'm still honest."

"We wouldn't be speaking to you if you weren't," said Dimitrios.

"Then I'm still missing something."

"You're missing a lot," said Matilda. "Sit back, relax, and make yourself comfortable, because I'm going to spend an hour or more filling you in."

Dimitrios studied Tchanga intently as Matilda explained who and what Santiago really was, what he had done, how he had hidden his true purpose from the Democracy, and why the string of Santiagos had ended the day the Navy "pacified" Safe Harbor.

"It's time to call him forth again," concluded Matilda. "The time is ripe for him to return. The Democracy is abusing and plundering the Inner Frontier again, colonists have almost no rights, aliens have even less. The Navy goes where it wants and takes what it wants. It protects us from a hostile galaxy, but there's no one to protect us from *it*."

There was a long silence. Finally Tchanga spoke.

"I'm more honored than you can imagine that you came to me. But I'm a used-up old man whose time is past. I'm no hero, no leader of men. I'm still holding a pulse gun, but if either of you made a sudden motion, I'd be more likely to duck than to fire it." He paused. "There was a time when I might have been the man you seek, but that time is long gone."

"You don't have to be a hero," said Dimitrios. "There's no holograph or video of Santiago anywhere in the Democracy's records. *He* didn't go out on raids, or face Democracy soldiers himself. He ordered his men to do those things."

Tchanga shook his head. "That may be so, but he *might* have gone with them from time to time. He *could* have. I can't. And I can't order men to do things I myself won't do."

"Generals don't fight in the front lines," said Dimitrios.

"They also don't run and hide when the shooting starts," replied Tchanga. "You need a Santiago who commands respect, and I am no longer that man. I wonder if I ever was."

"You were," said Dimitrios with certainty. "And you can be again. You can redeem your life and your reputation through the single act of becoming Santiago."

"I appreciate your words," said Tchanga, "but Santiago is too big. He blots out the stars. The ground trembles when he walks. He does not exist for me to redeem myself. You belittle him by suggesting that."

Dimitrios turned to Matilda. "Aren't you going to say anything?"

"What is there to say?" she replied. "I agree with him."

"Perhaps Santiago isn't a man at all," suggested Tchanga. "Perhaps Santiago is a woman."

"It's possible," she agreed. "But not *this* woman. I'm just someone who needs a little more protection from the Democracy than I've been getting."

"I hope you find your Santiago and get your protection," said Tchanga. He got to his feet and walked to the door. "You'd better be going. If he's as hard to find as I think he'll be, you haven't any time to waste."

They arose and walked out the door.

Dimitrios pointed to the pulse gun. "Is that thing even charged?"

Tchanga looked out across the vast field of mutated corn. "You see that scarecrow?"

Dimitrios squinted into the distance. "That one about five hundred yards off to the left?"

Tchanga nodded. "That's the one." In a single motion the old man spun, aimed his pulse gun, and fired. The scarecrow burst into a ball of flame.

"My God!" exclaimed Dimitrios. "That was more than a quarter mile away! I couldn't do that on the best day I ever had!" He turned to the old man. "Can you hit it every time?"

"Just about," said Tchanga. He paused, and a look of infinite sadness crossed his face. "Unless I thought it might fire back at me."

"Jesus!" said Dimitrios as he and Matilda walked toward their vehicle. "What he must have been as a young man!"

"He still is."

Dimitrios shook his head. "No. Like he said, he's all used up."

"Don't look so sad for him," she said. "He'll be all right."

"I was feeling sad for *me*, not for him," Dimitrios corrected her.

"For *you*? Why?"

"Because that's my fate, probably the fate of every bounty hunter, if we live long enough." He paused. "I hope I don't."

"Don't what?"

"Live long enough."

They reached their vehicle, and neither of them saw the tear that rolled down the Rough Rider's withered face as he tried unsuccessfully to remember what it felt like to face an armed man with no more fear than he felt when facing a scarecrow.

13.

Alien face and alien ways,
Alien thoughts and tribal lays.
Alien appetites, strange and cold,
Blue Peter's sins are manifold.

The Rhymer actually met Blue Peter before Matilda did.

He was on Bowman 17, which was actually the third planet circling its star but the seventeenth opened up by a member of the Pioneer Corps named Nate Bowman, who exercised his Pioneer's privilege of naming it after himself. It was an outpost world, with a single Tradertown consisting of a bar, a brothel, a weapon shop, an assay office, and a jail. That last was unusual for any Frontier world, especially one as underpopulated as Bowman 17.

Dante Alighieri was sitting in the bar, relaxing with a drink, when Virgil Soaring Hawk approached him and asked for a loan.

"What for?" replied Dante. "There's nothing to spend it on."

"I have to make a friend's bail."

"You've got a friend locked up on Bowman 17?"

"Yes."

"Who is it?"

"He's more of a what than a who," answered Virgil.

"Worth a verse?" queried Dante, suddenly interested.

"Maybe two or three."

"Santiago material?"

Virgil chuckled. "Not unless the job description has changed in the last couple of minutes."

"All right," said Dante. "Tell me about him."

"You ever hear of Blue Peter?"

"No."

"He's an alien," said Virgil. "I have no idea where his home world is. He's the only member of his race I've ever met."

"He's blue?"

"Skin, hair, eyes, teeth, probably even his tongue."

"How did you meet him?"

"It'll just embarrass you," said Virgil.

"Jesus!" muttered Dante. "Is there anyone on the Frontier that you *haven't* slept with?"

"You."

"Thank heaven for small favors." Dante finished his drink and lit up a smokeless cigar. "What's your friend in jail for?"

"Unspecified crimes against Nature," answered Virgil.

"What does he do when he's not assaulting Nature?"

"You mean for a living?"

"He's got to pay to feed himself, and to get from one world to another. How does he make his money?"

"He does whatever anyone pays him to do."

"Outside of being a rather twisted gigolo, what does that entail?"

"Robbery. Extortion. Murder. Things like that."

"Sounds to me like he's right where he belongs," said Dante.

"You won't loan me the money?"

Dante shook his head. "We have no use for him."

"*I* do."

"I don't want to hear about the use you'll put him to."

"You really mean it."

"I really mean it."

Suddenly Virgil smiled and picked up a chair. "Well, if you can't bring Mohammed to the mountain . . ."

He hurled the chair through a window, then threw two more out into the street before the Tradertown's solitary lawman came over from the jail, trained a screecher on him, and escorted him to the jail. Dante had seen Virgil in action before, and never doubted for an instant that the Injun could disarm the lawman any time he wanted—but of course he didn't want to.

Dante made a very happy Virgil's bail the next morning, spent a few minutes visiting with Blue Peter, and left the jail feeling uncomfortable that something like Blue Peter would soon be free. He wrote the poem that afternoon, and never saw Blue Peter again.

But Matilda did.

It was on Gandhi III, which wasn't as peaceable a world as its name implied. Dimitrios was there on business—another ladykiller with a price on his head—and Matilda had accompanied him. She had no reason to be there . . . but then, she had no reason to be anywhere in particular. She was looking for a perhaps nonexistent man who embodied a complex concept, and there was no more reason to search for him anywhere else than here, and at least here she was under the protection of Dimitrios of the Three Burners.

Dimitrios spent the day gathering information about Mikhail Mikva, the man he was after, while Matilda stayed in her room watching the holo and catching up on the galaxy's news. The Democracy had opened up nineteen new worlds. The Navy had been forced to pacify the native population of Wajima II, which had been renamed Grundheidt II after the commander of the Sixth Fleet. Contact had been made with four new species of sentient life; three had joined the Democracy, and the fourth was learning just how effective a quadrant-wide economic embargo could be. The Democracy had moved the planetary populations of Kubalic IV and V and their attendant flora and fauna to new worlds before the star Kubalic went nova. Lodin XI had voted to withdraw from the Democracy, but its resignation had not been accepted and the Fifteenth Fleet was on its way to Lodin to "peacefully discuss our differences." Five new cross-species diseases had been discovered; medical science announced that they would have vaccines and antidotes for all five within one hundred days.

She deactivated the holo at twilight, wondering why she ever bothered with the news. All it did was reinforce her decision never to visit the Democracy again.

The door opened and Dimitrios entered.

"Any luck?" she asked.

"If he's here, he's well disguised. No one's seen him."

"Could they be lying to you?"

He stared at her.

"No, of course not," she said. She got to her feet. "Shall we go out for dinner?"

"Yeah. I won't start searching the bars and drug dens for another couple of hours."

They left the hotel and went to one of the small city's half-dozen restaurants, one that advertised real meat rather than soya products (though it didn't say what kind of animals supplied the meat).

They had sat down, ordered, and begun chatting about the news from the Democracy when they became aware of a blue alien standing outside and staring at them through the window.

"You'd think he'd never seen a Man before," grumbled Dimitrios when the alien kept watching them.

"That can't be it," said Matilda. "There are thousands of Men on Gandhi."

"Then what's his problem?"

"I think he's about to tell you," replied Matilda as the alien suddenly walked to the door of the restaurant, entered, and began approaching their table.

The blue alien stopped a few feet from them.

"May I join you?" he asked.

"Do you know Mikhail Mikva's whereabouts?" asked Dimitrios.

"No."

"Then no, you may not join us."

"But you *are* Dimitrios of the Three Burners, are you not?"

Dimitrios stared at him. "What's it to you?"

"We are in the same poem."

"Do you know the Rhymer?" asked Matilda suddenly.

"I know Dante Alighieri, who calls himself the Rhymer. It is he who put me in his poem."

"Sit down," said Matilda, ignoring Dimitrios' obvious annoyance.

The alien pulled up a chair and sat on it.

"Who are you?" asked Matilda.

"My name when I walk among Men is Blue Peter. And who are you?"

"My name is Matilda."

Blue Peter stared at her. "Waltzin' Matilda?"

"Sometimes."

"How very interesting that three of us from what is, after all, an obscure little poem so new almost no one has encountered it should find ourselves on the same planet."

"Dimitrios is here on business. May I ask why *you* are here?"

"I was requested to leave Bowman 17, and since most of your spaceliners will not carry non-Men, I booked passage on a cargo ship. This was as far as my money took me."

"So you're stuck here?" asked Matilda.

"Until I obtain more money."

"How will you do that?"

"There are ways," said Blue Peter. He turned to Dimitrios. "I am pleased to make your acquaintance."

Dimitrios stared at the alien with an expression of distaste, then got to his feet. He turned to Matilda. "I'm going back to the hotel for a couple of hours before I make my rounds."

He walked out of the restaurant.

"He does not like me," said Blue Peter.

"He doesn't like most aliens."

"He has much in common with the rest of your race."

There was a momentary silence.

"I hope you're not waiting for me to apologize for him," said Matilda at last.

"No. I am wondering why you are here, since none of the establishments has advertised the presence of a dancer."

She looked at him, then shrugged. "What the hell, why not tell you? I'm looking for someone."

"You have become a bounty hunter too?"

She shook her head. "No."

"Who do you seek?"

"I don't know."

Blue Peter stared at her expressionlessly, his deep blue alien eyes unblinking. "That *does* make it harder," he said.

"You've seen many men on the Frontier," she began.

"That is true."

"Which of them is the most dangerous?"

"I am not sure I understand," said Blue Peter.

"The most deadly. The one man you would fear to fight more than any other."

"I fear to fight all men," said Blue Peter with an obvious lack of sincerity. "I fear Dimitrios. I fear Tyrannosaur Bailey. I fear Trader Hawke. I fear Mongaso Taylor. I fear Jimmy the Nail."

She sighed deeply. "Forget it. I'm sorry I asked."

"I fear the Plymouth Rocker. I fear Deuteronomy Priest."

"You can stop now," said Matilda.

"But above all others," continued Blue Peter, "I fear the One-Armed Bandit."

"Oh?"

"Yes. He is the most terrifying of all Men."

"Why do you think so?"

"Because he is the deadliest."

"Tell me about him."

"I just did," said Blue Peter.

"Do you know where he is?"

"I know where he is when he is not elsewhere."

She frowned. "You mean his headquarters—his home planet?"

"His headquarters," agreed Blue Peter. "I do not think anyone except the One-Armed Bandit himself knows his home planet."

"And of all the men and women you've seen on the Inner Frontier, you consider him the most dangerous?"

"Yes."

"Even more dangerous than Dimitrios?"

"There is no comparison. If Dimitrios is your friend, pray that he never has to face the One-Armed Bandit in combat."

"He sounds interesting," said Matilda.

"He is deadly."

"The man I'm looking for must be deadly."

"You are already traveling with a deadly man," noted Blue Peter.

"Still, I'd like to meet this One-Armed Bandit."

"I will give you the location of his headquarters," said the alien. "I will not accompany you there. He has promised to kill me the next time he sees me."

"Why?"

"I did something to Galpos that he disapproved of."

"Galpos? Who's he?"

"Galpos is a world," said Blue Peter. "Or, rather, it was."

She stared at the expressionless alien and decided she didn't want to know the details. "Where can I find him?"

"If he is not elsewhere, he will be on Heliopolis II."

"Thank you, Blue Peter. Can I buy you a drink?"

"My metabolism cannot cope with human intoxicants." He got to his feet. "There is a tavern that caters to non-Men. I was on my way there when I recognized Dimitrios of the Three Burners."

"I'm sorry you have to go alone," said Matilda.

"I will not be alone for long," Blue Peter assured her.

He stood up and walked to the door. Matilda was about to follow him out when she realized that she'd been left with the check. She placed her thumb on the table's computer, waited for it to okay her credit and transfer payment, and then returned to the hotel.

Dimitrios was sitting in the lobby when she arrived. She walked over and stood in front of him.

"What did the little blue bastard want?" asked the bounty hunter.

"He just wanted to meet us," she replied. "He's all alone here."

"Don't go feeling too sorry for him. He was kicked off Bowman 17, in case that got by you."

"I know." She paused.

"And he had two, maybe three, screechers hidden under that baggy outfit he was wearing."

"I know. I spotted them all."

"Five'll get you ten there's a price on his head."

"Probably," agreed Matilda. She paused. "What if you don't find Mikva tonight?"

He shrugged. "There are four more cities on Gandhi III. I'll check them out, one by one."

"That could take a while."

"I've got plenty of time."

"I don't."

Dimitrios looked up at her curiously. "What are you getting at?"

"I'm leaving here first thing in the morning," answered Matilda.

"Where to?"

"Heliopolis II."

"That's a couple of hundred light-years away—and you came here in my ship," he noted. "Just how do you plan to get to the Heliopolis system?"

"I'll get as close as a spaceliner will take me, which is probably the mining colony on Gregson VI."

"And then?"

"Then I'll rent or charter a small ship," said Matilda.

"You think you've found a candidate?"

"I've found one worth looking at."

"Care to tell me who it is?"

"The One-Armed Bandit."

"Yeah, I figured you'd go out after him sooner or later," said Dimitrios.

"Do you care to tell me anything about him?"

"I never met him. But they say he's formidable."

"So I hear."

"Well, as soon as I find Mikva, I'll hook up with you again."

"I'll look forward to it," she said, knowing full well that even if he found the man he was hunting for, some new ladykiller would take precedence over his joining her on Heliopolis.

Still, it didn't really matter. The Frontier needed a Santiago more than she needed a traveling companion. Maybe this would be the one.

14.

Heliopolis is its name;
Death and mayhem is its fame.
Death of hope and death of dreams,
Death of men and all their schemes.

That verse was true a thousand years before the first man set foot on Heliopolis II. It was true when Matilda arrived there. It was true when Dante Alighieri visited the place. It would be true a thousand years after both were dead. That's the kind of world it was.

To begin with, it was hot. The daytime temperature often reached 135 degrees Fahrenheit. At night it cooled down to a bone-melting 100.

It was heavy. At 1.18 Galactic Standard gravity, it meant you felt like you were carrying an extra eighteen pounds for every hundred pounds of actual body weight.

It was thin. The oxygen content was eighty-seven percent of Galactic Standard. Even strong, fit men often found themselves gasping for breath, especially after exerting themselves in the Heliopolis II gravity.

It was dusty. The wind whipped across the barren surface of the planet, causing dust devils to rise hundreds of feet high as they swept through human and alien cities alike.

It was dry. Oh, there was *some* water, but hardly enough for the planetary populace. The natives made do with what was there; a water ship landed twice a week to make sure that the Men didn't run out of the precious stuff.

It was hostile. The native inhabitants, a humanoid race known as the Unicorns, doubtless owing to the single rudimentary horn that grew out of each forehead, didn't like each other very much, and they liked Men even less. Almost everything Men did seemed to give offense, and no matter how often they lost their battles against the humans, they never tired of regrouping and fighting again.

So why did Men risk their lives and sacrifice their comfort to stay on Heliopolis II?

Simple. It possessed two of the most productive diamond pipes in the galaxy. The diamonds couldn't be mined with water, of course, not on Heliopolis II, but they could be separated from the rocks in which they were embedded by carefully focused bursts of ultrasound. It was a delicate operation: not enough strength in the bursts and nothing was accomplished, too much and even the diamonds could be shattered.

It never occurred to the miners that the ultrasound, which was beyond human hearing, might be what was driving the Unicorns to such violent states of aggravation—and, in truth, it probably wasn't, since they were a violent sort even before Men began mining. Probably the ultrasound merely served to remind them that Men were still working on the planet, and that knowledge was more than enough to work them into a killing frenzy every few weeks.

Matilda hadn't spent as much as five minutes researching Heliopolis II before she decided to rent a ship. It was more expensive than chartering one, but at least she would have the comforting knowledge that the ship was there if she needed to leave in a hurry.

As she approached the planet, she wondered why the One-Armed Bandit was there. Was he there to rob the mines? Well, if he was, she had no serious problem with that. The Democracy owned the mines, which meant he'd be robbing the Democracy, just as Santiago had done so many times more than a century ago.

Of course, if he was there to rob the mines, he'd probably accomplished his mission already and gone on to some other world. After all, her information wasn't current; all she knew was that he'd been on Heliopolis II six days ago.

On the other hand, the mines could be so well guarded that he was still casing the job, still studying the opposition. If that was the situation, she'd have a chance to see how he performed against overwhelming odds.

She was still considering all the possibilities when her ship touched down and she approached the robot Customs officer.

"Name?" asked the machine.

"Matilda."

"Last name?"

"No."

"Matilda No, may I please scan your passport?"

She held her titanium passport disk up to its single glowing eye.

"Your passport is in proper order, but your name is not Matilda No. Please step forward so that I may scan your retina."

She stepped forward and looked into its eye.

"Thank you," said the robot. A swordlike finger shot out, and its needle-thin extremity touched her passport. There was a brief buzzing sound. "I have given you a five-day visa. If you plan to stay longer, you will have to go to the Democracy consulate and have it renewed."

"Thank you," said Matilda, starting to step forward. The robot moved to its left, blocking her way.

"I am not finished," it said, and she could have sworn she detected a touch of petulance in its mechanical voice. "The world of Heliopolis II accepts Democracy credits, Far London pounds, New Punjab rupees, and Maria Theresa dollars. There is a currency exchange just behind me that can convert eighty-three different currencies into credits."

"I have credits and Maria Theresa dollars," replied Matilda.

"You will almost certainly be using personal credit for your larger expenses," continued the robot. "The machines at all the commercial ventures on Heliopolis II are tied in to the Bank of Deluros VIII, the Bank of Spica, the Roosevelt III Trust, and the Far London Federated Savings Bank. If you have not established credit with one of these banks through their thousands of planetary branches, you will be required to spend actual currency. Should you try to leave Heliopolis II without settling all your bills, your ship will be impounded and you will be detained by the military police until a satisfactory settlement has been arranged."

"Is that all?" asked Matilda.

"No," said the machine. "Will you require adrenaline injections while you are here?"

"No," she said. "At least, I don't think so."

"Do you wish to have your blood oxygenated?"

"No."

"Will you require intravenous injection of fluids?"

"No."

"Should you change your mind, all of these services are available, for a nominal fee, at the military infirmary. I am required to warn you that Heliopolis II, while habitable, is considered inhospitable to the race of Man."

She waited for the robot to continue, but it fell silent and moved back to its original position.

"Is there anything else?" she asked after a minute had passed.

"I am finished."

"What do I do now?"

"Pass through the disease scanner just beyond my booth, and then arrange for your accommodation."

"I'd rather go into the city first and see what's there."

"You will not want to walk from one hostelry to another. You can examine three-hundred-and-sixty-degree holographs of all of them right here in the spaceport. Then you will hire a vehicle, enter it, instruct the governing computer where to take you, and emerge only after the vehicle is inside the climate-controlled hostelry. After that you are free to do whatever you wish, but I am programmed to warn you not to go outside unless it is essential."

"Thanks."

She walked to the disease scanner, passed through it without incident, checked the holograms of the human city's seven hotels and chose one called the Tamerlaine, then walked to a row of vehicles. The first in line opened its doors as she approached. Once she was seated it slid the doors shut, asked her if she was the woman who had booked her room at the Tamerlaine, and then raced forward. Just as she was sure it was going to crash into a wall the entrance irised just long enough to let the vehicle through, then snapped shut behind her.

They sped across the dry, dusty, reddish, featureless countryside. As they circled a small hill a heavy rock, obviously thrown, probably by an irate native, crashed down on the windshield and bounced off without leaving a mark. She suspected that nothing short of a pulse gun could put a dent in the vehicle, and relaxed during the rest of the ten-minute trip. The vehicle approached the Tamerlaine, and just as at the airport, the wall spread apart at the last instant to let it enter, then shut tightly behind it.

She emerged into the cool, dry air of the Tamerlaine's garage, instructed a liveried robot to carry her luggage to the front desk, then fell into step behind it. She found the gravity oppressive, but manageable.

The reception clerk was ready for her. He'd already run a credit check through the spaceport, and had assigned her a room overlooking the garden behind the hotel.

"Have my bags put in my room," said Matilda. "I'm going to take a look around first."

"Outside?" said the clerk. "I wouldn't advise it."

"I won't be long," she assured him.

She walked to the elegantly designed airlock that passed for the front entrance, and found she couldn't get the outer door to open until the door behind her had sealed itself shut.

Two steps outside the door she knew why. The heat was oppressive, the air almost unbreathable. Her dancing had kept her in excellent shape, but she found herself panting before she'd walked thirty paces. The air was as thin as mountain air at three thousand meters, the heat was like an oven, and the gravity pulled fiercely at her.

Still, while Heliopolis II was horribly uncomfortable, it wasn't deadly. After all, she told herself, men worked here every day. (Between the conditions and the Unicorns, she hoped they were getting hazard pay.)

She decided to continue her tour of the small city while she was still relatively fresh, turned a corner—and found out what a Unicorn looked like close up.

There were eight of the creatures walking in her direction. Each stood about seven feet tall, though they were so stocky and muscular that they looked shorter. Their arms were jointed in odd places, but bulged with muscles. Their thighs were massive, as they would have to be on beings that had evolved in this gravity. Their heads were not quite humanoid, not quite equine, ellipsoid in shape, each with a rudimentary horn growing out of the forehead. They didn't wear much clothing, but they were loaded down with weapons: pistols, swords, daggers, a few that she'd never seen before but that looked quite formidable.

She stepped aside to let them pass. They paid her no attention—until one of them brushed against her shoulder as he walked by. He immediately halted and spoke harshly to her in his native tongue.

"I can't understand you," said Matilda.

He said something else, louder this time.

"I left my T-pack at my hotel," she replied. "Do any of you have a Terran T-pack?"

Suddenly the other Unicorns joined the one that was yelling at her. Three of them began talking at once.

She pointed to her ear, then shook her head, to show she couldn't understand what they were saying.

This seemed to anger them. One of them approached her ominously, growling something in his own tongue. When she made no response, he reached out and shoved her. She gave ground, barely keeping her balance in the unfamiliar gravity.

She looked up and down the street. There were no Men in sight.

Another alien pushed her.

This is ridiculous. I'm going to die on this godforsaken world, not because I'm a thief with a price on her head, but because I left my T-pack in my room.

They formed a semicircle around her and began approaching her again—

—and suddenly a man she hadn't realized was there stepped forward and stood in front of her, pushing her gently behind him.

"Stand still, ma'am," he said.

"It's all a misunderstanding," said Matilda. "I left my T-pack in my room, and they don't understand me."

"They understand every word you're saying," said the man. "Please step back a couple of feet. If they charge, I may not be able to hold my ground." He looked at the Unicorns. "But I'll kill the first three or four of you who try."

Matilda noticed that the man was unarmed.

Great! I'm being attacked by aliens and protected by a lunatic.

"You've had your fun," said the man. "Now get the hell out of here."

The Unicorns didn't move—but three other Unicorns, seeing the tense little scene, came over to join their brethren.

"What will you do now?" grated one of the Unicorns in a guttural Terran.

"We will kill both of you!" growled another.

"And when we are through, we will find more Men to kill."

"No you won't," said the man, never raising his voice. "You'll disperse right now, or the survivors will wish you had."

"Death to all Men!" screamed one of the new arrivals.

"Don't let them frighten you, ma'am," said the man softly. "If you're carrying a weapon, don't let them see it. It's better that they concentrate on me."

I have no problem with that. But what am I going to do after they kill you?

"Move to the right, ma'am," he continued without ever taking his eyes off the Unicorns. "The one on the left looks the most aggressive. He'll be the first to charge."

And almost as the words left the man's mouth, the Unicorn on the far left, the one who had initially yelled at Matilda, launched himself at the man.

The man pointed a finger at the Unicorn—and suddenly the Unicorn literally melted in midcharge. The other Unicorns began screaming, and two more charged. The man pointed again; this time energy pulses shot out of his hand, embedding themselves in the Unicorns' chests.

Then the man was striding among them. Two fell to sledgehammer blows, another to a karate kick. He simply pointed to all but one of the remainder and fried them instantly.

He walked up to the last Unicorn, planted his feet firmly, and looked into the creature's eyes.

"I'm letting you live," he announced. "Go tell your friends that this lady is under my protection. To offend or threaten her is to offend or threaten me, and you saw what happens when you offend or threaten me." He paused. "Nod if you understand."

The Unicorn nodded.

"Now go back to your people and give them my message."

The Unicorn literally ran down the street and disappeared around a corner, as the man turned back to Matilda.

"Are you all right, ma'am?" he asked solicitously.

"I'm fine," she said. "You were awesome!"

"All in a day's work, ma'am," he replied.

"My name's Matilda," she said, extending her hand. "I want to thank you for saving my life."

He took her hand and shook it. "I'm glad I was here to do it." He gestured to the restaurant behind her. "I saw them harassing you from in there. By the way, my name's—"

"I know who you are," she said. "The One-Armed Bandit."

He smiled. "You're well informed, ma'am."

"What should I call you?"

"I've got more names than I can remember," he said. "Why not just call me Bandit and be done with it?"

"I'll be happy to." She stared at him. "That's some set of arms you have!"

He flexed his right arm. "This one's real." He tapped his left arm with the fingers of his right hand; it made a drumming sound. "This one's the fake. I lost the original arm in the war against the Sett."

" 'Fake' is a feeble word for it," enthused Matilda. "It's the most impressive weapon I've seen! What can it do?"

"I don't like to talk about it," he said uncomfortably. "Most people think I'm some kind of freak."

"Not me," Matilda assured him. "And I do have a reason for asking."

He shrugged. "All right, ma'am," he said. "Depending on how I manipulate my wrist and fingers, it can be a burner, a pulse gun, a screecher, or—if I'm carrying the proper munitions—even a laser cannon."

"Amazing!" she said. "And you act as if the heat and gravity don't even affect you!"

"Oh, I feel 'em, ma'am," he said with a smile. "I just don't like to let *them* know it."

She looked at the bodies littering the street. "I'm surprised the law hasn't shown up yet."

"They don't have any reason to," said the Bandit. "Someone'll be along presently to do a body count and dispose of them."

"A body count?"

He nodded. "It's really quite oppressive out here, ma'am," he said. "You may not be aware of it, but I can see that you're gasping for air and having trouble swallowing. Let's go back into the restaurant and get you something cold to drink."

"Yes," said Matilda, suddenly dizzy. "I think that would be a good idea."

She turned to open the door and found herself falling. The Bandit caught her in his arms, set her back on her feet, and escorted her into the restaurant.

"Ah, that's much better!" she breathed as they sat at a table. Not only was the temperature comfortable, but she could tell that the oxygen content of the air had been increased.

"Your eyes look like they're focusing again," he noted.

"Yes, they are." A robot waiter brought two glasses of water to the table. She took one, soaked her napkin in it, dabbed her face and neck, and then took a sip of what was left. "Aren't you having any?"

"I'll get around to it," the Bandit assured her. "Right now I'm more concerned with you."

"I'll be fine."

"I don't know how long you plan to stay on Heliopolis II, ma'am," he said, "but if I were you I'd be very careful about going outside until I'd adjusted to the air and the heat."

"And the gravity," she added. "Am I that obvious a newcomer?"

He smiled. "I'd remember anyone as pretty as you."

She returned his smile, then took another sip of water. She could almost feel the precious liquid spread through her body. Finally, when she felt certain that she wasn't going to black out again, she looked across the table at the Bandit.

"You mentioned something about a body count?" she said.

He jerked a thumb out the window, where a pair of robots were picking up each Unicorn corpse and placing it carefully on a gravity sled. "They'll report it to the authorities."

"And then what?"

"And then I'll get paid."

"They pay you to kill the native inhabitants of Heliopolis II?" she asked, far more curious than shocked or outraged.

"A diamond for every Unicorn," said the Bandit.

She let out a low whistle. "You must have quite a pile of diamonds."

"A few."

"Why don't you just turn your laser cannon on their cities, or wherever it is that they live?"

"I don't believe in genocide," he answered. "I'll protect the men who work the mines, and I'll keep the streets safe, but I'm not going to wipe out an entire race, not even for diamonds."

All good answers so far. You have the greatest arsenal on the Frontier, you don't believe in genocide, you even protect damsels in distress. Maybe, just maybe, you could be Him.

"Why are you called the One-Armed Bandit?" she asked. "I understand the One-Armed, but why the Bandit?"

"It was a term for a type of gambling machine. A few people still use it."

"So are you a gambler?"

"No. I work too hard for my money to lose it at a gaming table."

"Then are you a bandit?"

"I won't lie, ma'am. I've been a bandit in the past. I may be one again in the future. But I've never robbed anyone who came by their money honestly. At least, I've tried not to."

Better and better. You're willing to be an outlaw under the right circumstances.

"And," he continued, "sometimes it's just practical. I'd have no moral qualms about robbing the diamond mines here, given all the abuses the Democracy has committed."

"Then why don't you?" she interrupted.

He smiled guiltily. "I wouldn't know how to find a diamond in a mine, or how to extract one. And why should I want the Democracy after me when it's so easy to let them pay me for killing Unicorns?"

"Your logic is unassailable," agreed Matilda. She paused. "How long is your contract for?"

"Contract?"

"For, how shall I phrase it, policing the planet?"

"I can leave whenever I want," he answered. "As a matter of fact,

I was thinking of leaving in the next week or two. A month in this hellhole is plenty." Suddenly he smiled at her. "But I'm willing to stay here as long as you need protection, ma'am—and on Heliopolis II, that translates to as long as you're on the planet."

"I appreciate that, Bandit," she said. "Where were you planning to go next?"

"I don't know. Wherever they might need someone like me."

"I might be able to help you out with that," said Matilda.

"Oh?"

"I have to speak to a friend first."

"Is he here?"

"No—but he can get here in a day or two."

"Well, I'll look forward to meeting him," said the Bandit. He pushed his chair back and got to his feet. "And now, if you'll excuse me, ma'am, I think it's time for me to go collect my commission." He paused awkwardly. "Perhaps you'd like to have dinner tonight?"

"I'd enjoy that very much," said Matilda. "I'm staying at the Tamerlaine."

"Fine. I'll call for you about an hour after dark. It'll still be oppressive, but it'll be a little more tolerable."

"I'll see you then," said Matilda.

He left the restaurant, and she ordered a very tall very cold drink, then another. Finally ready to face the planet again, she paid her tab and passed through one of the airlocks that seemed omnipresent on all the human buildings on Heliopolis II, walked back to the Tamerlaine, and went right to the bar for another cold drink the moment she arrived.

Finally she went up to her room, filled the tub with cool water, got out of her sweaty clothes, and carried the subspace radio into the bathroom. She set it down on a stool right next to the tub, then climbed in and luxuriated as the water closed in around her body.

After a few minutes, feeling somewhat human again, she put through a call to Dante Alighieri. It took about ten minutes for him to answer, and there was static whenever he spoke, but she was able to converse with him.

"How are you doing?" she asked.

"All right, I guess. I've incorporated eight more men and women into the poem. How's Heliopolis?"

"It's enough to make you get religion and walk the straight and narrow," said Matilda. "Now that I've experienced Heliopolis II, I don't ever want to go to hell."

He chuckled. "So where are you and Dimitrios going next?"

"Dimitrios isn't with me, and I'm not going anywhere."

"Oh?"

"But you are," she continued. "You're coming to Heliopolis II as soon as you can."

"Why, if it's that horrible a world?"

"There's someone I want you to meet."

"And who is that?" asked Dante.

"Santiago."

Part 3

The One-Armed Bandit's Book

15.

From out of nowhere the One-Armed Bandit
Built his legend, honed and fanned it.
In the book of fate he burned it—
Watched it spread till all had learned it.

"I've heard about the One-Armed Bandit," remarked Virgil Soaring Hawk as their vehicle sped toward the city.

"So you've said," answered Dante Alighieri. "Why do you seem so unhappy about it?"

"What I've heard doesn't jibe with Matilda's description of him."

"Well, we'll meet him in a few hours and make up our own minds," replied Dante. "In the meantime, I've scribbled down a tentative verse about him."

"Let's hear it."

Dante read it to him.

"What's the Book of Fate?" asked Virgil.

"Poetic license."

"Read the first two lines again."

"From out of nowhere the One-Armed Bandit built his legend, honed and fanned it."

Virgil frowned. "The meter's wrong. You got too many syllables in that opening line."

"Orpheus never worried about meter when it interfered with truth."

"That was Orpheus," said the Injun. "And besides, you don't know what the truth is."

"Well, if it's anything remotely like what Matilda thinks it is, I'll polish the verse and maybe fix the meter." He looked out at the bleak landscape. "Considering that she didn't call me to check out Dimitrios of the Three Burners or the Rough Rider, this guy must be something very special."

"The Rough Rider?" repeated Virgil, surprised. "Is he still alive?"

"After a fashion."

"Damn! I'm sorry I missed him."

"One of your childhood heroes?" asked Dante.

"After a fashion." Suddenly Virgil grinned. "I always wondered how he'd be in bed."

"If he doesn't share your unique sense of adventure, I imagine he'd be quite deadly."

"Yeah, probably. Still, it would have been fun to find out for sure."

A couple of rocks bounced off the vehicle.

"Stop!" commanded Dante.

The vehicle stopped.

"Open the doors!"

"My programming will not allow me to open the doors when doing so might put you at risk," answered the mechanical chauffeur.

"We're all at risk right now!" snapped Dante. "If someone's going to try to kill me, I want to be able to shoot back."

"Correction, sir," said the chauffeur. "This vehicle is impregnable to any weapon currently in the possession of the Unicorns. You are *not* at risk, and will not be unless you step outside."

Dante alternated his glare between the chauffeur and the shadows on the nearby hills.

"May I proceed, sir?"

"Yeah, go ahead," muttered Dante. "No sense staying here."

"What would you have done if it had let you out?" asked Virgil. "There could be a hundred of them up in those hills."

"And there could be two."

"Even so, do you think you're capable of taking even two of them?"

"Maybe not," admitted Dante. "But *you* are."

"I've got nothing against the Unicorns," said Virgil. "Besides, I'm a lover, not a fighter."

"Is that so?" responded Dante irritably. "You've killed four people since you hooked up with me."

"But I've been to bed with eleven of various genders and species," answered Virgil, as if that ended the argument.

Dante stared at him for a long moment, couldn't think of a reply, and realized with a wry smile that the argument was indeed over.

The rest of the journey to town was unremarkable. The landscape appeared dull, but from the comfort of their vehicle they could only guess what it felt like to walk through that heat and gravity while breathing the thin oxygen.

"I wonder what the hell he's doing here," remarked Dante.

"The place is supposed to be lousy with diamonds," said Virgil. "What better reason is there?"

"You know, I could get awfully tired of you and your worldview."

"You just don't like the fact that it's so defensible," answered the Injun.

"Maybe I'll change my name back to Danny. Then I won't need a Virgil at all."

"But your Santiago, when you anoint him, is going to need a Virgil, a Dante, a Matilda . . . all the help he can get."

"It's not up to me to anoint him," said Dante.

"Sure it is," replied Virgil. "If you write him up in your poem, he's Santiago, and if you don't, he isn't."

"It's not that simple."

"It's precisely that simple."

Dante was about to argue, realized that he didn't really give a damn what Virgil thought, and fell silent. They reached the city in another minute, and were soon climbing out of the vehicle in the Tamerlaine's basement.

"Well, let's go get our rooms," said Virgil, walking to the airlift as the vehicle turned and sped through the garage doors and began racing back to the spaceport.

"Not just yet," said Dante as they floated up to the hotel's lobby.

"Why not?"

"Matilda sounds more than impressed with the One-Armed Bandit," said Dante. "She sounds half in love. It may be coloring her judgment, so I want you to nose around and see what other people have to say about him. And find out where he's staying, if you can, just in case I want to speak to him alone."

"You might have told me before the fucking vehicle left," muttered Virgil.

"Yeah," agreed Dante. "But then you'd be so fresh and full of energy that you wouldn't do what I asked until you'd bedded half a dozen men and women and probably tried to make it with the robot chauffeur as well."

Virgil frowned. "I think I liked you better when you were an innocent."

"I was never an innocent," the poet corrected him. "I just didn't know you as well as I do now."

"Comes to the same thing," grumbled Virgil, walking through the airlock as Dante went up to the desk to register.

"Mr. Alighieri, right," said the clerk. "Two rooms?"

"That's correct." He paused. "Do you have any rules about visitors in your rooms?"

"No."

Dante tossed a twenty-credit cube on the desk. "Tell my friend you do."

"Yes, sir, Mr. Alighieri," said the clerk, pocketing the cube. "Will there be anything else?"

"You're got a guest named Matilda. I'd like to know what room she's in."

"That's against the regulations, sir."

Dante tossed another twenty-credit cube on the desk. "She's expecting me."

"What is her last name?" asked the clerk, pocketing the cube.

Dante frowned. "I'll be damned if I know," he admitted.

"I don't know how I can help you, then, Mr. Alighieri."

"Check your guest list for a single name: Matilda. If she didn't give her last name to me, she sure as hell wouldn't give it to you."

The clerk checked his computer, then looked up, surprised. "She's in 307."

"Let her know I'm on my way up," said Dante, walking to the airlift. He got off at the third floor, followed the glowing numbers that seemed to float a few inches in front of each door, and stopped when he came to 307. He was about to knock when it slid away from him.

"Come in," said Matilda, sitting on a chair by the window.

"Thanks."

"Did you have a good trip?"

"That depends."

"On what?"

"On whether you've found our Santiago."

"I think I have," she replied.

"I've heard of him here and there," said Dante. "I thought he was an outlaw."

"His name," she said, nodding.

"So you're saying he's *not* a bandit?"

"He's been an outlaw," she answered. "He's not one right now."

"What's he doing on Heliopolis II?"

"Providing protection to the miners."

"If these mines are so damned valuable, why doesn't the Democracy protect them?"

"Because he's better at it."

"Than a whole regiment?"

"Probably. And he's very reasonable." She smiled. "He charges them one diamond per Unicorn."

"Let me get this straight," said Dante. "He kills Unicorns and gets a diamond apiece?"

"Yes."

"That's very much like murder, isn't it?"

"He only kills those who attack or harass miners or other humans," she said.

"From what I understand, that could be a lifetime's work," remarked Dante. "What makes you think he'd quit to become Santiago?"

"Have you been outside yet?" asked Matilda.

"No."

She smiled. "Go outside for half an hour and then ask me that question."

"Point taken," he conceded.

"He's a wonderful man," said Matilda. "Just the kind of man Santiago should be."

"So when do I get to meet him?"

"Well, I was hoping we could have a drink right now—I knew you were due in early afternoon—but the Unicorns killed a miner this morning, and he's out there making sure they think twice before they do it again." She paused. "I don't know how he puts up with the conditions. I can barely walk a block. He goes for miles, and fights at the end of it."

"He's a formidable man."

"And at the same time he's the gentlest, best-mannered man I've come across on the Frontier," she enthused. "It's hard to believe those manners can go with those accomplishments."

Dante stared at her, trying to assess just how much her emotions had influenced her. She stared back, and it was as if she could read his mind.

"It has nothing to do with my feelings for him," she assured him.

"I didn't say that."

"But you were thinking it."

"I was wondering how detached your judgment was. There's a difference."

"He should be back before dark," said Matilda. "We'll meet him for dinner and you can make up your own mind."

"Fair enough." He walked to the door. "I might as well take a nap until then."

"Where's Virgil?" she asked. "Didn't he come with you?"

"He's out enjoying the climate."

"Good God, why?"

"There were a couple of things I wanted him to do." He grimaced. "I just hope he does them before he makes a pass at a Unicorn."

"You told me how you hooked up with him," said Matilda. "But for the life of me, I can't understand why you let him stay with you. You may have needed him the first few days you were on the Frontier, but surely you don't need him any longer."

"That's true."

"Well, then?"

"When we find our Santiago, he's going to need all the help he can get. Including Virgil."

"What makes you think he'll obey Santiago's orders?"

"He obeys *me*, and I'm no Santiago," answered Dante. "He needs an authority figure."

"He needs to be castrated and lobotomized!" said Matilda passionately.

"Well, that too," agreed Dante with a smile.

"He makes my skin crawl."

"He'll leave you alone."

"What makes you think so?"

"I told him to."

"And that will make him leave me alone?" she said dubiously.

"I told you: he obeys me."

"Why?" persisted Matilda.

Dante shrugged. "Who knows? Maybe he's really hung up on this Virgil/Dante thing. Or maybe he just wants a couple of more verses in my poem."

"Wait'll you meet the Bandit!" she said, her enthusiasm returning. "You'll give him a dozen verses!"

"I already wrote one," said Dante.

"May I see it?"

"Not until I've met him. I wrote it based on your messages. I may want to change it."

"You won't," she said with absolute certainty.

"I hope you're right," he said, walking to the door, then turned back to face her.

"But?" said Matilda. "There's an unspoken 'but' there."

"But I can't believe finding Santiago will be this easy."

He walked to the airlift, went up to the fifth floor, found his room, notified the desk that the robot bellhop had mixed his luggage up with Virgil's, waited a few moments until the problem was sorted out, and then lay back on the bed. It seemed that he had just closed his eyes when the desk clerk called to tell him that Matilda was waiting for him in the lobby.

He got to his feet, walked to the sink, muttered "Cold," and rinsed his face off. He considered changing clothes, but he didn't have anything better than he was wearing, so he left the room and took the airlift down to the lobby.

"Is he here?" asked Dante as he approached Matilda.

"We're meeting him at the Golden Bough," answered Matilda. "It's a restaurant three blocks from here."

"From everything I've heard about this world, it ought to be the Diamond Bough." He stopped by the desk. "Has my friend checked in yet?"

"Virgil Soaring Hawk?" responded the clerk. "No, Mr. Alighieri."

"Thank you." Dante escorted Matilda to the airlock. "Well, either he's dead or he's shacking up with a Unicorn. We'll find out which tomorrow."

They emerged from the hotel, and he noticed that the gravity had become much heavier.

"I hadn't realized just how much the Tamerlaine had spent to approximate Standard gravity," he remarked. "Why don't we ride instead of walking?"

"The Democracy gets fifty percent of the take from the vehicles that go to and from the spaceport," she explained. "They want the same from city transportation, and so far no one's been willing to give it to them. A couple of men set up a taxi business a couple of years ago; the Democracy came in and turned their vehicles to rubble. I think they killed one of the men, too. Anyway, since then, we walk. It's reached the point where the miners are proud of being able to cope with the climate and the gravity."

"Every goddamned Frontier world I've been to has a story like that," said Dante. "I hope to hell you've found our man." He grimaced. "Damn! It feels like each foot weighs fifty pounds."

"I don't mind the gravity as much as the thin air," she said.

"I don't think I'm especially enamored of the temperature, either," he added.

"It's much better now. Before sundown it's a lot hotter."

"And the Bandit fights Unicorns out here?"

"That's right."

"Well, he's Santiago or he's crazy," said Dante. "I vote for the latter."

"The conditions don't seem to bother him," said Matilda. "He's not like us."

"I'll vouch for that. Let's step it up a little and get out of this goddamned heat and gravity."

She locked her arm in his and gently restrained him. "You don't want to exert yourself in this thin air. You could black out before we reach the restaurant."

Dante slowed down and didn't admit that he was just a bit dizzy. "And he chases Unicorns up and down those hills! Amazing!"

"Don't keep talking," she instructed him. "Save your strength until we're inside the restaurant."

His limbs felt heavier with each step, and he fell silent and walked at her pace. The blocks seemed longer than they were on most Frontier worlds, but that could simply have been because he wanted them to be shorter.

Finally they came to the Golden Bough, and he gratefully entered the airlock with her. His lungs filled with oxygen, and the temperature dropped until it was comfortable if not cool—but his arms and legs still felt like the floor was tugging at them.

"There's no artificial gravity in here," Matilda noted. "I suppose it must cost too much for anything smaller than a hotel."

"Remind me not to order a soufflé," he replied wryly.

They were escorted to an empty table by the robotic headwaiter.

"So where's the Bandit?" asked Dante as they sat down.

"He'll be here."

"Yeah, I don't suppose you can kill Unicorns by the clock." He touched a small screen and summoned a waiter.

"How may I help you, sir?" asked the robot in a grating monotone.

"I'd like a beer. A very cold one." He turned to Matilda. "How about you?"

"Make it two," she told the robot.

"Would you care to order?" asked the waiter.

"No, we're waiting for a friend to join us."

The waiter walked to the bar, returning a moment later with their beers.

"You could work up one hell of a thirst walking around this town," commented Dante. He took a long swallow, closed his eyes, and sighed. "God, that's good! I don't think I ever appreciated beer before this evening."

"You'll find you need twice as many fluids as usual if you're going to spend any time outside," said Matilda.

Dante suddenly became aware of the fact that they were no longer alone. A tall man with wavy black hair, his clothes covered by red dust, stood next to their table. Matilda smiled when she saw him.

"Dante Alighieri," she said, "I'd like you to meet the man who saved my life—the One-Armed Bandit."

Dante stood up and shook the man's massive hand. "I've heard a lot about you," he said.

"Ditto," said the Bandit. "Matilda's told me all about you, Mr. Alighieri."

"Won't you sit down?"

"Thank you," said the Bandit. He signaled to the waiter. "Iced water, please—in the tallest glass you've got."

"How did it go today?" asked Matilda, lowering her voice enough so none of the other diners could overhear her.

"It went all right."

"That's all you've got to say?" she demanded.

"I wouldn't want Mr. Alighieri to think I was a braggart, ma'am."

"I won't," Dante assured him. "And I'd also like to hear what happened."

"There's really not much to tell," said the Bandit. "I took a land vehicle out to the mine, and when I didn't see any Unicorns there, I just went farther and farther into the desert until a few of them started throwing rocks at me the way they do. I waited until one of them charged, and before he could reach me I took out the hill where his friends were hiding so there was nothing left of either—the hill *or* the Unicorns. Then I melted the sand between the one surviving Unicorn and me, so he couldn't walk across it, and I told him that what I'd done was retribution for their killing that miner this morning. Twelve of them for one of us. I told him next time it'd be thirty for one, and then I let him go to spread the word." He paused uncomfortably. "I'm sorry I'm late, but the Democracy won't take my word for how many I killed, so I had to load them onto a couple of airsleds and attach them to the back of my land vehicle."

"And you did that in this gravity and heat!" said Dante admiringly.

"The trick is to not let them see that it bothers you, Mr. Alighieri," said the Bandit.

"Please, call me Dante."

"All right."

"And you killed twelve of them?"

"That's right, Mr. Alighieri."

"Dante."

"I apologize," said the Bandit. "That's the way my mother brought me up, and those early lessons stay with you even out here on the Frontier."

Dante seemed amused. "You don't have to apologize for being polite."

"Thank you," said the Bandit. "I'd call Matilda Miss something-or-other, but she won't tell me what her last name is."

"Welcome to the club," said Dante wryly.

"Dante has become the new Black Orpheus," said Matilda.

"So you told me, ma'am."

"Maybe if you'll tell him about some of your more exciting exploits he'll put them in his poem."

"Oh, I don't think any of 'em are worth putting in a poem," said the Bandit. "Certainly not the kind Orpheus used to write. Those verses were about important people."

"*You're* important," said Matilda.

"Thank you for saying so, ma'am, but I'm really not."

"You *could* be," said Dante meaningfully.

"I don't think I follow you, Mr. Alighieri," said the Bandit.

"I'm here on Heliopolis II for a few days," said Dante. "We'll talk about it before I leave. Tonight let's just get to know each other."

"Whatever you say, Mr. Alighieri."

"Dante."

"I'm sorry," said the Bandit. "Sooner or later I'll get it right."

The robot waiter trundled up and took their orders.

"Matilda's told me all about that arm of yours," said Dante as the waiter glided away. "It's quite a weapon. What made you decide to create it?"

"My father was a successful banker back on Spica II," said the Bandit. "He died just about the same time that I lost my arm in the Sett War. I suppose I could have just packed it in and lived on the interest from my inheritance, but I wasn't ready to retire from living yet. The war had kind of aroused my interest in seeing new worlds, so I took every last credit my father left me and found a team that could create this arm for me. I field-tested it in the Canphor VII rebellion, and then came out to the Inner Frontier."

"Why did you leave the Democracy?" asked Dante.

"I felt . . . I don't know . . . *constricted*. Too many rules and regulations, and I didn't like the way the Democracy enforced them, so I decided to come to where there weren't any rules at all."

"And now *you* enforce them," said Matilda. "That really does belong in Dante's poem."

"I never looked at it that way, ma'am," admitted the Bandit. "Still, I think Mr. Alighieri should stick to the important people, the ones who make and shape the Frontier."

Dante stared at him. *Can you be for real, or is this all just an act?*

Their dinner arrived, and they spent the next few minutes eating, while Matilda tried to make small talk.

When the meal was done, Dante lit a smokeless cigar and offered one to the Bandit, who refused.

"What are you doing tomorrow?" asked the poet.

"I won't know until tomorrow happens," said the Bandit. "I don't have any definite route or anything like that. If the Unicorns don't bother anyone, I'll stay in my hotel most of the day."

"If you're available, I'd like to have a serious talk with you."

"Sure."

"Aren't you curious?"

"You'll tell me when you're ready to," said the Bandit.

"Where are you staying?"

"Over at the Royal Khan."

"Fine. I'll be there about noon."

They got up to leave. As they walked past the bar, they came to a man whose face was swathed in bandages.

"Hello, Mr. Durastanti," said the Bandit. "Welcome back."

"They let me out this afternoon," said the man, his voice muffled by the bandages. "Lost an eye, and they're going to have to build me a new nose."

The Bandit reached into his pocket and pulled out twelve perfect diamonds. He took hold of the man's hand and carefully placed the diamonds in it.

"What's this?" demanded the man.

"Just in case the Democracy doesn't cover all your medical expenses, Mr. Durastanti," said the Bandit.

"You don't have to—"

"It's an honor to, Mr. Durastanti," said the Bandit, gently closing the man's hand on the diamonds and then guiding it to his pocket. "Don't drink too much tonight, and take those to the assay office in the morning. I'm sure there are identifying marks on them, but I'll stop by first thing and let them know I gave them to you . . . that you didn't steal them."

"As if I could!" said the man with a dry, croaking, humorless laugh.

"Take care, now," said the Bandit, accompanying Dante and Matilda out into the hot, uncomfortable night.

"What was that all about?" asked Dante.

"That's Mr. Durastanti," explained the Bandit. "He's a miner. The Unicorns killed his partner and laid a false trail for me to follow. By the time I realized it and doubled back, they'd already ripped half his face off."

"That's hardly your fault."

"I was supposed to protect him, and I failed." He paused, then continued with genuine regret. "I spoke to the doctors. He inhaled a lot of dust and he lost a lot of his face. They don't think he'll ever work again."

"Were those the diamonds you picked up for the Unicorns you killed today?"

"Yes."

"That's a lot of diamonds to give away."

The Bandit shrugged. "He needed them more than I did."

By God, thought Dante, *we* did *find Santiago after all!*

16.

He counts other people's money,
He mouths other people's words,
The Grand Finale hates his life,
And envies the free-flying birds.

Dante had been so fascinated by the One-Armed Bandit that he completely lost track of Virgil Soaring Hawk. That lasted until the middle of the night, when Virgil lurched into his room and poked him in the ribs.

"What the hell is it?" demanded Dante, sitting up.

"It's me," slurred the Injun. "I'm a he, not an it."

"Go away," said Dante, lying back down. "You're drunk."

"What's that got to do with anything?" retorted Virgil. "I've got a recruit."

"Who are we at war with?" muttered Dante, covering his head with a pillow.

"The Democracy."

"Go recruit eighty billion more and maybe you'll stand a chance," said the poet. "Now go away and leave me alone."

Virgil poked him in the ribs again.

"What the hell is the matter with you?" snapped Dante.

"I told you: I've got a recruit."

"All right, you've got a recruit," said Dante, now thoroughly and grumpily awake. "So what?"

"So I think you should talk to him."

"In the morning?"

"Now. He's downstairs in the hotel bar. And he wants to meet you."

Dante got up and started getting dressed. "This recruit of yours—does he have a name?"

"Probably. Hell, he's probably got a bunch of them. These days he calls himself the Grand Finale."

"Sounds like an actor with an inflated ego," said Dante disgustedly.

"He's waiting."

"I know. You told me." Dante slipped into his shoes and ran a comb through his hair.

"He's a gray-haired guy. Smaller than you. Kinda skinny. White mustache. You can probably find some of his dinner in it."

"Why are you telling me this?" said Dante. "We'll see him in just a minute."

The Injun lay down on the poet's bed. "I thought now that you know what he looks like, I'd take a little nap."

He was snoring by the time Dante reached the door.

Dante went down to the lobby, then turned to his left and entered the small bar. There was only one customer, and he looked exactly as Virgil had described him.

Dante walked over and stood in front of him. "You're the one who calls himself the Grand Finale?"

The old man looked him over critically. "So you're the new Orpheus?"

"So to speak. I gather you want to meet me?"

"Not as much as you want to meet me," said the old man. "Have a seat, Rhymer."

Dante sat down and ordered a beer.

"I'll have another," said the Grand Finale to the mechanical waiter. He turned to Dante. "I'm charging my drinks to your room. I hope you don't mind."

"I'll let you know after you tell me why I want to meet you."

"Because even Santiago can't function without a man like me," said the Finale.

"You don't look that formidable to me," remarked Dante.

"That's because you're thinking along the wrong lines, Rhymer," said the old man. "You don't need another soldier half as much as you need someone to pay for the bullets."

"Keep talking."

"I used to be a banker. A very exotic one: I arranged financing for terraforming worlds. I helped the Democracy bring recalcitrant worlds to their economic knees and helped rebuild them once they'd fallen into line. And I was *good*, Rhymer—there wasn't a trick I didn't know, a law I couldn't circumvent." He paused. "I was too good to stay in a legitimate business. It wasn't too long before the Kalimort bought me off."

"The Kalimort?" repeated Dante.

"They were a planetary criminal organization on Pretorius III that was about to expand to half a dozen other worlds. They needed financing, and they needed to know how to double their money while they were preparing to move."

"And you showed them how?"

"For a few years. Then they were absorbed by Barioke, one of the major warlords on the Rim, and I went to work for him. Over the years I've worked for half a dozen organizations that needed to hide and, at the same time, maximize their resources." He smiled. "The one you dubbed the Scarlet Infidel tells me you may be putting together another one."

"It's possible," said Dante. "Who are you working for now?"

"I'm between jobs," said the Grand Finale, looking uncomfortable for the first time.

"They caught you with your hand in the till," said Dante. It was not a question.

"Why should you think so?"

"Because we're as far from the Rim as it's possible to get. There's the Rim, then the Outer Frontier and the Spiral Arm, then the Democracy, and then the Inner Frontier and the Core. Why else would you be a couple of hundred thousand light-years from your warlord? How much did you run off with?"

"Not enough," admitted the Finale, unable to hide his bitterness. "I thought I'd never have to work again. I forgot how much it costs to live when you're in hiding."

"Yeah, it gets expensive," agreed Dante. "How long have you been the Grand Finale?"

"A few months." He grinned guiltily. "I saw a bakery on Ribot IV called the Grand Finale."

"Silly name."

"Well, I'm hardly likely to call myself the Banker or the Accountant when I'm trying to hide my identity."

"True enough," said Dante. "What's your real name?"

"Wilbur Connaught."

"If we decided to invite you to join us, Wilbur, what is it going to cost us?"

"It varies."

"Explain."

"I don't work for a salary. I'll take some living expenses as a draw against what I earn, but you'll pay me three percent of the profit I make with the money you give me to work with."

"Three percent doesn't seem like very much for a man with your credentials," said Dante. "What's the catch?"

"No catch. After a couple of years, you'll find yourself resenting how much you pay me."

"Give me an example of what you do."

"Let's say you give me a million credits, to name a nice round number," said Wilbur. "And let's say you don't need it for a year."

"Okay, let's say so."

"I'll use my sources to find those planets that are suffering from hyperinflation. They can't be just *any* planets; their economies have to be backed by the Democracy." He paused. "With more than fifty thousand worlds to choose from, it won't be too hard to find three worlds that are returning one hundred percent per annum on deposits, again using a nice round number."

"Okay, so you can double the money."

Wilbur snorted contemptuously. "Any fool can double the money. Just for the sake of argument, let's say each world has a twenty-four-hour day. I'll set up a computer program that transfers the money to each of the three worlds every eight Standard hours. Figuring simplistically, this will quadruple your money in a year, but actually, given compounded interest, it'll come much closer to quintupling. There's no stock market in the galaxy that can guarantee you an annualized five-hundred-percent return, and we'll do this with the full faith and backing of the Democracy. If any of those banks fail, the Democracy will step in and make good their debts."

"Very interesting," said Dante. "I'm impressed."

"That's kindergarten stuff," said Wilbur. "I just used it for a simple-to-understand example. There are investments and machinations that can give you a tenfold return in half the time. You'll need to pay an army, to supply them with weapons and ships, to keep lines of communication open. It all costs money. You need *me*, Rhymer."

"I'm sold," said Dante. "But it could take a while before we're ready for you, before we have anything for you to invest."

"I'm not going anywhere," said Wilbur. "I hate Heliopolis, but I'm probably safer hiding out in this hellhole than anywhere else." He sighed. "Almost makes me wish I'd stayed a banker."

"And we won't have an army, not in the normal sense of one."

"Neither did the Kalimort—but they sure killed a lot of people."

"That doesn't bother you?"

"My job is making money. I'm not responsible for what you do with it."

"That's a refreshing attitude," commented Dante.

"But if you use it against the Democracy, I won't be unhappy."

"Why should that be?"

"There's been a price on my head ever since I worked for the Kalimort," said Wilbur. "I've got two grandchildren in the Deluros system that I'll never see. That's reason enough."

"How will I get in touch with you?"

"I'm at the Royal Khan." The old man looked at him. "Have you found your Santiago yet?"

"I'm interviewing a very promising candidate tomorrow," said Dante.

"I didn't know they could apply for the job."

"They can't."

"But you just said—"

"He doesn't know what I want to talk to him about," said Dante.

"Well, if you're here for anyone, it's got to be the One-Armed Bandit," said Wilbur.

"What's your opinion of him?"

"You could do worse."

"That's all you've got to say?"

"My job is making money," said Wilbur. "Your job seems to be deciding who I make it for. I wouldn't let you tell me how to go about my business; I don't propose to tell you how to go about yours."

"You're going to be a pleasure to work with, old man."

"If you really think so, Rhymer, you might put me in a verse or two next time you're working on your poem."

"I might, at that."

The Grand Finale got to his feet. "I'm going back to my room now. No sense waiting til the sun starts coming out. It's hot enough as it is."

"We'll talk again soon," promised Dante.

"Not necessary," replied Wilbur. "I've told you what I can do and you've agreed to hire me. Contact me again when you're ready for me."

He walked out of the bar, crossed through the lobby, and went out the airlock while Dante sipped his beer and watched him bend over as the force of gravity hit him.

The poet considered going back to sleep, but decided that he didn't feel like wrestling the Injun for his bed, so he activated the bar's holo set and watched news and sports results from back in the Democracy until the first rays of the huge sun began lighting the streets.

He checked his timepiece, decided it was still a couple of hours too early to visit the Bandit, and walked out to the lobby.

"May I help you, sir?" said the night clerk.

"Yeah. Where do I go for breakfast around here?"

"We have our own restaurant."

"I know. But it doesn't open for another hour, and I'm hungry now."

"It's against our policy to recommend any other restaurants, so I am not permitted to tell you that the Deviled Egg is an excellent establishment and is located sixty yards to your right as you leave the Tamerlaine," said the clerk with a smile. "I hope you will forgive my reticence, sir."

Dante flipped him a coin. "All is forgiven and forgotten," he said, walking to the airlock.

The heat hit him the second he stepped outside. So did the gravity. He had a feeling he was adjusting to the thin air, because he walked the block to the restaurant without panting.

He walked through the near-empty Deviled Egg, found a table in the corner where he could look out through the front window and observe the few people who were out on the street, and ate a leisurely breakfast.

He sipped his coffee, checked his timepiece again, and decided that it was almost time to leave for the Royal Khan. He wondered if he should have Matilda come with him, but decided against it. He couldn't help feeling that she was a little bit in love with the One-Armed Bandit, and while he had no problem with that, he felt he'd rather present the proposal alone, with no emotional undercurrents distracting the Bandit.

He paid his bill, got up, and walked back into the hot, humid, thin Heliopolis air. The Royal Khan was half a block away, and he headed toward it.

A young woman was walking in his direction. As they passed each other she veered slightly and brushed against him. He thought nothing of it until he reached the lobby of the Royal Khan. A human waiter seemed to be charged with the task of bringing every person who entered the lobby a cold drink, and Dante reached into his pocket to grab a coin and tip him. Instead, he found a folded piece of paper, which the woman had obviously placed there. He unfolded it and read it:

*I know why you are here. The Scarlet Infidel thinks you will
be raising an army, but that's not the way Santiago fought in
the past, and it's not the way to fight now.*

"That goddamned Injun's got a big mouth," muttered Dante. He
continued reading.

*I have no love for the Democracy. If you would like to discuss
matters of mutual interest, fold this up and put it back in your
pocket, and I will contact you after you speak to the man you
came to Heliopolis II to see.*

Virgil hadn't known he'd be seeing the Bandit this morning.
Which meant she'd figured it out herself. It didn't make her a genius,
but it made her bright enough to talk to. Dante carefully folded the
note and replaced it in his pocket.

He looked around to see who was watching him. The lobby was
empty and there was no one in the street outside, but somehow he
knew that his action had registered with *someone*.

He tipped the waiter, who had waited impatiently while he'd read
the note, and then went to the airlift. He was going to the Bandit's
room as the successor to Black Orpheus; he had every hope that he
would leave as the creator of Santiago.

17.

A blossom, a petal, an odor so nice,
The flower of Samarkand's sugar and spice.
She eschews the moral and practices vice,
With a passion that's hot, and a heart cold as ice.

The door slid open and Dante entered the room. It was a little larger than his room at the Tamerlaine, but the air-conditioning didn't seem to be working as well. Then he found himself gasping for breath, and he realized that the window was half open.

"You sure you want to bring the outdoors in?" he asked, pointing to the window.

The One-Armed Bandit, who was floating a few inches above the ground on an easy chair that constantly remolded itself to his body's movements, glanced at the window.

"You can shut it if you like, Mr. Alighieri."

Dante walked over and commanded the window to close. It sealed itself shut an instant later.

"Don't you find the heat uncomfortable?" asked Dante curiously.

"Of course I do."

"Then why—?"

"Because then I find the outdoors a little less uncomfortable, and that's where I do most of my work."

"Makes sense," said Dante. He looked around and saw an empty chair by the desk. "Do you mind if I sit down?"

"You're my guest, Mr. Alighieri," said the Bandit. "You can have *this* chair if you like."

"The desk chair will be fine," said Dante, as he walked over and sat down. "I take it you're free for the day?"

"My services aren't needed." The Bandit paused. "So far, anyway."

"I think you're wrong," said Dante. "I think your services are needed more than you can imagine."

"Have the Unicorns—?"

"This has nothing to do with the Unicorns," said the poet. "Shall I continue?"

The Bandit nodded.

"What do you know about Santiago?"

"Not very much," admitted the Bandit. "They say that he was King of the Outlaws, and that he died more than a century ago. Why?"

"He was an outlaw, all right," said Dante. "But what if I told you that it was just a cover?"

"A cover?" said the Bandit, frowning. "For what?"

"That's what we're going to talk about," said Dante. "You want a cold drink? This is going to take some time."

"Later."

"Good. Now let's talk about what Santiago really was, and why he lasted so long."

Dante spent the next two hours giving the Bandit the full history of Santiago as he understood it. He explained in detail how Santiago made war against the excesses of the Democracy, but always hid it behind a cloak of criminality, because while the Democracy was content to send bounty hunters after the King of the Outlaws, they would have spared no expense hunting him down had they known he was actually a revolutionary. He explained that the first Santiago had trained his successor, and the next three had done the same, that the various Santiagos had included a farmer, a bounty hunter, a thief, even a chess master. Finally, he told the Bandit how the last Santiago and his infrastructure had been wiped out by the Democracy, which didn't even know he was on the planet of Safe Harbor when they turned it to dust.

"All that happened more than a century ago," said the Bandit. "It's interesting, Mr. Alighieri, but what does it have to do with me?"

"More than you think," said Dante. "The Democracy's abuses have grown since Santiago vanished. They confiscate property, they illegally detain and kill men and women, they destroy planets that pose no threat to them."

"I know all that," said the Bandit. "That's why I'm here on the Inner Frontier."

"But the Democracy's forces are here on the Inner Frontier, too."

"True."

"Well?"

"What do you expect *me* to do about it?"

Dante smiled. "I thought you'd never ask."

The Bandit stared at him. *"Me?"* he said at last.

"Why *not* you?" Dante shot back. "You're as decent a man as I've met out here. You're absolutely deadly when you feel you must be, yet you're not bloodthirsty or you'd have wiped out the Unicorns. You disapprove of the Democracy. You're generous to a fault; I saw an example of that last night. I have a feeling that you've never met anything that frightens you."

"That's not so," admitted the Bandit uncomfortably. *"Failure* frightens me."

"So much the better," said Dante. "I consider that a virtue."

"But—"

"We've been waiting a hundred and six years for Santiago to reappear. Are you going to make us wait even longer?"

"I wouldn't know how to go about *being* Santiago."

"That's what you'll have me and Matilda for, at least until you're comfortable with it."

"Just the three of us against the Democracy?" asked the Bandit, looking at him as if he was crazy.

"There's more. I found us a financial wizard last night."

"Why?"

"Money is the mother's milk of revolution. We'll need this man to set up and fund a network throughout the Frontier. Dimitrios of the Three Burners will work for the cause. So will Virgil Soaring Hawk."

"I've heard of Dimitrios."

"Virgil's in the poem as the Scarlet Infidel."

"Well, if you thought enough of him to write him up . . ." said the Bandit.

"There are more. And that's without any of them knowing we have our Santiago."

The Bandit was silent for a long moment, then another. Finally he looked up at Dante, his face filled with self-doubt. "What if they won't follow me?"

Dante smiled. "Why wouldn't they?"

"I'm just . . . just *me*," said the Bandit. "I'm nothing special, that men should die for my cause."

"It's the cause that's special, not its leader," said Dante. "Though he's special too," the poet amended quickly. "He has to be a man of his word, a resourceful man—and he has to be a man who won't back off from doing what's necessary. He has to know that if his cause is just, it doesn't matter that every citizen of the Democracy thinks he's an outlaw or worse; in fact he has to strive for that to protect his operation and his agents." Dante paused. "I think you're such a man."

"I think you're wrong."

"Santiago must also be a modest man, even a humble one—a man who *thinks* he's nothing special, when it's apparent to everyone else that he's very special indeed."

"I'll have to think about it, Mr. Alighieri."

"Think hard," said Dante. "Think of the difference you could make, the things you could do." He paused. "I can't rush you. There are no other candidates for the job. You're the man we want. But the sooner you agree, the sooner we can put everything in motion."

"I understand, Mr. Alighieri."

"Dante."

"I appreciate your confidence in me," said the Bandit. "I'll give you my answer tonight."

"When and where?"

"There's a restaurant called the Brave Bull. Meet me there for dinner, an hour after sundown."

"I'll see you then," said Dante. He walked to the door, then turned back. "Do you want me to open the window again?"

"No," said the Bandit. "I'm going down to the lobby to have some coffee."

"I'll join you."

"I'd rather you didn't. I've got a lot to consider, and I do my best thinking when I'm alone."

"Whatever you say," replied Dante. He turned and walked out the door, then took the airlift down to the main floor.

A very pretty woman was smiling at him. It took him a moment to place her; then he realized that she was the same woman who had bumped into him and placed the note in his pocket.

He walked over and stood in front of her. "Good morning," he said. "My name is—"

"I know who you are, and I know why you're here."

"Of course you do," he said. "But I don't know who you are or why you're here. Perhaps you'd care to enlighten me?"

"First things first. Did he agree?"

"I think he will."

"Good. Let's go back to your hotel."

"Why?"

"So we don't distract him," said the woman. "I've been studying him for weeks. Whenever he needs to think out a problem, he comes down here and drinks coffee."

"All right, let's go," said Dante, leading her to the airlock. He took two steps outside and felt like melting. "My God, it's even worse than yesterday."

"If you plan to stay here for any length of time, you really should go to a doctor for help or acclimatization—adrenaline, blood oxygenating, muscle stimulants, the whole works."

"I have high hopes of leaving Heliopolis II in a day or two and never seeing it again," Dante assured her as they began the seemingly endless two-block walk to the Tamerlaine. "And now, who are you?"

"My name is Blossom."

"Very pretty name," said Dante. "Where are you from?"

"Samarkand."

"Where the hell is Samarkand?"

"It was a city back on old Earth, or so they tell me," she replied. "In my case, it's a planet in the Quinellus Cluster."

"Okay, Blossom," he said, and found himself gasping for breath again. "I'll wait until we're at the hotel to talk to you. I think I'm going to need all my oxygen just to get there."

"I could give you a pill."

"Don't bother," he rasped. "We'd be at the hotel before it had a chance to take effect."

They trudged down the block in silence. Dante stopped at a corner, leaned against a building until his head stopped spinning, and then walked the rest of the way to the Tamerlaine without any further incident.

"The Bandit must keep some doctor in business, considering how much time he spends outside," said Dante when they'd passed through the hotel's airlock and were back in comfortable gravity and temperature.

"He doesn't take any medication," answered Blossom. "He doesn't believe in it."

"He doesn't believe it works?"

"Oh, he knows it works. He doesn't believe in putting any foreign substances in his body."

"Better and better," muttered Dante, taking her to one of the lounges and collapsing in a chair. She sat down opposite him. "All right, Blossom—suppose you tell me why you sought me out and what this is all about?"

"I had a long talk with Virgil Soaring Hawk last night," she began.

"I didn't know he *talked* to women," interrupted Dante. "I thought he just pounced on them."

"He tried." She showed off a steel-toed boot. "He'll be walking bowlegged for the next few days."

Dante smiled his approval. "Good for you."

"Anyway, he told me that you found Black Orpheus' manuscript, and were taking his place."

"I'm continuing his work," Dante corrected her. "That's not quite the same thing."

"Close enough," said Blossom. "Anyway, he mentioned that you were looking for a new Santiago to write about."

"I'm looking for a new Santiago because the Inner Frontier is in desperate need of him," said Dante, idly wondering if he was telling the truth, and then wondering if all writers had that particular problem. "My being able to write about him is very unimportant compared to that."

She stared at him for a moment, making no effort to hide her disbelief, and finally shrugged. "Your motivation is no concern of mine," she said at last. "I just want to know when you've found him."

"Why?"

"Because I want to offer him my services."

"And just what *are* your services?" asked Dante.

"Whatever the job requires."

"We're not dealing with nice people."

"I know that," said Blossom.

"The job could require you to sleep with some men you can't stand the sight of, or perhaps even kill them."

"As long as it hurts the Democracy, I'm in."

"Just what do you have against the Democracy?"

"My parents were missionaries. The Democracy had a chance to evacuate them before they pacified Kyoto II. They didn't. The first attack killed them." She lowered her voice, but continued talking. "My husband's mother was a diplomat; he grew up on Lodin XI. His closest friend was a Lodinite. They were like brothers. During the Lodin insurrection, the Democracy killed my husband's friend for unspecified crimes, none of which he had committed, and then they executed my husband for being a collaborator." She paused, her jaw set, her face grim. "You just tell me what I have to do, and if any member of the Democracy suffers because of it, I'll do it."

"It's not up to me to tell you anything," replied Dante. "I'm just a poet. Santiago will decide what needs to be done, and by whom."

"You'll tell him about me?"

"Of course."

"Do you think he'll let me join him?"

"We're just starting out. He'll need all the help he can get." He sighed. "Hell, he'll need all the help he can get fifty years and a hundred victories from now. This is the *Democracy* we're going up against, even if they're not allowed to know it." He pulled out his pocket computer. "Where can I get hold of you, Blossom?"

"As long as you've assured me that Santiago will be giving me my orders, I'll reserve that information for him."

"But—"

"Don't worry," said Blossom. "Neither you nor he will leave Heliopolis before I speak to him—but there's no sense doing that until he makes it official, is there?"

"It might help him decide."

"If I'm what it takes to make him decide, then you picked the wrong man for the job." She got to her feet. "I'll be watching, Rhymer."

"It shouldn't be long," said Dante.

She turned and left, and he watched her make her way through the lobby and the airlock. It seemed difficult to believe that such a gorgeous woman could have suffered so much—and then he realized that he was thinking in stereotypes. Santiago would know that it was the suffering that mattered, not the appearance of the sufferer.

Hurry up and make up your mind, Bandit. The Frontier is filled with Flowers of Samarkand. Someone has to step forward and make sure that the Democracy doesn't make any more of them suffer as this one has.

18.

He's the king of the outlaws, the crème de la crème,
He's clever, he's deadly, he's knavery's gem.
He sups with the devil, he revels in pain.
He kills and he plunders—humanity's bane.

Dante wrote that verse just before he went to visit the One-Armed Bandit and learn his decision. Black Orpheus had never mentioned Santiago by name; he simply assumed that no one else could possibly fit the verses he wrote about the King of the Outlaws and that his readers would know that.

Dante followed suit for a number of reasons, not the least of which was that he wasn't at all sure that the Bandit would agree to become Santiago. He was so moral, so out-and-out *decent*, that there was some doubt in Dante's mind that he could do all the unpleasant things that were required of him.

Dante tried to visualize the Bandit ordering his men to wipe out a Navy convoy filled with brave young men whose only crime was that they had been drafted to serve the Democracy. He tried to imagine the Bandit ordering Blossom to sleep with a degenerate man who had information Santiago's organization needed. He knew that Santiago would have to commit some actual crimes, some robberies and murders, if only to leave a false trail and convince the Democracy that he was an outlaw and not a revolutionary. All the previous Santiagos had blended in, had been able to hide out in the middle of a crowd—but none of them had the Bandit's reputation, or his easily recognizable prosthetic arm.

So do I want him to say yes or don't I?

Yes, he realized, of course he wanted the Bandit to say yes. There would be problems—but that was precisely why there was a need for Santiago. *I need you, yes,* thought Dante, *but the Frontier, maybe even the galaxy, needs you even more. I could look for a couple of lifetimes and not find a better candidate than you, so please, please say yes.*

He checked his timepiece, decided it was time to get his answer, and walked out into the crushing gravity and hot, thin, dusty air.

The first thing we do when we get the Democracy off our backs is get some public transportation here.

He stopped halfway to the Royal Khan to buy a cold drink, then forced himself back outside to complete the journey. Once inside the Bandit's hotel he found that his shirt was drenched with perspiration, and he stopped by a public bathroom to dry himself off. He looked at his face in a mirror, marveled at how tanned he'd become from the few days in which he'd been exposed to the blazing red sun, and finally, feeling a little more comfortable, went to the airlift and rode it up to the Bandit's floor.

As usual the door slid open before he could knock. This time, instead of using the floating, formfitting easy chair, the Bandit was sitting on a window ledge, his shoulder pressed against it, glancing out to the street every now and then.

"Good evening, Mr. Alighieri."

"Dante."

"I'll get it right sooner or later."

"And who am *I* saying good evening to?" asked Dante.

"Me."

"And who are you—Santiago or the One-Armed Bandit?"

"We'll talk a bit, and then I'll tell you."

"Do you mind if I sit down?"

"Suit yourself," said the Bandit.

Dante walked over to the easy chair. As he sat down, it seemed to wrap around his body and began rocking him gently. The rocking became a swaying as the chair rose and hovered a few inches above the ground.

Dante felt a grin of pleasure cross his face. "I've wanted to sit in this thing from the first minute I saw it."

"You look comfortable," observed the Bandit.

"I may never get out of it again," said Dante, still grinning. "Okay, I'm ready to listen if you're ready to talk."

"I have a few questions for you," said the Bandit.

"Shoot."

"You tell me there were five Santiagos."

"Right. The last one died when the Navy destroyed Safe Harbor."

"Did all five die violently?"

"I won't lie to you," said Dante, the grin gone. "Yes, they did."

"What was their average age?"

"I don't know as much about the first two as I should. I really couldn't say."

"It's not important anyway. The real question is: what was their average tenure as Santiago?"

"Maybe ten or twelve years. Less for the last one."

"And these were the best men the prior Santiagos could find, and they each inherited a massive organization." It was a statement, not a question.

"Except for the first," noted Dante. "He had to create it—and the legend, and the misdirection—from scratch."

"And even with those organizations, none of them lasted fifteen years, not even a man as accomplished as Sebastian Cain."

"That's right."

The Bandit frowned and fell silent. After a moment he turned and looked out at the street again.

"You're not afraid of dying in ten or twelve years, not with the odds you face almost every day," said Dante. "What's the real reason you're being so hesitant?"

The Bandit turned and faced him. "I don't know if I can accomplish enough before they kill me," he said. "You might be better off with some criminal kingpin or even a disgruntled military commander, someone who's already got an organization in place."

"Is *that* what this is all about?" asked Dante, suddenly relieved.

"I don't want to be the Santiago that failed," said the Bandit. "Is that so hard to understand?"

"I'm sure every Santiago had his doubts."

"Do you really think so?"

"I'm certain of it," answered Dante. "If you say yes to our offer, you'll become not only the most feared man in the galaxy, but the most hated as well. And you won't be hated just by the Democracy. You'll be hated by every decent, law-abiding, God-fearing colonist that you're trying to protect. You'll be hated and envied by the men and women who work for you, and most of them will be the scum of the galaxy. You'll only be able to leave your headquarters—I won't use the word 'hideout,' but that's what it'll be—if you're heavily disguised. You'll send decent men and women to their deaths. The Democracy will put a huge price on your head, and it'll get higher every month. You won't even be mourned when an underling or a bounty hunter finally kills you, because we can't let anyone know that Santiago is dead." Dante paused. "Don't you think the other Santiagos had their doubts?"

The Bandit sighed heavily. "When you put it that way, I guess they must have."

"Of course they did," said Dante. "And each of them thought the cause was worth it." He stared at the Bandit, studying his face. "You do a lot of good, and you're a hero." The Bandit was about to interrupt, but Dante held up a hand. "No, don't deny it. You're an authentic, bona fide hero. What we're asking is for you to do ten times, a hundred times as much good—and be thought of as a villain for the rest of your life. In the end, that's what it boils down to. Which is more important to you—being a hero or doing good?"

"You don't pull your punches, do you, Mr. Alighieri?" said the Bandit wryly.

"I'm asking you to become the most feared and hated man in the galaxy," replied the poet. "I don't know how to make it sound like anything other than that." He paused. "And there's something else."

"What?"

"If I *had* to couch it in diplomatic terms, then you're not the man we're looking for."

"Oh, I'm the man, all right," said the Bandit with another deep sigh. "I just wanted to make sure I knew what I was getting into, because there's no turning back."

"You're right about that. Once you're in, you're in for keeps." Dante paused thoughtfully. "Have you got any family?"

"Not much. A brother somewhere. I haven't kept in touch. Maybe a distant cousin or two. My parents are dead, and my sister died in the same battle where I lost my arm."

"No wife, no kids, no romantic attachments?"

The Bandit shook his head. "I never found the time for it. I always planned to someday."

"Forget about it. To you they'd be a wife and kids; to millions of men and women, they'd be targets."

The Bandit nodded thoughtfully. "Yes, I can see that."

"How about your arm?" continued Dante. "Does it need servicing?"

"Never has yet. Why?"

"We couldn't let your doctors know, or even guess, that they were working on Santiago."

The Bandit frowned. "You'd kill them?"

"Not me," said Dante. "I'm just a poet."

The meaning of Dante's statement was reflected in the Bandit's face. "I see."

"Could you order it done?"

The Bandit stared at him, unblinking. "I'd have to."

"That's right—you'd have to."

"I don't imagine decisions like that get any easier to make over the years."

"Not if you're the man we hope you are," agreed Dante.

"Okay, I've asked my questions," said the Bandit. "What do we do now?"

"Now we meet the members of your organization that are currently on Heliopolis II, and we start making plans."

"There's really an organization?"

"The start of one."

"Are they down in the lobby?"

"No," said Dante. "I told them I'd contact them if and when you committed."

The poet pulled out a communicator, and a moment later had made contact with the four people he sought.

"This is Dante," he said. "We have plans to make. I expect to see you all in"—he paused, then smiled—"in Santiago's room at the Royal Khan in half an hour."

"Santiago's room," repeated the Bandit. "I like the sound of that."

"That's who you are. The One-Armed Bandit ceased to exist three minutes ago."

Dante spent the next few minutes telling him tales of the previous Santiagos, tales he hadn't told the day before. The Bandit was most interested in how they died.

"Violently," answered Dante.

"I know. But *how?*"

"The first was killed during a raid on a Navy convoy," said Dante. "The second one died from injuries he received in prison. The third—"

"They had Santiago in prison?" interrupted the Bandit.

"Yes," answered Dante, "but they didn't know who he was. Many men were tortured to death without telling them." He paused. "The third was killed by a bounty hunter named the Angel. The fourth, who I'm convinced was Sebastian Cain, was assassinated by another bounty hunter, either Peacemaker MacDougal or Johnny One-Note. The last of them, a former thief known as Esteban Cordoba, died when the Navy vaporized his world." Dante paused, almost overwhelmed by the litany of violent deaths. "None of them died in bed."

"Except maybe for the second one."

"It's not a death you'd want. I gather they mutilated him pretty badly."

"There are so many worlds on the Frontier, literally millions of them. I'm surprised none of my predecessors could stay in hiding for as much as fifteen years."

"Probably they could have."

"Then why—"

"Because each of them seems to have reached a point where he decided not to run again." Dante shrugged. "I don't know. Maybe being Santiago affects your judgment after a decade or so. Maybe because you've held off the best killers the Democracy could throw against you, you start feeling that you can't be killed, that you're somehow immortal."

"The first might have felt that way," said the Bandit. "The others had to know better."

"Then you'll have to tell *me* someday. I sure as hell don't have any better explanation."

"I didn't mean any offense, Mr.—"

"*Stop!*" said Dante harshly.

"What's the matter?" asked the Bandit, surprised.

"Two things," said Dante. "Santiago doesn't call anyone *Mister*, and he never apologizes."

"I'll try to remember."

"See that you do," said Dante. "I'm serious about this. Any sign of deference or regret will be viewed as weakness not only by your enemies, but, worse still, by the men who work for you. Santiago bows to no one, he apologizes to no one, he defers to no one. Never forget that, or you'll be long buried when I want to ask you that question a decade from now."

"I'll remember," amended the Bandit.

Dante stared at him for a long moment.

"What's wrong?" asked the Bandit.

"Ordinarily I'd suggest cosmetic surgery, a whole new face, maybe prosthetic eyes that can see into the infrared and ultraviolet and retinas that aren't on record anywhere, but . . ." He let his voice trail off.

"But what?"

"But there's no way to hide or disguise your arm. I don't know that we'd want to, anyway. Once people know what it can do, just threatening to use it may win us a couple of bloodless battles." He got to his feet and started pacing back and forth. "I suppose what we'll have to do is find a sector of the Frontier where you've never been, where no one knows you, and build our organization from there. We'll have to fake the One-Armed Bandit's death, and make it spectacular, so everyone knows about it."

"Why?" asked the Bandit. "Sooner or later they're going to figure out who I am."

"You're Santiago."

"You know what I mean."

"Santiago can't be anyone except Santiago. That's why everyone has to know that the One-Armed Bandit's dead. Perhaps he was Santiago's friend. Maybe he even saved Santiago's life, and Santiago had his real arm removed and this prosthetic weapon installed in its place as a tribute to the Bandit, or because its power and efficiency impressed him. But the thing you can never forget is that Santiago is more than a man. He's an idea, a concept, a myth. He can't be bigger than life if everyone knows who he used to be."

"It sounds like you've considered all this pretty thoroughly," remarked the Bandit.

"I'm as close to a biographer as you're ever going to have," said Dante, "so I have to know everything there is to know about Santiago."

There was a knock at the door.

"Open," said the Bandit.

The door slid back and Matilda, Virgil, Blossom, and Wilbur Connaught entered the room.

"I know you," said the Bandit to Matilda. He turned to Blossom. "I've *seen* you." He gestured to Virgil and Wilbur. "These two I don't recognize at all."

"They work for you," said Dante. "Time for the introductions." He laid a hand on each of their shoulders in turn. "This is Matilda. This is Virgil. This young lady is Blossom. And this gentleman is Wilbur."

"No last names?" asked the Bandit.

"You'll learn them soon enough," said Dante. He walked over to the Bandit and turned to face the four of them. "And this is Santiago. He has no past, no history. He is a spirit of the Frontier made flesh. That's all you have to know about him, and all you will ever tell anyone else. The One-Armed Bandit is no more, and will never be referred to again until we are free to talk about his untimely and very public death. Is that clear to everyone?"

The four agreed.

Dante turned back to the Bandit. "Dimitrios of the Three Burners has committed to our cause. We'll get word to him that we're ready to have him join us."

"Let him continue to do what he does best," said the Bandit. "When I have an assignment for him, that'll be time enough to meet him."

Dante stared at the Bandit. *You look larger, somehow. Can you possibly be growing into the part right in front of my eyes?*

"Well, let's get down to work," said Dante. "As money comes in, we'll turn it over to Wilbur. He'll have to open his books to me or to Matilda if we request it, but only Santiago can fire him."

"How much are we paying you?" asked the Bandit.

"Three percent of everything I make."

"That seems fair. Wait here a moment." He walked into the bedroom, then returned a moment later with a small cloth bag. "Here," he said, handing the bag to Wilbur. "There are sixty-three diamonds in it. Get what you can for them—probably you'll have to go into the Democracy for the best price—and put the money to work for us. There's no sense having you wait around until we start generating cash. And Wilbur?"

"Yes."

"Those diamonds belong to every underprivileged, abused colonist on the Inner Frontier. If you or they should disappear, I will personally hunt you down and make you wish you'd never been born."

"You didn't have to say that, Santiago," said Wilbur in hurt tones.

"The One-Armed Bandit didn't have to say it," replied the Bandit. "Santiago did."

By God, you're really him! thought Dante. Aloud he said, "I think our first duty is going to be to find a headquarters world, someplace parsecs away from anyone who's ever seen you in action."

"It makes no difference to me what world we choose," said the Bandit. "Any suggestions?"

Dante turned to Matilda. "You're far more familiar with the Inner Frontier than I am. What do you think?"

"Let me think about it for a day," she replied. "Probably someplace in the Albion Cluster. You haven't been there, have you, Santiago?"

"Just once, ma'am, a long time ago—before I lost my arm."

"I think that's probably long enough," said Dante.

"Besides, his arm's his most distinctive feature," added Blossom. "It's what people remember."

"Okay, check out the Albion Cluster and come up with a safe haven by tomorrow." Suddenly Dante smiled. "Well, now I know how Safe Harbor got its name."

"What can *I* do?" asked Blossom.

"Come to the Cluster with us," said the Bandit. "When I decide where I want to strike first, I'll send you ahead to be my eyes and ears until I arrive."

"Now, once we've got a headquarters world, we'll start building an organization from the ground up," said Dante. "We'll recruit whoever we need, and we'll come up with some kind of battle plan." He paused. "Correction: *Santiago* will come up with a battle plan." He looked around the room. "Has anyone got any questions, or anything else to say?"

No one spoke up.

"Then I guess that's it," said Dante. "We'll meet again tomorrow when Matilda has come up with some worlds for our consideration— though again, we can only suggest and advise. It's Santiago's choice."

They began walking to the door, and then the Bandit spoke: "Before you leave, I want to say something."

They stopped and turned to him.

"You've given me an honor I don't deserve, and at the same time you've given me a challenge I can't refuse. From this moment on, I am Santiago, and the only thing that matters to me is protecting the colonists of the Inner Frontier from the Democracy. I realize that we will never overthrow it, and we wouldn't want to if we could—it serves its purpose in a galaxy where we're outnumbered hundreds to one—but we will devote our lives to reminding it with whatever degree of force is required that we of the Inner Frontier are Men, too, and that we are not the enemy." He looked at each of them in turn. "I pledge to you that I will never give you any reason to be ashamed of me."

There was a moment of silence, and then Dante began applauding, and soon all the others had joined in. Finally they walked out to the airlift and descended to the lobby. Matilda, Blossom, and Wilbur all left to go about their business, but Virgil made a beeline to the bar, and Dante joined him a moment later, sitting down next to him.

"You didn't say a word up there," noted the poet. "Not a single word."

"I didn't have anything to say."

"And do you now?"

"Not really."

"No comment on Santiago at all?"

"None," said the Injun. "What do *you* think of him?"

"He's humble, he's decent, he's polite, he's the deadliest man I've met but he only kills when he has to, and he seems to be adjusting to the role he's going to play."

"He only kills when he has to?" repeated Virgil.

"That's why he hasn't wiped out the Unicorns. He could, you know."

"Well, I'll tell you something," said Virgil. "While you were busy indoctrinating him, I went out and got some facts and did a little math."

"And?" said Dante.

"You know how many people our Santiago has killed?"

"I haven't the faintest idea."

"Thirty-seven men and an unspecified number of aliens, thought to exceed the thousand mark," Virgil paused and looked at the poet. "Do you think they *all* needed killing?"

"If *he* killed them, yes," said Dante sincerely. "Hell, he'd be justified in killing ten thousand Unicorns, the way they attack humans at every opportunity."

"If you say so."

"Listen to me, Virgil," persisted the poet. "This guy is the hero every kid wishes he could be. He's well-mannered. He's humble. He's moral. He's almost too good to be true."

"That's the gist of it," agreed Virgil.

"I don't follow you."

"It's been my experience," said the Injun, "that when you come across something that seems to be too good to be true, it usually *is* too good to be true."

19.

Gloria Mundi, born on Monday,
Gloria Mundi, died on Sunday,
Gloria Mundi, rose on Tuesday,
Which qualified as a bad news day.

No one ever knew her real name. The betting is that she herself had long since forgotten it. It didn't make any difference. What really matters is not *who* she was, but rather *what* she was.

Gloria Mundi had been a beggar woman, living out her life in squalor in the slums on Roosevelt III—until the day (and yes, it was a Sunday) that she was struck by lightning. It killed her, but because of the thousands of deaths and casualties caused by the Sett War, which had reached the Roosevelt system two weeks earlier, they didn't have time to perform a postmortem or prepare the body for a funeral. They were working around the clock, saving the wounded and trying to identify the dead, so Gloria's body was shunted aside until they finally had time to work on it.

And, miraculously, two days later she woke up, found herself in a room with dozens of corpses, and began screaming. She kept the screaming up for a very long time, until they finally found and sedated her.

When she awoke from the sedative, she claimed to remember what she had experienced while dead. A number of the medics felt she had merely been in a deep coma, that no one comes back from the dead after thirty-six hours . . . but when they checked the records of the medical computers and sensors that had examined her, they had to admit that yes, she really had been dead for a day and a half.

The moment that fact was made public, a number of news organizations offered her millions in exchange for her exclusive story. But before she could choose among them, or even adjust to the fact that she no longer had to worry about where her next meal was coming from, suddenly there were more people out to kill her than ever went after Santiago. And if the would-be killers weren't fanatical priests, ayatollahs, ministers, rabbis, and shamans themselves, then they were in the employ of such men. Publicly they all believed that their religion was the only true one, and that Gloria Mundi would confirm it . . . and privately their first thought was to make sure she didn't reveal any experience she might have had or knowledge she might have gained that would confirm the truth of a rival religion.

As for Gloria herself, she never spoke about what she had experienced. Somehow she eluded her assassins until they finally decided she had died of old age or at the hands of another killer, or their employers gradually lost interest in her.

And so, at age eighty-six, Gloria Mundi found herself on Heliopolis II, temporarily (and, for all she knew, permanently) safe from the men who had tried to hunt her down. Her health was gone—she had just about every disease of the aged except senility, and her brain hadn't functioned all that well since she had revived—but she kept to herself, didn't bother anyone, and seemed likely to live out her few remaining months or years in some semblance of peace.

She was far from everyone's thoughts when they met at the Bandit's rooms the next morning. Matilda had come up with Beta Cordero II, a world in the Albion Cluster, and she was extolling its virtues to the group.

"Standard oxygen, temperate climate, ninety-four-percent Standard gravity. No indigenous sentient races."

"None?" said Dante.

"Well, there were two—one humanoid, one not—but the Navy went a little overboard pacifying them about six hundred years ago. There are a few remnants on other planets who claim ownership of the world, but none of them have returned."

"Why not?" asked the Bandit.

"It only became safe for habitation a couple of years ago," answered Matilda. "Prior to that there was too much radioactivity. The water just passed inspection five weeks ago, so this is a perfect time to establish a presence there."

"What are the nearest major worlds?"

"The biggest trading world in the sector is Diomedes. There's a military outpost on Jamison V, but it's pretty small. A few nearby farming worlds that supply about sixty mining worlds within, oh, perhaps five hundred light-years."

"It sounds promising," said Dante. "Has the Democracy staked any legal claim to it?"

"No," answered Matilda. "I'm sure they'd claim it was within their sphere of influence, but there are no ownership claims."

"When was the last time the Democracy or its representatives set down on it?"

"They sent a drone ship thirty-two days ago to test the radioactivity level. As far as I can tell, no member of the Democracy has actually set foot on Beta Cordero II in more than six hundred years."

"Sounds good to me," announced the Bandit. "We'll set up shop there as soon as we can."

"Fine," said Dante. "Now we'll need a name for it."

"It *has* a name," replied the Bandit. "Beta Cordero II."

"That name's on every star map created during the past millennium, maybe longer," explained Dante. "We need a name to give to our agents, a name that if overheard won't tell the Democracy where we are."

"That makes sense," agreed the Bandit. He lowered his head in thought for a moment, then looked up. "We'll call it Valhalla."

"Valhalla it is," said Matilda.

"When shall we leave?" asked Blossom, speaking up for the first time.

"Not much sense going there until we've got some shelter," said Dante. "We'll have to send some people ahead to build us whatever we need—once Wilbur can raise some money. In the meantime, I guess we'll stay here."

"That's unacceptable," said the Bandit. "It's time to start making a difference."

"Well, I suppose there are still some buildings standing, but after six centuries, I don't know . . ."

"We're not going to use ancient buildings that are probably ready to collapse the first time someone sets foot in them, if indeed they're still standing," said the Bandit firmly. "And we're not going to wait for Wilbur to work his magic with the diamonds I gave him yesterday."

Good, thought Dante. *You're showing us what Santiago is supposed to do and be.*

"I don't see what you're getting at," said Blossom.

"Santiago is the King of the Outlaws, isn't he?" replied the Bandit.

"And this is a mining world, run by the Democracy. What better place for us to announce that Santiago is back?"

"You're going to rob the assay office?"

He shook his head. "I'd just get a few diamonds they hadn't transferred to the bank yet, and then we'd still have to wait for Wilbur to convert them into cash." He paused. "Santiago is going to rob the Heliopolis branch of the Bank of Deluros VIII. We'll pick up a few million credits in half a dozen currencies, money we can use immediately." He turned to Matilda. "Valhalla hasn't been worked in more than half a millennium. I think rather than posing as a farmer, perhaps I should be a reclusive sportsman, or maybe a trapper."

"I'll check and see if any animals are left on the planet."

"If there are, maybe they've mutated into something worth hunting," said Dante.

"No one has a problem with this?" asked the Bandit.

There were no responses.

"You," he continued, indicating Virgil. "You never speak. Why not?"

"I've got nothing to say," answered the Injun.

"There have been times when you couldn't shut him up," added Dante.

"If your silence is disapproval," said the Bandit, "now's the time to cut and run. I won't hold it against you. But once Santiago makes his presence known, I won't tolerate disloyalty."

"I'll stick around," said Virgil.

"You approve of Santiago, then?"

"I couldn't care less about Santiago," said the Injun. "My fate is tied to the poet's."

"In what way?"

"He's Dante, I'm Virgil," said the Injun, as if that explained everything.

"I don't understand."

"Neither do I, really," admitted Virgil, "but I know that it's my destiny to lead Dante through the nine circles of hell to the promised land."

"I don't know what you're talking about."

"What difference does it make? I serve the poet and he serves you, so therefore *I* serve you."

The Bandit considered his answer for a moment, then nodded his approval. "Okay," he said at last. "I can accept that."

"When are you going to hit the bank?" asked Wilbur.

"We need the money, so I might as well do it right now."

"I don't know," said Dante.

"What's your problem?" asked Matilda.

"We can't stay on Heliopolis once he robs the bank, but nothing will be ready for us on Valhalla."

"So we'll make our way there in slow, easy steps, while I send a crew ahead to prepare our headquarters for us."

"The Democracy's not going to pursue us in slow, easy steps," said Dante.

"The Democracy will be looking for Santiago," said Matilda. "What do *you* think he looks like? What are his identifying marks? How big is his gang?"

"Point taken," said Dante.

"Can I help?" asked Blossom.

"Are you any good with a burner or a screecher?" asked Dante.

"No."

"Then you might as well stay here, where you'll be safe."

"If you want to come, you can come," interrupted the Bandit. "There will probably be enough loot that we'll need all the help we can get just to cart it away."

"How will you carry it from the bank back here without being seen?" asked Matilda.

"We won't," answered the Bandit. "We'll summon transportation to take us right from the bank to the spaceport."

I don't know how well thought out this is, thought Dante, *but you're the boss. Let's see what happens, and if you're making a blunder, at least you're making it on a minor world and not on Binder X or Roosevelt III.*

"I'll handle the fighting," said the Bandit. "Whoever's with me is just there to cart out the money. I don't want to have to keep an eye on you once the shooting starts, so stay well behind me. Are there any questions?"

"Back in the Democracy," said Dante, "it's standard operating procedure for one or more of the bank's employees to have an implant that reads their blood pressure and adrenaline and is tied in to the bank's computer."

"What if the clerk is just reacting to a pretty girl?" asked Virgil.

"If the reading goes more than ten percent above normal, the teller's computers will register it. Then he's got about ten seconds to disable it, which means it *was* a pretty girl, or an insect sting, or something like that. If he *doesn't* disable it in ten seconds, it sends a signal to the police station."

"I didn't know that," said the Bandit.

"You've never robbed a bank before," said Dante with a smile. "I have. There's no reason to believe the technology hasn't spread to the Frontier. We can still do the job, but we'll have to act *fast*."

Silence.

"All right, then," continued the Bandit. "I'll give you each an hour to collect whatever you plan to take along to Valhalla and load it into your ships or mine." He gave them the location, ID number, and computer code to his ship. "Mine is big enough to carry all of us, but if we split up we should be harder to spot, in case anyone gets a good description of us." He turned to the Grand Finale. "Wilbur, you might as well leave right now. If we come away with cash, we won't need you to convert it for us, and if you wait a day or two, security at the spaceport will be much tighter and they'll almost certainly find the diamonds I gave you." He paused. "Meet us on Valhalla. We'll probably get there first, so radio us before you land and we'll give you coordinates. If we come away with some diamonds as well as cash, we'll turn them over to you and send you back into the Democracy with them."

Wilbur nodded his agreement. "Good luck," he said, and left the room.

"Okay," said the Bandit. "I'll see you at the bank in exactly two hours."

He sat down and lit up a smokeless cigar.

"Aren't you taking anything out to your ship?" asked Blossom.

"Just me. Anything I take might be too easy to identify."

"That makes sense," said Dante. "If this holdup works, we can all afford to buy whatever we need. If not, it won't matter anyway."

He sat down next to the Bandit.

"Well, if everyone feels that way, we might as well get started," said Blossom.

"Sit," said the Bandit.

"Why?"

"We've got to give Wilbur time to collect the diamonds, get out to the spaceport, and take off."

"Shit!" she exclaimed. "I hadn't thought of that."

"It's not your job to think of that," said the Bandit.

"What if they alert the spaceport after we're on our way there?" asked Blossom.

"Then we'll improvise," said Dante.

"They won't alert the spaceport," said the Bandit with such conviction that no one challenged him.

The five of them waited in silence for almost two hours. Finally the Bandit got to his feet.

"It's time," he announced.

The others got up and followed him to the door. They took the airlift down to the main floor, then were about to walk out through the airlock when Dante stopped by the desk, spoke in low tones to the clerk, allowed the cashier to scan his retina and then rejoined the party.

"What was that all about?" asked Matilda as they emerged into the hot, oppressive Heliopolis day.

"I paid for the Bandit's room for another month."

"That was stupid," said Virgil. "He's leaving today, and who cares who knows it?"

"If two Democracy soldiers hang around waiting for him to come back, that's two less that'll be on our trail once we leave Heliopolis," answered Dante. "As for the money, I'll take it out of what we steal from the bank, or I won't need it anyway."

"I approve," said the Bandit. "That's good thinking, Rhymer." He turned to Matilda. "Are you sure you want to be part of this, ma'am? You can wait in the ship if you prefer."

"If things get rough, she'll be more help to you than I will," Dante assured him.

The Bandit shrugged. "Your choice."

The bank was two hundred yards away. The Bandit walked with an easy spring to his stride, as if he was walking down a thoroughfare on Deluros VIII or Earth itself. The others struggled to keep up with him.

"It might be best for you four to wait outside," he said when they finally arrived at their destination.

"Not unless you make it an order," said Matilda.

"It was just a suggestion. The only order is: stay behind me, and make sure none of you gets between me and anyone else."

They entered the bank, the Bandit first, then Dante and the two women, and Virgil bringing up the rear. It was a small building, tightly bonded titanium beneath a wood veneer. There were a couple of coat closets, a huge water bubbler, a quartet of chairs carved from some alien hardwood, and holograms of the bank's founders on the walls. There were three tellers—two human, one robotic—behind a counter, and a well-dressed executive in a glassed-in office. Six customers were lined up at the windows, five miners and a small, wiry, eighty-six-year-old woman—Gloria Mundi.

The Bandit waited until one of the tellers' windows was open, and then approached it.

"Yes, sir?" said the clerk, a middle-aged man. "What can I do for you?"

"You can start by emptying out the drawer in front of you," said the Bandit calmly.

"I beg your pardon?"

"This is a holdup. Give me all the money you can reach without moving your feet. Then we'll go to work on the rest."

"I know who you are," said the clerk nervously. "You work *for* Men, not against us. This is some kind of joke, right?"

Disable him now, thought Dante. *Your ten seconds are almost up!*

"Give me your money," repeated the Bandit. "I won't ask again."

Suddenly lights started flashing and alarms began ringing. Metal bars appeared where open doors and windows had been. Two screechers suddenly appeared in the robot teller's hands. The clerk whose adrenaline readings had precipitated all this ducked down behind the counter, completely out of sight.

The Bandit whirled and sent a laser burst into the robot teller. It knocked the robot back against the wall, melting one of its arms, but didn't totally disable it. Another burst took the robot's head off its body, and it collapsed to the floor.

The Bandit then fired through the barrier where the clerk was hiding, and the man's body fell over with an audible thud. Next came two holo cameras and the third teller. A laser blast just missed him, and the Bandit turned and pointed a deadly finger at the executive.

"You'll never get away with—" yelled the executive, but the Bandit's lethal arm fired again and his sentence ended with a moist gurgle.

The Bandit looked at the carnage. No one was left alive except two customers, a man and a woman.

"Get in that corner," he ordered, indicating where he wanted them to go. Finally he turned to his confederates. "All right," he said. "Start collecting the money—fast! Concentrate on Far London pounds, Maria Theresa dollars, New Stalin rubles, and other Frontier currencies. Only take credits that haven't been bundled; there are too many ways for the bank to have marked the others."

Dante and the others quickly went to the tellers' windows, removing large wads of cash from them.

Two police officers burst into the bank. The Bandit fired at one, killing him instantly. Virgil straightened up and shot the other with a screecher, firing through the teller's window.

"Where the hell's the safe?" asked Matilda, staring at the blank wall behind the windows.

Dante looked around. "It's got to be in the office." He raced into the room and couldn't spot it.

"It's a bank—it *has* to have a vault!" said Matilda.

"Of course it does," said Dante. "Let me think." He examined the office. "Something's wrong here. No one has two coat closets, not on Heliopolis II." He opened the first. Nothing but a fresh white shirt. Then he tried the second—and hit pay dirt.

"Santiago!" he called out.

"What is it?" answered the Bandit.

"Got a helluva complex lock here," said Dante. "It'll take me the better part of twenty minutes to break the code."

"Step back," said the Bandit, entering the office.

Dante stepped away from the safe. The Bandit made a swift adjustment to his arm, and then he fired—and the door to the vault simply vanished amid a cloud of acrid smoke.

"Get to work!" said Dante, racing into the vault just ahead of Matilda and Blossom.

Dante found a pair of cloth bags and tossed them to the woman. Then he quickly rummaged through the office until he found a briefcase and began filling it with cash. After about two minutes they'd emptied the vault of all its cash.

"Where are the safety-deposit boxes?" asked Matilda.

"Don't bother with them," said the Bandit.

"We need all the money we can get!" she objected.

"There's a Democracy garrison four miles east of town. It's almost certainly tied in to the alarm. They figure to be here any second. It's time to leave."

Matilda ceased her objections instantly, and raced to the door.

"No vehicle," she announced.

"I put in a call for one," said the Bandit.

"Let's hope it arrives ahead of the soldiers," said Matilda.

Dante took a quick look out the door. "No such luck."

"They're here already?" asked the Bandit, more surprised than alarmed. "They were faster than I thought."

"What are we going to do?" asked Blossom.

"Stay calm," said the Bandit. "I'll handle this."

He waited until the two military vehicles that were approaching the bank pulled to within fifty yards, then made another quick adjustment to his arm and pointed it at them—but just as he was about to fire, the male customer launched himself at the Bandit's legs, knocking him to the floor. The Bandit brought his real hand down on the back of the man's neck, a killing blow that resulted in a loud *crack!* Then he got to his feet, stood in the doorway, pointed at each vehicle in turn, and calmly blew both of them away.

"That should discourage anyone from playing the hero before our transportation arrives," he announced.

"How will they know what happened or who to blame?" asked Blossom.

"We'll tell them," answered the Bandit. He pointed at the wall behind the cashiers and carved out the name SANTIAGO with a laser beam.

"That should do the trick," agreed Dante.

The old woman spoke up for the first time. "That will fool no one," said Gloria Mundi. "I know who you are."

"I'm Santiago," said the Bandit.

"You're the One-Armed Bandit," she replied, "and I'll tell everyone I know who you are. Santiago's been dead for more than a hundred years."

"I'm sorry you feel so strongly about that, ma'am," said the Bandit regretfully. He turned to her and pointed his finger between her eyes.

"Wait!" shouted Dante,

"What is it?" asked the Bandit.

"Santiago doesn't go around killing old ladies!"

"Santiago doesn't leave witnesses who can identify him."

"She's a crazy old woman who thinks she saw God once," persisted Dante. "No one will listen to her!"

"She's a threat to our continued existence," said the Bandit. "She's got to go."

"I agree," said Matilda.

"Is that how you want it to begin?" demanded Dante. "With Santiago killing a half-crazed beggar woman?"

"How do *you* want it to begin?" she shot back as the empty airport transport pulled up, avoiding the smoking shells of the two Democracy vehicles. "With a description of each of us on file with every soldier and bounty hunter on the Inner Frontier? We need the Democracy to be searching for clues *here* while we're setting up shop in the Albion Cluster."

"This isn't the way we're supposed to start," said Dante bitterly.

"We're in the revolution business," replied Matilda. "This is a war. There are always civilian casualties."

"What war?" croaked Gloria Mundi. "You're a bunch of bank robbers, working for the One-Armed Bandit!"

"That's it," said Matilda. "We have no choice. She has to die."

"What if she promises not to tell the authorities what she saw?" asked Dante.

"Would you believe her if she *did* promise it?" asked Matilda, staring at Gloria Mundi.

"No," admitted Dante, his shoulders slumping. "No, I wouldn't."

"Well, then?"

"Damn it, Santiago doesn't kill helpless old ladies!" repeated Dante.

"I hope you don't think I *want* to do this," interjected the Bandit. "But it was you yourself who pointed out all the unpleasant choices Santiago would have to make and all the unsavory things he would have to do."

"I didn't mean *this*."

"We both know Santiago will have to do far worse things before he's done," said the Bandit.

Suddenly they heard a humming sound and turned to see the source of it. Virgil Soaring Hawk had just aimed a burst of solid light between Gloria Mundi's eyes and left a smoking hole in the middle of her forehead.

"Enough talk," said the Injun. "Let's get the hell out of here."

Not an auspicious debut, thought Dante as he stepped over the old woman's corpse and carried his briefcase out to the vehicle. *Not a promising start at all.*

20.

Candy for the billfold, candy for the nose,
Candy for the client, as the business grows.
Candy by the bushel, candy by the ton;
The Candy Man supplies it, come and share the fun!

If he had a name, no one knew it. If he had fingerprints, they had long since been burned off. If he had a retinagram on file, it was rendered meaningless when he replaced his natural eyes with a pair of artificial ones, which had the added advantage of being able to see far into the infrared.

They say he began his career out on the Rim, and later moved to the Spiral Arm. No one knew how many addicts he had created, and no one knew how much money he had made, but estimates of both were astronomical.

He began with cocaine and heroin, both grown on his own farms on the Rim, then moved to more and more exotic designer drugs and hallucinogens. He finally stopped when he got to alphanella seeds, but only because there was nothing more addictive—and expensive—in the entire galaxy.

There were warrants for the Candy Man all across the Outer Frontier, up and down the Spiral Arm, and throughout the Democracy, so it made sense that he eventually turned up on the Inner Frontier, the one place where there was no price on his head.

That lasted about three Standard months. By then he'd taken over a rival drug lord's territory, and had killed three of the enemy and a pair of the Democracy's undercover agents. There was no place left to run to, so instead of running he surrounded himself with a quasi-military operation. Only the very best, the very wealthiest clients ever got to see the Candy Man face-to-face. He rarely did his own selling, and even more rarely did his own killing. (He *did* do his own accounting, and no one in his employ ever got to see his data files.)

He divided his time among half a dozen worlds, and even his most trusted underlings never knew when and where he'd show up next. He owned an impregnable mansion on each world, and three meals a day were prepared for him at each of them, just to confound any potential assassins. As an ambitious young man on the way up, he'd taken all kinds of chances; now that he was no longer poor and no longer in such a hurry, he saw no percentage in taking any chances at all.

The Bandit and his party had never heard of the Candy Man when they touched down on Beta Cordero II. They had spent a leisurely month getting there, approaching it by a wildly circuitous route to give the crews Matilda had hired time to build what appeared to be a large, luxurious private hunting lodge. There was no way the casual, or even the acute, observer could spot the three subspace antennae, or the generator that not only supplied light and power for the lodge but for its underground computer complex. There were three guest houses; two were what they seemed, and the third was an arsenal, currently four-fifths empty but soon, they hoped, to be filled with whatever weaponry Santiago needed to accomplish his goals.

The Bandit walked quickly through the lodge, ignoring the huge living room with the four-way fireplace crafted out of shining alien stone, checked his sleeping quarters, and declared it acceptable. He then summoned Dante and Matilda to the cozy paneled room he had claimed as his private office.

"I don't see any reason to waste time," he announced. "We might as well get to work."

"Have you something in mind?" asked Dante.

"There's no sense building an organization when we can simply take one over," answered the Bandit. "Find the biggest drug and smuggling rings in the sector."

"They might not be anxious to join us," said Dante.

"They won't have a choice. You just find them; I'll handle it from there."

"Whatever you say, Santiago," replied Dante.

"You don't need me for that," said Matilda. "I think I could serve you better by contacting some of the people I know and recruiting them."

The Bandit nodded his approval. "Keep in touch," he said, dismissing her. She left the room and he turned back to Dante. "Will you need to spread any money around to find out who's in charge of each ring?"

"Almost certainly."

"Take whatever you think you'll require. We're going to get it back anyway."

"You're going to kill the leaders?" It wasn't really a question.

"My job is protecting the citizens of the Inner Frontier," replied the Bandit. "They are preying on *my* people."

"We might be able to buy them off, get them on our side," suggested Dante.

The Bandit stared at him expressionlessly. "We don't want them on our side. They're parasites, nothing more."

Which is precisely what we'll become when we take over their organizations. I wonder how you rationalize that—or does Santiago just not consider such things?

"Killing their leaders will be an object lesson to the rank and file," continued the Bandit. "No one rises to a position of authority in such an organization without being totally ruthless. This will convince them that Santiago is an even more ruthless killer. That should impress them and keep them on our side."

Why do I feel uneasy about this, wondered Dante. *This is exactly what Santiago is supposed to do, so why does it worry me when you talk about doing it?*

"That's all," said the Bandit, dismissing him. "Let me know when you have the information."

"Yes, Santiago," said Dante, getting up and leaving the office.

Matilda was waiting for him in the corridor. "Well," she said as they walked past a number of holograms of savage alien animals to the living room, "what do you think?"

"About what?"

"About *him*," said Matilda. "He's growing into the role exactly as we'd hoped."

"If you say so."

"You don't think so?"

He shrugged. "I don't know."

"What's bothering you?" she asked.

"I can't put my finger on it," said Dante.

"He was right to want to kill the old woman, you know," said Matilda. "It would have been suicide to have left her behind."

"There were alternatives."

"What? Take her along for a month and then turn her loose? She'd still have betrayed us."

"Nonsense," he replied irritably. "All he had to do was turn to me or Virgil, address us as Santiago, and ask if we wanted him to do anything else."

She stared at him, surprised. "Hey, that's not bad."

"Yeah—but *he* didn't think of it."

"Not everyone's as devious as you are."

"You asked, I answered." He paused. "Also, he really gets into giving orders. The 'misters' and 'ma'ams' vanished pretty fast."

"He's Santiago. It's his job to give orders."

"I know, I know—but good manners ought to last a little longer."

"He's adaptable. And he's a born leader. Look at his decision to rob the bank, and burn Santiago's name into the wall. Look at the other ideas he's had." She paused. "What does he want you to do?"

"Find the biggest smugglers and drug runners in the sector."

"Whom he'll then proceed to kill?"

Dante nodded. "And take over their operations."

"Isn't that precisely the kind of thing that Santiago is supposed to do?"

"I suppose so. I just don't like it."

"That's why you're the Rhymer and he's Santiago."

"Probably you're right," he said.

"Then let's get going," said Matilda. "We both have work to do."

Dante sought out Virgil and handed him a wad of credits and Maria Theresa dollars.

"What's this for?" asked the Injun.

"The best drugs you can buy."

"That's my job?" asked Virgil with a happy smile. "I could really get into working for this guy."

"Just buy them, don't take them," said Dante.

"I'm ambidextrous," said Virgil. "I can do both."

"You heard me," said Dante firmly. "Buy it, and see if you can find out who sells it."

"The guy I buy it from."

"Find out who he works for, as high up the line as you can go."

"But I can't take any of the drugs?"

"That's right."

"This fucking scheme was a lot better when it just had *me* thinking about it," muttered Virgil.

"And let me know where you're going, so we don't visit the same worlds."

"You're buying drugs too?"

"That doubles our chances of finding the headman."

"Do you get to take any?"

"You can have mine when this is all over and we've got our man," said Dante disgustedly.

Virgil grinned. "That's more like it!" he said, and headed off toward the newly poured slab that housed all their ships.

Dante stopped by his room, packed a small bag, made sure he had enough money left, and then walked to the tiny landing slab. He fired up the pile on a one-man ship, climbed into it, had the navigational computer throw up a globe of the sector and its populated worlds, and decided on Alabaster, about sixteen light-years distant. He radioed his destination to Virgil to make sure they didn't both visit the same planet, and then took off. He hit the stratosphere about ninety seconds later, then jumped to light speeds.

He slept through most of the voyage, and awoke when the ship's computer told him he was in orbit around Alabaster. The world was almost totally covered in the fleecy white clouds that gave it its name. The ship turned over control of its functions to the spaceport's landing tower, and touched down without incident.

Dante emerged, passed through Customs, and caught a subterranean monorail that took him into the underground city of Snakepit. There were too many cyclones and tornadoes on the surface, so Man had built this commercial outpost where none of the planet's weather could bother him.

Snakepit extended about two miles in each direction. Since the planet had never been inhabited by a sentient race, the native quarter— the exclusive domain of offworld non-Men—was a little smaller and more upscale than usual. There were a number of banks—all far more heavily guarded than the one on Heliopolis II—and the usual array of traders, assay offices, hotels, brothels, casinos, restaurants, subspace stations, holo theaters, and permanent residences.

Dante checked into a hotel and then decided to take a look around and get the feel of the place. The first building he passed was a grocery selling fruits from Pollux IV, vegetables from Greenveldt and Sunnyblue, mutated beef from Alpha Bezerine IV, even some wine from distant Altagore.

He continued walking, came to a grubby bar, and entered it. He studied the faces he found there. These weren't the hard men who traveled the Frontier, living by their wits and their skills. These men weren't traveling anywhere, and such skills as they had once possessed were long gone.

You're the bottom of the food chain. There will be too many connections between you and the man I'm after.

He turned and left, ignoring the catcalls that followed him, then began looking into store windows until he found one that sold formal wear. He went in, purchased the finest outfit they had, waited while the robot tailor shortened the sleeves and took in the waist, then returned to his hotel and napped until dinnertime.

Then he donned the formal outfit, changed some of his larger bills at the hotel desk so that his roll of money would look even bigger, and had the desk clerk direct him to the most expensive restaurant in Snakepit. He wasn't very hungry, and found the food mediocre and overpriced, but he stayed long enough to be seen by a goodly number of people. Then, after he paid his bill with cash, flashing his huge roll of money, he went off to the Golden Flush, the most expensive casino in town.

He made quite a production of peeling bills off his roll to bet at the craps table, broke even after half an hour, then wandered over to the *jabob* table (the one alien game that had taken hold in the Frontier's casinos), and dropped a quick fifty thousand credits.

Next he went to the men's room, ostensibly to rinse his face off, actually because it was the most private spot in the casino and the one where he was most likely to be approached. And sure enough, a blond man with almost colorless blue eyes followed him in.

"I saw you at the tables," he said.

There was a long silence. Dante wasn't going to make it any easier on the man. He'd sell harder if Dante offered him no encouragement.

He hadn't asked any questions, so Dante offered no reply.

"You look like a man with money to spend," continued the man. "You ever spend it on anything besides the tables?"

"From time to time," replied Dante.

"How about tonight?"

Dante finished wiping off his face, then turned to the blond man. "The only thing I buy is seed, and I don't buy it from flunkies."

"I'm no flunky!" said the man angrily.

"Bullshit," said Dante. "I can smell a flunky a mile off. You go tell your boss I'll make a buy, but only from him."

The man seemed to be considering his answer, and whether to admit that he even had a boss. Finally he said: "He doesn't deal with the customers."

Dante pulled his wad out. "I've got two million credits here. I have another million Maria Theresa dollars back on my ship. I'm going to spend it on seed. Now, I can spend it with your boss, or I can buy it from someone else, it makes no difference to me." He paused. "But it'll make a difference to you, because I'll pass the word that you're the reason I went elsewhere."

"Maybe I'll just kill you and take your money," said the man menacingly as he stepped closer and loomed over the much smaller Dante.

"Just how dumb do you think I am?" said Dante, allowing his contempt to creep into his voice. "See this diamond stickpin I'm wearing? It's a miniaturized holo camera. Your face, your voiceprint, everything you've said since you came in here are already in half a dozen computers."

It was a lie, but told with utter conviction, and the blond man hesitated uneasily. "Why should I believe you?" he demanded.

"Because we're alone in a bathroom on your turf, and if it wasn't true I'd be inviting you to blow me away. Is everyone in your organization as stupid as you?"

"You call me stupid once more and I'll kill you, camera or no camera!" snarled the blond man.

Don't push it too hard. These guys shoot first and ask questions later.

"Okay, we're at an impasse. I've got millions to spend, your boss has millions to unload. You know I won't deal with anyone else. Do you take me to him, or do I spend my money somewhere else? It's getting late; I need a decision."

The blond man frowned. Finally he said: "It may take a while to reach him."

"That's not my problem. All he has to know is that my name is Dante Alighieri, and I'm staying at the Cheshire Hotel. He can find me there." He walked to the door, then turned back to the man. "I'm leaving in the morning. If I don't hear from him by then, I won't be back."

He walked out of the men's room without waiting for a reply, kept walking past the bar and tables of the Golden Flush, and didn't stop until he reached his suite at the Cheshire a few minutes later. Then he considered his situation. By now they'd checked out his identity and his ship's registration. They wouldn't be able to find out where he got his money, but they'd be able to assure themselves that he was who he said he was, that he wasn't a Democracy undercover agent. It would take a few hours for the man to round up some muscle and come to the hotel. He had time to get out of his uncomfortable formal outfit, take a quick Dryshower, and get into his regular clothes.

He finished dressing and had spent the next two hours hovering a few inches above the floor on a form-adapt chair, staring out his window at the city, watching the artificial lights play on the rough underground walls, when the Spy-Eye alerted him that he had visitors and showed him holograms of the seven humans who were standing at the door to the suite. He ordered it to open, then had his chair turn until he was facing his visitors.

The muscle entered first. What surprised him was that the muscle that seemed to be in charge were both women. They were hard-featured, hard-muscled, hard-eyed, and heavily armed, one with long auburn hair, the other with short blond hair, otherwise almost identical. They and the four men spread out and began searching the suite, examining it for hidden microphones, hidden cameras, hidden killers. Finally, satisfied, they stood aside and a stocky man entered with them. He was dressed in colorful silks and satins out of a previous, more spectacular galactic era, and he wore a hat with a huge feather in it, which he soon took off, revealing a colorfully tattooed bald head.

"Allow me to introduce myself," he said, showing no inclination to offer an exquisitely gloved hand. "I am known as the Candy Man."

"Pleased to meet you," said Dante.

"Are you really?" asked the Candy Man. "In fact, why are you meeting me at all? You were told I don't deal directly with the customers."

"And I told your man I don't deal with flunkies."

"Of course you do. Every single time."

"And yet here you are."

"You act like a rich, foolish man, Mr. Alighieri, and yet based on what my associate told me, you are not foolish at all. Since you seem to be pretending to be something you are not, I thought we should meet. I just happened to be on Alabaster today"—he stared hard at Dante—"or did you already know that?"

"All I know is that I came here to buy some seed. How much can you supply?"

"Subtlety is not among your virtues, Mr. Alighieri," said the Candy Man.

I'm glad you think so. I must be a better liar than even I thought.

"I'm in a hurry. Have you got any seed, or am I wasting my time?"

"I have more than you could use in half a dozen lifetimes," said the Candy Man.

"Prime?"

"The best."

"That's what they all say," replied Dante.

"You show me the color of your money, I'll show you the color of my seed."

"Money is my other favorite subject," said Dante. "How much are we talking about?"

"How many seeds are we talking about?" shot back the Candy Man.

"Fifty now, more later."

"You'd better go easy on them, Mr. Alighieri. Use them up in less than half a Standard year and there won't be any later."

"How I use them is *my* business," said Dante irritably. "Yours is selling them to me, and you can't do that without naming a price."

"For fifty? Are we talking credits, or New Stalin rubles, or . . . ?"

"Whatever you want."

"Most of my clients use credits," said the Candy Man. "Fifty seed will cost you two and a half million."

"You've got to be kidding!" exclaimed Dante.

"Do I look like I'm kidding?"

"I can get fifty prime seeds for an even million on Beta Cordero II!"

"Nobody lives on Beta Cordero II."

"Somebody does now."

"And they're selling seed at fifty for a million?" demanded the Candy Man.

"Right. Are you going to match their price, or am I going to walk?"

"Walk if you want, Mr. Alighieri, but I guarantee you won't be dealing with anyone on Beta Cordero II."

"Why not?" said Dante.

"Because I don't take kindly to people poaching in my sector. When I'm done with them, Beta Cordero II will be unpopulated again."

"Maybe this guy is thinking of coming to Alabaster and taking over *your* operation," said Dante. "It makes no difference to me, as long as I get my seed."

The Candy Man threw back his head and laughed. "I like your sense of humor, Mr. Alighieri! I'm so well protected that not even Santiago himself could lay a finger on me."

Dante returned his smile. "Not even Santiago?" he repeated. "That must be a comforting thought."

He was still smiling when the Candy Man went off to plot his next move against his newest rival.

21.

One is the Blade, one is the Knife,
One takes your money, one takes your life.
They're never alone, they're never apart,
Stay on your guard or they'll cut out your heart.

Dante followed the Candy Man's female bodyguards—one tall and auburn-haired, one tall and blond—down the streets of Snakepit until they stopped at an elegant restaurant. He waited to make sure they were there to eat rather than extort money or perhaps meet their boss, and then he entered and approached their table.

"Good evening," he said. "We met briefly at my hotel last night. May I join you?"

Their expressions said they'd just as soon kill him as look at him.

"I just want to talk to you for a few minutes," he said. "Tell you what: if you don't like what I have to say, I'll pay for dinner."

They exchanged glances, and then the auburn-haired one nodded her assent.

"Sit," she said.

"Thank you." Dante pulled up a chair and sat down.

"What do you want?" said the blonde.

"I told you: I want to talk to you."

"You'd better make it good," said the blonde. "You've already lied to the Candy Man."

"Me?" said Dante, surprised. "About what?"

"You've never chewed a seed in your life."

"Why would you say something like that?" asked Dante with mock indignation.

"Because they were delivered to you this morning, and you're still clear-eyed and clearheaded," she said. "No seed chewer in the galaxy could go all day without chewing one, and once they do that, they're in their own world for days."

"I have excellent self-control."

A waiter approached, and the blonde waved him away. He bowed obsequiously and went off to serve a table at the far end of the restaurant.

The auburn-haired woman suddenly laid a screecher on the table next to her fork. "If you lie one more time, Mr. Alighieri, I'm going to kill you right here, right now. I assure you this is not an idle threat. Now tell us why you are here."

"What makes you think—?" he began, and her hand closed on the sonic pistol. He stopped and sighed. "I followed you here because I want to talk a little business with you."

"And you've never chewed a seed, have you?"

"No, I never have."

"All right, Mr. Alighieri," said the blonde. "You have a business proposition for us. We're listening."

"If we don't like what we hear," added the auburn-haired one, "we can always kill you later."

"Just relax," said Dante. "You're going to want to thank me, not kill me."

"I hope so for your sake," said the blonde.

"Before I begin, I'd feel much more comfortable if I knew your names," said Dante. They exchanged glances again. "How can it hurt?"

"I'm the Knife," said the blonde. She gestured to her partner. "She's the Blade. That's all you have to know."

"Interesting sobriquets," commented Dante.

"Get on with it," said the Blade impatiently.

"All right," said Dante. "Let me begin by saying that the Candy Man has an impressive organization, not the least of which are you two."

"Flattery will get you nowhere," said the Blade.

"Except an early death," chimed in the Knife. "Now either tell us what you came to tell us or we'll kill you."

He stared at them. They had lovely faces, but there was no compassion in them, no trace of mercy at all. These ladies were not ambivalent about killing.

"As I was saying, the Candy Man has a good organization, as well he should. He's the biggest fish in a small pond—but a bigger fish has come to the Frontier. Not to put too fine a point on it, your boss's days are numbered."

"Explain," said the Knife.

"Santiago has set up shop in this sector. It's as simple as that. Your boss is a walking dead man."

"Santiago?" repeated the Knife, frowning. "What are you talking about?"

"Santiago has been dead for centuries!" added the Blade.

"A popular misconception," replied Dante. "He's alive, he's nearby, and he will not tolerate any competition. His organization dwarfs what the Candy Man's set up, and he's getting more powerful every day. You wouldn't believe some of the people who've joined him."

"Like who?" said the Knife dubiously.

"Like Waltzin' Matilda. Like Dimitrios of the Three Burners. Like the Rough Rider." He paused after each name for it to sink in, then added the clincher. "Like the One-Armed Bandit."

The Blade looked impressed. The Knife looked dubious. "If he's got all that firepower, why did he send *you*?" she demanded. "In fact, why are we still alive?"

"That's what I'm here to discuss with you."

"Why we're alive?"

"Why he's allowing you to live," said Dante. "There's a reason. Would you like to hear it?"

"We're listening," said the Blade.

"Santiago's got his fingers in a thousand pies on ten thousand worlds," said Dante. "He can't be bothered with the day-to-day operation of one obscure little drug ring that only covers half a dozen systems."

Suddenly the Knife's eyes widened.

Good, thought Dante. *You've figured it out.*

"Are you suggesting he wants *us* to take it over?" she said.

"He prefers to promote from within," said the poet. "Who knows the clientele and the routes better than you? Who can defend it better while he's occupied elsewhere?"

"Why doesn't he try to buy off the Candy Man?"

"Because it would be a demotion for the Candy Man, a step down no matter how you cut it. He couldn't help but be resentful, and a resentful partner isn't a loyal one. Santiago demands absolute loyalty from his partners." He paused while the words sank in. "But it wouldn't be a step down for you two. There'd be more money, more authority, more autonomy."

There was a moment of silence.

"What's he offering?" asked the Blade at last.

"Half—which is a hell of a lot more than you're making now," Dante pointed out. "I should add that we have a man who will audit you regularly. Santiago has no use for people who try to cheat him."

"Half?" repeated the Blade.

"Half," agreed Dante.

"Just for standing aside while Santiago kills the Candy Man?"

"He's going to want a little more than that as a token of your good faith," said Dante.

"Oh?" said the Knife suspiciously.

"He wants to know that you're fully committed to him and his organization," said Dante.

The Knife looked blank, but not the Blade. "Are you telling me he wants *us* to kill the Candy Man!"

"That's right."

"What's to stop us from killing the Candy Man and *not* splitting with anyone?" asked the Knife.

"You wouldn't live out the day," said Dante, amazed that he could lie with such absolute conviction. He leaned forward. "You're looking at it all wrong. Join him and you'll be millionaires within a Standard month, and you'll have the protection of Santiago's galaxy-wide organization if you should ever need it. As long as you're Santiago's partners, no outsider will ever be able to do to you what you're going to do to the Candy Man."

"What about insiders?" asked the Blade. "There will be people who already work for the Candy Man who may think *they* should be running things."

"This is a test of your leadership abilities," said Dante. "If you can take this organization over and run it successfully, Santiago will help you go on to bigger and better things."

The Blade picked up her screecher and tucked it back in her belt, then stood up.

"We have to discuss this. In private."

"I can wait outside for you," said Dante.

"That won't be necessary." She turned to her blond companion. "Come on."

The Knife got up and followed her to the women's bathroom while Dante ordered a Cygnian cognac. He had just about finished it when they returned and sat down opposite him.

"All right," said the Blade. "It's a deal."

Dante looked at the Knife. "Yeah," she said, "it's a deal."

"Fine. I think you've made a wise decision. You'd gone as far as you could with the Candy Man. You'll advance much farther with Santiago."

"So now you'll tell Santiago we're in business?"

"No."

"No?" demanded the Blade.

"He'll know it when he hears that the Candy Man is dead," said Dante.

They finished the meal, and Dante returned to his hotel. The next morning the entire city was abuzz with the news that the Candy Man had been murdered.

Dante paid for his room, went to the spaceport, and was soon on his way to Valhalla. He contacted the Bandit en route and told him what had transpired.

"Amazing!" said the Bandit.

"What are you referring to, sir?"

"They actually believed you, without any proof to support what you said. You must be one hell of an accomplished liar."

"Well, I *am* a poet, sir," replied Dante.

22.

Jackrabbit Willowby, lightning fast,
Built an empire made to last;
Sold his soul for works of art—
Fast he was, but not too smart.

Jackrabbit Willowby had never actually seen a jackrabbit. In fact, he'd never been within sixty thousand light-years of Earth. But he knew that the jackrabbit was one of the very few animals that wasn't extinct more than three millennia after the dawn of the Galactic Era, and that it survived because of its fecundity. Willowby himself had forty-three children from thirty-six mothers, all of which he neglected, and took his name from that prolific animal.

He didn't have an abundance of virtues. He was an agent of the Democracy, in charge of monitoring the black market in a fifty-world sector that included Beta Cordero II. He was in charge of close to a thousand men spread across those worlds, ready to respond to his commands.

In most cases, those commands were exactly what the Democracy wanted—but in a few cases they were not. Willowby and a handful of carefully chosen confederates were happy to look the other way for a consideration, which averaged some twenty-five percent of the black marketeer's take. They afforded the very best protection, and no one who dealt with them ever had cause to regret it. Similarly, those few that they approached who chose not to deal with them soon found themselves serving long jail terms or else were mourned by their friends.

Willowby developed a taste for expensive works of art, which led him to expand his operation, reaching more and more worlds, even those not officially under his control, finding new routes for contraband material, and protecting those routes with the full force of the Democracy. Before too many years had passed he was worth tens of millions of credits, and none of his employees had any cause for complaint. He understood the need to keep them all happy—and loyal—and while his crew was far from the most honest on the Inner Frontier, they were unquestionably the wealthiest and most contented.

He had only one rule: no one retired. He wanted his team to work in the shadow of the gallows until the day each of them died. He never wanted any to lose contact, or feel they could make their own deal with the Democracy and supply evidence against their confederates. You could get filthy rich working for Willowby, but that was the price you paid—there was no end to it. Most of his employees had no problem with that. The few who did didn't live long enough to cause any serious complications.

Dante had heard rumors about Willowby, and he knew it was just a matter of time before he showed up and made his pitch. The sudden death of the Candy Man could only hurry the day, and Dante was anxious for the meeting to take place.

"We don't want anything to do with him," said the Bandit when Dante brought up the subject. "He works for the Democracy. That makes him the enemy."

"True," answered the poet. "But this one has a ready-made organization that could bring in fifty times what we're going to make from the Candy Man's operation."

"If we deal with enough Democracy members, we'll be no different than they are," insisted the Bandit.

"I think you're looking at it all wrong, sir," said Dante. "If we can put Willowby to work for us, or somehow take over his organization, we'll be plundering him of millions every week, money that would eventually be spent or invested in the Democracy. Think of the good we could do with that money! Think of the hospitals it could build."

"You're getting ahead of yourself," said the Bandit. "First we need a Frontier-wide organization. *Then* we'll worry about hospitals and everything else."

"Even the original Santiago didn't have that big an organization," said Dante. "He just made it *seem* like he did."

"What good are hospitals and schools and whatever else you want if I can't defend them?"

"It's not what *I* want," protested Dante. "It's what *we* want. And it's not just hospitals and schools. Hell, there's two hundred alien races living in fear and poverty out here on the Frontier. They need our help."

The Bandit stared at him, seemed about to reply, then decided to remain silent.

"So can I tell the Knife and the Blade to send Willowby here if he starts making any inquiries?" continued Dante.

"Yes," said the Bandit.

"Alone, I presume?" said Dante. "Or just with his personal muscle?"

"Whatever makes him happy," said the Bandit. "It makes no difference to me."

Dante leaned back and relaxed. He'd been half afraid that the Bandit had planned to kill Willowby, and while he had no moral problem with killing the enemy, it made a lot more sense to coopt this one and leave him in place. The Candy Man worked just a handful of systems, really just six planets, and the Knife and the Blade knew all of his contacts. But from everything Dante had been able to learn, Jackrabbit Willowby's organization encompassed hundreds, perhaps thousands, of worlds, and if they killed him, there'd be no way they could keep his organization intact, or even find out who belonged to it.

Dante spent the next two days working on his epic, reworking the verses, honing the language, making lists of the colorful characters he'd heard about that he wanted to meet and include in the text.

Then Virgil checked in, stoned out of his mind. He'd found the drugs, which was admittedly the easy part of his assignment, but he couldn't remember where he'd gotten them or who he'd purchased them from. Dante checked the computer log of Virgil's ship, found out that the Indian had visited Nestor III, Lower Volta, and New Waco, and decided to send Blossom off to see if she could find out where Virgil had purchased his drugs, and from whom.

"And don't be a hero," he cautioned her. "We've already got one, and he'll handle any dangerous situation."

"We're *all* heroes, Rhymer," she said adamantly. "Everyone who fights the Democracy is a hero."

"Let's keep it to ourselves," said Dante. "The less people who think we're heroes, the less often we'll have to prove it. Remember: what we're doing only works as long as the Democracy thinks we're outlaws. Once they figure out what we're really about, that's the end of Santiago and everyone who has anything to do with him . . . so just make some *very* discreet inquiries, try not to call any attention to yourself, and then come back with whatever information you can get."

"Why should I listen to *you*?" she demanded. "I work for Santiago."

"And I speak for him," said Dante.

"I thought you were supposed to be a poet."

"I am. Don't make me write about how you turned Santiago down the first time he needed you."

She considered his remark, and finally nodded her assent. "But next time I want to hear it direct from *him*."

"All right, next time you will."

She left, and Dante spent another half hour working on his poem until he was summoned to the Bandit's office.

"What's up?" he asked upon arriving.

"I just heard from the Blade. Jackrabbit Willowby is on his way to Valhalla."

"Alone?"

The Bandit smiled. "Hardly."

"What is that supposed to mean?"

"He's coming with a little display of force to impress me."

"How little?"

"Twenty men, maybe twenty-five."

"I'm impressed already," said Dante. "Where do we put them all?"

"I'll meet them outside," answered the Bandit. "I might as well show them I have nothing to hide."

"You can meet them there, but you'll want to deal privately with Willowby in your office. You don't want anyone else to hear your negotiations. You might have to get tough with him."

"Don't worry," said the Bandit. "I just want them all to see me, since they're going to be dealing with me from now on."

Dante shrugged. "Okay, if you're sure that's the way you want to do it."

"I'm sure."

Dante waited in his quarters until he heard Willowby's ship approaching the landing strip. He looked out a window as it came into view and soon settled gently on the slab.

Twenty men emerged from the ship and formed two lines. Five more climbed out, went to the end of the lines, and fanned out, ready to handle trouble from any direction.

Then, after a wait of perhaps three minutes, Jackrabbit Willowby came out of the hatch and climbed down to the ground. He was a short man, elegantly dressed, and he moved with an athletic grace. Dante couldn't spot any weapons on him, but then, with all those bodyguards, he didn't need any.

Dante noticed that everyone's attention was directed toward the lodge. He turned and saw that the Bandit had walked out the front of the compound and was approaching Willowby.

Six of Willowby's men moved to form a living wall between them. The Bandit came to a stop and looked expectantly at Willowby.

"Good day, sir," said Willowby, parting the men with his arms and stepping forward to stand between them. "To whom do I have the pleasure of speaking?"

"You know who I am," said the Bandit.

"They told me your name was Santiago, but that is either a joke or a lie."

"I'd be careful who I called a liar, Jackrabbit Willowby."

"You see?" said Willowby. "You know *my* name. It's only fair that I should know yours."

"You do," said the Bandit. "My name is Santiago."

One of the men walked over and whispered something to Willowby.

"I'm told that you are actually the One-Armed Bandit."

"You've been misinformed. I am Santiago." The Bandit stared at his visitor. "Are we going to spend all afternoon arguing about my name, or do you have some reason for being here?"

"You're a very brave man, to speak to me like that when I'm surrounded by my men."

"You haven't answered me."

"Of course I have a reason for being here," said Willowby. "You deal in contraband materials. I work for the Democracy."

"So you're here to arrest me?"

"Putting you in jail won't do either of us any good," replied Willowby easily. "I'm here to negotiate a fine with you."

"A fine?"

"If I put you out of business, someone would just replace you next week or next month, the jails would have one more mouth to feed, and what purpose would be served? Let's be totally honest: there is a continuing demand for the goods you sell. *Someone* is going to satisfy it; it might as well be you."

"I'd call that very reasonable of you," said the Bandit.

"I can see we understand each other," said Willowby with a smile. "How does twenty-five percent sound to you?"

The Bandit seemed to be considering the offer for a moment. Finally he shook his head. "No, that's not enough."

Willowby looked confused. "Not enough?" he repeated.

"I think a third makes more sense."

"You'd rather pay me a third than a quarter?"

"No," said the Bandit. "*You're* going to pay *me* a third."

"What are you talking about?"

"I want a third of your business. Give it to me and you can leave here alive."

"Are you crazy?" snapped Willowby. "I've got twenty-five men with me!"

"You mean these men?" asked the Bandit, waving an arm in their direction. As he pointed, a laser beam shot out of his finger and mowed them down before they knew what was happening. The last seven or eight had time to reach for their weapons, but the beam was replaced by an exploding energy ball, and an instant later Willowby was the only member of his party still standing.

"Who *are* you?" he demanded.

"I told you: my name is Santiago. And you are a member of the Democracy. That's all I need to know."

The Bandit pointed a deadly finger at him, and an instant later Willowby fell to the ground, dead.

"That was stupid!" yelled Dante, rushing over to join the Bandit. "I told you—we needed his organization!"

"He worked for the Democracy," said the Bandit calmly. "The Democracy is our enemy."

"You were always going to kill him, weren't you?"

"That's what Santiago does to his enemies."

"Yeah, well, Santiago could use his brain every now and then!" snapped Dante. "You've cost us billions. *Billions!*"

"I don't deal with the enemy."

"Then next time let me!"

The Bandit turned to him, and for just an instant Dante thought he was going to aim his lethal arm at him.

"You're a poet. Go write your poems. I'm Santiago. Let me handle my business in my own way—and don't ever stand between me and the enemy." He turned to one of the men who had run out of the house. "One of them is still alive. The fifth from the left."

"You want me to finish him off, Santiago?" asked the man.

"No," said the Bandit. "If I'd wanted him dead, I'd have killed him myself. Treat his wounds, drop him off on some colony world, and make sure he knows that it was Santiago who did this. Let him pass the word about what happens to anyone who stands against me." He turned to Dante. "Does that meet with your approval?"

"Hell, no!" said the poet bitterly. "What the fuck does *he* know about running an organization that spans a hundred worlds?" He tried to control his temper. "If you were going to let someone live, why not Willowby? He'd have been just as impressed as that poor bastard."

"Yes, he would have," agreed the Bandit. "And next time he'd have sent two hundred men, or five hundred, or a thousand, and he'd have stayed away until it was over. He'd never give me another chance at him once he knew what I could do, and he couldn't let me live after I'd grabbed a third of his empire. If he'd shown any weakness of resolve, his own men would have been dividing the rest of his business."

"You could have negotiated," complained Dante. "Ten percent would still have been worth hundreds of millions."

"You don't negotiate with officers of the Democracy," said the Bandit coldly. "You kill them."

"But he was a *corrupt* officer, damn it! We could have reached an accommodation."

"They're *all* corrupt," said the Bandit, turning and heading back to the compound. "This conversation is over."

Dante watched him walk away.

Maybe you're right. Maybe you can't deal with representatives of the Democracy, even thoroughly corrupt ones. But damn it, you sounded a lot more reasonable when you were still just the One-Armed Bandit.

23.

Come inside the Blixtor Maze;
Spend your money, spend your days.
Nameless pleasures lie in wait—
Come along and meet your fate.

The Blixtor Maze was the brainchild of an alien architect named Blixtor. No one was quite sure what race he belonged to. Some said he was a Canphorite, but others said no, the Maze wasn't rational enough to have been created by a native of Canphor VI or VII, that he must be a native of Lodin XI. Still others said it was actually created by a human, but that his computer had crashed and he'd given up on the project, and other races built it based on what they could reconstruct from his shattered modules and memory crystals.

This much is known: no one ever succeeded in mapping the Blixtor Maze. It was said that parts of it went off into the fourth dimension, and other parts were so complex that not even a theoretical mathematician could explain them. It was approximately one mile square. No one knew how many levels there were. The only thing that was certain was that no one had ever walked from one end to the other in less than a week, and even homing wolves, those remarkable domesticated creatures from Valos XI, were unable to retrace their steps.

It took four centuries to build the Maze on the isolated world of Nandi III. Legend has it that the original Maze was to be four miles on a side, but two crews got lost and starved to death. Nobody believed it—until they tried to find their way out of the Maze. There were some who felt the Maze was constantly moving, or rotating in and out of known dimensions, because you could wander into an antiquarian chart shop or a drug den, and when you walked out the same door nothing was where it had been. Further, if you had left something behind, you could turn and attempt to go back and retrieve it, only to find that the establishment you thought was two paces behind you was nowhere to be seen.

There were no warning signs as you approached the Maze, because the authorities operated on the reasonable assumption that you wouldn't be on Nandi III if you didn't have business there. Far from banning weapons, visitors were encouraged to enter the Maze heavily armed, since no lawman or bounty hunter was likely to respond to any entreaties coming from within the Maze. All laws were suspended the moment you took your first step inside the Maze. Murder was no longer a crime; neither were any of a hundred other actions that could get you executed or incarcerated in the Democracy, or the half dozen that were still illegal across most of the Inner Frontier.

Dante was unsurprised to learn that Virgil was guilty of at least three of them. He was contacted by Blue Peter, who explained that Virgil was being held inside the Maze, that a group of permanent residents had him under what passed for house arrest, and that it was going to take a guide to find him and a lot of money to bail him out.

"How did *you* get out?" asked Dante over the subspace radio.

"The Maze spit me out," answered the alien. "It didn't want me."

"It spit you out?" repeated Dante.

"Come to Nandi," said Blue Peter. "It'll make more sense once you see it."

Two days later the Bandit's ship touched down at the Nandi spaceport. He and Dante passed through Customs—both used false IDs and passports—and took a room in a run-down hotel that was fifty yards from the entrance to the Maze.

Blue Peter was waiting for them.

"I'm glad you got here," he said. "Who knows what they're doing to him?"

"Whatever they're doing, he's probably so grogged up on bad booze and worse drugs that he's totally unaware of it," said the Bandit.

"Shouldn't we go get him?" asked Blue Peter as the Bandit walked into the hotel's restaurant.

"First we'll eat dinner," answered the Bandit. "We'll leave our gear here, get a good night's sleep, and go after him in the morning." He paused. "And tonight, before we're through eating, you'll tell us what you know about the Blixtor Maze."

"Nothing," said the alien. "Well, almost nothing."

"How could it spit you out?" asked Dante.

"That might be the wrong term," admitted Blue Peter. "I hid in this warehouse right across the street from the jail where they were holding Virgil. I planned to wait until it was dark and then see if I could break him out." He paused. "When the sun set, I waited an hour and then I stepped out, ready to cross the street—and somehow I wasn't facing the jail. In fact, I wasn't even in the Maze. I was standing on the road that borders the north side of the Maze. I looked for the door I'd come through, but there was nothing but a solid wall for hundreds of yards." He smiled an odd alien smile. "The Maze didn't want me. That's when I knew I'd have to contact you if he was ever to get out of there."

"I can see the entrance to the Maze from the front of the hotel," said the Bandit. "Can you find him if we go through it?"

"Yes," said Blue Peter. Then, "No." Finally, "Maybe."

"Explain."

"It's never the same twice," said the blue alien. "If it's the way it was the last time Virgil and I entered it, and nothing inside the Maze has changed, I can find it—but the odds against that are thousands to one. I've been in the Maze a dozen times, and it's never been the same twice. I've talked to people who live in the Maze, who have been there for years, and they never know what they'll see when they walk out their front door."

"How do they keep finding their front door when it's time to go home?" asked Dante.

"Oh, if the Maze wants you to find something, you will," Blue Peter assured him. "It might even move things around just to accommodate you."

"You make it sound sentient."

"It's not sentient—I mean, how could it be?—but it's tricky as hell."

The Bandit stared at him for a moment, then walked to a table and called up the menu. The other two joined him, and they ate the meal in total silence.

"I'll see you in the morning," said the Bandit when he was through. He got to his feet. "Sunrise, right here."

He left and headed toward the airlift as Dante turned to Blue Peter.

"Just what the hell was Virgil doing that got him incarcerated?" asked the poet. "From what I know of this world, I'd have thought nothing was illegal. Certainly it couldn't just have been drugs."

"It wasn't."

"Well, then?"

The alien looked at him for a long moment. "I don't think I'm going to tell you."

"Why not?"

"Because you will want to work with him again, and if I told you, you might leave him here forever."

"It was that bad?"

"Let us say that it was that *unusual*."

"Were you involved?"

"I think I've told you everything that I'm going to tell you," said Blue Peter. "Good night, Rhymer. I'll see you in the morning."

"What's your room number?"

"This hotel is for humans only," said the alien with no sign of bitterness. "I am staying a few blocks away."

"See you in the morning, then," said Dante as Blue Peter left the restaurant and walked out the front door of the hotel. He spent a few minutes sitting at the table, staring at his empty wineglass and trying to imagine what new perversion Virgil had discovered. Finally he got up and went off to his room.

His bed woke him gently just before sunrise, as he had instructed it to do, and he showered and dressed quickly, then went down to the restaurant. He decided he couldn't stand the smell of food that early in the day, so he sat in the lobby and waited for the Bandit to finish. Blue Peter joined him a moment later, and the two of them sat, half asleep, until the Bandit emerged from the restaurant.

"Okay," he said. "Let's go get him."

The three of them went out into the cool dry air of Nandi III, turned right, and rode the slidewalk past a row of low angular buildings to the entrance to the Maze.

"This is it?" asked the Bandit.

"That's right," said Blue Peter.

"If everything moves around, how are we going to find him?" asked the Bandit.

"We'll hire a guide."

"A guide? You mean someone knows his way around the Maze?"

"It's not that simple," began Blue Peter.

"Somehow it never is," interjected Dante dryly.

"There is an alien race, almost extinct now, that can usually find what you're looking for. Not always, but usually. Rumor has it that they were imported to Nandi III centuries ago to help build it. These are their descendants. No one knows what world they originally came from."

"Can they find their way back out?" asked the Bandit.

"Frequently."

"How do we make contact with one?"

"We'll just enter the Maze," answered the alien. "They'll start contacting us."

"What do they look like?"

"They're humanoid," said Blue Peter. "Perhaps four feet tall. Covered with fur. Their colors differ markedly from one to the next."

"Has the race got a name?"

"Probably," said Blue Peter. "I mean, all races have names, don't they? Inside the Maze, though, we call them Lab Rats, since they're the only ones who can find their way around with any degree of accuracy."

"Lab Rats?" said Dante with a smile.

"Your face just lit up," said Blue Peter. "You're going to use them in your poem, aren't you?"

"How could I not write about a race known as the Lab Rats?" responded Dante.

The Bandit stared at the entrance, which was a broad archway.

"We just walk in, right?" he asked.

"That's right."

"Okay, let's get on with it."

He strode forward, and Dante and the alien fell into step behind him. Ten feet into the Maze he stopped and looked behind him.

"The entrance is still there," he noted.

"Yes, it is," agreed Blue Peter.

"Maybe you were exaggerating a little bit?"

"I wasn't," said the alien adamantly.

They followed the street for fifty yards, until it dead-ended against a large modular triangular building built of imported alien alloys.

"Let's try the left," said the Bandit, walking off in a new direction.

They followed him. The street narrowed until the buildings were so close together that he couldn't fit through the opening.

"So much for that," he muttered. "All right, let's go in the other direction."

He turned and backtracked, but when they came to the triangular building, everything seemed different.

"Something's wrong," he muttered, looking around.

"What is it?" asked Dante, who was bringing up the rear.

"That alley," said the Bandit, pointing. "It wasn't there before." On a hunch, he turned to his right, toward the entrance. It was gone.

"Okay, so you weren't exaggerating."

Suddenly a creature the size of a child emerged from the shadows and approached them. It was covered by dull gray fur, and its face was long and angular, with wide-set green eyes and a broad purple nose.

"Need a guide?" it hissed in a sibilant whisper. "Need a girly-girly house? Need a trip to Dreamland? Like to make a bet? I take you anywhere you want for 20-credits-20."

The Bandit tossed a coin to the Lab Rat. "Tell him," he ordered Blue Peter.

"I'm looking for a friend," began the alien.

"No blue girly-girly houses in the Maze."

Blue Peter shook his head. "This is a human friend. He's been locked up. His name is Virgil Soaring Hawk. I want to find him."

"I must search," said the Lab Rat. "I tell you soon."

"Should we wait here?" asked the Bandit.

"Go wherever," said the Lab Rat. "When I am ready, I find you."

He shambled off and scuttled around a corner.

"No sense following him," said Blue Peter. "When you get to the corner and look for him, he won't be there."

"Then let's walk around and see what the Maze is like, as long as he says he can find us," said Dante.

The Bandit agreed, and the three of them set off. The farther into the Maze they got, the stranger it became. Streets ended inside buildings, or curved and twisted back onto themselves. Buildings were all shapes; some seemed to blink in and out of the men's dimension, though when they approached them they seemed solid enough. There were doorless, windowless buildings from which peals of human laughter emanated, and stores that sold objects that were totally unfamiliar to Dante. There were brothels showcasing males and females of a dozen different races, and gambling dens with long, winding, seemingly endless tunnels leading to individual games. They followed a corridor, found a room with aliens playing *jabob*, retraced their steps, and found themselves inside an alien shrine that featured an altar stone still wet with blood. They walked out the exit, and found themselves blocks from the gambling den, on a four-level avenue covered by a building that rose from the ground on both sides of the street, leaned toward the middle, and joined about ten feet above the top level, forming a huge triangular arch.

"This gets weirder and weirder," said Dante.

"This is the ordinary part," said Blue Peter. "It gets really weird about three blocks from here."

Another Lab Rat, this one light tan with large black spots on its fur, approached them. *"Psst!"* it hissed.

"Go away," said Blue Peter. "We've already got a guide."

"*Psst!*" it repeated. "Your guide has deserted you. I will never do that. I offer the unusual, the exotic, the bizarre. All for only twenty credits."

"Not interested," said the Bandit.

"For you, fifteen credits," said the Lab Rat. It pulled its thin lips back in a distorted smile. "Eat at Joe's."

"If we want a restaurant, we'll find one without your help," said Blue Peter irritably.

"Not like Joe's," said the Lab Rat. "Your meal is lightly basted and still alive. You can listen to it scream as it slides down your gullet."

"Forget it."

"It is forgotten," said the Lab Rat. "*Psst!* Girly-girly house of cyborgs, only twelve credits."

Their own guide suddenly appeared. He stared at the other Lab Rat and growled deep in his throat. The new Lab Rat hissed at him. A moment later they were roaring and screeching, jumping up and down and making threatening gestures. Finally, as the noise reached a crescendo, they both stopped at the same instant, and the new Lab Rat raced away.

"Do not let my brother disturb you," said their guide. "I will kill him later."

"He's your brother?" asked Dante.

"Probably" was the answer.

"Did you find Virgil Soaring Hawk?" asked the Bandit.

"Ah, the unfortunate Virgil," said the Lab Rat. "Yes."

"Why 'unfortunate'?" asked Dante.

"He is guilty of sins for which they have not yet created any names," replied the Lab Rat. He turned to Blue Peter. "You helped."

"Take us there," said the Bandit.

"They will not release him."

"That is not your concern," said the Bandit, tossing him another coin. "Just take us there and then leave."

"If I leave, you will never find your way out."

"That is *our* concern," said the Bandit.

"You will die of old age here, all but the blue one," warned the Lab Rat.

"Why not me?" asked Blue Peter.

"The Maze finds your presence offensive. It will throw you out."

"How do you know?"

"The same way I know how to find Virgil Soaring Hawk," replied the Lab Rat, as if that answered everything.

"But—" began Blue Peter.

"Shut up," said the Bandit. He turned to their guide. "No more talk. Take us to Virgil."

The Lab Rat stared at him, gave a shrug that rippled down its entire body, and headed off down a dank, twisting alley. The Bandit and his companions fell into step behind the furry creature, following as it turned one way and then another, seeming to follow no rational course—but they noticed that while they were constantly backtracking, they never passed the same street or building twice.

Finally the Lab Rat ascended two levels, walked a block, climbed back down to the pavement, and waited for his party to assemble.

"Here we are," he said.

"*Where* are we?" said the Bandit.

"You wanted to find Virgil Soaring Hawk, didn't you?"

"Yes."

The Lab Rat pointed to an unmarked door. "Just walk through there."

"There are fifty identical doors on this block," said the Bandit. "How do you know it's this one?"

"Because."

"All right. Open it."

"I am done. You are not paying me to stay."

"I paid you to find Virgil Soaring Hawk. You're not done until I know he's inside."

The Lab Rat turned to him. "Have I ever lied to you?"

"You haven't said five sentences to me."

"There. You see?"

"Open the door."

"I weep at your distrust."

"You'll do more than weep if he's not in there."

The Lab Rat stared at him for a long moment. "This door," it said, walking to a door next to the one it had originally indicated.

"I thought it was the other door."

"I changed my mind."

The Bandit opened the door and turned to Dante. "Keep an eye on him until I make sure that Virgil's here." He entered the building.

"What's behind the first door?" asked Dante.

"Open it," said the Lab Rat.

"Just tell me."

The Lab Rat forced his lips into another smile. "That would spoil the surprise."

"I notice your Terran has become a lot more fluent since our first meeting," noted Dante.

"That's because it is noon in the Maze."

"It gets better or worse depending on the time of day?"

"And the weather."

Dante was about to reply when the door opened and the Bandit reappeared.

"Okay, let him go and follow me."

Dante turned to tell the Lab Rat to leave, but it was already gone. He walked forward and entered the building, followed by Blue Peter. They walked down a narrow arched corridor that curved to the left, and after a moment came to a lighted room. There was a strange multi-level desk with a small, olive-skinned man seated behind it.

"This gentleman," said the Bandit, indicating the man, "seems to be in charge of the place."

"I *am* in charge."

"It's not a jail and it's not a stockade, right?"

"That is correct."

"And yet you freely admit that you have incarcerated Virgil Soaring Hawk here."

"The Maze is used to aberrant behavior," said the man. "It is used to perversions that I hope you cannot begin to imagine. And yet your friend has performed acts that offend not only the inhabitants of the Maze but the Maze itself."

"And the Maze told you that, did it?" asked Dante.

"Not in so many words, but if you live here long enough, you know how to interpret its moods."

"I am sorry our friend has offended you," said the Bandit. "Tell me how much we owe you for damages, I'll pay his tab, and we'll be on our way."

"The same perversions, performed on another world, will be no less offensive," said the man.

"But since you won't know about them, they won't offend *you*," the Bandit pointed out.

"The Maze says he must stay. He will not be harmed, he will be well treated—but he will be confined alone for the rest of his life."

"He belongs to me," said the Bandit. "I'm taking him away with me."

"Do *you* indulge in similar sins?" demanded the man.

"What I do is no one's business but my own."

"And I suppose you're going to tell me that what Virgil Soaring Hawk does is no one else's business?"

"That's right."

"That's wrong. Two men and a female Tellargian have been taken to a psychiatric ward after spending less than half the night with him."

"What the hell did he do to them?"

"We have no idea, but it is our duty to make sure that he never does it again."

"Enough talk," said the Bandit. "Name your price and I'll pay it. Just turn him over to me and we'll leave."

"That's out of the question."

"Nothing is out of the question for Santiago. Now, where is he?"

"He's quite safe, not only from his own urges, but also from delusional intruders who think they're Santiago."

"I'm only going to ask once more," said the Bandit. "Where is he?"

The olive-skinned man glared at him and offered no response.

The Bandit looked around the room, turned to the wall at the far end of it, and pointed his finger. A laser beam shot out, and soon cut a doorway through it.

"Rhymer," he said, purposely avoiding mentioning Dante's name, "go see if he's there."

Dante stepped through and found himself in what seemed to be a haberdasher's storehouse. He stepped back into the room.

"No, there's nothing there."

The Bandit turned back to the olive-skinned man. "I'm going to count to five," he said, "and if you haven't told me where I can find Virgil Soaring Hawk, I'm going to melt one of your fingers to putty. Then I'll count again. When we run out of fingers and toes, I'll melt more vital things. Look into my eyes and tell me if you think I'm bluffing."

The man stared into the Bandit's eyes and swallowed hard. "You're not bluffing."

"Then save yourself a world of pain and tell me what I want to know."

"I'll take you there," said the man with an air of defeat.

He got up and led them back down the corridor through which they had come, but instead of letting them out into the street, it dead-ended at a metal door.

"He's in there?" asked the Bandit.

"Yes."

"Open it."

The man uttered a code that was half mathematical formula and half song. The door vanished and Virgil, who had been lying on a floating pallet, got to his feet.

"Well, fancy meeting you here," he said.

"Shut up and get out of there," said the Bandit.

The Injun quickly exited his cell.

"Made my bail, huh?"

"So to speak." The Bandit turned to the olive-skinned man. "How do we get back to the street?"

"You don't."

The Bandit pointed a deadly finger between the man's eyes. "Do we have to go through all this again?"

"I'm not kidding. The Maze doesn't want him freed."

"The Maze doesn't have a vote," said the Bandit. "We're leaving this planet."

"You can try," said the man.

"Let's start by going back to your office."

The man led the way, but when they arrived, it was no longer an office, but a stone cell with iron bars on the windows. A heavy door slammed shut behind them.

"I told you," said the man. "The Maze will never let you leave."

"Don't bet every last credit you own on it," said the Bandit. He made a slight adjustment to his artificial arm, then stepped back and pointed at the wall with the iron bars. A pulse grenade shot out and exploded when it hit the wall, and a moment later there was a huge gaping hole.

The Bandit stepped through it, followed by his party. They found themselves in a walled courtyard, and the Bandit shot another grenade at a wall.

The Maze responded, entrapping them again, and it became a battle of attrition. The Bandit would explode or melt any barrier the Maze created, and the Maze would use all its resources to find a new way to imprison them.

After an hour the Bandit turned to Dante. "I don't have unlimited supplies of energy or ammunition," he said. "I'm going to have to put an end to this."

"What are you going to do?"

"Watch."

He made one more adjustment to his arm, then pointed to the sky. Something shot out, something small and glowing with power. It reached its apex at a thousand feet, then whistled down at the very center of the Maze. There was no explosion, no sense of heat, no tremors of the ground beneath their feet—but suddenly the Maze began to vanish, starting at its core and radiating outward. Buildings disappeared, streets and sidewalks vanished, thousands of Men and aliens popped out of existence without a sound.

Dante thought whatever the Bandit had precipitated would gobble them up as well, but it stopped about thirty yards away.

"What the hell was that?" asked the poet, trying to keep his voice calm and level and not succeeding very well.

"A little something I commissioned a Dinalian physicist to create for me," answered the Bandit. "It works on the same principle as a molecular imploder, but it creates a chain reaction."

"You could have killed us!" said Blue Peter.

"I know its physical limits," answered the Bandit.

"As it was, you probably killed a few thousand Men and aliens," said Dante.

"They would háve stopped us if they could," said the Bandit. "That makes them our enemies."

"Bullshit!" snapped Dante. "Ninety-nine percent of them didn't even know you were here and couldn't care less."

"Then this will add to the legend. Try to understand: Santiago has no friends in the galaxy, just enemies and hirelings."

"So we're just hirelings?" demanded the poet.

"I didn't mean you, of course."

"The hell you didn't!"

"I saved your life. This is no time for an argument."

"You saved my life at the cost of thousands of the lives you were *created* to save."

"It was a value judgment," said the Bandit. "Don't make me decide I made a mistake."

"It wasn't an either/or situation," said Dante. "There were half a dozen alternatives. Santiago—a *real* Santiago—would have found one!"

The Bandit turned to the olive-skinned man, who had been listening intently, and burned a deadly hole between his eyes.

"What was *that* for?" shouted Dante.

"It was your fault," said the Bandit angrily. "You implied that I wasn't Santiago. I couldn't let him hear that and live to pass it on."

"So you killed him, just like that?"

"*You* made it necessary."

"How the hell did you get so warped?"

"There's nothing warped about it," said the Bandit. "It goes with the job."

Dante snorted contemptuously.

"What do you know about it?"

"What do *I* know?" repeated the poet. "I *made* you!"

"You *found* me," replied the Bandit. "There's a difference."

Dante was about to reply, but something about the Bandit's expression convinced him to keep silent. A few days earlier he had told the Knife and the Blade that everyone in Santiago's organization was expendable, but he never really believed it.

Until now.

24.

Dante never wrote a verse about the Madras 300. He tried several times, but it never came out right.

But then, neither did the Madras 300.

It began a week after their experience in the Blixtor Maze. Dante, who had felt uneasy ever since they returned, was sitting alone in the dining room very late at night, sipping a cup of coffee, when Virgil Soaring Hawk approached him.

"What are you doing up?" asked the poet.

"Couldn't sleep."

"Why not?"

"Probably because you're using the strongest stimulant on the planet," said the Indian with a grin.

"I'm not interested in your habits or your perversions," said Dante.

"That's what I want to talk to you about."

"I just told you: I'm not interested."

"Neither is Santiago."

"Is that supposed to mean something to me?"

"It should."

"Virgil, it's halfway through the night and I don't know what the hell you're talking about," replied Dante. "I'm not in the mood for guessing games, so if you've got something to say, say it."

"I just did."

"Go away."

"You're not paying attention," said Virgil.

"I must not be, so spell it out for me."

"Look, Rhymer, I know why you came after me in the Maze. We're joined at the soul, you and I."

"The hell we are."

"It's an historic inevitability. Dante has to have his Virgil. But why did *he* come along?"

"You work for him," said Dante. "We all do."

"All I've done is buy drugs for him," said Virgil. "That's hardly an indispensable job."

Dante stared at him. "You think he *shouldn't* have come after you?"

"Maybe so, maybe not. But I know what I am and what I've done, and he at least knows some of it. So why did he destroy the Maze and maybe kill a couple of thousand people just to free me? I'm probably just going to get arrested again on the next world I visit for crimes against God and Nature. You know it, I know it, *he* knows it."

"Let me get this straight," said Dante, frowning. "Are you telling me you wanted him to leave you there?"

"I didn't *want* him to. I want to be free! But what kind of Santiago frees one lone redskin pervert at the cost of all those lives?"

"He's reestablishing the legend," said Dante uneasily. "He has to let people know how powerful he is."

"By killing the people he's supposed to protect? Hell, *I* could do that. He's supposed to do something better."

"I don't know what you want."

"It's not what *I* want," said Virgil. "I work for you—"

"You work for *him*," interrupted Dante.

"No!" said Virgil firmly. "Everyone else around here works for him. I work for *you*—and it's my job to tell you that I think you put your money on the wrong horse."

"And you reached this conclusion because he saved your life at the expense of others?"

"How much more honest can I be?" retorted Virgil.

Dante finished his coffee and sat in silence.

"So what do you think?" persisted the Indian.

"He's only been Santiago for a few weeks, and we're redefining the job."

"That's no answer."

"It's the best I've got," said Dante. "Hell, *he's* the best I've got."

"You found him very fast. Maybe you should have looked a little longer."

"Maybe I should have. I don't know. But the Frontier needs him *now*."

"It needs *help* now," agreed Virgil. "That doesn't mean it needs *him*."

"What do you suggest?" said Dante irritably. "Who has the authority to fire him? Who has the skills to kill him?" He sighed heavily. "Hell, he's doing what he thinks is right. Who am I to challenge that? I'm just a small-time thief turned poet. I don't have a monopoly on right or truth."

"All right," said Virgil. "You're the boss."

"I'm *not* the boss, damn it!"

"You're *my* boss. I won't bring it up again."

The Indian turned and left Dante alone with his thoughts and his doubts. By morning he had convinced himself that both of them were wrong, that this was a century and a half after the original Santiago and different times called for different approaches.

Then came the Madras raid.

Word came from an informant that a small Navy convoy was shipping gold bullion to their base on Madras IV, a mining world some 132 light-years distant.

The Bandit knew he didn't have the firepower to take on the Navy in space, so he waited until they landed and most of the ships departed. Then he touched down on Madras with Dante, Virgil, and three new hirelings.

The moment they emerged from their ship they were captured by an armed patrol. The Bandit meekly surrendered, the others followed suit, and shortly thereafter they found themselves incarcerated in an otherwise-empty stockade, surrounded by a sonic barrier that became intensely painful every time anyone got within four feet of it.

"I wonder how long they plan to keep us here?" mused one of the new men.

"Not long," said the Bandit. "They'll want to know what we're doing here."

"Well, it *is* a mining world," said Dante. "We could say we're here to consider investing in one of the mining complexes."

"We'll tell them the truth," said the Bandit.

"That we're here to rob them of their bullion?"

"That's right."

"You could save a lot of ammunition that way," said Virgil dryly. "Given our position, they just might laugh themselves to death."

"You mean this cell?" asked the Bandit. "I can leave it whenever I choose to."

"Then what are we doing here in the first place?" continued Virgil.

"Wasn't this easier than searching the whole planet for their headquarters?" said the Bandit.

"Now that you've found their headquarters, why are we still incarcerated?" persisted the Indian.

"So far all we've seen are the guards. I assume we'll be questioned by someone higher up the chain of command, someone who might know exactly where the bullion is."

"You know they're probably monitoring every word we say," put in Dante.

"So what?" replied the Bandit. "Sooner or later they're going to have to talk to us—and if it's too much later, I'll destroy the stockade and initiate the conversation myself."

"I don't know why you didn't do it in the first place," muttered Virgil.

"If I'd just walked in and blown them away, no one would know who was responsible. I plan to answer all their questions honestly, especially who I am, and let them inform the Democracy exactly who it was that robbed them."

"Isn't this a little early in the game for that?" suggested Dante. "Shouldn't we accumulate a nest egg and some more manpower before we start taunting the Democracy?"

"How much is enough?" replied the Bandit. "The sooner we begin our mission, the better."

A quartet of armed guards suddenly appeared, flanking an officer with a chest full of medals.

"So you want the Democracy to know who you are?" said the officer. "I think we can arrange that."

"I am Santiago," said the Bandit.

The officer laughed in amusement. "Can you spell 'delusional'?"

"I'm here for the bullion," continued the Bandit. "Where is it?"

"I admire your sense of humor," said the officer. "I can't say as much for your grip on reality."

"I'm only going to ask you once more. Where is the bullion?"

"In a safe place," said the officer. "We've run retina scans on all of you. You're the One-Armed Bandit. This one here is Virgil Soaring Hawk, the one on your left is a thief and murderer called Danny Briggs, the one directly behind you is—"

"I am Santiago," repeated the Bandit.

"We've got a holo recording of your intention to rob the bullion," said the officer. "You can be the One-Armed Bandit or Santiago or Peter Pan, for all I give a damn. You might as well call yourself Methuselah, because you're going to spend one hell of a long time in this stockade."

"You've had your chance," said the Bandit. He waved his arm at the officer and the guards, and a moment later all five lay dead on the shining, multicolored floor.

Then he stood back, pointed to the tiny control panel on the far wall, and melted it. The sonic field vanished, and they walked out.

"If it was that easy, why are any of the rest of us here?" asked Virgil.

"Four of you are here to carry the gold, and the Rhymer's here so he can chronicle my exploits," said the Bandit. "The stockade is at the far end of the compound. As we were brought in, I saw a barracks, a mess hall, and an office. I'll handle the opposition. You search every inch of the compound until you find the bullion."

The Bandit didn't wait for them to respond, but walked out the door and straight to the barracks. Dante heard some screams, and then all was silent. He went to the office and began to search through it. There was a safe with a complicated computer lock that took him almost thirty minutes to disable, but there was no bullion in the safe, nor even any money, just a handful of coded crystals that presumably showed the disposition of Navy ships in the sector.

"Any luck?" asked Virgil from the doorway.

"Not yet," said Dante, sitting at a computer and examining the crystals. "How about you?"

"Not a thing."

"Wait a minute!" said Dante, sitting at a computer and examining a decoded crystal. "Hey, Santiago—I've got it!"

The Bandit appeared in the doorway a moment later.

"What did you find?"

"There's a school about four miles from here. The bullion is hidden there."

"Why?" asked Virgil.

"Probably to safeguard it against what just occurred," said the Bandit. "Did it give the bullion's location at the school?"

"No, just that it's there."

"There were some vehicles out front," said the Bandit. "Let's go."

A moment later they were racing toward the school. It turned out to be a boarding school, with a pair of dormitories and a large cafeteria.

"No guards," noted Virgil.

"Guards would call attention to the place," replied Dante. "This way no one will assume there's anything here that *needs* guarding."

The Bandit got out of the vehicle. "Unload the airsleds," he instructed Virgil. "The bullion's going to be heavy."

"I wonder where it's hidden?" said Dante. "This is a pretty large complex."

"Let's find out," said the Bandit. He pointed at a window, and a second later it crashed into a hundred pieces. Ten more windows, chosen at random, followed.

Suddenly a number of adults—obviously teachers—burst out of the school's entrance.

"What the hell is going on?" demanded one of them, a gray-haired woman who seemed to be in charge.

"This is a robbery," said the Bandit calmly. "We're here for the bullion."

"Bullion? What are you talking about?"

"Please don't waste my time by feigning ignorance. We have just come from the military compound. We *know* that they stored their bullion here."

"We don't have any bullion!"

"I told you not to waste our time," said the Bandit. "I tell you now that if you don't immediately agree to produce the bullion, I will take out the east wing of your school, regardless of who might be in it."

"You wouldn't dare!" said the woman. "There are three hundred children in that wing."

The Bandit turned and pointed toward the east wing.

"No!" yelled Dante, hurling himself at the Bandit's arm and trying to hang on to it.

The Bandit shrugged and Dante went flying through the air. By the time he'd hit the ground, there was a deafening explosion and the east wing was no more.

"The bullion," said the Bandit calmly, "or the west wing goes next."

"Don't!" cried the woman. "I'll show you where it is!"

The Bandit nodded at Virgil and the three other men. "Follow her and bring it back out."

As they disappeared inside the school, the Bandit turned to Dante, who was still sprawled in the dirt.

"I will not tolerate another display of disloyalty," he said coldly.

"Goddammit to hell!" spat Dante. "Do you realize what you've done?"

"I got us the bullion."

"You killed three hundred kids!"

"They were Democracy children," said the Bandit with an unconcerned shrug. "Why wait until they grow up to exterminate them?"

Dante stared long and hard at his handpicked Santiago.

My God—what have I done?

Part 4

Silvermane's Book

25.

There are those who will swear he's a hero,
Born to fulfill mankind's dreams.
But listen to those who now are his foes:
Santiago is not what he seems.

The door opened and Matilda entered her room.

"Lights," she said, and instantly the room was filled with light.

She turned to walk to a closet, then jumped as she saw Dante Alighieri seated in a chair by her desk.

"What the hell are you doing here?" she demanded.

"We have to talk."

"I've spent two weeks on the road recruiting members for the organization. I'm tired. We'll talk tomorrow."

"Now," he said, and something in his voice convinced her to sit on the edge of her bed and face him.

"All right," she said, staring at him. "What's up?"

"We've made a terrible mistake."

"What are you talking about?"

"The Bandit."

"You mean Santiago?"

"He's no more Santiago than I am," said Dante. "He never was."

"Just because he doesn't fit your image of—"

"Shut up and listen!" snapped Dante.

Again she stared at him. "Just what the hell did he do?"

"What would you say if I told you he killed three hundred kids for no reason except that someday they'd grow up to be members of the Democracy?"

"Did he?"

"Yes. On Madras IV."

"He must have had some reason."

"I just gave it to you."

She frowned. "Three hundred children?"

"In cold blood." Dante paused. "You and I can argue about whether he should have killed that crazy old lady back on Heliopolis. After all, she was a witness to a crime and could describe Santiago. But these were just kids. They never saw us, we never saw them."

"That doesn't seem like him."

"The hell it doesn't. He killed a couple of thousand people in the Blixtor Maze. This isn't the same guy we knew three months ago—or if it is, then we were terrible judges of character."

"Of course he's the same man. We didn't set out to select an angel."

"We don't want an angel," agreed Dante. "But we want someone who can discriminate between a Democracy officer or bureaucrat and a child who lives in the Democracy."

"Maybe we defined the perameters of the job wrong," suggested Matilda. "Maybe he thinks—"

"You're not paying attention," interrupted Dante. "Fuck the definitions. Do we want a Santiago who'll wipe out three hundred kids for any reason at all?"

She sighed deeply. "No," she said at last. "No, we don't."

"Part of it is my fault. I told him to lose the 'sir's and 'ma'am's, and never to apologize, that Santiago didn't do that. But he's gone overboard. I should have known it would happen before we ever set foot on Madras."

"How could you?"

"Virgil's helped me out of some tight spots, and introduced me to some people I wanted to meet . . . but let's be honest: he's a lying, drug-addicted killer who's probably sent half a hundred bedmates to the psycho ward. Whatever he is to me, he's nothing to Santiago—and yet thousands of men and aliens died in the Blixtor Maze just so the Bandit could set him free. That's not loyalty; that's out-and-out crazy."

"All right," said Matilda. "When you put it that way, I can't disagree with you."

"I don't know where it started going wrong," continued the poet. "I never met a more decent, more humble man than the One-Armed

Bandit. He practically reeked with concern for his fellow man. How could just calling himself Santiago change him so much?"

"You can ponder that for the next few years," she answered. "The more immediate question is: what do we do about him?"

"I don't know," admitted Dante. "We certainly can't take him out by ourselves. I've seen him wipe out twenty hired guns without working up a sweat." He paused. "Besides, there probably aren't half a dozen men on the Frontier who can kill him. Do you want someone that formidable, that potentially uncontrollable, to become our Santiago? We'd just be replacing one problem with another."

"If we can't tolerate him and can't remove him, just what do you propose to do?" demanded Matilda.

"I don't know. That's why we're talking."

"I suppose we can wait until there's an opportunity . . ." began Matilda.

"To do what?"

"To kill him, of course," she replied. "He doesn't have any reason to suspect we're turning against him. Sooner or later he's got to drop his guard, relax, turn his back, do *some*thing to give us a chance."

"And then what?"

"Then we find another Santiago, or you go back to writing your poem without him and I go back to being the best thief on the Frontier." She stood up and began nervously pacing back and forth across the room. "Hell, I just wanted a Santiago so the Democracy would have a bigger target than me. If I can't have one, I can't have one. I was doing just fine before I met you, Rhymer; I can do fine again."

"It's more than my poem," said Dante. "The Inner Frontier needs Santiago. Hell, the human race needs him."

"Even if he kills three hundred innocent children?"

"He's not Santiago."

"He is now. Just ask him. Or your ladyfriends from Snakepit. Or the survivor from Jackrabbit Willowby's little army. Like it or not, Santiago is abroad in the galaxy once more, all thanks to us."

"We created him," agreed Dante. "We have to find some way to uncreate him."

"Short of finding an even better killer, I don't know what we can do," said Matilda. "We've given him an organization. We've set him up in the drug trade, and robbed millions from a bank. We've supplied him with Wilbur's services, and that's probably doubled his money already. We've hired two dozen guns, and we've got a couple of ladies like Blossom who'll do anything, no matter how perverse, if it's for the good of the cause. We did more than create him; we made him successful."

"Some of them might leave if we give the word," said Dante with more conviction than he felt.

"Name one, besides Virgil," she challenged him.

He grimaced. "I can't."

"I know."

"Still, we have to do something. Somehow, in his mind, he's equated being against Santiago with being *for* the Democracy. The originals knew the difference. They didn't expect anyone to thank them, or to understand what they were doing. Santiago didn't get to be a myth that's lived for over a century by killing children and old ladies."

"You really feel you can't reason with him?"

"He's armored in his . . . I was about to say his ignorance, but that's not it. He's armored in his *righteousness*—and it's been my experience that there's nothing more difficult to reason with than a righteous man."

"So what do we do?"

"We keep in touch, we talk whenever we're alone, we try to keep him from doing any more harm until we can come up with a solution, and we hope we don't cause even more unnecessary deaths by waiting." He paused. "I know this started out as a way for me to add to my poem and you to get the heat off you—but it's much more than that now. He'd still be killing Unicorns back on Heliopolis if it wasn't for us. I don't even blame him; he can't help being what he is, and Lord knows he didn't apply for the job. It's our fault he's here, doing what he's doing, and we've got a moral obligation to put an end to it."

"I never thought I'd hear you argue in favor of moral obligations," she noted wryly.

"Neither did I," he admitted. "I certainly don't think of myself as a moral man. But we've unleashed something very dangerous, something uncontrollable, and I think it's our duty—mine, anyway—to do something about it."

At that moment the door burst open and three recently hired men entered the room, burners in their hands.

"What the hell's going on?" demanded Matilda.

"He wants to talk to you," said one of the men. He turned to Dante. "To *both* of you."

"Who does?" asked Dante.

The man looked amused. "Guess."

Dante and Matilda walked out of her room, down the corridor to the living room, and then to the office. The Bandit was sitting at his desk.

"That will be all," he said to the three men. "You can leave now."

"Are you sure, Santiago?" asked the spokesman.

"I am quite capable of protecting myself," he said in a voice that brooked no opposition.

The three men left without another word, and the door slid shut behind them.

"What do you want?" asked Matilda.

"Yeah," said Dante. "We were just about to get romantic."

"Spare me your lies," said the Bandit.

"Who's lying?"

"Just how stupid do you think I am? I heard every word you said."

"What are you talking about?" said Matilda.

"I had both your rooms bugged."

"Why?"

"How can you ask that when I just told you I've been listening to you since Matilda entered her room?" said the Bandit irritably.

"All right, you heard us," said Dante, deciding that further denials were futile. "Now what?"

The Bandit looked from one to the other. "I thought you were more perceptive than you are," he said at last. "You have absolutely no concept of what Santiago is, what I must do if I am to succeed. We don't live in a humanistic universe. There is absolute good and absolute evil abroad in it. The Democracy is the evil, and we can never compromise with it, can never appease it, can never show it any more mercy than it would show to us if it were given the opportunity."

"You're talking about the Democracy, and I was talking about the three hundred kids you killed," said Dante. "How evil were *they*?"

"Can't you understand?" replied the Bandit. "That's three hundred armed men who won't be coming after us in fifteen years."

"That's three hundred kids who might have grown up to be doctors, who might have saved a million lives, including some right here on the Frontier."

"They belonged to the Democracy. They would have been trained to be the enemy."

"That's a crock," Dante shot back. "For all you know, it was a religious school, training ministers to come out to the Frontier."

"No more word games," said the Bandit. "My problem is not what to do with members, however young, of the Democracy. It is what to do with *you*." He paused. "I should kill you, as you would kill me if you had the chance. That is the only logical course of action, do you agree?"

Dante and Matilda stared at him, but made no reply.

"Well, at least you don't disagree." The Bandit rubbed his chin thoughtfully with his real hand. "On the other hand, I wouldn't have become Santiago without you. I owe you something for that."

"If you can solve this moral problem, you can solve others," said Dante. "Maybe there's hope for you yet."

"Shut up," said the Bandit, making no attempt to hide his annoyance. *Not anger,* noted Dante. *We're not important enough to arouse his anger. He's just annoyed, as if we were insects that were bothering him on a hot summer day.*

The Bandit was lost in thought for another moment. Finally he looked up at Dante and Matilda. "I know I can never again trust you, that you will kill me if you are given the opportunity. By the same token, I can't trust anyone you recruited; I don't know where their loyalties lie. So this is my decision: I will give the two of you, as well as Blossom and Virgil, one Standard day to get off Valhalla. If you are still here when the day is over, I'll kill you. I will contact Wilbur and tell him to transmit all my money to an account of my choosing, and that if he doesn't do so within that same Standard day he's a walking dead man."

"Maybe he can't do it in a day," suggested Matilda.

"He'll find a way, or he'll wish he had." The Bandit got to his feet and faced them. "One day and one second from now, we are at hazard. If you don't act against me, I won't seek you out—but know that starting tomorrow, I will kill each and every one of you the next time we meet."

26.

They sat in their ship—Dante Alighieri, Waltzin' Matilda, Virgil Soaring Hawk, and the Flower of Samarkand—half a dozen light-years from Valhalla, and discussed their situation.

"I don't believe you've told me everything," said Blossom angrily. "What did you do? Why has he turned against us?"

"He hasn't turned against us so much as he has turned against Santiago," said Dante.

"You keep saying that," protested Blossom. "How can he turn against Santiago? He *is* Santiago!"

"No," said Dante. "He's a man we've been calling Santiago. There's a difference."

"Maybe he had a point about those children," she said. "At least they won't be gunning for him in ten or twelve years."

"Are you saying that if he had the ability to kill every child in the Democracy, he should?" asked Matilda.

"No," said Blossom. "But there are billions, maybe hundreds of billions, of children. He killed three hundred. Is that any reason to turn against him?"

"If he'd killed one, that would be reason enough," said Dante.

"Didn't all the other Santiagos kill people?" she demanded. "Innocent people as well as guilty?"

"Yes, they all killed people," answered Dante. "And sometimes innocent bystanders were killed. That's the fortunes of the kind of war Santiago has to wage. But no Santiago ever went out of his way to kill innocent bystanders when it could be avoided."

"How old are you?" said Blossom. "Thirty? Thirty-five? How do you know what Santiago did more than a century ago?"

"I know what he was."

"That's no answer!"

"It's the best you're going to get."

"Which is a roundabout way of saying that you don't know for a fact whether or not any Santiago killed innocent children."

"If they did," said Dante, "then we're going to improve upon the originals."

"Who made you the arbiter of what Santiago does and doesn't do?" continued Blossom. "You're just a poet."

"Not even a very good one," admitted Dante.

"So?"

"I'm carrying on the work of a very good one," said Dante. "In the cargo hold of this ship are thousands of pages of his manuscript. I've studied it until I damned near know it by heart, and that means I know what Santiago did and what he meant to the Frontier. The One-Armed Bandit is no Santiago."

"Where does it say that he has to be? That was *your* idea, not his."

"It's his now," said Dante. "But he doesn't understand the concept. He's made it too black and white. He's the good guy and all the members of the Democracy are the bad guys—but it's not that simple. It never has been. Most members of the Democracy are just men and women who are trying to get through each day without rocking the boat or hurting the people they love. Not only don't they have any interest in the Democracy's abuses, they don't even have any knowledge of them. As for the Democracy itself, we don't want to get rid of it; it's all that stands between us and a hostile galaxy. What we want to do is limit its abuses, and remind it who it's supposed to be protecting out here on the Frontier. The Bandit would destroy it; Santiago just wants to straighten it out. Neither will ever succeed, but the Bandit will kill more innocent people with each passing day, and eventually bring down destruction on all the people he's fighting for, because he's going to commit some abuses that the Democracy can't ignore."

"Santiago committed abuses," said Blossom. "That's why he was King of the Outlaws."

"Santiago committed *crimes*," said Dante. "That's why the Democracy put a price on his head and left it to the bounty hunters to find him. If he'd gone to war against innocent Democracy citizens, the whole goddamned Navy would have come out to the Frontier, two billion ships strong, and blown away every world they came to until they found him. *That's* what the Bandit's asking for."

Blossom sighed deeply. "All right. Maybe you're right, maybe you're not—but it's all academic now anyway, since he's banished us and plans to kill us on sight. So what do we do now?"

"I don't know," said Dante. "Find the true Santiago, I suppose."

"While this one's killing people right and left and telling everyone Santiago's to blame for it?" asked Virgil.

"What do you suggest?" said Dante.

"Kill him."

"Who's going to do it?" Dante shot back. "You? Me? Matilda? You've seen him in action. Even Dimitrios of the Three Burners wouldn't stand much chance against him."

"There must be someone out there."

"So you find a better killer," said Matilda. "Then what?"

"Then you hope he's more reasonable than the Bandit," replied Virgil.

"We're going about this all wrong," said Dante. "Santiago is more than merely a competent killer. We chose the Bandit not just because of his physical abilities, but because we thought he was a moral man."

"He is," answered Virgil. "Too moral. Sometimes that can be as much a fault as not being moral enough."

Dante turned to Matilda. "Have you got any suggestions?"

"He's not an evil man," she began.

"But he's done evil things, and he's almost certainly going to do more."

"Let me finish," she said. "He's not an evil man. He's wrong-headed in some respects, but he's willing to put his life on the line for the cause—as he perceives it—every day, he's willing to be hated and feared and mistrusted by all the people he's trying to defend, he's willing to do everything required of Santiago. The problem isn't that he's a shirker, but that, because of his misconceptions, he's willing to do too much, not too little."

"What's your point?" said Dante.

"I think it's more practical to educate him than replace him," she said. "After all, he's already set up shop as Santiago. Even if you found a way to kill him, there's no guarantee that the next one would be as moral, or as self-sacrificing."

"How are we going to educate him if he's going to shoot us on sight?" demanded Dante in exasperation.

"*We* aren't," said Matilda. "That much is obvious."

"So . . . ?"

"So we find someone who can."

"You're saying we get someone to join his organization and try to influence him?" asked Dante. "That strikes me as a pretty slim hope."

"Do *you* want to kill him?"

"You know we can't."

"Anyone can be ambushed. We're smarter than he is. It wouldn't be that hard—especially now, before he builds a truly formidable organization." She stared at him. "Now answer my question."

"No," he admitted. "No, I don't want to kill him."

"Then we have two choices: we can hope someone else kills him, or we can try—by proxy—to change the way he looks at things."

"Do you have anyone in mind?"

"Not yet."

"I don't want to cast a pall of gloom here," volunteered Virgil, who looked only too happy to do so, "but you're the guys who chose the Bandit in the first place. What makes you think you'll do any better this time around?"

"If we don't find a replacement, who will?" asked Dante.

"Me."

"You have a candidate in mind?"

"Yeah. I figure the easiest way to make the Bandit accept our candidate is to send him someone with a reputation, someone with bona fides, so to speak—but a freelancer, not someone who proposes to share his business out of the blue."

"All right," said Dante. "Who is it?"

"You ever hear of the Black Death?"

"He's a killer for hire?"

"Everyone's a killer for hire," said the Injun. "The difference is he don't make any bones about it."

"And what makes you think he can influence the One-Armed Bandit?" asked Matilda.

"He owes me a couple of favors."

"Sexual, of course," said Dante distastefully.

"Personal, anyway," said Virgil noncommittally.

"Can you trust him?"

"Probably."

"Just 'probably'?" asked Matilda, frowning.

" 'Probably' is as high a rating as I'd give the Rhymer here," retorted Virgil, "and he and I are connected at the soul."

"The hell we are!" snapped Dante.

Virgil grinned. "You see? My closest friend in the galaxy, and he's pissed that I cherish our friendship. One of these days he'll sell me out for thirty pieces of silver."

"Two pieces of lead alloy would do it," muttered Dante.

"Get back to the point," said Matilda. "Can we trust the Black Death?"

"As much as you can trust anyone," answered Virgil.

"*Can* he kill the Bandit if he has to?"

"Hell, *I* can kill him when his back's turned. How many times did he turn his back on you in the past month? A hundred? A thousand?"

"So your friend shoots people in the back?" said Dante.

"Not really, though I'm sure he'd have no serious objection to it." Virgil lit a smokeless cigar. "His job is killing people. He doesn't care if you subtract points for form."

"Where can we find him?" said Dante. "I'll want to talk to him before we agree to this."

"Not a good idea," said Virgil.

"Why not?"

"He doesn't like being hemmed in. Let me talk to him one-on-one."

"Not a chance," said Dante.

"Why not?"

"Not to put too fine a point on it, you're a moral dwarf compared to the Bandit. I don't want you telling anyone how we want the Bandit to behave."

"You really know how to hurt a guy, Rhymer," said Virgil with an obvious lack of sincerity. "Say that in public and someone might think you disapproved of my lifestyle or my ethics."

"There's nothing wrong with either that castration and a couple of decades in solitary confinement wouldn't cure," said Dante. "Now tell me where we can find this Black Death."

"He's not like the Tyrannosaur," replied Virgil. "He doesn't have his own world, and he doesn't stand out in a crowd—at least, not the way you'd think. He's a freelancer. It might take me a few days to track him down."

"Start."

"Start how? We're eight light-years from the nearest inhabited planet."

"Get on the subspace radio. Ask your contacts. Pass the word that you've got a lucrative job for him."

"I'll ask around, but you don't want me to lie about a paycheck. He might take it as an insult."

"Just get your ass over to the radio and do what you have to do," said Dante irritably.

Virgil started to say something, thought better of it, and went over to the subspace radio, where he tried to track down the Black Death.

"We can't just sit around and hope this works out," said Dante. "If I know Virgil, this Black Death is more likely to kill for the Bandit than persuade for us."

"So what do you want us to do?" asked Blossom, who had been silent for the past few minutes.

"I'm glad to see you're talking to me again," said Dante dryly. "And to answer your question: we'll keep looking."

"For what?"

"I wish I knew. Some way to educate or depose the Bandit." He stared at her for a long minute. "If we can't come up with something, maybe we'll send you back."

"He'll kill me!"

"What if you contacted him and convinced him that we made you leave against your will, that you believe in him and everything he's doing and you want to come back?"

"Which probably isn't too far from the truth," commented Matilda.

"He won't care about the truth," said Blossom. "You know how rigid he is. He's already said he'll kill us. He never changes his mind."

"Well, it's something to keep in reserve," said Dante.

"Fuck your reserve!" snapped Blossom. "I believed in him, and now you've fixed it so he'll kill me the next time he sees me! I want out. The next planet we touch down on, you go your way and I'm going mine."

"I can't stop you," said Dante.

"You're damned right you can't," she replied. "You're a fool, you know that? You've got a saint on Valhalla, and that's not good enough for you. You want a god."

"I just want Santiago."

"The *real* Santiagos were killers and thieves. You want yours to walk on water!" She got to her feet. "I'm going to my cabin. Leave me alone until we land."

She walked through the galley to the cabins and entered the nearest of them.

"Well, I handled that with my usual aplomb," said Dante bitterly. "Virgil, the Bandit, and her." He grimaced. "Sometimes I wish I'd never found that goddamned poem."

"Sometimes I wish I were Queen of the Universe," replied Matilda. "Tell me when you want to stop talking drivel and get back to business."

"I think you'd make a rather nice queen."

"You heard me."

"I heard you. I just don't see any viable options." He sighed deeply. "Maybe the kids were an aberration. Maybe he'll work out after all."

"Maybe he will."

"Except it wasn't just the kids," complained Dante. "It was all those people in the Maze. And the old lady at the bank, too—and the fact that he couldn't think his way out of it, couldn't come up with a lie that would allow him to let her live."

"I know," she agreed. "At first I thought he was right, but after I heard you explain how we could have avoided killing her, could even put her to use explaining that we all worked for Santiago, I knew he was wrong." She paused. "He's just not very quick on his mental feet."

"Most fanatics aren't," said Dante.

Suddenly Virgil stood up and turned to them. "It's all arranged," he announced. "Lay in a course for Tosca III."

"What's on Tosca?" asked Dante.

"The Black Death."

27.

The Black Death comes, the Black Death goes,
The Black Death can be bellicose.
So friend, be on your guard today—
His blood is up, he lives to slay.

As Dante became more comfortable with his epic, he began using poetic license here and there. The first time was when he wrote of the Black Death.

He was writing about heroes and villains so big they blotted out the stars, so memorable that children would be telling their stories decades after he wrote them, and once in a while he came across such an aberration that he felt free to embellish or, in this case, to out-and-out falsify.

Not that the Black Death wasn't every bit as deadly as Dante said. In point of fact, he was even deadlier. Not that he didn't deserve the three verses Dante gave him, or that he wasn't feared wherever he went—once he was recognized.

The interesting fact is that he was almost never recognized.

Until it was too late.

The name itself conjures up fantastic images. A tall, muscular black man clad in muted colors, plain blazers or screechers in worn holsters, shopworn shoes or boots.

Or perhaps a slender man, looking like Death itself, wearing a black frock coat, his clothes and his drawn skin absorbing all color and reflecting only the total absence of color.

You can picture an unforgiving face, cold lifeless eyes like those of a shark, a thin-lipped mouth that never smiles. Some kind of hat or headpiece so that the sun never illuminates that death-mask countenance.

Expensive gloves that never slip off the handles of his weapons, that leave no fingerprints, that never expose his surprisingly delicate fingers to prying eyes.

That's the image of a man called the Black Death—and yet the only thing it had in common with the *real* Black Death was the gloves.

His name was Henry Marston, hardly a name to roll off frightened men's lips. And he wasn't black. He was a pale, chalky, sickly white; what pigment his skin had once possessed was almost totally gone.

He stood five feet seven inches, when he was strong enough to stand. His weight varied between 110 and 125 pounds; it had never in his life been more than 136.

His clothes were nondescript, wrinkled, a bit faded. The left elbow was patched, the right cuff frayed. He wore no primary colors; everything was neutral.

The only belt he wore held his loose-fitting pants up. It housed no weapon of any kind. There were no telltale bulges pinpointing hidden knives or pistols anywhere on his body. His boots were so old they were past the point of holding a polish, and the large toe of his left foot poked out through a crack in the inexpensive material.

And there were the gloves.

They went halfway up his forearms, totally functional, totally unstylish.

There was also the mask. It was transparent, and covered his face from the bridge of his nose down to his Adam's apple, then all the way around to the back of his head.

If there was ever a man who looked less than formidable, it was Henry Marston.

So it was probably God's little cosmic joke that he was the deadliest man alive, far more dangerous than Dimitrios or the One-Armed Bandit or Tyrannosaur Bailey, with a sobriquet that was more accurate than most.

"No matter what you think," Virgil told his companions as they waited patiently to pass through Customs at the Tosca III spaceport, "he's everything I've said he is."

"Why shouldn't we believe you?" asked Dante.

"Well, he doesn't make a good first impression," admitted Virgil. He paused thoughtfully. "Come to think of it, his second and third impressions aren't much of an improvement."

"We came here on your say-so," said Dante angrily. "If you've been wasting our time, maybe you'd better tell us right now."

"Everything I said about the Black Death is true," said Virgil. He spat on his hand and held it up, palm out. "I give you an Injun's solemn oath on that."

"There's something you're not telling us," continued Dante.

"It'll probably be better if you find out for yourself."

"Why?"

"Because if I tell you any more about him, you won't want to meet him."

"He's that ineffectual?" asked Matilda.

Virgil smiled. "I told you: he's the deadliest killer out here—at least the deadliest I've ever seen."

"Then why won't we want to meet him?"

"You'll be afraid to."

Dante glared at him. "Just how much seed have you been chewing today?"

"None," Virgil assured him. "I'm depressingly sober."

"Then shut up," Dante ordered him. "The more we talk, the angrier I'm getting with you. Just take us to meet this Black Death and let's get it over with."

"You're the boss," said Virgil. They passed through Customs without incident. "By the way," added Virgil as they walked to a hovering limo, "call him Henry."

"Why?"

"Because that's his name. And he hates being the Black Death."

"You mean being *called* the Black Death," Matilda corrected him.

"That, too," agreed Virgil.

The limo took them into Red Dust, the nearest of Tosca's three towns. The buildings showed the effects of the wind constantly blowing the dust against them, and two of the slidewalks were closed for repairs, also owing to the omnipresent dust.

The limo announced that they had reached the municipality of Red Dust and asked for a specific destination.

"Take us to the Weeping Willow," said Virgil.

"Done, sir," replied the limo so promptly and formally that Dante decided that it must be frustrated at its inability to offer a snappy salute.

The Weeping Willow was a nondescript tavern, small and unimpressive, filled with secondhand and oft-repaired chairs and tables. There was no back room for gambling, no upstairs rooms for sex, nothing but a small selection of mediocre liquor from various points on the Inner Frontier, an unused alien dart game hanging on one wall, and a much-dented metal bar in addition to the tables.

Dante glanced around the tavern. A small, sickly-looking man sat at a table in the corner. Two oversized women, smoking alien cigarettes and drinking alien whiskey, sat at another, playing a complex game using hundreds of cards with unfamiliar markings. The only other person in the place was the tall, muscular bartender, who looked hopefully at them when they entered, then lost interest when he saw they weren't there to drink.

"Your information was wrong," said Dante. "He's not here."

"Yes he is," answered Virgil calmly.

Dante looked at the small man with the transparent mask and the long gloves. "Is this some kind of joke?" he demanded.

"Why don't we talk to him, and then you can tell me if it's a joke or not," said Virgil, approaching the small man's table.

Henry Marston looked up and tried to smile at Virgil. It was evidently too much of an effort, and the smile froze halfway across his face, then vanished a few seconds later.

"Hi, Henry. It's been a while."

"Hello, Virgil," said Henry, stifling a cough. "What brings you to a little dirtball like Tosca?"

"I'd like you to meet two friends of mine—Dante and Matilda."

"I hope you'll forgive me if I don't get up," said Henry in a weak, hoarse whisper.

"I heard you were on Tosca," said Virgil, pulling up a chair and motioning for his companions to do the same. "Got a job to do here?"

"It's done," said Henry.

"Then why are you still here?"

"I was paid to kill her," was the answer. "I have to stick around and make sure she died."

Wonderful, thought Dante. *The old man's such a lousy shot he doesn't know if his victim will live or die. Why are we wasting our time here?*

"Excuse me for interrupting," said Dante, frowning, "but are you really the man known as the Black Death?"

"It's not a name of my own choosing," said Henry.

"I mean no disrespect, but you look like you're half dead yourself."

"I am."

Dante turned to Virgil. "And this is the guy you think can take out the Bandit?"

"If he has to," said Virgil. "But I thought the plan was for him to ride herd, to kind of redirect him."

"Ride herd?" repeated Dante. "No offense, Henry, if that's your name, but he can barely sit up in his chair. What the hell got into you?"

Virgil chuckled. "Nothing got into me. That's why I'm still alive."

"I think your friend deserves an explanation, Virgil," said Henry.

"Yeah, I suppose so," agreed Virgil. "Too bad. I just love to watch him when he's confused."

"Is one of you going to tell me what this is all about?" said Dante, trying to control his temper.

"It's *him*," said Matilda, nodding her head toward Henry.

Henry smiled. "You're very perceptive, my dear."

"I'm getting really annoyed!" growled Dante. He turned to Matilda. "What do you know that I don't know?"

"You're not the Black Death at all," said Matilda, staring at Henry. "That may be what they call you, but that's not what you are. You're its carrier."

"What are you talking about?" demanded Dante.

"Look at him," said Matilda. "That mask isn't there to protect him from unfiltered air. It's to protect *us* from *him*. Look at his gloves. You can't touch him and he can't touch you." She paused. "What disease are you carrying, Henry? *Ybonia?*"

"*Ybonia* takes weeks to act," replied Henry. "I'm a carrier for *Bharzia*."

"How fast does it act?"

"If I touch you, you're dead within an hour. If I breathe on you, it could take up to two days. They are not days you would wish on anyone."

"I've heard about *Bharzia*," said Dante. "There's no cure for it."

"Not yet," agreed Henry. "Maybe in another ten or twelve years."

"I thought it killed everyone that was infected," continued Dante. "That once it showed up on a planet it decimated the whole population. How come you're still alive?"

"No one knows," said Henry. "Genetic sport, probably. I haven't had a healthy day in two decades, but I don't die. There are days, oh, thousands of them, when I *wish* I was dead, but it never happens."

"How did you decide to become the Black Death?" asked Matilda.

"I figured that if God has such a vicious sense of humor that He'd leave me alive when all I wanted to do was die, the least I could do was even the score by killing men and women He wanted to live."

"An interesting philosophy," commented Dante.

"What do you do with your money?" asked Matilda.

"What *can* someone like me do?" responded Henry. "I spend some of it on moral lepers like Virgil, who allow me to vicariously experience some very out-of-the-ordinary things. And I donate millions to research. Without me, they'd be thirty years from a cure."

"It doesn't sound like much of a life."

"It's the only one I've got."

"Maybe you'd like to do something meaningful with it," said Dante.

"Are you suggesting that killing hundreds of men and women isn't meaningful?" said Henry sardonically.

"I'm being serious."

"All right, let's be serious," said Henry, staring back at him through watery eyes. "Who do you want me to kill?"

"Hopefully no one."

Henry looked amused. "My only skill is killing people. If you want me to let them live, that could run into real money."

Dante was silent for a long moment, studying the old man. Finally he spoke. "I'm sorry for wasting your time, Henry. You're not the man we want."

"I don't even know what the job is," complained Henry.

"It doesn't matter," said Dante. "It requires a man with a stronger moral compass than you possess."

"I resent your drawing moral and ethical judgments on my character before you've had a chance to know me," said Henry.

"Okay, you resent it," said Dante. "What are you going to do— take off your mask and breathe on me?"

"It's a possibility."

"That's why we can't use you," said Dante. "Killing the man in question was a last resort . . . but killing seems to be your *only* resort."

"You do what you're good at," replied Henry bitterly. "This is what *I'm* good at."

"I don't mind that it's what you're good at," said Dante. "I mind that it's *all* you're good at."

Henry stared at his gloved hands for a long moment. "Just out of curiosity, what would the job have paid?"

"I don't know."

"You don't know?" repeated Henry unbelievingly.

"It's too complicated to explain. You'd have been working for someone else."

"The man you wanted me to kill?"

"The man I hoped you wouldn't have to kill."

"This is getting very complicated," said Henry. "I'm a simple man. Show me who you want dead and I'll kill them. Show me who you want to live and I'll leave them alone. Black and white makes sense to me. I don't like grays."

"That's the problem, all right," said Dante. "I'm sorry to have bothered you."

"No bother at all," said Henry. "Leave two hundred credits at the bar."

"Why?"

"For my time. I didn't ask for this interview."

Dante considered it, then nodded his agreement. "Fair enough."

"If you ever decide what you really want, come on back and we'll talk some business," said Henry.

"If you're still alive," said Virgil with a smile.

"Oh, I'll be alive," Henry assured him. "If God wanted me dead, the son of a bitch would have taken me out twenty years ago."

"Well, I'll see you around," said Virgil, as the three of them got to their feet.

Henry was about to reply when a single gunshot rang out. The old man fell over backward in his chair, a bullet buried deep between his eyes.

Dante turned to the door to see who had fired the shot, then blinked his eyes very rapidly and shook his head. Maybe it was simply because Henry has been referring to the deity, but for just an instant it seemed to the poet that he was looking at God Himself.

28.

He's a master of each weapon, and he's got a lion's heart.
He turns mayhem into science, and then science into art.
He's Silvermane the hero, and there isn't any doubt:
If you go and break the law he will surely call you out.

He was the most beautiful man Dante had ever seen. Not beautiful in a feminine way, but rather every-feature-perfect, the kind of beauty Michelangelo had striven for and never quite achieved.

He stood six feet eight inches tall, but so balanced were his proportions, so catlike the grace with which he moved, that he seemed smaller. His eyes were a clear and brilliant blue, his nose straight, his teeth porcelain smooth, his jaw firm without being overly square. His shoulders were broad, his waist and hips narrow, his legs long and lean.

His most distinctive feature was his hair. He had a huge thick shock of it, and it was silver in color—not black streaked with white to form a bright gray, but actual silver, every strand the purest color. It hung down his back, the longest section of it reaching his waist, and gave the impression of a huge, heavily maned lion.

He wore a matched set of projectile pistols, and the belt that supported his holsters held perhaps a hundred bullets. A knife handle peeked out from the top of one of his polished boots. His clothes were black and silver, and fit him as if they'd been designed by the finest tailor back on Deluros VIII. He wore no jewelry of any kind, not even a ring.

A thousand of the best commercial artists over the eons had tried to capture his likeness on the covers of adventure books and magazines, and had never succeeded. Heroic statues had always fallen short of the mark. Dante had a feeling that when women thought of their ideal man, they would have traded whatever their imaginations came up with for the man standing in the doorway of the tavern, putting his pistol in his holster.

The man stared at Dante and his two companions curiously, as if expecting a reaction.

"You know who that was?" said Dante at last.

"The Black Death," said the man in a strong, clear baritone.

"You meant to kill him?"

"I hit what I aim at."

Dante moved his chair away from Henry's corpse. "Well, you might as well pay the insurance."

"Pay the insurance?" repeated the man, frowning.

"Put a bullet in his ear, just to be on the safe side."

"I told you: I hit what I aim at."

"You never miss?"

"Never." The man noticed that a trickle of blood had rolled down the side of Henry's head and was moving slowly toward Dante's boot. "I'd move if I were you. His blood is probably as deadly as the rest of him."

Dante quickly stood up and walked a few steps away. "Thanks. Are you a bounty hunter?"

The beautiful man shook his shaggy silver head. "No."

"The law?"

The man smiled. "There isn't any law out here."

"Let me guess. You just didn't like the way he looked?"

"You don't strike me as a fool," said the man. "Don't say foolish things."

"I'm just trying to find out who you are and why you killed the man I was talking to."

"Then you should ask."

"Consider it done."

"My name is Joshua Silvermane, and I killed that man because he didn't deserve to live."

"Silvermane," repeated Dante. "I've heard of you. Dimitrios thinks very highly of you."

"Dimitrios of the Three Burners?" asked Silvermane.

"Yes."

"He's right."

"He never mentioned your modest streak," said Dante sardonically.

Silvermane stared at him without making any reply, and suddenly the poet became very nervous. Finally the tall man spoke. "I don't trade witticisms."

"I know why *I* think the Black Death deserved to die," said Dante, quickly changing the subject. "Why did *you* think so?"

"He killed a woman who had never done him any harm, a woman who was far better than he was."

"Your lover?" asked Matilda.

"I never met her."

"Someone paid you to hunt him down and kill him," concluded Dante. "That's pretty much like bounty hunting."

"No one paid me anything."

Dante frowned. "Then I don't understand."

"She had just married a friend of mine. A very bitter and unsuccessful suitor commissioned the Black Death to pay her a visit."

"And you hunted him down for your friend?" said Dante. "I'd call that a noble thing to do." He paused. "What do you do when you're not hunting down killers for your friends?"

"I right wrongs."

"For whom?"

"Sometimes you don't worry about that. Sometimes you just see something that's wrong, and no one is doing anything about it, so you have to."

"Why you?"

"Because someone has to."

"That's not much of an answer."

"When I was seven years old," said Silvermane, his perfect face reliving the event, "I was walking down the street of a Tradertown on Majorca II with my father. There was a fight in a building we were passing, and a stray laser beam caught him in the neck. He dropped to the ground, bleeding profusely, and for an hour I begged people to help him while they just walked around him or crossed the street and ignored him. He died before anyone helped get him to a doctor, and I swore that I would never walk past someone who needed help, would never be one of the ones who looked away."

"A not-for-profit avenger!" said Virgil, amused. "How do you pay your bills?"

"Sometimes people pay me out of gratitude," said Silvermane. "I've never asked for money, and I've never felt bitter or cheated when it wasn't given—but it comes often enough to feed and clothe me, and keep me in bullets."

"Why bullets?" asked Virgil. "I haven't seen half a dozen projectile pistols in my life."

"They make a bang," said Silvermane. "People aren't used to the noise, and it sometimes freezes them into immobility for a second or two. That's usually more advantage than I need. Also, my pistols never run out of power. I know how many bullets I have left in each and in my belt, and I don't have to constantly check my power packs."

"You know," said Dante, staring at him curiously, "Sebastian Cain used bullets, too."

"Never heard of him."

"He died a long time ago," said the poet. "I think you may have a lot in common with him."

"Interesting," said Silvermane with no show of interest whatever. He turned to the bartender. "Find me a waterproof groundsheet or something else that's airtight and doesn't leak and I'll take the body off the premises."

"Coming up," said the bartender.

"Have you got a burner?" continued Silvermane.

The bartender reached beneath the bar and produced a small laser pistol.

"Good," said Silvermane. "After I get the body out of here, take that thing and fry every drop of blood you can find on the floor."

"Was something wrong with him?" asked the bartender.

"More than you can imagine. Just do it."

"Right." He disappeared into a back room, then returned a moment later with the requested groundsheet, which he carried over to Silvermane.

"Have you got a trash atomizer out back?" asked the tall man.

"Yeah," said the bartender. "Just walk around the building. You can't miss it."

"I'm going to use it," announced Silvermane, bending over and wrapping Henry Marston's body in the blanket while being careful not to touch it with his bare hands, then hefting it to his shoulder as if it weighed almost nothing. "Even dead, this fellow is too dangerous to bury."

"Be my guest," said the bartender, as Silvermane walked out the front door.

Dante turned to his companions. "Are you thinking what I'm thinking?"

"I don't know," said Matilda, a troubled expression on her face. "We've been wrong once already."

"And the Bandit seemed a lot more tractable than this guy," added Virgil.

"But the Bandit's a fanatic," said Dante. "We couldn't know that up front."

"And this guy travels around the galaxy risking his life righting wrongs for free," Virgil pointed out. "Doesn't that seem a little fanatical to you?"

"Maybe," said Dante. "Maybe it's noble." He signed deeply. "It's almost as if Black Orpheus himself is telling me that this is the one. He uses bullets, just like Cain did . . ."

"But four other Santiagos didn't," said Matilda.

"I know," said Dante.

"Now why don't you admit the real reason you're considering him?" continued Matilda.

"And what is that?"

"The same reason *I'm* considering him," she replied uncomfortably. "He's the first man we've seen who might actually have a chance against the Bandit."

"What if he wins?" asked Virgil. "Are you really sure you want to replace one fanatical killer with an even more formidable one?"

"I don't know," said Dante. "I've just got this feeling."

"Take deep breaths and think pastoral thoughts," said Virgil. "It'll pass."

At that moment Silvermane reentered the tavern and approached their table.

"The three of you are witnesses to a killing," he announced. "If you're going to report it, let me know, and I'll stick around and give my side of it. I don't intend to be a fugitive."

"Report it to *who*?" asked Virgil.

"I don't know," admitted Silvermane with a shrug. "I just got here half an hour ago. I don't know if they have any local law enforcement."

"My guess is that they don't even have any local laws," said Dante. "Anyway, we're not reporting anything. The man you killed was scum and we all know it."

"Good," said Silvermane. "Then I'll be on my way."

"I'd like to buy you a drink first," said Dante.

"I know you would," said Silvermane.

"You do?"

"Of course. You could only have one reason for talking to the

Black Death, and now he's dead." He turned to the bartender. "Bring me a beer. A cold one." Then it was back to Dante. "Who did you want him to kill, and why?"

Dante uttered an embarrassed laugh. "I wasn't ready for such bluntness."

"There's a lot of evil abroad in the galaxy, and life is short," said Silvermane. "I have no time to waste. Who's your target?"

"It's not that easy."

"It never is—but I can't help you if you don't tell me what you want."

"I want someone to stand up for people who can't stand up for themselves," said Dante.

"That's what I do best," said Silvermane.

"So you say."

"Who's the enemy?"

"The Democracy."

Silvermane stared long and hard at him. "You don't look like a traitor."

"I'm not."

"Continue."

"There's a difference between being a traitor to your race and being opposed to the excesses of your government," continued Dante.

Silvermane stared at him and offered no reply.

"Well?" said Dante, uneasily breaking the silence.

"Well what?"

"What I said. Does it sound like something that might interest you?"

Silvermane continued staring at him. Finally he spoke. "Do you seriously expect me to believe that you were recruiting the Black Death to go to war with the Democracy?"

"No. I was interviewing him about eradicating a mistake—but he wasn't the man for the job. We were just about to leave when you showed up."

"What is the mistake?"

Now it was Dante's turn to stare in silence for a long moment, as he tried to decide how much to tell the tall man. "We chose the wrong man for the job."

"The job you're offering me?"

"The job I'm willing to discuss with you. I'm not offering anything yet."

"All right. Who did you choose originally?"

"A man known as the One-Armed Bandit."

"I've heard of him."

"Everyone has," Virgil put in.

"I heard he vanished from sight a few months ago," continued Silvermane. "I assumed he'd been killed. Eventually that happens to just about everyone in our line of work."

"The One-Armed Bandit is no more," said Dante. "But the man who *was* the One-Armed Bandit is still around."

"Oh?"

"These days he calls himself Santiago."

"The King of the Outlaws," said Silvermane. "If he wanted to attract attention, he couldn't have chosen a more obvious name. Tell me about it."

"We convinced him that it was time for Santiago to return to the Inner Frontier, to walk among Men again, to harass and harry the Democracy."

"The way I heard it, Santiago harassed and harried everyone for profit," said Silvermane.

"That's the way he *wanted* people to hear it," said Matilda.

Silvermane didn't have to be force-fed the proper assumption. "Okay, so he was a revolutionary. He didn't get very far. We've still got a Democracy."

"We need the Democracy," said Dante. "No one's trying to overthrow it."

Again the tall man surprised them with the speed with which he could assimilate what was being said. "So he was trying to lessen their abuses out here, and of course he had to convince them he was an outlaw. Even Santiago couldn't have held off the Navy."

Dante and Matilda exchanged looks.

He's awfully fast on the uptake. Maybe, just maybe . . .

"That's it in a nutshell," said Dante.

"And what's the problem with the One-Armed Bandit?" asked Silvermane. "Has he gone overboard on the outlaw part?"

"I wish it was that easy," admitted Dante with a grimace.

"What is it, then?"

"We were on Madras a couple of weeks ago . . ." began Dante.

"That was *him*?" said Silvermane. "That made the news everywhere on the Frontier, as well as the Democracy. More than three hundred kids slaughtered."

"That was him."

"What the hell got into him?"

"He says that's three hundred kids that won't grow up to be three hundred members of the Democracy."

"He's a fool," said Silvermane. "Ninety-nine percent of the Democracy is just like the men and women who walked past my father when he was dying. They're not heroes or villains, they just don't want to get involved. Hell, they're what the Democracy's there to protect. If you've got a problem with the Democracy, eventually you emigrate and come out to the Frontier." He paused. "You've got yourself a real problem, and of your own making. I assume that without you, there'd be no Santiago."

"I was part of it," interjected Matilda. "It wasn't just him."

"We've been a century without Santiago," said Silvermane. "A trillion people have been born and died in that time, maybe more. Why is it that you two have decided to resurrect him?"

Matilda gestured to Dante. "He's the new Black Orpheus."

"Self-appointed?"

"I've got the original's manuscript," said Dante. "That's how I was able to find out what Santiago really was. I'm continuing his work—and if it's to be about anything besides a handful of misfits and losers, if there's to be any balance in the galaxy, then we need a Santiago."

"So you want me to become Santiago because it'll make a satisfying poem," said Silvermane noncommittally. He turned to Matilda. "What about you?"

"I'm his great-granddaughter."

"You want me to plunder the Frontier and then die so you can claim your inheritance?"

"It's simpler than that," she answered. "I need Santiago to take the heat off me, to give the Democracy a bigger target."

Silvermane smiled. "I was wondering if we'd ever meet, Matilda."

"I haven't told you my name."

"You didn't have to. I heard that Waltzin' Matilda was traveling with the new Black Orpheus. And you just told me as much yourself: if only Santiago can draw the Democracy's attention away from you, you have to be Waltzin' Matilda." The smile vanished as he stared at her. "I've been hearing about you for years. Given your accomplishments, you're younger than I expected."

"I started early."

Silvermane turned to Virgil. "What about you?"

"I'm with him," said Virgil, jerking a thumb in Dante's direction.

"Why?"

"It's too complicated to explain—or maybe too simple."

"Try."

"He's Dante. I'm Virgil."

"How many circles of hell have you led him through so far?" asked Silvermane.

"Sonuvabitch!" exclaimed Virgil, obviously impressed. "You've read it!"

"It seems to me there's an awful lot of poetry going on around here," said Silvermane. "But it seems that these days even poets wind up relying on the sword."

"Maybe the two aren't mutually exclusive," suggested Dante. "Maybe it's the pen that must direct the sword."

Silvermane patted his pistol. "Maybe I'm writing history with my own pen."

"Are you ready to write an epic?" asked Dante. "Or are you going to keep writing little unrelated pieces that will all be forgotten?"

"I'm happy curing the ills of the Frontier one by one," said Silvermane. "I don't know how I'd feel about trying to cure them wholesale."

"I can't make you," said Dante. "I just want you to think about it."

"You say that, but what you mean is that you want me to think about killing the One-Armed Bandit—who, I should point out, wouldn't need killing if you hadn't chosen *him* to be your secret hero."

"I really don't want him killed if it can be avoided, if we can find some other way."

"How many deposed tyrants are walking around these days?" asked Silvermane. "If he's got the bit between his teeth, if he believes in what he's doing, there's only one way to replace him, and we both know what that is."

"You're a cold son of a bitch, you know that?" said Dante irritably.

"I'm in a cold business."

"You're not in a business at all. You don't demand pay for what you do." Dante paused and studied him carefully. "How do we know you won't be as much of a fanatic as the Bandit is?"

"You don't."

"What do *you* think?" said Dante.

"I have no idea," admitted Silvermane. "I don't think I'm a fanatic, and I don't think I can be corrupted—but until you give me a cause I'm willing to die for and combine it with absolute power, how can I answer your question with any certainty?"

"You just did," said Dante. "I trust you."

"I thank you for your trust, but I haven't said I'm interested in the job yet."

"I know. Take some time and think about it. We'll explain how we're setting up an organization, what connections we've established so far." Dante paused. "But don't take too long. If he goes and slaughters another three hundred kids, I'll have to take him on myself, and I don't have the chance of a snowball in hell."

"Then why do it?"

"Because he's my responsibility," answered Dante. "Because those kids would be alive if it wasn't for me."

"If I agree to become Santiago, I think we're going to get along just fine," said Silvermane.

"When do you want to learn about the operation?"

"The first thing you'd better tell me about is the One-Armed Bandit," said Silvermane. "On the not-unreasonable assumption that he has no intention of resigning, he's the first obstacle, and if he can't be overcome, none of the rest matters. I've heard about that prosthetic arm of his, but I don't really know anything about it. Just how lethal is it?"

"Depending how he's using it, he can pinpoint a target no bigger than a coin at six hundred yards, or he can take out a city block."

"Is he inclined to shoot first or talk first?"

"Once upon a time he talked first," said Dante. "These days I don't know."

"Left arm or right?"

"Left."

"Any vision problems?" asked Silvermane.

"Not to my knowledge."

"Okay, I'll think about it."

"Where will we find you?"

"I'll be leaving for New Patagonia in an hour. That's about sixteen light-years from here. You can find me at the Jong Palace."

"That's a casino?"

Silvermane smiled. "A hotel."

"With Henry—that's the Black Death—dead, we have no reason to stay here. We might as well go to New Patagonia with you."

"There's no room in my ship."

"I meant that we'll leave Tosca when you do."

"All right. I'll see you there." He walked to the door, then turned back to them. "If I decide to do it, you won't regret asking me. I'll be the best Santiago I can be." Then he was out in the street.

"Jesus, I hope so!" muttered Dante.

29.

Simon Ten Broek loves to draw attention;
Simon Ten Broek spent years in bleak detention;
Simon Ten Broek, with crimes too vile to mention;
Simon Ten Broek won't live to see his pension.

New Patagonia was everything that Tosca was not: green, temperate, pleasant, crisscrossed by rivers, framed with snowcapped mountains. It had been developed into a resort world by the cartel that had laid claim to it. They erected a ski lodge atop the snowiest mountain, then leased out the rest of the range, until the place was dotted with ski facilities. Next they expanded downward, building half a dozen fishing camps along the meandering rivers. Soon a quartet of towns sprang up, and before long the secluded little world was actually bustling with permanent and transient populations.

The largest of the towns, quickly approaching city status, was Belvidere, and it was there that Dante and his companions found the Jong Palace. After registering for a room, Virgil immediately went off by himself in search of a little professional love, hopefully from a different species, and Dante and Matilda sat down in a corner of the lobby while a small furry alien loaded their luggage onto an oversized airsled and carefully guided it up to their rooms.

"Have you done any further thinking about it?" asked the poet when he was sure no one could overhear them.

"That's *all* I've been thinking about," answered Matilda.

"Me too."

"And what have you concluded?"

"If the Bandit goes out and kills more innocent bystanders, kids or adults, it makes no difference. We'll have to stop him, and like it or not Joshua Silvermane is the only weapon we've got."

"I keep thinking that if we found the Bandit and Silvermane in less than four months, maybe we could find the perfect Santiago in a year or two," said Matilda.

"Maybe we could," admitted Dante. "Or maybe we found him already."

"Silvermane?"

"Maybe."

Matilda frowned. "Surely you're not referring to the Bandit?" she said.

"I don't know. Maybe I was a little too full of myself when I thought this thing up. What special insight do *I* have into what it takes to be Santiago? Hell, maybe killing them off before they grow up to be soldiers and cops and bounty hunters is the right way to go about it."

"You don't believe that for a moment," she said firmly.

"I don't know what I believe anymore," he admitted. "Except that maybe it was a bit presumptuous, trying to force my will on the history of the Inner Frontier. No one told the first Santiago that it was time to become Santiago. He wasn't manipulated. He just did it, because it was his destiny." He sighed deeply. "Hell, I don't even know what *my* destiny is. Why am I screwing around trying to tell them theirs?"

She stared long and hard at him. "I don't like it when you're like this."

"Like what?"

"Full of self-doubt," said Matilda. "From the outset, you've always known what you wanted to do, and how you planned to do it. This isn't like you."

"I stood back and took a good look at what I've done," he replied. "A lot of people are dead who wouldn't be if it weren't for me."

"You didn't kill them."

"They're dead just the same. Not just the children, though that's the worst of it—but I killed the Candy Man and Jackrabbit Willowby just as surely as if I aimed the weapons and pulled the triggers."

"They deserved to die."

"I'm not arguing that," said Dante. "But the fact remains that if I'd stayed on Bailiwick and never come to the Frontier, they'd still be alive. I'm the reason they're all dead, maybe the only reason."

"So are you quitting?"

"No, I'm not quitting. But I've got to be *certain* this time. I can't keep choosing the wrong man and turning him loose on the galaxy."

"It just means you care, and that you're giving it a lot of thought."

"It means I've got a lot to make amends for." He looked at her. "And it means that I can't make any more mistakes."

"If it was anyone's mistake, it was *mine*," she protested. "Don't forget—I'm the one who got you to come to Heliopolis to meet the Bandit in the first place."

"And I'm the one who approved him."

"There's enough guilt to go around," said Matilda.

"Yeah, I suppose so," agreed Dante. He got to his feet. "Come on. I'll buy you a drink."

"You're on," she said, relieved that the conversation was over.

"In fact," he continued, "instead of going to the hotel bar, why don't we go out for that drink and take a look around town? I've never been to New Patagonia before, and I'll probably never come back. It'd be a shame not to spend at least a couple of hours getting the flavor of the place."

"Sounds good to me," said Matilda, taking his arm and walking out into the street with him.

"It's really quite a lovely world," said Dante approvingly. "Fishing, skiing, skating—they probably even have hunting safaris."

"And even though there's snow surrounding us, it's still very pleasant down here in the valley," she added.

"Let's walk up and down the street and see what kind of shops they have."

"What are you looking for?"

"Anything I can steal." She looked annoyed, and he smiled at her. "Oh, don't worry, I won't—but a lifetime's habits are hard to lose. I still like to look."

They walked down the block, reached a corner, and were about to cross to the other side of the street when Dante heard a familiar voice behind him.

"Hi, Danny boy," it said. "You've led me on one hell of a merry chase."

"*Shit!*" muttered Dante, freezing.

"Turn around very slowly," continued the voice, "and keep your hands out from your body."

Dante did as he was ordered. "You're a long way from home, Commander Balsam," he said when he finally was able to face his antagonist.

"It's just plain Balsam now," said the big man, aiming his burner between Dante's eyes. "Things got so dull back on Bailiwick after you left that I quit my job and became a bounty hunter." He paused. "You've been a busy boy, Danny. I've been on your tail for months now, but all I keep finding are dead bodies."

Matilda began edging away from Dante, and suddenly Balsam trained his weapon on her. "That's far enough."

"You want *him*, not me," said Matilda.

"You're with Danny Briggs," said Balsam. "That's enough for me. You're going to stay with us until I find out if there's any paper on you." Dante took a tentative step toward him. "Watch it, Danny. You're wanted dead or alive. It makes no difference to me which way I bring you back."

"You've really been following me since I left Bailiwick?" asked Dante.

"A few weeks later," said Balsam. "You leave an awful easy trail to follow."

"I'd totally forgotten I was wanted back in the Democracy," admitted Dante. "I've had more important things on my mind."

"Always thinking—that's my Danny." He paused. "Where's the Indian?"

"What Indian?"

"Don't play stupid, Danny. It's unbecoming, and it doesn't fit you at all." Balsam looked around. "My information says that you usually travel with an Indian."

"I don't see one," said Dante. "Do you?"

"No, but after I take possession of that poem you're supposed to be writing, I'll figure out who he is and find him." He smiled. "Am *I* in it?"

Dante shook his head. "I only write about interesting people."

"You cut me to the quick," said Balsam with mock pain. Suddenly he laughed. "Hell, I'll write myself into it after I take it away from you."

"You're not touching it," said Dante firmly.

"We'll see about that," said Balsam. Suddenly he grinned. "You're only worth sixty thousand credits this month, Danny. How much is it worth to you if I let you keep your damned poem and you go deeper and deeper into the Frontier?" He paused. "I'm not saying I'll never come after you again, but I'll give you a sixty-day head start. How does that sound?"

Dante looked past Balsam and saw Joshua Silvermane exit a restaurant and step out into the street. The tall man stopped and surveyed the little scene calmly, an armadillo watching ants bickering.

"You haven't answered me, Danny."

"I don't deal with blackmailers."

"View me as a liberator," said Balsam.

"You don't want to know what I view you as."

"I'm running out of patience, Danny. I can kill you or I can take you back alive or I can let you go—but one way or another I'm going to make myself sixty thousand credits. Now, do I do it the hard way or the easy way?"

"Why not make a trade?" said a strong baritone voice.

"Who the hell are you?" demanded Balsam as Silvermane approached them.

"My name's Joshua Silvermane."

"I never heard of you."

"That's okay," said Silvermane. "I never heard of you, either."

"What kind of trade are you talking about?"

"Just a moment," said Silvermane, walking to the entrance to a drug parlor about forty feet away.

"Where are you going?" said Balsam suspiciously.

"Stay where you are. I'll be right back."

Silvermane vanished into the drug den's interior. A moment later there was a deafening *crash!*, and an instant after that a body literally flew out through a window and landed with a sickening *thud!* on the street, where it lay, twitching feebly.

Silvermane emerged and approached Balsam again.

"That's Simon Ten Broek," he said, not even deigning to give the moaning man a glance. "There's paper on him all over the Frontier. He's worth a hundred thousand credits back on Spica VI, even more in the Roosevelt system."

"What the hell did he do?"

"Rape. Arson. Torture. Murder. Three jailbreaks. You name it, he's probably done it."

"Okay, he's a wanted man. So what?"

"I'll trade him to you for the poet and the lady," said Silvermane. "You'll come out at least forty thousand credits ahead."

"What if I say no?"

"Then I'll kill Simon, and when I'm done, I'll probably kill you too."

Balsam aimed his weapon at Silvermane. "You forget who has the advantage here, friend."

"Put that burner down or I'll take it away and cram it up your ass," said Silvermane with no show of fear or apprehension.

The grin vanished. Of all the answers Balsam had expected, that was the least likely, and it troubled him. "How do I know that's really Simon Ten Broek?"

"How do I know you're really a licensed bounty hunter?" Silvermane shot back.

"This is ridiculous!" snapped Balsam, his courage slipping away in the face of this totally confident stranger. "I've wasted enough time! You want a trade? All right, we'll trade! Just take them and get the hell out of my sight."

"You've made a wise decision," said Silvermane. He turned to Dante and Matilda. "Come on."

They fell into step behind him as he began walking back to the Jong Palace. As they did so, Balsam went over to Simon Ten Broek and delivered a powerful kick in his ribs. "Get up!" he bellowed.

Silvermane was beside Balsam before he realized it. "And *that*," he said, "was a foolish decision." He grabbed Balsam's wrist before he could reach for his weapon. They stood motionless for a moment. Then there was an audible *crack!*, and Balsam screamed. Silvermane released his grip, and Balsam dropped to one knee, holding his wrist.

"I gave you a prisoner, not a toy," said Silvermane sternly.

"You broke my wrist!" snarled Balsam.

"You'll have time to think about abusing your fellow man while it heals."

"Abusing my fellow man? *You* threw him through that fucking window!"

"*I* met him on equal terms," said Silvermane. "You didn't. If I hear he was further abused, I'll come looking for you. You'll live a lot longer if I don't."

Silvermane stood and stared down at the bounty hunter.

"I heard you," grated Balsam.

"Make sure you remember."

Silvermane turned and walked to the Jong Palace, followed by Dante and Matilda.

"Thank you," said Dante once they were inside.

"There's no need," said Silvermane. "I took an instant dislike to your officious Democracy associate. Besides, it makes no difference whether I kill Simon here or they put him to death back in the Democracy. The important thing is that he dies."

"What did he do?" asked Matilda.

"More than I hope a lovely lady like yourself can imagine," said Silvermane.

"He's the reason you came to New Patagonia?"

"He's the reason."

"What will you do now?"

"I haven't decided."

"Have you thought about what we discussed last night?" asked Dante.

"Why else would I save you from a bounty killer?" replied Silvermane with an amused smile.

"And have you reached a decision?"

"I'm working on it."

30.

Billy Green-Eyes, bold and brave,
Would never be a hero.
And now our Billy seeks the grave:
His prospects total zero.

Silvermane announced that he had one more world to visit before he made his decision. It was the mining world of Trentino, the seventh planet in the Alpha Bellini system, and they had no choice but to follow him in their own ship.

The journey took three days. Virgil opted for seventy hours in the Deepsleep pod, but Dante and Matilda chose to remain awake most of the time, discussing their options, wondering if they'd found their Santiago or if they could do better with a little more searching.

"It doesn't really make much difference if there's a better man out there," said Matilda after they'd gone over the possibilities for the tenth time. "We have an immediate problem, or we wouldn't be here. We've got to stop the Bandit before he kills more innocent people."

"We could hire an assassin if that's all that matters," responded Dante. "I think our original idea was right. We just chose the wrong man."

"Maybe it's not time," said Matilda. "Maybe events choose the man. You and I are just people, not events. Maybe it's simply not yet time for Santiago to cast his shadow across the galaxy."

"How much worse do things have to get?"

"I don't know. But do you ever get the feeling that we're like journalists who stop reporting the news and start creating it?"

"I'm not a journalist, and neither are you."

"You know what I mean. Maybe we're not supposed to handpick a Santiago. Maybe he'll step forward on his own. Maybe until he does, until it's *his* idea to be Santiago, we're being premature about the whole thing."

"I thought you *wanted* a Santiago," he said accusingly.

"I did," she said. "And I got one. And look at what's happened."

"That's because he's *not* Santiago."

"Make up your mind. Is he Santiago because you say he is, or because we set him up in the Santiago business, whatever that is—or is he Santiago because he's an historic inevitability at this time and place?"

"Oh, come on. Next you'll be telling me that only God can anoint him."

"I'm just saying that maybe God is working on a different deadline, and that He might do a better job of choosing a Santiago than we've done."

"We have it within our grasp to do some good, to make a difference," said Dante adamantly. "You don't get more than one or two such opportunities in a lifetime. I'm not turning my back on it."

"It's not a question of turning your back, but of pursuing it too vigorously," replied Matilda.

"Damn it!" exploded Dante. "Whose side are you on, anyway?"

"The Frontier's," she answered. "And I want to make sure that what I do doesn't bring it even more hardship and misery."

He stared at her for a long moment. "It's time. In fact, it's past time. Santiago's reign ended on a fluke. To this day the Democracy doesn't even know they killed him."

"You're absolutely sure you're right?"

He paused for just an instant. "I'm absolutely certain that I hope I'm right."

"Maybe he'll take the decision out of our hands and turn us down," she said hopefully.

"He won't."

"What makes you so sure?"

"I've been watching him. He's not a fanatic, he's no One-Armed Bandit—but he's got an ego as big as all outdoors. The more difficult we make the job sound, the more we explain that he'll be fighting a holding action, that he can never hope to overthrow the Democracy, the more he'll want to prove that we're wrong, that he can bring the whole thing down."

"And you want that quality in a Santiago?" she said dubiously.

"The odds are a billion to one against him," said Dante. "He's got to be a bit of an egomaniac even to consider taking the job on."

"Well, I've never known you to be wrong about anyone," she said. Then she added: "Except the Bandit. How did you miss what he would become?"

"You don't want to know."

"Yes, I do."

"I let your opinion influence me," said Dante.

"Bullshit!"

"You vouched for his character, so all I concentrated on was his ability. And he *does* have the ability; otherwise we wouldn't be trying to find ways to stop him."

"So the One-Armed Bandit is *my* fault?" she said heatedly.

"No. I'm the one who made him the offer and hired Wilbur and Blossom and set up the drug deal with the two ladies from Snakepit. If I made the wrong decision, and I did, I have no one to blame but myself."

"So what do we do now?"

"Wait. The offer's on the table. The next move is Silvermane's."

"He's almost too good to be true," she remarked.

"Virgil had something very wise to say about things that were too good to be true," said Dante wryly.

"What was it?"

"It's not important." Dante got to his feet. "We'll be landing in an hour. I think it's time to wake Sleeping Beauty."

He went to the Deepsleep pod and spent the next five minutes bringing Virgil to wakefulness.

"How are you feeling?" he asked when the Indian finally climbed out of the pod.

"Stiff."

"That's normal," said Dante. "You haven't moved in almost three days."

"And hungry."

"You haven't eaten in three days either. We'll go back to the galley and get something for you."

"How soon do we land?"

"Less than an hour."

"I'll wait," said Virgil.

"I thought you were hungry."

"There's nothing like the taste of galley food to kill an appetite. I'm an hour from a real restaurant. I can wait."

Dante shrugged. "Suit yourself."

He stopped by the galley, got a cup of coffee, rejoined Matilda in the command cabin, ordered the ship's computer to respond to any questions from the planetary authorities, and relaxed until they touched down.

"Where are we staying?" asked Virgil as they rode the slidewalk to Customs.

"I haven't bothered to reserve any rooms," answered Dante. "The way Silvermane operates, I figure we'll be back on the ship before nightfall."

"He doesn't waste his time, that's for sure," said Virgil. "He could be a little friendlier, though."

"He saved my life," said Dante. "How much friendlier does he have to be?"

"Okay, so I used the wrong word. He could be a little warmer."

"I don't think it's a job requirement."

"Have it your way," said Virgil, losing interest in the conversation.

They reached the Customs station, and found themselves facing a uniformed woman rather than the usual robot.

"Welcome to Trentino," she said. "May I ask the purpose of your visit?"

"Business," answered Dante.

"Precious stones or fissionable materials?"

"Neither."

"Those are our only two industries."

"We're here on personal business," said Dante.

"I must insist that you be more explicit, Mr. Alighieri." She stared at his titanium passport disk. "That's very odd. It's such an unusual name, and yet I could swear I've encountered it before." She frowned, shrugged, and looked back at him. "Why are you here, Mr. Alighieri?"

"To confer with a business associate named Joshua Silvermane, who either landed within the past few hours or will be landing shortly."

"Ah, Mr. Silvermane!" she said, her face lighting up. "What an absolutely beautiful man! And what wonderful manners!" She checked her screen again. "What is the nature of your business with him?"

"I don't believe I'm required to divulge that information," said Dante. "But if you have any doubts that he is expecting us, just contact him."

"That will not be necessary," conceded the woman. She glared at the poet. "You cannot pass through here without purchasing visas."

"What are the shortest visas available?"

"One week. They cost one hundred credits apiece."

"You don't have anything for daytrippers?"

"We don't get daytrippers on Trentino."

Dante pulled the cash out of his pocket and gave it to her. She encoded the visa on each of their passports.

"I am required to warn you that the atmosphere of Trentino is inimical to human life. As you pass through the spaceport, you will emerge into a domed, enclosed area that is approximately one mile long and a quarter of a mile wide. You must be a registered miner to pass beyond the dome, and if you attempt to do so without a protective suit no attempt will be made to hinder you—but the air, such as it is, is eighty-three percent methane, and the temperature is minus ninety-two degrees Celsius, which is to say you will not survive for even a minute." She paused. "I am also required by law to ask you if you understand my warning."

"Perfectly," said Dante.

They had begun walking past her station when a metal bar shot out, stopping them.

"You may not answer for your companions. Each of them must answer for themselves." She turned to Matilda. "Did you understand my warning?"

"Yes."

And to Virgil: "Did you understand my warning?"

"Right. I just didn't care about it."

"Welcome to Trentino," she said with an expression of distaste. "You may pass through now."

The three of them walked past the Customs station, made their way through the spaceport, and soon found themselves outside the facility but still enclosed by the huge dome.

"So where do we go from here?" asked Matilda.

"He wouldn't tell me who he's after," replied Dante. "I suppose we might as well wait here. I mean, hell, you've seen him in action. Can you imagine it'll take him more than an hour or two to find whoever he's looking for and take care of business?"

"That seems so . . . passive," she said. "He's a very distinctive man. Perhaps we should ask around. He's not the kind of man people forget."

"If that's what you want," said Dante. He turned to Virgil. "You wait here by the spaceport entrance, just in case we miss him."

"How will I know you've missed him?"

"He'll come back alone. If he does, tell him we're here and that I want him to wait for us."

"Fine."

"We really have to talk to him," said Dante. "No booze and no drugs, and no fucking any stray pets that pass by."

"What fun is that?" said Virgil with a smile.

"I'm not kidding."

"Neither am I."

Dante was about to say something further, changed his mind, then turned and began walking down the major thoroughfare with Matilda at his side.

"Where do we start?" he asked. "Bars, I suppose."

"You're in a rut," she replied. "For all we know, he's after a stockbroker or an incompetent doctor."

"I can't walk into every brokerage house and infirmary and ask if they've seen this tall silver-haired guy who's here to kill someone."

"Okay," she conceded. "You've got a point."

"If he's looking for someone, and doesn't know anything except that he's on Trentino, I imagine he'd stop at the first bar he came to and ask about him. And if he didn't get any answers there, he'd stop at the next one, and so on down the line."

"Why not drug dens or whorehouses?"

"A man's likely to visit a bar more often than the other two. And if he's chewing seed or with a woman, they may not want to disturb a good client, so they'd lie and say they didn't know him. I think a bar's the likeliest spot."

"I'll give you this much," she said. "You've always got a sensible answer."

"God didn't give me Silvermane's abilities, and medical science hasn't given me the Bandit's, so I have to use what I've got."

They stopped by a bar about half a block away, and Dante described Silvermane. He got as far as the hair and the height.

"Yeah, absolutely, he was here maybe half an hour ago," said the bartender. "Couldn't mistake him for anyone else. He was looking for Billy Green-Eyes."

"Where would we find Billy Green-Eyes?" asked Dante.

"Same place as always. Go two blocks down, turn left, and you'll come to a small park built around a fountain. Check the first bench you come to."

"It sounds simple enough," remarked Dante. He turned to Matilda. "Let's go. The fireworks should be all over by now."

They followed the bartender's directions. When they turned and approached the park, they saw Silvermane standing, hands on hips, talking to an emaciated man who was seated on the bench.

As they drew near, they could see that the man was horribly mutilated. He was missing his left arm, his right leg, and his left eye. Part of his left ear was gone, burned off by a laser beam. He was dressed in rags, and a cheap pair of crutches were balanced against the back of the bench.

Silvermane looked up and nodded a greeting.

"Hi," said Dante. "Where's Billy Green-Eyes? Have you found him yet?"

"You're looking at him," said Silvermane.

"Him?" said Dante, startled. *"He's* what you came to Trentino to kill?"

"He's not quite the man he used to be," said Silvermane with a grim smile. "Are you, Billy?"

The man on the bench muttered something unintelligible.

"What the hell did he do?" asked Matilda.

"About seven years ago a plague broke out on New Damascus, way out in the Belladonna Cluster. Billy-boy here stowed away on the ship that was racing the vaccine to them, killed the crew, and held them up for a few million credits before he delivered the vaccine. Thousands died during the negotiations." He paused. "Sweet man, our Billy."

"So what happened to him?"

"Six of the survivors happened to him," continued Silvermane. "Billy killed them all, but not before they did what you see. He'd blown all his money on seed, and his deeds made him a pariah even among the scum he associated with, so no one would help him or give him money to go back to the Democracy for the necessary prosthetics. Hell, even if he'd managed to borrow the money, they'd have jailed and executed him the second they spotted him. So Billy has been rotting out here for the past few years, isn't that right, Billy?"

Another unintelligible answer.

"He lives in the filthiest corner of the filthiest warehouse on Trentino. Each morning he comes out to the park and sits here, hat in hand, begging, but of course everyone knows he's the man who extorted millions for the New Damascus vaccine, so he probably takes in about three credits a week, all from newcomers. We've just been discussing his situation, haven't we, Billy?"

Billy glared at him balefully with his one remaining green eye, but said nothing.

You cold son of a bitch, thought Dante. *Whatever he's done, I don't know how you can shoot a helpless old cripple who can't lift a finger to defend himself.*

"And now we're all through discussing it," concluded Silvermane.

"All right," said Dante uncomfortably. "Shoot him and let's get it over with."

"I'm not shooting anyone," replied Silvermane.

"Oh?"

"Four thousand men, women, and children died on New Damascus while Billy was negotiating a price for the vaccine. Killing's too easy for him."

"So what *are* you going to do to him?" asked Dante.

Silvermane stared at the emaciated one-eyed, one-armed, one-legged beggar. "Not a thing," he said. "Have a long life, Billy." He turned and began walking back to the spaceport.

Jesus, you're even colder than I thought, mused Dante. And then: *Still, that's very much like justice.*

"I hope he lives another century," said Silvermane.

"He deserves to," agreed Matilda.

"Still, I'll give him credit for facing those New Damascans. There were six of them, and he stood his ground, for what little good it did him."

"You sound like you admire him."

"I admire the trait, not the man," explained Silvermane. "I suspect there's a lot to admire about your One-Armed Bandit as well."

"There is," she admitted.

"Seems a shame," he continued. "From what I've heard, he's a moral man doing the best he can."

"His best isn't good enough," said Dante firmly. "He can destroy what we're trying to build."

"I know," said Silvermane. "That's why I've decided to accept your offer."

31.

The Plymouth Rocker mourns a love
That used to be and is no more.
He curses to the skies above—
A most unhappy troubadour.

Bodini II wasn't much of a world. Small, flat, green, agricultural, dotted here and there by impenetrable thorn forests. It had a trio of towns, each with a small spaceport where the local farmers and agricultural cartels brought their goods to ship to the nearby colonies and mining worlds.

It was here that Silvermane took Dante, Matilda, and Virgil when they left Trentino. They passed through Customs without incident and stopped for a quick lunch in one of the spaceport restaurants.

"Couldn't you just send this guy a subspace message telling him to join us?" asked Dante.

"Not the Plymouth Rocker," answered Silvermane.

"And we really need him?"

"He's the one I want."

"What makes him so special?"

"I trust him." Silvermane paused. "There aren't many men I've trusted over the years. He's the best of them."

"I heard a lot about him maybe ten, fifteen years ago," volunteered Virgil. "Not a word since then. I figured he was dead."

"Why?" asked Dante.

"When you stop hearing about people out here, especially people like him, you just naturally assume someone or something caught up with them."

"I heard someone mention him not too long ago," said Matilda. "Dimitrios, maybe, or perhaps the Bandit."

"He had quite a reputation back then," said Virgil. "What happened to him?"

"To *him*?" replied Silvermane. "Nothing."

"The way you emphasized that," interjected Dante, "something happened to *someone*."

"You're a perceptive man," said Silvermane. "I suppose that goes with being a poet."

"So what happened?" said Dante, ignoring the compliment.

"He had a woman," answered Silvermane. "Lovely lady. Mind like a steel trap. Totally fearless. Devoted to him. They made a hell of a team."

"Did she have a name?" asked Dante, pulling out a stylus.

"She had a lot of them, depending on the situation," said Silvermane. "I first knew her as Priscilla, so that's the way I think of her. They did everything together, Priscilla and the Rocker. I don't remember ever seeing them more than eight or ten feet apart. He'd start a sentence and she'd finish it, or the other way around. If you were with them for any length of time, you finally appreciated what the term 'soulmate' really means."

"What did they do?"

"A little of everything. They were actually law officers together back in the Democracy, two of the best. They worked the entire Quintaro Sector, and they put one hell of a lot of bad guys away." He paused thoughtfully. "I think they did a little bounty hunting when they first moved out here. Then they spent a couple of years bodyguarding Federico Bogardus when he was King of New Lebanon. Just the two of them . . . but that was enough to scare off any potential assassins."

"How did she die?" asked Dante.

"What makes you think she died?"

"You said he *had* a woman. Past tense. You don't leave a woman like that—or bury yourself on an obscure little world like this one. Not without a reason."

"You're good, poet. We're going to work well together." Silvermane paused for a moment, staring sightlessly into the past. "She was quite a woman, that Priscilla. Been dead about a dozen years now."

"What happened?"

"She died," said Silverman noncommittally. "The Rocker left Prateep a few weeks later, and he's spent the last few years on this little backwater planet."

"Is he a farmer?"

"No. He just rents a house from an absentee landlord."

"What *does* he do, then?" asked Dante.

"He hides."

"From what?" asked Matilda.

"From the past. From his memories." The tall man smiled grimly. "They always find him."

"And this is the man you want by your side?"

"Nobody fights by my side," said Silvermane with what Dante thought was just a touch of arrogance. "But this is a man I want for our organization."

"Why should he be willing to rejoin the world?" asked Matilda curiously.

"Because I know him better than he knows himself," said Silvermane.

"I still don't see why you couldn't have just sent him a message to join us," said Dante.

"It's been years since he's seen any action," said Silvermane. "I want to make sure he's in good enough physical and emotional shape. A decade of seclusion and mourning can change a man beyond all recognition."

"Well, let's hope it didn't."

Silvermane got to his feet and threw some Maria Theresa dollars on the table. "Let's go find out."

Dante and the others joined him, and a few moments later they were rapidly skimming a few inches above a dirt road in a sleek limo.

"Beautiful country," remarked Dante, looking out across the green fields.

"Dull country," said Silvermane. "Beautiful country has hills and mountains and valleys and makes lousy farmland. You need an expanse of flat characterless land like this to grow anything in quantity."

"I grew up surrounded by mountains and valleys," said Dante. "We paid a premium for the food we imported." He smiled wryly. "Maybe that's why I appreciate farmland."

"Take a look at *that!*" said Matilda, pointing to a huge cow that stood a good ten feet at the shoulder. Suddenly another enormous cow came into view, then a whole herd of them. "Aren't they remarkable?"

"Mutated," said Silvermane. "Cost a bundle to create them, but once they began breeding true they've more than paid back their cost."

"You sound like you've been here before," noted Matilda.

"Once, about eight years ago."

"You didn't get him to come with you back then. Why should this time be any different?"

"I didn't ask him to come with me then," answered Silvermane.

"What were you doing here?"

"I'd been wounded, and I needed a place to stay while I healed. The Rocker gave it to me."

"He sounds like a good friend."

"He was, once."

"Maybe he still is."

"We'll know soon enough," said Silvermane.

They rode the next half hour in silence, and then the limo came to a halt, hovered for a moment, and lowered itself gently to the ground.

"We have arrived at our destination," announced the navigational computer.

Silvermane climbed out of the limo, then helped Matilda out. When Dante and Virgil had also emerged, he turned and faced the farmhouse a short distance away.

The door irised and a burly man stepped through. He took one look at Silvermane and a broad smile crossed his sallow face.

"Joshua!" he called out. "How the hell are you?"

"Just fine this time," answered Silvermane, approaching him. The man trotted forward and threw his muscular arms around Silvermane.

"Damn, but it's good to see you!" He backed away a step. "Who are your friends?"

Silvermane introduced each by name. "And this is the notorious Plymouth Rocker," he concluded, indicating the man.

"It's been a long time since I was notorious," said the Rocker. Then: "Come on into the house. You must be thirsty after your trip out from the spaceport."

"One of us sure as hell is," volunteered Virgil, stepping forward.

The Rocker took them back to the farmhouse, and a moment later they were inside it. The walls of the foyer were covered with holos of a lovely woman, who Dante knew must be Priscilla. They passed to the living room, which had still more holos, plus a dozen little remembrances of her: a favorite book of poetry, a gold-handled hairbrush, a crystal wineglass that had stood empty for more than a decade.

"It's like a goddamned shrine to her," Dante whispered to Matilda.

"It must be wonderful to be loved the way he loved her," she whispered back.

"Wonderful or stifling," whispered Danny. "Either way, it had to make losing her almost unbearable."

The Rocker brought out beer for everyone, then invited them to sit down on the various chairs and couches.

"So, what brings you to Bodini?" he asked Silvermane when they were all settled.

"You."

"I'm always glad to see you, Joshua," said the Rocker. "But I'm out of the business."

"What business?" asked Silvermane with mock innocence.

"*Any* business."

"You can't bury yourself here forever."

The Rocker pointed to an elegant urn with gold inlays that floated in an antigrav field near his fireplace. "That's what remains of my Priscilla," he said. "When I die, I've left orders to cremate me and then mix our ashes together. I won't have it any other way." He paused. "I don't want to die on some other world and be separated from her forever."

"Whatever you say," said Silvermane.

"*That's* what I say."

"Still, it seems a shame."

"That I can't go killing bad guys with you?" said the Rocker with a smile. "You don't need me. You never did."

"It's a shame," continued Silvermane, as if the Rocker hadn't said a word, "that you can't avenge her death."

"What are you talking about?" demanded the Rocker, suddenly alert. "No one knows who killed her—you know that. How can I avenge her?"

"You've been looking at it all wrong. You don't know which individual killed her. But you know he worked for the Democracy, that he represented it."

"So what?" said the Rocker bitterly. "How do you go to war with the whole Democracy?"

"That's the easy part. You join me."

"Just you and me against the whole Democracy?"

"You and me—and them," said Silvermane, indicating his companions. "And the whole of Santiago's organization."

"How can Santiago have an organization?" said the Rocker in exasperated tones. "He's been dead for a couple of hundred years, if he ever really existed at all. You're not making any sense, Joshua."

"Santiago is alive," said Dante.

The Rocker turned to him. "Another quarter heard from."

"Santiago is more than a man," continued Dante. "He's an ideal, and he changes outfits just the way you and I do. Today he's wearing Joshua Silvermane."

"Well, I'm sure that's very interesting, but it doesn't make any sense," said the Rocker.

Dante was about to explain, but Silvermane cut him off. "It doesn't have to," he said. "All you have to know is that you can punish the Democracy for what they did to Priscilla, or you can stay here and mourn her and never do anything about it. It's your choice."

The Rocker stared at Silvermane for a long moment. Dante thought he was actually going to take a swing at him, but instead he finally got to his feet.

"I'll only come if I can take Priscilla with me," he said at last.

"If that's what you want."

"It's not negotiable. Wherever I die, she's got to be there or they'll never mingle our ashes."

"Have you considered living?" suggested Silvermane.

"Not lately," admitted the Rocker. "But now you've given me a reason to, even if we only last an hour—which, I might add, seems optimistic." He walked to a closet, pulled out a very old pulse gun, and tucked it in his belt. Then he tenderly took the urn in his arms. "Okay, I'm ready. Let's go."

"Don't you want to take anything else?" asked Dante.

"Like what?" asked the Rocker.

Dante shrugged. "I don't know. Some clothes, maybe, or perhaps another weapon?"

"I'll buy 'em when I need 'em."

A few moments later they were racing back to the spaceport, as Dante and Silvermane took turns filling in the newest member of their organization.

32.

They didn't all leave Bodini II together, since they had come in a number of ships. Dante, Silvermane, and the Plymouth Rocker took off first and landed on Brandywine, a lovely little world in the Spinos system, where Silvermane had a mountain retreat. He hadn't visited it in close to three years, but it had a full-time staff—a husband-and-wife team, plus a groundskeeper—and it was in perfect repair. Dante left messages to Matilda and Virgil to meet them there. He wasn't sure how far he could trust Blossom, so he kept her out of the loop.

"Nice layout," commented the Plymouth Rocker, walking through the rustic retreat. "Build it yourself?"

"I appropriated it from someone who didn't need it any longer," replied Silvermane.

"Who was it?"

"Nobody very important," answered Silvermane in tones that made it clear the subject was closed.

"Well, Joshua, what's our next step?" asked the Rocker.

"We're about to decide—and call me Santiago."

"Sorry."

"I've been thinking about it," said Silvermane. "And it seems to me that there's no reason to build a new organization when it's so much easier to take over the One-Armed Bandit's. How many men does he have working for him now?"

"I'm not sure," answered Dante, settling down in an angular chair of alien design that was more comfortable than it looked. "He has people recruiting all over the Frontier. I would think he's got between seventy-five and a hundred by now, maybe even more."

"That proves my point. It could take us months to get that many men—and then we'd have to go to war with *his* men. Much better to just take over what he's got."

"Won't the One-Armed Bandit have a little something to say about it?" asked the Rocker.

"Not if we work it right," said Silvermane.

"You're not talking about walking right in and killing him?" said Dante. "We don't have any idea what defenses he's installed since I left—not that he needs very many."

"No, I don't plan to confront him on his own world," replied Silvermane. "I may be brave, but I'm not suicidal."

"So the trick is to get him off Valhalla," said the Rocker.

"That's right."

"How?"

Silvermane turned to Dante. "I thought our resident poet might have an idea. It seems that he's never short of them."

"Are you being sarcastic," asked Dante, "or are you really asking for suggestions?"

"Both."

Dante lowered his head in thought for a moment, then reached into a pocket and pulled out a notebook and a stylus and began scribbling something.

"What's he doing?" asked the Rocker.

"I'm sure he'll tell us when he's done," said Silvermane, watching the young poet as he crossed out words, wrote in new ones, and stared off into space, obviously thinking. Finally he looked up.

"Here's how we do it," he announced, and then read aloud:

> *"Women scream and children shake,*
> *Lawmen hide and strong men quake.*
> *The world is turning upside down—*
> *The One-Armed Bandit's come to town."*

"What the hell does *that* have to do with anything?" asked the Rocker.

Silvermane smiled. "You're on the right track, Rhymer."

"Would someone explain what's going on to me?" said the Rocker.

"Dante is the new Black Orpheus," said Silvermane. "He's the reason that Santiago is being resurrected in the first place. The One-Armed Bandit knows this. Do you start to follow?"

"Okay," replied the Rocker. "So the Bandit sees the poem, and he realizes that Dante is telling the Frontier that he's not the hero he's cracked up to be. So what? From what you tell me, he's already going to kill Dante the next time he sees him."

"He's calling himself Santiago these days," said Silvermane. "He's done everything he can to separate himself from his identity as the One-Armed Bandit. He's going to make enough enemies as Santiago; he doesn't need the ones who have reason to kill the Bandit."

"That's not enough," said the Rocker. "Are you telling me he's going to drop everything he's doing and come after Dante here just because he writes one lousy stanza calling the Bandit a villain?"

"Use your imagination," said Silvermane. "This is the opening shot, the Bandit's wake-up call." He turned to Dante. "Am I right?"

"You're right."

"Okay," said the Rocker. "What comes next?"

"I find a remote planet maybe a hundred thousand light-years from Valhalla," said Dante, "and I start printing poems in the classified section of its major newsdisk—and each poem is more explicit. I point out who he deals with, what he looks like, where he lives. I start naming his key people. Then we get a third party to transmit all this to the Bandit. How long do you think it'll be before he comes after me himself?"

"Why wouldn't he simply send one of his killers?" asked the Rocker.

"Because I know too much. He's got to be *sure* he shuts me up, and that means he'll do the job himself."

"And once we know he's left," concluded Silvermane, "you and I will pay a visit to Valhalla and take over the Santiago business."

The Rocker turned to Dante. "And then you come back from the planet before the Bandit can reach it?"

"I'm not going to it at all. I don't have to be there to put the ads in. We'll have to send *somebody* there, because he'll check to see if they were inserted locally, but I'm the only one he'll recognize, and I'm no more suicidal than Santiago here."

"Okay," said the Rocker. "Now that you've explained it, I don't see any reason why it shouldn't work." He paused. "I'm not stupid, no matter what you think. I'm just not used to dealing with a devious bastard like yourself."

"I'll take that as a high compliment," said Dante, forcing a smile.

He spent the next three days writing the verses that would convince the Bandit to leave his headquarters and travel halfway across the Frontier. In the meantime, Silvermane contacted a friend who owed him a favor and had him to go Hadrian II, a distant, isolated Frontier world that had a large enough population to support a hugely popular newsdisk.

Matilda showed up the day after Dante finished the poems, and Virgil arrived two days after that. Blossom radioed them that she had decided to return to Valhalla and beg the Bandit to take her back.

"Stupid," said Dante.

"Maybe he *will* take her," said Matilda.

"She's signed her own death warrant," said Dante. "If he doesn't kill her, *we* probably will. After all, there's no question now where her loyalties lie."

"You recruited her," said Matilda. "Can't you unrecruit her, just send her back to Heliopolis?"

"She practically worships the Bandit. Do you think she'll just pack up and leave peacefully if we kill him—or if we take over while he's gone and haven't killed him yet?"

"No," she admitted, "I suppose you're right. I'm just sorry about it."

"If I were you, I'd worry about how many more innocent bystanders the Bandit will kill before we depose him," said Dante. "At least Blossom knows the score and made an informed choice. Stupid, but informed."

Even at light speeds it took Silvermane's friend eight days to reach Hadrian. Dante could have sent the poems via subspace radio while the man was en route, but he couldn't be sure the man wouldn't just transmit them on, and the whole purpose was to make certain that if the Bandit or any of his people traced the poems to their source, there could be no doubt that they came from Hadrian II itself.

Finally the man landed on that distant world, the poems were transmitted, and within two days the first four had appeared on the newsdisk, which had a new edition every eight Standard hours.

Then came the question of how best to get the poems into the Bandit's hands.

"It's too obvious to send them directly to the Bandit," said Dante. "I mean, hell, if they come from an 'interested friend,' he might try to find out who the friend is before he races off to Hadrian."

"What do you suggest?" asked Silvermane.

"I've been thinking about that," said Dante. "We'll use Wilbur Connaught."

"Santiago's accountant?" said Silvermane, surprised. "The one they call the Grand Finale?"

"That's the one."

"Why him?"

"Because I can give him a reason for reading the classified section of the Hadrian newsdisk," answered Dante. "He told me once that he used to work for Barioke, one of the major warlords out on the Rim. That was a long time ago. Barioke's probably dead by now; he's certainly not a warlord any longer."

"So?"

"So we run a classified saying that Barioke needs to speak to Wilbur about a very private matter, and that since he's lost track of him he's trying classifieds all over the galaxy." Dante paused. "Then we put the same ad in twenty other newsdisks, but we wait two days to insert it. Since Wilbur has to get into the Democracy now and then to keep an eye on Santiago's investments, he's still got a Democracy ID, which means all of Barioke's messages will be routed to his code no matter what computer he's using. But the one we want him to read will get there first—the others are just to convince him he's not being used—and we'll make sure that it appears right next to the poem. He'll see it, and bring it to the Bandit's attention. The Bandit may make sure the poem originated on Hadrian, but I don't think he'll check Barioke's message, or even read it."

"Sounds good to me," said Silvermane. He looked around. "Does anyone have any objections to it?"

No one did—until Matilda burst into Dante's room three days later, a worried expression on her face.

"What's up?" he asked, looking up from the stanza he was working on.

"You'd better get your ass out to Hadrian II *quick!*" she said. "The Bandit's probably got a half day's start on you. You have to beat him there!"

"What are you talking about?" said Dante. "I'm not going anywhere—and we *want* the Bandit to go to Hadrian."

"You don't understand!" snapped Matilda, tossing a computer cube across the room to him.

"What is it?" he asked.

"The Hadrian newsdisk," she replied.

"The ads are there?"

"Yes."

"Well, then?"

"That's all anyone else read," said Matilda. "But I read the whole damned thing. Do you know the name September Morn?"

"Sounds like a painting, if memory serves."

"Screw memory! She's the poet laureate of the Questada Cluster, and she lives on Hadrian."

"I didn't know they had a poet laureate."

"There are a lot of things you don't know," said Matilda. "For example, I'll bet you don't know that she's won an award for a poem about Santiago."

His eyes widened. "You're kidding!"

"Do I look like I'm kidding?"

"Oh, *shit!* He's going to think *she* wrote it!"

"Almost certainly."

"We'll contact her via subspace and tell her to get the hell off the planet!"

"Do you think the Bandit will stop looking for her if she's gone when he gets there?" asked Matilda.

"No," said Dante. "No, of course he won't. But what the hell do you expect *me* to do if I get there ahead of him?"

"I don't know, but this was your idea. I think you owe it to her."

"To do what?" he yelled in frustration.

"You're the big thinker," said Matilda angrily. "Think of something."

"All right, all right," he said, getting to his feet. "Give me ten minutes to pack some things, and tell Virgil I need to borrow his ship. It's faster than mine."

She nodded her assent. "Anything else?"

"Hell, I don't know." He paused. "Yeah. See if you can contact Dimitrios of the Three Burners and have him meet me there. Tell him I *really* need some help."

Nine minutes later Dante took off from Brandywine, convinced that he probably wouldn't live to see it again.

He turned control of the ship over to the navigational computer and began preparing the Deepsleep chamber.

I don't know how it happened, he thought. *Suddenly everything's falling apart. Three hundred children are dead because of events I initiated. I don't know if Silvermane can beat the Bandit, or even if he's the right man for the job. And now I've endangered a brilliant poet who I didn't even know existed half an hour ago, and if I luck out and find her, then I'm going to become the prime target of the most competent killer I've ever seen.*

He lay down in the pod, and as consciousness left him, he had time for one final thought:

I wish I'd never found that goddamned poem.

Part 5

September Morn's Book

33.

He's not what he seems, he's not what he claims,
He's as fake as his phony arm.
He lives on Valhalla, playing his games,
And he means you nothing but harm.

That was the second poem to appear in the Hadrian newsdisk. The first was the one Dante had written while Silvermane was watching him.

The third one made it clear that there was a real Santiago, and that he would soon take his vengeance upon the One-Armed Bandit for impersonating him.

The fourth and fifth named two of the Bandit's most trusted henchmen.

The next half dozen told more details, details the Bandit would gladly have killed to keep secret, and, Dante was sure, would now kill to punish the poet for making public.

By the time the Deepsleep chamber gently roused him from his sleep to inform him that he was in orbit around Hadrian II, twenty-two stanzas had appeared, and there actually wasn't much more to reveal.

Dante lay still for a moment, his brain coming back to life more quickly than his body. Then he sat up, climbed out of the pod, realized that he was starving, and headed off to the galley, where he assuaged his hunger. He took a Dryshower, changed clothes, and finally went to the control cabin, where he found that his navigational computer had already answered all of the spaceport's questions and was preparing to break out of orbit and land.

The radio hummed to life. "May I speak to the captain, please?" said a voice.

Dante took over manual control of the radio and opened a channel.

"This is Dante Alighieri, captain of the *Far Traveler*, registration number R-two-six-S-M-three-six-two, five days out of Brandywine. What's the problem?"

"Your ship is registered to Virgil Soaring Hawk."

"Contact him on Brandywine. He'll confirm that he loaned it to me. In the meantime, let me land, and you can hold the ship until you speak to him."

A brief pause. Then: "Agreed."

"I also need a favor."

"How may we help you, Mr. Alighieri?" said the voice at the other end of the transmission.

"I'm supposed to meet a business associate on Hadrian. If he's already landed, it would surely be within the past six Standard hours. He travels under two names—the One-Armed Bandit and Santiago— and I don't know which he's using. Can you tell me if he's arrived yet?"

"Santiago? He's got a sense of humor."

Dante ignored the comment. "Has he landed?"

Another pause. "Let me check. . . . No, no one of either name has landed."

"All right," said Dante. "I need one more favor. I'm a writer, and I'm supposed to interview one of your local poets, a woman who called herself September Morn. Can you tell me where to find her?"

"We can't give out addresses or even computer ID codes," came the answer. "I can transmit your message to her and have her contact you."

"Tell her I'm staying at . . ." He checked the computer screen. "At the Windsor Arms, wherever the hell that is. And tell her I've got to speak to her at her earliest convenience, and not to make her presence known to anyone else."

"You're making this sound more like espionage than an interview," commented the voice sardonically.

I can't tell you the truth. If you even hint that you know why the Bandit is coming to Hadrian, if you make any attempt whatsoever to protect her, he'll blow the whole spaceport to kingdom come.

"There's a rival reporter coming out to interview her," said Dante, making it up as he went along. "It's the man I asked you about, the one who writes under the pen name of Santiago. If he gets to her first, I could lose my job." He paused. "Please. This means a lot to me."

There was a final pause.

"All right, Mr. Alighieri, we'll do what we can to help you keep your job."

"Thank you," said Dante. "And I can't overstress the need for speed and secrecy."

"You journalists!" said the voice, half amused, half disgusted. "You'd slit each other's throats for a scoop. Signing off."

Dante leaned back and watched the viewscreen as the ship approached the surface. There were six cities spread across the face of the planet, more than usual for a colony world, especially one on the Inner Frontier, where small Tradertowns were the order of the day. He had no idea which city September Morn lived in, but then, neither did the Bandit, and he was getting here first, so with any luck he'd make contact with her first. If nothing else, he was sure the Bandit wasn't subtle enough to fabricate a story about why she should seek *him* out.

He touched down and cleared Customs. To make things go more smoothly he identified himself as Danny Briggs; the ID would check, and no one on the Frontier except the occasional bounty hunter would give a damn if the Democracy had put a price on his head. Finally he hired a limo to skim above the surface and take him into Trajan, the planet's capital city, which was home to the Windsor Arms Hotel.

He stopped at the desk to register, took an airlift up to the eighth floor, found his room, waited for the security system to scan his retina and compare it with the scan he'd just undergone downstairs, and finally entered the room as the door dilated to let him pass through.

The first thing he did was walk across to the desk that was positioned by a corner window and activate the computer that sat atop it.

"Good morning, Mr. Alighieri," said the computer in a soft feminine voice that startled him. "How may I help you?"

"I need to find a woman named September Morn. I know she lives on Hadrian II," replied Dante. "Check all the vidphone directories and see if she's listed."

"Checking . . . No, she is not," announced the computer. "This means that she either does not possess a vidphone, or else she possesses an unlisted number."

"Tie into the Master Computer on Deluros VIII and access any information it has on her."

"That will be an extra charge of five hundred credits, or one thousand two hundred twenty-eight New Kenya shillings. Press your left thumb against the spot indicated on my screen if you agree to the charges."

Dante pressed his thumb against the screen, then waited almost two minutes for the computer to address him again.

"The only information the Master Computer possesses is that September Morn is a writer residing on Hadrian II, that she has sold four novels and two volumes of poetry, and that her poem entitled *The King of the Outlaws* won this year's Questada Prize for literature."

"Contact her publisher and see if you can get her address, or her ID, if she's got one."

"Contacting . . . It is against their policy to give out such information."

"The local newsdisk must have a morgue with all prior issues. See if you can find any information on how to contact her directly."

"That could take as much as ten minutes, Mr. Alighieri."

"Why so long?"

"They use a primitive filing system, and I will have to reaccess it by year."

"Don't go back more than four or five years. I need current information."

"Understood."

"One more thing. Let me know if a man named either Santiago or the One-Armed Bandit lands at the spaceport."

"Yes, Mr. Alighieri. Is there anything else?"

"No."

"My screen will go blank, and I will not speak until I have finished my assignments, but although I will appear to have shut down all systems, this is not the case, so please do not mistakenly report me as broken or inactive to the management."

"No problem," said Dante. The computer went dead so quickly he wasn't sure it heard him.

He ordered the wet bar to pour him a beer, and had just taken his first swallow when there was a knock at the door.

"Open," he ordered, and the door dilated again to reveal Dimitrios of the Three Burners.

"I got Matilda's message," he said, entering the room. "What the hell's going on?"

"To borrow an ancient saying, we put our money on the wrong horse."

"So he's turned pure outlaw instead of helping the Frontier?" asked Dimitrios.

"It's not that simple," replied Dante. "He's become a fanatic. If it has anything to do with the Democracy, it can't be permitted to survive."

"Isn't that the purpose of the exercise?"

"He just slaughtered three hundred children who might have someday grown up to be Democracy soldiers or bureaucrats."

"Ah," said the bounty hunter. "I see."

"The original plan was for me to lure him out here and never even show up myself—but everything's gone to hell. If we can't find some way to stop him, he's going to kill a woman who doesn't even know he's alive, let alone after her."

"Back up a minute," said Dimitrios, frowning. "Why did you want to lure him here in the first place? What's so special about Hadrian II?"

"It's about as far as you can get from Valhalla and still be on the Inner Frontier."

"Valhalla. That's the planet where he's set up his headquarters, right?"

"Right."

"So what is supposed to happen while he's gone?" asked Dimitrios.

"His successor will move in and take over, and present him with a fait accompli."

"And who is this successor?"

"Joshua Silvermane." Dante couldn't help but notice that Dimitrios grimaced at the mention of the name. "Do you disapprove?"

"He's as good a symbol as you could ever find," began Dimitrios. "He looks like a statue, and he's certainly as good with his weapons as the Bandit."

"But?" said Dante. "You look like there's a 'but.' "

"But he's a cold, passionless son of a bitch," continued the bounty hunter, "and he's so self-sufficient that he doesn't inspire much loyalty, if only because it's apparent he doesn't need it or want it."

"But he's a moral man without being a fanatic."

"He's a man of his word," agreed Dimitrios. "He's so beautiful and so deadly that people will watch him in awe, but I don't know if he's the kind of man other men will follow." He paused. "I guess you'll find out—if the Bandit doesn't go back and kill him once he's done here. Exactly what's drawing him here in the first place?"

Dante explained his plan, and even quoted a few of the poems to Dimitrios.

"Sounds fine to me," said the bounty hunter. "What went wrong?"

"Just a stroke of bad luck," replied Dante. "Of all the goddamned planets on the Frontier, this is the one that's home to a woman who just wrote an award-winning poem about, of all things, Santiago."

"Suddenly things make a lot more sense."

"Her name is September Morn," Dante concluded. "And we've got to find her before he does."

"Well, on your behalf, you couldn't know she'd gone and won a prize for a poem about Santiago," said Dimitrios. "It was a hell of a good idea except for that."

"Thanks," said Dante with grim irony.

"Problem is, you've endangered this woman, and we don't know how to reach her to protect her or warn her off."

"Neither does *he*," Dante pointed out.

"That's one thing in our favor. If we're starting out even, I'll put my money on you to outthink him."

The computer suddenly hummed to life.

"I am sorry, Mr. Alighieri," it said, "but the newsdisk morgue gives no indication of how to contact September Morn. All I could learn is that as of two years ago she resided in Trajan."

"Well, that's a start," said Dante. "What's Trajan's population?"

"One hundred and ten thousand, four hundred and sixty-three at the last census."

"So much for going door-to-door." The poet paused. "Thank you, computer. You may deactivate until I need you again."

"This contradicts your order that I alert you if a man named Santiago or the One-Armed Bandit lands on Hadrian II," the computer reminded him.

"I forgot that," admitted Dante. "All right, do that and nothing more."

"Understood."

The machine seemed to go dormant again, but Dante knew it was monitoring the spaceport.

"So what do you suggest we do?" asked Dimitrios. "I'm at your disposal."

"I asked the authorities to contact September Morn and let her know I had urgent business with her," replied Dante. "And I gave the Windsor Arms as my address. I don't think we should leave the place until I hear from her."

"I haven't eaten today," said Dimitrios. "I saw a restaurant in the hotel, just off the lobby. Let's grab a bite there. If she tries to contact you by vidphone or computer, the hotel can transfer it to our table, and if she shows up in person they can point us out to her."

"I don't see any harm in that," agreed Dante, getting to his feet. "Let's go."

They took the airlift down to the main floor, and were soon sitting in the restaurant. Dimitrios ordered a steak from a mutated beef animal. Dante just had coffee.

"You're not hungry?" asked Dimitrios.

"No."

"Don't be so nervous. We'll find her."

"We'd better."

"Get some calories into you," said Dimitrios. "Maybe they'll get that brain of yours working again."

"All right, all right," muttered Dante irritably. He called up the menu and placed a finger on a hologram of a pastry.

"They have wonderful meat," said Dimitrios.

"You said calories. This has calories."

"What the hell—do what you want," said the bounty hunter with a shrug.

They ate in silence, got up, and were walking to the airlift when Dante glanced out the window and suddenly froze.

"Do you see her?" asked Dimitrios.

"I don't even know what she looks like," replied the poet. "I saw *him.*"

Dimitrios walked to the window. "I don't see anyone. The street's empty."

"He's in the hotel right across the street. Probably looking for her."

"Or you."

"Or me. If he sees me here, that lets her off the hook. He'll know I wrote those verses."

"You're not seriously considering walking out there?" demanded Dimitrios.

"I can't let him kill her."

"Are you going to challenge him to a thinking match?" said Dimitrios angrily. "Or maybe a poetry contest? They're the only two things you can beat him at."

"What do you suggest?" snapped Dante. "I don't want to die, but I can't let him find and kill September Morn!"

"What do I suggest?" repeated Dimitrios. "I suggest you step aside and let someone face him who's at least got a chance!"

And before Dante could stop him, Dimitrios had stepped out into the street. He stood there patiently for a few seconds, and then the Bandit came out of the hotel.

"Dimitrios?" said the Bandit, surprised. "It's been a long time. What are you doing here?"

"I'm here on business," replied Dimitrios.

"Who is he? Maybe I know him."

"I'm sure you do. He wiped out a schoolhouse on Madras."

"Forget your business," said the Bandit. "You're a good man, and you're no friend of the Democracy. Go in peace."

"You're a good man, too," said Dimitrios. "But you've gone a little overboard. We should talk, Bandit."

"My name is Santiago," the Bandit corrected him.

"Not anymore. That's what we have to talk about. You can work for him, you can help him, but you can't *be* him."

"Stand aside, Dimitrios. I'm only giving you one more chance to walk away."

"I can't," said Dimitrios.

"I know," said the Bandit sadly. He pointed a finger at Dimitrios. The bounty hunter went for his burners, but never got them out of their holsters. An instant later he was dead, a black, bubbling, smoking hole in the middle of his forehead.

"*Shit!*" muttered Dante. "He'll kill the whole fucking city if he doesn't find what he's after."

He walked to the hotel's doorway and stepped outside.

"I knew I'd find you here," said the Bandit.

"You killed my friend."

"I'll kill more than your friend if I don't find the woman who writes poems about Santiago."

"She only writes about the *real* Santiago," said Dante. "*I* wrote the ones you read."

The Bandit stared at him. "Why?"

"To lure you out here."

"Still why?" asked the Bandit, frowning and scanning the area for hidden gunmen.

"To get you away from Valhalla. You'll find some changes when you get back." Dante smiled grimly. "Dimitrios was telling the truth. You're not Santiago anymore."

"We'll see about that when I return to Valhalla," said the Bandit, pointing his finger at Dante. "In the meantime, I told you that the next time we met I'd—"

Suddenly he stopped speaking. A puzzled expression crossed his face. He opened his mouth, but only blood came out. Then he pitched forward on the street, stone-cold dead.

As he fell, the figure of a woman was revealed. She was standing behind him, a burner in her hand.

Dante stood motionless, finding it difficult to believe he was still alive.

The woman approached him. "I believe you were looking for me," she said. "I'm September Morn."

34.

She sings, she dances, she writes novels too.
There's nothing that she isn't able to do.
Just set her a task that all have forsworn:
Of course she can do it—she's September Morn.

They were sitting in the restaurant, which management had closed to all other customers. A lone waiter stood in the most distant corner, awaiting their pleasure.

September Morn poured Dante a stiff drink. "Take this," she said. "You look like you need it."

"Thank you," said Dante, swallowing it in a single gulp, then watching as she poured him another. "I owe you my life. If there's ever anything I can do for you . . ."

"You can tell me why he came here to kill me," said September Morn.

"I will," said Dante, looking out the window to where medical crews were removing the two corpses from the bloodstained street. Finally the last vehicle raced away, bearing the Bandit's body, and he turned back to her. "But shouldn't we be expecting a visit from the authorities any minute now? I mean, you *did* kill him out there in broad daylight. I'll testify that you were saving my life, but surely they're going to want to ask us both some questions."

She shook her head. "Don't worry," she said. "They won't bother us."

Dante downed a second drink, and felt the tension finally ease. "Why not? There are two dead men out there."

"It's very complicated," replied September Morn. "Let's simply say that I'm not without a certain amount of cachet here on Hadrian."

"Oh?" He stared at her, waiting for her to continue, and finally she did.

"I'm the only native who ever won a major award for anything, and they're very proud of that. When I considered moving to the Binder system, they passed a law declaring me a living monument. My mortgage was canceled, all my outstanding debts were paid, and by definition I cannot break the law—within reason, of course." She grimaced. "All that's on the one side. On the other is that I can't leave the system without a military escort whose sole purpose is to see that I return."

"So no one's going to hassle you for shooting the Bandit?" he said.

"*Was* he a bandit?"

"No. That was just his name—the One-Armed Bandit. He lost his left arm years ago. You saw just a minor demonstration of what his prosthetic replacement could do."

"He called himself Santiago," she said.

"I know."

"There has to be a connection. I wrote about Santiago, and he thought he *was* Santiago." She paused. The waiter mistook it for a signal and instantly walked over to their table. She glanced at him and gestured him away. "But even if he was delusional, what did that have to do with me?"

"It's a long story." Dante leaned back, and his chair changed shape to accommodate him. He realized that he could no longer reach the table and eat his food comfortably, and he moved forward again.

"I've got all the time we need," said September Morn. "And it's about my two favorite subjects—Santiago and me."

"All right," he said, sampling a mouthful of mutated shellfish in a cream sauce, and deciding she had good taste in restaurants. "But let me begin with a question. When did Santiago die?"

"No one knows." She learned forward confidentially. "But do you know what I think? I didn't even put it in my poem, but I think there were *two* Santiagos!"

"Do you really?"

"And I'm almost certain the second was a bounty hunter named Sylvester Cain."

"Sebastian Cain," he corrected her, taking a sip of Belarban wine from a crystal goblet. "And he was the fourth, not the second."

"How do you know?" she demanded sharply.

"I've read Black Orpheus' original manuscript."

Her eyes widened with excitement as she considered his revelation. "You've actually *seen* it?"

"I own it."

"How do you know it's authentic?"

"First, because the style of the verses that no one's seen match those that we all know. Second, because everything he says in those verses checks out."

"Checks out how?"

"I know his great-granddaughter. She's verified a lot of it. Others have verified other parts. And my ship's computer tells me the paper is more than a century old."

She was silent for a long moment.

"So the Songbird was the fourth Santiago!" She looked directly into his eyes. "Do you want to repay me for saving your life? Let me see the poem!"

"It's on Valhalla."

"So what? We'll go to Valhalla."

"I thought you couldn't leave the planet without a bodyguard. Santiago's people will blow them out of the sky if they approach Valhalla."

"For *this* I'll find a way to leave them behind," she said. "Now tell me everything you know about Santiago. There were four, you say?"

"No, I didn't say that," replied the poet. "I said Cain was the fourth. There were actually five. The last one died in 3301 G.E."

"*Five?*"

"That's right."

"There couldn't have been that many!"

"I can give you names and dates of death for the last three, and I can prove to you that none of them can possibly have been the original Santiago."

"And only you know it?" exclaimed September Morn, her face and her voice reflecting her excitement. "We've got to find a way to make the poem public. All the lost verses, the apocrypha, everything!"

"There's thousands of pages."

"All the better."

"We'll talk about it," said Dante. "But I'm still waiting for you to ask the operative question."

"And what is that?"

"How many Santiagos have there been *since* then?"

"What are you talking about?" she asked, confused.

"After I found the poem, I thought my calling was to continue it, to bring it up to date, to continue describing the adventurers and misfits who come out from the Democracy—and in a way it was. But the more I delved into it, the more I realized that it was time for Santiago to come back to the Inner Frontier, that conditions were ripe for him. The Democracy was still oppressing and overtaxing the colonists out here, aliens were still being treated like animals, rights were being violated, and it was apparent to me that we needed Santiago more than we ever had . . . so it became my mission to find him." *Talk about hubris,* he thought; *listen to me!* He grimanced in embarrassment. "So I went looking for him," he concluded lamely.

"And the One-Armed Bandit was your candidate?"

"We were wrong."

" 'We'?" she repeated. "Then you're not alone in this?"

"No."

"Good. It was too big a blunder for one man to make all by himself." September Morn stared at Dante. "So what will you do now? Go back to whatever you were doing before you found the poem?"

"Not a chance," he replied. "I was a small-time thief with big-time dreams who was going absolutely nowhere. I'm not going back."

"Then what?"

"Santiago's story isn't over yet," said Dante. "I'll keep writing it."

"What are you talking about?" she said. "He's dead. I just killed him."

"He wasn't Santiago," answered Dante. "He was just the One-Armed Bandit."

Her eyes widened. "You mean you've got another one?"

"Yes. That's why the Bandit was on Hadrian."

"I don't understand."

"We'd built him an organization, a couple of hundred strong. I found him the best financial brain on the Frontier to manage his money. He had a great-granddaughter of one of the original Santiagos helping him. Even Dimitrios of the Three Burners, the man he just killed, was part of the organization."

She placed a hand on the bottle. "Do you want another?"

"No, I'm okay now," answered Dante. "Anyway, there were two alternatives once we knew the Bandit had to go. Silvermane, our new candidate, could meet him face-to-face . . . but you saw what just happened to a top-notch bounty hunter who tried that. One or the other was bound to die, and we couldn't be sure which. The other option was to lure the Bandit thousands of light-years away from his headquarters and take control of the organization before he got back, to make the place impregnable. We felt there was even a slim chance that he might be willing to become the One-Armed Bandit again and work for Santiago. After all, he still believed in the cause."

"All right, I follow you so far," said September Morn. "But what does that have to do with me?"

"He knows ... knew ... that I've been continuing Orpheus' work," explained Dante. "I thought the best way to get him out here was to run some stanzas in the local paper that revealed secrets about the organization."

"I never saw any."

"They ran in the classified section."

"I never read the classified ads. Most people don't. So why run them there?"

"It's very complicated, but believe me, it was the surest way to bring them to his attention. I figured when he saw the information was in verse form, he'd know it was me, and he'd come out here to kill me." Dante sighed deeply. "I never planned to come within fifty parsecs of Hadrian. I was going to stay with Silvermane when he took over Santiago's organization. The one thing I never counted on was that there'd be a prize-winning poet on Hadrian II, and that you'd have won your prize for a poem about Santiago. As soon as I learned that, I knew I had to come out here and try to stop him before he killed you for writing the stanzas that *I* actually wrote."

"Now it all makes sense," said September Morn. She stared admiringly at him. "You're a very brave man, Dante Alighieri. You were willing to sacrifice your life for a woman you'd never even seen."

"It was guilt, not bravery," answered Dante, shifting uncomfortably on his chair. "I've been responsible for the deaths of enough innocent people."

"Whatever the reason, you went out there unarmed and faced a man who had just killed a skilled bounty hunter. That's the kind of courage I wrote about in my poem."

"I have to admit I haven't read it. I'm sorry."

"I'll give you a copy," she promised. "It's a Romance, with a capital R. There are heroes and villains, high adventure, Good and Evil in juxtaposition, and a man who isn't without fear but finds the strength to overcome it, which in my opinion is *real* bravery, the kind you displayed."

"What led you to write about him?"

"A feeling that we'd forgotten his values, that in the overpowering shadow of the Democracy we'd conceded one liberty after another for more and more security until we had no liberties left to give, and one day we woke up and found we needed protection from our protectors. I never thought of Santiago as a role model—I mean, whoever thought he might come back again?—but I felt it was time to remind people that the ideals he embodied didn't have to die with him." She smiled. "And here I was, just writing my daydreams about it, while you were actually going out and *doing* something about it."

"An awful lot of people have died because I went out and did something," said Dante grimly. "You were almost added to the list."

"This is real life, not a book or a play," answered September Morn. "Things don't always work out the way men of virtue hope they will, and sometimes the effort is every bit as important as the results."

"It sounds good," said Dante, "but right about now I'd say we need some results."

"It would be nice," she said. "The Frontier could use a Santiago again." A pause. "To tell the truth, *I* could use him more than most."

"Oh?"

"There are some serious disadvantages to being a living monument," said September Morn as the waiter cleared the table and brought them their dessert pastries and coffee.

"So you told me," replied Dante, watching the waiter retreat in utter silence to the kitchen.

"You mean having to stay here?" she said. "That's a minor annoyance."

"What's the major one?"

"When word of my official status got out, it didn't take long for anyone who heard about it to conclude that if they could steal me away, the government of Hadrian would pay quite a ransom to get me back."

"Have there been many attempts?"

"There have been a few. Nothing I couldn't handle." She paused. "Until now."

"Who's after you now?"

"Something even more formidable than your One-Armed Bandit," answered September Morn.

"I don't think there *is* anyone more formidable, except maybe Joshua Silvermane."

"I said some*thing*, not some*one*."

"Exactly who or what is it that's after you?" he asked, curious.

She took a bite of her pastry. "Fabulous stuff," she said. "You should try it."

"I will," he said. "But first tell me what's after you."

"Have you ever heard of Tweedledee and Tweedledum?"

"Dimitrios mentioned them once," said Dante. He chuckled and took a sip of his coffee. "Those names aren't exactly designed to strike fear into one's heart."

"Don't laugh!" she snapped angrily. "Their names may be childish, but there's nothing childish about them. They're the most dangerous creatures on the whole Frontier!"

His smile vanished. "What makes them so dangerous?"

"They conquer whole planets, just the two of them."

Dante frowned. "You're telling me these two aliens can defeat an entire military force?"

"Yes."

"And they're after you?"

"That's the word that's reached the planetary authorities," she replied. "That's why I was carrying the burner. When I heard that both you and the Bandit wanted to find me, I thought one or both of you worked for them."

"They work as a pair, this Tweedledee and Tweedledum?" he persisted.

"Yes."

"What do they look like? What makes them so formidable?"

"I don't know," admitted September Morn. "I've never actually seen them. All I know is what I've heard and read—and based on that, I hope I *never* see them. They conquer entire worlds, just the pair of them, and nobody who's tried to stand up to them has lived to tell about it." Her expression hardened. "And now they're after me."

Dante reached across the table and placed a reassuring hand on hers. "You saved my life," he said. "The least I can do is return the favor. No one's going to harm you."

She looked questioningly at him.

"I'll get Santiago to protect you," promised Dante. "The *real* Santiago."

35.

Mongaso Taylor, churchmouse poor,
Bites the hand that feeds him.
Embittered man, he will not save
The family that needs him.

Dante sat alone in his room, waiting for Silvermane's face to reappear. For almost a minute it had been popping into and out of existence, terribly distorted. Finally the signal came through, and his perfect features took shape.

"I got your message," he said. "I'm sorry about Dimitrios of the Three Burners."

"So am I," replied Dante.

"And the Bandit is really dead?"

"That's right." Dante smiled wryly. "The girl I came here to protect killed him and saved my life."

"I'm almost sorry," said Silvermane. "I was looking forward to meeting him."

"To killing him, you mean."

"If it had been necessary." He paused. "Well, you might as well come back to Valhalla. There's nothing to keep you there now, and I've got plenty of work for you here."

"I can't."

"Why not?"

"The girl," said Dante.

"The one who saved your life?"

"Right. She's in danger."

"Just a minute," said Silvermane, frowning. "I thought you told me the Bandit was dead."

"He is. But—I'm not quite sure how to put this—she's the most important person on the planet. Or maybe I should say the most popular, or the most revered, or—"

"I get the picture," interrupted Silvermane irritably. "What about it?"

"The planetary government would pay any amount to get her back if she was kidnapped."

"Are you suggesting we kidnap her?" asked Silvermane, who didn't look unduly upset by the proposition.

"She killed the Bandit," Dante pointed out, lighting up a smokeless Antarean cigar he had picked up in the hotel's gift shop. "She's on our side. We *owe* her."

"Okay, you're my man on the scene. If you feel we should protect her, go ahead and do it." A pause. "Have you got any idea who's after her?"

"A pair of aliens—I gather they're called Tweedledee and Tweedledum."

Silvermane's expression darkened noticeably. "You're sure?"

"That's what she tells me."

"Get off the planet right now."

"I don't know if I can do it that quickly," said Dante. "She's been declared a living monument, whatever the hell that means, and there's all kinds of red tape, and—"

"I'm not talking about *her!*" said Silvermane sharply. "Get your ass off Hadrian II right now!"

"I can't."

"Trust me, you're not in their league, Rhymer," said Silvermane. "You can't even protect yourself from them, let alone your ladyfriend."

"Then send help."

"I'll send someone. Just get the hell out of there."

"Not without her," said Dante, fighting back a surge of frustration. "She stood up to the Bandit and saved my life. I can't desert her."

Silvermane sighed deeply. "All right," he said at last. "I can't argue with that kind of loyalty."

"Thanks."

"And arguing with that kind of stupidity hasn't gotten me anywhere," he added sharply. "Where are you staying?"

"The Windsor Arms Hotel."

"I know a man who's not too far from Hadrian, a man who owes me a favor. He's probably not up to taking the aliens either, but at least he'll buy you some time. I'll have him leave for Hadrian today; he should be there in two days' time, maybe sooner."

"Has he got a name?"

"Mongaso Taylor."

"I've heard that name before. I think maybe Dimitrios mentioned him."

"Could be," said Silvermane. "He used to be a hell of a commando for the Navy, back when he lived in the Democracy. They dropped him behind enemy lines on Cyrano IV during the Sett War. He took out eighteen of the purple bastards and blew an ammunition dump all by himself."

"He sounds like he should be all we need."

"He hasn't got a chance," said Silvermane. His voice began crackling with static. "He'll buy you some time, that's all. Do your red tape or whatever's necessary, but get off the planet before Tweedledee and Tweedledum show up."

"It's difficult to take them seriously with those names," remarked Dante.

"Don't let the names fool you," said Silvermane. "I was eager to go up against the Bandit. I've no desire to ever find myself in the same sector with those two."

"Your picture's breaking up," said Dante. "Is there anything else?"

The hologram vanished before Silvermane could reply.

Dante went over to the bathroom, muttered "Cold," rinsed his face off in the flow of water, ordered the blower to dry him, ran a comb through his hair, and prepared to leave the hotel room.

"Open," he said as he approached the door.

The door remained shut.

"I said open."

The mechanical voice of a computer answered. "I must bring to your attention the fact that you have not shut off the water in the bathroom, and that if you leave it will continue running until you return. If that is your desire, say so and I will instruct the servo-mech not to disrupt the flow when it cleans the room. If it is not your desire, I will be happy to shut it off."

"Shut it off and let me out of here," said Dante.

He heard the water stop flowing as the door dilated and he stepped through to the corridor. He took the airlift down to the main floor, then climbed into a robotic rickshaw and had it take him to September Morn's house on the outskirts of town.

It was an old stone building that had a couple of additions grafted onto it, obviously signs of her success in the world of letters. The gardens were carefully tended, filled with flowers he had never seen before. Avian feeders abounded, and several leather-winged little creatures watched him curiously as he approached the front door. He answered a series of questions from the security system, and finally the door dilated. He entered the living room, where September Morn was waiting for him.

The walls were covered with holographic prints of pastoral artworks by human and alien artists alike. One small section held some holos of September Morn accepting various honors. There was a false fireplace, and the mantel was lined with trophies and awards.

"Where are all the books?"

"I actually have very few books," she replied. "They cost too much. My library consists mostly of disks and cubes."

He held up the thin book he'd been carrying. "I wonder if you'd autograph this for me."

"What is it?"

"*The King of the Outlaws.* I bought it last night at the hotel's gift shop."

"I'll be happy to," she said, producing a stylus as he carried the book over to her. "What did you think of it?"

"It depressed me terribly," said Dante.

She looked concerned. "Oh? What didn't you like about it?"

"I liked everything about it," said Dante. "I realized about three pages into it that the wrong person is trying to be the new Black Orpheus." He paused. "I envy the way you use words. I just write these little stanzas. You create textures and tapestries that I can only marvel at."

"I'm flattered. But what I write is far removed from the way Black Orpheus wrote. The person who carries on his work should write in his style."

"That's generous of you to say so, but you can write rings around me in any style you choose and we both know it." He took the book back and looked at the autograph. "I'll cherish this. It's one hell of a piece of work."

"I don't know how many times I can thank you before it starts sounding false," she said with an embarrassed smile. "So please stop praising me."

"All right."

"Besides, we have more important things to discuss."

He nodded. "I spoke to . . . Santiago."

"And?" said September Morn.

"He can't come himself, but he's sending help."

"Good."

"But he wants us off Hadrian as soon as possible."

"This is my home," she replied adamantly. "I'll leave it when *I* choose, but I won't be threatened or frightened into running."

"You're sure?"

"If I run once," said September Morn, "I'll run every time I'm threatened, and then every time I think I *might* be threatened, and one day I'll look around and realize I've spent most of my life running away from things rather than *to* them. That's not a life I care to live."

"All right," said Dante. "If I were a little bigger and a little stronger, maybe I could tie you up, sling you over a shoulder, and carry you to my ship. But one thing I know is that I'm not about to win an argument with the wordsmith who wrote the poem I just read."

"Thank you," she said. "And for what it's worth, you couldn't tie me up and carry me off even if you were twice your size."

"Probably not," he admitted.

"So I'm staying right here. I'm a crack shot, and I'm not afraid. I know how dangerous they are; they have no idea how dangerous *I* can be. My sister and I will be safe here."

"Your sister?" said Dante.

"Yes."

"I didn't know you had one. It's not in your bio," he said, holding up her book. "Does she live here?"

"Sometimes." He looked at her curiously, and she continued: "We don't get along very well. I suppose a lot of siblings are like that. But when push comes to shove, blood is thicker than . . . than whatever those aliens have coursing through their veins. She'll stand up and be counted if they come after me."

"Well, that's you, me, your sister, and Mongaso Taylor," said Dante. "Maybe it'll be enough."

"I doubt it," she said.

"So does Santiago."

"But even if we can't beat them, maybe we can convince them that kidnapping me is more effort than it's worth."

"We can try," agreed Dante.

"All right, we've covered that about as thoroughly as we can until your man Taylor gets here," she said. "Make yourself at home. I'm going to get us some drinks, and then you're going to spend the rest of the day telling me about Santiago—*all* the Santiagos."

It was a pleasant afternoon, and the next morning she showed him around the town of Trajan. They had just finished lunch at a local restaurant when his hotel paged him and told him he had a visitor.

"That's got to be him," said Dante. "Go home and lock all your doors, and don't let anyone in unless he's with me."

"You're overreacting," said September Morn. "They might be twenty systems away from here."

"And they might be twenty minutes away," answered Dante. "It doesn't hurt to play it safe."

"All right, I'll do what you say," she replied. "But I won't *keep* doing it. I value my freedom too much to stay locked up in my house."

"It's your freedom we're trying to protect," he said, getting up and walking out of the restaurant.

He reached the Windsor Arms in five minutes, and looked around the lobby. Standing by the artificial fireplace, his back to the desk, was a tall, slender, almost emaciated man dressed in muted shades of gray. There were a pair of telltale bulges under his tunic.

Dante approached him. "Mongaso Taylor?" he asked.

The man turned to face him. His face was long and lean, like the rest of him, and he had a thick handlebar mustache. "You must be Dante . . . Dante something. I've forgotten your last name."

"It's not important," said Dante. "The important thing is that you're here."

"I *had* to come," said Taylor bitterly. "I needed the money."

"Silvermane's *paying* you? I thought he told me you owed him a favor."

"I don't owe him a big enough favor to put my life on the line without money—five thousand credits up front, twenty more when I'm done."

"Well, that's between you and him. I'm just here to lay out the situation for you."

"You can buy me a drink in the bar while you're talking."

"I thought he just paid you five thousand credits," said Dante with a smile.

"That's more than I've seen in two years," said Taylor. His eyes became unfocused, as if he was looking back across the last few years. "You back out of one goddamned fight . . ."

He fell silent, and while Dante was curious, he decided it would be best not to ask any questions at present. He led Taylor to the bar and let the newcomer order for both of them.

"A pair of Dust Whores," Taylor told the bartender. "Light on the smoke." He turned to Dante. "Okay, I'm paid and I'm here. Who does Silvermane want me to kill?"

"Hopefully no one. But there are two sisters who live on the edge of town, and one of them seems to have become a prime kidnap target."

"You got to have more information than that," said Taylor. "I can't just hang around until some local makes a move. It could take months."

"We're not worried about locals."

"Offworlders?"

"Aliens," said Dante.

"Lady must be worth a bundle," said Taylor, rubbing his chin thoughtfully.

"Don't even think of it. You don't want Silvermane after you."

"You've got a point," admitted Taylor with a sigh. "So who are the aliens—Canphorites? Lodinites?"

"I don't know what they are. I've never seen them, and I don't think the ladies have either."

"Have you got *anything* I can go on?"

"Just their names—Tweedledee and Tweedledum."

Taylor didn't reply for a full minute. Finally he downed his drink, placed the empty glass on the bar, and turned to Dante.

"Nice to have met you," he said.

"What do you mean?"

"I mean I may be poor, but I'm not crazy." He reached into a pocket and pulled out a wad of banknotes. He counted through them, and placed a pile on the bar. "That's three thousand credits. You tell your boss I'm keeping the rest for expenses. If he doesn't like it, he can try to take it back."

"You can't just leave!"

Suddenly Dante was looking down the barrel of a screecher. "Are you gonna stop me?" asked Taylor softly.

"No, but—"

"Then get the hell out of my way."

And with that, he was gone.

Wonderful, just wonderful, thought Dante. *I've got a woman who's too proud to leave and a gunman who's too scared to stay. What the hell do I do now?*

36.

The little sister, fortune's bane,
Wishes she had not been born.
Filled with rage and hate and pain,
There she slinks—October Morn.

"He did *what*?" demanded Silvermane's image.

"You heard me," said Dante, sitting in the pilot's seat of his stationary ship and staring at the hologram that appeared just above the subspace radio. "That's why I'm not transmitting from my room. I don't think anyone's watching me, but if they are I don't want this to be overheard."

"He can't get away with this! I don't give a damn about the three thousand he returned."

"I don't care about the money either," replied Dante. "I'm still here with a woman who's a target for these two aliens. What are we going to do about it?"

"Get off the planet," said Silvermane. "I told you that the last time we spoke."

"And I told you that it's not that easy."

"If she's still there when I get there, *I'll* convince her to leave," said Silvermane confidently.

"Then you're coming to Hadrian?" said Dante, relieved.

"Eventually. First I have to hunt down Mongaso Taylor and make an example of him, or others will think they can break their word to Santiago."

"Goddammit!" shouted Dante. "He's nothing but a has-been killer who's lost his nerve! *I'm* the one who made you Santiago, and I need your help right now!"

"Nobody *made* me Santiago," answered Silvermane coldly. "You merely pointed out the fact of it."

"And nobody made your fortress on Valhalla and presented you with two hundred loyal men and women, and nobody killed the Bandit for you!"

"You didn't kill the Bandit," was Silvermane's calm reply. "*She* did."

"And now she needs your help."

"Everything in its proper order—first Taylor, then Hadrian."

"What do we do in the meantime?"

"You're the bright one," said Silvermane. "Use that brain of yours."

Dante broke the connection, cursed under his breath, then left the ship and returned to his hotel. Once there, he tried to raise September Morn on the vidphone. There was no answer.

"Damn it!" he snapped to her holo-message tape, making sure his face looked properly grim. "I told you not to leave your place without me!"

He went out, had lunch, and returned to his room, where he tried again without success to contact her. He checked his timepiece; it was only an hour and a half since his first attempt. He left another message about staying put, then lay down and took a nap.

He awoke in late afternoon and called September Morn a third time. The result was the same.

He went down to the lobby, had the desk clerk summon a robotic rickshaw, and took it out to her house.

The door was missing.

Not broken, or melted, or shattered. Missing. As if it had never been there.

He wished he had a weapon of some kind. He looked cautiously into the interior, took a tentative step inside, then a second and a third.

The place was as neat as ever. Nothing was out of place. There were no signs of a struggle. There were no messages, written or transcribed.

And there was no September Morn.

He spent half an hour scouring the house for clues. There weren't any. Finally he sat down on a chair in the living room to consider his options.

He'd been sitting there pondering the situation for perhaps five minutes when he heard footsteps approaching the house.

"Who's there?" he said.

Suddenly the footsteps began retreating. He jumped to his feet and raced to the door, just in time to see a feminine figure racing away.

"September Morn!" he shouted. "Wait!"

The figure kept running, and he took off after her.

"Damn it! Wait for me!"

The figure kept ahead of him for perhaps two hundred yards, then began slowing noticeably, and finally he was able to reach out and grab her by the arm.

"Stop!" he snapped. "What the hell is—?"

He stopped in midsentence as the girl turned to face him. There were similarities to September Morn—the same high cheekbones, the same light blue eyes, the same neck, the same rounded shoulders—but this girl had a stronger jaw, a broader mouth, and was between five and ten years younger.

"You're the sister," said Dante. It was not a question. "Why did you run away?"

"I wasn't sure who you were."

"Who did you think I might be?"

She wrenched her arm free. "I don't have to talk to you!"

"You have to talk to me now or Santiago later," he lied. "I'm a lot more pleasant."

She glared at him without answering.

"What's going on?" continued Dante. "You saw that the door was gone. That didn't frighten you. *I* frightened you." Still no reply. "But I'm not a frightening guy—at least not until you know me better—and besides, you didn't see me. You were frightened by who you *thought* I was." He gripped her arm harder. "Suppose you tell me who you were expecting?"

"No one!"

"Let me reword that. I know you expected to come home to an empty house. But if it wasn't empty, who did you think would be waiting for you?"

"None of your business!" she snapped, trying to pull her arm free.

"I told you: it's Santiago's business, and he has very unpleasant ways of getting what he wants."

"Fuck off! He's been dead for a century!"

"The king is dead, long live the king. He's back, twice as big and three times as deadly. If you don't tell me what I want to know, I'll turn you over to him." He paused. "You won't enjoy it, take my word for it."

"Why should I believe you?"

Dante shrugged. "Okay," he said, pulling her by the arm. "We'll wait for him at your place."

"Stop pulling me!"

"Stop dragging your ass."

She stared at him. "He really exists?"

"I just told you he does."

Another pause. Then: "All right, I'll tell you what you want to know."

Thank God for that. I don't know what I'd have done if we got to the house and you hadn't given in.

"Let's start with names," he said. "Mine is Dante. What's yours?"

"It depends on who you talk to."

"I'm talking to you."

"It's Belinda—but ever since my sister got famous, they call me October Morn."

"I take it you don't like the name?" said Dante.

"I hate it!"

"You don't like her much either, do you?"

"That's an understatement."

"She likes you," said Dante.

"She told you that?"

"In essence."

"Then she's an even bigger fool than I thought," said Belinda.

"Next question," said Dante. "Why did you run from the house?"

"I thought it had been broken into."

"One more lie and you can tell your story to Santiago." He continued pulling her toward the house. "Why did you run?"

"I thought they had come for me."

"They?" asked Dante.

"The aliens."

"Tweedledee and Tweedledum?"

"Yes." She came to a stop.

"Why would they come for you?" he asked. "Your sister's the one who's worth all the ransom money."

"I thought she had tricked them," said Belinda.

"Explain," said Dante, taking her hand and once more leading her to the house.

"I told them where we lived, when she was likely to be home, what she looked like, and—"

"You sold your sister out to aliens?" Dante interrupted.

"I didn't take any money!"

"Then why—?"

"Because I hate her!" yelled Belinda as they reached the house and entered it.

"Okay, you hate her and you gave her to the aliens. Why did you run?"

"She's smart, smarter than anyone suspects," said Belinda bitterly. "I was afraid she'd convinced them that she was me and I was September Morn. When I realized someone was inside the house, I was afraid they'd come back for me."

"Where would they have come back from?" asked Dante.

"I don't know."

"How did you contact them?"

"Through an intermediary."

"Who?"

"I can't tell you," she screamed, panic reflected in her face. "He'll kill me!"

"And I'll kill you if you don't," said Dante harshly. "I'm a lot closer to you at the moment than he is. I want you to consider that very carefully."

"If I tell you who, you've got to protect me from him!" whimpered Belinda.

"The way you protected your sister?" he asked.

"She never *needed* any protection or any help! She was always the smartest and the prettiest and the most popular and . . ." Her words trailed off into incoherent sobs.

"She needed protection from the aliens," said Dante coldly. "It may have been the only time in her life she needed help, and you betrayed her." He stared contemptuously at her. "I think Santiago and I are going to let you live, just so your sister can take her own revenge on you."

"If my sister isn't dead already, she will be soon."

"Don't bet on it," said Dante. He paused. "We're going to rescue her."

"Why?" asked Belinda, the tears suddenly gone. "What did she ever do for you?"

"She saved my life."

A look of fury crossed Belinda's face. "That figures. She's just the type."

"It's an admirable type," said Dante. "Certainly more admirable than an overgrown petulant brat who sells her sister out to aliens."

Belinda glared at him but made no answer.

"I'm still waiting," said Dante after a moment.

"For what?"

"The name of the man who can contact Tweedledee and Tweed-ledum."

She considered the question. "You'll protect me?"

"I'll let you live," said Dante coldly. "That's enough of a bargain."

She seemed torn, and finally slumped in resignation. "It's Moby Dick."

"Moby Dick?" he repeated. "Someone's really walking around with that name?"

"Yes."

"You know what will happen to you if you lie to me?"

"Yes, goddammit!" she snapped.

"Where do I find him?"

"The Fat Chance. It's a casino."

"Where is this Fat Chance in relation to the Windsor Arms?" asked Dante.

"A block north, two blocks west."

"Does Moby Dick work for the aliens?"

"He works for himself," said Belinda.

"What does he look like?"

"You'll know him when you see him."

"All right," said Dante. "I'm off to find him." He checked his timepiece. "You've got two hours to clear your stuff out of here."

"This is my house too!"

"You forfeited your right to it. I want you and all your possessions gone today, and I don't want to see you back here. If you disobey me, you'll have to answer to Santiago. Is that understood?"

No answer.

He took a step toward her. "Is that understood?" he repeated ominously.

"Yes," she muttered.

"Then get going."

"I wish you as much luck with Moby Dick as Ahab had!" she said as he turned and headed off to the Fat Chance.

37.

He's bigger than big, he's whiter than white,
He's got an IQ that's plumb out of sight.
Moby Dick is his name, and his talent is vast:
He changes the future and toys with the past.

The Fat Chance wasn't like any casino Dante had ever been in. There were no craps tables, no roulette wheels, no poker games in progress. All but a handful of the customers were aliens—Canphorites, Lodinites, Mollutei, plus a few species he'd never seen before—and all the games were of alien origin.

There was a long, polished metal bar, manned by two robot bartenders. Given the clientele, Dante hated to think of what was in all the oddly shaped containers displayed behind the bar.

The poet stepped further into the casino, looking around, and finally he saw the man he knew had to be Moby Dick. He was a big man, big everywhere—he stood almost seven feet tall, and weighed close to five hundred pounds. The wild part, decided Dante, was that he'd be willing to bet there weren't twenty-five pounds of useless fat on the man. He was huge, but he was hard as a rock, and despite his weight he somehow managed to look fit.

His eyes were a dull pink, his lips were thick, his ears small, his head almost bald. When he opened his mouth, he revealed two rows of shining gold teeth.

But the thing that drew Dante's immediate attention, even more than all his other features, was the fact that the man was an albino. It wasn't hard to see how he'd come by his name.

The man sat alone at a table, a drink in front of him, watching the action at a nearby *jabob* pit. Dante approached him slowly, and came to a stop a few feet away.

"You gonna stand there all day?" asked the albino. "Or are you gonna sit down and tell me why you've come looking for me?"

"I'll sit," replied Dante. The huge man snapped his fingers, and a chair floated over and adjusted to the poet's body. "And I'll have something to drink, too."

"Do I look like a bartender?"

"No," said Dante. "You look like a white whale."

Moby Dick smiled. "Most people are afraid to say that, even though it's true." He paused. "I like you already."

"Good," said Dante. "I wouldn't want anyone your size taking a dislike to me."

This time Moby Dick laughed. "Okay, you've ingratiated yourself enough. Now tell me why you want to see me—and don't deny that's why you're here. No human comes to the Fat Chance to gamble."

"Then why are *you* here?"

"I own the place."

"A casino just for aliens?"

"My own race doesn't go out of its way to make me feel wanted," said the albino. "So I repeat: why are you here?"

"I need some information," said Dante. "My name is Dante Alighieri, and—"

"How divine is your comedy?" interrupted Moby Dick.

"I beg your pardon?"

"Never mind. You're not the same one."

"But I chose his name for my own."

"Do you write poetry?" asked Moby Dick.

"After a fashion."

"Then it's a fine name for you. Unlike Herman Melville, I don't write epics about whaling. But I'm a whale among men, I'm whiter than any of them, and I'm ready to kill any one-legged man named Ahab." He smiled again. "Haven't found one yet."

"Maybe you'd like to go hunting more dangerous game?" suggested Dante.

The table glowed, and the albino stared at a holocube. "That's his limit," he said to it. "No more credit for him until he makes good his losses." He turned back to Dante. "Why do I think you have someone in mind?"

"Maybe because I haven't got a poker face."

"Go home, Dante Alighieri," said Moby Dick. "You don't want any part of them."

"Any part of whom?"

"We've finished the social niceties," said the albino. "I'd really appreciate if you didn't play stupid with me."

"All right," said Dante. "October Morn told me you can contact Tweedledee and Tweedledum."

He chuckled. "The little bitch would love to see them kill the pair of us."

"Probably," agreed Dante. "But was she telling the truth?"

"Yeah, I can contact them," said Moby Dick. "But you don't want me to."

"Why not let me be the judge of that?"

"Because you've never met them, and your courage is born of ignorance" was the reply. "Believe me, no sane man wants to mess with them."

"The man I work for does."

"Then the man you work for's not long for this plane of existence," said the huge man.

"Nevertheless."

One of the *jabob* pit bosses, a Lodinite, waddled up and showed a slip of paper to Moby Dick. He grunted, signed it, watched the alien waddle away, and then looked at Dante. "Maybe I should talk to your boss myself."

"He'll be here in a few days' time," said Dante. He paused. "His name is Santiago."

Moby Dick seemed amused. "Why not Caligula or Conrad Bland, while he was at it?"

"Because he *is* Santiago."

"Somebody's been feeding you a fairy tale, Dante Alighieri," said the albino. "Santiago died seventy or eighty years ago, maybe even longer than that."

"A galaxy that can produce you and Tweedledee and Tweedledum and some of the aliens walking around this casino can produce a man who doesn't age and die like other men. I work for the King of the Outlaws."

Moby Dick was silent for a long moment, analyzing what he'd heard. Finally he spoke. "If he really is on his way to Hadrian, I'd like to meet him."

"I thought you didn't believe in him half a minute ago," noted Dante.

"I don't necessarily believe in him now," said Moby Dick amiably. "All the more reason to want to meet him."

"In the meantime, can you set up a meeting between the two aliens and me?"

Moby Dick shrugged. "I can ask. What should I tell them you want to talk about? The lady poet?"

Dante considered his reply for a moment. "Tell them Santiago's coming to kill them, but I might be able to bargain for their lives. I might be able to convince him to take September Morn and hold her for ransom if they'll turn her over peacefully."

"They can't laugh," said Moby Dick. "They're physically incapable of it. But if they could, they'd laugh in your face."

"Just deliver it."

"You're bluffing, of course," said the albino. "Or out-and-out lying. It won't work. They don't understand bluffs. They'll believe what you say."

"I want them to."

"No you don't," said Moby Dick. "I keep telling you: you don't want any part of them. Neither does your boss, whoever he is."

"How is it that you alone know how to contact them?" asked Dante, changing the subject.

"Lots of people know how. I might be the only one currently on Hadrian, or the only one the little bitch sister knows, but there are lots of us."

"Why are you and this small handful of men and women so favored?"

"There are only two of them in the whole damned universe," answered Moby Dick. "There's just so much they can do, so they rule through handpicked men and women."

"And they picked you?"

The huge man shook his head. "Do I look like a ruler? I'm just a supplicant. If things work out, they may toss me a couple of crumbs someday."

"Would I be correct in assuming one of those crumbs will be Hadrian II?" asked Dante.

"Why not?" Moby Dick shot back. "They can't live everywhere. They can't *be* everywhere. Someone has to bring order to their empire."

"How many planets do they control right now?"

"Maybe eight or nine."

"That's not much of an empire. The Democracy controls about a hundred and fifty thousand worlds, and they influence at least that many more."

"It's a start. Even Man started out with just one world, you know," said Moby Dick.

"So you're going to fight for them?"

"They may never ask me to, and if I do it'll be without much enthusiasm," answered Moby Dick. "Show me a better side to fight for."

"I intend to," said Dante. "Order something to drink. This is going to take a while."

For the next two hours, Dante filled the huge albino in on what had been transpiring for the past few months, about the poem, and Matilda, and the Bandit, and Silvermane, and—always—the ideal of Santiago. When he finally finished, Moby Dick stared at him for a very long time, and then spoke:

"It's an interesting idea," said the albino. "If you had the right Santiago, I'd join up this minute. But you don't."

"You haven't even met him."

"I don't have to. You've described him. That was the giveaway."

"The giveaway?" repeated Dante, puzzled.

"Yeah. You described his gun and his bullets, you told me how tall and graceful he is, you told me that he looks like some artist's dream, you told me about his silver hair. You told me almost everything I need to know about him—except who and what he is."

"I told you: he's Joshua—" began Dante.

"You described a very beautiful and efficient killer," interrupted Moby Dick. "And except for being very beautiful, I don't see much to differentiate him from your last killer, the Santiago you and September Morn . . . ah . . . deposed right here on Hadrian II."

"He's *totally* different," said Dante. "For one thing, he's not a fanatic. For another, he really does understand what being Santiago means, what's required of him."

"I don't know," said Moby Dick. "I think they're both dead ends."

"Would you care to explain that?"

"Sure. But first let's generalize a bit. What causes a species to evolve?"

"What are you talking about?" asked Dante irritably.

"You heard me," said the huge albino. "What makes a species evolve?"

"How the hell do *I* know?"

"You would, if you were using your brain. If you don't, you're just like them."

Dante stared at him, but made no reply.

"The answer," continued Moby Dick, "is that evolution is a response to environmental need. Are the branches of a tree too high? Grow a long neck. Is the sun too bright? Grow bigger eyes and better ears and sleep all day. Are you too small to kill prey animals? Develop opposable thumbs and a brain, and learn to make weapons."

"You *are* going to get to the point sooner or later, aren't you?"

"The point is obvious. You found two of the most efficient killers on the Frontier, maybe *the* two best. But because they've always been able to get anything they wanted with their weapons and their physical skills, why should they develop social skills, or be adept at teamwork, or inspire loyalty when they've never required any help before? I'm sure your Silvermane is a dangerous man, and I'm sure he wants to be Santiago—but based on what you've told me, I don't think I'd be inclined to lay down my life for him, or to follow him into battle if the odds were against us."

"You wouldn't be asked to risk your life—or lose it—for *him*," said Dante, "but for the cause."

"The two should be indistinguishable," answered Moby Dick. "And I get the distinct impression that neither of your Santiagos could describe the cause in terms that would make people willing to die for it."

"All right," said Dante. "So you won't join us. Will you at least help us?"

"You really want me to contact them, even after what I've told you?" asked the albino.

"She saved my life. I owe her."

"Noble," commented Moby Dick. "That's not a trait I see much of out here—nobility."

Another pause. "Then you'll do it?"

"I'll do it. Where can I reach you?"

"The Windsor Arms."

"Wait for me there. I'll be in touch."

Dante got up. "Thanks."

"It's a pity," said Moby Dick.

"What is?"

"I like you, Dante Alighieri. You're a little too noble for your own good, but I really like you. I hate to send you and your boss to your deaths."

"I've got to at least *try* to save her," answered Dante simply.

"I know."

Dante turned and left the casino, window-shopped his way back to the hotel, and took the airlift up to his room, where he found a message from Virgil waiting for him.

"I'm on Laministra IV, encouraging a couple of drug dealers to voluntarily join our network of freedom fighters"—a nasty grin—"and I realized I'm just a hop, skip, and a jump from Hadrian, so I thought I'd pop over there and take my ship back if you're through with it. See you in the morning."

Dante wiped the message, waited a few minutes for Moby Dick to contact him, and finally lay down on the bed and closed his eyes.

He didn't know how long he'd slept, but his computer awoke him by gently repeating his name over and over. Finally he sat up groggily.

"All right, I'm awake," he mumbled. "What is it?"

"A Mr. Dick is attempting to communicate with you, Mr. Alighieri."

"I don't know any—" Suddenly he straightened up. "Put him through!"

Moby Dick's image flickered into existence above the computer.

"I've contacted them," he announced, staring straight at him.

"And?"

"As I told you, they can't laugh—but they *did* seem amused."

"Will they meet with me?"

"No. I gave them the message, exactly as you worded it. They'll meet only with Santiago."

"Where?"

"Kabal III."

"Never heard of it. How far away is it?"

"Perhaps ten light-years."

"Is it an oxygen world?"

"Yes," replied the albino. "That's their only concession to Santiago."

"Concession?" repeated Dante, surprised. "Don't they breathe oxygen?"

"I'm not aware that they breathe anything at all," answered Moby Dick.

"Why would they choose this particular world?"

"It's a deserted colony world, with a couple of empty Tradertowns. There won't be anyone there to interfere."

"Which means they'll have time to booby-trap every inch of it."

"They won't need to," said Moby Dick. "Try to understand: these are aliens who conquer entire worlds with no help from anyone. You have no conception of their powers, no idea what they're capable of."

"So tell me."

"I don't know the specifics. I just know that time after time they accomplish the seemingly impossible with no visible effort."

Thanks for nothing, thought Dante. "I want you to get back to them and tell them Santiago will only meet them on a world of our choosing."

"If you insist, but . . ."

"But what?"

"But *they* have September Morn. It would seem to be a seller's market."

"Tell them anyway. If they don't know what a bluff is, they might think Santiago won't come under any other conditions. I mean, hell, he's never even met her. He has no reason to walk into a trap to try to save her."

"Whatever you say. Stay there."

Moby Dick broke the connection, and contacted him again twenty minutes later.

"Well?" demanded Dante.

"No deal. They may not know how to tell a lie, but they know how to spot one. They'll only meet him on Kabal III."

"At least we tried."

"What now?" asked Moby Dick.

"It's obviously a trap. We can't let him go there alone." Dante did some quick mental calculations. "I can have half our men here in six days' time. Let's set the meeting for then."

Moby Dick's expression said it was a hopeless request, but he agreed to pass it on. He was back in communication with Dante ten minutes later.

"Big mistake," he said. "We gave them a time frame. Now they say that if Santiago's not on Kabal III in one Standard day, they'll kill September Morn rather than continue holding her for ransom."

"Shit!" muttered Dante. "She's going to die, and it's my fault! If I'd left it alone, the goddamned government would have come up with the money!"

"Don't blame yourself too much," replied Moby Dick, not without sympathy. "You didn't know who or what you were dealing with."

"Excuse me, Mr. Alighieri," said the computer, "but there is a priority communication coming in from a Mr. Santiago."

"No problem," said the albino. "I'll talk to you tomorrow. You can let me know what he said then."

He cut the connection, and an instant later Silvermane's visage replaced his.

"I found him," he announced.

"Mongaso Taylor?"

"That's right." Something in his manner precluded any questions about what had happened. "I should reach Hadrian II in about thirteen Standard hours. I'll meet you in Trajan just before noon." He paused. "Did you talk any sense into the lady poet?"

"We have to talk about her. I'll go to my ship and get back to you in half an hour."

"I'm getting tired of that," said Silvermane. "Do you have any reason to think someone is monitoring this?"

"No, I'm just trying to be safe."

"Then talk to me now."

Dante sighed deeply. "The aliens kidnapped her."

Silvermane seemed unsurprised and unconcerned. "I *told* you to get her off the planet." He sighed. "Well, they'll pay the ransom and that'll be that. I hope you learned your lesson."

"It's not that simple."

"Oh?" asked Silvermane, suddenly alert.

"I made a terrible blunder," said Dante. "I tried to bluff them, to scare them with your name."

"Tell me about it."

Dante filled him in. "And their last message is that they've got her on Kabal III, and they'll kill her if you don't show up tomorrow."

"What are they asking for her?"

"You're not seriously thinking of going there?" demanded Dante. "It's a trap!"

"Of course it's a trap."

"I'm glad we agree on that," said Dante, relieved.

"I don't think my pistols will be much good against them. I can stop by Hadrian on the way to Kabal. Can you hunt up a molecular imploder by tomorrow morning?"

"What the hell are you talking about?" shouted Dante at the holographic image. "They're waiting there to kill you, and it's *their* world! They know every inch of it!"

"You don't seem to understand. They've called me out."

"So what?"

"This goes with the job, poet," explained Silvermane. "If I back down now and get away with it, I'll be tempted to back down again and again. What kind of Santiago would I be then?"

"A live one."

"Don't bury me just yet," he said wryly. "I plan to make a hell of a fight of it—and I've never lost."

"You told me once that you didn't ever want to be in the same sector with them," Dante reminded him.

"That was Joshua Silvermane talking," said the image. "I'm Santiago."

"Surely there's something I can say, something I can do . . ." said Dante.

"There is," replied Silvermane. "Make sure you have the imploder ready for me."

He broke the connection, though Dante stared at the spot where his image had been for a full minute before turning away.

He's going to die, and there's nothing I can do to prevent it, he thought miserably.

He walked over to a mirror and stared at the face that confronted him, searching for all the hidden flaws that he knew must be lurking there.

We're going to lose another Santiago, and it's going to be my fault again, just like the last one. I don't understand it. I try so hard to do the right thing. Why am I as good at getting them killed as I am at finding them?

Part 6

Santiago's Book

38.

He's proud and he's arrogant, fearless and bold;
If you travel with him you'll never grow old.
Those who oppose him have drawn their last breath:
He's the king of the outlaws—his partner is death.

Moby Dick stood in the corridor, waiting for the security system to identify him and inform Dante of his presence. Finally the door dilated and he stepped into the poet's room.

"Did you get it?" asked Dante anxiously.

"No problem."

"No problem?" repeated Dante disbelievingly. "Molecular imploders are outlawed on almost every planet in the galaxy, including out here on the Frontier."

"I am not without my connections," answered the albino with a smug smile.

"So where is it?"

"Back at my casino," replied Moby Dick.

"But I told you that Silvermane needs it this morning!"

"He'll have it—but I'm coming along with it."

Dante stared at him sharply. "Why?"

"Because I agree with you that it's time for another Santiago, and I want to see how this one measures up."

"We're not holding auditions," said Dante. "He's *it*."

"Right now he's just a name, and I don't follow names. If I'm going to join your crusade, I want to see just who it is I'm joining."

"I don't know if he'll let you come along," said Dante.

"He will if he wants that imploder," said Moby Dick.

"He's going to be hard-pressed enough without having to protect you as well."

"I don't need any protecting. They won't bother me. I've dealt with them, remember?"

Dante shrugged. "Have it your way. It's his decision anyway, not mine."

"Good," said Moby Dick, approaching the largest chair in the room. It expanded to accommodate his bulk, then wrapped its arms partway around him and began rocking very gently. "When it's all over, I'll let you know how it went."

"You won't have to," said Dante. "I'm going."

"Didn't you just tell me that he likes to fight alone?" asked the albino.

"I'm not fighting. I'm there to write it up, and hopefully bring back September Morn."

"He could bring her back himself, you know."

"He's never met her," said Dante. "What if they've got twenty women imprisoned there?"

"Then he'll bring back all twenty and you'll tell him which one she is."

Dante listened politely, then uttered a two-word response: "I'm going."

The security system blinked. Moby Dick began laboriously to lift his five-hundred-pound bulk from the chair, but Dante gestured him to stay seated.

"It's not him," he announced.

"Who is it, then?"

"The friend whose ship I borrowed."

"Are you sure this is a hotel room and not a public meeting place?"

Dante smiled. "Not as sure as I was fifteen minutes ago." He muttered a code to the door and it irised, allowing Virgil to step through it.

"How are you doing, Rhymer?" said the Indian. "You don't look any the worse for wear." A pause. "So the Bandit is really dead?"

"Really and truly."

"You know, I didn't believe it when I first heard the news. I didn't think anyone or anything except maybe Silvermane could kill him." He chuckled. "So it was the lady poet that shot him down?"

"That's right."

"Doesn't sound to me like the kind of woman who needs rescuing," said Virgil.

"She needs it from *these* captors," said Moby Dick.

"Yeah, that's what everybody who knows them says," agreed Virgil. He stepped forward and extended a hand. "Virgil Soaring Hawk. Pleased to meet you."

"Moby Dick."

"Not the Moby Dick who used to live in the Carnasus system?" said the Indian.

"No, that was another one," replied the albino. "He was the wrong color, but the right mutation. The way I hear it, he was born with gills, and he could breathe in the water just as easy as in the air."

"I didn't know whales could breathe water," said Virgil. "Of course, there ain't been any around for a couple of thousand years, so what do I know?"

"They can't breathe water," agreed Moby Dick. "But my namesake could."

"He still alive?"

"I don't think so."

"Someone harpoon him?"

Moby Dick shook his head. "Got shredded by a pleasure craft's motor, or so I heard."

"Serves him right for spending all his time in the water when he could have been chasing the ladies—or the gentlemen, for that matter," said Virgil with his usual single-mindedness. He turned back to Dante. "Silvermane hasn't shown up yet, I take it?"

"Not yet. And call him Santiago."

"Yeah, I know—I keep forgetting."

"How did things go on Valhalla?" asked the poet.

"Pretty smoothly since word reached them that the Bandit wouldn't be coming back." He paused, then smiled. "Matilda's put together a team she calls the Thieves' Carnival."

"Catchy name. Any reason for it?"

"There's half a dozen of them, they work together, and she sent them to Calliope."

"That's the carnival planet, isn't it?"

"That's the place," said Virgil. "Ten million vacationers any given day, all of them with money. You couldn't ask for a better world for Santiago to pick up operating funds." He glanced out the window. "When's he due here?"

"He's late already," answered Dante. "I expected him right after sunrise."

"Maybe he's not in such a hurry to die," offered Moby Dick.

"Are you saying he won't show up?" demanded Dante heatedly.

"What's the point? He can't defeat them. Whole armies have tried and failed."

"Anyone can be defeated," said Dante. "It's just a matter of coming up with the right strategy."

"Nonsense," said Moby Dick. "You're a minnow. I'm a whale. You can't defeat me. All you can do is escape to live another day."

"That's a defeat of sorts," answered the poet. "And if I tell *all* the other minnows how, and we all escape every day, you might find yourself growing a little weaker and a little slower, which will make you weaker and slower still, until you starve to death."

"By God, I *knew* I liked you!" said Moby Dick with a sudden laugh. "Santiago's got himself a hell of a biographer, young Dante Alighieri."

"I'm not his biographer," answered Dante. "Well, not exactly. Not primarily. I'm just carrying on what Black Orpheus started."

"Isn't it about time you stopped kidding yourself?" said the albino.

"What are you talking about?"

"From everything I can tell, just about the only thing you've done since you found that poem is try to find a new Santiago."

"What the hell do *you* know about it?" said Dante irritably. "I've written hundreds of verses, and I've spent days and weeks honing and revising them."

"What's more important to you?" asked Moby Dick. "Writing your poem or making sure that there *is* a Santiago?"

"What's more important to you—eating or breathing?" Dante shot back.

Virgil grinned. "Do you still like him?" he asked Moby Dick.

"Hell, yes!" said the albino. "He's as good at evading questions as answering them. That's a rare talent."

"Flatter me any more and I might take an axe to you," said Dante. "Or worse still—I might lock you in here with Virgil and not come back for a day or two."

"Promises, promises!" muttered the Indian.

Dante was about to reply when the security system told him that Silvermane was at the door. He commanded it to dilate, and the tall man, immaculate as usual, strode into the room.

"Who are you?" he demanded, staring at Moby Dick.

"And I'm pleased to meet you too," said the albino.

Silvermane did not look amused, and Dante immediately stepped between them. "This is Moby Dick," he said. "He's the one who's supplying the imploder."

"Then I thank you," said Silvermane sternly. He looked around. "Where is it?"

"It's in a safe place," said Moby Dick.

"Get it. I don't have any time to waste."

"Once we reach an agreement."

Silvermane glared at him. "How much?"

"No money."

"Then what?"

"I'm coming along."

"I won't protect you," said Silvermane.

"I don't need protecting," said the albino.

"Against these two, *everyone* needs protecting."

"Not me," said Moby Dick. "I have an arrangement with them."

Silvermane looked at the huge man as if he was the lowest form of life, but he made no reply.

"Well, we *don't* have an arrangement," interjected Dante. "Maybe we could use some help." Silvermane turned to him. "This whole planet loves September Morn, practically worships her. Give me a day. I'm sure I can gather a few hundred men and women to come along and—"

"Santiago doesn't beg for help," said Silvermane.

"But he doesn't have to turn it down if it's freely offered," urged Dante.

"They didn't challenge Hadrian II. They challenged *me*."

"That's your final word?"

"It is."

"At least let *me* come with you," said Dante. "You don't know what she looks like. If they have more than one captive and they've done them any damage, you won't know which one's her."

Silvermane frowned. "Just how stupid do you think I am? I've pulled up a dozen holograms of her from the local newsdisk."

"Then consider this: if you're good enough to kill the aliens— aliens she felt could not possibly be defeated—she may find you so terrifying that she won't want to put herself in your power."

Silvermane considered what Dante had said for a moment, then nodded his head almost imperceptibly. "All right, you can come." He looked at Virgil. "But not the Indian. I don't like him."

"I go where he goes," said Virgil.

"You're staying here."

"I'm not one of your sycophants," said Virgil. "I don't take my orders from you. I work for the poet."

Suddenly Virgil was looking down the barrel of Silvermane's pistol.

"When I tell you to do something," began Silvermane, "you'll do it!"

"Stop!" yelled Dante, so suddenly and so loud that everyone froze. "Is this the way Santiago treats his allies? I thought you saved your bullets for your enemies."

Silvermane looked uncertain for just a moment, then holstered his gun.

"All right," he said to Virgil. "But stay clear of me, in the ship and on the planet." He turned to Moby Dick. "I've wasted enough time. Let's get the imploder."

He walked out the door, followed by Virgil.

"Four heroes off to slay the monsters," said Moby Dick to Dante, so softly that the other two couldn't hear him. A sardonic smile crossed his face. "I wonder how many of us will still be alive when we get there?"

39.

Oh, Tweedledee and Tweedledum,
The parts are greater than the sum.
They send their foes to kingdom come,
Do Tweedledee and Tweedledum.

Kabal III was a dark world, considering how close it was to its yellow sun, dark and bleak and gray. Rocky surfaces with jagged edges covered the surface. Undrinkable water created small canyons as it wound through the landscape. Opaque clouds crawled slowly across the sky.

"I don't like the looks of this place," said Dante, studying the viewscreen as the ship took up orbit around it.

"Nobody asked you to come," answered Silvermane, who sat in the pilot's chair, meticulously oiling and cleaning his pistols and checking his ammunition.

"I've never seen them," said Virgil, "but based on all the stories I've heard, you're wasting your time. The most a bullet or two will do is make 'em angry."

"Probably," agreed Silvermane. "But if the imploder doesn't function or doesn't work, I need fallback protection."

"Mine would be: run like hell," said the Indian.

"That's why I'm Santiago and you're not."

Dante hadn't taken his eyes off the screen. "Seven degrees Celsius, one-point-one-seven times Standard gravity, not much oxygen." He sighed deeply. "So you can't use your speed, you can't stand a sustained battle, and you're not going to be able to work up a sweat. Are you sure you don't want to wait until I can mobilize some of the people on Hadrian?"

"If *I* can't defeat them, *they* can't either."

"I see that being Santiago is not necessarily conducive to modesty," noted Virgil wryly.

"They've destroyed entire armies," shot back Silvermane. "There's no reason to believe two hundred yokels from Hadrian will turn the tide of battle. I'm the best there is. Either I can beat them or I can't." He turned to Moby Dick. "It's about time you told me what you know about them."

"I know they're undefeated," said the albino.

"So is every man out here who carries a weapon."

"They don't carry weapons."

"Oh?" said Silvermane. "What did they do to get you to work for them?"

"Nothing."

Silvermane's face mirrored his contempt. "You gave in without a fight?"

"They didn't conquer me," answered Moby Dick. "They dealt with me."

"And you dealt with the enemy."

"I thought the Democracy was the enemy," said Moby Dick. "Or is the enemy whoever you're mad at this week?"

"You're here under sufferance," said Silvermane coldly. "Don't forget it."

"Fine," said the albino. "Give me back my imploder and I'll leave."

Silvermane stared coldly at him but made no reply.

"Got it!" said Dante, still looking at the screen. "Increase the image and sharpen it," he commanded, and suddenly a small fortress came into view. It was made of local stone, poorly constructed, unimpressive from any angle. "Bring that up in three dimensions, and give us a three-hundred-and-sixty-degree view of it, then give us an overhead."

"That doesn't look like it'd keep anyone out," remarked Virgil, studying the image.

"It won't," said Moby Dick.

"Then what—?"

"They have hostages," interrupted the albino. "It was built to keep *them* in."

"Computer, take us down," commanded Silvermane. "Land us four hundred yards due south of the fortress that's on your screen."

"The terrain is too uneven," replied the ship. "There is a flat area that will accommodate my bulk four hundred and twenty-seven yards south-southeast of the fortress. Will that be acceptable?"

"Do it."

The ship broke out of orbit and headed toward the planet. A few moments later it touched down on the precise spot the computer had pinpointed.

"Computer," said Silvermane, "I want you to analyze the area immediately surrounding the ship."

"Done."

"I oxygenated my blood just before we took off from Hadrian II, and I have injected adrenaline into my system. I've let you take readings of both. Is there anything else I should do to prepare myself for extreme physical exertion on the planet's surface?"

"Please wait while I scan you. . . . Done. I recommend the following vitamins and amphetamines . . ." The computer reeled off a small catalog of pills.

"Get 'em ready," said Silvermane, getting up and walking toward the galley. A small packet of pills appeared and he swallowed them all, washing them down with a mouthful of distilled water.

Then he turned to his three shipmates.

"I didn't want you here," he said, "and I won't waste any effort protecting you. If you have any survival instincts at all, you'll remain on board." He looked at each in turn. "I can't force you to behave intelligently. Just know that if you climb down onto the planet's surface, you're on your own—and I don't want any of you near me."

"Agreed," said Moby Dick.

"I got no problem with that," added Virgil.

Dante was silent.

"I'm waiting, Rhymer," said Silvermane.

"If there's a chance to rescue September Morn, I'm going to try."

"No."

"That *is* what we're here for," insisted Dante.

"We're here for me to face the aliens."

"Only because they kidnapped September Morn," said Dante. "There's no other reason for you to be here or to have ever contacted them."

"I'm here because no one challenges Santiago."

"Yeah," said Dante, unimpressed. "Well, *I'm* here because they've kidnapped the woman who saved my life."

Silvermane stared at him for a long time. It was a stare designed to make him back off. Dante stared right back, unblinking.

Finally the tall man shrugged. "Have it your way," he said, breaking eye contact. "Just make sure you don't get between me and them."

"I don't intend to."

Silvermane turned back to Moby Dick. "And there's nothing more you can tell me about them?"

"Their conquests are a matter of record. I didn't require any demonstrations."

"Maybe you should have. Then at least I'd know exactly what I'm going up against."

"Well, if I'd known you felt that way," replied the albino, "I'd have asked them to level Trajan so I could tell you what to expect."

Silvermane glared at him. "You're not much help."

"I gave you the imploder," Moby Dick shot back. "Show me anyone else who's helped you as much."

Silvermane made no reply. Instead, he picked up the molecular imploder, checked his pistols one last time, then commanded the hatch to open, and ordered the stairs to transport him to the planet's surface.

Dante was about to follow him when he felt Moby Dick's hand on his arm.

"Let him get a few hundred yards ahead of you," cautioned the albino.

"Then you *do* know what their powers are!" said Dante accusingly.

Moby Dick shook his head. "No, I truly don't. But if they're formidable enough to conquer an army, you really don't want to be standing next to him."

"I'll be careful," Dante assured him. "I'm not here to fight anyone. I just want to rescue September Morn."

"You may not have any choice once you leave the ship."

"If Santiago risks his life, how can his followers do any less?"

"That man's not Santiago," said Moby Dick with absolute conviction.

"He's got to be," said Dante. He gave the albino a weak smile. "We're all out of candidates." He turned to Virgil. "Are you coming?"

"It all depends," said the Indian.

"On what?"

"On you," replied Virgil.

"On me?" said Dante, surprised.

"*Him* I don't follow; *you* I do."

"He's *my* leader," said the poet. "I'm going out."

"Then I guess I'm going out too," said Virgil unhappily.

"Then I guess you are," said Dante. He turned to Moby Dick. "How about you?"

"They won't harm me. I work for them, remember?"

"Then let's go."

Moby Dick looked out. "He could have set it down closer. That's a long way to walk in *any* gravity."

"What are you talking about?" said Dante. "We're only a quarter of a mile away."

"When you're built like me, a quarter of a mile is too much even at Earth-Standard gravity," muttered Moby Dick unhappily. "I should have brought a gravity mat."

"It's too late now," said the poet.

"You two go ahead," said the albino. "I'll follow along at my own pace."

Dante and Virgil stepped through the hatch, waited until the top stair gently lowered them to the ground, looked around to get their bearings, and spotted Silvermane walking toward the fortress. The poet wasn't inclined to wait until the tall man got there before starting to cross the planet's surface, so he headed off to his right on the assumption that he'd be just as safe, or unsafe, two hundred yards to Silvermane's right as two hundred yards behind him.

There was no sign of life in the fortress, and Dante began wondering if it was a trap.

He must have said it aloud, because Virgil responded: "Of course it's a trap. I just don't know what kind. If the place is as deserted as it looks, it could be rigged to blow up the second Silvermane sets foot in it."

"His name's Santiago," muttered Dante, never taking his eyes off the fortress.

And suddenly, standing in front of it, was a large blue being, some ten feet tall, vaguely humanoid in shape, very broad and heavily muscled, totally nude. Its eyes were large and glowed a brilliant yellow, its nose was a quartet of horizontal slits, its mouth seemed to be filled with scores of brownish, decaying teeth, its ears were shaped like small trumpets. It wore no weapons.

"Where the hell did *that* come from?" whispered Virgil.

"It just materialized."

"So is it Tweedledee or Tweedledum?"

"How the hell do I know?" snapped Dante.

Silvermane took a step closer. "You wanted me," he said. "I'm here. Where's the woman?"

The creature made no reply, and suddenly the imploder was in Silvermane's hands, aimed at the blue being. Its lips still didn't move, but the four humans seemed to hear a deep voice within their heads.

"I am the Tweedle," it said. *"You have intruded upon my world."*

"There are two of you," said Silvermane, looking around. "Where's the other one?"

"He is here when I need him," said the Tweedle.

"Turn over the woman, or you're going to need him pretty damned soon," said Silvermane.

"You think to impress me with your talk?"

"No. I think to kill you with my weapon."

"Alone, I am a target," said the Tweedle. *"But I am never alone."*

And suddenly it seemed to split right down the middle. An instant later there were two identical Tweedles, both confronting Silvermane. They moved a few feet apart as they spoke, silently but in unison, with similar though not identical telepathic voices.

"I am the last of my kind," said the Tweedles. *"All the others died in warfare or of disease or old age. I alone have survived, for I alone have learned how to release my doppelganger, and by freeing him I have freed all the powers that lay dormant within myself and every other member of my race. Together there is nothing we cannot do. Does the terrain hurt your tender feet? Then behold."*

The Tweedles moved their left arms in a theatrical gesture, and suddenly the ground between the fortress and the ship was totally flat.

"Do you peer in the darkness with dilated pupils?" continued the Tweedles.

Suddenly the area was bathed in light, so bright that the humans had to squint to adjust to it.

"Perhaps you shiver with the cold."

Another gesture, and suddenly the temperature was a pleasant 22 degrees Celsius.

"We would change the gravity and the atmosphere, but it would deleteriously affect you after the various medications that we see you have taken into your body." They smiled at him. *"Do you still wish to match your strength and skills against ours?"*

"All I've seen are some parlor tricks," said Silvermane, trying his best to sound unimpressed. "You could have rigged them all before we arrived. But if you will produce the woman and turn her over to me, and promise never to bother her or her planet again, I will leave in peace."

"Is he crazy?" whispered Virgil to Dante.

"He's bluffing," answered the poet just as softly.

"You can't bluff these two," said Moby Dick, who had just joined them seconds ago. The albino was panting heavily from his exertions.

"You are a very courageous being. But we have killed courageous beings before."

"You've never faced Joshua Silvermane before," said the tall man.

"Moby Dick was right," muttered Dante. "He'll never be Santiago."

"Makes no difference," whispered Virgil. "They're going to kill him no matter what name he gives them."

Silvermane aimed the imploder at the being on his left. The weapon hummed with power, but had no effect.

He instantly dropped the imploder, drew his pistols and began emptying them, one into each of the Tweedles.

The bullets didn't pass through them, for the Tweedles weren't transparent images with no substance. The bullets entered them, left discernible entry holes, but had no more effect that the imploder. Their bodies simply absorbed whatever he threw at them.

Then each of the beings slowly raised an arm. Nothing more than that. But Silvermane dropped to his knees, obviously in agony. The pistols dropped from his hands and clattered noisily on the rocky ground.

The one on the left made a sudden gesture, and blood began pouring out of Silvermane's ears. He staggered to his feet to face his attackers. The one on the right slowly closed his hand into a fist, and Silvermane clawed at his chest, as if the alien were squeezing his heart.

Finally, with one last effort that took all his remaining strength, Silvermane pulled a knife out of his boot and hurled himself at the creature on his right—and froze in midair, his body suspended four feet above the ground, his knife hand extended, his perfect face filled with hatred. The two creatures made one final gesture in unison, and Joshua Silvermane fell to the ground, headless. His head wasn't severed; it simply vanished. His body twitched once or twice, then lay still as bright red blood gushed out of it.

"Jesus!" muttered Dante. "Did you ever see anything like that?"

"Only during bad trips," answered Virgil, unable to tear his eyes away from the scene.

Moby Dick stepped forward. "I tried to warn him," said the albino.

"That is because you are a rational being, and hence a coward. It stands to reason that you could not dissuade this Silvermane, who was a brave and hence irrational being, from confronting us."

"That's not quite the way I would have worded it," said Moby Dick.

"How you would have worded it is of no interest to us." The

creatures turned toward Dante and Virgil. *"Who are you, and why are you here?"*

"I am a friend of September Morn," said Dante. "I want to be sure that she is in good health, and is being well treated."

"I'm with him," added Virgil.

"She is healthy."

"May I see her?"

"No. We will permit you to gather your companion's body and leave Kabal III with it. You may not return."

"Before we do, I have a question," said Virgil.

All eyes turned to him.

"Which of you is Tweedledee and which is Tweedledum, and how can I tell you apart?"

"We did not choose those names."

"I'd like to know anyway, just out of curiosity."

"Your curiosity is of no concern to us."

And, as quickly and easily as they had split in two, they now joined in a fraction of a second and became simply the Tweedle once more.

"What do you propose to do with September Morn?" persisted Dante.

"We will give Hadrian II twenty Galactic Standard days to ransom her for five billion credits."

"That's a lot of money," said Dante. "What if they can't come up with it?"

"Then we shall kill her."

40.

He felt the call to serve his God,
His indiscretions quickly ceased.
Now sinners all are threatened by
Deuteronomy Priest.

"Do you get the feeling we're back where we started?" asked Virgil, as he sat in the Fat Chance with Dante and Moby Dick, sipping a drink and watching a trio of Canphorites squabbling over the result of a nearby *jabob* game. "We don't have a Santiago, we don't have September Morn, Dimitrios is dead, and who the hell knows where Matilda is? Maybe we should have anointed Tyrannosaur Bailey and let it go at that. Look at the time we could have saved."

"Shut up," said Dante.

"Every time I've opened my mouth since we got here you've told me to shut up," complained Virgil.

"I'm thinking."

"Leave him alone," said Moby Dick. "Your friend's at his best when he's thinking."

"I don't notice that thinking's done us any good," said Virgil.

"That's because you're a fool," said the albino.

"Could be," agreed Virgil. "But what gives you the right to say so?"

"You've still got an organization. You've got millions of credits. You've got a couple of hundred operatives. And from what I can tell, you've eliminated two unsuccessful candidates for the top job. That's not bad for six or eight months, or however long the poet's been out here."

"We're not in the business of eliminating Santiagos," said Virgil. "We're trying like all hell to find one."

"One will manifest himself," said Moby Dick. "And if not, you can still plunder the Democracy six ways to Sunday."

"That's more or less my own line of thought," said Virgil. "We've been spending too much time searching and not enough plundering."

"Shut up," said Dante.

"Just what the hell is your problem, Rhymer?" demanded Virgil angrily.

"We need a diversion," said Dante to no one in particular.

"What are you talking about?"

"September Morn."

"Forget her. You saw Tweedledee and Tweedledum. There ain't no way you're going to get her back without five billion credits. Either the planet antes up or she's dead meat."

"Shut up."

"Fuck you!" snapped Virgil. "Now that I know what you've been thinking about, I don't feel any need to kowtow to you. Even if you steal her back, all you've done is sign a death warrant for the whole goddamned planet."

"You're a fool," said Dante.

The Indian looked annoyed. "Maybe you should talk to the whale here, since that's all either of you can say to me."

"Do you really think you can rescue her without catastrophic repercussions?" asked Moby Dick.

"Of course," said Dante distractedly. "Avoiding repercussions is the easy part."

"No more drinks for him," said Virgil. "He's had enough."

"Shut up," said Moby Dick.

"Are you guys brothers?" said Virgil disgustedly.

"Go out back and molest one of the servo-mechs," said Moby Dick. "I'll let you know if you're needed."

Virgil stared at him. "You're kidding, right?"

"Am I smiling?" replied the albino.

"I never had a servo-mech before," said Virgil. "How does one ... ah ... ?"

"You're a creative sort of pervert. You'll figure it out."

Virgil got to his feet. "Talk some sense into him while I'm gone." He headed off toward the back door, and a moment later was out of the building.

Moby Dick ordered his chair to glide closer to Dante's. Once there he laid a hand on the poet's shoulder. "Take a break, Rhymer. All you're going to do is give yourself a headache. There's no way to beat the Tweedle."

"Oh, I know how to do that," said Dante distractedly. "It's the other details I'm having trouble with."

The albino stared at him. "You *really* think you know how to defeat them?"

"Yeah—but I have to go to Kabal III first."

"Go back? Why?"

"I've got to get September Morn off the world before I do anything else." Dante paused, still staring at his untouched drink. "*That's* the tricky part. Everything else follows from that."

"If you know how to kill Tweedledee and Tweedledum, kill 'em first and then get the girl."

Dante shook his head. "I can't."

"I don't suppose you'd care to tell me why?"

"Wait until I work it all out," said Dante. "Damn! I wish Matilda was here. She can spot the flaws in a scheme quicker than anyone."

"So send for her."

"It'll take her seven or eight days to get out here, and if I'm wrong, we don't have time to come up with a different scheme. They gave Hadrian twenty days to come up with the money—and that was two days ago."

"You can talk to her on the subspace radio," suggested Moby Dick.

"I will, once I work out all the details."

"Just how the hell many details are there? Either you can rescue her or you can't."

Dante finally looked up, as if paying attention to him for the first time. "You don't understand," he said at last.

"Enlighten me."

"Rescuing September Morn is just the first step."

"And killing the aliens is the last, I know."

Dante shook his head. "No, that's just another step along the way."

"What the hell are you talking about?" asked Moby Dick.

"I came out here to accomplish something," said Dante. "I've been so busy trying to do it piecemeal that I lost sight of the whole."

"All right," said Moby Dick. "I know better than to argue with a genius when he's working."

"I'm no genius," said Dante. "I'm just a guy who doesn't want to go back to being Danny Briggs."

"Who's Danny Briggs?"

"An unimportant thief who never did a memorable thing in his life."

There was a brief silence.

"You mentioned a diversion before," said the albino. "What kind of diversion? Is there some way I can help?"

"I need something or someone that can entice the Tweedles a few hundred miles from their fortress," replied Dante. He grimaced. "That's going under the assumption that they can't teleport. If they can change locations instantaneously, then I can't save her."

"Or kill them."

Dante looked annoyed. "Killing them is the easy part."

"There are a couple of million corpses strewn around the Frontier that would disagree about killing them being the easy part," said Moby Dick.

"They went about it wrong," said Dante. "If I can get them three hundred miles away, maybe they won't see me land. Even if they *can* teleport, they have to have a reason to do so. If they're far enough away, they won't have one."

"We can fly low and drop some explosives three hundred miles away," said the albino. "Or five hundred, or eight hundred, if that's what you want."

Dante shook his head. "Then they'll come after the ship. I have to get them to leave the fortress and give me time to get September Morn out."

Suddenly Moby Dick smiled. "I think I've got the solution to your problems."

Dante looked at him expectantly.

"Did you ever hear of Deuteronomy Priest?" continued the huge man.

"No."

"He preaches all over the Inner Frontier. Last I heard, maybe three weeks ago, he wasn't too far from here. I think I can have him on Hadrian in two Standard days, maybe less if his preaching has taken him in this direction."

"Then what?"

The albino grinned. "Then we turn him loose on Kabal III."

"There's got to be more to it than that," said Dante. "Tell me about this Deuteronomy Priest."

"He's a hellfire-and-damnation preacher the likes of which I'll wager you've never seen. Used to be a male prostitute, of all things. Then he got the call, and now no sinner is safe from his ministrations, which mostly take the form of rather unpleasant predictions about the particularly nasty afterlife awaiting you if you don't repent." Moby Dick paused. "And since almost no alien has ever been baptized, they've become his special project."

"Let me get this straight," said Dante. "He's a preacher. He's not a bounty hunter, like legend says Father William was. He doesn't carry weapons, just invectives?"

"You got it," said Moby Dick. "If we land him next to the fortress, they'll probably kill him before his ship touches down. At any rate, you won't be able to sneak in." Suddenly he grinned again. "But what if we program his ship to land a thousand miles away, give it a state-of-the-art communication system, something that'll carry his voice a hundred miles or more, and tell him to start preaching?"

"The Tweedle would want to see what the hell's going on," continued Dante excitedly. "And once he got there, he'd probably be more curious than deadly. He'd want to know what this guy is carrying on about before he kills him." He closed his eyes, did some quick calculations, then looked at the albino. "Even if the Tweedles can get there in five minutes, if Priest can keep them amused or interested or even just curious for another five minutes before they kill him or leave him alone, that's bought me a quarter of an hour. If we monitor them, I can land when they're halfway to Priest. The fortress isn't that big. I'll bring sensors, she can yell, one way or another I can find her in a couple of minutes, and I can blast her out of any cell she's in." Suddenly he frowned. "Only one problem. Will the Tweedle show up on our ship's sensors? Is he so alien that it won't be able to read where he's at? After all, Silvermane's ship didn't find any sign of life when we landed."

"I didn't think of that," admitted Moby Dick.

"It's not your job to," said Dante. "All right, we'll just have to assume the Tweedles become aware of him almost as soon as he lands. Now, will they go there immediately, or will they stay put and see if he's waiting for allies?"

"They don't worry about losing battles," said Moby Dick. "I think they'll go right away."

"I agree," said Dante. "If they can't teleport, how soon can they get there?"

"The planet's got a heavy atmosphere. Whatever kind of vehicle they're using, if they go too fast they'll burn up. Let's land him a thousand miles away and give them six minutes to get there. Maybe it'll take them an hour, but I sure as hell doubt it."

"Okay, I'll just have to assume they act like rational beings and show a little curiosity."

"And if they don't?"

"Then I'll have to do some mighty fast talking when they ask me what I'm doing there," said Dante.

"Is there anything else?"

"Lots," replied the poet. "But let's see if your preacher's available first."

"Let me get to the radio and I'll contact him," said Moby Dick, relaxing as his chair gently changed shapes and helped lift his huge bulk onto his feet.

Dante suddenly realized that he hadn't slept the night before, that he'd been sitting here at the table for almost twenty hours working out all the ramifications of his plan. Suddenly he could barely keep his eyes open, and he went back to his room at the Windsor Arms. He didn't even bother taking his clothes off or climbing under the covers. He just collapsed on the bed, and was asleep ten seconds later.

When he awoke, he felt like he'd just come out of the Deepsleep pod. All his muscles ached, and he was starving. He looked at the timepiece on his nightstand: he'd been asleep for twenty-two hours.

His mouth felt dry and sour, and he wandered into the bathroom, drank a glass of cold water, threw some more on his face, took a quick shower, rubbed a handful of depilatory cream on his face, climbed into the robe the hotel had supplied, and went back to the bedroom. He put on fresh clothes, and was considering having breakfast delivered to his room when the security system told him he had visitors. The moment he saw that one of them weighed in excess of five hundred pounds, he commanded the door to dilate.

"I trust you slept as well as you slept long," said an amused Moby Dick, stepping into the room.

Accompanying him was a pale, thin, almost emaciated man with piercing blue eyes, an aquiline nose, and thin lips above a pointed chin. He was dressed all in black, except for a glowing, diamond-studded silver cross that hung around his neck.

"Dante Alighieri, allow me to introduce you to Deuteronomy Priest," continued the albino.

"Pleased to meet you," said Dante, staring at the strange-looking man.

"More pleased than this fucking alien will be, I can promise you that," said Deuteronomy Priest in a vigorous voice that seemed much too powerful for his body. "The blue bastard will never be the same. Once I convert the fuckers, they *stay* converted!"

Dante looked at Moby Dick with an expression that seemed to say: *Is this a joke?*

Moby Dick grinned back so happily that Dante knew it wasn't a joke at all, that this was the person September Morn's—and his own—life depended on.

"You got anything to drink?" asked the preacher, looking around the room.

"Sorry," said Dante.

"What the hell kind of hotel doesn't supply booze for its guests?" groused Deuteronomy Priest. He looked up. "How about drugs?"

"I don't have any."

"What the hell are you good for?" muttered the preacher. He walked to the door. "I'll be back in the casino. Let me know when we're ready to read the riot act to this alien bastard."

And with that, he was gone.

"I wish you could see your face right now!" chuckled Moby Dick.

"Is this guy for real?" said Dante.

"He's perfect for the job," answered the albino. "Nothing in the world can shut him up or scare him. Once he touches down, he's the one person you can be sure won't be tempted to cut and run when the Tweedles confront him. Hell, he might actually convert them!"

"Just keep him sober enough to stand up and talk once he gets there."

"When are we leaving?"

"Not for a week, maybe even a bit longer."

"That long?"

"We've got a lot of work to do first."

"We do?"

"Matilda and I have built a formidable organization. In Santiago's absence, I'm going to put it to work—and you're going to help."

"Just who are you going to war with, besides the Tweedle?" asked Moby Dick.

"No one. The key to survival is avoiding wars, not fighting them."

"Then what are you going to do?"

"Arrange a war between two other parties," answered Dante.

41.

He killed a man by accident, then two, then six, then ten.
He's got to where he likes it, and longs to kill again.
His name is Accidental Barnes, he cannot lose that yen—
His weapon is the crossbow, his game is killing men.

Dante arranged for the hotel to give Deuteronomy Priest the presidential suite, and put Moby Dick in charge of him. Then he went back to his own room and raised the Grand Finale on the subspace radio.

"Well, hello, Rhymer," said Wilbur Connaught's image as it flickered into existence. "I haven't heard from you in a while. How are you?"

"I'm fine, thanks," replied Dante.

"What's all this I hear about someone called Silvermane taking over?"

"Forget it. He's dead."

"Then I still report to the Bandit?"

"He's dead, too."

Wilbur frowned. "Who's left?"

"Until we find another Santiago, you'll report to me," said Dante. "But that's not what I'm contacting you about. You've been operating inside the Democracy for a few months now. Have you got three or four men or women, also within the Democracy, that you can trust?"

"Four for sure. Maybe five."

"Stick to the sure ones."

"Okay," said Wilbur, lighting a smokeless cigar. "What do you want them to do?"

"I want them to spread out, thousands of parsecs from each other. And I want each of them, independently, to report to the Navy that an alien entity that calls itself the Tweedle was responsible for slaughtering all those children in the Madras system, that it's been bragging about it all across the Inner Frontier."

"Didn't the Bandit do that?"

"That's one crime Santiago doesn't need the credit for," answered Dante. "Once the Democracy has someone to blame, they'll be out in force."

"Okay, so we'll lay the blame on this alien. I assume you have a reason?"

"I do. Now listen to me, and capture and save this conversation, because if you mess up the details you've killed me." Dante paused. "Are you ready?"

"Shoot."

"I want you and each of your people to inform the Navy, all independently of each other, that no one knows where the Tweedle lives, but they know it will be on Kabal III, on the Inner Frontier, six days from now, for a payoff. It's a very cautious creature, and it travels with its own army. It will arrive at a fortress that's at latitude thirty-two degrees, seventeen minutes, and thirty-two seconds north, and longitude eight degrees, four minutes, and eleven seconds east. It will show up exactly two hours after sunrise at the fortress—my computer tells me that's 1426 Galactic Standard time, keyed to Deluros VIII; make sure you tell them that—and it'll be gone ten minutes later. The planet is uninhabited. The only way to defeat the Tweedle is to pound the whole fucking planet until there's nothing left of it."

"You're giving yourself an awfully small window, Rhymer," noted Wilbur.

"Any earlier and they'll kill me and someone who's working with me. Any later and the Tweedle almost certainly *will* be gone, and I hate to think of what it'll do to Hadrian if it gets away from Kabal."

"I'll take your word for it."

"Can you convince the Navy to do it?" asked Dante. "Everything depends on that."

"Probably. I'm not without my connections—and you haven't been back here since Madras. It's still in the news every day. They've been looking for the culprit ever since it happened. Our pal the Bandit didn't leave any clues."

"I'll be in touch with you in five and a half days. I can still call it off then, if you don't think the Navy's bought your story."

Dante broke the connection, then left the room, took the airlift down to the main floor, and took a slidewalk over to the Fat Chance. Moby Dick was sitting at his usual table, and Dante quickly joined him.

"Is your preacher going to hold up for six days?" he asked by way of greeting.

"He's been abusing his body with bad booze and worse drugs for the better part of thirty years now," answered the huge albino. "I don't imagine another few days will make much difference."

"I hope you're right," said Dante. "I've got another job for you."

"What is it?"

"Find me an engineer. I want to be able to operate Priest's ship from a thousand miles away."

"What's the matter with autopilot?"

"Nothing, once he's taken off. In fact, I want it programmed to take him to some uninhabited world—but I have to be able to make it take off when *I* want it to."

The albino frowned. "Why an uninhabited world?"

"If my plan goes wrong, the Tweedle is going to be chasing one or the other of us, and I don't intend for either of us to lead them to Hadrian or any other populated world."

Moby Dick grinned. "He's gonna be that pissed, is he?"

"That's a pretty fair assessment," agreed Dante.

"I take it you're really going to go back for September Morn?"

"That's right."

"How much time do you think you'll have before the Tweedle knows you're there and tries to stop you?"

"I don't know. Five minutes. Ten at the outside."

"Then I want you to take a friend of mine along."

Dante looked sharply at him. "Oh?"

"He's as brave as they come, he can help you look for her, and if it gets rough, he'll be another distraction. It might just buy you the extra few seconds you need."

"I'll be taking Virgil."

"Take my friend, too," urged the huge man. "You're telling me you've only got five minutes. The more people you have trying to find where he's stashed her, the better."

"I hope *you're* not going to volunteer, too," said Dante with a smile. "It'd take you ten minutes just to get from the ship to the fortress, even if I land right next to it."

"I know my strengths and I know my weaknesses," said Moby Dick. "I'm staying right here."

"All right. Who's your friend?"

"Did you ever hear of Accidental Barnes?"

"It sounds like a joke."

"There's nothing funny about him."

"It's the name that's amusing."

"He killed his first man by accident," said Moby Dick. "He killed his next thirty on purpose. If things get nasty, you'll be glad you've got him with you. He's certainly more use than that goddamned Indian." He grimaced. "You know, none of my servo-mechs have worked since yesterday."

Dante chuckled. "I seem to remember you suggesting that he pay them a visit."

"Only because I never thought he'd do it!" snapped Moby Dick. Suddenly all the alien gamblers stopped what they were doing and stared at him. "Go back to your games," he said in a more reasonable tone of voice. "Nothing's wrong." He turned back to Dante. "I don't know why you let him hang around. He's useless."

"That useless man may possess some tastes that you and I disagree with," answered Dante, "but he's as deadly a killer as Dimitrios was. And he's totally loyal to me. If there's a better reason to let him hang around, I can't think of it."

"Point taken," acknowledged Moby Dick.

"Now, where is this Accidental Barnes?"

"He's staying at your hotel. He arrived while we were off visiting the Tweedle."

"What's he doing here?"

"Gambling," said the albino. "He doesn't need the money, but he enjoys the challenge."

Dante looked around. "So why isn't he here?"

"This casino is for aliens."

"Nobody's ever stopped me from entering."

"He can enter it any time he wants, but we don't have any human games, and he prefers them." Moby Dick signaled to a Mollutei, which ambulated over and stood in front of him. The albino spoke in an alien tongue for a moment, and then the alien left the casino. "I've just sent for him. He should be here in a few minutes."

They waited in silence, and five minutes later a short, stocky man with spiky blond hair and a bushy beard, blond but streaked with white, entered the casino. He looked around, spotted Moby Dick, and walked over.

"Dante, this is Accidental Barnes, the man I was telling you about."

Dante extended a hand, which Barnes accepted.

"Got a job for you," continued Moby Dick. "How would you like to ride shotgun on a rescue mission against Tweedledee and Tweedledum?"

"Tweedledee and Tweedledum?" repeated Barnes. "Nice to know you're not thinking small. What's it pay?"

"Nothing if we fail, bragging rights if we win," said Dante.

"You're asking me to go up against the most dangerous pair of aliens on the Frontier," said Barnes. "And I didn't hear any mention of money."

"You're not going to. They've kidnapped a woman. I plan to rescue her. We'll be in and out in five minutes, or we're dead. Moby Dick volunteered you. I don't *need* your help, but I'd like it."

"And you're not paying anything at all?" said Barnes.

"The woman is September Morn," said Moby Dick.

Barnes's entire demeanor changed. "Why didn't you say so in the first place? I'm in."

"You know her?"

"She's as close to royalty as this sector has produced," answered Barnes. "If the Inner Frontier ever gets civilized, it's going to be because of people like her, not you and me."

"The question is whether we *want* it to be civilized," interjected Moby Dick. "Most of us came out here to get away from civilization."

"We came here to get away from the Democracy, which isn't the same thing," replied Dante.

"I agree," said Barnes. "And whether the whale here likes it or not, sooner or later we *are* going to get civilized." He turned to Dante. "Where are Tweedledee and Tweedledum keeping her, and when do we strike?"

"I'll tell you the planet as soon as I know where it is," said Dante. "We'll leave in four or five days."

"Count me in." Barnes got to his feet. "Nice meeting you. You can find me at the Windsor Arms."

Barnes left the casino.

"Why didn't you tell him she's on Kabal III?" asked Moby Dick.

"You heard him. He thinks she's royalty. He wanted money until he found out we're after September Morn, and now he's willing to risk his life for free. If I tell him where she is, I don't think he'll wait until I'm ready."

"So what if he goes early?"

"He'll get us all killed," answered Dante firmly.

"Are you sure this is going to work?" asked Moby Dick.

"No," said the poet. "If everyone does what I tell them to do, I'm sure it *ought* to work, but that's not the same thing."

Dante went back to his room, contacted a few more people he knew and trusted in the Democracy, and gave them the same instructions he'd given to Wilbur.

He then spent four days trying not to think about what was coming. He arose each day, ate breakfast, and took long drives through the countryside, avoiding Virgil, Moby Dick, and Accidental Barnes whenever he could, and just trying to relax and ease the tension that was gnawing at his stomach.

Finally, on the morning of the fifth day, he contacted Wilbur again.

"How are we doing?" he asked.

"So far so good," answered the accountant. "I had to spread a little money around, just to be on the safe side. As things stand now, they'll blow the whole fucking planet at exactly 1435 Standard time. You got any more instructions?"

"One very important one," said Dante. "I'm flying a four-man Silver Meteor, registration GF-five-three-one-four-GL. I want you to alert the Navy that I'm the guy who located the Tweedle, and that I'll be taking off like a bat out of hell just a minute or two before they're due to strike. I don't want them jumping the gun while I'm on the planet, and I don't want them mistaking me for the Tweedle and blowing me out of the sky while I'm racing away from Kabal. Can you do that?"

"Easy."

"I want you to be very sure, Wilbur. If you screw this up, you'll kill me."

"Trust me," said the accountant. "I haven't let you down yet, have I?"

"So far all you've done is make money. This is a little more important to me."

"I'll take care of it, Rhymer."

"If you don't, I'll haunt you from the grave."

"If I don't, there won't be enough left of you and your ship to put in a grave."

"All the more reason to do it right," said Dante. "Oh, one more thing. There's another ship that will be leaving when mine does. It belongs to a preacher named Deuteronomy Priest, and they're not to fire on it, either. I'll get back to you with the registration number later today. Over and out."

He walked over to the Fat Chance and roused Moby Dick from his formfitting support chair.

"Get the preacher over to the spaceport," he said. "His ship is programmed to land on Kabal, one thousand miles due south of the fortress, at exactly 1408 Standard time. It won't activate the communicators until then." He paused. "I know your engineer gave me a remote control for his ship. Is there anything I need to know about it?"

"Just press the yellow button," said the albino. "Easy as that."

"Okay, get him onto his ship."

Moby Dick went to the hotel to pick up Deuteronomy Priest, and Dante allowed himself the luxury of one last breakfast at a real restaurant before he was reduced to eating the food from his ship's galley.

Then he contacted Virgil and Barnes and told them to meet him at his ship. When they arrived Dante stared at Barnes' weapon.

"What the hell is *that*?" he demanded.

"A crossbow."

"I thought they were obsolete four or five millennia ago," said Dante.

"That was before we were able to create bolts with nuclear devices in their tips," said Barnes, lovingly patting his quiver.

"Okay, bring it aboard."

They took off a few minutes later, and came to a stop when they were half a light-year from Kabal.

"Let me check one last time and make sure everything's on schedule," Dante announced. He contacted the Grand Finale and his other agents, received positive reports from them, and finally shut down the radio. He ordered the ship to resume flight, and instructed the navigational computer to land as close as possible to the fortress at precisely 1416 Standard time—ten minutes after the preacher landed, and ten minutes before the Navy arrived. He considered arming himself, but decided any weapon he could carry would be useless against the Tweedle.

The three of them spent the next hour with their eyes glued to the chronometer. Finally the ship began descending to the planet's surface. Dante had the sensors try to pick up any form of life other than Deuteronomy Priest, who had landed six minutes earlier, but nothing showed up.

"You'd better be right about where they are and how fast they can travel," said Virgil, also staring at the sensor panel.

"If I'm not, we'll know it soon enough," answered Dante, passing out communicators. "Make sure to keep in constant touch with each other. We haven't got much time."

The ship touched down fifty yards from the fortress, precisely on schedule.

"Well, at least he's not perfect," commented Dante.

"What do you mean?"

"We're right next to the fortress," he said. "Last time we were here he leveled the ground just to impress us, and he's forgotten to let it revert to its natural jagged surface."

He stepped through the hatch, waited impatiently for his companions to join him, and let the platform lower them to the ground.

"I'll take the west side. Virgil, you take the east. Barnes, you're riding shotgun, just in case there's something waiting for us. If there's nothing there, walk straight through and check the north end."

They entered the fortress, half-expecting to bump headfirst into the Tweedle. It seemed deserted.

"September Morn!" he yelled as he turned to his left and entered a darkened corridor. "If you can hear me, speak up!"

No answer.

"It's Dante Alighieri!"

Silence.

"I'm in a corridor on the east side," said Virgil. "There aren't any doors."

"No opposition," said Barnes, checking in. "I'm heading to the south wall."

Dante continued walking, afraid to spend too much time examining his surroundings and simultaneously afraid that if he went too fast he could go right past September Morn.

"Virgil here. Still nothing."

"Ditto," said Barnes.

"Damn it!" said Dante. "We've only got seven or eight minutes left."

"I'm going as fast as I can," said Virgil. "It's not exactly a maze, but I still can't find any doors."

"Me neither," said Barnes. Then, suddenly: "Wait a minute! I think I've got something!"

"Where are you?" demanded Dante.

"About eighty feet from the west wall, and ten feet from the north wall. In the open—there doesn't seem to be a roof here."

It took Dante almost a minute to find it. Virgil arrived a few seconds later. Barnes was trying to move a circular slab of rock from where it sat on the ground.

"It's too perfect a circle," grunted Barnes. "Nature never made anything like that on a world like this."

Dante knelt down next to him. The two men strained to no avail, and then Virgil lent his strength, and finally the rock moved a bit, revealing a darkened chamber beneath it.

"Thank God!" said September Morn's voice.

"Hang on!" said Dante. "We'll have you out in a couple of minutes."

"Better make that less than a minute," said Virgil, his face flushed with the effort he was putting forth on the slab. "I've been counting."

The three men finally moved the slab about two feet. Then Virgil, the tallest of the three, lay on his belly and extended his arm down.

"Can you reach my hand?" he asked.

"I can't see," she said. "My eyes haven't adjusted to the light. Let me feel around."

There was a moment of tense total silence.

"Got her!" said the Indian suddenly. He began pulling her up, and suddenly stopped. "Give me a hand. I can't pull her any higher."

"Just don't let her go!" said Dante sharply, as he and Barnes stood over Virgil and slowly pulled his torso up until September Morn's hand was visible. Than Dante grabbed it and pulled her the rest of the way out, and a moment later she was standing next to them, a little weak and wobbly on her feet.

"I didn't think I'd ever see a human again," she said. Suddenly she smiled. "I'm too relieved even to cry."

"Are you strong enough to run?" asked Dante. "We haven't got much time."

"I don't know."

"Then I'll have to carry you." He picked her up. "Barnes, lead the way! Virgil, protect my back in case anything comes after us!"

"Where's the Tweedle?" she asked as Dante began running toward the ship.

"Let's hope he's hundreds of miles away," said Dante, as they raced out of the fortress.

When all four were inside the ship, he ordered the hatch to close, and then took off. He counted to thirty and pressed the yellow button that would lift Deuteronomy Priest's ship off the surface if it still existed.

"How did you manage it?" asked September Morn, still trying to focus her eyes.

"Mostly luck," answered the poet.

"Won't they be coming after us?" she asked.

"Not if things go according to plan," said Dante. "Computer, show us Kabal III on the viewscreen." He turned to her. "Can you see it?"

"Yes. My pupils are finally adjusting. I'd been down there a long time."

"Then keep an eye on the planet," said Dante.

And no sooner had he spoken than the Navy bombarded it with all the terrifying power at its disposal, and suddenly Kabal III was nothing but a spectacular light show. When the Navy left a few minutes later, nothing remained but a cloud of swirling dust.

"Is the Tweedle dead?" she asked.

"He's got to be."

"I wish I could believe that, but I don't know . . ." she said, shuddering at the thought of the creature. "It could be invulnerable to all that. For all we know, it's floating in space, already planning its revenge."

"He's dead," said Dante.

"How can you be so sure?"

"He had nostrils," said Dante. "I don't think any living being could stand up to that pounding, but even if he could, his nostrils mean he has to breathe. There's no planet, which means there's no atmosphere. He's dead, all right."

"I never thought of that!" said Virgil.

"Of course not," said September Morn, staring at the poet with open admiration. "You're not Dante Alighieri."

42.

His mother was a cosmic wind,
His sire an ion storm.
His army charges straight from hell,
A filthy obscene swarm.
His shout can level mountains,
His glance can kill a tree,
His step can cause an earthquake,
His breath can boil the sea.

September Morn wrote this verse, because Dante Alighieri was much too busy to work on the poem. She imitated his style and rhymes, which were much more austere than her own lush, rich, metaphor-filled poetry, but she wrote an eight-line stanza to differentiate it from his work.

They had been back on Hadrian II for less than a day when word reached them that Wilson Tchanga, the Rough Rider, had been robbed and killed on his farm on Gingergreen II. Dante immediately sent for Virgil, who showed up in the poet's room a few minutes later.

"What's up?" asked the Indian.

"The Rough Rider's dead—murdered."

"Big deal," said Virgil. "From what I hear, he was over the hill anyway."

"As sensitive as ever," said Dante sardonically.

"I never met him" was Virgil's explanation.

"I don't care," said Dante. "I want you to get your ass out to Gingergreen II."

"What's on Gingergreen II?"

"That's where he lived."

"It's a waste of time," said Virgil. "Whoever killed him is long gone."

"Shut up and listen," said Dante. "I want you to go to Gingergreen and spread the word that Santiago robbed and killed the Rough Rider. I'm going to have Wilbur send you a hundred thousand credits, and I want you to bribe or buy three or four men who will swear they saw Santiago making his getaway from Tchanga's farm."

"What did Santiago look like?" asked Virgil. "Artificial arm or silver hair?"

"One of your men will swear he was tall, thin, and bearded. The second will say he was short, fat, and clean-shaven. And the third will claim he was an alien, eleven feet tall, with orange hair." Dante paused while Virgil assimilated his instructions. "If the locals won't put up a reward, put up one yourself. Make as much noise as you can, and when you're done on Gingergreen, hit every neighboring world with the story and the offer of the reward."

"How much should I offer?"

"It doesn't matter. Nobody's going to claim it."

"I don't understand any of this," complained Virgil.

"You don't have to understand it," sand Dante. "You just have to do it."

"How soon do I leave?"

"As soon as you can get to the spaceport."

"Well," said the Indian, "you usually know what you're doing. I suppose this will make sense to *some*one."

He turned and left.

Dante had a cup of coffee, then went down to the lobby and had the desk clerk summon a robotic rickshaw, which he took out to September Morn's house.

"Hi," he said, when she ordered the door to dilate and let him pass through. "How are you feeling today?"

"Much better, thank you," she replied. "I had to buy a new door, but otherwise the house seems intact." She paused. "My sister seems to have packed up and left. Would you know anything about that?"

"I seem to remember her expressing some interest in seeing the galaxy."

September Morn smiled. "You're a lousy liar."

"Let's hope you're a good one," said Dante.

"What are you talking about?"

"I notice that Trajan has a police department. Do they have a Neverlie Machine?"

"I suppose so. Most police departments do," said September Morn. "Why?"

"I want you to submit to it, turn it up to lethal, and make a holodisk of yourself swearing that Dimitrios was killed by Santiago."

"You're crazy!" she said. "It'll fry me in an instant!"

"No it won't," he corrected her. "You'll be telling the truth. The Bandit *was* Santiago when he killed Dimitrios."

A look of comprehension crossed her face. "He was, wasn't he?"

"Right. Can you do it?"

"I'll do it twice. Once at minimum voltage, so it just gives me a little jolt if it thinks I'm lying. Once I'm convinced that it's safe, I'll do what you want."

"Good. I'll send Accidental Barnes with you, to make sure none of the police play any games with the machine while you're in it."

"I assume there's a reason for this?"

"Just bring me the holodisk when you're done."

"All right."

He left and went back into town. Before the day was out, a huge man, taller than Silvermane and almost as broad as Moby Dick, wandered into the Fat Chance, looked around, spotted Dante sitting at a table with the albino, and approached them.

"You've come a long way and accomplished a hell of a lot, Rhymer," he said in his booming voice. "I've been hearing about you all the way back on Devonia."

Dante jumped to his feet. "Tyrannosaur Bailey!" he said. "I never thought I'd see you again."

"I never thought I'd leave Devonia—but when I heard that you killed Tweedledee and Tweedledum, I decided that you actually did what you set out to do and found Santiago, and the time had come to take a stand. You point him out to me, and I'll sign up to follow him."

"I can't," said Dante. "We've had a couple of unsuccessful candidates. But the organization is intact, and we could sure use you on our side."

"There's no Santiago?"

"At the moment."

Bailey shrugged. "What the hell—I'm here."

"Then you'll join us?"

"Yeah, I'll join you. Truth to tell, I was starting to feel a little claustrophobic back on Devonia." He paused. "So what do I do now?"

Dante stared at him for a long moment, then spoke.

"Do you really want to help?"

"I said I did."

"Then I want you to go back to Devonia—"

"I just left!" interrupted Bailey.

"Just for a short time," continued Dante.

"And what do I do once I get there?"

"Burn your tavern down."

Bailey stared at him as if he was crazy. "Do *what?*"

"You heard me. Burn it down."

"Just go home, burn it down, and leave?"

"And tell everyone who will listen that Santiago did it, and you want his head." Dante paused. "I especially want you to tell that to any member of the Democracy, or anyone who might soon be traveling to the Democracy. Can you do it?"

"Of course I can do it!"

"Good. Can you leave tonight?"

"I just got here. I plan to eat, shower with real water, and sleep in a real bed. I'll go back in the morning."

"Fair enough."

"What about you?" asked Moby Dick after Tyrannosaur Bailey had gone off in search of a meal. "You're sending everyone else off on missions. What do *you* do now?"

"Go back to Valhalla, I suppose, and see what needs taking care of," said Dante. "Matilda and the Plymouth Rocker are still there, and they probably need some help." He paused. "You might as well come along."

"Me? I've got a business to run right here."

"It'll get by without you, and we may need you to use your alien contacts on our behalf."

"For how long?"

"I don't know. A few days. Maybe a week."

"All right," agreed the albino. "I don't suppose there's any sense backing out now that we've already beaten the Tweedle."

"We'll leave in the morning."

"How about tonight?" said Moby Dick. "I've got nothing better to do. We might as well get started."

Dante shook his head. "I want to stick around to make sure Bailey leaves for Devonia. Then we'll go."

Moby Dick shrugged. "You're the boss."

"In the meantime, get hold of Deuteronomy Priest and convince him that Santiago is the Antichrist."

"And then what?"

Dante smiled. "Then turn him loose."

They took off in midmorning. During the flight, Dante contacted Wilbur Connaught and had him transfer half the money he'd raised to a numbered account on Far London. Then he climbed into a Deepsleep pod—Moby Dick was already ensconced in one—and didn't wake up until they'd broken out of orbit around Valhalla and were about to touch down.

Matilda was waiting for him, as were the Plymouth Rocker, Accidental Barnes, Blue Peter, Virgil Soaring Hawk, and dozens of other members of the organization. Even Tyrannosaur Bailey, possessed of a faster ship, was there.

"I hear you've been a busy man," said Matilda. "You look like you've lost a little weight."

"I'm lucky that's all I lost," he replied.

"The Rhymer's done pretty well to hang on to his life when so many men and aliens were trying to relieve him of it," agreed Moby Dick.

Dante introduced the albino to the assembled group, then went off to the office with Matilda, who'd gotten a description of Silvermane's death and the destruction of Kabal III but wanted all the details.

"I just love the fact that you had the Navy kill the Tweedle!" she said when he was done.

"I think it was an elegant solution," replied Dante. "They were the only ones with sufficient firepower to destroy the planet—and not only did they do our dirty work for us, but the one crime we didn't want laid at Santiago's door has been officially blamed on the Tweedle."

"And now you're getting Santiago blamed for crimes he *didn't* commit."

"We lost sight of that along the way," said Dante. "He's got to be a criminal, important enough for the Democracy to be aware of his activities, and yet not enough of a threat for them to go after him with the full force of their military might."

"The Bandit was right," said Matilda.

"About what?"

"You've got a wonderfully devious mind."

"Thank you," said Dante. "I think."

Nine days later, word filtered back to Valhalla that Devonia had posted a 500,000-credit reward for Santiago. Gingergreen II upped it to 750,000 credits the next day, and a week after that September Morn showed up, having eluded her bodyguards, with word that the Hadrian system was offering a million credits for Santiago, the killer who had murdered Dimitrios of the Three Burners in the streets of Trajan.

Before the month was out, the Democracy itself announced a reward of two million credits for the notorious Santiago, dead or alive.

"Well, everything seems to be working out," announced Dante to the rest of them at dinner that evening. "Now all that remains is to actually find our Santiago."

Moby Dick laughed.

"What's so funny?" asked Dante.

"He's right here," said the albino.

"What are you talking about?"

"Santiago," added Matilda. "He's been here all along. We've just been too blind to see it."

Dante looked around the table curiously. "Tyrannosaur?"

"How can you be so foolish when you're so smart?" said September Morn.

"You think better, risk more, and work harder than anyone," added Matilda.

"Me?" said Dante with an expression of disbelief.

"They're right, you know," said Virgil. "It's always been you."

"Always," echoed Matilda.

43.

His name is only whispered,
His face is never seen,
He's King of all the Outlaws,
He's hungry and he's lean.
Nothing ever hinders him,
And nothing ever will—
For he is Santiago,
And he lusts for money still.

Dinner had been over for almost ten minutes, yet no one had left the table. They were all waiting for Dante, who had not moved or uttered a word, to speak.

Finally he looked up.

"You're all wrong," he said, looking at all of them. "I wish you weren't, but you are. I'm a poet, and not even a very good one at that."

"*I'm* a poet," said September Morn, "and you're right—I'm a damned sight better than you'll ever be. Starting today, I'm going to be writing the poem."

Dante was about to object, but he found that he agreed with her. She *was* a much better poet. Which meant he was out of a job.

"We discussed this among ourselves before you arrived," said Matilda, "and the conclusion is obvious. We just didn't see it until now."

"I appreciate your confidence," he said, "but I'm just a thief. I've never done anything worthwhile in my life."

"You saved me," said September Morn.

"And me," said Virgil.

"And you found a way to kill the Tweedle," added Matilda.

"Anyone could have done that," he said with a self-deprecating shrug. "You're not paying attention. Santiago is a leader of men. No one will follow me."

"I will," said Moby Dick.

"Me, too," chimed in Barnes.

"And me," added Bailey.

And suddenly he was overwhelmed by a dozen more pledges of allegiance.

"I've only been on the Frontier for a year," he protested. "I don't know anyone. I wouldn't begin to know who to contact."

"You've done pretty well so far," said the Plymouth Rocker.

"I'll be your liaison," offered Matilda.

"And I'll act as your go-between with the aliens," said Moby Dick.

He stared at them for a long minute. "You're sure?"

"We're sure," said Matilda. "You've changed every one of our lives, and always for the better. Who but Santiago could have done that?"

"All right," he said, feeling an almost tangible warmth flowing from them to him. "I'll give it my best shot."

"That's all anyone's asking," said September Morn.

Late that night he was sitting in the office, going over the figures Wilbur had transmitted to him, trying to decide the best way to put the money to use, when Matilda appeared.

"It's late," she said. "You don't have to do it all your first night on the job."

He sighed deeply. "There's so much work to do. I've got to get started."

"If I can help, let me know."

"You can tell me this isn't all some cosmic joke," he said.

"I don't understand."

"An unimportant little thief is leading an army made up of a foul-mouthed preacher, an Indian whose goal is to copulate with every race in the galaxy, an albino who's so huge he needs help just to get on his feet, a prize-winning poet, a killer who uses a crossbow of all things . . ." He shook his head as if to clear it. "What the hell kind of army is that?"

"Exactly the kind Santiago would have," she said.

"You think so?"

"Of course I do," said Matilda. "You're Santiago, aren't you?"

"Everyone seems to think so." He paused. "If I am, then when did I become him?"

"Like I told you: you always were."

Just before he went to bed, he looked into the bathroom mirror and studied the face that confronted him. For the first time, he noticed the tiny lines of character, the firm set of his jaw, the openness with which the image stared back at him.

"Well, I'll be damned," he said to the face that no longer bore any trace of Danny Briggs, and was fast losing the look of Dante Alighieri. "Maybe she was right."

EPILOGUE

He's back from the dead,
He's back from the grave;
He's clever, he's cunning,
He's ruthless, he's brave.
Fear is unknown to him,
Mercy is too.
His name's Santiago—
And he's coming for you!

There was a lot of work to do, a lifetime or more, and they soon got busy, each in his own way—for as Santiago explained, everything that had been done up to this point merely put the pieces in place. It would be years before the Democracy truly realized that the King of the Outlaws was back, defying them at every turn.

September Morn never returned to Hadrian II, but remained on Valhalla, where she added another two thousand stanzas to the poem, while still writing her own works.

Moby Dick opened a chain of Fat Chance casinos all across the Inner Frontier, each catering exclusively to aliens, and spent most of his time covertly helping Santiago.

Deuteronomy Priest spent the rest of his life warning anyone who would listen that Santiago was the devil in disguise, and that as long as he remained in human form, he was fair game for any God-fearing Christian with a weapon and a strong sense of moral outrage.

Accidental Barnes and Blue Peter crisscrossed the Inner Frontier, quietly recruiting human and alien foot soldiers for a ragtag army whose existence would always remain a secret from the Democracy.

The Plymouth Rocker did what he was told, went where he was sent, and proved to be every bit as good a majordomo as Silvermane had predicted.

The Blade killed the Knife and took over the Candy Man's operation, but continued to send Valhalla its percentage.

Tyrannosaur Bailey led the first successful raid on a Navy convoy in more than a century. And the second, and the third.

Wilbur Connaught never left the Democracy to live on his beloved Inner Frontier again, but he channeled tens of millions of credits to the organization that fought in secret to defend that Frontier.

Virgil Soaring Hawk realized that he no longer had a Dante to lead through the nine circles of hell. He stayed on Valhalla for a time, but eventually he wandered off to satisfy his unholy appetites, and was never seen again.

Waltzin' Matilda continued to practice her criminal trade, at which no one was better, but this time it enriched the coffers of her organization rather than her own bank account.

As for a small-time thief named Danny Briggs who had once operated on the world of Bailiwick, he was never seen or heard of again. After a year had passed the Democracy assumed he had been killed, canceled the reward, and closed his file.

And that is the story of how Santiago came back to the Inner Frontier.